WITCHY
KINGDOM

BAEN BOOKS by D.J. BUTLER

Witchy Eye
Witchy Winter
Witchy Kingdom

To purchase any of these titles in e-book form,
please go to www.baen.com.

WITCHY KINGDOM

Secrets of the Serpent Throne

D.J. BUTLER

WITCHY KINGDOM

This is a work of fiction. All the characters and events portrayed in this book are fictional, and any resemblance to real people or incidents is purely coincidental.

A Baen Books Original

Baen Publishing Enterprises
P.O. Box 1403
Riverdale, NY 10471
www.baen.com

ISBN: 978-1-4814-8415-2

Cover art by Daniel Dos Santos
Map of the Palace of Life by Bryan G. McWhirter
Map of the Hudson River Republic by Bryan G. McWhirter

First printing, August 2019

Distributed by Simon & Schuster
1230 Avenue of the Americas
New York, NY 10020

Library of Congress Cataloging-in-Publication Data

Names: Butler, D. J. (David John), 1973– author.
Title: Witchy kingdom / D.J. Butler.
Description: Riverdale, NY : Baen, [2019]
Identifiers: LCCN 2019017288 | ISBN 9781481484152 (hardcover)
Subjects: | BISAC: FICTION / Fantasy / Historical. | FICTION / Fantasy /
    Epic. | FICTION / Alternative History. | GSAFD: Fantasy fiction.
Classification: LCC PS3602.U8667 W585 2019 | DDC 813/.6—dc23 LC record
available at https://lccn.loc.gov/2019017288

Pages by Joy Freeman (www.pagesbyjoy.com)
Printed in the United States of America
10   9   8   7   6   5   4   3   2   1

For Margaret Barker

and Frances Yates and Robert Graves

and all my other heroes who have been willing to
look long and deeply down unmarked paths.

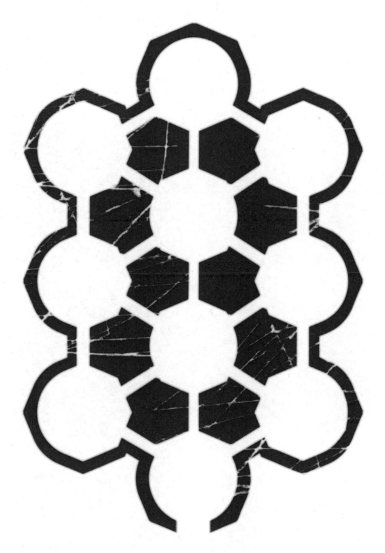

Palace of Life

"Three may keep a secret, if two of them are dead."

———⋅◆⋅———

CHAPTER ONE

Sarah lay against the wall of the long nave of the Temple of the Sun, gazing at the naked Serpent Throne across a space that should have been veiled. She had a long Imperial dragoon's wool coat pulled over her as a blanket against the chill night breeze wafting into the Temple through the open door.

It was night, and the Temple was dark. Sarah was here because she couldn't sleep elsewhere, hadn't been able to catch a moment's sleep anywhere but atop the Great Mound since the moment she had seen her father's goddess on the Sunrise Mound.

William Lee had told Sarah that her father occasionally slept in trees. Was it some experience like this that had caused him to do so?

Or was it a taboo he had *chosen*?

Sarah dozed in and out. When she was awake, her mortal eye saw nothing but gloom and shade. Through her Eye of Eve, though, she had visions.

She saw smoke and pollution. Something was wrong, she saw; not with the throne itself, but with how it had been treated. But beneath the mists of darkness, light shone. It was the brilliant blue light of the eternal Eden into which Sarah had briefly set foot, and yet it had a warm, golden glow, as well.

It reminded her also of the light she'd seen inhabiting the Serpent Mound above the confluence of the Mississippi and the

1

Ohio Rivers, where her father's acorn, planted, had grown into a tree that was in some sense also her father himself.

The light was power.

Sarah had come far, leaving her childhood home in Appalachee at the word of the monk Thalanes to search after the lost heritage of her father and the stolen wealth of her mother. She had made her journey less for those things than for the sake of the kin she had learned she possessed—a brother and a sister she had never known.

She had found her brother. Her sister was still missing, though, and Sarah and her people were penned within the wall of her father's city, Cahokia, by hostile Imperial forces. She had seen Eden, the land of her father's goddess, but only barely set foot in it and had not mastered its power. That power now winked at Sarah tantalizingly through a veil of pollution and wrongdoing.

Sarah needed to get access to that power if she and her people were going to survive.

The throne had an occupant. At least some moments, drifting in and out of troubled sleep, Sarah thought she saw a woman— *the* Woman—sitting on the throne. Was she smiling at Sarah?

But at other times, she seemed to see a second figure, standing behind the goddess: a tall, green, heron-headed man. Was she seeing the Heron King through her Eye of Eve, or in her dreams? He wasn't consistently there, and Sarah's uncertainty built up in her heart as dread.

The Heron King rested one hand on the Serpent Throne, and it seemed to Sarah that the hand sat also on the shoulder of the goddess. In his right hand, the Heron King held a sword.

The one Sarah had given him.

Had that been a mistake? With the Heronplow she had gained in return, she had rescued one of her two siblings, and she had, once, saved her father's city from an incursion of rampaging beastkind.

Was that enough? Did that make the trade worth it?

Uncertainty became fear, but Sarah was so exhausted that she continued to drift in and out of sleep, fear notwithstanding.

"Beloved." The Heron King stretched forth his hand. "Beloved."

He touched her shoulder.

Sarah shrank and cried out—

"Beloved, you're dreaming"—

and woke up.

Pale light crept in through the temple's door. Sarah looked immediately to the throne, seeing the light and the pollution, but neither the goddess nor the Heron King.

"Beloved." Maltres Korinn knelt beside her. He'd positioned himself carefully, so that the light shone on his face and revealed his identity. That face wore an expression of concern. "Forgive my touch, Beloved. You were crying out."

"I ain't made of glass." Sarah shivered and sat up, pulling the coat up around her neck. "I can stand some handlin'. Iffen I had my choice, I'd rather you shake me than call me that title."

Korinn didn't take the bait, but she knew he wasn't about to stop calling her *Beloved*.

"Beloved, the Handmaid Alzbieta told me you had disappeared from her home. The wardens and I have been looking for you."

Sarah took a deep breath and exhaled, trying to force the fear and uncertainty out with the air. It didn't work. "I can't sleep there. I can't sleep anywhere, except here. It's the damnedest thing."

"Or the most blessed."

"You try it for a week, and then tell me that."

Korinn nodded. "I'll talk with Alzbieta. I believe there's a solution."

"Maltres," she said, "how did you end up here? I don't mean looking for me this morning. I mean, how did you end up as Regent-Minister?"

Maltres Korinn eased himself into a cross-legged sitting position. "I love this land. I love the city, too, though I long to be in my own brambles and groves in the north. But this is the city of my goddess, it was the city of my king, and now it's the city of my queen."

"I ain't queen yet."

"In time. So when your father died and a group of the city's leaders asked me to take care of the city until a successor was chosen, I couldn't say no."

"Leaders, meaning the wealthy?"

"Some of them were wealthy. Others held important titles, like Royal Companion and Notary and Archivist. Or military rank—Jaleta Zorales was one of them."

"It didn't occur to you to use their support to just take the throne for yourself."

"But that wasn't what they asked me to do."

Surrounded by Imperial troops and caught between a god of destruction and a cold-blooded necromancer, it touched Sarah's heart to be reminded that there were still people in the world who acted out of duty, and for love. "I never hear you talk about a wife, or children." Sarah softened her Appalachee twang, not wanting to sound hostile. "Does that mean you're...you're not the marrying kind?"

Korinn laughed. "It means that my wife died, and my children are grown or mostly grown. They have lives of their own, and are not here in the city. But when I can get back to Na'avu, along with harvesting blackberries and cutting dead wood out of the forest, I will read with my daughters and ride with my sons and sit beside my wife's grave to tell her of my adventures in the big city."

"Sounds like a good plan to me." Sarah rose creakily to her feet. "I guess that's all the sleep I'm going to get tonight, though. Time to go fight the good fight."

"Foxes have holes," Etienne Ukwu said, "and birds of the air have nests; but the Son of Man hath not where to lay his head."

He spoke loudly, the opening words to a quick sermon. He stood atop a wooden crate he had placed on an angle on the boardwalk in the Vieux Carré, and he wore neither his black vest, with its Vodun patterns, nor his episcopal garb. He wore his black trousers and a simple white shirt. He counted on his reputation to tell people who he was.

His reputation, and the Brides.

The women within earshot noticed him first, turning to look at him as the Brides touched their souls and their bodies. The men took only moments longer.

Etienne had chosen this corner because there were no gendarmes in sight. Still, they would hear of his appearance and they would come. He had to speak quickly.

"A keen-eared critic will say, 'ah, this Ukwu compares himself to Jesus,' but no. I am not the Son of Man, but only the son of *a* man, the son of a poor man who served this city. And I, too, have tried to serve the city, and look at me now. The fox of a chevalier has a hole. The vulture bishop, my former beadle, has a nest. And I, the son of your poor servant?"

A crowd was forming. There were nods and murmurs of agreement.

At the back of the mob, someone ran off—to fetch the constabulary, most likely. Etienne had only moments left.

"Do not give the robber what he demands!" Etienne shook his fist in the air and several women fainted. "The only way to defeat this beast is to starve it!"

"Starve it!" someone yelled.

"No more taxes!" Etienne cried. "Justice for the bishop!"

"No more taxes!" the crowd roared.

"No more taxes!" he shouted one last time and then jumped down from the box. The gendarmes were coming.

As Etienne slipped down an alley to disappear, he thought he heard someone whistle a jaunty and familiar tune behind him.

Thomas discreetly touched the Jupiter ring on his right hand as he followed Temple Franklin into the Walnut Street Prison. He always walked with an erect posture—it strengthened his air of command—and he consciously threw his shoulders back and his chin up.

He wasn't wearing his Town Coat because he didn't want to be recognized. Instead, Temple had brought a three-chinned, eight-fingered gramarist from the College to ward him with hexes of protection. The magician had done his job efficiently in the library at Horse Hall, repeatedly invoking both St. Reginald Pole and also the Dagda. He had not sat down, had kept his back to the corner at all times, and had politely declined Temple's offer of a drink.

The College feared Thomas. Excellent.

Now Thomas and Temple, both wearing brown coats and brown tricorn hats such as any Philadelphia burgher might don, walked from cell to cell. Temple had the ring of keys, and they stopped to open random doors and look at the men behind them. No light came through the high, tiny windows of the cells because of the late hour; in addition to the keys, Temple carried a fat taper.

"The problem with these men," Thomas said, "is that they're not warriors." He gestured with disdain at three unshaven, foul-smelling prisoners. Emaciated and filthy as the men were, they still had the soft look of clerks and merchants.

The gesture itself hurt him. He had been shot in the shoulder by Wilkes the actor. Thanks to the ministrations of College magicians, the wound had almost entirely healed, but he still ached when he made certain motions with his arm.

Thomas shut the door and they moved on.

"I see that as an advantage." Temple fluttered his fingers, a gesture vaguely reminiscent of a cheap stage magician's theatrics.

"I see it as a sign that we have drained our prisons of their most brutal and dangerous men, and now we are reduced to scraps. I want more marauders for the Ohio, Temple. Look at these fellows—they're bankrupts and frauds, not cutthroats."

"They're men with families." Franklin smiled.

They opened another door. Here too, the prisoners were ragged scarecrows whose hair had not been cut in weeks and perhaps months, but they bore sure signs of middle class Pennslander living: they still had teeth in their mouths, for instance, and Thomas had yet to see a tattoo or a ritual scar.

Thomas considered, then dismissed an idea. "But they're in prison because their families can't pay their debts. There's no ransom to be had here, Temple."

"No ransom," Franklin agreed. "But men with families won't desert, or turn against you. Children and wives of men released from prison via your benevolent work-release program—"

"Fight-release," Thomas said, "let us be honest. Or even better, pillage-release."

"Even better," Temple agreed. "If your father is released from prison and brings home plunder from war, do you not feel benevolently toward the emperor who released him?"

Thomas thought about that possibility. "You, there," he called to the nearest prisoner, a man whose belly fat had not been completely drained by Walnut Street. "What say you? If you could be released from prison and also be paid to fight for your Emperor, say, in the Pacification of the Ohio, would you do it?"

The prisoner raised a befuddled face into the greasy yellow light of Franklin's taper. "Would you consider advancing me some of the money on credit?"

"An enlistment bonus, eh?" Thomas snorted. "The Emperor's shilling? But if I am to pay in advance, I could have free men.

Let us go, Temple. These fellows have clearly not been in here long enough."

"But," the prisoner said. "But—"

Temple Franklin slammed the door shut.

They followed the acorn.

The acorn had apparently been wrapped inside Nathaniel's ear when he was born, and the Cavalier Captain Sir William Johnston Lee carried it with him along with an enchanted, milk-giving rag from Philadelphia to the home of the Earl of Johnsland, not far from Raleigh. The earl had kept the acorn and rag all Nathaniel's life, clutching it to himself through years of madness. Now Nathaniel had both objects, in a small wooden box, and his sister, a Firstborn witch named Sarah, had enchanted it to lead him to their third sibling.

Nathaniel had only met Sarah in a visionary-transcendent state he experienced as a starlit plain, but which might be something like heaven, but he had rescued her from one kind of prison and she had rescued him from another, and he felt deeply connected to her.

The acorn didn't point them toward specific paths, but when Nathaniel held it in his cupped palms and thought about his sister—Margaret Elytharias Penn—the acorn rolled to show them which way to go. It always rolled in a consistent direction, northward and eastward.

When Jake held it, the acorn did nothing.

The acorn didn't do this of its own accord; it was a spell Sarah had cast, and the birth-bond that linked the acorn to both Nathaniel and Margaret was an essential piece of the gramarye.

They had tried other methods first. Nathaniel had ridden across the starry plain of the sky on his drum-horse, listening for a voice that sounded like it might be Margaret's, and he'd never heard one. He'd heard the rattling voice of Robert Hooke once or twice, and that had given him pause. He'd heard the voice of the wiindigoo Ezekiel Angleton, the dead Yankee Wizard who had attacked him in Johnsland, too.

The voices had settled into Nathaniel's heart as cold fear. The three fresh scars on his neck, cut by Angleton's long nails, burned.

Sarah had gifts of sight that Nathaniel couldn't fathom. She'd tried using them to find Margaret, and they had also failed.

Something hid their sibling from them. But the acorn, for whatever reason, pointed the way.

Perhaps, coming from their father as they did, the acorns were the most powerful bond holding the siblings together.

Jake and Nathaniel walked. Nathaniel could *only* walk; flesh and blood horses shied away from him and, though he couldn't explain it at all, he shied away from them, too. In the same way that his body didn't feel right holding a knife anymore, or wearing his coat right side out or his hat forward, he didn't feel right sitting astride a horse.

Nathaniel's inside-out coat and backward hat were the reason they trampled through so many brambles and forests. On the road, but especially in towns, Nathaniel drew too many stares. He smiled and, if asked, told people he was a juggler with a circus. When Jake was asked, he said that Nathaniel was touched in the head.

They avoided saying anything at all by staying off the larger roads. Jake didn't complain and Nathaniel didn't have to insist.

Jake carried a small sack of coffee beans he said he'd been given by Sarah. Twice a day, each of them chewed and swallowed a single bean, and after eating a bean, Nathaniel wanted to run. Without conscious thought, he tapped his fingers lightly on the large drum he wore slung over one shoulder—that, too, seemed to speed his feet and alleviate his fatigue.

Jake's hands shook, except when he thumbed through his fraying, water-warped and -bloated deck of Tarocks. He asked Nathaniel many questions and, when Nathaniel asked, he told his own story. Mostly it was the tale of a deaf-mute from New Amsterdam who'd grown up as an unloved errand boy working in his uncle's merchant venture, but from time to time that tale shaded into something darker and more violent. Sometimes, when Jake told tales of being that terrible god, Nathaniel thought he heard distant screaming. It was as if the Dutch ship-boy had dreamed of being a god of chaos and destruction, and then had matured into a man who couldn't remember which had been real, the ships or the cataclysms.

This was a reason Nathaniel should enter the starlit plain again, to find healing for Jacob Hop.

But he didn't dare.

Another reason to enter the plain of the sky would be to

locate Ezekiel Angleton. Ma'iingan, the Ojibwe man who had rescued Nathaniel when he'd been abandoned in the forest and then helped him find his way into the sky and a meeting with Ma'iingan's manidoo, his personal demigod, had called the man a *wiindigoo*. Sarah had known Angleton from earlier battles. The man had raised the dead to attack Nathaniel, and might now—*must* now—be on Nathaniel's trail. If he entered the plain of the sky and listened, Nathaniel thought he'd be able to find Angleton, the better to flee the man.

But whenever the darkness of the forest shadows or the bitter bite of the January wind made him consider doing so, Nathaniel remembered sinking in Robert Hooke's warm, amber pool, hands trying to drag away his soul for eternity. He'd only been rescued from that attack by Sarah's intervention, and the enchanted slate that had allowed her to intervene had been shattered in the act.

He felt Sarah's eye on him, from time to time, and even without leaving the mortal world he could sometimes hear her. She might not be able to rescue him again, but he believed she was following his progress toward finding their sister.

During the brief periods when Nathaniel lay trying to sleep, he thought he also heard Margaret. He thought the voice belonged to Margaret because it sounded like *his* voice, and Sarah's.

Mostly, he heard Margaret weeping.

"Don't worry, Margaret." He huddled deep into his inside-out coat, the wrong-turned collar chafing his neck. "We're coming."

Bill hobbled on two crutches toward the *Mimir's Well*. The *Well* was a tavern just inside the western wall of Cahokia, whose signboard depicted a cup of some dark red liquid with a one-eyed crow perched on the rim. It had survived the fires on the night of the Heron King's assault, despite being an aboveground building of half-timber construction with a thatched roof. Good luck on the proprietor's part, or maybe a hex against flame. The warehouses and receiving offices built in the manner of the children of Eve around the *Well* had mostly burned down and had not yet been rebuilt.

The mounds were much less damaged, the wood of their structures being sunk into the cold winter earth.

Even if the neighborhood hadn't burned in the assault, it would have been quiet. The docks on the other side of the Treewall were destroyed by rampaging beastkind, and the beastkind still prowled the frozen riverbank, cutting off river traffic into Cahokia. The Treewall's western gate, called its Mississippi Gate, was shut, warded by Cahokia's too-few wizards, and watched by armed men from the ramparts above. So were its Chicago Gate (on the north side), its Ohio Gate (on the east), and its Memphis Gate (on the south). The Imperials cut off traffic on these three sides, bottling the city up and forcing her to live on stores that had already been meager to begin with and were now running out.

Children, skinny but bright-eyed, played across the street and sang:

> *I'll sing you seven, O*
> *Green grow the rushes, O*
> *What are your seven, O?*
> *The spirit of the Lord*
> *And it ever more shall be so*

The words didn't sound right to Bill, but it had been a long time since he was a child, innocently singing Christmas shanties.

It was also a long time since he'd seen a goat or a chicken. He hadn't seen a horse or a dog in a week. Come to think of it, he couldn't remember the last time he'd seen a rat.

The Treewall had been scorched as well, but it had grown new bark and leaves. That was Sarah's doing. Bill had been fighting elsewhere, but he'd heard from Maltres Korinn how Sarah had run the Heronplow around the entire city. That spell had restored life to the wall and stopped the raging of the beastkind still within it.

The thought reminded him that he wasn't alone.

Bill turned to Chikaak. The beastman warrior, a man-sized and man-shaped coyote who stood on his hind legs, was Bill's sole remaining sergeant. Faithful Calvin Calhoun had fled after committing sacrilege against Sarah's goddess, and Sarah had sent the odd Dutchman Jacob Hop after her other siblings. The Firstborn counselor Uris had died at the hands of Cahokian wardens, bribed by a traitor. That left Chikaak, bound by a magical oath upon Cahokia's Sevenfold Crown, an oath that Bill knew could be disrupted by a thing as small as the physical application of a bit of silver.

Bill felt dangerously exposed.

"I shall not require your assistance here, Sergeant," Bill told the beastman.

Chikaak didn't move. With his tongue lolling out his mouth, the damned fellow looked as if he were grinning. "You're seeking relief from pain."

"Hell's Bells, yes, I am. My legs are both broken beyond healing. I shall never run again and I walk only with difficulty. My... *physician*," he had almost said *lady*, which would have been closer to the truth, though Cathy Filmer had been a Harvite novice and was the closest thing to a doctor he'd seen in years, "tells me I am likely to feel pain the rest of my life. Yes, Sergeant, I would like a little relief, and some of us are not constituted so as to be able to lick our own wounds."

Chikaak's expression didn't change.

"You're not following my instruction, suh," Bill growled.

"You're my commanding officer," the beastman said, "but my oath is to the queen."

Dammit. "Very well, then. Come watch me drink."

Bill stumped into the *Well*. Years of walking into taverns had conditioned him to expect the smell of food, and his mouth was watering even as he pulled the door open. The bitter gush around his tongue sharpened the pang in his stomach as he realized that the tavern smelled only of sweat and candle wax.

No food.

There was drink, at least. Men huddled over tankards and cups at the *Well's* scarred tables, sipping without speaking. And there was music: a man huddled beside the fire plucked slowly at a lute that seemed to be missing strings—this, too, likely an effect of the siege—and sang an English ballad.

> It's been a long, hard journey
> > since Peterborough burned
> Many a good man buried,
> > many bitter lessons learned
> I'm sunk up to my shoulders
> > in this thick black Ely mud
> My eyes are full of chainmail
> > and my heart is full of blood
> I'm not the last man
> I'm just the last man standing

It was an English tune, and after a moment, Bill recognized it. It was a ballad about Hereward the Saxon, last resisting warrior against the Norman invasion of England in the eleventh century. It was a fitting song for soldiers trapped and determined to fight to the end.

> *I've seen the girls of Flanders dance*
> > *in taverns by the way*
> *And English girls on alder trees*
> > *by Norman nails did sway*
> *We fired the wall, and William's witch*
> > *fell broken all apart*
> *My oath on Etheldreda's bones*
> > *goes dancing through my heart*
> *I'm not the last man*
> *I'm just the last man standing*

Bill would be the last man standing, if need be, but right now the mere *thought* of standing pained him. He dragged his carcass across the floor to a table beneath two smoked-paper windows. Hurling his crutches into the corner, he crashed onto the chair; it wobbled, and so did the table, but they held.

Chikaak had the wit to remain skulking by the door, out of Bill's way.

The serving boy who approached was skinny but clean. He had the milk-white face and teeth of a pure-blooded Wallenstein, and hair so blond it nearly glowed.

"Whisky." Bill tried not to growl. "Please."

"No whisky." The boy had a hint of a Chicago V in his W, and he smiled hopefully. "Wine?"

"Dammit." Bill sighed. "Wine."

By habit, he had sat with his back to the wall, facing the tavern's door. The sight of Chikaak, tongue dangling, waving away the serving boy and staring at Bill, brought up a wave of impotent rage, so Bill dragged himself around the small table until he faced the corner. That left his back exposed, but if Chikaak was bound and determined to stand and watch Bill drink, he could rely on the beastman to sound an alarm if anyone attacked.

Besides, Bill was in priestly, mystical, alien Cahokia, not stab-you-in-the-back New Orleans.

The wine came in a wooden cup carved with German images: a tree, a serpent, a squirrel, a bird. Bill deliberately ignored the smell and drained half the cup in one long gulp.

It tasted more of vinegar than of wine.

"Heaven's footstool, what have I come to?" he muttered.

A man stepped past Bill and sat at the same table. Chikaak bore down on them both, growling, but Bill raised a hand to restrain the beastman. The stranger looked Firstborn in the fineness of his facial features, though with darker skin than usual, as if he had Indian or Africk ancestors. He wore a green tunic with gold abstract patterns embroidered around the neck and sleeves, and he smiled at Bill.

"The man is unarmed," Bill said to his sergeant. "At ease."

Chikaak withdrew, snarling, and the Firstborn smiled again. "Thank you, Captain Lee."

Bill instantly regretted calling off the beastman. "You have the advantage of me, suh."

"You must surely recognize that *you* are well-known in this city. A few—myself among them—remember your days of riding in the Missouri with Kyres the Lion, but everyone has heard of your part in driving the Imperial Ohio Company militia from Cahokia."

"So that we may starve," Bill said. "What a hero I am."

"There is still wine."

"Two parts water, at least."

"Only two? I'd have guessed four, by now. My name is Gazelem Zomas."

"Zomas." Bill sighed. "The eighth kingdom. Deep in the Missouri, or beyond it, the white towers of Etzanoa built by those who would not accept the rule of the great Onandagos, or some such tale?"

"That is one story. Another story is that the man who should have been King of Cahokia was driven out by Onandagos, and built Etzanoa as a refuge for all Adam's children who could find no other home."

Bill shrugged. "As you like. We are speaking of the same place."

"Did you know that the southern gate of this city was once called the Zomas Gate? Relations have not always been hostile."

"And yet now it is the Memphis Gate."

Zomas shrugged. "You haven't been to my home, I take it."

"I've seen the towers from afar. Kyres Elytharias did not regard the King of Zomas as his friend."

"He and my uncle were rivals in the Missouri. Some of what Kyres saw as doing justice, my uncle saw as interfering in the affairs of another man's realm."

"I was there." Bill took a sip of the wine, tasting it more this time and regretting that fact. "You can go to hell."

"But Kyres and I were friends. I served him, after my fashion."

Bill wasn't sure whether to feel offended, curious, or friendly. He resolved his uncertainty by grunting.

"You were injured in the battle." Zomas nodded at Bill's crutches.

"I've been injured in more than one. I fear my legs have finally lost the power to recuperate."

"You must be in great pain." Gazelem Zomas furrowed his brow in a compassionate expression. "I'm very sorry for that. I doubt *Mimir's Well* has enough wine in it to ease your suffering even for an hour."

Bill grunted again. "I intend to test that proposition. I shall tell you what I learn."

"What if I could offer you another solution?"

Bill's heart leaped at the thought. "I hadn't heard that Zomas was famous for its healing magics."

"We aren't," Zomas admitted with a faint smile. "We're famous for our thoroughly creoled population, and for our hounds, for being the biggest market for Comanche slavers raiding Texia and New Spain, for guarding the overland route to New Muscovy, and for the standing bounties we pay on beastkind. But I myself am, among other things, an apothecary. What do you know of the Paracelsian Tincture?" He produced a small glass bottle full of a dark liquid from under his tunic.

"Laudanum? That it is costly, and I have no money. That it is given to hysterical women, of which I am not one." Bill eyed the bottle. Laudanum eased coughing and diarrhea, and for that reason was sometimes given to the small children of the New Orleans wealthy, but it also relieved pain.

"It is also given to wounded soldiers, of which you *are* one, sir." Zomas set the bottle on the table between them. "And I am wealthy enough, and grateful enough, that I will give this to you as a gift."

Bill looked at the bottle without touching it. "How do you profit from the gift?"

"Ah, direct. A soldier's vice." Zomas smiled. "But you're right. Sarah has defeated me, and all seven claimants putting themselves forward at the solstice in hopes of becoming the goddess's Beloved. But Sarah needs help still, if she is to free the city from the Imperial chokehold."

"You hope that if you help her, she will help you?"

Zomas nodded.

"Help you what?" Bill asked.

"Help me win the right to return home."

Bill's legs stabbed him; he had little interest in the details of the man's exile, at least at the moment. "I have heard that some soldiers come to depend on the tincture."

Zomas nodded. "As other men come to depend on liquor or coffee. All things in moderation, Captain. If I were you, I would not plan on taking the drops my entire life, but only until the siege is lifted and a better medicine can be found. Or until a healer more talented than our queen can come to your assistance."

Was Gazelem Zomas's offer much different from Bill's own plan? He had come to the *Well* hoping to get drunk on whisky, and when that plan had failed, had set about trying to achieve the same thing with watered-down wine.

Surely, if he used the Paracelsian Tincture sparingly, the bottle would last him a long time and be no more dangerous than wine.

"I think you'll find that a drop or two of the solution will cause the suffering to go away," Zomas said. "Or if not, it will cause you to no longer be troubled by the pain."

"God's teeth, suh, that sounds like the same thing to me." Bill took the bottle and glared at it, tiny and dark in his big hand. "What do I do?"

"It has a bitter taste," Zomas told him. "And in large quantities it can kill. You put only a single drop into a drink, say, that glass of wine. If one drop doesn't give you relief, try a second."

Bill had enough experience with apothecaries to know they never properly accounted for a man's size when recommending a dosage. He carefully poured three drops into the wine glass. Without looking at Zomas to see the man's reaction, he drained the cup. Then he closed his eyes.

"Give it a minute," he heard Zomas say.

Bill took a deep breath. The aftertaste of the laudanum on his tongue was bitter and vegetable, though there was also a pleasing touch of brandy. He inhaled again and felt the tincture's fumes burn in his nasal cavity and the back of his throat.

He felt lightheaded, as if he were floating.

"I can still feel the ache in my legs." His voice sounded far away. "But it is lessened. It no longer feels urgent."

"You may be tempted to try walking without the crutches," Zomas said. "Don't surrender to that temptation. Precisely because you don't feel the pain, you can do more damage to your body by pushing it too far. Try to enjoy the blessing of Paracelsus without attracting his curse."

"If that doesn't describe all of life in a single sentence, I don't know what does." Bill opened his eyes and saw Zomas smiling at him. "Thank you. Will you share a glass of watered-down wine with me, as a small expression of my gratitude?"

"It is I who am grateful to you, Captain," Zomas said. "However, I will happily share a glass of wine as an expression of mutual respect."

Bill raised a hand to summon the serving boy again. He determinedly ignored Chikaak, who stared from the *Well*'s doorway.

When the wine came, Bill put the Paracelsian Tincture away in his coat to resist the urge to add a few drops to his drink.

"You are not young," Temple Franklin said.

The two men sat in Thomas's carriage outside an immense stone house glittering with light.

"I'm not *old*," Thomas shot back. "And if *I'm* old, you're *older*."

"Yes," Temple agreed. "Which is why I'm so very concerned about generating heirs. If I do not marry and have heirs before I die, my bastard nieces and nephews with whom I am at war will inherit my vast wealth and undo my works. They will squander it on their strange Cahokian goddess rather than on feeding the poor and building highways in my name and in the name of my illustrious ancestor. My empire will not hold together, but will fall apart, to exist as separate little fiefs or be swallowed up by the New Spanish or cut to pieces by the Free Horse Peoples. I have done so much in life, and it must not be undone!"

"You bastard," Thomas said drily. "How long is the list?"

"Seven."

"Seven women who wish to meet the dashing Lord Thomas."

"That's one way to think of it. Or seven fathers who hope to trade their daughters for family advancement."

"Cynic."

"It won't do to be idealistic or squeamish about this. Very few people are able to live the romance of a Hannah Penn in this world."

"Including Hannah, at the end." Thomas remembered for a moment the bloodied, dying face of his sister and forced it from his mind. "I'm far from squeamish, Temple."

"Good." Temple pushed open the carriage door and eased himself out onto the cobblestones between two waiting footmen. "Then let us go ravish some maidens."

He must ignore the attractions of their persons, Thomas knew. Even the power of the ladies' families was only a secondary consideration, as were many kinds of wealth—land, for instance, or illiquid shares in a joint-stock company.

What he needed was ready cash, and a steady source would be preferable to a large pile. Though best of all would be both, combined.

It was time for another payment to the cutthroat Chevalier of New Orleans. Now, of all times, Thomas did not want the circumstances of the death of Kyres Elytharias coming to light, and his own cash resources were strained by the costs of raising an Imperial army to march into Cahokia. The increased tariffs the Electors had approved would eventually defray some of the heightened expense, but they had only just begun to be collected. Any raised tax pushed some citizens at the margin into tax evasion and other forms of lawlessness.

Franklin knew all of it.

Franklin stepped aside to wait as Thomas straightened his cravat and then rattled his Mars-sealed dress saber once in its scabbard for luck. Then the counselor followed Thomas through the wide front door. The building was the Philadelphia house of one of the great cattle-driving grandees of Ferdinandia and New Spain, His Excellency Felipe Albanez, Marqués de Miami. Cattle was a business that generally consumed as much cash as it generated, and in bad years more, which made the Marqués's daughter Alejandra an unlikely candidate even if she had been pretty. Unsightly Dago clabbernapper that she was, she—

"Buenas tardes, Señor Thomas!"

Thomas leaped aside as the very lady he had been contemplating thrust herself into his view, and very nearly into his embrace.

"Lady Alejandra! I have not seen you since your quinceañera, and you are even more lovely than I remembered!" This was literally true, inasmuch as a thick plaster covered all three of the birthmarks Alejandra bore on her face. Nevertheless, they were striking enough for Thomas vividly to recall their locations, and the plaster did nothing to ameliorate a nose that resembled nothing so much as an oversized bobbin.

"And you are so vital! On behalf of all the ladies of the Empire, I must beg you to reveal your secret, Lord Thomas—you do not appear half your age!"

Thomas tried not to furrow his brow. "And how old do I appear, then, Doña Alejandra?"

"Not more than thirty!" she cried, trilling an exuberant R that would have been the pride of Madrid.

Not more than thirty? Half his age? How old did she take him for? *Focus on the cash*, Thomas reminded himself. *There is no room here for your vanity.* Felipe was powerful enough to be a fit ally and father-in-law, an Elector as well as possessor of some sort of title under Napoleon's Spanish puppets. How much cash did he have?

"You are too kind," Thomas said. "How fare the herds, my lady?"

Alejandra made a sour face that thrust her cylindrical nose downward. "The winter has been only ordinarily bad, of course, but this rampaging of the beastkind has interrupted the transport of beef to important markets. My father says that they shall eat cheap beefsteak in Knoxville this spring, and expensive pork in Chicago! Praise God, he always has more land he can sell!"

"Praise God!" Thomas agreed, with the biggest smile he could muster. "Would that God granted your father a herd of pigs to match the size of his wealth in beef!" He swung easily into a ninety-degree pivot, and a long step that would take him out of the hidalga's clutches.

Franklin swooped down on him and clung to his shoulder like a sorcerer's bat familiar. "That was one," Temple said. "How did you find her?"

"She's cash-poor and she's too honest to hide it. What are you thinking?"

"That there are only so many decent choices."

"You cannot quote one of your grandfather's tiresome sermons at me and say 'beggars can't be choosers.' I'm not a beggar, I'm the Emperor."

"Yes, but what you have asked for is a woman who is connected with both cash and Electoral votes."

"More importantly, the cash."

"Still, that is a small field, and the winner may not be as impressive in her person as you would wish."

"Let us see the other horses, Temple. But no more ambushes, I beg you. No, I *command* you. There is a gazing pavilion in the garden behind the house. I shall conceal myself there; if asked, say I am contemplating difficult issues of state. Bring the ladies out one at a time to meet me. Do not send one until I have sent back her predecessor."

"I could have brought them to you at Horse Hall on such terms."

"Yes, but now the Marqués will be able to say that I attended his soirée. And others will remember having seen me. Besides, Venus is strong for me tonight, and what better place to capture the influence of Venus than at a ball?" In answer to Temple's slight disapproving cluck, he added, "I am wearing my Town Coat, Temple. This is hardly more dangerous than attending the theater."

The pavilion was what some were beginning to call a *gazebo*, though Thomas hated the new-fangled word for its macaronick Latinity. It was a wooden pavilion encircled by inward-facing benches, creating a space for lounging on a summer evening. The Marqués, anticipating guests' expectations or perhaps hoping to show off the large magnolias of his garden, imposing even in the leafless winter, had had a brazier heaped with burning wood placed beside the pavilion.

Thomas stood in the pavilion, at the edge of the circle of light and heat, and waited. When the women began to come to him, he counted down.

Six was plain, but scholarly. Her Cavalier father in Henricia—or as some called it, pining for England's last Stuart king, *Carolina*—had trained her in the Classics and left her utterly without preference as to gods. She launched a rapid series of apothegms at godar and bishops alike, in which Thomas joined with great amusement until she inadvertently reminded him that her father's vast fields were planted with tobacco, cotton, and maize. She lauded the fertility of the river-bottom soil, the size of the cotton bolls and the natural juiciness of the tobacco leaves, but Thomas's answering smile was completely formal.

No cash.

Five was an Ottawa princess. At least, she was a princess in Thomas's imagination, and when she told him of her love of dancing and swimming, her lithe physique informed his imagination vividly. Her people's wealth was in furs: beaver, hare, marten, and fisher. Thomas knew well that a shipload of New World furs brought to market in London, or even in Philadelphia, could make a man's fortune.

He also knew that the business was risky, both on the supply side—which could be physically dangerous as well as subject to the vagaries of climate—and on the demand side, which was enslaved to the whims of fashion. His own Imperial Ohio Company was already driving down the price of furs with the huge volume of beaver pelts it was currently bringing to market.

The best reason to marry Five would be to induce her people to stop selling their furs. While that would help Thomas by driving up the price of Company fur, it would impoverish the Ottawas. With visions of divorce and war against a confederation of cheated Algonks, he sent her back.

Four was a younger sister of the King of Oranbega. Her Firstborn features were softened with an obvious strain of hearty blonde German, and she brought with her a queer three-stringed guitar no longer than her forearm, flat, and fretted diatonically. When she had finished singing a lilting ballad about the love of some queen who died as her realm was flooded by the sea, she reminded Thomas of her land's wealth in coal and salt deposits, as well as its famously fertile soil.

But it was no good. Thomas would have the wealth of Oranbega in any case, by the relentless working of the Pacification. And the shade of William Penn had insisted he show no mercy to the Firstborn. Could Thomas hope for success in ruling his grandfather's empire if he began by traducing his grandfather's will?

When Thomas shook his head and invited her to go back into the house, the Firstborn princess boldly pressed her body against his and lifted her lips in the most elemental of pleas for grace.

But Thomas was fixed of purpose. He was gentle as he steered the young woman back toward the ball.

Three was an Igbo woman from Birmingham. She disavowed that she had any connection with the Lord Mayor there, who was the Elector, though that was a vote that was often cast by proxy. While lovely, she was the oldest of the seven, and also the calmest. She smiled, recited a lengthy poem in Igbo when asked, and talked about how much she missed the weather on the Gulf coast. When Thomas grew tired of equivocation and directly asked her about her family's wealth, she would only admit to owning a fishing boat.

By this time, Thomas had grown short-tempered. "Very well, then!" he snapped. "Enjoy the remainder of the ball!"

She smiled as she left.

At the door, Thomas met Temple Franklin. "What were you thinking?" he demanded. "She says she doesn't even *know* the Elector!"

"You said cash was more important!" The spectacles quivering on the tip of Franklin's nose made him look as if he were about to fall over under the force of Thomas's irritation.

"What cash?" Thomas snorted. "The woman owns a boat!"

"A boat?" Temple guffawed. "That's what she said to you?"

Thomas waited for Temple's rolling belly-laugh to end.

"That woman," Franklin finally explained, "is John Hancock's sole trading partner in Birmingham."

"She's a smuggler?"

"A very wealthy one."

"Who either didn't want to admit it, or isn't interested in an alliance with me."

Temple arched his eyebrows. "Shall I bring her back?"

"No," Thomas said quickly. "I was impolite, and she is uninterested. Bringing her back will only compound the offense by making me look stupid as well. Bring out the next lady."

Thomas instantly knew Two was Acadian from her growled Rs and pure vowel sounds. She was a cousin of La Fayette and her father was a banker. She claimed a talent for language, and without further provocation launched into a monolog that would have been at home among the workmen of Babel, shifting language every three sentences as she recounted her travels to London, Paris, and elsewhere with her father. Thomas followed her through English, French, and German with satisfaction, and then endured five minutes of gibberish that nearly left him unconscious.

He had finally convinced himself that he could tolerate this woman as a wife, especially if she would agree to stay in Quebec most of the year, when she concluded her oration on the delighted note that her father would be so pleased to see her make an alliance with the Penns, especially with the capitalization problems his banks had had in the last few years.

Thomas wished her and her father good luck, concealing the white knuckles of his clenched fists behind his back.

He recognized the last young woman with a shock, though he could not remember her name; she was the oldest daughter of Kimoni Machogu, Prince of Shreveport. She had her father's fierce stare and the curve of his lip that hinted at his piratical ancestry. Thomas listened to her genealogical recitation along with a surprisingly detailed inventory of facts about the cotton wealth of Shreveport and several songs. Finally, he wrapped both her hands in his and looked into her eyes.

"Please tell your mother and your father that I am trying very hard to marry a wealthy woman, so that I can bring as much help as I can to Shreveport, as quickly as possible. Are you going back home?"

The girl's hands trembled as she shook her head. "No, I am staying here, with my sisters."

"Good," Thomas said. "For now, that's wise."

Temple Franklin found him a few minutes later, leaning his forehead against the cool trunk of a magnolia tree and sinking his nails slowly into its bark.

"I take it none of them was a match," Temple said.

"You do so many things well," Thomas said slowly. "It turns out that finding a suitable bride for me is not one of them. Did you try the Lord of Potosí?"

"He's so wealthy, he's not interested in you."

"What about the silver miners in Georgia?"

"Ben Yehuda said he'd be willing to talk. How do you feel about wearing a little round cap and giving up pork?"

"I suppose I'd be willing to wear a cap."

"I rather think it's the other requirement that is non-negotiable."

"Next, he'll be wanting to discuss circumcision." Thomas sighed. "Well then, Temple, I think our course of action is obvious." He straightened, stretching the muscles of his back and looking up into the night sky for guidance. Obscured by winter clouds and the lights of Philadelphia, the stars gave him nothing. His burdens felt, if anything, heavier.

"I haven't yet consulted with the Anakim," Temple pointed out.

"The wealthiest of them will be the one with the largest pile of lake fish and otter's bones," Thomas said. "Not a help, however interesting it might be to make love to an eight-foot-tall red-headed woman with hands like coal scuttles and a bed perched atop a pole. No, our solution is rather nearer to hand, in New Amsterdam."

"You have someone in mind?"

Thomas nodded. "It's time to settle a lawsuit."

The Marqués's city house blazed with light, and Thomas couldn't bring himself to go back inside. Crossing abruptly to the edge of the garden and ignoring sudden yelps from Temple Franklin, he climbed the tall iron fence and vaulted over into the alley beyond.

He stalked across Philadelphia alone, with his Town Coat and his dress saber to protect him.

Three streets from Horse Hall, he collided with a staggering drunk. The man vomited on Thomas's shoes, then emitted an odor like that of a charnel house and something that might have been an apology, rolled into a single belch.

Thomas beat the man until he stopped moving.

He would marry, by damn. He would pay his bills. He would pacify the Ohio. He would hold the Empire together.

He would live up to the hopes of William Penn.

Ahmed Abd al-Wahid rose from prayer in the mamelukes' simple chamber, adorned only with mats for sleeping and prayer. Omar and al-Muhasib rose with him.

In the hall, Ravi sat with his face in a book. When Abd al-Wahid emerged, the Jew stood.

"The poet says, 'I have been a seeker and I still am, but I stopped asking the books and the stars. I started listening to the teaching of my soul.'" Abd al-Wahid smiled. "What are you reading?"

Ravi showed him the cover, with the English title embossed in silver: POOR RICHARD'S SERMONS.

"Is that Christian, O son of Isaac?" Abd al-Wahid was surprised at the thought that after all these years of exposure to the true faith, his Jewish companion might become a follower of the man from Galilee.

"Yes, O son of Ishmael, these are famous sermons written by a famous Christian priest of Philadelphia. But fear not, I have no interest in his words."

"What possible reason could you have for reading a book, if not the words contained therein?" Omar al-Talib asked. "When I read every book in al-Qayrawan, was it not for the sake of their words?"

"Your question about al-Qayrawan is fascinating," al-Muhasib said. "Tell us more about that experience. Which book was your favorite?"

"Who can love one star more than another?" Al-Talib shrugged. "Who can truly say that one flower has a more delicate scent than another?"

"I like lilies," al-Muhasib said.

"I read this book," Ravi said, "not for its words, but for its language." He switched suddenly to English. "'Love your enemies, for they tell you your faults.' 'Three may keep a secret, if two of them are dead.'"

Omar, who knew no English, frowned.

Al-Muhasib clapped Ravi on the shoulder and spoke in English as well. "Very good, my friend! I like the way you talk!"

Abd al-Wahid returned the conversation to Arabic. "And there is even wisdom in the words you have chosen. Well done, Ravi."

He turned and led them to the chevalier's audience chamber. The other three followed.

Omar snorted. "If I did not read the words in one of the books of al-Qayrawan, then the words cannot contain wisdom worth learning."

"'The way to see by faith,'" Ravi declared in English, "'is to shut the eye of reason!'"

"And the way to learn by hearing," Abd al-Wahid told him, "is to shut the jabbering mouth."

Ravi fell silent, but his smile was contented.

"How long do we remain here?" al-Muhasib asked. Al-Muhasib had two wives in Paris, and one of them was quite young.

"I've received a letter from the Caliph's secretary," Abd al-Wahid told him. "We are instructed to kill this Bishop Ukwu and then come home."

It was no longer a matter of Ahmed's own deal with the chevalier. Implied in the Caliph's missive: do not come home until you have killed the bishop.

Abd al-Wahid had no feeling about the matter; he didn't hate the young bishop. But he would do as he was ordered.

Only as he thought about the task, he realized that he *did* have a feeling; he felt camaraderie. He had chosen the mameluke warriors to come with him for their skills and by reputation, but, to his surprise, he found he had begun to think of them as his friends.

"If you had told me this before we began our attempts on this man's life, I would have pronounced it an easy task," Omar said. "Now, I am not so certain."

"A dagger between any man's ribs will bring his days to an end. Probably, Ravi's Richard the priest even says so in one of his sermons. It can only be a matter of bringing the dagger to the man."

They entered the audience room of the Chevalier of New Orleans. The discovery of the Vodun curse doll—and whatever the mambo had done to counteract its efficacy—had restored color to the chevalier's face and breath to his lungs. He looked up as the mamelukes entered with a folded letter with a large, official-looking seal.

He saw it only for a moment, but he thought the seal showed the eagle, rattlesnake, and cactus of New Spain.

"Thanks be to God," Abd al-Wahid said. "You are looking well."

"Thanks be to *you*," the chevalier answered.

"The witch also should receive credit," Abd al-Wahid said.

"I have been considering the challenge we face with our enemy, the bishop," the chevalier said. "And trying not to repeat previous errors."

"'Today is yesterday's pupil!'" Ravi blurted out in English.

The chevalier squinted at the Jew. "Are you quoting Bishop Franklin to me?" he asked, in the same language.

"Yes." Ravi grinned. "I am sorry."

The chevalier laughed. "You have been here too long. We must end this now. The challenge, as I see it, is that in destroying the cathedral, we have driven the beast from its lair rather than kill it. Now it stalks free in the woods, and we do not know where to seek it."

"We must make it come to us," Abd al-Wahid said.

"Agreed," the chevalier said. "And I believe I know just how to do that. In addition to you, my plan has two components. First, these men." He raised his voice and called out, "Come in!"

The door behind his desk opened and four men trooped in. They were unarmed, and they trooped slowly up to stand beside the mamelukes, one Frenchman with each mussulman warrior.

Abd al-Wahid saw it and laughed with immediate approval.

A few moments later, his comrades began to bob their heads up and down as they too began to understand the chevalier's thinking.

"And what is the other component, O Chevalier?" Abd al-Wahid asked.

"We only need one other thing, which is the bait. The thing to which the beast must come, sooner or later."

"And do you possess this bait?"

The chevalier laughed and rubbed his hands together. "Yes I do, my friend. Yes I do."

"He's not a hypocrite. And many love him."

—⊷•⊶—

CHAPTER TWO

Monsieur Bondí sang.

> *L'évêque s'en va-t-en guerre*
> *Mironton, mironton, mirontaine*
> *L'évêque s'en va-t-en guerre*
> *Ne sait où dormira*
> *Ne sait où dormira*
>
> *Il dormira par terre*
> *Mironton, mironton, mirontaine*
> *Il dormira par terre*
> *Ou dans la Pontchartrain*
> *Ou dans la Pontchartrain*

Etienne set down the hot pepper he was gnawing and laughed; to his own surprise, the song brought a lightness to his heart.

"Yes, that is the tune I heard. Poor John Churchill," he said, "that a beggar such as I should steal his glory second hand."

The two men sat in a dark room in the *Onu Nke Ihunanya*, a hotel within sight of Etienne's casino. Only a few days earlier, the chevalier's mamelukes had launched an attack on Etienne from this very room, with the assistance of a captive mambo.

The irony gave Etienne grim amusement, but it was the

direction of the Brides that brought him here. Through slitted shutters, he and Bondí watched as those same mamelukes stood watch on the street outside the casino. They were hidden in shops and taverns, no longer dressed in their scarves and black pourpoints, but Etienne knew them by their beards and their lean, staring faces.

They watched for Etienne.

"You aren't stealing it." Bondí shook his head. "The people are giving it to you. And you know what they are calling the song?"

"It should be 'L'évêque s'en va-t-en guerre,' no?" Etienne suggested. "As the original is 'Churchí s'en va-t-en guerre'?"

A third voice joined the conversation unexpectedly. "They call it 'Le sou de l'évêque,'" Onyinye Diokpo said, her eyes twinkling like the eyes of a grandmother on Christmas morning. "The Bishop's Penny. It is the penny you give them in lieu of the taxes the chevalier demands."

"Say rather that my father gives it to them." Suddenly, despite the fire the peppers stoked and the constant alluring susurrus of the Brides, Etienne felt exhausted. "They loved him."

"But he is dead," Diokpo said, "and you are fighting. He may be a saint, but only you can be a leader. Only you can wear the Big Crown—or *be* it."

Etienne laughed out loud at the hotelier's literal translation of his name. *Etienne* came from Greek *stephanos*, which was a crown; he knew no Greek, but his father, as former theology student, then as deacon, and finally as bishop, had repeatedly told him the name's meaning, urging his son to seek Paul's crown of rejoicing every day and after death, Peter's crown of glory.

It had been his mother, a mambo devotee of the loa Ezili Danto and Ezili Freda, and frequently their horse, who had never given up her faith, who had told him that the other name he had from his father—Ukwu—meant *big*. "Be big, Etienne," she had whispered to him as he sat on her lap in services in which his father officiated as deacon, "be great."

"Stephen Big." He chuckled. "Don't tell the Irishmen. They'll never let me hear the end of it."

"How long?" Onyinye asked. A member of New Orleans's City Council, she had joined the revolt against the chevalier's taxing authority; in response, the chevalier had ordered the council disbanded. Now Renan DuBois and Holahta Hopaii increasingly stayed away, avoiding New Orleans entirely, leaving Onyinye and Eoin Kennedie effectively as the City Council, working with Etienne clandestinely. "How long do you think the chevalier will allow the casino to continue to operate?"

Etienne shook his head. "He won't shut it down. For the moment, he hopes to flush me from hiding. When he gives up on that, he'll be too anxious for revenue to destroy the casino. He'll try to take control of it instead."

"Also," Onyinye said by way of concurrence, "he won't want to offend the casino's clientele."

Etienne ruminated on that thought.

"You're not going to let him have that money, are you?" Bondí said.

"You could move the gaming activities into my hotels," Diokpo suggested. "I do not fear the chevalier. My god is as great as his."

"It is not a question of gods," Etienne said. "The only thing that protects your wealth from the chevalier right now is that he can't be sure which hotels belong to you. As it is, how many has he discovered and seized?"

"Too many."

"Too many. Let us not attract attention to the others by setting up casino operations in their foyers."

"Or, for that matter," Onyinye said, "mass."

"Tents and street corners will suffice for church services," Etienne said. "But we control the rebuilding of the cathedral."

Bondí grunted agreement. "We'll want to make sure that whoever does the accounts of the casino reports to us."

"A corrupt accountant," Etienne said. "St. Bernardo de Pacioli forbid."

Bondí chuckled. What neither of them said, because Onyinye Diokpo didn't know it and didn't need to know it, was that an underground passage connected the casino and the cathedral site. If Etienne could control the accounting of the casino, he could easily smuggle cash out through the church.

"This is a savage game," Onyinye said. "Who will starve to death first, the chevalier or the bishop?"

"Oh no," Etienne corrected her, "it is considerably more savage than that. The chevalier and I each have a hand on the other's throat and we are crushing each other's windpipes. His hand is brutal force, exercised in the name of good order; my hand is corruption, fostered under the auspices of heaven. One of us will die of suffocation sooner or later."

"If neither of you manages to stab the other in the belly first," Onyinye concluded.

"And we definitely intend to stab the chevalier in the belly. I am, after all, houngan asogwe of the Société du Mars Vengeur. Vengeur, not Mars Danseur or Mars Frivole. But speaking of savage games, Onyinye...I have had a question about you in my mind for a few days now."

Onyinye arched an eyebrow of acknowledgement. "Tell me."

"Your man who died in this hotel," Etienne said. "He had his throat slit, as if by ambush. And yet, the ambush was ours, perpetrated upon the mamelukes."

"Are you asking whether I killed my own cousin?" Onyinye smiled.

"Yes."

"In that case, I have a question for you, Stephen Big."

Etienne nodded his consent.

"The Synod appointed you bishop very quickly upon your father's death. And I have heard it said that they were doing your bidding."

"Are you asking whether I was seeking the office while my father was still alive?" Etienne asked.

"Yes."

Etienne smiled. He didn't want to explain that his mother, his gede loa, had urged him to take steps to become bishop even while his father was alive. He didn't want to reveal his connection with her, or with the Brides, unless necessary.

So instead, he laughed. Onyinye laughed with him.

"So we both have questions," Etienne said. "How goes your work with the pawnbrokers, Monsieur Bondí?"

"It goes," he said. "We must choose our candidates carefully."

"But you have good prospects?" Etienne asked.

"I like a certain Frenchman. And I think there's a Jamaican who might do. He certainly has the enthusiasm for the job. It's still far too early to tell."

Etienne nodded. "The pious, I think, are with me." He felt the Brides stirring within him. "Ironically. They are for me because they were for my father. I should like to have more of the wealthy on my side."

"Perhaps you should think about establishing another casino, then," Bondí suggested. "We could keep it secret. Or we could put it in a tent, as well. Or outside the city, on a boat."

"I think you had it right the first time," Etienne said. "I think it's time for me to think about who is sleeping in the Pontchartrain."

"Party from Philadelphia for you," Schäfer said. He was a good agent, a Youngstown German with a keen eye for quality in beaver pelts. Behind him in the open tent door stood Dadgayadoh, a Haudenosaunee tracker and factor who wore a red blanket over his shoulders and a silk top hat on his head. Director Notwithstanding Schmidt trusted these men more than she trusted the militia under her command; they were Company men, and had been with her for years.

They'd been with her longer than Luman Walters, the magician she had briefly made her aide-de-magie, before the combination of his impatience and her desire for a stronger wizard had driven him away. She had gotten her stronger magician, in the form of the walking corpse Robert Hooke.

Whom she trusted least of all.

"Courier?" She set aside her quill pen and carefully placed her hands to either side of the book of accounts, so as not to smudge the ink.

Dadgayadoh shook his head. "Hotgö'."

"Wizards," Schäfer added, rather more helpfully.

"Earlier than I expected." Schmidt stood and strode from her tent.

Her men were accustomed to her brusque pace. Schäfer immediately pointed in the direction of the Imperial arrivals, away from the Mississippi and the alien Treewall of Cahokia. Both traders paced the director step for step, one on either side of her.

Schmidt had learned two lessons early in her days with the Imperial Ohio Company. The first was that she must give direction early and often, and ask for it almost never; the second was that she must move quickly and show energy at all times. If she failed to do those two things, men saw her as a heavy woman and expected her to be slow, torpid, and passive.

If she succeeded in doing those two things, she took men by surprise. She much preferred taking men by surprise.

Always.

In a way, it was a lesson she had first learned from her father. After attaching himself to one charismatic prophet too many, he'd been disfellowshipped by the Ministerium. He promptly began redistributing the pain he felt from the separation, inflicting it on his wife and daughter by physical beatings. His wife had faded, died inside, and taken the beatings with little complaint. Her daughter had resisted the beatings and being called *knothead* in grim silence for years before she tried to run away.

He'd chased her and brought her back once, and then a second time.

The third time he chased her to bring her back to more pain and insult, he'd found her camped along the banks of the Wabash with a man named Joe Duncan. This time, Notwithstanding had stolen all the money she could on her journey and had hired Duncan, a man of no morals or fixed abode, to be her bodyguard. At her instruction, Joe Duncan had taken her father by surprise and killed him, sinking an Arkansas Toothpick into his belly.

That same night, when Duncan had tried to force Notwithstanding to submit to his lecherous attentions, she had surprised and killed him in turn. She'd hit him in the head with a horseshoe, something she never could have brought herself to do to her father.

She had buried the two men in a single muddy grave.

Notwithstanding Schmidt called her canoe or her horse—her principal means of travel—*Joe Duncan* as a perpetual reminder. Freedom was necessary. Power was necessary.

Even if the means to acquire them was a crime.

She looked about as she crossed her camp. On three sides of Cahokia, she and her Imperial forces had besieged the city. Its gates were shut. Its gray-caped defenders glowered down from the tops of its wooden Treewall, their cheeks pitted by hunger. A hundred yards of mud- and blood-stained snow surrounded the city's wall, and beyond that lay the trenches Schmidt's men had dug.

Warfare of any kind was not Schmidt's métier. She had had the trenches dug after the turncoat Imperial artillerists within the walls had demonstrated their ability to kill her men with impunity. Within the trenches, huddling in shadow during daylight hours, were corpses. Walking dead. Not Lazars like Robert Hooke, who seemed preserved and was articulate, but shambling, moaning draug who rotted, festered with worms, and fell apart. Their preference for avoiding direct sunlight meant they drove all but the strongest-willed and -stomached of her men from the trenches during the day; at night, the draug dragged themselves about the base of the city's walls, groaning and scratching like homeless burrowing beasts.

Behind the trenches were tents, and in the tents, milling restlessly about, were the Imperial Ohio Company militia. The best of these men were used to protecting markets in border towns and guarding caravans from Wild Algonk or Comanche depredation, and had never participated in anything like a siege.

The worst of them had been prisoners only two months earlier and could hardly be kept from knifing each other over the bad roll of a sheep's knucklebone. They were far better put to use as marauders and looters in the seven Sister Kingdoms.

The only reason the Cahokians hadn't broken the siege was that they themselves were few and poorly organized, a town watch or the private bodyguards of the city's wealthier citizens. Also, on the fourth side, the city faced the river. The river and its banks teemed with braying and howling beastkind. What had once been an ordered and thriving array of wharves lay shattered like split kindling, obscured by the steam rising from the bodies of slinking beasts.

Because of the marauding beastkind, Imperials had to approach their camp overland. Schmidt had commandeered and then expanded the docks of a fishing village five miles downstream, protecting it with one of her best militia corps; she now reached the head of the path that led to that village and found the arrivals from Philadelphia.

"I had expected gramarists," she said. "University men. Who are you?"

Three young men—no older than sixteen, and maybe not that old—gazed serenely at her. Their heads were all shaven and bore the same swirling tattoos in bright blue ink. They wore a uniform that was unmistakably Imperial without bearing any insignia whatsoever: Imperial blue breeches, waistcoats, coats, stockings, and shirts.

Their faces were identical.

Then they opened their mouths and spoke in unison. "WE ARE THE PARLETT QUINTUPLETS. LORD THOMAS SENDS US."

Behind the three young men stood a squad of Imperial soldiers. They looked as nonplussed as Schmidt felt. Their officer, a long-limbed man with thick eyebrows and a high, nearly vertical forehead, stepped forward. "Are you Director Schmidt?"

Schmidt nodded.

"Captain Onacona Mohuntubby." The captain saluted. "I've brought the Parletts here safely, and I'm ordered to place myself under your command."

"Cherokee?" Schmidt asked. It paid to recognize names, kinships, and peoples of the Empire. Those were the unofficial and invisible networks of capital and power that lay alongside the more formal structures of courts, companies, and Electors.

Mohuntubby nodded.

"Quintuplets means five," Schmidt said. "Looks to me like you lost two of them."

"WE ARE TWO IN PHILADELPHIA," the Parletts announced. "AND THREE IN THE OHIO."

"You are the means by which My Lord President will communicate to me?" Despite the heavy blue coat over her shoulders, the winter chill bit into Schmidt's flesh. She resisted the urge to shiver by sheer force of will.

The three Parletts abruptly changed facial expression, the vacant serenity replaced by a grimace that would have looked more at home on the face of an old curmudgeon. "DIRECTOR SCHMIDT," they growled, their voices changing tone as well, "THIS IS TEMPLE FRANKLIN. DO YOU REMEMBER ME?"

Captain Mohuntubby took an abrupt step backward and dropped his hand to the sword hilt at his belt.

Schmidt nodded. "I remember you." Franklin had no official title or form of address; he was Thomas Penn's éminence grise, his Machiavel.

The Parletts laughed, a sound like a rusted hinge swinging slowly. "THE PARLETT QUINTUPLETS WERE GIVEN BY THEIR PARENTS TO THE IMPERIAL COLLEGE OF MAGIC AT BIRTH."

"I'm not good at dealing with children," Schmidt said. "I can never remember their names."

"THE PARLETTS DO NOT HAVE INDIVIDUAL NAMES. I AM INFORMED BY COLLEGE GRAMARISTS THAT THEY DO NOT EVEN HAVE INDIVIDUAL SOULS. THEIR SHARING OF

A SINGLE MIND IS WHAT WILL ENABLE OUR COMMUNICA-
TION OVER THE GREAT DISTANCE THAT SEPARATES US."

"And I will deal with Lord Thomas through you?"

"OR THOMAS HIMSELF MAY SPEAK WITH YOU THROUGH
THE PARLETTS. THEY ARE IN A SAFE PLACE, A PLACE TO
WHICH ONLY HE AND I AND A FEW TRUSTED SERVANTS
HAVE ACCESS."

Horse Hall? But it didn't matter. "I assume you have two of
the quintuplets?"

"WE BELIEVE THAT IF ONE DIES, THE OTHERS WILL
SURVIVE AND REMAIN IN CONTACT. WE HAVE KEPT TWO
HERE TO GIVE US A MARGIN OF SAFETY, IF SOMETHING
SHOULD HAPPEN TO ONE OF THEM."

"And I get three because the Ohio is the more dangerous end."

"CONSIDERABLY MORE DANGEROUS, DIRECTOR. AND
IF THE MIMICRY OF THE PARLETTS IS TO BE BELIEVED,
YOU ALSO HAVE A CONSIDERABLY MORE MELODIOUS
VOICE THAN I." The Parletts twisted their faces into something
that might have been a leer.

Schmidt laughed. "Then they are liars through and through,
Franklin, and you had better come up with another means to
stay in touch."

The Parletts bellowed their raucous imitation of Temple
Franklin's laughter.

"LORD THOMAS IS SENDING THE PROMISED REIN-
FORCEMENTS."

"More than this one squad, I hope. Competent as Captain
Mohuntubby appears, I think he'll have his hands too full protecting the Parletts to be able to effectively besiege Cahokia."

"INFANTRY AND MOLLY PITCHERS."

"Good. We have a wall to batter down."

"THE MILITARY WILL BE UNDER THE COMMAND OF
GENERAL SAYLE."

"The Roundhead? The cannoneer? I hate a fanatic."

"SAYLE IS NOT A FANATIC. YOU WILL HAVE DIRECTION
OF THE CIVIL GOVERNMENT ONCE CAHOKIA CEASES ITS
REBELLION AND SURRENDERS."

Schmidt managed not to sigh. Sayle *was* a fanatic; if not for
a saint, then for a strategy. "The company has the experience to
manage that."

"AND *YOU* HAVE THE EXPERIENCE, DIRECTOR SCHMIDT. LORD THOMAS BIDS ME TO TELL YOU THAT HE IS PLEASED. AND ALSO THAT . . . HE DOES NOT BELIEVE THE COMPANY TRULY NEEDS FIVE DIRECTORS."

Schmidt kept a calm face, though her heart leaped. "I understand."

"DO YOU NEED ANYTHING ELSE FROM US AT THIS TIME?"

"No," Schmidt said. Should she mention her connection with Robert Hooke and his shuffling undead soldiers? "Nothing that can't wait. I assume I can contact you through the Parletts at any time?"

"SOMEONE WILL ALWAYS BE LISTENING ON THIS END. PLEASE ARRANGE THE SAME ON YOUR SIDE."

"Understood." Schmidt turned to her own men. "Schäfer, Dadgayadoh—put the Parletts in a tent adjoining mine, and make sure they have all the necessaries. Food, clothing, cots and blankets . . . dolls, hoops, pull-horses, whatever they need. If you need to send marauders back through the lands we've sacked looking for toys we left behind, do so. I'll want one of you with them at all times. If they start talking as they did just now, I want to know about it immediately. Captain Mohuntubby, I'll leave it to you to provide for security."

Shouts from the direction of the besieged city's eastern gate caught her ear. She turned as the Cherokee officer and his men followed her two traders back toward camp. At the militia barricade over the eastern road milled a knot of people in robes that had once been white but had been stained gray and brown by winter and travel. A blue cordon of Imperial uniforms held back the knot, which seemed to be trying to make its way into the city.

Schmidt approached the scene at her usual brisk pace.

She counted twelve robed travelers, all on foot, all men. None of them younger than forty, by her guess. Eleven of them stood, leaning on walking sticks. Their backs were bent by fatigue, but the light of conviction burned in their eyes.

The twelfth knelt.

He had been kneeling for some time, by appearances. His robe had been torn to shreds by walking on his knees; the knees themselves were purple and covered with skin so thick and callused that they wouldn't have looked out of place on a camel. His eyes were sunken into deep wells flanked by bony cheeks and gnarled brows; both ears and nose looked half again too large for his face. Long gray hair and a gray beard hung back over his shoulders, presumably so he wouldn't pull his own face into the frozen mud by kneeling on the hairs of his chin.

Schmidt sighed.

She whistled sharply around her fingers as she stomped up, which was enough signal for the militiamen to clear a space for her. The mud-spattered apostles in white cleared a space opposing, and she abruptly found herself looking down at the filthy old man kneeling in the snow. All twelve men in white were unarmed.

"You don't look dangerous," she said. "If you're hungry, I can arrange for you to get a meal."

The old man laughed slowly. "I look like a beggar." His eleven companions laughed with him.

"Yes," Schmidt said flatly.

"I don't want your crusts and pottage." The old man pointed at the Treewall. Gray-caped shoulders and shining sallet helmets visible over the ramparts suggested Cahokian interest in the conversation. "I only want passage."

"I am besieging the city."

The old man raised his arms. "My name is Zadok, though most call me Metropolitan Tarami, or simply Father. Do I look like a threat to your siege?"

Schmidt hooked her thumbs into her broad leather belt. "Not all threats are visible. Who are you?"

At that moment, Robert Hooke arrived. The eleven standing men in white shrank from his presence; the militiamen, freed murderers, road agents, and rapists, by and large, grinned in appreciation.

He stinks of piety, the Lazar's voice rang in Schmidt's mind, *but not of gramarye.*

She had no way of knowing whether others could hear Hooke's words, so she kept her nod discreet.

"I am the kingdom's ranking priest," Zadok Tarami said. "Or ranking secular priest, at least. I preside in the Basilica and, when they are Christian, I hear the confessions of the kings and queens of Cahokia."

When they are Christian? Schmidt refrained from laughing out loud, thinking of the wild paganism of Cahokia's temple. The serpent-tree behind the open veil, the star mosaics. "Does the Metropolitan of Cahokia ordinarily travel about on his knees, in

winter? I understand the Moundbuilder kingdoms are impoverished in these sad times of revolt and Pacification, but I thought
they could at least afford *feet.*"

"I return from pilgrimage," the priest said. "I have come the
entire road of the great Onandagos, from the borders of the Talligewi to the hill where the prophet finally pinned the serpent
and stole its crown."

"Your sense of geography is confused, cleric," Schmidt said.
"This is the flattest place on the continent. The only hills are the
ones you people *built.*"

"God tells me that you will admit me. Your heart is touched,
I can see."

Schmidt frowned. "Did you travel the entire road on your
knees?"

Tarami nodded. "I have seen all seven kingdoms. I have lain
quartered twice on the crosses of the earth itself. I have done
this not for myself, but begging heaven for its blessing upon my
people."

He can only hurt the serpent's daughter, Hooke whispered into
her mind. *It does no harm to admit these fools. At the very least
they are more Firstborn mouths to feed.*

Unexpectedly, Schmidt found herself missing Luman Walters.
Hooke's advice rang true, but it bore a hard edge of arrogance.
Also, it completely lacked the warmth and humor of her banter
with Walters.

Whither had her Balaam gone? In the confusion of the beginning of the siege, Notwithstanding Schmidt hadn't followed the
magician's movements. He might have gone upriver or down or
across the water into the Missouri, or even into the city itself
for all she knew.

She could ask Hooke, but Luman's whereabouts seemed none
of the Sorcerer's business.

"You eleven," she said, addressing the standing men. "I will
give you your bowl of curds, and then you must leave. Take any
road you like, but go away." The men looked relieved; had they
expected her to kill them on the spot?

"And I?" Zadok Tarami asked.

"No pottage for you," she said. "But if the Cahokians will
take you in, you are welcome to enter the city."

✧   ✧   ✧

Flanked by Alzbieta Torias and Cathy Filmer, Sarah looked down from the height of the Treewall. The soldiers in blue retreated into their trenches—which also crawled, she knew, with dead abominations no less repulsive than Robert Hooke himself, though mute and rotting—or into their tents beyond. A single figure in gray was left on the road.

Kneeling.

On his knees, he then continued his approach alone.

"Who is that?" Sarah raised the bandage from her Eye of Eve and saw the soul of the approaching man as the shining blue aura of one of the Firstborn, the children of Wisdom.

Only she now knew that Eve and Wisdom were the same person.

Or did she know that, after all?

The more she learned, the more the world seemed an insoluble enigma.

"That can only be one man." Alzbieta's voice was sharp. "He undertook a difficult journey, and I was beginning to be optimistic that it had killed him."

"An enemy of yours?" Cathy's voice was always cold when she spoke to Alzbieta.

"An enemy of Kyres Elytharias," Alzbieta said.

Sarah looked quickly at the priestess and found honesty visible in her soul. "A pretender?"

Cathy laughed. "No, that would be Alzbieta Torias."

"A priest. A rebel." Alzbieta lowered her head humbly. "Your grandfather...your father's father...became king at a very young age. He fell under the influence of certain thinkers, men who were powerful and...dissatisfied."

"Dissatisfied how?" Sarah asked. If this was some would-be rival, at least he was approaching on his knees. She could have him shot easily, if she had good reason for doing so. "You alluded to this once, as we rode to Cahokia together. You said my father's father tried to eradicate priesthoods and secrets."

"Dissatisfied with the goddess. Dissatisfied with the constitution of the kingdom. Dissatisfied with the spiritual life of Cahokia. Dissatisfied with the way the tale of the great prophet-king Onandagos had always been told. Dissatisfied with the differences separating us from the children of Eve."

"These men were priests?" Sarah asked.

"Some of them, yes. Including the leading priests of the

Basilica, which to this day continues to harbor and train more priests who think this way. But some were also wealthy men, men with land, men in the royal family. Philosophers. Poets. And there were influential men in the other six Sister Kingdoms who felt the same way. We were drawing closer to the Cavaliers and the Roundheads and the Ferdinandians and others in those days. Appalachee was becoming less a barrier and more a highway. The ghosts of the Kentuck were fading into oblivion. It seemed likely that some sort of close alliance was going to come to pass, perhaps even union, and it was felt that our differences might stand in the way of that consummation."

"Differences such as...?" Cathy pressed.

"The goddess," Sarah said. "Or really, the throne. It's one thing to read the Bible in a private way and tell each other that Wisdom or the Spirit or the Serpent refer to your goddess. It's something else to have a golden serpent in a temple."

Sarah had done much thinking about that throne.

Cathy nodded.

"It is indeed...something else." Alzbieta's face was grave and her voice quiet. "These would-be reformers thought we would be seen like Odin-worshippers of Chicago and Waukegan, pagans and unbelievers. They felt shame, perhaps. Fear. Lack of confidence."

The kneeling figure had covered a third of the ground from the trenches to the gate. Soon, Sarah would have to make a decision.

Were those streaks of blood behind him in the snow?

She looked to the barbican tower over the gate and saw the men within it gazing back at her, waiting for a signal.

"But the Serpent Throne still stands," Sarah said. "No one tore it down. No one burned down the temple."

"Not for want of trying. This was before my day, of course, but I heard the stories. Men with torches and pry bars assaulted the temple. Its groves were uprooted and burned to ash, the ashes trampled underfoot. Cahokia's two great priesthoods—the one serving Father and Son, and the one serving the Virgin—split as they had never split before. Blood was shed. Women of great honor were humiliated and enslaved."

"The veil," Sarah said.

"The great veil was torn down," Alzbieta agreed. "Your father later hung a new one in its place. He never closed it. Presumably, the goddess told him not to."

"Why would She do that?" Sarah asked.

"Perhaps we are not yet ready for Her presence." Alzbieta shook her head. "Perhaps this is what you can accomplish here, Beloved."

"But the... rebels," Sarah continued. "They couldn't deny the goddess, surely? Where do they think they come from?"

"Most men don't experience their gods as you have been privileged to do, Beloved." Alzbieta spoke slowly, and her use of the title Beloved underscored the fact that Sarah too was a priestess of Alzbieta's goddess, a goddess they both had seen.

A priesthood about which Sarah knew practically nothing. But something about Sarah's priesthood, her status as the goddess's Beloved, or her vision of Eden, had changed her.

Sarah's stomach turned at the mere thought of meat, and she could not bring herself to touch it. And, no matter how tired she became, she could only sleep atop the Great Mound.

What had happened to her?

"Then... the stories you told me of the great migration west, the building of the temple and the church side by side?"

"The rebels tell another story, about a flight west plagued by a demonic serpent. About a race of men descended from the serpent, who bear its mark on their very souls to this day, and whose blood boils because of the serpent's corruption still flowing within them. About a king who slew the serpent and sat upon her to crown himself, not as a sign of solidarity and kinship, but as a mark of conquest and redemption from his corrupted birth. About a line of kings whose great triumph is to keep serpents at bay. About a people who had outgrown the serpent throne, and all their former private, sacred things."

"That makes the rebels sound heroic," Sarah said. "A little like Moses, breaking up the golden calf and forcing the sinners to drink it."

"But Moses raised the serpent," Alzbieta pointed out.

"Maybe a little like the New Light," Cathy added, her voice softening.

Alzbieta shrugged. "The Campbells and Barton Stone may have taken some inspiration from the rebels against the goddess of Cahokia. I don't know. But the children of Adam have never had a shortage of men who wish to tear down all that prior generations have built, in the name of freedom, or virtue, or progress, or conscience. And in that tearing down, Peter Plowshare was pushed away and the truths we knew about him were forgotten. Our children were taught the language of William Penn, rather than the language of Onandagos. And many important things were lost."

Sarah pointed down at the crawling figure. "And that man? Is he a man of conscience?"

Alzbieta was slow to answer. "He's not a hypocrite," she finally said. "Many love him."

"And what's the difficult journey he undertook?"

"The Onandagos Road. It's a sunwise path that crosses all seven Sister Kingdoms, beginning at the far edge of the Talega lands in the north and east, and touching at points where important events are believed to have taken place in the life of the great prophet. It finally enters Cahokia through the eastern gate—the Ohio Gate, though before your grandfather's time, it was more commonly called the Onandagos Gate. The true final length of the Onandagos Road travels from the Onandagos Gate to the Temple of the Sun, though I think he will not finish his pilgrimage that way."

"No?" Sarah asked.

Alzbieta shook her head. "He will go to the Basilica. The comfortably pious make that journey on horseback. The path is not straight, and travels some eight hundred miles, weaving north and south as it pushes continually westward. Only the truly religious do it on foot."

"And am I to understand that this man traveled the Onandagos Road on his knees?" Sarah asked.

"He's not a liar," Alzbieta said.

Sarah watched the crawling man crossing the last thirty yards to the Ohio—or Onandagos—Gate. "What's his name?" she asked.

"Zadok Tarami," Alzbieta said. "Father Tarami. He's the Metropolitan of Cahokia. The Basilica is his church. Tradition would have him your confessor. He would have been your father's confessor, only your father insisted on his Cetean friend, in defiance of his father."

"Zadok doesn't sound like a Firstborn name."

"It's a Hebrew name. The name is that of David's priest in the Old Testament. He took the name on his ordination to the priesthood. Many of his party take old Hebrew names. The names of priests and prophets—Josiah, Jehu, Hezekiah, Elijah—are all popular."

"The breakers of idols," Cathy murmured.

"It is how they see themselves."

"He's not old enough to have been tearing down veils in my grandfather's time," Sarah said.

"He's of the generation that came after. More compassionate, maybe. No less principled or dogmatic."

"The generation my father fought against?"

"Yes. Your grandfather was chosen as the Beloved as a child, but later the goddess abandoned him. It was a shocking thing, unheard of."

Sarah's heart hurt even imagining such a loss. "She abandoned him during the rebellion?"

"*Because* of the rebellion, some said. Others convinced themselves that there had never been such a thing as the Beloved, that it was only a silly old idea they had all believed in because their fathers told it to them."

"And the subsequent Beloved must have been a woman," Sarah said. "She alternates in Her choice, does She not?"

Alzbieta nodded. "Your grandfather was followed by a cousin of yours. She was a learned and kind Handmaid of the goddess, who after becoming the Beloved lived out her life in fear and seclusion. All Cahokia—all Cahokia that still believed—knew she was the Beloved, and it availed her nothing. She lived in darkness and died a failure. She never wore the crown."

Alzbieta's voice was wounded.

"Did you know her?" Cathy asked.

Alzbieta hesitated. "She was my mother. From a young age, I never left her side and we never left the temple. When she died, she was mad. Some whispered of poison, but I think that seclusion would have been enough."

Sarah blinked back sudden tears in the corners of her eyes. "And then the goddess chose my father. Unexpectedly."

"He was young and reckless. Some regarded him as a fool and an adventurer, a dashing younger son who might make a good career as a soldier but could never be a statesman. Some expected the goddess's choice to fall on an older brother. Others expected that there would be no more Beloveds. But Kyres proved them all wrong. He became Beloved and king."

"He didn't drive out the rebels against his goddess."

"He drove them from Her temple. And his virtue and prowess

silenced them. Who would raise his hand against such a king, a dealer of justice and a hero in war, a man who could ride to far Philadelphia and marry an empress? And then he was gone."

Questions piled into Sarah's mind, but most of them would have to wait. "And Tarami. Why did he travel the Onandagos Road?" she asked.

"*The Law of the Way* says 'Blessed is he that walketh the sunwise road of the king, for he shall be given the grip of peace.'"

"He wrecked himself like that . . . for scripture?" Sarah found the idea hard to believe.

Alzbieta shrugged. "Who can guess what's in a man's heart? A pilgrim making such a journey accrues fame and experience and may make interesting alliances on the road. Perhaps he hoped his pilgrimage would re-ignite the fires of rebellion, or at least inspire others to follow him. I can tell you that on his departure, he prayed publicly that God would lift the Pacification."

"Don't let him in," Cathy Filmer said. "Men of too strict principle are dangerous."

"I agree," Alzbieta said. "Zadok Tarami is not your friend. With the Imperials camped around the city, you have every reason to bar his entry. For all you know, he could have been corrupted by your Uncle Thomas. He could be a spy, or a traitor."

As he reached the great eastern gate of the city, Zadok Tarami reached forward to touch the wood. Losing his balance, he fell on his face in the snow and the mud.

Sarah raised her arm and gestured to the men in the barbican. "Open the gate!"

New Amsterdam sprouted like a disordered hedge along the opposite shore of the Hudson River. Kinta Jane Embry shivered, huddling deep into the wool cloak around her shoulders. As the ferry bumped against the wood of the dock, the yapping beagle on its broad deck fell silent. It stared at Kinta Jane with wide eyes, wrinkled its nose as if smelling something offensive, and then bolted to the far side of the vessel.

"Are we in Pennsland still?" she asked Isaiah Wilkes in a whisper.

They both wore disguises, of a sort. Wilkes had stained the skin of his face and hands a reddish brown, and for days he had responded to all attempts to communicate with him by grunting and shaking his head. It worked; even real Indians took him for members of some tribe they didn't know and left him alone after an attempt or two. Kinta Jane, meanwhile, wore a false beard made of horsehair the actor had given her, and pretended she was deaf and mute.

It was an easy charade.

They stood now on a boardwalk over the ice-choked Hudson with the flow of traffic disembarking from the ferry out of earshot. Still, they looked out over the river so no one could see their mouths move and they spoke in low voices.

"Farther up, starting at the Tappan Zee, the Republic straddles both sides of the river. Here, you and I still stand on this land at the sufferance of Lord Thomas. It was not far north of here that William Penn, on a day dictated by the stars, began his miraculous walk that convinced the Lenni Lenape and others that the land grant to him was ordained of heaven, as well as by the ruler of England."

"Lord Thomas." Kinta Jane grunted. "Whom you called *Brother Onas*."

Isaiah Wilkes turned slightly to her and smiled. "You've been patient."

"Was it a test?" she asked. "If so, it was an easy one. You know I was trained not to ask some questions."

"You experienced Franklin's Vision," he said. "Do you remember much of it?"

"Mostly the sensations," she admitted. "Chaos and doubt at the return of Simon Sword, fear of death, a world turned upside down and then destroyed before it can be reborn."

Wilkes nodded. "Many remember less than that. Let me tell you the story of Brother Onas."

Kinta Jane waited.

"Once there were three brothers," Wilkes began. "They were neighbors as well as brothers, and they all lived on land that belonged to the same landlord."

Kinta Jane frowned. "Not the Penns."

Wilkes snorted. "Not the Penns. The landlord was a kind and benevolent ruler. When one of the brothers arrived from a distant land, he brought illness with him. The illness would have struck down the other two brothers, but the landlord was a magician of serious power, and he healed them."

"What kind of brothers were these, if one came from a distant land?" Kinta Jane asked.

Wilkes continued. "Their names were Onas, Anak, and Odish-kwa. They were brothers, though they shared no father and no mother. One day, their landlord's wife died, and in grief he went mad. He tore up the brothers' paths and shattered the boundaries between their lands. He planted hatred between them and brought them to blows. He drove one brother into the swamps, the second to the frozen lands of the far north, and the third deep into the woods to hide. The brothers and their families skulked separately, eating carrion and berries and hoping the landlord would die.

"But he didn't die. Instead, he grew more and more terrifying. He took the brothers' women. He ate their children, after sacrificing them on stone altars to himself, and he engulfed all his land in a perpetual storm so great that it made the very earth tremble."

"Well, *now* he doesn't sound like one of the Penns," Kinta Jane said.

"Rivers ran uphill. Fire froze and water burned. The air was too heavy with smoke to breathe, and the ash was so thick on the ground that nothing would grow. Finally, one of the brothers saw that the landlord would have to be confronted. He set out in the blighted world and after many obstacles he managed to gather his two brothers to his side again."

"Which brother was it?" Kinta Jane asked.

Isaiah Wilkes chuckled. "The story is told three different ways, so maybe it is all the brothers. For our telling's sake, let us say it was Brother Onas. And Brother Onas's great insight was that the landlord could be calmed again if he were to remarry. Only the landlord was of noble birth and couldn't marry just anyone; he had to marry a princess of the same lineage as his first wife.

"While two of the brothers fought the landlord to distract and delay him, the third brother—we shall say it was Brother Onas—crept into the halls of the landlord himself. There he found imprisoned a princess of the lineage to which the landlord was bound. Freeing her, he brought about the landlord's marriage, and the landlord regained his sanity."

"In a ruined world," Kinta Jane pointed out.

"But you are forgetting what a great magician the landlord

was," Wilkes said. "By his art, the brothers' wives rose from the dead, and their children sprang whole and unsacrificed from the altars. The land was healed and reborn. Some even say that such a death and rebirth is necessary for the land, just as a death and rebirth is necessary for the children of Adam."

"Do you mean baptism?" Kinta Jane was surprised to hear religious talk from the Franklin.

"That's one possibility," Wilkes said. "And so the brothers, fearing the return of the landlord's madness, swore an oath. The brother from a distant land—Brother Onas—was granted by the other two as much land as he could walk in a day. Fortified by the restored landlord, he walked a great distance. The brothers agreed they would tell their sons the tale of the landlord's loss, illness, and redemption, in such a manner that if the landlord went mad again—and some say it was inevitable that he would do so—there would always be a Brother Onas, a Brother Anak, and a Brother Odishkwa with the lore and the will to restore the natural order."

"Franklin's Vision is the landlord's madness," Kinta Jane said.

"And Brother Onas has forgotten his lore and his will."

"Are Brother Anak and Brother Odishkwa in New Amsterdam?"

"No, they are north and west of here." The Franklin's face softened into a smile. "There is a meeting place, at the edges of the Acadian city of Montreal. Beneath a column of rock shaped like a centaur is a hidden chimney, and through that chimney lies a cave where the three brothers meet. We are going to that cave, Kinta Jane, and we will signal Brothers Anak and Odishkwa that we wish to meet. But our way lies through the Hudson River Republic. If we are fortunate, we may find allies to help us."

"Why on earth do you need me?" she asked, feeling small in the face of these strange stories. "You know the lands and the tales and the people. You are a master of disguise. What can I possibly do to help?"

"For one thing," Isaiah Wilkes said, "you speak French."

"You speak ill of the dead."

———◦———

CHAPTER THREE

Luman Walters was hungry.

Not metaphorically hungry. Not hungry with the desire for knowledge, which was part of what had driven him to leave his mostly effective and reasonably comfortable working relationship with Notwithstanding Schmidt and slip within the walls of Cahokia, just before the gates had all been raised.

He was physically hungry.

There was food within the Treewall, but very, very little. Private stores were being rationed out. Animals were kept indoors by their owners, until those owners themselves were prepared to slaughter them.

Children, as yet, were permitted to be outdoors. Given the snow that blocked the streets, most of them stayed inside. Those who were outside traveled in ragged gangs. Luman did his best to avoid them . . . just in case.

Luman felt guilt at the thought of taking food from any Cahokian mouth. He had no right to be here. He had resolved that he would both fight to defend the city, when the time came, and also not consume its resources.

He had eaten one rat, trapping it himself with a bit of braucherei. It had a sour flavor, but Luman was hungry enough that he'd have done it again, if he'd seen any more rats.

He hadn't.

Instead, he repeatedly sang a short braucher prayer that was supposed to ease hunger, thirst, and fatigue. It mostly worked, though Luman found himself growing thinner.

He slept on the cot in the *King's Head*, paying for the room by performing minor magic for the landlord, a slow-talking Talegan with obvious Lenni Lenape features named Zo'es Collins. Spells to stop fire. Spells to secure income. Before the milk gave out, Luman had carefully placed the Collins's Bible atop his full butter churn, to keep the butter from going bad. But he spent most of his waking time either in the Basilica, helping Mother Hylia and the secular priests there care for the refugees, or in the streets of Cahokia, watching the actions of the city's strangest and most fascinating inhabitant, her would-be queen, the half-Eldritch, half-Pennslander, all-Appalachee witch who stared at the world through mismatched eyes. The refugees knew Luman as the stranger who had driven the marauding beastkind from the church; they didn't know how he had done it. A few of the younger Missourians, more wildly afflicted with inflamed imaginations, whispered that he was a gunfighter, or that the pockets of his long coat were full of exotic weapons. Regardless, his word became authoritative, and Luman found himself settling disputes and easing fears.

The rat had been an occupant of the Basilica. Luman calculated that the rat's death was only just punishment for the pages of the hymnals the rodent had apparently eaten. He'd roasted it over a fire made from the splintered rood screen. Holy wood, holy fire, holy meat. On crude but undeniable magical principles, he'd felt as if the flesh of the rat were some sort of consecrated host.

He eyed the white doves that flocked on the high roof of the Basilica, but they were too hard to catch by hand, and Luman wasn't yet hungry enough to actually shoot one of the church's birds. It felt too impious, too close to shooting an angel.

But if I am hungry enough...

The witch Sarah Elytharias—no one in Cahokia called her by the name *Penn*—knew Luman, so he was careful not to come too close to her. He didn't want to be taken for an Imperial spy. But her movements were generally accompanied by an entourage of priestesses, ministers, and even beastkind soldiers, so he could watch much of what she did from the slopes of the Basilica Mound, peering through his spectacles and even sharpening his eyesight and hearing by minor charms, when occasion suggested.

He would like to get closer to her. He needed his next magi-cal mentor, some access to an initiatory path, a new source of power. None of the priests in the Basilica would admit to any such thing even existing, and Mother Hylia maintained her dif-fident evasions, no matter how many times she saw Luman play the Good Samaritan with the wounded travelers of the Missouri.

He stood on a bright morning in early January on a large east-west avenue, the road that most directly connected the large eastern gate with the Great Mound and the Basilica. The witch Sarah stood atop the eastern wall looking intently at something outside; whatever it was also captured the attention of the wardens and Pitchers and other warriors on the wall, because they stared and murmured.

Before Luman could recite any spells to hear what Elytharias and her two female advisors were saying to each other, the gate opened. The iron grill rose, and the iron-studded wood on the other side slowly dropped. Luman saw first the Imperial camps—larger than they had been a few days earlier—then the militia, then the trenches and earthworks.

And then a single man with long white hair and beard, lurch-ing forward on his knees.

Long-cloaked Cahokians standing all around Luman on the avenue gasped as one.

They knew the man.

Luman watched the old fellow creep forward. His knees were scabbed and callused, his once-white robe tattered, his skin blue from the cold. A thousand eyes stared at him, but he didn't look back, not at a single face.

Instead, he looked up and forward.

Luman didn't need to turn to know what the old man was fixed on. He was staring at the Basilica.

Luman retreated ahead of the old man, keeping an eye on his forward progress. Sarah, he noticed abruptly, had descended from the wall, but he couldn't see where she'd gone.

The old man trembled and left streaks of blood behind him in the snow. Could he even *reach* the Basilica?

The crowd closed in around him, nevertheless leaving a straight, narrow aisle ahead. They knew where he was going.

Who was he?

Could this be the mentor Luman was hoping for?

Crossing a plaza, the old man's knees slid out from under

him on a patch of ice. Hands reached out to elevate him and he pushed them away. Unsteadily, he rose to all fours...waiting, breathing hard as a frozen breeze snatched the tatters of his robe away, revealing a sunken chest that was also frozen blue...and then dragged himself to his knees and advanced again.

With the last coins of his Imperial salary, Luman bought a half-full cup of watered-down beer at a tavern. He asked for a crust of bread as well, but the drooping man behind the bar only frowned and shook his head. Luman then positioned himself at the foot of the Basilica Mound, holding the cup before him.

Watching the crowd mill about him, thickening the walls of the pilgrim's aisle, he found Sarah Elytharias again. She and the two women stood on Cahokia's other sacred mound, in front of the Temple of the Sun, watching.

From the conversation about him, Luman gleaned the pilgrim's name: Father Tarami. He was a priest of the Basilica, and he was returning from a long pilgrimage, something called the Onandagos Road.

When Tarami reached the foot of the mound, he sat back on his own heels and looked up. Luman tried to catch his eye with a smile and a flourish of the cup, but Tarami ignored him. The old man's breath came with effort, his lips were cracked, and Luman could hear the rumbling of his belly.

Tarami began to climb.

With each ponderous movement forward, the priest muttered some prayer under his breath. Luman heard the syllables clearly, but didn't know the language and had no charm to decipher it. Throwing a sharp elbow into the belly of a tall, black-bearded Ophidian with sooty hands, Luman turned and seized the position immediately behind Tarami. Muscling his way with each step and pushing away other enthusiasts, he held the spot.

All together, like ants swarming a hill in their queen's wake, the crowd climbed the hill with the old man.

His steps grew more labored. He left more blood behind on the stones. Luman saw the old man lose two large toenails when his foot struck a step at a bad angle.

And then, a few steps from the top, the old man collapsed.

Weeping erupted from the crowd. Luman feared they might riot. In defense of his own life as well as that of the priest, he pushed the mob back.

"Let him breathe!" he shouted.

Sarah Elytharias must see his actions. What would she think of them?

What would the pilgrim think?

He knelt beside the old man, feeling his feeble breathing scarcely disturb the air and watching his eyelids and blue lips flutter.

"You're almost home," he said to Father Tarami. "Drink this."

The old man shook his head.

"Come now." Luman smiled as gently as he knew how. "Even our Lord took a cup of wine at the end. Or the beginning, as it were."

The priest's eyes opened and his chest heaved. Luman feared he was suffering a heart attack, but then the old man's cracked lips split into a grin and Luman recognized laughter for what it was.

"Mixed with gall," Tarami wheezed.

"Yes, well, once you've tasted this, you might wish you were drinking vinegar, too."

Tarami's smile grew wider, revealing bleeding gums and sores on his tongue. Luman put an arm under the old man and raised him to sitting position, allowing him to slowly drain the contents of the cup.

The mound-climbing crowd stared.

Missourians, clustered around the front door of the Basilica, beneath its sculpted vine, thick with cooing doves, watched with wide eyes.

Luman tucked the cup into one of his many pockets and lowered himself onto his knees. "I would carry you as the Cyrenian carried our Lord, but I think you will not have it."

Tarami turned and knelt. "If you would accompany me, I will not turn you away."

They finished the climb together. The combined crowd of Cahokians and Missourians widened the aisle to accommodate both of them. By the time they reached the Basilica door, where Mother Hylia stood waiting, Luman's knees hurt. The cooing of the doves overhead sounded like a taunt.

How had this old man crossed the entire city?

And how far had he come before that? Luman thought he had heard someone in the crowd mention Oranbega, but that was *hundreds* of miles away.

The rubble left by the beastkind assault a few days earlier had been cleared away, but the damage to the rood screen and the pews was still very visible. Father Tarami ignored it, as he ignored the people clustered to either side of the nave, and focused on the altar in the apse.

His movements became more vigorous, each knee forward reaching farther than the one preceding. Luman found himself racing to keep up.

As the two men approached the altar, Luman held back. The assembled crowd seemed to hold its breath; Luman had rarely heard a more complete silence, despite the hundreds of people crowding the nave.

Abruptly slowing again, the old man stretched himself out on the paving stones in cruciform shape: arms extended to his sides, feet together and straight back, face pressed to the floor. He lay there long enough that Luman was beginning to wonder whether the old man had arrived at his destination and died, but abruptly he moved, raised his face slightly from the floor, and kissed the stone.

Crawling forward, he kissed the stone of the altar, too.

Then dragging himself up, Father Tarami stood on his two feet. He wobbled unsteadily and sucked air into his lungs with a look of surprise on his face, but he remained standing.

To Luman's astonishment, the crowd broke into song:

> *Crown of iron, heart of flesh*
> *Shaker's Rod and feet of clay*
> *Lord of harvest, ere you thresh*
> *Send a light to guide our way*

> *Chariot rider, god of war*
> *Mankind's father, son of peace*
> *Shelter us from foes of yore*
> *From all trial grant surcease*

Should he imitate the pilgrim and throw himself on the floor? Should he kiss the altar? If he did, surely others in the crowd would follow him. Would the priest himself regard that as presumption?

But Luman did neither of those things, and the moment passed.

A metallic ringing harsh as thunder cracked the air inside the Basilica, and Maltres Korinn stepped into view from the apse. He leaned on a black wooden staff with a metal horse's head at the upper end and a metal cap on the bottom; it was the staff whose noise rang so loudly. Korinn had been the Regent-Minister, but after siding with Sarah Elytharias during the tumultuous events on the night of the solstice, he had emerged as Vizier. He still wore black and carried the staff without other sign of office, except that if anything his facial expression had become even more dour.

"Zadok Tarami," Korinn said.

The old man spread his arms wide. "I am returned from my journey."

"You are summoned to the throne." Korinn looked to Luman. "You'd better come too, Imperial."

Sarah was good at keeping her composure, but to Cathy's experienced eye there had been signs of increasing agitation as the pilgrim Zadok Tarami had crossed Cahokia and ascended the Basilica. Those signs would have looked like anger on another person—narrowed eyes, less mobility in the mouth, the twitch of a jaw muscle. In Sarah, they betrayed cussedness, and mentally digging in.

Which suggested she felt the *need* to dig in.

Maltres Korinn was shrewd enough to limit the priest's ability to make further spectacle. He neither chained nor dragged the man, but simply descended one mound and ascended the other with as little ceremony as possible.

With them came the Imperial wizard, the man with eyeglasses and a long coat.

At Sarah's instruction, Cathy stood to one side with Yedera the Podebradan. Sarah stood directly in the open doorway of the Temple of the Sun. On her left hand stood the eight slaves who had once been Alzbieta's palanquin bearers, and now that she walked on the earth like a normal woman, still followed her around as a bodyguard. On Sarah's right stood the spell-less Polite wizard Sherem, Alzbieta herself, and, once he'd regained the height of the mound, Maltres Korinn.

Cathy didn't know the logic of the arrangement, though she noticed that it made an array of twelve people.

Zadok looked small even beside the Imperial wizard, who was a man of average height. The two men stood, breathing hard from their climb.

Sarah said nothing.

It was a raven that finally broke the silence with a single baritone croak.

"You're Elytharias's daughter," Tarami said. "God has told me of your coming."

"The goddess told all Her children," Sarah said slowly.

"I'm glad you're here," Tarami said. "You're the answer to my prayers, as I can be the answer to yours."

"What prayers?" Sarah asked him.

"Surely, you pray for wisdom. You pray to know what you should do in this situation, and you are surrounded as never before by a bewildering confusion of conflicting information." Tarami smiled. "The fact that you are the daughter of Kyres Elytharias doesn't give you any great gift of inborn knowledge, does it? One thing you will learn, if you haven't learned it already, is that being Kyres's daughter means that there are many people who are very willing to tell you lies."

The wizard looked as if he'd been struck.

"You've been traveling, priest," Sarah said. "How's the weather in the rest of the Ohio?"

"Cold." Tarami's voice was a bass drone, a surprisingly deep sound to come from such a thin frame. "Our people starve. Not just in Cahokia, but all our people. They need leadership, too. They need righteous kings, Cahokia needs a righteous king, to guide it through the narrows. Thomas is misguided, he may even be wicked, but God will give a penitent king the wisdom and the power to bring peace."

"Bring peace?" Sarah laughed, a shrill wedge that pierced the bass wall. "That's what Thomas says he's up to. Isn't that right, Balaam?"

At the name, the wizard started. "My name isn't *Balaam*... my lady."

"You may call her *Beloved*," Alzbieta said.

"Beloved," the magician repeated. "Director Schmidt called me *Balaam* to mock me. My name is Luman Walters."

"*She* has a name, too," Tarami said. "To call her *Beloved* is to give credence to her pagan nonsense, which I know you cannot believe."

"To tell truth," Sarah said, "I'm not all that comfortable with the title myself. For now, how about I call you 'Luman' and you call me 'Sarah'?"

Walters nodded acquiescence.

Sarah removed her eyepatch, fixing her witchy eye on the Imperial magician. "Tell me why you came here, Luman."

Walters stepped back, looking surprised. "I came with Director Schmidt."

"I know that. Tell me *why* you came here."

"It was my job. I worked for the Imperial Ohio Company. But I've walked away, I've quit."

"I know that too, Luman. This is your last chance, now, so I think you need to tell me the truth. All of it, the hard part, the truthiest truth you don't want to tell me right now. Why did *you* come here?"

Luman Walters took a deep breath. "I came here to steal."

Zadok Tarami put a hand on the wizard's shoulder. "There are thieves in paradise, my son."

"There's the truth," Sarah said. "But that leaves me with at least two riddles, Luman."

Luman Walters shook his head, looking chagrined. "I'm pleased not to be *entirely* transparent, Sarah."

"One," Sarah said, "you're a thief and you know it, but you have the most earnest soul a thief ever had. How is that?"

Walters shrugged and looked at his feet.

"And two, you've got a pocketful of angels. What on earth is that?"

Walters straightened up his back. "I'm a wizard, Sarah. I'm not some Philadelphia gramarist or a Polite scholar, I'm what you might call a hedge wizard. In a place like Youngstown or Knoxville I might make a decent living reading palms and hexing cattle against the murrain. Here... well, I will trade you. I will tell you all about my pocketful of angels in exchange for the knowledge you have."

"I can see you want to be my apprentice, Luman." Sarah's voice was gentle. "Only I don't know very much myself. And as I learn more things, I expect I'm not going to able to talk about most of them. That seems to be the way of things around here."

"These are not the ways of God," Zadok Tarami protested. "God is openness and light."

"The gods are light, alright. Is that why you went to Oranbega, Father? To follow the ways of God?" The way Sarah said the word *Father* made it sound almost like an insult.

"I walked the Onandagos Road on my knees," Father Tarami

said. "Not your allegorical Way of Adam, not your mystical non-sense and mumbo-jumbo allusions to a road that exists only in your head, but the real road, with roots and stones and all. I did it begging at every step that God would send salvation to my people, and He has done it. Here you are, a wizard, a seer even, of great power. God brought you here, and He gave everyone in the city to know of your arrival, as He informed me. You are the answer to my prayers, Sarah Elytharias, and the answer to the prayers of all our people. I will guide you, I will clarify for you your own experience. Yes, I went to Oranbega for the ways of God. For myself, and also for you."

"I believe in God," Sarah said. "But the one I saw was a goddess. I saw Her and Her realm in a vision of glory, and She chose me."

Tarami shook his head. "I pray it isn't so. She is an old deceiver, and this land is the land of those who have conquered Her."

Alzbieta Torias stepped forward. "I entered Eden Unfallen, the eternal home of Wisdom. There I saw the goddess and heard Her voice, and She chose Sarah Elytharias Penn as Her true Beloved."

"No," Tarami groaned.

The Polite Sherem stepped forward, shoulder to shoulder with Alzbieta. "I, too, entered Eden, and I, too, am witness. The Mother of All Living chose Sarah."

Maltres Korinn joined them. "I entered Eden. I saw the goddess and heard Her voice. Sarah is Her Beloved daughter."

"You are deluded!" Tarami cried. "You share a madness, but it's madness still. This is blasphemy! This isn't a goddess, it's a demon that has been bound in hell, and yet has never ceased to plague this land, this city, and the descendants of Onandagos. It seeks all our destruction as its revenge! Korinn, I expected better from you!"

As one, Alzbieta Torias's eight slaves advanced a step.

Tarami threw his hands skyward. "What, you too? Am I to hear that a gang of chained laborers went to this impossible non-place, Unfallen Eden, and met the goddess?"

"We did not go Eden," one of the ex-bearers said. "We stood at the foot of the Sunrise Mound in the snow on the morning of the solstice. We saw light in heaven. We heard the angel choir. And we heard the voice of the Mother of All Living, declaring that Sarah Elytharias was Her Beloved daughter."

If Sarah had arranged these witnesses, Cathy had had no advance hint. Or had Cahokia's goddess done this?

"But do you see what you are doing?" Tarami's words were urgent, but he wasn't yelling. He pleaded with Sarah. "You were not raised among us, and may not know all our books, but you must know Matthew. 'Ye shall know them by their fruits,' the evangelist wrote. 'Do men gather grapes of thorns, or figs of thistles?' Well, then? What does your pretended goddess give you thus far? The grapes and figs of prosperity and freedom, or the thorns and thistles of siege and starvation?"

"I accept." Sarah's words and her face were calm, but Father Tarami staggered back as if struck.

"You accept *what*?" he asked.

"The test," she said simply. "Ye shall know them by their fruits. It is a fair test. It should be a test acceptable to you, since you quote it to me as scripture."

"It is God's test," Tarami said.

Sarah reached into her satchel, the satchel that had once belonged to her mentor monk, Father Thalanes, and removed from it the Heronplow. Zadok Tarami and Luman Walters both gasped.

"What is that?" Walters asked.

Tarami seemed to recognize it, and feel fear.

Sarah set the Heronplow to the frozen ground and leaned heavily onto it. With all the weight of her small body, she pushed until the tooth of the plowshare bit just a little into the frozen soil of the moundtop.

"It will take more than an act of magic to convince me," Tarami told her.

"Fear not. I will show you more than an act of magic." Sarah held the dull iron Orb of Etyles cupped in her left palm and knelt, placing her right hand on the Heronplow. Taking a deep breath, she shouted an incantation: "*Maxima mater! Rogo ut hoc aratrum pelleas!*"

The Heronplow started forward.

Cathy had heard from others—Sherem and Maltres, since she couldn't bring herself to talk to Alzbieta as friends—about the Heronplow's activation of the Treewall on the solstice. What she saw sounded like the tale she'd received. The plow sank into the earth and sped back and forth across the flat top of the mound. The land here was already plowed, and the Heronplow followed the existing furrows. It broke the ice and snow, which melted into living water instantly in its wake. The water sank into the furrows, and scant feet behind the Heronplow as it progressed, green shoots sprang from the earth.

Tarami tore at his beard and wept.

Luman Walters fell to his knees.

Corn and beans and squash raced skyward in intertwined vegetable towers. Wheat exploded to maturity, heavy heads pulling the stalks downward before they had even reached full height. Peaches, apples, and grapes ripened in the space of a few breaths as Cathy watched.

She heard a grunting sound and looked to Sarah. The young woman's eyes were closed and she was sweating despite the cold. Cathy rushed to throw her arms around the girl and held her.

"It's enough," Cathy whispered.

"Not...yet..." Sarah ground through clenched teeth.

The Heronplow touched the end of the final furrow on top of the Great Mound and sank into the earth out of sight.

All eleven of Sarah's witnesses gasped.

Luman Walters spun on his heel and stared down at the side of the mound.

And then the plow broke from the earth on the east-facing slope of the temple and raced downward. It paralleled the steps in its course, and as it traveled, trees grew in its wake. They were impossible trees, trees that couldn't grow in the cold Ohio, much less in its winter—persimmons, oranges, dates, bananas, olives...and figs.

It was nonsense as a garden or a forest, a luxuriant glossolalia of vegetation.

As an act of fertile power, it was shocking.

A cry of astonishment and joy rocked the mound from below.

"This doesn't come from your demon, child!" Tarami cried. "This comes from heaven. This is an act of God! This is how the Lord answers my thousand miles, my bloodied knees, my hundred thousand prayers, the million prayers of his children! Abundance means peace! May He bless Lord Thomas and his house as gloriously as He now blesses us!"

"No," Sarah croaked.

Tarami ran down the steps of the mound.

Luman Walters sat, breathing rapidly and burying his face in his hands.

"Stop him!" Sarah fell forward onto one forearm, clutching the Orb of Etyles to her breast. "Stop the priest!"

The others looked at each other in surprise, but Maltres Korinn sprang forward. "Stop, Father!" he bellowed.

Cathy quickly lost the ability to make out the words of the vizier or the priest under the tumult of yelling that rose from the city. She could see the movement of the Heronplow around Cahokia by the growth of vegetation that rose from the ground in its wake, filling the avenues and plazas, turning every mound into an island of snow surrounded by a sea of fruit-bearing plant life.

Shouts of joy mingled with weeping of relief.

She watched Father Tarami move through the crowd that parted for him, crossing to the Basilica Mound. There he stood on the mound's lowest steps and shouted, waving his arms and leaping as if in dance. He fell to his knees and had his arms stretched heavenward as if he were personally calling down rain when Maltres Korinn and half a dozen of Cahokia's gray-caped wardens seized him.

The crowd tried to free the priest.

"No," Sarah groaned, trying to drag herself forward and failing.

The wardens beat the mob back with their batons, but not before two of their number were knocked to the ground. The crowd picked up sticks and stones and was gathering to charge again when the priest Tarami threw up his arms to stop them.

Cathy couldn't hear his words, but whatever he said, the crowd stepped back. They dropped their weapons and merely stared at the vizier as he dragged the old man away under guard.

Cathy took a deep breath.

"This is the most astonishing thing I have ever seen," Luman Walters said.

"He'll need help." The Polite Sherem, jolted out of paralysis, descended the mound.

The entire city had become a garden.

"People won't need instructions to feed themselves," Walters said. "But they should be organized to collect all the food they can and store it."

"Why?" Alzbieta said. "Wisdom has provided this. And Her Beloved. Don't you trust them to provide again?"

Sarah collapsed to the ground.

✧   ✧   ✧

Maltres Korinn locked Zadok Tarami into the same cell deep in the Hall of Onandagos that had held Sarah and Calvin Calhoun a few days earlier. Tarami was no magician, as far as Maltres knew, but the silver-bound construction of the cell would help prevent any magical rescue attempt from the outside.

He stationed a dozen wardens to watch the prison cells. When Sherem produced two Polites in red as volunteers to join the guard—a sleepy-eyed woman with short graying hair and a thin man with surprisingly heavy jowls—he promptly accepted, asking them to take turns, so as to always leave a gramarist on duty.

Later, under cover of darkness and perhaps with the assistance of the Polites, Maltres planned to relocate the priest to a more secret cell.

The Imperial hedge wizard Luman Walters also volunteered. Maltres sent him away.

What to make of the exchange between Walters and the Beloved? That Walters was a thief, but earnest and with angels in his pockets?

It was Zadok Tarami who prevented any real violence in his arrest. After telling the crowd that God the Father and his Son Jesus Christ, as revealed by the prophet in his true book, *The Law of the Way*, had sent this heavenly bounty to sustain the people of Cahokia and turn their hearts toward peace, he had submitted to arrest. He had begged the Cahokians to set down their sticks and stones and submit as well, telling them that Korinn and Sarah Elytharias were only misinformed, and that the miracle of food had been sent for their benefit as well, to convince them of the error of their ways.

Maltres Korinn knew better. Whatever the priest could say, he had seen the Mother of All Living in her Unfallen Eden. He knew She lived, and had chosen Sarah Elytharias Penn as Her Beloved.

He would bear witness to those truths, and if need be, he would do it with the sword.

In due time, the Beloved would become Queen. And then, he hoped, the Duke of Na'avu would be allowed to return home.

Still, he was grateful that, for the moment at least, the people of Cahokia weren't tearing each other to pieces in riots.

For the collection and storage of food, Maltres knew he'd need to deploy the wardens. Having been underfed for weeks, he feared his people might respond poorly to the sudden bounty. Deploying the wardens to oversee food collection would mean taking them off the Treewall, so Maltres sought out Captain Sir William Johnston Lee.

He found him on the wall, attended by the coyote-headed beastman named Chikaak. It was only on emerging from the wooden stairs encased within the living wood of the Treewall onto the ramparts that Maltres realized that the wall, too, had borne fruit. Not one kind only, but several: a nut like a chestnut, encased in a prickly shell; something that looked like a bright orange quince; clusters of green berries.

The wardens atop the wall had lain spears and rifles down and were stuffing fruit into their mouths as fast as they could. Maltres looked along the rampart and saw the same scene repeated each time.

The beastkind warriors on the wall, on the other hand, stood still and stared fiercely down at the Imperials below.

The Imperials—Maltres looked and saw men pointing at the wall. They saw, they knew.

What would they do about it?

"Sir William," he said.

"Mmmm," the Cavalier answered.

Maltres thumped the Earthshaker's Rod on the wood under his feet. "Sir William, are you concerned about discipline?"

Chikaak made a small sound like a whimper.

"I am always concerned about discipline, suh," Sir William said. "The children of Adam are by nature such unruly beasts."

The Johnslander turned his face to Maltres and smiled. His eyes were oddly glassy.

"You could use some sleep, Sir William."

"So could we all."

"I need to borrow the wardens for at least a few hours, and maybe longer."

"Outbreak of crime?"

"An outbreak of fruit!" Maltres thumped his staff again. "Haven't you noticed? Look below you! Look at the Treewall! The goddess has blessed us, but I fear riots and theft will lead to violence if we don't prevent it."

Sir William shook himself and looked about. "Hell's Bells, you're right. The goddess, you say?"

"May I borrow the wardens?" It wasn't entirely clear that Maltres had to ask; the wardens had been exclusively under his command until a few days earlier. Now, though, they were one of four more or less well-organized segments of Cahokia's defense, the other three being the household troops of the Elytharias family and those of Cahokia's other great families, the corps of Molly Pitchers that had defected to Cahokia, and Sarah's personal retinue of beastkind. The wardens and household troops reported to Valia Sharelas and the artillerists to Jaleta Zorales, former rivals of Sarah for the Serpent Throne, who had given her their allegiance upon her being called as the goddess's Beloved. At least while on military duty, they all answered to William Lee—the beastkind answered to him directly—and they called him *General*.

Many details were yet to be decided, but the organization worked. If the crisis holding them together passed, Maltres doubted the organization was yet solid enough to stand on its own.

Lee nodded. "We beasts shall hold the wall, suh! You may place your trust in us."

Something was wrong, but Maltres didn't have to time to find out what. He banged his staff on the floor a third time and raised his voice. "The next man I see putting fruit into his mouth gets hanged!"

That put a sudden end to the gorging. Grabbing the nearest officer, Maltres passed on clear, concise orders—the peace to be kept, all household to be entitled to one basket of produce of any kind per person, the remainder to be collected into the city's storehouses.

As he descended the stairs, he heard the barked commands that heralded the beginning of his instructions' implementation.

He returned to the Great Mound.

The Podebradan Yedera stood before the temple door.

"Where is she?" Maltres asked.

"Beneath. Where she can sleep. With the priestesses."

"With the *other* priestesses, you mean."

The Unborn inclined her head slightly.

"She lives?"

"She lives. She rests."

"She has saved us. For now, at least."

The Podebradan nodded again. "A doubter, such as Zadok Tarami, will say that she has destroyed us in the long run."

"Do you doubt?"

Yedera shook her head. "I hold true to all the things of my mothers, Vizier. Their ways, their beliefs, their stories, their gods. It would take more than a desire to join any man's empire for me to topple the Serpent Throne. It would take more than a fear of death for me to abandon the children of Wisdom."

"I wish we had twenty thousand like you."

"In this city, I doubt you have twenty. Perhaps not ten. Ours is not a society that organizes monthly meetings."

"Each of you sworn to a different noble family?"

"I am the only Oathbound attached to the family of Alzbieta Torias and Sarah Elytharias."

The Unborn Daughters of St. Adela Podebradas were elite warriors whose field of action was not generally war. They were named for the Serpentborn queen of the old world who had rejected her Imperial husband, a son of Eve, in divorce, and who had eventually been executed for her temerity; or rather, they were named for the daughters it was imagined she would have had. And their behavior in some ways suggested they were people outside the common sphere of descent from Adam. They didn't marry; they ignored taboos and social conventions; they celebrated no feast days. During the recent Christmas celebrations, Yedera had stood apart in every meeting and refused all invitations. The seven Sister Kingdoms acknowledged and legitimated their setting apart, exempting the Unborn from taxes, military service, and other forms of mandatory contribution. They were bodyguards and temple defenders, they were paladins, they carried out sworn acts of vengeance and punishment, they were even assassins. They were fiercely loyal to their kind and sworn to serve a single family.

Battlefield warriors or not, Maltres Korinn wished there were more of them in the city.

"And if Sarah Elytharias required the death of a single troublesome person?" he asked.

She didn't inquire whom he meant. "Inside or outside of these walls, I stay true to the things of my mothers."

They stood awhile in silence.

"I take it I'm not to be allowed in?" he asked.

"Cathy Filmer tends Sarah with her healing arts. Alzbieta Torias is also in attendance." Unexpectedly, Yedera cracked a lopsided smile. "Between the two of them, the Beloved may feel she is surrounded by more than enough noise already."

Maltres leaned on his staff. His inclination was to look north-ward, toward his own estates. Instead, he looked westward to the river and the wooden shore beyond, teeming with bloodthirsty, maddened beastkind. The emissaries of the Heron King had prom-ised him destruction, and his footsoldiers were certainly trying their hardest. Beyond the Great Green Wood, on the borders of the Missouri, lay Zomas. One of Maltres's hopes in dealing with the claimants for the throne of Cahokia was that if Gazelem Zomas had won, the split kingdom might have been reunified, or at least reconciled. An ally on the Heron King's other flank could have been very useful.

Perhaps he should talk to Gazelem anyway. Perhaps he still might be able to facilitate an alliance.

Maltres shook his head and shifted his stance, looking to the east.

"A heavy part, to wear a crown."

"I wear no crown," he said immediately.

"I agree, My Lord Duke," Yedera answered, looking at his face intently. "And yet standing here, looking at our enemies on either side, you think the thoughts of one who does."

"Say rather that I think the thoughts of one who would offer good counsel," Maltres said. "I would be for the Beloved daughter of Wisdom what Uris was for your mistress."

"An old man who talked too much, schemed too quickly, and died of his own mistake?"

"You speak ill of the dead."

"I am a Podebradan."

"Uris's failure was mine. We both stood against Sarah Elythar-ias, not knowing that the goddess had chosen her."

"*Had* the goddess chosen her? Or did the goddess choose her *afterward*, once she had defeated you and Uris?"

Maltres considered. "I don't know whether it matters."

"I don't think it does, now. Either Sarah was always the god-dess's choice, and once the goddess made Her will known, you followed Sarah's banner, or Sarah *became* the goddess's choice, at which point you aligned yourself with her. The Virgin forgives. Either way, you're with the goddess and Her Beloved now."

"Or I'm on the side of a malevolent serpentine demon that plagues the descendants of the priest-king Onandagos and their people, seeking revenge for a primeval imprisonment."

"Yes," Yedera agreed. "Or that."

"In the meantime, if you find any way to introduce a plague of weevils into Cahokia, by all means do so."

———◆———

CHAPTER FOUR

No one told Dadgayadoh to keep an eye on the Sorcerer Robert Hooke, but you didn't climb the Imperial Ohio Company ladder under Director Schmidt by sitting around waiting for the rain to fall, and Dadgayadoh was determined to climb. His first encounter with the Company had been as a boy, selling the furs of animals he'd trapped to Company agents at the headwaters of the Ohio. He'd envied their new long guns, the bright colors they wore, and the confidence with which they walked through the woods, and he'd decided he'd be one of them.

It had been easy enough; he'd acted as guide on a few journeys into Haudenosaunee territory, Oranbega, among the Talligewi, and one small battle with the gloomy, slow-talking giants, in which he'd saved two agents' lives by burying them, along with himself, in a bog for three days. When the victorious Talligewi had finally grown bored of looking for the missing agents and gone back their pole-borne houses, Dadgayadoh had pulled all three of them from the mud and led them home.

Even if he hadn't known the name, it was obvious that there was something wrong with the fellow—a deathly illness or a curse—and Dadgayadoh was mistrustful. As it happened, he knew enough English history—learned from campfire songs, mostly—to know the name *Robert Hooke*, and to understand that the man was some sort of necromancer, a walking corpse.

When the Sorcerer left camp to ride around the besieged city, Dadgayadoh followed him. He made a point of leaving his silk top hat and his red blanket behind in his travel chest, wearing instead a nondescript gray wool coat such as you might see anywhere along the Ohio, on any person, or such as he might wear to hunt.

Hooke caught Dadgayadoh's attention splitting wood. He did it himself, by hand, using something that looked like an obsidian wedge. The tool was sharp enough that it split the skin of the Sorcerer's hands repeatedly, leaving smears of black ichor on his work and on the snowy ground.

Hooke asked for no help and accepted none; when two agents, evidently recognizing him from his interactions with Director Schmidt and seeking to curry favor, tried to offer the Lazar a long-handled ax, he took it from them and beat them both so severely with its handle that they spent the next three days moaning on their bedrolls.

Hooke started with a single trunk, a tall, straight pine that he felled himself. He didn't seem to care about the bark, but he smashed off all the branches and kicked them aside, leaving the straight naked bole. Then, over the course of a day and a half, he reduced the trunk into two large lengths of timber and many small ones.

He did all this within the company camp. Dadgayadoh could pretend to be about various errands while keeping an eye on the Sorcerer.

Heaping all the unused branches and needles onto a canvas, Hooke lit it on fire. He stood watch through the night, warning off anyone who approached his blaze. Dadgayadoh drifted in and out of sleep in a small stand of pine beside the canvas wall of a commissary tent, always waking to find the black silhouette of the dead Englishman standing against the orange blaze. The next day, when the fire had finally died, Hooke collected the ashes in a basket.

He then piled all the cut timber in a wagon.

Dadgayadoh watched from the tent he and Schäfer shared with the Parlett children as Hooke finished loading the wagon, hitched it to two horses, and then rolled out of camp. He quietly saddled a horse without a light; the moon was just a tiny waxing sliver, but it was enough for Dadgayadoh, who grew up in the deep, tangled forests of Iroquoia looking for the marks of hoofprints in soft earth and shooting at distant deer.

Then he followed.

Hooke drove slowly. He sang in a language Dadgayadoh didn't know, so it wasn't Haudenosaunee, French, or English. It didn't sound like German, Dutch, or Talligewi, either. He drove the wagon with one hand, holding the other hand off the side constantly like the single wing of a cumbersome bird.

Puzzled, Dadgayagoh slipped ahead in a copse of trees to get a better look. The Sorcerer took a handful of ash from the basket and held it to one side, slowly letting the powder fall from his fingertips. When his hand was empty, he filled it with ash again.

He was leaving a trail of burnt wood.

A couple of miles from camp, Hooke stopped the wagon and climbed down. Taking two of the short lengths of wood, he pounded one stake, three feet long, into the ground. He then tied a second stake across it at a right angle; the second stake sat just inches from the ground and was as long as Dadgayadoh's forearm.

He rubbed a line along each piece of timber with the pine ash.

When he was done, Hooke chanted more in his strange language, remounted the wagon, and continued his ride, leaving Dadgayadoh staring in puzzlement.

His people had fiercely rejected the preaching of Anne Hutchinson and every other preacher Christendom had thrown at them since. Still, he had seen enough of the Ohio to know that a cross—two pieces of wood joined at a right angle, with the downward-pointing length longer than the other three—marked a Christian place of worship, book, or image.

What did an upside-down cross mean?

Hooke was English. Maybe this sign meant something to the followers of Thunor and Herne. Dadgayadoh had never been to the Crown Lands, and what little he knew of the Cavaliers and their gods had come at second hand.

The Lazar rode a slow circuit around Cahokia, planting the small upside-down crosses at regular intervals and connecting them all with faint trails of ash.

As dawn approached, Dadgayadoh rode behind a long screen of trees to get ahead of the magician, fearing to be spotted if he continued to trail. He rode along Cahokia's shattered wharves and under the eyes of the defenders on its walls, stopping only twice to be sure that Hooke continued his method of planting the queer crosses. He planted two along the river, both tightly against large poles sunk into the bank to support docks. That positioning made the crosses harder to see, and maybe protected them against traffic.

Beastkind slunk among the ruined docks. Dadgayadoh's rifle was loaded, and he kept his long knife bare and in his hand. The misshapen, monstrous semi-people of the Great Green Wood left him alone. An otter the size of a bear, with a reptile's eyes and tail, came close, but Dadgayadoh hissed at it and brandished the knife, deliberately trying to catch the light with the blade. Whatever the otter-crocodile saw, it was enough. It turned and crept away under the smashed hull of a keelboat.

Strange barriers, the walls of Cahokia. His people knew the Firstborn of the eastern Ohio, who built differently—mounds and thatched buildings. This palisade was something else. It had appeared to be made of the trunks of dead trees, branches and all, when Dadgayadoh had first arrived with Notwithstanding Schmidt. A few days later, on the day the Company and its traders and militia had all been driven out of the city, the wall had sprouted leaves.

Now, its branches were thick with fruit.

Dadgayadoh rode ahead and secreted himself in an irrigation ditch halfway between the river and camp. At this point, he was watching only for the sake of confirmation. Hooke did as expected, pounding two more of his upside-down crosses into the ground.

Dadgayadoh thought, as Hooke was hammering into place the last of the small crosses, a mile or so from camp, that the Sorcerer looked up and stared in his direction.

Dadgayadoh froze in place and shivered. He sneaked two fingers to the ornately beaded charm that hung around his neck on a snakeskin thong. It had always served him against witches. Would it be strong enough to defend him against the Sorcerer?

At a tiny knoll just outside the company camp, Hooke poured out the remainder of the ashes. There he finally took the two large timbers from the wagon and used them to build one final upside-down cross. This was identical to the others in shape and proportion, but was significantly larger, jutting straight up from the earth perhaps nine feet, with a six-foot crossbeam.

Dadgayadoh cared nothing for either Christians or Wodenists

and their respective piety, but the Sorcerer Robert Hooke had put an enormous amount of work into this arrangement of upside-down crosses. Whatever purpose he tried to imagine the crosses might serve, Dadgayadoh felt unsettled.

He resolved to tell Director Schmidt. She would see the large cross anyway, but at least she would know that there was more than that most obvious portion of the arrangement.

Also, she would know how diligent Dadgayadoh had been. A hard worker, a self-starter, a real Company man.

Sarah awoke to the cinnamon-like smell of incense. She also smelled thyme and something that wasn't very familiar, but might be basil or oregano.

Oil lamps burned faintly within niches sunk into plain stone walls. She lay on a flat bed, firm almost to the point of being hard, under a sheet that felt like cotton to her fingertips.

Her Eye of Eve was unbound, and through it her surroundings all glowed a faint blue. The scene had the sort of aura that suggested it was located *within* the flow of a ley line.

Her mortal eye would not have noticed for the gloom, but her Eye of Eve clearly saw two women sitting on stools beside the room's single entrance: Alzbieta Torias and Cathy Filmer. Cathy's aura shone with the bright white of the children of Eve—in this setting, she was the striking thing, the thing that stood out.

"Am I inside the Temple of the Sun?" Sarah asked.

"If you're thinking this is a crypt, be at ease," Cathy said. "You're alive and well. Alzbieta neglected to tell you that there are sleeping chambers underneath the temple."

"But Alzbieta did tell me that my father's people bury their dead in jars." Sarah pivoted to the edge of the bed and dropped her feet to the floor. The stone was cool to the touch, despite the warm air. "With live snakes."

"The serpent is a creature that can travel between worlds," Alzbieta said. "As you have cause to know. Also, it's a creature that is perpetually reborn, and it belongs to our goddess."

"I ain't sayin' it ain't an interestin' practice," Sarah cracked. "I'm jest sayin' iffen you buried me alive by mistake, I'd expect to wake up curled into a ball, with a snake ticklin' my bum." She pondered for a moment her father's burial, but before she could fully articulate any idea, Cathy interrupted her thoughts.

"Does Zadok Tarami approve of jar burials?"

"We call such an interment a *burial to life*," Alzbieta said. "And no, I think he must not. Sarah's grandfather, at the direction of the Basilica priests in his day, dug up all the kings of Cahokia from the field of life and buried them again in box-shaped coffins, and in a different place."

"And without the snakes, presumably," Sarah said. "In a better world, I'd add that to my list of wrongs to correct. In this world, that's such a tiny problem, it doesn't rate. The fact of there being two warring priesthoods who don't even believe the same set of facts about God might not even be worth my attention. I have a siege to break, a people to rescue, and land rights to reclaim. And hell, the only reason I came here was to rescue my siblings, one of whom is still lost."

"But one is found," Cathy said.

"I ain't sayin' I'm a *total* gump."

"Speaking of warring priesthoods," Alzbieta continued. "There's a petitioner to see you."

Sarah stood. Her legs quivered, but held. She felt parched. "Tell me it's not the Metropolitan."

"He is locked up in the Hall of Onandagos," Cathy said.

"Same place I was locked up?"

"Same place." Alzbieta nodded.

Sarah sighed. "That can't possibly be a good idea."

The other women said nothing.

"Well, tell me about this petitioner, but get me something to drink, too. Water will do in a pinch, but if possible, I'd love to have something with a kick to it. Coffee, fruit juice, small beer. How long have I been asleep?"

Cathy slipped from the room.

"Not long," Alzbieta said. "The remainder of the day and most of the night. It's not yet dawn. And you're in one of the chambers *beneath* the Temple of the Sun. There are living quarters for one sept of priestesses at a time, and for the monarch. Ordinarily, only priestesses are allowed here."

"I appreciate you making an exception for me and Cathy."

"*You* are not an exception. You're the Beloved of the goddess. And Cathy . . . at the moment, the Temple is unconsecrated. Defiled. It is no trespass against the sacred for anyone to be in these chambers now, though it is a breach of tradition."

Cathy returned, a cup in her hands. Sarah smelled coffee and thought with a pang of her lost friend and mentor, Thalanes. "You two still at war?" she asked them.

Neither said anything. She sighed. Cathy handed her the cup and she drank.

"Alright, then. The petitioner—who is it?"

"You've met her. She's the Lady Alena, a priestess of the order."

"Vow of silence." Sarah remembered. "Talked through a eunuch, a real mouthy sack of toads."

"She broke her vow of silence the night of the solstice," Alzbieta said. "She comes asking you to renew it."

"She certainly has my permission to shut up," Sarah said. "Her eunuch has my permission to shut up, too. In fact, I'd kind of like to *command* him to close his mouth. I don't see that it concerns me at all."

"You are the Beloved," Alzbieta Torias said. "You are the footprint of the goddess upon the earth. You are the seal upon every binding vow, your word binds the goddess on earth as in heaven, you—"

"Stop!" Sarah abruptly felt very old, and very small. She finished the coffee, sipping it slowly and blowing on it to avoid burning her tongue, and then handed the cup back to Cathy. "Where are my things?"

Cathy pointed. Sarah's vision had adjusted to the low light enough that even her natural eye now saw a high-backed chair beside her bed and, hanging from the back, her shoulder bag.

She stretched to limber up her arms and legs, then took the bag and slung it over her shoulder. She wished she were wearing something more elaborate than a shift, but the women had seen fit to undress her before tucking her into bed.

So be it. She'd just have to be priestly in other ways.

Sarah straightened her back and nodded.

"Where shall we see her?" she asked. "Is there a traditional place? A reception room?"

Alzbieta shook her head. "In the Hall of Onandagos there is. And there is space in the Basilica."

"Lady Alena waits in an anteroom just down the hall," Cathy said.

"We'll do this here. Bring her in."

Should she wear the Sevenfold Crown? That didn't feel quite

right, in that she wasn't queen . . . not fully . . . yet. Sarah took the Orb of Etyles from the bag and held it in her right hand.

The tall, white-haired Alena entered slowly, with hands clutched together before her and head bowed. The wide-hipped man with serpents painted on his face followed in the same posture. They both wore plain white tunics and kilts, which made them look like supplicants.

She was glad they hadn't crawled in on their knees.

Sarah groped for an opening line. *Good morning* didn't feel quite right. "Welcome, Lady Alena," she finally said.

"I apologize and I beg forgiveness," Alena said, not looking up. "I didn't know—"

"Enough," Sarah said. "Accepted." Her eye caught the light of the oil lamp as she spoke, and something completely unexpected nearly made her choke on her own words: within the oil-fed flame crouched a salamander. She had seen such a flaming lizard at the feet of the Mother of All Living, in Her Eden. Were there salamanders in every fire, and she simply hadn't noticed before? Or only special fires, like the fires in the Temple of the Sun? Was she seeing the salamander now because she was the Beloved? Did the salamander bring her a message? As Sarah spoke words of acceptance and mercy, the salamander danced as if for joy. "You are forgiven," she managed to say.

Alena continued. "I humbly ask—"

"Wait." Sarah turned to the eunuch. "What about *you*?"

"Me?" The eunuch's eyebrows raised in surprise. "I am but a mouthpiece."

"No," Sarah said. "Sometimes, you're pretty clearly a mouth. Are you a mouth with nothing to say for itself?"

"I—I—I also, I beg forgiveness."

"Remember one thing, eunuch." Sarah raised a warning finger.

The mouthpiece stared. "What's that?"

"I can make 'em grow back."

Now the eunuch did fall to the floor, groveling. Sarah was happy to let him cower.

"Beloved," Lady Alena said softly. "I humbly ask to reinstate my former vow of silence."

"Tell me what you do," Sarah said. "Your sacred duties."

"With my sept, I attend the throne. I dust it; I light the lamps."

"If the veil were closed, would you be allowed behind it?"

Lady Alena nodded. "I and I alone, on the day of my tendance. The day also known as Monday. And because I am allowed behind the veil, in certain circumstances, I . . . dress the goddess."

She looked at Sarah piercingly for a moment, and then looked away.

"She means *you*," said a voice that was bass and yet feminine. "She would dress you at the four corners of the year, if they happened to fall on her cohort's day."

Sarah looked into the oil lamp and realized that the salamander was speaking to her.

None of the other people in the room responded to the voice.

"I understand." Sarah kept an eye on the salamander to gauge its reaction. She also reached through the orb into the Mississippi's ley and drew mana from it, filling her words with energy and destiny. "Lady Alena, this land is riven by enough dissension and threatened by more than sufficient foes. May the priesthood of the goddess be strong, stable, and powerful, and a force for the healing of ills rather than for inflicting them.

"I restore all things to you.

"Your oath, for good and ill, binds you again.

"You resume your responsibilities and your authorities all as formerly. Between you and me, there is peace. If there is any cause for strife between you and me, you will come to me promptly to resolve it. Understood?"

Alena knelt and touched her forehead to Sarah's bare feet. The salamander leaped in a graceful circle inside the fire.

"By our lives and by the life of the goddess," the eunuch said. "We so swear."

Sarah hadn't intended to make this an oath. After her experience with Alzbieta and the beastkind, she wanted to avoid the swearing of oaths. But so be it.

She reached down with her free hand and raised the Lady Alena up. Tears streamed down the older woman's cheeks and she smiled.

"Lord Thomas, the Parletts are speaking!"

Thomas barely heard the words. Philadelphia's network of brick-lined sewer tunnels, built by John Penn and the old Lightning Bishop, had become inadequate, and it was up to Thomas to find a solution for the pools of fetid wastewater now settling into filthy ice in three Philadelphia crossroads. He stood at a table in his personal library, with a stack of papers and a heart full of doubts.

He pored over plans the Imperial Engineering Corps had delivered to him, plans that required the construction of a pumping station at a hill called Faire Mount. This looked like a considerably more expensive proposition than the alternative proposal, which involved the Imperial College of Magic constructing something that would allegedly strain all the filth from the waste water. On the other hand, Thomas was nervous that any solution to the city's cloacal problem that depended on a wizard could be fickle, subject to dispelling by the interference of a rival wizard, or simply too good to be true. And what if a stray shilling were to come in contact with the proposed runic inscriptions?

But to build the pumping station and the expanded tunnel system would require money. His mines and farms didn't generate enough.

Why could people not see that if they simply gave him the power, he could make their lives better?

Why, especially, could the stubborn Electors not see it?

"Lord Thomas, the Parletts are the children who put us in contact with Director Schmidt."

Thomas shook off his reverie. His valet Gottlieb stood holding the door open, an urgent expression on his face.

"Ah." Thomas set down the plans and followed Gottlieb, who led him up a nearby staircase toward the usually vacant rooms in Horse Hall where the Parlett boys had been housed. "Temple wishes me to see his device."

"I understand it's more than that," Gottlieb said. "I believe there is news."

"Either unusually good or bad," Thomas said, "or Temple would handle it himself and inform me later, to make all the Empire's great accomplishments sound like minor feats he nonchalantly accomplished without assistance."

Gottlieb had no comment.

The two Philadelphia Parletts lived in two adjoining chambers, a bedroom behind a sitting room. They stood in their identical blue uniforms (made from a single roll of felt, Temple had assured him proudly, which appeared to be part of the web of connections that kept the Parletts constantly in contact with each other), backs straight and mouths turned down at the corners.

They appeared to be mimicking a jowly person, and they spoke to Temple Franklin.

Temple sat in one of several upholstered chairs that faced the Parletts. He looked tired.

"Is it Sayle?" Thomas asked, deliberately adopting a flippant tone. "He is defeated, or he has lost his way entirely and found himself in Georgia instead. Though that doesn't look like an imitation of Sayle's face."

"THIS IS DIRECTOR SCHMIDT, MY LORD PRESIDENT," the Parletts said. "I HAVE SEEN NO SIGN OF SAYLE YET, BUT I DIDN'T EXPECT HIM THIS EARLY. THERE IS A DEVELOP-MENT IN THE CITY OF CAHOKIA."

"I expect you to handle all developments until Sayle arrives. Frankly, given how long we've been starving the Ohio already, I expect you may well resolve the siege before Sayle gets there, in which case you'll go from being the commander in chief of the besieging forces directly to acting as the leader of the civil government."

"I WOULD HAVE SAID THE SAME. HOWEVER, WE HAD INDICATIONS YESTERDAY THAT CAHOKIA HAD DISCOV-ERED A NEW AND UNORTHODOX FOOD SOURCE. I HAVE CHOSEN NOT TO REACH OUT TO YOU UNTIL I WAS ABLE TO GET INFORMATION FROM SPIES ON THE INSIDE, TO DETERMINE THE SCOPE OF THE PROBLEM."

"What are you talking about?" Thomas laughed. "It's an entire city. Unless they've corralled half their own people into slaughtering pens to feed the other half, how can they possibly have any food source large enough to be relevant?"

"TEN DAYS AGO, THE TREEWALL OF CAHOKIA SPROUTED LEAVES. YESTERDAY, IT SPROUTED FRUIT AS WELL. WE LOST A MAN IN THE PROCESS, BUT WE MANAGED TO OBTAIN SOME OF THE FRUIT—PERSIMMONS AND ALMONDS. EDIBLE."

Thomas put his face in his hands. He would never expand Philadelphia's overtaxed waste water system. He would die of old age bogged down by the impossible task of trying to dig a fifteen-year-old girl out of her tree fort, while Philadelphia slowly sank beneath an ever-expanding lake of shit.

"MY LORD PRESIDENT?"

"I'm still here."

"IT'S WORSE. TODAY A SPY WE HAVE INSIDE THE CITY

REPORTED THAT IT WASN'T ONLY THE TREEWALL THAT BLOOMED. IT WAS THE WHOLE CITY. IT GREW NEW TREES AND CROPS. ALL THE SPACE WITHIN THE WALLS BECAME A SINGLE ENORMOUS GARDEN, WE'RE TOLD. THE CITY HAS SPENT AN ENTIRE DAY HARVESTING FOOD, AND THE TREES AND BUSHES AND GRAINS LOOK LIKE THEY'LL GROW MORE."

"Enough to feed the city perpetually."

"MAYBE."

"In which case, no siege can succeed."

"THIS IS PRECISELY WHAT I FEAR."

"Do we have any idea what caused this abominable multiplication of the persimmons?"

"Magic," Temple Franklin said.

"Good Lord," Thomas said, "but I am grateful to have such an insightful Machiavel in my employ. But for your insight, I might have guessed this was the work of Robin Goodfellow."

"It is the sort of thing folk tales associate with Peter Plowshare," Temple Franklin said. "Surprising fertility, impossible abundance."

Thomas's head throbbed. "If you tell me a folk tale, I shall kick you in the face. Even if I have to run at you horseback to do it."

"I've summoned experts of the Imperial College. They'll be here tomorrow to discuss."

"Experts in what? Almonds? Peter Plowshare? Food magic, what would that be? I failed Greek at Harvard. Sitos? No, that's wheat. Trophos-something? Trophomancy?"

"That would be the art of prophesying by food. Trophurgy would be the magical art of working in food, by analogy with thaumaturgy," Temple Franklin said.

"It is an ugly neologism, and suits this ugly situation." Thomas ground his teeth. "When they get here, let's reach out to Director Schmidt again. I'll wager you all of Johnson City that it will be at least three weeks before the College can reach a combined opinion, much less agree on a course of action."

"UNDERSTOOD." The expression on the Parletts' faces was solemn. "I HAVE MY BEST MEN WATCHING THE PARLETTS AT THIS END."

"The Ohio Parletts," Thomas said.

"THE OHIO PARLETTS. I'LL BE INFORMED IMMEDIATELY, ONCE YOU'RE READY."

"Very good. In the meantime, if you find any way to introduce a plague of weevils into Cahokia, by all means do so."

Luman was poring over one of the books in the Basilica's library when Zadok Tarami appeared at his shoulder.

"Do you read our language?"

The priest hadn't changed his clothing. He smelled like a pilgrim, sour with sweat and crusted with filth. In his white robe torn to shreds below the thigh he looked like a beggar. His straight back and unassuming smile communicated power and confidence, though. He had a comfort in his own skin that Luman had seen in the best of the company's leaders, including Notwithstanding Schmidt.

A comfort that Luman himself had never felt.

Luman had discovered a small library of books at the back of the apse while cleaning up the wreckage of the beastkind attack. They had been stored in a locked cabinet that had been shattered in the incident. Once the Missourians saw they were only books, they lost interest. Mother Hylia and the secular priests didn't object to Luman examining them.

Sadly, he wasn't able to learn much.

"No," Luman admitted, running his finger over a golden swirl at the center of the page. "That's why I picked the one with pictures." The book was illuminated. Like other medieval manuscripts Luman had seen, the initial letters were larger and picked out with gold and scarlet paints; strange figures and miniature scenes filled the margins. Occasionally, an entire half-page was dedicated to illustrating a story.

Unlike old Greek, Latin, and German texts he'd seen, the Eldritch book's writing started at an apparently random point on each page and spiraled out in large swirls of looping and knotted lines, swarmed by dots, swoops, and dashes on either side. Some of the illustrations followed the spiraling text, and a single story seemed to circle up from the depths of the page.

"Many of our books have been translated into German. There is a story that the Winter Queen translated all of them into English at Heidelberg, but if she did so, most of that translation was lost in the Serpent Wars. Perhaps the translation was part of the cause of the wars. Who can tell? A conspiracy is a terrible way to bring a book to light. Fragments of the so-called Heidelberg

Bible turn up from time to time, but outside of universities, there is little interest. The Firstborn have never been much for proselytizing."

"I have seen copies of *The Law of the Way* in the stock of traveling pedlars," Luman said. "Many copies, actually. It's an easy book to come by. I've seen none of the others, to my knowledge."

Tarami smiled a knowing smile. "You bought a copy of the *Law* because you knew it was an Ophidian text and you hoped it would contain spells."

Luman coughed. "Actually, I *stole* a copy."

Tarami laughed.

"I was poor at the time," Luman said. "I tried to make it up later with extra kindness to other book pedlars."

"I'm not sure that's how it works."

"I'm pretty sure it isn't."

"And what magic did you learn from *The Law of the Way*, then?"

Was the priest taunting him or testing him? "If there are spells in the *Law*, my eyes are not opened to see them."

"Mother Hylia told me this about you."

"That my eyes aren't opened?"

"That you hope they will be."

Luman closed the book carefully. "I think it's wrong to covet riches. I think it's wrong to covet power and seek to scratch the itches of the flesh and flaunt your wealth in clothing. I do not believe it is a sin to seek knowledge. I seek knowledge above all other things. And if the *Law* says it is a sin, I missed that passage."

"You're teasing me, wizard. We are commanded to seek knowledge, and you know it. Indeed, your words are nearly a paraphrase of the passage that commands it."

Luman smiled.

"*Nearly*," the priest said. "Here are the words of the prophet-king Onandagos, in his final testament, as recorded in the twenty-eighth through thirtieth chapters of the *Law*: 'Seven things it is wrong to seek, and the seeking thereof shall lose a man his soul: power, unless it be to do justice; wealth, except that wealth must be sought to clothe the naked; the satisfaction of the flesh, except that it is commanded to enjoy the flesh for the expression of love and for the generation of life; the life of another, except that it is given to you to take life in defense of the life of your people; loud singing, only you must raise your voices in acknowledgement of your debts to God; fine clothing, except it be the fine clothing you must wear for the giving of glory to God; and knowledge, unless it be true knowledge of the way of God and His creation, which you must seek above all other things.'"

"That sounds like a *prohibition*." Luman smiled. "You said we were *commanded* to seek knowledge."

"But what is knowledge of the way of God and His creation, if not the knowledge of all things? And if the exception enjoins us to seek the knowledge of all things, then what is the prohibition?"

"You're certainly doing very well on the clothing part of the commandments," Luman said.

Zadok Tarami snorted, then laughed.

"Why is it so easy to come by copies of the *Law* in English?" Luman asked.

"We have made it easy." Tarami was still chuckling. "The *Law* and its contents are the thing we most wanted John Penn and Ben Franklin and their Electors to know of us."

"Was it Elizabeth who translated it?"

Tarami's laughter ended in a sigh. "No, she didn't possess it."

"Because it was a new world document?"

"In part, perhaps. *The Law of the Way* was dictated by Onandagos at the end of his great career, other than a codicil at the end that simply notes who took dictation and that Onandagos died and was buried. The book recounts his great journey west, including lists of his enemies and his allies. It tells his battle with the serpent of our people, and how he finally defeated it. It defines the bounds of the seven kingdoms of the Ohio, and the two places where four kingdoms meet. It gives final commands and prohibitions, and then a prophecy about the fate of the *Law* itself."

"What is the fate of the *Law*?" Luman in fact had little interest in ideas about the end of the world, but if the priest was a member of an esoteric brotherhood, anything he said might contain clues, so it was valuable to keep him talking about his sacred things.

"The Prophecy of the *Law*'s Rebirth has in fact already been fulfilled," Tarami said. "Again in his final testament, Onandagos said: 'In that day the serpent shall be reborn. My very words shall be eaten by the serpent and forgotten, and the children of my people shall fall into a deep sleep, in which sleep they shall dream great dreams of sin. They shall again scar their bodies as of old, and worship the serpent who seduced their father. But in the heart of the city whose foundations I have laid, the children of my people shall find again my words. My words shall restore them to the true way of God.'"

"You say this prophecy came true already." Luman's head was spinning. He had never cared much to learn about the cult practices and beliefs of the Firstborn, and now he was finding it considerably more complex that he could have imagined.

"For centuries, *The Law of the Way* was lost, and the children of the people of Onandagos languished in sin. The worship of the serpent returned."

"They scarred their bodies?"

"Circumcision," Tarami said. "A gleeful reminder of the days when the serpent-demon demanded that all men in Her service be castrated."

"Jesus was circumcised," Luman said.

"An old lie whispered by a djinn into Luke's ear." Tarami smiled ruefully. "Paul knew better. As did Onandagos."

"And then, what did you say? In the heart of the city?"

"In the days of Sarah Elytharias's grandfather," Tarami said. "He ordered renovations in the Basilica. There was found a hollow space within the wall, a place into which sacred texts had been discarded, to avoid desecrating them by destruction after their pages had moldered and their ink faded. Most of these were texts we had long possessed, but we also found *The Law of the Way*."

"How did people take it?"

"The king, for all his youth, grieved. He tore his hair to realized how sinful his people had become. He ordered the Temple of the Sun torn down, and the serpent's priestesses slain."

Luman raised his eyebrows in surprise. "Those things didn't happen."

Tarami shook his head sadly. "There was war in the streets. A great number of the people of Cahokia, and especially of the people of the land—peasants, farmers, slaves, ordinary people—refused to surrender their goddess. But in the compromise that the king forced on the serpent's daughters, they agreed to tear down their veil and lay open their secrets. And even Kyres Elytharias, for all his wicked attempts to bring back the cult of so-called Wisdom, never re-veiled the serpent throne."

Luman felt exhausted. "And your pilgrimage... you asked God to overthrow the serpent?"

Tarami turned a shocked face to him. "No! Understand me, I have prayed every day of my awakened life for the end of the serpent's cult. I have done that since I first learned to pray, as a child rescued from the slavery of the goddess by the learned Metropolitan Father Ahijah, and of course on my pilgrimage I continued to remember the blight that scars my land.

"But I did not crawl the Onandagos Road to fight against the serpent. I begged God at every step to raise the Pacification of the Ohio. I undertook the pilgrimage to beg for peace with the Emperor Thomas Penn." Tears trickled down the old man's cheeks.

"Of course, forgive me. I was so caught up in your tale of apostasy and restoration, I simply forgot." Luman hesitated. "I don't wish to sound impertinent, but... did it ever occur to you that maybe Father Ahijah, or whoever was Metropolitan before him...?"

"Yes?" Tarami asked.

Luman struggled to find a way to articulate his doubt without offending the priest. "No one had ever heard of *The Law of the Way*. No living person, I mean. And then, who should find it but priests, who use the book to push for change."

"Repentance and reform," Tarami said. "What are you suggesting?"

"I'm asking... how can you be sure Onandagos wrote the book? How can you be sure it wasn't someone like Father Ahijah who wrote *The Law of the Way* to put forward his own ideas, but then claimed Onandagos had written it?"

"What, so people would pay attention?"

"It doesn't sound insane to me."

"He was the Metropolitan. People already heeded his word."

"Not everyone," Luman pointed out. "Even with Onandagos to back him up, not everyone agreed with him. And from what little I've heard, even just from what I've heard from *you*, it sounds like the... serpent-worshippers, let's call them, have different ideas about Onandagos than you do."

"*The Law of the Way* is completely consistent with everything we know about Onandagos." Tarami's voice was stiff.

Luman realized that his curiosity had led him away from

his objective. If he offended the Metropolitan, the odds the man would invite him into any esoteric tradition of which he was a member declined to zero. "I'm sure you're right."

Tarami continued. "Of course, the serpent-worshippers claim otherwise. They have written themselves an Onandagos in their own image, a worshipper of the serpent rather than its foe."

"What about Moses?" Luman asked cautiously. "I only want to be instructed, Father Tarami. Didn't Moses raise a brass serpent on a rod?"

"To show the serpent's defeat!" Tarami snapped. "And with the defeat of the serpent, the children of Israel were healed!"

"I see." Luman nodded, careful to avoid smiling. He was afraid any smile would look like a doubter's smirk.

"I understand you did the Basilica a great service on the night of the beastkind's assault," Tarami said.

Luman shrugged. "I did what anyone would have done. I was lucky, and the beastkind thought I was more dangerous than I am. They fled before they could do any serious damage."

"I have no secrets to offer you, Luman Walters," the Metropolitan said. "I am no wizard, and Father Ahijah taught me no grips or passwords. The only Onandagos Road is the one I have walked, and God's commandments are all light and openness. But I am grateful for your defense of the house of God. And I am happy to satisfy any curiosity you have, about *The Law of the Way* or anything else. And you are welcome to sleep here, with me and the other refugees."

Luman was hesitant to ask, but his curiosity got the better of him. "Might you tell me how you read the windows of the Basilica?" he asked. "I seem to see two different versions of the creation, and two versions of the story of Adam and Eve, spelled out in one church. And one version of the creation shows a goddess, exhaling angels."

Tarami smiled patiently. "Ah, you touch on the deep things of Christian philosophy."

Does he mean esoterica? "I'd be grateful for whatever you could tell me."

"You know from the Bible that God created man in his image, male and female."

Luman spoke carefully. "Wouldn't some say that suggests there is a goddess?"

Tarami shook his head. "*The Law of the Way* is quite clear on this. 'Woman is in the image of God, and so is man. God is neither man nor woman, but is life and spirit, and all flesh is in the image of God.'"

"The image of the creating woman is...an allegory?"

"A reminder that we should not think of God as an old man, looking down on us from the heavens. And the twin stories of Adam and Eve are there to remind us that we can tell that story with great sorrow and regret, but we can also tell it with joy and gratitude."

"Nor is God an old woman," Luman added.

"Nor a serpent." Tarami smiled.

"Priests. Shoot me now."

———◆———

CHAPTER FIVE

"Madam Director! Madam Director!"

In her sleep, the shouting came from a crowd of Philadelphia's wealthiest and most influential, applauding her as she stood in the deep well of a theater. Notwithstanding Schmidt had brought order to the Ohio by applying the necessary amount of brutality and nothing more, and in that order there had flourished trade and prosperity. She deserved the accolades, as well as her inclusion on the Imperial honors list, and the new building for moral and economic philosophy Harvard was going to name for her.

"Madam Director!"

Schäfer was shouting. He wasn't touching her, he knew better than that, but he stood over her cot and shouted.

"Madam Director!"

"I'm awake." Schmidt sat up, throwing aside the wool blanket. The vigorous action, plus the sudden assault of frozen air on her calves, brought her to full wakefulness.

The brazier that had started the night with a merry orange fire now cradled an armful of dusty red embers.

"It's Dadgayadoh!" Was Schäfer sobbing? In the darkness, she couldn't see his face.

"What has Dadgayadoh done?" The Haudenosaunee was a dependable man and a hard worker. Schmidt was surprised to hear a complaint, much less a hysterical one. She stepped into cort-du-roy britches, tucking in her long nightshirt and groping in the darkness to find her coat again.

"He's been killed!"

Schmidt grabbed the brace of loaded pistols from beneath her cot. She had liked to mock her former wizard Luman Walters for sleeping with loaded guns, but only because he thought it kept away evil spirits.

She slept with loaded guns for much more prosaic reasons.

Like the death of one of her better traders.

She pushed through the canvas flaps into the frozen corner of earth bounded by her tent, the Parletts', and a supply tent, and then into the tent of the three quintuplets. Schäfer followed close on her heels. Had Dadgayadoh died defending an attack on her communication link with Philadelphia?

Dadgayadoh lay on his back, half-covered by furs and wool blankets. He held his hands in front of his eyes, twisted into claws with his fingers forward, as if some beast had leaped on him, attempting to bite his face.

In one hand he held the shredded remains of a beaded Haudenosaunee amulet.

His mouth was open in an expression of fear. There was no blood on him, no sign of any visible injury.

Piled about him like stacked wood were the bodies of Captain Mohuntubby and his soldiers. Schmidt prodded the captain with a pistol grip and was rewarded with a sleeping groan. The soldiers were asleep—ensorcelled? The company trader was dead.

There was no sign of the Parlett children.

The day before, Dadgayadoh had come to her to report the strange behavior of Robert Hooke, circling the city of Cahokia with wooden crosses. Was this death punishment for his spying?

After sunset, she had noted that mobile corpses shambled along the line of crosses.

"Find Hooke," she said, but she already guessed where he was. "Get everyone up. Find the Parletts." She raced out.

Just beyond the edge of her camp glowed a blasphemous light. It was wrong, backward. It was black, and though her eyes saw the black glow where Robert Hooke's largest cross stood on a low mound of earth, her mind could not quite process it.

She felt as if she were seeing a hole in the world. The fabric of the cosmos had split, and something shining and terrible lay on the other side.

The black light didn't wake the camp. Or had the camp been spelled into sleep?

Why was she awake?

She cocked the pistols and approached.

"Hooke!" she shouted.

A figure in the black light turned toward her. She heard a sound as it moved, or an anti-sound, in the same way that the darkness was an anti-light. She could make out the pale face and the white, black-rimmed eyes of Robert Hooke, and then she heard his dry laughter in her mind.

I bid thee good morning, Director.

"You killed Dadgayadoh. I'll have you answer for that."

He would not sleep, and he tried to stop me. As thou wouldst have done, as even Thomas would have. And I am one who will do the necessary thing.

And thou, Madam Director?

She now saw beyond him. Two of the Parletts stood at the foot of the mound, mouths open in shock, eyes rolling back in their sockets.

Bang! Bang!

She shot the Sorcerer in the chest with both pistols. He staggered and collapsed back against the large cross, but when he stood again he was laughing.

I begin now, foolish woman. Out of charity I warn thee, that if thou steppest on this mound during my operation, thou diest. Nevertheless, do thou as seest fit.

Then Schmidt saw the third Parlett boy. He was naked and tied to the cross, head downward. His mouth was open in the attitude of a scream—

no, all three of them had their mouths open as if to scream.

No, they *were* screaming. Schmidt couldn't hear a sound, but they were screaming at the top of their lungs.

Hooke faced the cross. Schmidt now saw that the cross was the source of the black light, the tear in the cosmos. *Come thou, Lord Protector!* Hooke shrieked. *Manifest and strike down the hopes of thine enemies!*

The black light erupted into fire. The flames shot up from the ground in a wall and raced away from the cross in two directions. Schmidt narrowly missed being struck by the fire and she fell back.

She dropped the useless pistols. "Schäfer! Mohuntubby!"

The Cherokee officer stumbled toward her at the head of a ragged file of men. They looked baffled and embarrassed. Schäfer followed.

The wall of black fire curved away from Schmidt as it ran. It curved, she realized, as if to surround Cahokia. Following the line of ash Dadgayadoh had told her about?

She took a step back.

The fire enclosed a corner of the company's camp. Mules and horses caught within it brayed and whinnied in consternation, and men came running from their tents. Dismay painted their faces, but they lived.

Schmidt almost forgot Hooke for a moment, watching the fire race. It moved in both directions around the besieged city.

Silence.

And then the plants within the circle of black fire began to die.

Schmidt saw it first in a young pine tree, just two paces within the circle. Its needles turned brown, curled, and then fell to the ground, first one or two, and then a steady stream, and finally a single brown avalanche.

A white oak tree, already leafless from the winter, split in two with a loud *CRACK!*

She turned her gaze to the city.

The leaves fell from the Treewall in a storm of green. Thinking she saw a second light, Schmidt stepped through the wall of black fire—

it didn't hurt.

Once within the strange veil, she could see that a blue light emanated from the city. Had she never noticed it before? It must be new. But that light streamed out from the trees of the Treewall as if they were bleeding.

As if they were maples, being tapped for their sugar.

Thin streams of blue light arced over frozen ground until they struck the wall of black fire. Along the nearer sections of the wall, Schmidt could see that the blue light intersected the fire at the sites of the smaller upside-down crosses.

No, the blue light didn't *intersect*. It *entered*, and was *absorbed*.

The black fire rose higher into the night sky. With her rational mind, Schmidt didn't understand how she could even see the dark flames, but she did.

Enter thou this worthy vessel! Hooke wailed.

The Parlett on the cross writhed. His two feet were riveted to the upright timber with a single nail, with further spikes pinning him to the crossbar through each palm and also each wrist. He wasn't twisting to try to get away.

He moved as if something was behind him, pushing to pass him.

Or perhaps it was *inside* him, and wanted to get out.

Hooke knelt and gripped the Parlett boy's head with one hand behind his neck. That put Hooke's forearm alongside the boy's cheek and his open, howling mouth. With a black flake of obsidian, Hooke slit his own wrist.

Black ichor burst from the dead flesh and poured into the Parlett boy's mouth.

The screaming became a choking, writhing and violent convulsion.

The other two Parletts fell to their knees and began vomiting black blood.

What was happening in Philadelphia?

"Arrest that man!" Mohuntubby shouted. Not waiting for his soldiers, he leaped forward, drawing his sword—

CRACK!

A flare of black light struck Mohuntubby in his charge and knocked him and all his men flat on their backs in the snow.

Hooke stood and gripped the vertical timber of the cross in both his hands.

I give thee, Lord Protector, this tribute of life!

Arching his back, he snapped the cross. The Parlett boy fell to the ground, his face as white as the snow on which he lay. His two brothers collapsed as well.

The fire flickered, as if under a strong gust of wind.

Hooke moved slowly. He seemed tired. Producing two smaller pieces of wood and a strip of leather thong from inside his tattered coat, he formed a smaller upside-down cross and pushed it down into the earth beside the large one.

The black flames stopped wavering.

This barrier will limit the power of the witch queen, Hooke said. The black slime dripping down his forearm trickled along his long yellow nails and stained the snow. *Among other things, we shall not see again this trick of the eldritch spring. Thou must instruct the men of the company not to interfere with my markers.*

"I must do no such thing," Notwithstanding Schmidt said, but she said it softly and under her breath.

What had Thomas seen? What did Thomas know? What did Thomas want her to do?

Pacifying the Ohio by coercion sat uneasily on her conscience, but she had made her peace with it. But this?

However exalted the goal, was this a necessary means?

Captain Mohuntubby stood. "You killed that boy. I'll see you tried for it."

Hooke laughed. *I did not.*

Mohuntubby pointed at the boy's body, facedown in the snow, arms still nailed to the beam. "I know what I saw."

Dost thou?

At that moment, the crucified Parlett brother stirred. He drew his knees up underneath him in the snow. Arms still nailed to the timber, he got one foot beneath him, and then the other, rising into a squatting posture, face still looking down.

He stood, and as he stood he raised his chin to look at Captain Mohuntubby. The boy's eyes were completely white, and a thick, black fluid welled up at their corners.

Mohuntubby gasped and stepped back.

Schmidt heard the other Parlett children weeping. "What have you made him?"

The crucified Parlett turned his head to meet Schmidt's gaze. When his face was turned directly toward her, she seemed to see a different face overlaid upon the boy's features. It was an older man's face, with a long, somewhat bulbous nose, and curly hair falling down from a point high above his forehead.

She heard a voice in her mind, but where Robert Hooke's voice sounded like dry leaves, this voice sounded like breaking glass.

My servant Robert made the boy a glorious thing. Consider thou young Parlett the horse I ride, or the cup containing the wine.

Oliver Cromwell.

Or the glove masking the fist.

The Necromancer.

Bringing his arms down with abrupt force, Cromwell shattered the bar that bound his arms. The broken halves fell aside and pulled away from the wracked little Parlett body, leaving nails behind in the cold flesh.

Cromwell stepped forward, the nail prints in his feet leaving black spots in the snow.

I am come to break the city of the serpent.

Director Schmidt stood her ground. "Robert Hooke killed my man Dadgayadoh. I will let Lord Thomas demand recompense for the child's life, but Hooke must stand trial for the life of my agent."

Thine agent lives, Cromwell said. *Even now, he comes to thee.*

"Protect the director!" Captain Mohuntubby shouted.

As she turned to see where Cromwell was pointing, Schmidt found a half-circle of muskets forming around her. She found the fact somewhat comforting, though beneath her comfort was the nagging thought that a sorcerer who could kill the Treewall of Cahokia could sweep these men away with little trouble.

And that was just Hooke. What about Cromwell?

Silhouetted against the cool blue-white pre-dawn glow of the sky, Dadgayadoh walked toward her.

His confident, upright step had fallen into a slouch; he wore his red blanket and his silk top hat, but without his usual somewhat jaunty look. For a moment, Schmidt thought she must have been mistaken earlier. He must not have been dead, only sleeping, like Mohuntubby and his men. Awakened by all the noise, her excellent Haudenosaunee trader now rejoined her. He was tired, but alive.

Then she saw his bare feet, the black nails of his fingers and toes, leaving behind a scratchy, confused trail in the snow. His blank stare. His slack jaw.

"Poor Dadgayadoh," she said. "I'm so sorry."

The draug who had once been Dadgayadoh only groaned.

"Deu meu!" Miquel gasped as a wall of black flame raised to encircle the city. "What is that?"

"Fire, you idiot," Josep said.

The two men leaned on the taffrail of the *Verge Caníbal* to either side of Montserrat Ferrer i Quintana. The ship lay at anchor in the center of the Mississippi and slightly downstream of Cahokia's walls. This didn't put it out of reach of the beastkind—the *Caníbal's* crew had killed three of the creatures trying to swim, climb, or fly aboard their ship in the few hours they'd been there—but it put the smugglers mostly out of the beastkind's notice.

The keelboatmen in Baton Rouge had explained that the Mississippi was too shallow for the *Verge Caníbal,* and had insisted that the best way upriver was to be poled or pulled in one of their coffin-shaped punts. They boasted they could make as much as a mile an hour upstream.

At that pace, Montse had calculated that she may as well walk. After a brief flirtation with the idea of horses—but few of her crew knew how to ride, much less care for such an animal—she had found a rivermage.

The man was Dutch, and a smuggler. His name was Pieter, and he insisted on being called Piet. He had only seven fingers and considerably more than seven tattoos, which mostly consisted of images of fantastic creatures, including basilisks, a two-headed alligator, and a pair of mating krakens. He claimed to be an Ohio River hansard, and to be able to navigate the curves of the Mississippi in the dark even *without* the magic that allowed him to command his exorbitant rates. He also said he'd been up and down the river six times in the last twelve months. He claimed to know all the sandbars, including the newly formed ones, by heart.

Piet hadn't exaggerated. They'd come up the Mississippi on a strong wind and pushed through the shallows by Piet's incantations. They only had to drag the ship off a sandbar once—and that had been Montse's fault, when she'd ignored Piet's strong warning and tried to cut through an ox-bow lake.

They'd outrun a tax cutter of one of the cotton princes, and a couple of Imperial Ohio Company canoes. They'd fired on a third Imperial craft to warn it out of their way, and bribed a fourth when it caught them in a slack breeze.

They'd arrived in the middle of the night and had spent the last several hours trying to calculate their best approach into the city. On the one hand, an army of Imperial irregulars surrounded the city entirely on the landward side. On the other hand, beastkind prowled the riverbank.

They didn't just prowl, they rampaged. In addition to fending off several attacks themselves, Montse and her crew watched beastkind gore each other, kill small river creatures, and even tear to pieces someone who might have been a fisherman—or maybe a Cahokian scout or spy—leaping from hiding as the poor man tried to stow his coracle under a shattered dock. They'd seen two climbing beastkind with sloth arms and powerful hind legs get nearly to the top of the wall before finally succumbing to the bullets and arrows pouring from above.

Then the fire had encircled the city.

"It's an opportunity," Montse said. "Look."

She pointed to the riverbank, where beastkind squawked and hooted, racing away from the walls.

"This fire isn't made by the Firstborn." Josep sucked a lemon drop.

"Lower the boat!" Montse ordered, and her men raced to obey.

"You race into a besieged city that is now also on fire," Josep said. "Only you, Capità."

Montse took a coiled length of cord with a steel grapple on the end. Her insides still hurt when she moved. "Sail downriver. I'll come down and signal when I can."

"If only you were so anxious to race into my arms." Josep sighed. "At least take Miqui with you."

Miquel grabbed another line and grapple and patted the pistols in his waistband. The boy wore a heavy wool coat over his ridiculously light cotton clothing. None of them had been really ready for the Ohio's cold, and Piet's river-magery, as powerful as it was, only extended to navigating and sailing the ship. It would not raise the temperature. "If nothing else, we can get off two more shots before the beasts overwhelm us."

Montse raced down the ladder, not looking to see whether the boy followed her. "We go now!"

Miquel landed with the grace of a lifelong sailor as Montse pulled away with both oars. "Capità," he protested. "At least let me do the rowing."

Montse acquiesced, switching places and leaning forward in the graying light. She kept an eye fixed on the beastmen, who splashed into the river or hid in the wreckage of the docks.

The Imperials, peering from their trenchworks, seemed equally surprised, but they weren't running away.

"Speed is everything," she said to Miquel. "We run to the wall, throw the grapples up, and climb. The Imperial soldiers might shoot us, and the beastkind might come up after us. Move fast."

"Do you have any good ideas for preventing the Cahokians from shooting us?" Miqui asked.

Montse shook her head. "Do you know any good prayers? Maybe something from St. Robert Rogers?"

"Maybe we can smile as we climb."

Montse laughed. "For you, that would work. For me, I fear

my white teeth will only give them a target to shoot at. Are you ready?"

Miquel grunted assent as his last stroke on the oars drove the boat up the shallows and into the muddy bank of the river. Montse leaped ashore, shrugging out of the coiled line and freeing the grapple to throw it.

The great advantage they had was the strange nature of the Treewall. Montse had never seen it, but the wooden palisade with the natural branches at its height was legendary. She'd never seen the city of Hannah's husband, and she hadn't expected those branches to actually have green, living leaves on them.

Still less had she expected the leaves to fall out the very minute she hurled her grapple into the branches.

"Capità!" Miqui was only a moment after her, hurling the steel toward the top of the wall. "You have killed the trees!"

The grapples caught and both smugglers began to climb. The riverbank mud on Montse's boots made footholds trickier, but this was a climb to be accomplished by arm strength. She dragged herself up cursing, knees and toes banging against the bark of the wall. Green leaves fell about her, striking her in the face and threatening her grip.

Miquel whistled, the cheerful bastard.

Halfway up the wall, the leaf-fall ended and she began shouting. It was a calculated risk. Would she attract Imperial fire? Perhaps, but she hoped that the darkness, and the strange wall of black flame would spoil their shots. But she worried that if she simply vaulted over the top of the palisade wall without warning, she'd end her days impaled on a Cahokian spear.

"Sóc amiga!" she shouted. "Je suis une amie! Ich bin eine Freundin! Abu m enyi! I am a friend!" The words stole her breath and slowed her progress, but when she reached the end of her scant repertoire, she started it again from the beginning.

Miqui joined her as best he could. "Friend! Freund! Amigo!"

Steel Ophidian-style sallet helmets peeped through the branches at the top of the wall. The black fire gleamed dully on the metal, and also on the metal of what Montse took to be musket barrels.

"Friend!" she shouted.

Her rope went suddenly taut. Her feet lost their purchase on the wall and she slipped, catching herself only after sliding down several feet and burning the skin of her hands. Only a lifetime of clinging to ratlines in Gulf storms kept her from losing her grip entirely and falling.

Below her, something with a head like the rhinoceros she had once seen in a private garden in Miami, only covered with fur, leaped upward, climbing the rope.

Stupid. She should have pulled it up behind her.

Hooking one booted toe around the rope to stabilize herself, Montse grabbed the hilt of her saber—

bang!

The shot came from beside her, rather than from above.

The rhino-headed beastman lost his grip and fell back.

Bang! Bang! Further shots came, but these were from the Imperial trenches, rather than Miquel or the defenders.

"Go!" Miquel shouted. "Climb!"

He slid down past her, and she resumed her upward progress. In his hand, she saw the flash of steel as the young sailor pulled a knife. Her rope went taut again and shook as the rhino began again to climb—

and then Miqui cut the line, and the rhino fell.

"Go!" Miquel shouted. "Go!"

Her hands and her guts both torturing her, Montse flung herself up the wall. She heard shouting in Ophidian—of which she only knew a few words—and braced herself to be shot from above, but the attack never came.

More gunfire came from the Imperial trench, but then Montse was into the branches. She released the rope. As blood flowed into her hands again she felt the burning of her abraded skin more intensely.

She stopped on the lower branches and reached out a hand for Miquel.

The boy pulled himself up to within reach, gripped a branch and then took Montse's arm.

Bang!

Miquel fell. Montse jammed one boot into the crotch of a branch and pulled her sailor up, but he was heavy. She hit the branch behind her, heard a loud crack, and then she and Miqui began to slide.

"Help!" She flung an arm over another branch, trying to wrap her elbow around the wood and stop her motion, but her arm slid along the limb, and she and Miqui rolled toward the edge—

below, she saw the snarling rhino face—

would she even survive the fall?—

and then hands caught her from above. Two men grabbed her by the shoulders of her coat. Two more grabbed Miquel, by one leg and one arm. The crew of four rescuers dragged the two Catalans up and over the top of the palisade, dropping them gently on the wooden walkway on the other side.

"Gràcies," Montse said. "Thank you."

Then her rescuers stepped back and she saw what they were. Beastkind.

Farther away on the walkway stood men in the silver helmets the Cahokians favored, leaning on spears or holding muskets in the crooks of their arms. But the four who had rescued Montse all had animal features. The one who stood closest and now grinned at her had the head and upper body of a coyote and wore a pair of pistols in holsters hanging from bandoliers over each shoulder.

"Keep your hands away from your weapons," the coyote said in English.

"I'm a friend," Montse said.

"I heard you the first time." The beastman grinned. "My queen will know for sure. Until then, you're my prisoner."

Montse didn't resist as the beastman stripped her of her sword and her pistols, and disarmed Miquel.

"And my friend?" she pressed. "The boy? Do you have healers?"

"We'll look to his wound," the coyote said, looking over the wall. He seemed distracted and surprised by the wall of flames. "In due time."

Sarah sat at a table in the Hall of Onandagos, beneath the stained-glass images of tall vines. The last time she'd been in this room, she'd been the second of Alzbieta Torias, who had been one of the candidates to be chosen by the city's goddess as the next king or queen.

This time, she sat at the table and no one objected.

The other former candidates weren't present. The landowner Voldrich and the poisoner Gazelem Zomas were the two about whose whereabouts she knew nothing. The Lady Alena seemed to have fallen into line, and the two military women were both now working with Sir William.

Confirming and learning such details was the purpose of the meeting. Cahokia had continued to be governed as it had been before, lightly, and by Maltres Korinn (as Vizier now rather than as Regent-Minister of the Serpent Throne, though it wasn't clear to Sarah that either position was very clearly defined).

It was time for Sarah to exercise a little control. To do that, she needed to get a clearer picture of what the pieces were and how they worked.

Around the table were Maltres Korinn, Alzbieta Torias, William Lee, the Polite Sherem, and Cathy Filmer. In the door stood Yedera the Podebradan. Outside the door were several of Alzbieta's warriors.

"I don't want his arrival to surprise anyone." Sarah pointed at the one unoccupied seat as she started the meeting. "I've invited Zadok Tarami."

Sir William snorted and the Duke of Na'avu looked dubious, but Alzbieta nodded. "It's a wise move, Beloved. Show his followers that you respect him ... and them."

"Is it so wise, though?" Cathy asked. "Maybe he shouldn't be invited to all the meetings. Maybe we shouldn't say anything in front of him that can be used against you, Your Majesty."

"In what capacity are you here, Mrs. Filmer?" Alzbieta Torias asked. "Sir William leads our combined army. Maltres has been head of the civil government for years, and—forgive me, Maltres, if I give away secrets—is a well-connected Freemason. Sherem is connected with the wizards of Cahokia, in their various groups. I represent the Handmaids of the Virgin. Even Metropolitan Tarami's presence makes sense to me, representing the priests of the Basilica and those who worship with them. What constituency do *you* represent?"

Sarah knew by now that Cathy's perfectly still expression concealed rage.

"She represents *me*," Sarah said. "Cathy is here precisely because she is not connected to any of Cahokia's groups. She is here to be my second soul."

Cathy smiled faintly and nodded.

"I'm inclined to agree with ... Cathy, Your Majesty," Sir William said.

Maltres inclined forward across the table. "How are you feeling, Sir William?"

Sarah expected a droll quip or a fiery rebuff. Instead, Sir William seemed to shrink into himself. "Your question is reasonable.

I apologize for the state in which you saw me on the ramparts the other day, suh. I was *not* myself."

"And you are yourself now?"

Sir William fixed the Vizier with a steely green eye. "Yes I am."

Maltres nodded.

"I'm glad to hear it," Sarah said. "I need each of you to operate at full power and to be available to me at all times."

There was a round of general nodding.

"Beloved," Maltres Korinn said. "Might we begin by articulating the basis on which we are here?"

"We are the government of the kingdom," Cathy said.

"Yes," Maltres agreed. "Let us be clear about it. Sarah is the Beloved of Wisdom, First Handmaid of the goddess of Cahokia. Everyone in the city knows that."

"That is *not* what everyone in the city knows." Zadok Tarami spoke from the door. With a subtle show of her teeth, Yedera let him in.

"You weren't in the city," Alzbieta Torias said. "You didn't feel it."

Zadok Tarami took the empty seat. "By your account, you weren't, either. You were in a place I do not believe to exist, a magical land called Unfallen Eden, in which Adam's tragic decision was never made, and all the children of the primeval demon serpent Lilith worship her in happiness, surrounded by buzzing bees and purring lions."

Alzbieta shook her head. "Say rather that essential portion of Eden that was not affected by Adam's choice, where the goddess has always remained and will always remain, undiminished by the necessary echoes of her in this mortal world."

"Priests." Sir William leaned toward Cathy. Sarah barely heard him. "Shoot me now."

"What I have been told by my congregants," Tarami shot back, "was that at the rising of the sun on the solstice they felt a powerful feeling of love and wellbeing directed toward Sarah Elytharias."

"There you have it," Maltres said.

"I believe God has chosen her," Tarami said. "I believe He chose her in answer to my prayers and the prayers of the thousands of others who have begged for relief from the Pacification. I am honored to be included in this council, and I will do my best to help Sarah achieve God's purpose for her."

"And if I believe I am meant to become queen?" Sarah asked him.

"One can be chosen by God and fail. Our Lord himself chose Judas Iscariot." He looked at her with unblinking eyes. "My fellows and I will be happy to instruct you and advise you. Traditionally, the Metropolitan of Cahokia has crowned the land's kings."

Meaning Tarami thought he had a veto right.

"That is only the public coronation," Alzbieta said. "The second coronation takes place within the Temple of the Sun and is necessary for a person to truly take the throne."

"Last I heard, you and your sisters didn't even know of what the so-called second coronation consisted." Tarami's smile was warm and benevolent. "As much as we may hope for the blessed revelation of such a thing, for now, the coronation within the Basilica is all there is."

"Thank you for these competing views," Sarah said, cutting Alzbieta off. "This is precisely why I invited you all into this council. If you all agreed, your advice would not be useful to me."

Tarami smiled.

"Here is the situation as I see it," Sarah said. "Those who were with me know that the goddess chose me as Her Beloved."

"Amen," Alzbieta, Maltres, and Sherem said together.

She continued. "I am therefore titular head of an order of priestesses I scarcely understand. Also, all the Firstborn in the city at that time felt . . . something. That feeling is the basis on which I govern. I may have rivals, either among former claimants to the throne or from quarters as yet unseen. One thing I intend to do is consolidate my power by quickly accomplishing my coronation."

"There may be other reasons my Beloved would wish to take the Serpent Throne," Alzbieta said.

"Mmm," Tarami murmured. "Didn't John tell us that 'Jesus answered him, I spake openly to the world'?"

Sarah ignored the tension between her priestess and her priest. "I want to hear about the state of the city. I need you to teach me about Cahokia. And I want to hear about the claimants under the presentation. But there's something more urgent than that."

"The food supply is secure," Maltres said. "We harvested every grain, seed, melon, squash, fruit, and legume we could find in the bounty the goddess sent us."

Zadok Tarami opened his mouth; Sir William fairly leaped over the table to jab a finger at him. "Don't say it, suh. We all know what you think, and we'll take it as said. Do not waste my queen's time."

Tarami smiled and sank back into his chair. "Forgive me. I'm an old man and a debater of many years' experience. It's hard for a leopard to change his spots."

"I, too, am resisting old spots," Sir William told him. "Only I believe my spots are considerably more violent than yours."

"What happened this morning?" Maltres looked about the table at all the participants as he asked, but his gaze came to rest on Sarah.

They all knew what he meant. They all knew he was asking her. In the early morning, before dawn, the abundance of plants that had sprouted in the thoroughfares and plazas of Cahokia had entirely wilted. By midday, when they'd come together for this conference, the plants had begun to rot where they stood.

"The foliage and buds of a new crop of fruits and nuts fell from the Treewall," Sir William said.

Sarah nodded. "I would have guessed as much. I will tell you what I know, and what I guess.

"I was awakened before dawn with a feeling of intense pain. It was if all the blood in my veins had been sucked out in one moment, and I was instantly parched to dust. I sneaked out and climbed the wall—"

"You shouldn't get ahead of your bodyguard like that," Maltres said sternly.

Sarah laughed. "Iron Andy Calhoun is the best man between New Orleans and Philadelphia, and *he* couldn't keep me penned. You're welcome to try, Maltres Korinn, but you're going to have to get up really early in the morning."

Maltres and Alzbieta both looked embarrassed. They shouldn't feel that way; Sarah had used an *oculos obscuro* incantation, and there was nothing they could have done to stop her.

"You were on the wall," Sir William said. "Chikaak told me he smelled you, and I doubted him."

Sarah didn't love to hear that she had been *smelled*, but she let it pass. "A mighty spell has been cast in the Imperial camp."

Zadok turned his head sharply. "Walters?"

"No. Robert Hooke, I think. I recognize his . . . visual stink, so to speak." How much could she really tell them about the spell that forced her to kill Thalanes, that nearly killed Sarah and her brother Nathaniel both, the vortex of groping hands in a sea of amber death? "I think I know the enchantment he has worked. We're trapped inside a spell of his, a spell that kills."

"The whole city is trapped?" Tarami asked.

Sarah nodded.

Sherem sighed. "I ... fear I may know the spell of which you speak."

Sarah hadn't expected help, but she was happy to accept it. "Will it ... kill people?"

The Polite was slow to answer. "Maybe. Perhaps eventually? Perhaps it will close in and become more potent? Perhaps if the Sorcerer can channel additional power into it?"

"That's a lot of perhapses," Sir William growled. "If a subaltern offered me that many maybes, I'd break him down to a corporal, if not worse."

"This is gramarye." Sherem shrugged. "Not bricklaying. Perhaps the spell will do nothing. Perhaps we will merely starve to death when the supplies run out."

"At least the goddess has given us more time." Sarah shot a warning look at Tarami, and he said nothing. "Maltres, I'll need to know how much."

"There are many variables," he said. "I'll give you my best estimate."

"I am grateful for the fruits and nuts," Bill murmured. "But I would have been more grateful for behemoth."

Alzbieta Torias laughed. "To fight our battle for us, you mean?"

Bill frowned. "No, to eat. Behemoth means many cattle."

"Behemoth is a monster." Tarami glared at both Bill and Alzbieta.

"And yet that is not what I remember from Harmonszoon," Bill muttered. "The behemoth is beeves, I would swear to it."

"How are we doing on getting messengers out?" Sarah asked Maltres.

Maltres Korinn frowned. "Poorly. My men are being intercepted by the Imperials."

"Is that just bad luck?" Sarah frowned.

"Maybe," Korinn said. "Or maybe it's because the Imperial web is strong and thrown wide. And I am hesitant to send men out the Mississippi Gate. It seems certain death. We'll continue to try."

"I think for now I can forego a detailed description of city functionaries," Sarah said. "And I reckon we've all heard enough for today on the differences between the Temple Handmaids and the Basilica gang."

"We do more than operate the Basilica," Zadok Tarami said. "We run multiple charitable organizations and two schools."

"And *we* curate a large library," Alzbieta said.

Sarah nodded. "Understood. And I urgently want to know more about the arcane resources we may have at our disposal. But most urgently, I want to make sure we have something resembling an army coming together." She looked at Sir William and was gratified to see that he didn't flinch. "Joleta Zorales and Valia Sharelas. Are they with us? I think I could stand a rebellion of poets, but I want the cannons pointing away from me."

The Cavalier cleared his throat. "Zorales commands Your Majesty's artillery. The majority of the soldiers under her command are former Pitchers. They are also largely women and Firstborn, and I understand they are particularly enthusiastic for Your Majesty's cause."

Even Tarami laughed at that.

Sir William continued. "Valia Sharelas has also agreed to serve Your Majesty. With Your Majesty's permission, I should like to offer her the second position after myself, with the appropriate rank. She is acting in that capacity already."

"Of course. And our forces?"

"It is a small army," Sir William said. "Barely fit for the defense of a city, and certainly unfit for sallying forth to attack a larger enemy. We have artillery for the walls. Most of the wealthy families of the city have contributed some or all of their retinues. Along with the wardens and the beastkind, we are drilling the new recruits. Thank Heaven that, for the moment, the forces outside the walls are nearly as motley as ours."

Sarah breathed a sigh, if not of relief, exactly, then of a slight lowering of the tension that knotted up her spine.

"Still, to break this siege, we will need more forces than we presently have at our disposal. And one more thing, Your Majesty," Sir William added. "We have taken two prisoners this morning, climbing the western wall."

Sarah frowned. "Beastkind?"

Sir William chuckled. "Pirates, as it happens. And I think you should see them."

"Your father gave powerful gifts."

———◆———

CHAPTER SIX

Thomas carried the dead child in his own arms.

Temple had brought him in to see the boy shortly after dawn. The other Parlett quintuplet was alive, though unconscious and whimpering through some sort of nightmare. Gottlieb, whose duty it had been to watch the children through the night for any incoming messages, lay senseless on the floor, bleeding through his nostrils.

Thomas took the Parlett boy to Shackamaxon Hall. He wasn't traumatized by the child's death any more than he was shaken by the deaths of any of his dragoons or company factors or spies. People died for empire: men, women, and children. Thomas could not begin to hold himself responsible for each of them.

If the Parlett boys had come to him from their families rather than from the Imperial College, he might have sent their parents money, perhaps even arranged an annuity. He might very well have put all five Parletts on the honors list, once their work was done.

But he wouldn't shed a tear.

Once the other Parlett was conscious, Thomas would inquire whether Director Schmidt had any explanation. First, he would see what he could learn from his guiding ancestral genius.

The hall was cold. Since Thomas was the only person who used the hall, and that only infrequently, there was no point heating it. The vents that would have brought coal-heated air into the large room were shut, and the stones felt like slabs of ice under his knees.

He laid the boy on the floor.

"Grandfather," he said. "What happened?"

There was no answer.

"Grandfather," Thomas tried again. "This boy died under my roof tonight. He died for his empire and there's no shame in that, but there is something of a mystery. His brother lives, but raves, and the name that falls from his lips over and over again is Oliver Cromwell."

Nothing.

"The Lord Protector could not be allied with the Cahokian witch." Thomas pressed his forehead to the stone. "Please. I am trying to understand."

The Presence filled the hall.

Thomas's heart beat faster.

"My son," the apparition said in his voice of cutting wire and shattered glass. "You are troubled by death."

"The boy is nothing," Thomas said. "There are four others to replace him. But he died in my hall. Was it an attack? Did the boy take a blow that was aimed at me? Why does he repeat the Lord Protector's name, over and over?"

"Are you troubled by the name of Cromwell?"

Thomas considered. Was he? "No. The Lord Protector deeded Pennsland to my family. I owe him my wealth. And if perhaps he went astray later in his life, he did it for his land. He took power to benefit the people of his England."

The Presence took two steps forward, plate armor gleaming dully in the morning light. Thomas's heart beat faster; his grandfather was walking toward him. "He took power to benefit *all* the children of Eve, my son."

"But is it the Lord Protector who now attacks me?"

"The Lord Protector has no desire to bring down the House of Penn. On the contrary, together we shall work a mighty work. The Eternal Commonwealth that fell in England under the hammer of John Churchill may rise in Pennsland, protected by the sword of Thomas Penn."

Visions of an eternal Philadelphia filled Thomas's mind, a Philadelphia in which every building glowed with the warmth and light of permanent power, and not just the Lightning Cathedral. A Philadelphia in which Thomas had no need of the protection of his Town Coat, in which he didn't need to cadge shillings to fund the grinding pseudo-war of the Pacification, and in which the most noble and wealthy princesses of Europe came to seek his affection.

He shook his head. "Grandfather, strengthen my faith. You speak of glorious things, and I find that I am a bricklayer whose task it is to capture the continent's overflow of liquid feces."

Moments of terrible and majestic silence passed.

"I give you a sign, my son. Rise."

Thomas lifted his eyes, surprised that the Presence would command him to stand.

Then he realized that the order wasn't directed at him.

Lying naked on his back, the Parlett boy opened his eyes. A split second later, he gasped, sucking air into his narrow chest with a high-pitched whistle.

"God be praised," Thomas murmured.

"Life," the Presence said. "So fragile in the individual. So indomitable in its collective flow. Nowhere to be found when needed, and impossible to eradicate when it is not desired."

Thomas nodded.

Parlett sat up. The pallor fled from his cheeks and he shivered.

"The gift of God poured out uselessly on the undisciplined poor, and grudgingly withheld from the mighty."

The Parlett child climbed to his feet, swaying unsteadily.

"Even John Churchill doubted at the end," the Presence said. "Even the Hammer of Woden wondered whether he had sided with the powers of death, to the detriment of his beloved land."

Odd to hear his grandfather talk of Lucky John so, though of course they had been contemporaries. "I would bless my land."

"I know you would, my son. And yet you have no children to follow you. If you die today, who rules Pennsland? Whom do the Electors choose for the throne?"

Thomas sighed. "I know I fail you in this, grandfather. I am trying. I do not wish Hannah's rebel get to spoil what you built. What *I* have built. And I have years yet to take a bride."

Parlett tottered toward the door. Thomas turned his neck slightly to keep an eye on the boy.

"You may have more years than you think," the Presence said. "I preserve you with my power, my son. You will be vigorous and strong into an unusually old age, as you are faithful."

"I am faithful," Thomas said.

"And yet, I cannot extend your life forever," the Presence said. "My power is limited as of yet."

Parlett abruptly fell. As if he were a marionette and his puppeteer had cut the strings, the boy collapsed in a tangle of bare knees and elbows and lay still.

Should he rush to the youth's aid? But if his grandfather's power, sufficient to raise the boy earlier, could do nothing now, then surely Thomas was ineffective.

"What would you have me do?" he asked.

The Presence strode closer. His armored feet made no sound on the stone, and he cast no shadow. "When the Lord Protector granted the forests of the new world to William Penn, he installed Penn not merely as landowner, but as king."

"Yes." This felt right. This was what Thomas had always known in his heart.

"The ceremony took place on board Penn's ship *The Fox*. Penn eschewed a literal crown, but he knelt in a box of soil brought from the banks of the Susquehanna River and the Lord Protector anointed and blessed him."

Thomas shivered. His own accessions to power had been more prosaic: a legal document, drawn up after the fact, sequestering Hannah for madness; a deed transferring the family lands and properties; a grudging consent from the Electors to his regency, and another to his taking the throne. He had come to power with the blessing of lawyers. He envied his grandfather's more beautiful ascent.

"Yes," he said.

"This is no secret." The Presence gestured at the painting of the Fox Anointing on the wall. "It is as public as the history of the Walking Purchase, your grandfather's alliance with the peoples of the forest. But here are aspects of that history that are less well known."

"Yes." Curious that his grandfather spoke of himself so consistently in the third person.

"I will tell them to you now."

Thomas found he was holding his breath. He forced himself to exhale steadily and nod.

"In the anointing, Oliver Cromwell passed more to William Penn than just land. He placed himself into the landowner and traveled to the new world in Penn's breast."

"Do you mean a copy?" Thomas was confused. He had listened to lectures on the theory of gramarye at Harvard, but Ezekiel Angleton had sat all those exams for him. "A doppelgänger, or a simulacrum?"

"The copy stayed behind. John Churchill was rising, and the Lord Protector saw that his reign would be ended in England. He had to leave a shade, a mirror image of himself to act and rule in England, and that cost him much of his power. But his true self traveled to the new world with William Penn."

Thomas shook his head, not meaning to. Could this be true? "A sizar at Harvard reported such a rumor to me," Thomas said. "I had to pay a pretty purse to the Yankee he served after I killed the fellow in a duel."

"The rumors have at least a kernel of truth within them. Your family, my son, has prospered with the blessing of the Lord Protector. The blessing, and often the counsel as well."

Counsel? "What do you mean?"

The Presence stepped forward again and reached down to graze Thomas's shoulder with a mailed hand. "I am your ancestor William Penn. I am also Oliver Cromwell, the Lord Protector, great benefactor of your family. The loss of my other half to John Churchill was a crushing blow, and I have been regaining power slowly for decades. I guided you to the throne because it was imperative to keep the Firstborn from seizing its power. I will guide you now to take even greater power."

Thomas swallowed. His throat was so dry, the action hurt. "My sister . . . what did she know?"

"Nothing," the Presence said. "My power descends through the male line alone. She was the first landowner not to bear me in her breast, the first not to hear my wisdom in her ear."

"And my father? Did he see you?"

The Presence squeezed Thomas's shoulder, a sensation like a gentle breeze. "The men of the House of Penn have heard my voice in their hearts from William Penn through to you. They have taken me to be the Holy Ghost, or their own intuition, or the phantoms of dream.

"You are the first to see me."

"You appeared to me here." Thomas could never forget the moment he knew his grandfather had chosen him. His grandfather, who was also Oliver Cromwell. The shade had appeared to him in the empty field that would one day become the site of Horse Hall, the night before Hannah's installation as Empress. Thomas had seen the Presence sitting in a ghostly image of the Shackamaxon Throne, surrounded by a phantasmagorical Shackamaxon Hall.

That first conversation had started Thomas on the path that had brought him here.

"You will be the greatest Penn ever to sit the Imperial throne, my son. My power is recovered. The pieces are moving into position. The time is right."

"The stars favor us."

"You will unite your lands. Not as a loose coterie of squabbling fiefdoms, but as the true and eternal Empire of Pennsylvania, as it was always intended to be."

"Yes."

"You will crush your rebel niece and all her allies, grinding them beneath your heel and adding their lives to your honor and the glory of your house."

"I will."

"You will open up the shell of the Moundbuilders, and you and I shall drink their life. You will live forever, and all mankind will know you as their benefactor and great leader. Your name will be whispered with the names Moses, David, Cromwell, and Christ."

Thomas trembled.

"You will end death."

Thomas fell forward onto the stone. He pressed himself flat to the slab, arms extended before him.

"It is time I again took a body," Cromwell said. "Or rather, bodies."

Thomas turned his head slightly to watch. The Lord Protector—did Thomas think of Cromwell as *the Necromancer*, or was that the invidious slander of his enemies?—stepped slowly to the body of the Parlett boy.

"Turn him for me," Cromwell said. "Lay him on his back."

Thomas made slow, small, solemn motions. He rose to his knees, approached Parlett slowly, and then rolled the corpse onto its back. He arranged the arms by the boy's sides, straightened out his legs, as if he were preparing the boy for burial.

Then he moved back and knelt.

Cromwell in turn descended to his knees. He then lay on

the boy's body, stretching himself out to full length and intoning heavy syllables Thomas didn't understand.

Then Cromwell sank into the boy's body and disappeared.

Thomas gasped, despite himself.

The boy opened his eyes again, but they had changed—they were entirely white. As the boy stood, a dark gel began to form in the corner of his eyes.

The boy turned to Thomas. "This is not eternal life." His voice was the grating sound of church bells being ground to pieces, the Lord Protector's voice. He reached a hand forward to grip Thomas by the shoulder. This time Thomas felt flesh and bone, if not warmth. "This is puppetry. But eternal life will come."

"Yes." Thomas was surprised at how eager he felt. "Tell me what to do."

Calvin Calhoun's ride down the Mississippi was troubling.

An Imperial Ohio Company canoe intercepted the keelboat early and exacted a toll. After that, two Memphite barges threatened, though the keelboat captain and all his crew waved, smiled, and promised not to dock at Memphis, and the Memphites let them pass. But the perils of the river were not what disturbed Cal.

The work didn't bother him. He poled, he sang, he cooked grits and bacon to earn his keep, but Lord hates a man as don't know how to work when it's called for, and this was light going, by his standards.

The refugees carried by the boat were distressing. Cal heard tales of ravaged farms, of men impressed into the local militias or the military entourages of backwoods barons, leaving women and children defenseless when the beastkind attacked. A kingdom Cal had never heard of before, some kind of Firstborn land out beyond the Missouri, raided and stole from the farmers as well. It was as if something had driven all the beastkind mad, and their riot had knocked everything out of order, so everyone in the Missouri was fighting everyone else for land, food, and the joy of killing.

What had happened to start the frenzy of killing, Cal knew, was the death of Peter Plowshare and the coming to the throne of his son, or self, or alter ego, or shadow, or whatever—Simon Sword.

The refugees' stories broke his heart, and Cal gave half his food at every meal to the Missourians huddled in their match coats, blankets, and furs. When not poling or sleeping, he threw a line into the river and tried to catch fish. His success was limited, but the occasional bass or catfish he managed to pull from the water was expertly dissected by his knife, cooked at the boat's small stove, and then passed in chunks to wide-eyed, sooty-faced children.

The refugees didn't trouble him. If anything, they gave him the opportunity to show what the New Light meant to him.

He needed that, after what he'd seen and heard in the Firstborn city, Cahokia.

What troubled Cal were thoughts of Sarah. Was she queen of Cahokia now? Was she an angel? Was she some kind of Firstborn girl Jesus?

He didn't know.

He hadn't abandoned her; he'd been driven away. He would tell his grandpa, Iron Andy Calhoun, with a clean conscience, that he'd protected Sarah all along her road. He'd brought her to her throne, and there, to defend her rights, he'd killed a man.

And then she had rejected him.

Maybe she had to. Maybe the goddess had made her do it.

Maybe the necessary killing Cal had performed had left him unclean, and unfit for her company.

Still, it hurt.

If she'd come to the throne and the news had gone out, Cal was outracing it. He felt a pang of regret wishing he could meet his grandpa in the Elector's Thinkin' Shed and tell him proudly his foster daughter had become queen.

Still, he did have some astonishing things to report.

He also had something to show, something he'd been carrying close to his skin for weeks—a letter. It was a confession, written by Bayard Prideux, confessing to the murder of Kyres Elytharias.

The letter identified Thomas Penn as the man who had ordered the murder.

Cal disembarked by jumping into the river in shallow water and splashing ashore. He did it under cover of night and on land he knew belonged to the Clays. This was deliberate; he had personally lost cattle to Clay rustlers, taken from spring pasture. Cal had seen beasts he knew as well as he knew his own cousins, for sale in Knoxville in the autumn. The Clays were rustlers as much as the Calhouns, as much as Cal himself.

Not these particular Clays, of course, but the family.

That meant he didn't feel the slightest bit bad about stealing two of their horses.

They'd shoot him if they caught him, that was the game. But Cal was good at what he did. He had the patience to sit quietly for a long time, watching the movements of the farmhouse occupants, the beasts, and the moon. He had the self-discipline to count how many slugs that single guard had taken from his bottle, and wait until the man nodded off against the wall. He had half a catfish wrapped in a bit of wool to break into three pieces and throw to the rangy dogs when they raised curious muzzles at his appearance. He had the silent step to creep without being caught to the stable, the muscle control to freeze and escape notice when a late-night visitor to the jakes wandered by, and the wisdom to avoid opening hinged doors that might not be well-oiled.

Jerusalem, if the Clays were half as cunning as Calvin or Iron Andy, they'd deliberately not oil the hinges, precisely to catch rustlers and horse thieves.

So Calvin climbed over the door, a few feet from the sleeping guard, and let himself in. He picked two beasts that looked like fast runners and helped himself to a rope hanging on the stable wall. He cut off a length, tied it with a slipknot, and dropped the loop gently around the drunk and snoring guard.

Mounting up and leading the second animal, he opened the stable door.

With the loud *creak*, the Clay snoozing under his slouch hat stopped snoring and looked up.

Cal kicked the horses into a gallop. He yanked the rope with him and the Clay guard hit the ground and bounced, dragged in Cal's wake. He dropped the bottle and, more to the point, his rifle.

The man was too drunk, surprised, and knocked breathless to yell, at least for a few minutes. That was as Cal planned. He dragged the fellow eastward into the forest along a wide path for a mile. At that point, the fellow began to catch his breath and yell, "Horse thief, dammit! Horse thief!"

Cal cut him loose and rode faster.

A mile farther along, where the road plunged through deep shadow on a straightaway, Cal tied half his stolen rope across the path at chest level. He was just beginning to hear the sounds of pursuit behind him.

He tied the second half a mile later, in a bend in the road.

That would make the Clay boys peer really carefully into every patch of darkness before riding through, and take it slow.

Then Cal rode like hell.

He rode to the Memphis Pike. There was the risk he might attract Imperial Foresters, watchful to impose their tariffs and tolls on illicit commercial traffic, but even if he did, he didn't think they'd try to stop him. He wasn't carrying anything for sale. If they asked why he was riding so hard, he'd tell them he'd tried and failed to kidnap a bride, and now he had to worry about the girl's brothers.

He stuck to the paved pike for a couple of miles, and then plunged off into the forest again on a narrow trail he thought he recognized.

No pursuit short of the supernatural would follow his trail over those changes, and if the Clays were willing to use magic to track him, he wasn't going to get away. Another mile farther on and over the crest of a rocky ridge, Cal let himself slow down.

He rode up the approach to Calhoun Mountain two days and four trades later, riding only a single horse, and that one exhausted. At the foot of the defile leading up to the mountaintop, his fatigue was cracked wide open by familiar shouting.

"Calvin! Calvin Calhoun, hot damn iffen you ain't come back!"

Red Charlie took Cal's horse and Caleb gave Cal a shoulder to lean on as he hitched himself up the slope, one ragged step at a time. Caleb was full of questions, as were the younguns who bounced into view at the top, Young Andy at their head.

"You ain't brought back Aunt Sarah!" Young Andy hollered, announcing the obvious conclusion before anyone could beat him to it. "That mean she's Empress now?"

Cal grabbed his cousin by the ears and roughed up his hair. "Iffen you don't know too much, you know too little. I can't rightly say which it is. No, I don't expect Sarah is Empress."

"Queen of the Ohio, at least?" Andy insisted.

"Mebbe that," Cal conceded.

He crossed the meadows as briskly as he could manage, shooting a loving wave and a grin at every friendly face he saw on the way. When he reached the Elector's Thinkin' Shed, he was surprised to see two men standing on the covered dogtrot.

"Grandpa." Cal nodded to show his respect. "Mr. Donelsen."

Charlie Donelsen showed his missing teeth in a broad grin. "I heard of you afore, Calvin. I have boys as say you're a pretty impressive hand with a lariat."

"Lord hates a man as can't work for a livin'." Cal shrugged. "I'm right glad that horse I rode up on ain't wearin' a Donelsen brand, though."

"What brand was it?" Donelsen asked.

"I come up from near Memphis at a dead gallop, Mr. Donelsen," Cal said. "Wearin' out horses and tradin' down all the way. I set out with a pair of fine, fresh beasts. I didn't look too close, but I expect they mighta had Clay brands on their hides. The one I jest turned over to Red Charlie—and I reckon it's a miracle if she don't end up in the cookin' pot—looks like her brand's been stamped over three or four times."

"That won't be a Donelsen animal, then."

Cal shook his head. "I believe it's one of Emperor Thomas's. Used to pull a cook wagon for some Foresters as are camped out about thirty miles west of here, and are happy to git a younger beast."

Charlie Donelsen laughed. "Iffen it *had* been one of ours, hell, son, we got bigger fish to fry."

Iron Andy threw his one arm around Calvin in a tight embrace, dragging the younger, taller man up onto the wooden porch. "Sarah?" The lines in his face looked as deep as rivers.

"Alive," Cal said. "In Cahokia. Mebbe...mebbe queen, I can't say for sure. Jest as things was startin' to git interestin', I had to leave. Iffen she is, I reckon we'll hear soon enough. But she's with good people. William Lee, mebbe you heard of him. Dragoon captain. And the regent of Cahokia, he took her in. And one of the high-rankin' priestesses."

Cal felt worse than ever for leaving.

Iron Andy nodded. "And Thalanes? I ain't heard you mention my old friend."

Calvin felt a ball of lead in his belly. "He died, grandpa. Savin' Sarah from a sorcerer as tried to take her soul."

Iron Andy set his jaw in a straight line. "Full of pepper to the end, I expect."

"Yessir," Cal agreed. "Brave as e'er a feller could be, too."

Iron Andy Calhoun sighed. "Well, come on in, Cal. We got some thinkin' to do—little Tommy Penn wants a great big war."

Calvin pressed his hand to the Frenchman's letter to reassure himself it was still there. "In that case, Grandpa...I might have brought a solid cannonball to heave at the bastard."

"I like this one!" Charlie Donelsen laughed. "Tell me your name again, son."

They called themselves the Village of the Merciful.

Some had argued for Kingdom. There had even been a few votes for the idea that the community should name itself after Chigozie Ukwu—the Ukwites, or the Chigozi. Chigozie himself had pleaded against those options and in favor of a name that sounded more like a church: the Community of Christ, or the Church of Christ the Merciful.

Kort and Ferpa had argued energetically in favor of the word *Merciful*.

Though Kort never raised a hand in threat or raised his voice, the other beastkind that streamed to join Chigozie's followers all deferred to him. Was it size? Fearsomeness? A general air of charisma? A reputation he had earned with previous ferocity?

Whatever the source of his influence, Kort's view carried the day.

Within a week of Christmas, Chigozie had thirty followers. Many of them had been within the walls of Cahokia on the morning of the solstice, the same morning Kort had been there. Something had happened to them, though none of them could say what. Their madness subsided like a retreating wave, though the wave still carried many of their fellows with it.

And the madness didn't disappear entirely. When hungry, or afraid, or provoked, the Merciful could still react with energy and even violence.

But mostly, they reacted as Chigozie would have expected any child of Adam to react. Sometimes with mirth, sometimes impatiently, sometimes with a short temper, but mostly with a cheerful decency and a desire to get along. They came to join the Merciful of their own free will; they tried to live in peace.

It wasn't hard to find Chigozie. He didn't try to hide. On the hill with two springs of fresh water where they made their camp, he erected a twelve-foot-tall wooden cross. At dawn, the Merciful gathered to face eastward and sing the songs Chigozie taught them.

Many thought he should have a title. Again they tried King,

but also Lord, General, Prophet, and Duke. Chigozie demurred, though at the title Bishop his heart broke and he very nearly agreed to be called Priest...which, after all, he was.

But he held fast. "Call me Brother," he insisted, whenever anyone showed the slightest hint of an intent to do otherwise. "Brother Chigozie. As I call you Sister Ferpa, and Brother Kort, and Sister Lanani. We are all children of Adam. We are all creatures of the same God."

The hill was theirs to occupy because the village and castle adjoining had been destroyed. Chigozie resisted suggestions that he move into the remaining roofed rooms of the castle—instead, when any of the Merciful were injured or ill, he housed them there, beside a large fire. They came to refer to the three connected rooms (formerly a dining hall, a kitchen, and a pantry, though most of the stores had been depredated before the Merciful arrived) specifically and the ruined castle generally as the Houses of Healing.

Chigozie built a small shelter for himself to live in. It was simple, as he had no art in the matter, and he was only able to do it at all because he could salvage planks and tables from ruined houses of the village.

He lay down a rectangle of bricks. On top of that, out of flooring stolen from elsewhere—tabletops, and stray planks—he stitched together a rough floor. At this point, the Merciful ignored his insistence that he do it alone and helped him raise walls and a peaked roof. A salvaged iron stove provided warmth. Chigozie hung blankets and furs on all the walls, with a twice-folded wool blanket hanging in the doorway.

The structure had no windows. To circulate the air inside, Chigozie had to open the door to the winter's blast. But it gave decent shelter, and no one had been killed inside it.

After burying his club, Kort had lost his taste for theological dispute. He grunted assent to Chigozie's statements that they worshipped God the Son, God in the Bread, and after the morning hymn he drank from the bowl of blessed water and ate a fragment of the blessed loaf Chigozie passed around.

If they gained too many more adherents, he'd have to appoint a suffragan to help him with the morning liturgy. The thought gave Chigozie pause—it would introduce rank, something he'd been steadfastly resisting. Fortunately, the numbers of the Merciful grew slowly. After an initial influx of beastkind who had participated in the assault on Cahokia, they reached an essentially stable size.

Kort now seemed to live to do two things: serve his fellows with manual labor, and sing.

> Come, we that love the Lord
> And let our joys be known
> Join in a song with sweet accord
> And thus surround the throne
>
> Let those refuse to sing
> Who never knew our God
> But children of the heav'nly King
> May speak their joys abroad

Chigozie stood on a boulder on a low knob of earth two thirds of the way up the hill, facing the Merciful. They sang with a call and response technique, because other than the words to a few Christmas songs they'd worn out in the first week, Chigozie was the only one who knew any hymns.

> The hill of Zion yields
> A thousand sacred sweets
> Before we reach the heav'nly fields
> Or walk the golden streets

He was preparing to begin the song's fourth verse when a bugle interrupted him. To his surprise, soldiers in sallet helmets and red cloaks rode out of the forest at the base of the hill and began to climb. A pack of hounds accompanied them, racing ahead as well as following behind.

Several of the beastkind hooted and pawed the earth in anxiety, fear, or perhaps bloodlust.

"No!" Kort bellowed. "We are the Merciful."

Chigozie swallowed his own fear and waited.

The Merciful far outnumbered the men who rode to the edge of the gathering. Nevertheless, a thick energy burned below the surface among the beastkind as the newcomers arrived. They numbered twenty, and they were dressed like riders, with tall black boots, black trousers, and black coats, and then over the top a broad-brimmed red hat and a long red cloak. They wore breastplates and also armor on their thighs. The armor appeared to be carved of lacquered red wood. They carried a short rifle or carbine holstered alongside their saddles and pistols. They rode in two files—the second rider of one of the files carried a banner. Chigozie didn't recognize it, but thought the black image against a red field might have been a cuckoo wearing a crown.

The man to the right of the banner-carrier raised a bugle and blew his call again as the riders came to a stop. Their posture was alert but not threatening, close enough to attack the Merciful but far enough back to turn and ride away.

Curiously, the faces of the men might have been pulled from a New Orleans dance hall. Some had the pale features and dark hair of the Eldritch; others were Indians, though Chigozie could not have identified a specific tribe; still others looked like they might have Bantu blood in their veins.

He raised his arms and voice. "Welcome. Did you come to sing?"

One of the riders at the front of the troop took off his hat and wiped sweat from his brow. He had a broad face and wide nose, skin that was slightly dusky, and straw-blond hair. Some kind of German, or part-German Creole?

Chigozie couldn't place these soldiers, and that made him uncomfortable.

"We don't know the words, preacher."

"I sing them first, and then the congregation sings. You don't need to know words. You only—"

"Stop!" The rider waved Chigozie into silence with his hat. "This is Zomas land."

Chigozie pointed at the rubble on the adjacent hill. "Until three weeks ago, this land was claimed by a man calling himself Baron McClane."

The rider snorted. "Welcome to the Missouri, preacher. Any idiot who could pile one stone on another has been claiming noble status around here for decades. Well, no longer. My name is Captain Naares Stoach. Turim Zomas the second, Lord of the White Towers, sends me to tell you that you must vacate this land or submit."

A hound with wolfish features and a thick leather collar planted itself at the side of Stoach's horse and growled, as if in punctuation.

An angry mutter ran through the Merciful. Kort raised a hand and they fell silent.

"What does 'submit' mean?" Chigozie asked.

Captain Stoach replaced his hat on his head. "In a more peaceful time, it would merely mean 'agree to pay taxes.' One fifth of all your produce. We would begin by taking one fifth of what you now possess."

Chigozie stroked his chin. "That seems a little high. Though you might find the fifth part of what we currently possess to be disappointingly little."

"Understand that what you produce includes your young. If you submit to Zomas, we will begin by taking one in five of you to work in our slave camps."

A beastman with the upper body of an ape shrieked in protest. Kort spun and thrust his heavy face close into the space of his fellow, roaring a dull roar that left no room for disagreement.

Despite Kort's bellow, the beastkind shifted back and forth from one foot or hoof to another and grumbled. But Chigozie didn't want to provoke an open battle. The riders would simply shoot his people.

"I see," he said. "Since we live in a less peaceful time, does that mean you will leave us all our possessions and all our people?"

Captain Stoach shook his head. "We will return tomorrow. If you are still here, we will take one fifth of you into slavery. We are reasonable. We'll let you choose. We'll send the brutes, the idiots, those with the broadest shoulders and the tiniest brains into the slave camps to work the fields and the mines.

"The rest of you will join the Host of the White Towers. You will serve Zomas in this conflict that now overtakes us."

"We are peaceful people," Chigozie said.

Naares Stoach let his gaze wander over the Merciful. "You may be peaceful, but I think you could be terribly effective in combat. Since we battle to fight off rampaging beasts on our land, the Lord of the White Towers will be especially satisfied to have fighters such as you in his service. And consider that it would mean dependable food and warm places to sleep. And pay."

"And death," Kort rumbled. "And murder. We have no use for your pay."

"Don't be so quick to decide," Stoach said. "Have you been to Memphis, or New Orleans? Many enticing things can be had for money, even when the coin is iron rather than silver."

"We're not warriors, Captain," Chigozie said. "We're peaceful people. We're just looking for a place to be left alone."

"Then tomorrow morning, you'd better not be here. I'm a merciful man, but I'm willing to kill."

The Firstborn had treated Miqui's wound, pulling the bullet from his thigh and then stopping the bleeding with a linen bandage and heavy and thick yellow salve. The boy lay on a flat wooden cot hanging from a wall in the same cell as Montserrat, sleeping.

Montse eased up the edge of his bandage to peek at the wound; it was clotting and didn't look angry. The Ophidian healers knew what they were doing.

She looked up from the wound to see Kyres Elytharias.

No, not Kyres, though the girl standing outside her cell looked like Hannah's husband. She had his face and his thin build, but she was smaller, and the expression in her one visible eye was like the stab of a dagger. Her other eye lay beneath a strip of cloth.

This had to be one of the other two children.

"My name is Sarah Penn." The girl held an iron key ring in her hand. She was alone. "I guess maybe you know that."

She slipped the bandage from her head, revealing her other eye. It was white as ice and reminded Montse of the eye of a wild animal, or a bird of prey.

"I would have known you from a mile away," Montse said. "You have your mother's fire behind your father's face."

"Sir William says I should trust you, Montserrat Ferrer i Quintana. He says you're of an old noble house."

Montse nodded. "My family has earned respect, if not always wealth. Please call me 'Montse.' I loved your parents dearly."

Sarah paused long before her next words. "Especially my mother."

Montse's heartbeat was loud in her own ears. She nodded and looked away.

"Sir William also says you're a smuggler, a pirate, and a positive magnet for scandal."

Montse chuckled, the dry laugh rasping in her throat. "But more to the point, your mother entrusted me with the care of your sister at her birth. Hannah Penn trusted me, so you can do the same."

Sarah unlocked the door and stepped into the cell with the two Catalans. She gazed on Miqui for a few moments. "He'll recover."

"I think so," Montse agreed.

"I grew up in the mountains of Appalachee," Sarah said. "Thalanes placed me with Iron Andy Calhoun, who raised me as his daughter."

"You were watched over by good men."

"My brother Nathaniel was not so lucky. His foster father was the Earl of Johnsland, whose madness began at about the time he took Nathaniel into his care."

"Ah." Montse smiled slightly. "The Elector of the Birds. Thank you for telling me this. I saw you all at birth, and many times I have wondered."

Sarah nodded. "I can see your honesty and your loyalty."

"A vision that clear is a powerful gift."

"My father only gave powerful gifts. I think you knew him."

"Your father gave powerful gifts," Montse agreed. "I did not place your sister Margarida—excuse me, Margaret—into the care of another. I kept her. She came into life a princess, but she has lived as a smuggler and a wharf rat, a crew member of *La Verge Caníbal*, a notorious evader of stamp duties, a bearer of illicit goods, and sometimes a raider of the bounty of the Imperial treasury, or the treasury of the Chevalier of New Orleans."

"And a carrier of wanted persons."

"Even so."

Sarah fell silent and studied Montse's face. Was there something she wanted to ask?

What did she know?

"Perhaps it was your father who gave Margarida her most extraordinary gift," Montse said tentatively.

Sarah reacted with a brief look of surprise that she immediately smothered.

"You can see," Montse said. "Your brother?"

"He can hear. Which...has had surprising consequences."

Consequences? "Your sister has queer hair. When I tried to cut it in her childhood, she complained. Loudly. Later, when she consented to letting me cut it, her hair broke the scissors unless they were made of the strongest steel. It is a curly mass of hair, long and sprouting in all directions like a fern, and tangled into a ball on top of her head."

"The gift of magical hair is … not what I expected," Sarah admitted.

"When she is angry, and when she feels fear, that hair stands on end. And then she has the strength and the endurance and the hardiness of twenty men."

Sarah nodded slowly. Something was coming together for her. "But she isn't with you now."

"The Chevalier of New Orleans took us prisoner." Montse felt her face color with shame as she told of her defeat. "He hid her from me. I don't know where. I attempted to rescue her and failed. And the chevalier sent me to you with a strange message."

"Yes?" Sarah's face was impassive.

"I am the embassy you were expecting. He offers the gift of your sister's life." Montse hesitated. "May I ask what he means?"

"He means he would marry me and dominate me, own my lands in the east and despoil my father's kingdom, and in exchange he would set my sister free."

"You cannot give in."

Sarah's laugh began slowly, but quickly became sharp and loud—a cackle. With the splitting sound of her laughter and her gift of vision, she suddenly reminded Montse of Cega Sofía, the blind seeress murdered by the gendarmes of the chevalier. "Oh hell, no, Montse. Oh hell, no."

"Gather up all our gramarists.
It's time we made a decent counterattack."

———⊸•⊰———

CHAPTER SEVEN

"You carry two pistols," Etienne pointed out.

August Planchet smiled. One of the weapons was literally in his hand. Though it wasn't pointed at Etienne, it only needed to be raised an inch or two to aim at his chest. The second lay on the table, roughly pointed in Etienne's direction. "You are troubled by the thought of a bishop who is armed? Ironic."

Etienne waved a hand in dismissal. "Not at all. Only I believed the customary weapon of the clergyman was the stiletto, or perhaps the garrote. You are teaching me many interesting things, Your Grace."

The two men sat at a warped table in the corner of a tavern called *Le Charles Cronea*, in the Vieux Carré. Etienne didn't remember who Charles Cronea was—an obscure hero in the war against the Spanish, perhaps. Or, judging from the state of disrepair of the building, maybe a pirate. A struggling fire filled the greasy air with smoke; Planchet's two bodyguards, hired thugs from the same class of men as Bad Bill though without his history of rank, sat two tables away and glared at Etienne over their cups of cheap wine.

Monsieur Bondí was doing an admirable job of keeping quiet.

Planchet also sipped wine from a cup. Etienne sucked at a pickled hot pepper, feeling it stoke the fires within him.

"I have more things to teach you, *Your Grace*." The former beadle's eyes glittered.

"St. Paul never envisioned two such bishops as these, did he?" The thought amused Etienne, whatever the tentmaker of Benjamin would have thought.

"St. Paul?" Planchet frowned.

"'Not selfwilled, not soon angry, not given to wine, no striker,'" Etienne said, quoting Paul's Epistle to Titus. He left out "not given to filthy lucre," thinking it would be slightly too pointed, but then gestured at the common room with a sweep of his arm. "A lover of hospitality, though."

Planchet growled. "You sound like your father."

"Hectoring, you mean?" Etienne laughed. "Preachy? You're right, I have no ground to stand on in moral matters. I am the most inconstant of men. But you, Your Grace? Tell me what brings us together at this midnight hour and in this seedy place."

"You think to prick me," Planchet said.

"If it offends you that I address you as 'bishop,' I will stop."

"No, that's not it. That—between you and me, knowing men of the world—is mere humor. No, you call yourself 'inconstant.'"

"Then I prick myself, don't I?" Etienne bit into the pepper and enjoyed the feeling of chilled lightning on his tongue.

Planchet shook his head. "You call me inconstant, but only because you don't know me. You think my jumps from being the beadle to the bishopric to a willingness to betray the chevalier make one jump too many. You think me a weather-cock, a man of no principle."

"On the contrary," Etienne said, "I have always believed you to be the most constant of men."

"I am reassured." Planchet's tone was petulant.

Etienne continued. "What you love is your own wealth. When the office afforded you plentiful opportunity to embezzle, you were a diligent and diligently corrupt beadle. When it paid you more to be an honest beadle in my service, you did that. When becoming bishop paid better still, you took up the miter and chasuble."

"Yes," August Planchet said. "Exactly. I am predictable."

"I should have seen your betrayals coming."

Planchet harrumphed.

"I think there can only be one reason you've asked to meet me, one reason why we had to over-dignify this pissoir with the presence of two anointed bishops in the middle of the night, one reason why you so urgently wish me to know that you have things to tell me. You have learned something, August Planchet, and you believe it will make you wealthy."

"Clever," Planchet said. "And correct."

"I have been a gambler, a collector of debts, a gangster, and a priest in two traditions," Etienne told him. "I can usually read a man. Tell me, Planchet. What is it?"

Planchet licked his lips. "How do I know you won't cut me out?"

Etienne spread his hands. "I find that, on whichever side of the law a man stands, he convinces others to work with him by being trustworthy himself. If I were to betray associates lightly, they would in the future be reluctant to transact with me. A petty criminal or an amateur can be a man without shame or a code, but self-interest compels the *great* criminal to act with honor. Don't you find the same?"

Planchet nodded slowly.

"And I have learned that it's much the same with priests."

Planchet's laugh turned into a chuckle. "Very well, then. Yes. The chevalier is already taking the bishopric's money and mine. He commands me to live on a pittance and says that my stipend will be increased later."

"The bishop shouldn't receive a stipend from the chevalier." Etienne frowned. "The businesses and investments of the bishopric should support the bishop and generate a surplus for charitable works."

"Yes, but he takes that money. And I have no soldiers, no troops to counter his. As bishop, you had this advantage of me."

"I see you're in a grievous situation," Etienne acknowledged. "Have you considered taking to the pulpit to reprimand the chevalier? Call him to repentance?" With *this* question, Etienne was indeed needling Planchet. The mass of believers in New Orleans was with Etienne, not with the parish's former beadle.

Planchet didn't notice the barb. "That didn't work well for your father," the former beadle pointed out, "and he was a much better orator than I am."

"I don't know," Etienne mused. "My men tell me your sermons are improving. They particularly enjoyed learning that Jesus ate with publicans, and therefore, as the city's chief publican, the Chevalier of New Orleans deserves to be eaten."

"Deserves to be invited to our table! Would be invited by our Lord Jesus, were He among us!"

"Ah. That makes better sense."

"You're toying with me." Planchet set his pistol on the table and took the cup of wine in both hands. "I deserve it, I know."

"Forgive my pettiness. Please continue. What did you wish to tell me?"

"I have learned of a great sum of money our chevalier receives from the emperor on a regular basis."

Etienne considered this. "Do you mean a subsidy? Is the chevalier paid to maintain the port or dredge the river? Or keep the Texians in their place?"

"I mean that the emperor personally pays the chevalier every quarter a sum that is not transferred through the adjustment of bank balances, but instead moved in cash."

Etienne had wondered how the chevalier continued to recruit and train gendarmes. He acted as if he expected to continue to be flush with cash, even as the city's stamp duties, taxes, tolls, and tariffs received all dwindled—either because city residents refused to pay them out of outrage for the chevalier's murder of the former Bishop Ukwu, or because Etienne's men intercepted the payments before the chevalier received them.

Why would the emperor personally pay the chevalier? They weren't family.

"I'm still perplexed about the nature of this payment," Etienne said.

"As am I. But it is a secret payment. I think it may be in the nature of a bribe."

Curious. A bribe to do what? Could this have something to do with the recent presence of the Appalachee witch Sarah Penn in New Orleans? Was the chevalier being paid to attempt to capture her? Was it possible the chevalier had been paid to kill Etienne's father? "I would think such information would be known only to very few people," Etienne said.

"It's known to the chevalier." Planchet sneered. "And in his cups, the chevalier is a man who boasts."

Etienne took another pepper. "Did the chevalier in his cups give you any further details? I am thinking about the timing of the payment, the nature of it? A letter of credit or an endorsed deposit order will not be easily intercepted."

"The chevalier was not so indiscreet. But I am not entirely without resources, especially with regard to the movement of money." August Planchet's eyes twinkled. "The chevalier and the emperor are both men of the ancient world in their hearts, mistrustful of banks and the men who run them. The money comes hidden inside a cargo of coal, in the form of gold ingots. It is carried by Memphite barge."

Etienne stroked his chin. "What sort of division between us were you imagining?"

"Half each." Planchet smiled. "Naturally, I will wait until the night the barge arrives to tell you any more details. You must have men ready."

"Where will you go, afterward? You will need to flee the chevalier's wrath."

"New Amsterdam, I think. Or Paris. Some place where a man with money is respected. A place where the good life can be purchased."

August Planchet smiled, a weedy, corrupt snicker on his breath. Etienne took that as his signal—the man had nothing more to tell him.

Standing suddenly, Etienne raised the table with him. Cup and pistols flew aside, and the last Etienne saw of Planchet's face, the former beadle was gasping in surprise. Etienne pushed the table forward with his shoulder, pinning Planchet's head and chest to the wall behind him—

and leaving his belly exposed.

Etienne took his time pulling his knife from his sheath. "You see, Monsieur Beadle, the mistake that you made. You acted the petty criminal when you should have risen to be a great one. You treated me as if you'd never need me to trust you again, and now you see that a little trust between you and me might have accomplished impressive things. Tonight, it might have saved your life."

"Mmurmph!" The former beadle squirmed behind the table, arms and legs thrashing ineffectively. Etienne was the bigger, younger, and stronger man; moreover, he was fortified by the chilis and by the susurrus of the Brides, while the beadle-bishop was weakened by wine.

"Your thugs are dead." Etienne pressed the tip of his blade against Planchet's belly. "I tell you this to take away your last sliver of hope and to truly blacken your final moments with despair. No rescuer is coming for you, August. I am going to kill you."

August Planchet squealed like a piglet. Suffocation alone had nearly rendered him unconscious.

"Consider the honor, though. You are being killed by the Bishop of New Orleans."

Etienne cut horizontally across the former beadle's belly, a wide slash from hip to hip. His second crossed the first, from navel to sternum, and August Planchet's life splashed out of his body.

Etienne threw Planchet to the ground, dropping the table on top of him to hide him. Etienne had killed the man, but he took no pleasure in it.

Planchet kicked twice, made a burbling sound, and died.

Etienne walked to the table where Planchet's two thugs lay slumped forward, dead of poison. Sitting out of the beadle's view, they had died unnoticed as well as unmourned. Beyond them, the bartender met Etienne's gaze and nodded. He was Igbo, rather under average height, with broad shoulders and a narrow waist.

Etienne wiped the blood from his knife meticulously on the relatively clean shirtsleeve of one of the dead men, then resheathed it.

He heard a thumping sound from the corner where he'd been sitting. Turning, he saw a wooden panel of the wall repeatedly opening and slamming into August Planchet's corpse and table on top of it. Monsieur Bondí was trying to exit the secret passage where he'd been hiding.

"Push harder, Monsieur Bondí!" Etienne called. The Brides sang through every sinew, making his limbs tingle. "It's only a dead man blocking your path!"

Cursing and grumbling, Bondí threw his shoulder into it and knocked the door open. He stepped over Planchet's corpse cautiously, pointing his scattergun at the dead man.

"The plan was that *I* would shoot him," Bondí said. "I wanted to shoot him."

"I remember," Etienne said. "Only as we spoke, he said such infuriating things that I found myself missing my days of breaking legs and I decided that I wanted to do it myself. Did you know, my family name *ukwu* can mean *big* in Igbo, but it can also mean *leg*? It depends how you say it. I was Stephen Leg, who collected late interest payments by breaking the debtor's leg. I have never truly ceased being that man."

"August Planchet was a disgrace to the noble profession of accounting." Bondí frowned. "I looked forward to removing the stain from our honor. I regarded it as my duty."

"You may tell your numerically able brothers that you have removed the smirch from your collective escutcheon," Etienne said. "I don't need the credit. And anyway, even in the Vieux Carré, the boom of a blunderbuss doesn't go unnoticed. We have saved Onyinye the trouble of having to explain the shooting to her neighbors."

Onyinye Diokpo herself, who had come in from the tavern's kitchen, spoke. "I wouldn't worry about that, Etienne. My neighbors don't bother to explain *their* gunshots to *me*. But if nothing else, you have certainly reminded me that within the bishop there still lives a man capable of a stabbing, when the occasion calls for it." Her gray hair was hidden beneath a golden silk scarf, which was brilliantly set off against a bright purple tunic, embroidered with fantastical birds.

"Is that a good thing or a bad?" Etienne asked.

Onyinye shrugged. "It's a moment of clarity."

"Etienne," Monsieur Bondí said. "We could use the cash."

"We all could," Onyinye said. "Our businesses are being squeezed by the chevalier's gendarmes—all our businesses the chevalier knows about, in any case."

Etienne sat to think. "Could I have a glass of wine, Onyinye?" he asked. "Or better still, rum. Preferably without poison."

"Are you *capable* of being killed by poison, houngan?" She poured a large tumbler of black rum. "Or does the maryaj-loa protect you from such a death?"

"I try not to test my Brides' limits," Etienne said.

"Afraid to injure yourself in the experimentation?"

"Perhaps." Etienne took a gulp of the rum. "Or perhaps, when my time comes, I want my death to be a surprise."

"It could be a trick," Bondí suggested.

"If so, it was not August Planchet's trick. I don't think the beadle was a man to risk his own life." Etienne thought of the glitter in the man's eyes, the greed larding his voice like lust. "Planchet was sincere. He believes there is a Memphite barge carrying gold down the river to the chevalier. He thought we would capture it and give him half for the information."

"Greedy bastard," Bondí said. "And stupid. He should have known the finder asks for ten percent. Twenty at most."

Etienne nodded. "Do you know, I think I might even have been open to such an offer. I respect a man who can repent almost as much as I respect a man who can accurately gauge his own price. Perhaps there is a Christian within me yet."

"What do we do about this information, then?" Onyinye asked.

"We investigate. The docks are the most corrupt part of New Orleans—that makes them the best part. Bondí?"

The Creole nodded. "I'll see if I can identify that barge. What do we do about Planchet himself?"

"His Grace came to an unfortunate end while strolling in the Vieux Carré, as many have before him. The pious will interpret this as God's punishment upon a man who was willing to steal a holy office that did not belong to him."

"And the impious?"

"They will likely conclude on their own that I am responsible for Planchet's death. If they don't, you may give the appropriate wink and nod to give them the idea."

"So that half the city thinks you're a saint, and the other half thinks you're the devil."

"It was ever thus in New Orleans."

New Amsterdam was a city of docks.

Nathaniel knew the Dutch port was one of the great cities of the Empire—greater by far than Fort Nassau, the capital of the Hudson River Republic—but in his head, he had envisioned a city with paved streets and stone towers.

New Amsterdam had stone buildings, squat and crenellated, with arrow slit windows or no windows at all on the ground floor. On higher levels, the windows were covered with iron grates.

"That's a bank," Jacob Hop said, noticing his gaze. "Or the counting house of a joint-stock company, or a wealthy family."

But most of the city's buildings were brick or wood. Close to the river, the streets too were of brick, though within only a few streets, that brick disappeared, replaced by muddy snow.

Muddy snow lay heaped in piles about a circular church within shouting distance of the docks. The center of the building rose to a bell tower, also circular, with a pointed cap of a rooftop. Before the church stood a bronze statue of a man wearing a long perruque, with one hand on his hip and the other holding a rolled-up scroll.

"John Watts." Jake nodded at the statue. "After we signed the Compact, we were careful to send one English-speaking Elector to Philadelphia. I guess we didn't want to seem too foreign."

Nathaniel didn't have a great sense of the place's geography, but New Amsterdam straddled several islands at the mouth of the Hudson River. Entering the city was like approaching a hedgehog—first you had to make it through the spines. The shores of the city bristled with docks, and the docks swarmed with traffic. Sweating men of every description loaded and unloaded ships on the docks and carried the unloaded goods into the next layer of the city, a belt of warehouses.

These were tall, mostly wooden, and windowless. They had wide doors to allow wagons to drive right inside, and armed men stood at every one of them. New Amsterdam had no defensive wall, but it still had men on its ramparts, after a fashion.

Beyond the warehouses were the banks and counting houses. If the counting houses had armed men, they were inside and discreetly out of sight.

Beyond the counting houses, the island rose up in hills toward wooded parks and meadows. Intermittent boardwalks lined streets of tall, narrow stone houses with wrought iron fences. Carriages and riders passed up and down the long streets, not giving a second glance at Jacob, who was, however travel-stained, one of them—

but staring at Nathaniel.

"Could you reverse your hat?" Jacob asked. "Only until we get through the city?"

"This is the only way it fits," Nathaniel said.

Jacob shook his head. "Your skull looks very ordinary to me. I don't know why the hat should only fit backward. I think maybe you don't know how to wear a hat."

Nathaniel couldn't tell him that he *had* to wear the hat this way. The part of him that could cross the starlit plain forced him to wear his hat backward and his coat inside out.

Makwa. His bear-self, his bear-shadow, the part that stayed behind to protect his body. *Makwa* gave shape to his skull and body.

"And that's not to mention the travesty of my coat." Nathaniel shrugged. "I'm just not as fashionable as you, I guess."

Jacob Hop laughed. "Okay, I deserved that. What does the acorn tell us now?"

Nathaniel took the box from his breast pocket and held the acorn in his palm. It rolled to indicate a northerly route, toward the forested hills dominating the upper part of the island. "We must be close."

"Ja, on the island, I think. But unless we want to try to find her in the darkness, we should stop."

Nathaniel squinted at the scudding gray clouds overhead, growing dark with the arrival of sunset, and thought about the frozen feeling in his toes. "There are inns and taverns by the docks, behind us. Are there inns on the roads ahead?"

"There are inns on this island," Hop said. "And barns we could sneak into if we wanted to save a little money. But I want to stop here. That's my cousin's house, or it used to be. He's a preacher, so he knows a lot about what's happening in New Amsterdam and in the Empire. Hopefully he can give us information."

"About my sister?"

"Ja, maybe. Or about what is happening with the Pacification or the Electoral Assembly. Or if there is unusual Imperial activity here in the Republic."

"Why are we standing out here in the snow, then?" Nathaniel stamped his feet in turn, trying to drive blood into them. "Let's speak to your cousin."

"Ja, that's a good idea. We should do that." But Hop stood in place, staring at a sober brownstone house with a row of winter-bare maple trees in front of it.

Nathaniel put the acorn away. "Will your cousin welcome us?"

"He doesn't hate me," Hop said. "He's not angry with me, as far as I know."

"Then why are you hesitating?"

"He knows me as a deaf-mute," Hop said. "And the explanations I can give him for why I can now hear and speak... will not please him."

Nathaniel caressed the skin of his drum-horse and felt comforted. "I'll distract him with my display of high Philadelphia fashion. He'll be so stunned by my elegantly backward hat, he won't even notice that you're talking."

That joke kicked the Dutchman into motion. Hop skipped up the boardwalk and then the stone steps to the front of the house. The street was hazardous with mud and melting ice, but the boards and the steps were swept meticulously clean and dry.

Hop knocked.

Nathaniel heard singing within. He didn't understand the language, but he enjoyed the steady moving bass line sung by male voices and the rapid melody above it, sung by women and children. The whole harmonized very well with the faint background music Nathaniel heard all the time, the innate music of the world.

When Hop knocked a second time, the singing stopped. Moments later, the door opened and a bigger, broader-shouldered, redder-cheeked version of Hop bounced into view.

"Goedenavond," the Dutchman said. "Wat kan ik voor jullie doen?" And then his eyes opened wide. "Jacob!"

He turned and yelled a stream of rapid Dutch into the house.

"Ambroos," Jacob Hop said. "Stop. Wait. I know you're surprised."

Ambroos fell silent and stared at Hop, his mouth open.

"I was hoping we could stay the night here," Hop said.

Ambroos spoke slowly, with the slight stiffness that suggested he wasn't entirely comfortable with the language. "I don't know what's most astonishing, and there are so many possibilities. To see you at all. To see you with this...stranger. To hear you *speaking*. And to hear you speaking *English*."

"Let us in, Ambroos," Jacob Hop said, "and I'll tell you things that are more astonishing still."

"Who lives in a house such as this?" Kinta Jane Embry stared at the grounds about her. The tall white house was built of wood, with a gambrel roof, flaring eaves, and three chimneys. It stood only a few steps from tall limestone cliffs that dropped hundreds of feet into the Hudson River. Landward, the house was fenced in by thick screens of trees. If there was a road on the other side of all those gray trunks, Kinta Jane couldn't see it.

Kinta Jane and Isaiah Wilkes had sailed up the Hudson and approached the house from the other side. Their path up the cliff had been completely invisible from five steps away, and very nearly invisible even as they were climbing up it. They now emerged through a notch between two gray boulders, faintly silvered by the quarter moon.

"Adriaan Stuyvesant, Chairman of the Dutch Ohio Company as well as one of its significant shareholders. Also an investor in a dozen other well-known commercial ventures in the empire, and one of the Hudson River Republic's seven Electors."

Kinta Jane couldn't help herself. She broke into song:

> *Seven Electors Knickerbock*
> *Seven votes on the Tappan Zee*
> *Three Electors by joint stock*
> *Heads of three big companies*
> *The States-General choose another three*
> *The Stadtholder makes seven, see*

"Which one is he?" she asked. "One of the Joint-Stock Electors?"

"I believe you got that song exactly right," a man's voice said. "Now raise your hands over your head slowly. In this poor light, I'd hate to mistake your intentions and accidentally put a mustketball through your brains."

The speaker stepped forward, not entirely emerging from the shadow cast by two closely grown tree trunks. In the darkness, Kinta Jane could tell he was of middling height, but his head seemed enormous and misshapen. He held a musket at waist height, pointed at her and Wilkes.

"I'm here to see Adriaan Stuyvesant." Wilkes spoke slowly and distinctly. "On a matter relating to his three brothers."

There was a silence.

Then the man in shadow spoke. "I have two brothers. We each came from a different mother and father."

The hair on the back of Kinta Jane's neck stood up.

Wilkes answered, "Such brothers would be a marvel to remember until the end of days."

Then the Franklin stepped forward and offered his hand to the shadow. Kinta Jane knew when the men clasped hands they were exchanging recognition grips; Wilkes would offer one, and then the other man would counter and so on, until they had established not only shared belonging to the Conventicle, but respective rank.

Isaiah Wilkes certainly had the superior rank. Who was the other man?

"Dockery," he said, stepping further out of the shadow of the trees and revealing that what appeared to be a swollen and deformed head was a badger-skin cap. Together with his fringed leather jacket and the pouch at his hip decorated with a row of deer's dewclaws, it gave him the appearance of a trapper or a scout. He spat a stream of tobacco juice to one side.

"Isaiah Wilkes."

"I'm Kinta Jane Embry. This must be a back way into Stuyvesant's house," Kinta Jane said. "Expressly for the use of brothers."

"Oh?" Dockery turned and led them toward the big house at a steady saunter. As he pivoted, Kinta Jane caught a glimpse of a powder horn strapped to the side of his pouch; the horn was ornately carved with a floral pattern. Wilkes invited Kinta Jane to go second, and then brought up the rear.

"Otherwise, it's a ridiculous coincidence that we climbed up this goat path and ran into you."

Wilkes turned a half-smile on her and beamed.

"I got nothing to say to that," Dockery grunted. "Except I ain't sure I trust someone who feels compelled to say out loud everything she thinks."

"Kinta Jane only recently acquired a tongue," Wilkes said. "She is carried away by the novelty."

"Having a tongue is about the least special thing there is," Dockery said. "Knowing how to *keep* your tongue in your head is considerably less common, and worth a lot more."

"I went seven years without saying a word," Kinta Jane shot back.

"Hot damn, but weren't those the days?" Dockery said.

"Is Adriaan here?" Wilkes asked.

"I'm taking you to him. He might be expecting you—he's been saying for a few weeks how we need to be extra careful watching the river path."

"Dark things are afoot in the west," Wilkes said.

"Franklin's vision?" Dockery asked.

Thinking of the strange coin the Dutchman had given her aboard the *Incroyable*, Kinta Jane blurted out, "Yes!"

"And here I was, wondering whether my new best friend had seen Franklin's vision, and of course she's kind enough to show me. Kinta Jane. That make you Choctaw, I guess?"

"Now look who's showing off what he knows. And what about you? You talk something like a Cracker, only without the twang."

"I got Appalachee in me. A little German, too, and about half English, from two generations back or so. I'm a regular Creole, only all of it's pale-skinned. I came up in Pennsland, within musket-shot of Pittsburgh. My kin are what they sometimes call Mountain Alchemists in those parts."

"Moonshiners?" The phrase was new to Kinta Jane.

"Radical Christians," Wilkes said. "And counterfeiters."

Dockery nodded. "In parts where coin is scarce, the local clipper is sometimes the only person who brings ready money to the local economy. As a boy, I got kidnapped by Algonks and ended up learning their ways and tongue for a couple of years until my uncle bought my freedom. With counterfeit money, naturally. That give you enough biography, Woman With Tongue?"

Dockery looked up at an illuminated window on the second floor and fell quiet.

Suddenly, Kinta Jane found she was not especially eager to share her own life's story. "That'll do for now."

"Good. You got to realize that Adriaan Stuyvesant keeps a couple of men close to him who belong to the Conventicle, but his family and most of his folk just have no damned idea. Safest that way, and best you not upset the arrangement."

Kinta Jane nodded. "Understood."

"Excellent." Dockery stepped up onto a low porch at the back of the house. He struck a match, held it up to his face to illuminate it, and knocked gently on the glass of a window. "We're here."

Shutters on the inside opened a crack, revealing only darkness.

A few moments passed, and then a door several steps farther along the porch swung open. A turkey-necked servant with iron gray hair hanging in long loops around his ears brought them inside into the orange light of a kitchen with an open stove door and a six-armed candelabra. Handing Kinta Jane the candlestick, he pointed up a staircase, the passage barely as wide as Kinta Jane's shoulders and each step as high as the distance between her elbow and the tip of her finger.

Dockery stayed in the kitchen.

The staircase emerged into a high-ceilinged attic. Dark drapes hung where Kinta Jane assumed windows would be. In the center of the room sat half a dozen wooden slat-backed chairs in a loose circle. In one of the chairs sat the man who must be Adriaan Stuyvesant.

He was heavy, but he fidgeted as if he had too much energy. Even in the light that came from the candlestick in her hand, together with light from a similar candlestick standing on the floor beside Stuyvesant, she could see that his skin was pink and young-looking, like a baby's. He had the short-cropped gray hair of a man who ordinarily wore a perruque in public, and he was dressed in shirt tails and cotton breeks.

"Look—" Kinta Jane pointed at lines on the floor.

"Shh." Isaiah Wilkes motioned her forward.

She stepped to the circle of chairs and sat down. As Wilkes followed her example, she examined the lines on the floor. They were painted, permanent lines, whorls, and stars she did not recognize. Some sort of warding.

"Can we speak here?" Wilkes asked.

"If Van den Berg is to be trusted."

"Well, is he?"

"He's a cunning bastard," Stuyvesant said. "And ruthless. As you'd want in a wizard. And I believe he's loyal. If this circle isn't a safe place to speak, there's no safe place in all the Republic. I take it Thomas didn't respond as you'd hoped."

This room had no window. It was also too far off the ground to be the window Dockery had gazed at. What had he been thinking?

Kinta Jane shook her head and concentrated on the conversation at hand.

"*Hope* is too grand a word," Wilkes said, "for my flicker of willingness to believe there might be a possibility that the man who killed Hannah Penn would recognize and take up his ancestors' fight."

"There's no audience to bow for here, Wilkes. Use fewer words. He told you to go to hell."

"Tried to kill me, actually. Tried to kill *us*."

Stuyvesant lifted his candlestick to get a good look at Kinta Jane. "You're from the New Orleans cell, aren't you? I'm sorry about the challenges you've had. I knew Jackson."

"*She* didn't," Wilkes said.

"My brother was René du Plessis."

"Ah." Stuyvesant set down his candlestick again. "Poor bastard. Sorry to hear about him, too."

Kinta Jane mumbled inarticulate thanks.

"You ride north, then?" Stuyvesant asked.

"Anak and Odishkwa may yet remember their obligations. Can you help us?"

"I'll send Dockery with you. He's a solid frontiersman, years with the Dutch Ohio. Take all the supplies you need, and I'll send money as well."

"How prospers the Dutch Ohio Company?" Wilkes asked.

"Poorly." Stuyvesant harrumphed. "Elbows have always been sharp between us and the Imperial Ohio, even when it was just the Penn Ohio, but in the last decade the Imperials have gone from shoving us aside to stabbing us in the back. Slander, theft, destruction of our vessels, warehouses burned. The board and I claim compensation, but we are forever delayed in the simple battle to determine whether the case should be heard in Philadelphia or New Amsterdam—we never even get to the evidence or the real legal arguments. The shareholders have been patient, but the truth is the Dutch Ohio Company is going out of business."

"Is it bad enough that the Company is tempted to join in with the Pacification?"

"The bigger profits are always on the smuggler's side," Stuyvesant said. "So are the bigger risks. And yes, more than one member of the board has expressed the view that we should be offering to cooperate with Thomas rather than compete with him. Indeed, some think that's what his man Temple Franklin is coming to New Amsterdam to offer us this week."

Wilkes sat up straight. "Franklin?"

"I assumed you knew, since you just came from there. Maybe you outran the news. The board has agreed to a meeting with Franklin the day after tomorrow. He's specified that I'm to be there."

"Do you think he knows you're a brother?"

"To my knowledge, neither Franklin's son nor his grandson ever lifted a finger to bear Franklin's burden. I would be shocked if this has anything to do with the Conventicle."

"What, then?"

Adriaan Stuyvesant shrugged, a rolling gesture that shook his entire body. "The lawsuits were what the message referenced. But I assume the timing has to do with the Assembly's passage of new imposts and authorizing a Levy of Force. Thomas makes war on the Firstborn, and it grows expensive. Settling the lawsuits and ending the fighting will mean more profit in his company as well as mine."

"Will the board entertain offers to settle?"

Stuyvesant snorted. "They leaped for joy to hear Franklin was coming. I think if any sort of decent offer is made, I'll be hard pressed to resist it, or even delay acceptance."

They sat in silence for a moment.

Wilkes asked, "How can we get into that meeting?"

Sarah walked to the edge of the plaza atop the Great Mound, Sherem half a step behind her. The chill wind blowing over the city from the north warmed slightly around the Temple of the Sun, so with the step to the top of the slope, she felt the cold burn the skin of her face.

She looked eastward, over the massed Imperial forces. Were they growing? She huddled deeper into the Imperial dragoon's coat she still wore. Alzbieta and Maltres had both repeatedly offered her Cahokian-style cloaks and tunics, as well as knee-high boots and leggings, and she had turned them down. She liked her moccasins—she could feel the earth through them. She liked the coat; it reminded her of her uncle's threat to her, and her claims against him.

She had acquired the coat at the junction of the Mississippi and Ohio Rivers, at the grave of her father. It reminded her of him.

"Tell me what the arcane resources of the city are," she said. Hearing the harshness of her own voice, she added, "Please."

"There is no organization," Sherem said. "There is a small group of Polites, strictly informal. There are individual priests of the Basilica and Temple priestesses with some ability, none especially great. Some of the great families have magician retainers, scattered here and there. The city has a few eccentric individuals who have pursued magic for their own reasons: for commerce, as a personal interest, or a spiritual discipline. All together, they come to approximately thirty wizards. And there is Luman Walters, the Imperial hedge wizard. Or *former* Imperial, perhaps."

"And we have you."

"Are any of them by chance really powerful?"

Sherem scratched his head. "I don't know how to measure that. Six months ago, I would have told you I was one of the better wizards in the city. Maybe the best. And you snapped me like a twig, so that doesn't bode well for us."

"I caught you by surprise, Sherem. It was luck."

"No, Beloved. There was no luck involved."

Sarah sighed. The guilt didn't dissipate.

"I don't think we have the strength for a frontal assault," she said. "But maybe we can use our magicians as heralds. Maltres tells me Chicago has traditionally been our ally. Surely the kings of the other six sisters share our interest in rebuffing the Imperial fist."

"The sisters share our interest, yes. They also share our poverty. In fact, our location on the far side of the Ohio from Thomas Penn may mean we've suffered the least from raiders and pillagers. Chicago may come, and he is closely allied with some of the Algonk peoples."

"Might Memphis be willing to help us?" Sarah thought out loud. "Or the Cotton League? Or the Free Horse Peoples? They're all within striking distance."

"They are," Sherem agreed. "I wonder how much they suffer at the hands of the Heron King's beastkind."

"There's the Chevalier of New Orleans," Sarah said.

"Beloved," Sherem said. "There is a possibility for increasing our magical strength in battle."

"Or what about Zomas?" Sarah asked. "I understand there's bad blood, and believe me, in Appalachee we know about bad blood. Still, no matter how many horses the other family has stolen or how many of your cousins they've killed, sooner or later it comes time to bury the hatchet."

"Do you know the story of Jock of Cripplegate?" Sherem asked.

Sarah shook her head, but then remembered. "Wait . . . he's the one Cromwell experimented on. A thief, right?"

"A burglar. Cromwell killed him and demonstrated that Firstborn souls could be exploited as magical energy."

"I don't like where this conversation is headed."

"There's a Basilica priest named Josiah Dazarin. He's been preaching a devotion to St. Jock of Cripplegate."

"Thinks we should all become second-story men, does he?" Sarah bit her tongue. "Flippancy comes easy to me, Sherem. I apologize." She took a deep breath. "Does Dazarin suggest we should execute our criminals to fuel magical attacks?"

Sherem nodded. "Our criminals. Or our slaves. Or volunteers."

"We ain't there yet," Sarah said. "I hope we never get there, but for sure we ain't there yet."

She wasn't at all sure they wouldn't get there eventually, and maybe soon. The city had food for a few weeks at best—Maltres was still counting and calculating exactly how long the stores would last—and the ring of black fire encircling the city suggested that Hooke's sorcery was not finished yet.

The Imperial army was definitely getting larger. Larger, and more military-looking. The militiamen were being joined by regular soldiers, and behind the trenches, here and there, Sarah saw the noses of artillery pieces pointing at her walls.

"Chicago," she said. "And the sisters. And I want to talk to Gazelem Zomas as soon as possible—please find him for me."

She needed to talk with Montserrat Ferrer i Quintana, too. The pirate queen who had sneaked into the besieged city could help her to sneak out. Sarah didn't want to flee, but she wanted to speak with her father.

He might have keys to help her.

"And gather up all our gramarists. It's time we made a decent counterattack."

*"We're not Appalachee here, you know,
we don't kidnap our women."*

CHAPTER EIGHT

Jacob Hop found himself placing the cards around his plate. He'd managed to leave the Tarocks in his pocket through the hearty plate of stamppot—potatoes mashed in with cabbage and served alongside boiled sausages—but when the dried apples, raisins, and jonge kaas came out, and he no longer needed one hand for the knife and the other for the fork, he began dealing the cards out onto Lotte's best tablecloth in four columns. He was sorting the cards face-up—when he drew them randomly, only the Major Arcana appeared.

"You were possessed," Ambroos insisted. They spoke English for the benefit of Nathaniel Penn, who seemed to be paying close attention despite occasionally breaking into short bursts of hummed music.

"Ja, that's why I need your help."

"Only you weren't possessed by de duivel. You were possessed by a giant bird."

Ambroos's two daughters openly snickered, but Lotte looked troubled. Ambroos had three sons as well, but they were all serving their turn in the city watch this night.

Jake looked up at the blunderbuss Ambroos kept over his fireplace. The firearm was almost certainly loaded. Fortunately, it was out of Ambroos's reach.

"You've heard of the Heron King," Jake said. "I know you have."

"Naturally, yes. He's supposed to be some kind of creature who goes around the Ohio cursing people. But that's just an old Haudenosaunee story, Jacob, or maybe an Algonk tale. There's no such person."

"I think I prefer that you call me 'Jake.'"

"My aunt and uncle named their son Jacob."

"But Jacob was a deaf-mute. I am not completely that person any longer."

"So not only were you possessed by de duivel—you can stop right now this stront talk about the Heron King—"

"Ambroos!" Lotte flashed fierce eyes at her husband.

Ambroos paused, looked heavenward, and then crossed himself while his daughters pretended not to be amused. "Not only were you in Satan's grip, but you view that as some kind of baptism. Satan has made you a new person. Apparently one who can speak and hear."

"You see why I need your help," Jacob said quietly.

"*I'm* a healer." Nathaniel Penn looked down at his plate.

Jake had completed his four columns. He looked at what appeared to be four stories, laid out completely in pictures. The suit of Swords showed a man in hunter's garb, who traveled through the forest on a twisted path, crossed a stream, climbed a hill, stood in a ditch, and then embraced an unseen person. The suit of Lightning Bolts showed a man with the same face (and it looked a little like the face of Calvin Calhoun), or perhaps the same man, undertaking a different journey. This journey had him climbing a high mountain, and dealing with such trials as climbing a cliff, jumping a ravine, and taking eggs from an eagle's nest, he reached the top of the mountain and sat upon a throne. The suits of Cups and Shields showed strikingly similar journeys, only the protagonists depicted in these images were women.

Jacob still held all the Major Arcana apart in one hand; he had deliberately held them apart.

"You're a healer?" Ambroos pressed Nathaniel. "But you look like an orphan drummer boy. An hour ago you were telling me you and Jacob were looking for your sister."

"I *am* an orphan," Nathaniel said.

"Ambroos," Jacob said. "Would you not consider an exorcism? At this moment, beyond this table and those sitting around it, what I see is a bload-soaked scene of sacrifice and pillaging."

"I would want to bring together the community of faith." That was what he called his congregation. The Dutch had a habit of fragmenting into small church groups and arguing vehemently over religion. Ambroos, no sooner had he finished his studies, followed in that well-worn traditional groove. "If what you tell me is at all true, this is a serious matter and I should not attempt anything alone. I will begin my fast immediately."

Ambroos pushed his plate of apple slices and kaas toward his daughters, who fell on it like jackals.

"I will fast as well." Jacob pushed his last morsel of sweet white cheese to Nathaniel.

"It won't be tomorrow," Ambroos said.

"You have to gather the community?"

"Yes. And also, I have a board meeting."

"A board meeting. You mean that your community of faith has a board meeting?"

"No, the Ohio Company has a board meeting. I'm a director."

Jacob smiled, ignoring the black slivers he saw raining from the sky all around him. "A preacher and a trader, too. You must be busy. We're lucky we caught you at home."

"No, it's part of Van Heusen's reforms. All chartered companies above a certain size have to appoint independent directors. Clergymen and news-paper publishers are preferred, though why we should be lumped together with those schurken is a little beyond me. I'm one of the Hudson River Republic Ohio Company's three independent directors. I get paid from the Republic's coffers."

"Three is not a majority, hey?"

"No. The expectation is not that we will be able to outvote the others, it's that we will be able to report any secret wrongdoings."

"You were chosen because you're a professional loudmouth," Jacob said. "Like a news-paper man."

"Ja, dat klopt." Ambroos smiled.

"What do you do at the meetings? Set the price of beaver pelts? Decide wages?"

"Sometimes," Ambroos admitted. "And before you say anything, you're right, I know very little of the subjects with which we deal."

"But you know much of the heart, corruption, probity, and repentance." The Major Arcana felt like a brick in Jacob's hand. They wanted to be played on the four journeys, but Jacob didn't know how.

"But tomorrow's meeting is different. The Emperor Thomas has sent up a legate. We haven't heard his proposal yet, but we think the Emperor wants to drop a lawsuit. And possibly also wants to stop the underhanded methods of his traders that caused the lawsuit at the same time. Both things would be good for the Republic."

"I am certainly grateful that no *Dutch* trader ever engaged in underhanded methods." Jacob leaned over to Nathaniel and spoke in an exaggerated whisper. "This way, we always have the upper hand in these conversations."

"Don't worry, Jake," Ambroos said. "I'll be there to make certain the board behaves honestly."

The challenge of the disguise was that Temple Franklin had seen his face before. Perhaps that had been a mistake; perhaps he should have arranged matters so as to be invited into Horse Hall wearing a false visage.

But he hadn't.

Isaiah Wilkes's solution was to dress himself as a woman. Slight padding in the hips—too much would push the disguise into a grotesque parody and make him more visible, rather than less—and a more feminine walk comprised most of the disguise. He also thickened his eyelashes, made his complexion more Dutch, the color of spring cream, and shortened his height by adjusting his posture and walking with bent knees, hidden under a heavy skirt. And he wore scent, naturally, borrowed from Mevrouw Stuyvesant herself. It smelled like apple liqueur.

He also uglified himself with a false nose. Surely, Temple Franklin would have more interesting things to look at than the serving-women, despite his notorious lechery.

At Isaiah's request, Adriaan Stuyvesant promised that all the other servers would be nubile and lovely.

And tall. It wouldn't do for Isaiah to hulk over all the other servers, after everything else.

These were the skills Isaiah had learned for the stage, first as a standing-ticket punter in between grueling shifts setting type or hanging printed sheets for his exacting first master, the future Lightning Bishop, and then treading the boards himself. But they were the skills of the stage applied by a master hand to a more exacting standard than any stage could require, and with higher stakes.

He was awake all night with the patient work.

He didn't have the time or the need to do the same work on Kinta Jane. Instead, he hid her in an apartment not far from Wall Street in a hotel called *De Zwaard van de Stathouder*. The Stadtholder's Sword—it seemed appropriate enough.

The apartment belonged to Adriaan Stuyvesant. It contained both a well-appointed office—with paper, pens, and ink in abundance, though no record books of any kind in evidence—and a luxe bedroom, with a downy feather mattress on the four-poster bed beside the broad fireplace.

Isaiah didn't ask what Adriaan kept the apartment for, and Adriaan didn't offer any explanation. "I know you will be discreet," was all the Dutchman said.

Kinta Jane looked perfectly happy to take a nap.

And the staff of the *Zwaard* treated Isaiah Wilkes with the casual contempt that told him his disguise was effective.

The Hudson River Republic Ohio Company headquarters was less luxurious than Adriaan's rented chambers, though considerably more defensible. The building was a three-story fortress built of stone. Its walls came to a parapet two stories up, which was patrolled by Dutchmen in polished breastplates and helmets, with long muskets. This guard paced around a penthouse level set back from the outer wall for protection. The penthouse consisted of a single large room with wood-panel walls and tall windows. Through the windows, Isaiah could see the Hudson River and Pennsland on the other side, and in the other direction the wilds of Brooklyn.

Two staircases provided access to the penthouse. The directors came up the large spiral staircase made up marble and sat in the southern two-thirds of the room at a massive dark-stained oak table. There were twelve directors—a bit of a Cahokian number, but also a pious nod to the twelve apostles or the twelve tribes of Israel. Their number included two clergymen and a publisher of some kind—Isaiah recognized the manic look in the eye and the ink-stained fingers.

The rectangular table accommodated sixteen chairs, presently containing thirteen Dutchmen. The one non-director was the company's Secretary, a bony man with an iron bun of black hair behind his head, whose face looked as if he were perpetually sucking on a lemon. His name was Van Dongen.

While the directors waited, the company's kitchen staff prepared food. Pannenkoeken, appeltaart, dried fruit, fried poffertjes, oliebollen flavored with cinnamon, and a selection of light wines and liqueurs made the assortment more of a dessert than a meal. None of the directors had yet touched the food, though; they sat waiting and murmuring among themselves.

Van Dongen sharpened several quill pens and neatly ordered a bottle of ink and a thick stack of foolscap.

None of them knew what the emperor wanted, but they were very anxious to hear. "Franklin is just the sort of unofficial messenger who can be used to send a confidential offer," one director huffed.

"Confidential," another answered, "and completely deniable after the fact."

"Yes, yes," Adriaan Stuyvesant huffed. "We'll paper it up thoroughly afterward, when the time comes."

A clerk in a gray frock coat preceded the emperor's man. "Meneer Temple Franklin," he said simply, and then descended again out of sight.

"Meneer." Franklin chuckled and rubbed his belly as he climbed into view. He wore a blue frock coat whose gold thread suggested the Empire's colors; a kerchief peeking from a breast pocket was embroidered with the ship, eagle, and horses, as well. "How I enjoy the sound of that! So Republican, so egalitarian, and above all, so frugal... you pare not only your cheese, but also your titles. We are all meneers here, are we not?"

"There are the serving women," one of the preachers said. "We customarily refer to a woman as *mevrouw*, rather than *meneer*. I believe your Pennslander Germans would say *fräulein*."

Franklin cast his eye toward Wilkes and the young women. He curtsied along with them.

"Also, some of us are directors," Adriaan Stuyvesant said loudly. The brusqueness of the comment—even more pointed than the preacher's, and nearly to the point of being rude—recaptured Franklin's attention. "One of us is even a chairman."

"Oh, how embarrassing," Franklin said. "Forgive me my democratic aspirations."

"Your grandfather did indeed have such aspirations," Stuyvesant said. "Lord Thomas's grandfather may even have had them, agreeing as he did to the Assembly title of *Mr. Emperor*. But the man you serve is known for rather contrary inclinations."

Franklin spread his hands in a gesture of admission. "True. And yet I've come with olive branches in all my pockets, Mr. Chairman. And I am ready to commence the discussion when you are."

Stuyvesant nodded. "If we are to take any binding decisions, we shall have to embody the meeting in a formal written act. To that end, Meneer Van Dongen here will take notes of the conversation, and should we decide to proceed, will use those notes to draw up resolutions, as well as any necessary contracts or memoranda."

"Excellent!" Franklin sat. "Meneer Van Dongen, I shall try to be succinct."

Van Dongen bobbed his head once and dipped a quill into ink. The directors sat.

Isaiah Wilkes took a bottle of white wine and crept around the table with small, shuffling steps, offering it to each director in turn and filling glasses when asked.

"Understand that what Lord Thomas is proposing is a package." Temple Franklin stretched his shoulder and back and sank comfortably into his chair. "I am empowered to take a complete yes. I am not empowered to accept a partial yes, or to agree to any other terms."

"Do you take us for children?" Stuyvesant bellowed. "We know what you are, Franklin. We know the limits and powers of a creature like you."

"A creature? My goodness." Franklin smiled. "Some of your Dutch terms sound almost insulting when translated into good Penn's English."

Stuyvesant raised his eyebrows and waited.

Franklin began, raising fingers to count off terms as he listed them. "Item one, all existing lawsuits between the Imperial Ohio Company and the Dutch Ohio Company to be settled with a mutual release. No payment of damages by any party."

"That's outrageous!" an older director snapped. Isaiah thought he might have personally been on a ship that the Imperials had burned.

"Wait, Paul," Stuyvesant urged his fellow. To Franklin he added, "Go on."

"Item two, the release of claims between the two companies shall further provide that neither shall commence any lawsuit against the other predicated on any facts existing prior to the date of the agreement."

Paul blustered further, but the other directors looked thoughtful.

"We'll want some covenants," one murmured. "Disclosures."

"Yes, yes," Franklin agreed, "we'll let the lawyers at it once we've agreed, but on short leashes—nothing ruins a good agreement like a lawyer."

"Go on," Stuyvesant said again.

"Item three, for a period of ten years, renewable upon agreement of the parties, all Ohio markets to be shared and all prices to be agreed jointly by a steering committee of the two companies, having equal representation thereon."

"Existing markets and also new ones," Stuyvesant said.

"Naturally." Franklin nodded.

"Deadlocks to be broken by an arbitrator acceptable to both parties, to be located in New Amsterdam."

Franklin's nod was slower this time. "I believe that will be acceptable."

The directors were beginning to smile.

"Item four, all disputes between traders of the two companies to be settled by same steering committee." Franklin hesitated. "With the same arbitration provision."

Now the directors said nothing, but leaned forward over the table as if anxious to hear Temple Franklin's every word. And no wonder; what he proposed went well beyond settling lawsuits, and offered something that sounded like alliance.

Isaiah had come to the meeting knowing that Adriaan Stuyvesant would feel pressured to accept a good settlement. He now became concerned that Stuyvesant would in fact accept the offer.

And perhaps betray Isaiah as a sign of good faith?

Isaiah moved to the next director. "Witte wijn, meneer direktor?" he asked in his best contralto.

Van Dongen wrote furiously.

"Item five, and this is the last item, but, mark you well, it is the most important one." Franklin peered through his spectacles slowing around the table, meeting each man's gaze. Only Stuyvesant flinched. "The Emperor has decided to take a Dutch wife. How did you say it? A *mevrouw*. Naturally, she will have to come with a dowry no less excellent than that of any other imperial bride."

"You can only mean the dowry paid for Hannah Penn," Stuyvesant said slowly. "As I recall, that was three hundred thousand crowns."

"Five hundred thousand, actually." Franklin looked Adriaan Stuyvesant directly in the eye. "Yes, that's the appropriate amount."

"But...who on earth?" Adriaan looked green in the face and his words came haltingly. "Or rather, who on the Hudson River?"

"Yes. His Imperial Majesty feared you might have a hard time deciding, so he has taken the liberty of deciding for you." Franklin made a show of reaching into his jacket pocket to find a square of paper and then examining the name written on it. "Why, how curious! Lord Thomas has written here the name *Julia Stuyvesant*. Perhaps you know her, Meneer Chairman."

Nathaniel felt a little less nervous for the fact that Jacob Hop came with him.

They lay on the floor in the attic bedroom above Ambroos's house, and Nathaniel drummed them up seven steps and onto the starlit plain of the spirit world.

Jacob Hop stared at the sky and at the endless waves of grass and finally at Nathaniel.

"What do you see?" he asked. "What am I?"

"You're a Dutchman," Nathaniel said. "You look very much as you appear in the world of flesh and blood."

That news didn't seem to relax Jacob. "Sarah has said a similar thing, more than once. That she could see the Heron King when he was within me, and that she would know if he returned."

"You don't look like a heron," Nathaniel said. "Or a king."

"Then why do I feel that I am him?" Jacob asked. "Why do I have so many of his memories?"

Nathaniel looked at his companion and tried to find something to do. There was no second self out of place, no obvious injures; the Dutchman looked whole. "I'm sorry. Maybe I'm not the healer I thought I was."

"Maybe Ambroos will be able to help." Jacob laughed and cheered up visibly. "Maybe there *is* no help."

Nathaniel listened for the Sorcerer Robert Hooke. He heard the leaf-crackle laughter of the dead man, but it sounded ever so far away and Nathaniel relaxed. Slightly.

Then he listened for Ambroos, heard him nearby, and led Jacob Hop the short distance to his cousin. They found a castle that shimmered like gold as they approached. The knights standing guard the front door ignored Nathaniel and Jake, and when the travelers climbed the steps inside a circular tower toward Ambroos's voice, speaking from the roof, Nathaniel realized the construction was of something else entirely: paper.

The castle was made of paper, covered over entirely with ink. Nathaniel leaned in to examine the letters. He couldn't read them, but from close up the ink looked black. It was reflecting starlight on the long, looping lines of the characters that made the whole building shine and sparkle.

At the top of the circular stair they reached a clearing. Nathaniel saw thirteen men, including Ambroos, standing in a line on one side of a clearing; facing them and opposite, stood the man Franklin. Behind Ambroos's line stood a knot of women surrounding a single man, who lifted their skirts and crouched to hide behind them. Nathaniel and Jake witnessed the meeting Ambroos attended; Ambroos was the only one Nathaniel recognized, though he knew the name *Franklin,* and he gathered from the conversation that this Franklin was a grandson of the Lightning Bishop.

~Franklin,~ Jake murmured, over and over.

Something felt wrong to Nathaniel, but it was neither the location nor the gathering.

Something was wrong with *him.*

When Franklin finished his offer by saying, *~Perhaps you know her, Mr. Chairman,~* the clearing fell silent.

The person Franklin had been talking to, a florid and corpulent man named Stuyvesant, split abruptly into two. One Stuyvesant stepped forward and began to stammer out half-sentences. *~Well, I don't . . . Well, she really . . . We couldn't . . . There must be . . . ~* The second Stuyvesant sprang backward as if he had been bitten by a snake and screamed.

Eleven of his companions leaped upon both versions of him and dragged him away. Their words fell on Nathaniel like a storm, threatening to shatter his ears.

~We must discuss!~

~Such an interesting offer!~

~How would you feel about another young woman in her place?~

~How would you feel about my wife?~

~It must be Julia Stuyvesant, or I cannot accept the deal.~ Franklin seemed taller. *~And the dowry must be paid in cash.~*

Nathaniel and Jacob Hop followed the directors a few steps away. The man hiding behind women's skirts dropped to his belly and wriggled through the grass until he was close enough to listen, too. The twelve men huddled behind a short wall and began yelling at Stuyvesant.

~*Don't tell me you're going to be this selfish, Adriaan!*~

~*My own marriage was arranged! How would an arranged marriage with the Emperor Thomas Penn be a shameful or disappointing thing?*~

~*She'll live a wonderful life, you understand that?*~

~*But she's betrothed already!*~ Stuyvesant yelled back. ~*Do you really want me to break my daughter's heart?*~

~*YES!*~

~*This will save the company!*~

~*Half a million crowns?*~ Stuyvesant pulled at his own face in astonishment. ~*I don't have that money!*~

~*We'll lend it to you!*~ several shouted together.

~*You'll make back the money in three years. Think of the litigation costs saved! Think of the costs avoided by sharing markets with the Imperials! Think of the new buyers and additional revenue!*~

~*Think of the monopoly!*~

~*You aren't saving just the company. You're saving the Republic! If the company fails, the Republic's tax base withers, and then who will re-pave Wall Street?*~

~*You're saving the Empire! You were the one who told us about the Assembly, and how the Empire needs cash to send soldiers to fight the beastkind!*~

~*Don't be selfish!*~

A cunning expression came over Stuyvesant's face. ~*If I am asked to sacrifice my daughter for the Republic and the Empire, surely you can do better than lend me money for the dowry.*~

The man lying on the grass yelled. ~*No! Adriaan, no!*~

~*Shut up!*~ Stuyvesant yelled back.

The other men didn't notice the exchange. They looked back and forth at each other in surprise.

~*It would be a good interest rate, though,*~ one said.

~*The best,*~ a second added.

~*Don't be selfish.*~ Stuyvesant wagged his finger at the other directors. ~*If I'm to give up my daughter, you must be willing to pay the money.*~

~*I'm still willing to give up my wife,*~ one director said glumly. ~*Better my wife than my wealth.*~

~*Stop trying to sell your wife, Rijkert,*~ his neighbor said. ~*Franklin already turned her down.*~

Ambroos stepped forward. ~*Nobody is being asked to sell a daughter—or a wife—or to lose a daughter. The Emperor proposes a very honorable marriage and, if I understand you correctly, a marriage that will strengthen the company and the Republic financially.*~

~*That is correct,*~ Stuyvesant said to Ambroos. To the other directors, he said, ~*Do we have a deal?*~

~*No!*~ yelled the man on the ground.

~*Who is that?*~ Jake whispered to Nathaniel.

Nathaniel shrugged.

~*Wait,*~ Ambroos said. ~*Even an arranged marriage requires the consent of both groom and bride. We're not Appalachee here, you know, we don't kidnap our women. And you want me to tell the shareholders and the public that everything here was done above board, don't you?*~

The directors agreed, grumbling.

Adriaan Stuyvesant licked his lips. ~*If you agree that you will pay the half million—pay, not lend—and I mean you eight who have any money, I'm not going to hang this around the preachers' necks—then I will go ask my daughter to break off her engagement and marry Thomas instead. She's a good girl, I think she'll do it.*~

~*And the young man?*~ Ambroos asked.

~*I will handle him,*~ Stuyvesant said.

All around, the thirteen men nodded. They looked like chickens, clucking and bobbing their heads up and down, and then like chickens they waddled back around the low wall to meet with Franklin again.

The man lying on the ground stood up and crept away.

~*Alright,*~ Adriaan Stuyvesant said. ~*Let me speak with my daughter.*~

Franklin smiled. ~*I'll look forward to your answer tomorrow.*~

Jacob Hop pointed at the man creeping away. ~*Can we follow him?*~

Nathaniel wanted to say no. He felt ragged and exhausted, but he nodded.

Kinta Jane was knocked out of sleep by the slamming of a door. She had always been a good sleeper—able to fall asleep quickly, able to wake easily. It was a necessary skill for a working woman in the Faubourg Marigny, and it had served her well in the Ohio. On this day, it had allowed her to take an efficient nap beside the fire while Isaiah Wilkes attended the meeting with Adriaan Stuyvesant.

It was Wilkes who came through the door. He was still dressed as a woman, but before Kinta Jane's eyes he stepped up and out of his assumed woman's walk and into a longer, taller stride. Plucking the false nose from his face, he tossed it into the flames.

"You look angry," Kinta Jane said.

"I am . . . agitated. We leave immediately."

The Conventicle's Franklin certainly *sounded* enraged. "Where's Dockery?" she asked him.

"We leave without him. We'll take a different road."

A knock came at the door.

"Go away, Adriaan!" Wilkes yelled.

"It's my apartment, dammit!" Stuyvesant yelled back.

"Then open the door if you like!" Isaiah Wilkes tore the remainder of his disguise from his body and climbed back into his own clothing.

Stuyvesant came in. "I was being polite."

"Is that all?"

"Well, also I thought you might shoot me."

"I still might."

Kinta Jane's things were already collected in a single shoulder bag. She pulled on her winter walking boots and stood near the door, ready to move.

"Perhaps a marriage will put me in a position to influence the Emperor," Stuyvesant said. "Perhaps I can . . . awaken Brother Onas."

Wilkes shrugged into his coat. "Perhaps a marriage will put you in a position so that the Necromancer can corrupt you, as he has corrupted Thomas. Perhaps you will fall into the same sleep that plagues Brother Onas, and another wall of Franklin's bastion will collapse."

"I could never do that," Stuyvesant protested.

"And this morning," Wilkes said, picking up his shoulder bag. "What would you have said about Julia? Would you have said you were willing to break off her engagement?"

Stuyvesant said nothing.

"And yet now you propose to do it. For mere money, Adriaan. For money!"

The pink-faced Dutchman pounded one fist into the other hand's palm. "Yes, dammit, for money!"

"And you admit it!"

Stuyvesant roared suddenly to life. "It is easy for you to condemn me for doing something for money, when you are a man alone in this world! You can eat earth and drink air and never sleep because of Franklin's Vision that burns within you, but where are the children whose lives depend on *you*, Isaiah Wilkes? Where is your wife who did without a new dress for *twenty years* while you were making your fortune? Where are the employees who can only light their lamps and mend their roofs if you give them work to do? Where are the citizens of the Republic whose walls you are entrusted to defend, though you struggle to arm a single regiment or caulk the hull of a single warship, because of the rising cost of lead and tar! *Do not talk to me of your disdain for money!* It is cheap moralizing, coming from a man who has been so selfish as to live alone."

Wilkes recoiled as if he had been struck. "I was not always alone," he said slowly. "And I do not *choose* to be alone now."

Both men stood in silence.

Kinta Jane was baffled. What had happened?

"I keep my obligations," Stuyvesant said. "All of them, including my oath of office as Elector and my contracts with the Hudson River Republic Ohio Company. I can do this without corrupting myself, Isaiah. And I will give my daughter the choice."

"And if she says no?" Wilkes asked.

"Then perhaps the company declares bankruptcy. Perhaps the Republic sells land to the Penns, or to Acadia."

"And will *she* know what the risks are when you offer her the choice?"

Stuyvesant said nothing.

"I see. We're leaving, Adrian. We need to find Brother Odishkwa."

"Delay a few hours. I need you to help me."

Wilkes shook his head slightly.

"Please."

"What help do you need?"

"Take Dockery and the canoes. And take Julia's fiancé with you."

"What? Why? This is a bad way to distract a man whose heart you've just broken!"

Adriaan sighed. "Gert Visser is a good man. His family are

burghers, cloth merchants. But Gert is something of a hothead. And he's something of a bigot, and deeply in love. If Julia ends their engagement in person, he'll make trouble."

"This is not my problem, Adriaan."

"Imagine Gert Visser tracking down Temple Franklin and clobbering him with his big-knuckled fists. Or worse, imagine him and his friends tarring and feathering the Emperor's envoy."

"Still not my problem. And don't tell me that I have to help you or the bastion of Franklin's plan falls. Franklin's plan never depended on the Hudson River Republicans being able to wear silk."

"Gert Visser is a brother."

Isaiah Wilkes took a deep breath. "Of the Conventicle?"

Adriaan nodded. "He was to marry my daughter. She and he had been ... spending time together at the cliff house late one night, and he walked in on a meeting with me. I had to kill him or bring him in."

"So he could indeed make trouble. If not in person, how will you ask Julia to end her engagement?"

"By letter. Which I will consign to you. And I will ask you to give it to him at Ticonderoga."

"At which point, if he reacts as a hothead, I will have to deal with him."

"At which point, if he reacts as a hothead, I ask that you kill him."

"Who were those men?" Nathaniel asked. He felt ill and weak.

They had emerged from the star-strewn landscape into which Nathaniel had taken Jake and back into Ambroos's attic. As he considered his answer, Jake packed his gear into his bag. "Isaiah Wilkes and Adriaan Stuyvesant, you mean. I don't know. They might be friends."

"They don't seem even to be friends with each other."

"No, but they're brothers of some kind. I think they're in Franklin's Conventicle together."

"I look forward to finding out that some horrible folktale or ridiculous bugaboo or improbable rumor I heard as a child *isn't* true," Nathaniel said. "So far, I seem to be living in a nursery story."

"I'll ask Ambroos to bring together his community and attempt an exorcism on the way back," Jake said. "Right now, I want to get to your sister. As soon as possible."

Nathaniel put on his backward hat and shrugged into his coat. His drum was heavier than ever, but he managed to hoist it onto his shoulder. "What's changed?"

They descended the stairs, Jake leading quickly and Nathaniel faltering behind, leaning heavily on the wall. The house was empty. Snowflakes blew across the boardwalk as they checked the acorn, turned, and walked north again.

"Thomas is in motion," Jake said. "Of course he is. He's not sitting around waiting for Sarah to surrender to him, he's trying to kill her. Kill us. And the Dutch are about to give him a large pile of money, and more influence in the Assembly. And none of that is *really* new, but it's new information to *me*. And a good reminder not to sit around. And not to complain about a few headaches."

At the word *headaches*, Nathaniel rubbed his temples. "Now that you mention it, I've developed a splitting one." He felt he might pass out, and took deep breaths.

"Too much time in...that place?"

"I don't think so," Nathaniel said. "I think...I think my gift is not meant for use in spying."

Jake laughed. "You don't usually hear a strong man say his arms weren't meant for lifting or throwing, or a clever woman claim her intelligence wasn't made for a puzzle. What makes you think your gift has a purpose?"

Nathaniel was quiet for a few minutes. They passed beyond the stone buildings and into fenced farmland, furrows hidden beneath a blanket of white snow and the steam of animals' bodies rising from sheds and stables. "The manner of my getting it. Also, it felt wrong today. *I* felt wrong."

"You mean you have to be honest?" Jake asked. "The same way you have to wear your hat backward?"

"No, I think I can lie. But I left my body to be healed, and I can leave it to heal. Leaving it to do something else today... hurt my head." He didn't mention the sensation that he was on the verge of collapse.

"Too bad," Jake said. "I was beginning to think you'd be a terrific spy."

"I can do it, but it hurts. I wouldn't want to do it long, or often."

There was something in Nathaniel's hesitation that told Jake he was leaving something unsaid. "What else is bothering you, friend Nathaniel?"

"I'm also nervous about Robert Hooke."

Jake snorted. "Good. He *should* make you nervous. He makes me *terrified*."

"But we'll tell Sarah about those people. The Conventicle."

"We'll tell her."

Nathaniel pulled the acorn from its box again. To Jake's surprise, it rolled in Nathaniel's palm and pointed due east.

"She's moved," Nathaniel said. "Or we're arriving."

The next turn east was a broad lane that cut through more farms. Nathaniel kept the acorn in his palm and they watched it, only taking their eyes away to step out of the path of horses and the occasional sled.

The road took them to a village whose signpost identified it as HAARLEM. The acorn led them northward through the village, to a sprawling Dutch-style house atop a low, rocky hill.

"I supposed I could enter the starlit plain again." Nathaniel put on a cheerful smile, but it was forced.

"Your head still hurts?"

Nathaniel nodded.

"I have a different idea," Jake said. "You say you think you're able to lie?"

"My name is Randolph," Nathaniel said. "I'm from Georgia and I'm a horse trader. I come to New Amsterdam and Haarlem all the time, and I hate that fellow Jacob Hop." He shrugged. "I feel fine."

"Very good. Let's put that to a harder test."

*"This is magic we are talking about, after all,
and not hydraulics."*

———◆———

CHAPTER NINE

Chigozie and the Merciful left their hill the same day, in case Naares Stoach decided to bring his riders back early. There was no vote about what they should do, and very little discussion.

Shortly after the riders left, Kort asked Chigozie, "Where shall we go?"

"North of us are the plains of the Free Horse People," Chigozie said. "East lies Cahokia, which in better days might have been a place of refuge." Left unsaid was: *But in these days, the Heron King and his minions, your former brethren, devastate that land.*

"South of us is the City of White Towers. Etzanoa," Kort rumbled. "They've made their intentions toward us clear."

The Merciful within earshot all nodded and made braying, mewing, growling, or hissing sounds of agreement. They spent the morning and early afternoon gathering everything they could from the castle of the former Baron McClane and bundling it within furs and blankets. Each Merciful beastwife or beastman shouldering a bundle, they turned and trudged west.

Chigozie regretted leaving behind the buildings, even ruined as they were, as well as most of the furniture.

The beastkind weren't impervious to the cold, but they resisted the stinging northern blasts better than Chigozie did. His clothing had torn in climbing through brambles and on sharp rocks, it had frozen and snapped, and it had worn to threads rubbing on the ground, or on the wooden boards on which Chigozie slept. He had replaced it with a pair of wool trousers from the Baron's castle, supplemented with furs wrapped around his legs and held in place with leather strips. He wrapped a wool matchcoat about his shoulders and a long fur muffler that must have belonged to a fine lady around his neck. With all the fur on his body, other than the broad-brimmed beaverskin hat, he might have been a beast.

He might have been one of the Merciful, and that suited him just fine.

The blessing of the storms was that the snow must surely cover their tracks, so after two days of walking, Chigozie began to feel safe.

They stayed away from the Missouri River, because Chigozie feared the traffic that might travel on it. Instead, they followed its course in the hills above, sticking to the forests and avoiding towns.

Most of the settlements they passed were burned and trampled. The few that weren't bristled with muskets and the fiercely staring eyes of starving people.

The Merciful sang while they walked and fell asleep promptly once they were still. Chigozie had more difficulty getting to sleep. He thought of the last words he'd heard from the Zoman outrider: *I'm a merciful man, but I'm willing to kill.*

Chigozie had killed in the name of mercy, cutting short the lives of two women who were being ravaged by Kort and his troop, before they had returned to become the Merciful. As he thought back on those pulse-pounding moments, he was unsure what exactly he had seen in their faces at the last.

Gratitude at the cutting short of their suffering?

Anger that Chigozie should join their tormentors, rather than rescue the women?

Simple fear?

Chigozie Ukwu slept poorly.

On the fifth day, they found a place to stay.

The first sign Chigozie noticed was a reaction among the Merciful. Muzzles that had hung low and drooping shoulders began to raise. A low murmur of wonder and questioning ran through the line of marchers.

Then he saw steam rising from what appeared to be the flat

ground. "Could that be a cave?" he asked Ferpa, pointing. "Don't caves stay warmer than the surface in winter, as they are cooler in summer?"

Ferpa's negative answer sounded like the lowing of a tired cow.

"I smell water," a hound-headed beastwife said, immediately bounding forward into the snow.

Shortly thereafter, Chigozie found himself shrugging out of his furs and throwing the matchcoat over one shoulder as he climbed down a crack in the rock into a narrow valley. The valley had stone walls that rose sharply on all sides, as if some cosmic giant had created it by cleaving the range of hills in two with a sword. Several paths led up the cliffs, but for Chigozie they all looked like tricky footing and a strenuous climb.

The beastkind looked unfazed by the roughness of the trails.

Water flowed out of the valley through a crack in the walls barely wider than the stream, and not wide enough to ride two horses abreast or drive a wagon. The water wasn't frozen because it bubbled up beneath a rock overhang and beside a stone shelf in a hot spring. The spring was the source of the steam. As he climbed down into the valley, Chigozie noticed over the musky reek of the Merciful and the stink of his own sweat that the water smelled heavily of sulfur.

"We're grateful for what we have, Lord," he murmured. "We have nothing of our own merit, and everything of Thy bounty."

Above the spring and along the stream before the canyon narrowed grew several copses of trees and thickets of berry bushes.

Chigozie's legs burned and his knees wobbled with the effort of the last few steps down. To help keep his balance on the wet stones, he picked up a long, slightly curved piece of wood and leaned on it like a staff. Crossing the stream to the bench of stone, he threw down his furs and coat and stood above the spring.

The heat from the spring told him that the water bubbling up was quite hot. The sulfur was oddly sweet in his nostrils. He tried to raise his arms to address the Merciful, but he couldn't get his hands above his shoulders, and he gave up. Instead, he hugged his new walking stick and leaned on it.

He was more tired than he'd realized.

The beastkind who followed him—no, who *shared his journey*—stood ranged about the canyon. They had energy in their stance and excitement on their faces. Chigozie wanted to say something profound, but could think of nothing. He contented himself with quoting the Bible.

"The Lord is my shepherd," he said. "I shall not want. He maketh me to lie down in green pastures; He leadeth me beside the still waters. He restoreth my soul; He leadeth me in the paths of righteousness for his name's sake. Yea, though I walk through the valley of the shadow of death, I will fear no evil for Thou art with me; Thy rod and Thy staff they comfort me. Thou preparest a table before me in the presence of mine enemies; Thou anointest my head with oil; my cup runneth over. Surely goodness and mercy shall follow me all the days of my life, and I will dwell in the house of the Lord forever."

"Amen," the Merciful bellowed.

"These are the still waters," Kort said gravely. "Here we shall give great mercy."

"Amen."

"And Chigozie Ukwu shall be our shepherd."

"Amen!"

Chigozie had no strength left to resist. Besides, shepherd was a more modest title than king or priest.

Hadn't David been a shepherd? Didn't the kings of Memphis still carry the shepherd's crook as one of their staffs of office? And wasn't Christ himself the Good Shepherd?

The title had humility, but also antiquity and meaning.

"Amen." He bowed his head low. When he raised it again, he saw a hundred glittering eyes fixed on him. "Let us find food. And then let us build."

As they walked up the path to the front door between snow-shrouded flowerbeds, Nathaniel closed his fingers around the acorn and listened.

He heard the voices of the Lenni Lenape pining for their lost land. He heard the soft whispers of the sleeping trees and the heart-wild cry of animals who had died, killed by bullet, arrowhead, or claw. He heard the cheerful songs of hard-working Dutch traders and sailors.

And he heard a voice that sounded familiar. ~*Who am I? Where am I? Why do I know nothing?*~

"She's here," he said. "There's something wrong."

"Is she a prisoner?" Jacob asked. "Is she injured?"

"I can't tell. But she doesn't know who she is." Maybe that was why he had been unable to hear her before, when he had listened on the starlit plain.

"Do *you* know who *you* are?"

Nathaniel grinned. "I'm your deaf-mute lackey."

"*Lackey,* a very harsh word. You are my trusted body servant."

"Does that sound less harsh?"

"It does in Dutch. Remember to keep quiet, and don't react to sound." Jacob Hop thumbed through his Tarocks with shaking hands, looking at three cards in quick succession without laying them out.

Nathaniel nodded.

Standing on the wide porch, Jake knocked. Nathaniel examined the whitewashed boards, the red brick chimneys, the rough-hewn wooden bench and rocking chair sitting on the porch. At Jake's second knock—Nathaniel remembered to betray no sign that he actually heard the rapping—the door opened.

"Ja, wie gaat daar?"

Jake launched into a fervent conversation in Dutch. He sounded friendly and polite, and he also sounded as if he were begging. Nathaniel reminded himself to pretend not to hear the conversation, which was easy enough, since he couldn't understand it.

He smiled at the man behind the door and got a bare grunt in return. The man was squat and wide and wore an orange and gray uniform of thinning flannel that had been made for a taller, more slender man. The waistcoat looked stretched around his belly and about to lose buttons, and the sleeves of his jacket rucked up in tight wrinkles at the elbows.

The leafless trees at the foot of the plowed fields looked like skeletal arms. Beyond them, Haarlem puffed thin tendrils of gray smoke into a slate-gray winter sky.

He listed for the voice he thought belonged to his sister. ~*I'll do it, this doesn't hurt me. Who are these men?*~

Suddenly Jake grabbed his elbow and shook him. Nathaniel barely managed to avoid asking, "What?" At the last moment, he remembered to put on an oblivious grin and shake his head.

Jake said something in Dutch and pointed toward a dull red barn squatted at the other end of a field west of the house, just beyond a ditch. He pointed again several times, said something loud in Dutch, and then kicked Nathaniel in the seat of his pants.

Nathaniel stumbled away, turned—

and saw himself.

Not actually himself, of course, but through the open door behind the man in orange and gray, he saw a young woman who might have been Nathaniel, if Nathaniel wore an orange and gray flannel dress and had an enormous pile of thick, curled hair on top of his head. She carried a circular tray that held a coffee pot and white cups, and around her neck hung a medallion that looked like a lump of lead.

She met Nathaniel's gaze; her eyes were dull and confused.

Jake swung another kick at Nathaniel and missed, maybe on purpose. Nathaniel nodded and backed away, making moaning and grunting noises in the back of his throat. The man at the door leered, said something in harsh syllables, and laughed. Jake joined in the laughter, and then followed Nathaniel off the porch.

It occurred to Nathaniel that with his backward hat and inside-out coat, he looked like someone who was not only deaf and mute, but also an idiot. A deaf, mute, idiot drummer boy.

"No wonder they told us to sleep in the barn," he grumbled as they crossed the field. "I look like a madman."

"No, that's a good thing, hey?" Jake said. "The barn is ordinary hospitality for strangers around here. It's what I asked for."

"Did you see the girl?"

"I only saw the doorman."

Had he imagined her? Or heard her, with his astral ear, and interpreted the information as visual cues? But no, she had been quite solid.

"I saw my sister," he told the Dutchman. "She didn't react at all to seeing me."

"Maybe she didn't see you. Or maybe she was distracted by your sense of fashion. Was she a prisoner? A guest?"

"She wore the same colors as the doorman. She looked like a servant."

Jake looked over his shoulder and waved back at the house in the last light of the setting sun. "Let's get behind a closed door and discuss plans."

The barn was neatly ordered, with bales of hay filling half the high-roofed structure and farm implements the other. Jake shut the large barn door behind them.

"We can't stay here," Nathaniel said.

"It's a pretty warm barn."

"There's something wrong with my sister. Something...something is wrong with her spirit."

"Is she mad?"

Nathaniel considered. "No, I've known a madman, and he was nothing like this. And I don't think she's an idiot, either. But something has been taken from her, or hidden. Her identity, her memory."

"That could be madness."

"Or it could be a kind of prison. It could be gramarye."

Jake wore a very innocent look on his face. "Do you think she needs...healing?"

Nathaniel flinched. "Maybe."

"Then you might be the right person to help her."

Nathaniel nodded, trembling only slightly at the sudden thought of Robert Hooke's vortex of grasping hands.

"In any case, your point is that if she's a prisoner, the people in the house are the ones holding her captive. They are not to be trusted."

"And if the doorman noticed how much I look like her..."

"We should leave immediately." Jake made a beeline for the much smaller barn door in the back corner and Nathaniel followed.

They walked directly away from the farmhouse, keeping the barn between them and the building to screen them from view. It was easy—they just made sure the barn blocked the light coming from the house's windows.

Then they got onto a different lane from the one they'd traveled before, and followed it again into Haarlem.

"No one will think twice about you," Nathaniel said. "You're Dutch, this is the Republic. But I'm a Cavalier...well, I sound like one...anyway, I'm not Dutch. Do you know that the Ojibwe have this word, Zhaaganaashi, and it means people who speak English as their native tongue? Also, because of the way I wear my clothes."

"We could make a word like that. Engelsspreker. English-speaker. That kind of thing works for the Germans, anyway. I'll call myself Thijs," Jake said. "I'll get a room on the ground floor and let you in by the window."

They chose an inn called the *Benedito de Espinosa* and Nathaniel sneaked into the yard behind the inn to wait. In the shadow of a chicken coop, he counted three of the inn's guests who made it to the privy in the corner of the hard-packed dirt yard, two who never found the outhouse and made use of the back fence instead, and one who staggered in circles singing the same verse of a song Nathaniel didn't know over and over until he finally gave up and wandered back into the common room again. Nathaniel watched the back windows of the inn, waiting for one to open. He was beginning to grow impatient when he heard a hissing noise from above.

He looked up and saw Jake, leaning out a window on the second story and waving his arms. "Psst! Psst!"

Jake threw down a rope made of a knotted sheet and Nathaniel tied his pack to it. Jake hoisted the pack in through the window, and then lowered the rope again. Nathaniel climbed awkwardly, levering his feet against a lead drain pipe and against the frame of a window on the first floor, but when he was close enough, Jake grabbed him and dragged him in through the window.

"We said ground floor," Nathaniel gasped, lying on the floor.

"Those windows don't open," Jake said. "I think it's to force the burglars to work for their living. I had to go back and lie to the innkeeper and tell him I had said second story when we both knew very well I'd said first. Then I had to make this rope."

"We could have picked another inn."

"Or you could have worn your coat right side out and no one would look at you twice. But we didn't do either of those things, and now you're inside."

Had they wasted their time with elaborate precautions? He decided not. "We'll be happy if those people follow us into the village and go around asking for the odd foreigner in the turned-out coat."

"And think of the excellent practice you're getting, in case you decide you do want to become a spy." Jacob Hop was shuffling his Tarocks. "Let's do a casting."

"Why? We found my sister, and now I want to go heal her."

"Does that mean you're not nervous about Robert Hooke anymore? Your headache is gone?"

"Do the casting."

"Here's the question I have: what are the omens for Nathaniel Penn's journey to rescue his sister?" After the shuffling, Jake laid down three cards. "The omens are good."

"I don't know how you'd know," Nathaniel said. "Though at

least the Tarocks have pretty pictures. Astrologers cover a page
with simple dots and tell you it predicts the future. You've dealt
all . . . what do you call them?"

"Major Arcana," Jake said. "Yes, the Highway, the Virgin,
and the Serpent. I take these as good omens. The starlit plain
is the Highway you wish to travel and the Virgin is the sister
you'll rescue. The Tarocks acknowledge your plan. Your sister
Sarah is the Serpent, or your father is, or your goddess. Or *you*.
It's a good sign for your family. A negative sign would be the
Revenant or the Sorcerer, which I might take to indicate Hooke
himself, or Oliver Cromwell. Or Simon Sword."

"That seems unlikely, that all three cards would be from the
Major Arcana. There are twenty of those, and how many cards
total?"

"Seventy-six. On a random draw, twenty chances out of
seventy-six—call it one in four, to make the math easier—you
get one of the Major Arcana."

Nathaniel struggled. His mathematical training had been
rudimentary, and mostly expressed in terms of the number of
pheasants on a string, or miles to Richmond. "If you add one
in four to one in four, you get—half?"

"No." Jake shook his head. "If I draw one card, there is one
chance in four it's one of the Major Arcana. If I draw a second
card, the chances that both are from the Major Arcana is one
in four *multiplied by* one in four. And the odds of three cards
all being from the Major Arcana are one in four times one in
four times one in four."

"I don't know what that makes," Nathaniel admitted.

"One in sixty-four."

Nathaniel whistled.

"You think that's impressive, hey? Watch this." Jacob Hop
shuffled the cards thoroughly, putting the Serpent, the Highway,
and the Virgin back into the deck, and drew three cards again.

The Drunkard, the Virgin, and the Hanged Man.

Nathaniel stared.

"Six cards in a row is one chance in four thousand ninety-
six. But here's the thing—I've been turning cards for about two
and a half months, and they're *always* from the Major Arcana.
As long as I hold the cards in my hands, I can shuffle through
them and see them all, Minor Arcana as well as Major. The

minute I start laying cards down, only the Major Arcana come up. That's thousands of cards in a row, and I long since stopped calculating what odds that made. There are no odds here. This is fixed. Something is dictating what cards turn up."

"Is it just that deck?"

"I borrowed a deck in Johnsland, and the same thing happened. The man whose cards I borrowed couldn't believe it either, and when I handed it back to him, his deck worked normally again."

"Well, that answers my next question. And now I suppose I know why you haven't stopped fidgeting with those cards since I met you."

"There are other reasons," Jake said.

"Does it only affect *you*?" Nathaniel asked.

"It didn't affect that fellow in Johnsland."

"Let me try." Nathaniel held out his hand.

Reluctantly, Jake passed over the deck. Nathaniel shuffled them thoroughly and then dealt three cards: the River, the Virgin, the Revenant.

And again: the Horsemen, the Drunkard, the Highway.

He shuffled and dealt five more times, each time getting only Major Arcana. Each time, he felt more troubled and haunted, but to his surprise, Jake's expression looked like relief.

"It isn't only me!" Jake burst out at Nathaniel's final casting.

"Then what explains it?" Nathaniel asked.

"I worried it was me. That maybe my...connection...with Simon Sword made the cards not work."

"I don't have a connection with Simon Sword," Nathaniel objected.

"I think you do," Jake said. "Not the same connection I have—I hope—but your family is tied to the Heron King. And now that Simon Sword is in motion, for those of us who are connected to him, the New World Tarocks show only Major Arcana."

"You think this is some magic of Simon Sword's?"

"Maybe." Jake shrugged. "Maybe it's not something he intends, it's just something that happens. Or maybe it's some magic of Benjamin Franklin and John Penn. Maybe it's a warning system. Maybe when Peter Plowshare dies and Simon Sword ascends to the Heron King's throne, the Tarocks go mad as a way to let people know."

"But they don't go mad for everyone."

Jake shrugged. "For people who have crossed Simon Sword's path? Or who *will* cross his path? This is magic we are talking about, after all, not hydraulics."

"Well, I am grateful for the omens." In truth, Nathaniel did feel slightly better. He didn't especially trust the Tarocks to tell his future—he trusted them *less*, thinking that Simon Sword or Benjamin Franklin or someone else was manipulating what cards came up—but it heartened him to see images he thought of as positive: the Serpent, the Virgin.

The inn's room had a single bed and a narrow table, with no fireplace and only the single window. Two tall tapers in brass candlesticks sat on the table, lighting the chamber. Nathaniel sat cross-legged in the center of the floor and closed his eyes. He inhaled deeply and shifted his drum into his lap. But before he could focus his mind, he heard Jake sitting down facing him.

"I'm coming with you," Jacob Hop said.

"To spy?"

"No." Jake spoke with a straight face. "We're going to heal your sister. But if Robert Hooke comes to take you, I'll be there to help."

"What will you do?"

"I'll start by throwing Tarocks at him. If that doesn't work, I'll throw myself under his feet to slow him down so you can get away."

Nathaniel opened his eyes. "Don't do that."

"I don't serve you, Nathaniel Penn. I serve my queen, Sarah Elytharias, and she sent me to bring back her siblings. If I die and you live to return to Cahokia, then I have succeeded."

Nathaniel considered. "I understand. And still . . . don't do that. There will be another way."

"Not always," Jake said. "I'm closing my eyes now, I'm ready."

Nathaniel drummed and sang:

I ride upon four horses, to heaven I ride
I ride to seek my sister, horses by my side
I bring a true companion, by perils tried
I seek the land of spirits, to heaven I ride

He rose from his sitting position, pulling Jake behind him onto the back of his drum-horse and up onto the starlit plain. He listened for Robert Hooke and heard sounds of cursing and shouting, far in the west.

Good. Whatever made Hooke suffer should make Nathaniel glad.

He listened for Margaret and now—having heard her voice, he recognized it and could pick it out of the deeper song of the cosmos—he found her nearby.

~*You know,*~ Jake said. ~*In this place, your coat is rightside out and you wear your hat the right way.*~

Nathaniel checked his clothing and was surprised to find it was true.

~*Ha,*~ he said.

They rode across a short meadow and through a curling valley to find the house they'd left outside Haarlem shortly before. On the starlit plain, the white farmhouse appeared as a sagging warehouse painted a dark crimson.

~*They're smugglers,*~ Jake said. ~*They must be.*~

Nathaniel was pleased that his head didn't hurt, and he nodded.

~*Your vision is just as powerful as your sister's,*~ Jake said.

~*This isn't vision. This is . . . motion. Of an unusual kind.*~

They rode through the front door. Within, bottles of rum stood stacked around all the walls. Three men sat at a table, playing cards. Nathaniel rode closer and saw that the fronts and backs alike of the cards were blank.

~*Strange.*~ Jake produced his battered Tarocks and held them up for him and Nathaniel both to see. The usual images were on the cards, front and back.

Though on the faces of the Major Arcana, Nathaniel thought he saw a second set of images, ghostly as watermarks, lurking behind the colorful paintings he knew.

And was that music he heard, coming from the cards?

~*Put those away,*~ he told the Dutchman.

Later, they could examine the cards again.

~*Will Hancock pay us or will the Frenchman?*~ One of the card players asked the others. He was burly and lacked one ear. ~*The loss of a ship is no small thing to recompense.*~

A second card player, a thin man with a drooping nose, shrugged. ~*It's La Fayette's money either way.*~

~*They're talking about John Hancock,*~ Jake whispered. ~*He's the biggest smuggler north of Baltimore. And someone named La Fayette. Maybe the Marquis, the Acadian Elector?*~

~I understand them,~ Nathaniel whispered back. *~They're speaking English.~*

~No, they're not,~ Jake said, and then they both fell into thoughtful silence.

~I didn't mean that Frenchman. I meant Le Moyne. In New Orleans.~ One Ear played a card and the other two cursed.

~They're family,~ said the third card player, a man with burn scars on both hands. *~Same money.~*

~Yeah?~ Droop Nose asked. *~You and I are family, Luuk. I'm married to your sister. How about you pay off the note I owe old man Van Beek?~*

~Go to hell,~ Burn Hands said cheerfully.

~There's an upper floor,~ Nathaniel said. There had to be, the building was too tall to contain just this one room.

Though the starlit plain didn't exactly obey the ordinary rules of size and dimension.

~I don't see stairs,~ Jake said.

~We don't need stairs.~ Nathaniel sang:

> *I ride the winds of heaven, iron inside*
> *I shall not be resisted, my will denied*
> *No wall can stop my progress, she cannot hide*
> *I seek my sister Margaret, to heaven I ride*

With a liquid neighing sound and the thunder of an invisible drum, his horse leaped up and through the ceiling—

emerging through the floor above into a cell.

Margaret sat on a wooden chair and stared at a blank wall. Her face was just as expressionless as the wall; her hands were folded in her lap.

~Margaret,~ Nathaniel said.

No response.

Nathaniel heard a footfall and he spurred his horse aside, expecting to be dragged into Robert Hooke's amber pool, or get stabbed in the back.

Behind him stood another Margaret. This Margaret was identical, in an orange and gray flannel dress, except that her hair shot straight out of her head in all directions like a halo, and wiggled. She waved her arms at Nathaniel and her eyes bulged wide, but she held her lips tightly together and made no sound.

~What do you think your sister's gift is?~ Jake asked. *~Is this her work? Is she projecting an image of herself? Or which of these is the real Margaret? They appear identical.~*

~Not quite. Look.~ Nathaniel pointed; only the sitting Margaret wore the amulet.

Fire seized Nathaniel suddenly, knocking him to the floor. He fell tangled with Jake, and with his horse, which suddenly seemed to be a drum again.

The room around him flickered. The two Margarets faded in and out, and in their place he saw a single Margaret, lying on a small iron cot. Beside Margaret stood a bent-backed, unshaven man in an orange frock coat. He stared at Nathaniel and laughed.

"Who do we have here? Is it an Acadian wizard whose master doesn't want to pay for a ship his cargo sank?"

A third scene overlaid the first two, and at the same moment Nathaniel seemed to see the cell on the starlit plain, the second-story inn bedroom at the *Benedito de Espinosa*, or a windowless stone-walled chamber with a man in orange.

The room looked like a cellar.

"Or are you some adept from the Imperial College, chasing down the rumor of a lost Penn scion, who must be eliminated if Thomas is to sleep well at night?" The man in orange stood inside a circle chalked onto a stone floor. The circle completely enclosed Margaret's cot. Incense burned where he was—which must be somewhere in the white farmhouse, or beneath it—and he held an aspergillum in one hand. He shook the aspergillum in a circle around him, splashing liquid on the floor within the confines of the chalked space.

Fire fell on Nathaniel and Jake.

"Or are you someone else? Maybe you're with the pirate queen, and you want to steal back your hostage with this Talligewi sorcery." The orange-clad mage chuckled. "Today is not your lucky day, friend. Today's the day you go in the bottle."

The mage let the aspergillum fall to his side. It hung there, connected to his belt by a leather strap.

Nathaniel tried to bang his drum, but his fingers wouldn't respond. He tried to sing, but his parched throat emitted a cracked warble with no words and no power. The sleeping Margaret, he noticed, also wore the lumpy amulet. The same amulet worn by Margaret in the chair.

The mage reached into a coat pocket and produced a dark brown glass bottle.

The Margaret who could move, but not speak, wore no amulet.

Jake threw the Tarocks.

The cards burst into flame as they sailed through the air. Doing so, something in them was freed. Men and beasts and horses sprang from the cards as they disintegrated, and a stampede of Major Arcana rushed over the orange wizard. The images themselves took fire as they moved and a river of flame struck the mage, who dropped the bottle and raised his hands defensively—

Nathaniel could move.

He sprang toward Margaret. He saw three of her, so it took mental effort to shut out the sleeping Margaret on the bed and the frantic mute Margaret, and focus on Margaret sitting and staring at the wall.

He dodged beneath a flaming horse and was buffeted by a drunkard on fire, but he lunged across all three rooms and wrapped both hands around the amulet hanging around sitting Margaret's neck.

He yanked it off.

An intense surge of pain shot up both arms to his brain, and he fell to the ground, frozen.

Sitting Margaret stood and looked at frantic Margaret. Each took a step toward the other, and then a second, and then they melted into each other and became one. As the last of the burning Tarock images faded and the orange-wearing wizard turned and glared at Nathaniel, Margaret stepped in front of Nathaniel. Her hair flared and waved and she raised one warning finger.

"Now you're really going to get it," she growled at the wizard.

The mage's answering smile was unsteady. "Oh? I think you'll find I can deal with you on this plane just as easily as I can in Haarlem."

But as the wizard spoke, behind him in the farmhouse cellar, the flesh and blood Margaret stood. As she climbed to her feet, her hair rose and spread until it waved about her head like the white spores of a summer dandelion.

The wizard raised his aspergillum—

and flesh and blood Margaret tore it from his hand.

She pulled so hard, the strap broke and he fell to the ground. He yelped and when he hit the stone, his lungs emitted a high-pitched squeak.

Nathaniel tried to move, but was still frozen in place.

~Don't let him do any more magic!~ Jake yelled.

Margaret bent over the wizard as he struggled to catch his breath. *"Corporem—"* He grunted, and she shoved the handle of the aspergillum into his mouth, muting him instantly. She picked him off the ground entirely and slammed him to the stone again, forcing grunts of pain from the wizard.

Then she slid his body across the floor. Like a wet sponge run over a school slate, she smeared a large gap into the chalk circle.

Nathaniel tried to rise and couldn't. He tried to throw the amulet away and couldn't. He felt a cold stupor and an electric paralysis flowing from the lump in his hands through his entire body.

A hard, rapid knock came at a door. What door was that? Nathaniel thought it was in the inn. "Wie schreeuwt daar?" yelled a voice on the other side of that door. "Is alles goed?"

Another door opened. Did the room in the *Benedito de Espinosa* have two doors? No, this was a door in the cellar of the white farmhouse. It opened, and through it charged the three card-playing men. One Ear rushed in first and tried to grab Margaret.

She rose swinging a fist. Her punch connected, her fist sinking deep into One Ear's gut. He made a sound like a bellows squeezing out all its air in a single forced push and sank to the ground, blood pouring from his lips.

The other two men shouted incoherently. Margaret calmly picked up One Ear by the belt and tossed him. He whirled end over end, striking both the ceiling and the floor as he went, and plowed through both other men, knocking them down.

~The amulet!~ Jake shouted.

A fog began to creep over Nathaniel's vision, obscuring all three spaces at the same time.

When the two conscious smugglers stood, they were armed. Burn Hands had a truncheon and Droop Nose a knife, and they came at Margaret swinging.

But she had armed herself, too. She held the wizard by both ankles and she swung him around overhead like a lariat. The mage's skull and Droop Nose's connected with a loud *crack* and she dropped the wizard.

Nathaniel's vision was almost totally fogged over.

He heard the thudding sounds of someone trying to break into the bedroom at the inn.

Burn Hands swung his truncheon downward at Margaret's head—

she caught it with one hand.

"Kanker!" Burn Hand shouted.

With her other hand. Margaret casually punched him in the nose, knocking him unconscious.

~The amulet!~ Jake shouted again.

~The amulet!~ spirit Margaret also shouted.

Flesh and blood Margaret gripped the amulet around her neck with one hand and ripped it from her body. Smashing the lump on the floor, she stamped it under her heel and ground it flat.

The amulet in Nathaniel's grip disappeared, the fog lifted in an instant, and he could move.

The cellar and the inn room were beginning to fade.

~Where do I find you?~ spirit Margaret asked, stepping backward toward her flesh and blood self.

~Get out of the house!~ Jake shouted. ~There's a barn by the west fields. Hide there, we'll come within the hour!~

Spirit Margaret and flesh and blood Margaret fused, and flesh and blood Margaret raced out through the cellar door just as the cellar and the inn both faded from view.

~We're about to have visitors,~ Jake said.

Nathaniel pulled the Dutchman up onto his horse and turned to race back the way they'd come. In quick bounds, his drum-horse covered the long grass of the curling valley and descended the seven steps into the *Benedito de Espinosa*. Jake fell into his cross-legged body, Nathaniel melded into the shadowy form of his bear-self Makwa, and the horse became the drum across Nathaniel's lap.

The door caved in. A heavy Dutchman in a greasy apron charged through, caught his balance, and then began yelling at Jake.

Jake yelled back, all in Dutch.

Nathaniel considered jumping out the window. Instead he stood, slung his drum carefully over his shoulder, and walked out the door.

So much for secrecy and spycraft.

He heard the metallic jingle of coins behind him, and then Jake caught up.

They exited the common room into the streets of Haarlem.

"Well, people are going to talk about this. You're going to be so famous in Haarlem, you'll become a folktale."

"The innkeeper thought we were trying to steal from him?"

"Yes, he charges by the person, not by the room. Also, he thought we were lovers."

"What?"

"Apparently, we were screaming. And he said he doesn't mind that kind of thing, but we ought to keep it quiet. And if there are two of us, we both have to pay."

"That sounds like he really *does* mind."

"Or he was happy to have found opportunity to make a little more money."

"I heard coins," Nathaniel said. "Did you pay him? Even though we're leaving?"

Jake shrugged. "I thought it was better to pay him than risk having a jager sent after us."

"What's a jager?"

"A hunter. You know, someone who tracks down fugitives for money?"

"A bounty hunter." Nathaniel stopped in the middle of the frozen street and pointed at an orange light north of the village. "What's that?"

Jake looked, and then laughed. "We'd better hurry up and get there before anyone else does. Your sister lit the farmhouse on fire."

"I shall not visit thee in hell, Ophidian."

———◆———

CHAPTER TEN

Ezekiel Angleton, that was his name.

He had to remind himself from time to time, when the winter's chill drove the name from his head.

Winter didn't trouble his body at all. His new body, he reminded himself. His resurrected body. Like Elijah of old, Ezekiel had been taken into heaven and transformed without the necessity of death first.

His nails had grown black. His pale complexion, easily burned by the sun, had turned an impervious gray. His breath had grown sweet with the flesh of men.

This is my body which is given for you, the Lord had said.

Not Ezekiel's Lord, but his predecessor.

He had eaten men first, because men had attacked him. But he had learned that women and children were sweeter.

I am the resurrection, and the life.

Winter didn't trouble his reborn flesh, but it dulled his mind. It caused him to forget his name sometimes and, much worse, to forget Lucy.

Lucy. He must share this gift with her.

This day shalt thou be with me in paradise.

After being repulsed by the Earl of Johnsland, with his ferocious fire and his mounted men, Ezekiel had taken refuge in the hills. He had grieved his failure for several days in a crack in the earth, until hunger had finally driven him to move.

He had eaten, taking a child from outside a chapel. The boy was peeping in through a frost-glazed window during service, obviously disobeying his parents. Naughty child. Ezekiel had enjoyed the sense of being the instrument of justice that came when he broke the boy's neck, dragged him behind the hill, and devoured his flesh.

Men with torches had pursued him deeper into the hills, but Ezekiel didn't sleep and didn't tire. In the face of a north wind-riding blizzard, the posse comitatus had given up.

Ezekiel had turned into the teeth of the storm. Sometimes, he thought he was going home to Lucy. He knew where she was buried. He knew he could raise her from her grave; he believed his Lord would give her a perfected body like his own.

He had followed his coat to Johnsland, but there the coat had been destroyed.

Robert Hooke had once worn the coat, but Ezekiel realized that it must have had an earlier owner. The coat pulled him in the direction of the children of Kyres Elytharias, which must mean that it had once belonged to the Lion of Missouri. Had he lost it to enemies in the Spanish War? Had it been taken from the scene of his murder by Daniel Berkeley or Bayard Prideux, his murderers?

Somehow, in any case, it had come into the possession of the Lord Protector, who had given it to his servant Robert Hooke.

And then to his servant Ezekiel Angleton.

But now it was gone.

Ezekiel turned to old magic. The skills he had learned at Harvard seemed dry and dusty to him, but they worked. He stole a small glass bottle from a farmhouse window and filled it with spring water. He had once carried quicksilver on his person, but that had disappeared somewhere along the way. Carefully, he had scraped the packed grime from beneath three long nails of one of his hands.

That grime contained the flesh and blood of Nathaniel Elytharias, and he had formed it into a ball, compacting it with his gray fingers and his tongue and forcing it with his mind into a tight, solid object the size and shape of a pea, but black, and with the sweet odor of decay.

He dropped the ball into the bottle, then spoke a short incantation over it: *ani mechapes yeled*. He stoppered the bottle and held it up to examine: the ball inside swam steadily to one end of the container, pointing north.

He was his Lord's servant. He would be his Lord's best

servant, the one who killed the Elytharias children and ended the menace they represented.

There had been another. He had served another.

Thomas, that was the name. Thomas Penn.

He still served Thomas Penn, but Penn also served the Lord Protector. And he would be the Lord Protector's greatest servant.

Ezekiel. Ezekiel Angleton, that was his name.

His tongue fell out. He found he didn't miss it.

He'd wrapped his face in a long scarf and pulled the brim of his tall hat down to cross the Hudson River on a ferry loaded with Pennsland coal. He'd stalked across the island of Manhattan with his eyes fixed north and east, imagining the country churchyard in the Covenant Tract where his dead love lay.

What was her name?

Lucy. And he was Ezekiel.

He would raise her to eternal life. But first, he must kill the Unsouled.

How would their flesh taste?

Approaching a village on the east side of the island after dark, Ezekiel saw a house a few miles ahead of him burst into flame.

He hesitated, thinking of a burning tobacco barn in Johnsland where he'd failed to do his Lord's bidding, where he'd been rebuffed by mounted Johnslanders, Sarah Elytharias's Dutch servant, and an Indian wrestler.

He wouldn't be rebuffed again.

Thy kingdom come. Thy will be done.

He broke into a run.

Sarah gazed from the height of the Treewall at the ring of black fire. Had it advanced closer?

No, she could still see the crosses that gave it its shape. But neither had the fire retreated or faded, and her people would run out of food in two weeks' time if she did nothing.

The riders were prepared, messengers to race north, south, and east, through the city's Talligewi, Zomas, Mississippi, and Onandagos gates. Many of them were Alzbieta's former servants, who had learned a little horsemanship under William Lee—they would ride to call on friendly powers to come to her aid. At the risk of humiliation to herself and her people, Sarah had insisted on not limiting herself to known and traditional allies. Messengers were ready for Chicago, for

Calhoun Mountain, for Memphis, for the Igbo Cities, for Chicago, and for Johnsland—multiple messengers with multiple copies of the same message, in case some were struck down as they tried to escape.

Some would inevitably be struck down.

Sarah looked one last time at a copy of the message she had laboriously written, mostly rejecting but in a few cases accommodating suggestions from Maltres and Zadok.

> ~ *A CALL TO ALL LOVERS OF FREEDOM* ~
>
> *The usurper Thomas Penn has for years oppressed the honest folk of the Ohio, robbing their wealth, tearing down their walls, choking their highways, and restricting their public meetings, on the pretext of quashing a rebellion that did not exist. He has done this to innocent Cahokia and her six Sister Kingdoms—which Elector's lands will be next?*
>
> *On the pretext of madness that never existed, Thomas sequestered and then murdered his sister, Hannah Penn. Earlier, he treacherously slew her husband, Kyres Elytharias, King of Cahokia. Now, he has laid siege to Elytharias's city Cahokia in an effort to kill the only daughter and heir of Hannah Penn and the Lion of Missouri, Sarah Elytharias Penn.*
>
> *Defend your rights as Electors! Protect the integrity of the Philadelphia Compact and the legacy of John Penn! Steady the ark of Christendom! Resist the usurper Thomas! Cahokia calls you—send aid!*

The message had its faults. It contained at least one lie—that she was her parents' only daughter. It also left rather ambiguous Sarah's own status, which was at least honest, since Sarah's claims were only partially realized and her status was unclear. Alzbieta urged Sarah to include the indication that she was the Beloved of Wisdom, arguing that that was at least as important and as valid as claiming a bishopric, but Maltres reinforced Sarah's better instincts, and she pulled back from making that revelation.

If this didn't work, Sarah knew she could try to send flying messengers over the heads of her besiegers. She also knew what a toll that would take on her physically and how much it would dry up her resources, so she was loath to do it unless necessary, and she feared Hooke would have a means to trap any such highly visible heralds.

Could I make contact with someone outside the black fire by gramarye?

But with whom? And how?

And what would the fire do to me when I tried to cross it?

Somehow, messages must go out, and Maltres's earlier attempts had failed. Without aid, Cahokia would fall.

The riders massed within the gates on the last of the city's horses. More than one resident watched the animals with a hungry look. Sarah herself, though she could not longer stomach the thought of eating meat, was uncomfortable to see the last of the good edible flesh exit the city.

She folded the sheet of paper and tucked it into her satchel. From the shoulderbag she removed the Heronplow and the Orb of Etyles and held one in each hand. They were heavy, and the time she'd be able to hold both of them without tiring would be measured in minutes, not hours.

She should only need minutes.

In her Eye of Eve, the wall of fire looked much like it did with her natural eye: a negative light, a brilliance that was also black. She found the filthy aura of Robert Hooke, stalking the perimeter of reversed crosses. His shuffling dead stayed low in the trenches during the daytime. Sarah had deliberately chosen the hour of noon for that reason.

She also saw the aura of something or someone like Robert Hooke. From this distance, it seemed to be a short, naked person, but his or her aura had the same black and filthy appearance that Hooke's did. To Sarah's annoyance, this person—likely another sorcerer—stayed close to Hooke's largest cross.

This might be a problem for her.

"There is a second sorcerer," she told her fellow magicians on the wall. "He lurks near the cross."

Hooke's presence alone made her nervous; she had struggled enough to defeat him the last time, and had done so by ambushing him. The presence of a second sorcerer like Hooke ratcheted that nervousness into pure fear.

The wall was their target. Sarah believed that if she punched a hole—or at least, a big enough hole—in the wall of fire, the whole thing would collapse. She also hoped that the attack would shake her besiegers loose enough to allow some messengers through.

It had been a hard decision, whether to launch the attack at night—when the Imperial militia would have a harder time shooting at messengers—or by day—when the walking dead seemed generally to stay in their ditches. Sarah had chosen the latter.

No one had gainsaid her.

Sarah's cannons were prepared to fire to give support to the messengers. Sir William also had escorts of beastkind warriors ready to race ahead of the messengers. He suggested the beastkind for the mission because they were faster on foot than any of the children of Adam in the city, which made tactical sense to Sarah.

She didn't ask whether he regarded them as more expendable, or in some sense desirable to take as casualties early on, before their oath to Sarah could really be tested.

They had to make the attempt today. The Imperial forces were larger each successive dawn.

"Please, Maltres," she said. "For the last time, I beg you. If you stand here, you may be hurt."

"Beloved, I will refuse you very few things in this life." Maltres Korinn smiled, the unexpected curve to the lips breaking the harsh, pitted look of his face. "Today I do not leave your side."

"Nor I," Yedera said, standing to her other side. The Podebradan had become a more constant presence in Sarah's life as Sarah had spent more and more time with Alzbieta Torias, until one day she found that when Alzbieta left, Yedera stayed with Sarah.

"Very well, then," she said, and she nodded down the line at her magical corps. "Begin."

Sherem had gathered every magician in the city he'd mentioned to Sarah and discovered a few more, to boot. He stood at the end of the line to Sarah's right, still unable to cast a spell, but unwilling to leave, as was Alzbieta Torias, who stood at the left of the line.

All three of her witnesses, then. So be it.

Sherem had also agreed to act as Sarah's eye. Sarah had taken a tiny amount of consecrated lamp oil from the temple's stores—the oil that illuminated the lamps in the complex beneath the temple, and that would, with additional sanctification, be used in the right circumstances to light the lamps on the Serpent Throne—and anointed both their eyes.

"*Visionem coniungo.*"

Her vision was a complex overlay of three plates. She had grown accustomed to seeing through her natural eye and her Eye of Eve simultaneously, but now a third layer was what she saw out of Sherem's eye. It was slightly different from the view through her natural eye, being placed a hundred feet to the side.

Sherem leaned on a musket. A horn of powder hung at his side.

Stretching to either side of Sarah were the wizards: priests and priestesses, retainers of wealthy families, and scholars. Every wizard Sherem could find in Cahokia except Luman Walters.

The Imperial magician had volunteered, and Sarah had turned him down. He looked honest, but she didn't know whether he was dependable. And moreover, he'd called himself a hedge wizard. What would he really contribute to her plan?

The plan was three-part. Too many parts, Sir William warned her, would doom a plan to failure, but these three seemed necessary.

Her part came first. To employ a chess metaphor, she must tempt her opponent by exposing her queen.

Which was to say, herself.

Exposing, not sacrificing.

"Robert Hooke!" she cried. "I have had enough of your wall! Come out and do battle!" She willed a little energy into her voice and amplified it, shouting audibly across the entire Imperial camp.

Curiously, she felt energy flow into her from her right and left.

From her witnesses, it seemed. So perhaps their presence would be useful, after all.

Another Beloved, centuries earlier, had challenged the Philistines' best man to single combat. David had won, but God had been with him, or at least that's the way Samuel told it. And if not God, then serious luck.

Was God with Sarah? Or the goddess?

Or luck?

The Imperials heard her. She saw faces turning in her direction, eyes rising to stare.

"Come on, Hooke!" she shouted. "Arrogant bastard like you, you must be sore after I caught you out for a gump and shipped you off downriver! Let's settle this! Come on out, and I'll stuff you down your own lizard hole with that ugly hat pulled down around your uglier face!"

She could see him clearly by his aura, watching her from behind the flap of a large tent. After a moment's hesitation he stalked forward, crossing through the black flame to stand on bare snowy ground, just behind the Imperial trenches.

I hear thy mewling hiccup, serpentspawn! Hooke roared into her mind. And then the full weight of his amber sea of death fell upon her.

"Fire!" Jaleta Zorales shouted.

BOOM!

Cannons all along the wall went off. They had been modestly reinforced by the big guns from the west side of the Treewall, which had been dragged around under cover of darkness. Maltres forced out of his mind the possibility that the beastkind prowling the Mississippi might seize this opportunity to attack, or might simply be provoked to frenzy by the violence of the guns. It was a calculated risk.

The guns all lay aimed at the thickest knots of besiegers, nearest the roads. Korinn watched cannonballs plow into the dirt, bounce, and slam into the Imperial ranks. He saw a squad of militiamen behind a wooden barricade torn apart as two balls flew through their ranks. The men themselves exploded. Bits of bone and shattered rifle flew in all directions, inflicting further damage.

He didn't feel the slightest compassion for the dead men. They had brought this on themselves with their unlawful marauding and their wickedness.

This was not to be a sustained cannonade. Cahokia didn't have the powder and shot for that. It needed to conserve resources against the possibility of further battles. Three shots, that was the plan.

Behind the Imperial lines, Notwithstanding Schmidt rode back and forth, shouting commands. Perhaps Jaleta should have laid at least one gun pointing at the director's tent?

Crisply following Zorales's shouted commands, echoed by subordinates directing the fire on the south and north walls, the former Pitchers—now the Cahokia Cannon Corps—reloaded.

Maltres signaled to his two servants below. He'd explained the plan to the Podebradan, and they now locked eyes.

Thirty feet below, Maltres's men—a valet and a butler, two thirds of the total household staff he lived with here in the city, since most of his people were at home in Na'avu, where he would rather be as well—brought forward a net. It was the same net he'd used to arrest Uris, Alzbieta's counselor who planned her political position and managed her household while she thought of priestly matters.

Uris was dead, in part due to Maltres's miscalculations and mistakes.

Four wardens met Maltres's two servants and the six of them held the net ready. A seventh man stood by with a blanket that had been sewn to Korinn's very particular instructions.

Yedera nodded.

"Fire!" *BOOM!*

The three gates of the Treewall dropped.

A horn blew from the Great Mound. Alzbieta had objected to the impiety of directing an assault from the goddess's temple mount, saying it was a violation of ancient law. Maltres had joined Sir William in pointing out that the peak of the mound was the single best vantage point in Cahokia for seeing all three sallies, more or less from the same spot, arguing that the law might in this case be stretched. Atop the roof of the Temple of the Sun would have been even better, slightly, but even Maltres balked at *that* thought.

So had Sir William. Captain—no, *General* Lee—had suggested the rooftop himself, but then withdrawn the idea, saying, "But perhaps, Your Majesty... that's just a little bit more than the law will allow."

Alzbieta had looked prepared to dispute the point further, but Sarah had intervened at that point, directing Sir William to use the mound. She had a strange knack for impieties, the Beloved. It set her apart, although Maltres Korinn was hard pressed to articulate exactly why. Perhaps her will to trample sacred traditions and her ability to get away with it marked her as favored of the goddess? Perhaps her success in trampling the rules showed that she had a strong grasp of what was truly impious and what was merely conventional?

Perhaps Maltres simply wanted to believe that Sarah was doing right. Perhaps he wanted someone else to take on all the burdens of administration and leadership, so he could go home.

Sarah's beastkind warriors charged out all three gates. Immediately, a thicket of guns rose before each gate, and a tight volley exploded into the beastkind. Sarah's warriors were fearsome and huge, but they began to fall.

Had the Imperials been waiting for such a sortie?

Had they been warned?

Responding to the same signal horn, riflemen along the walls leaned forward into position. At that moment, the rest of the

Imperials returned fire. Farther down the line, Maltres saw first one warden, and then a second, take a musketball and fall wounded.

None of the magicians were shot. All of them had closed eyes and chanted Latin together except Sarah, who was feverishly mumbling incoherent syllables, locked in her own invisible battle, and two wizards from one of the kingdom's noble houses who waved their hands in front of each other repeatedly and shouted.

They were protecting the magicians.

Behind the beastkind came the riders. For the moment, they ran alongside their horses, staying low to minimize the chances that an Imperial musketball might abruptly end their commission.

Beastkind dropped here and there, too, shot by besieging rifles. As the beastkind reached the Imperial lines, the riflemen on the walls fired their first round. They, too, were restricted to three shots each. To ensure compliance, they had only been issued three paper cartridges.

The riflemen fired at the defenders on the roads. Three seconds later, the charging beastkind hit.

Maltres looked to the top of the Great Mound. Sir William leaned on his crutches and pressed a telescope to his eye, looking southward and eastward. One of his beastkind, a warrior with the head of an eagle, stood on the north side of the mound and waved a feathered arm to General Lee.

Sir William blew his horn again, a different collection of tones.

Sarah's mumbling grew more feverish.

The wedge of beastkind forcing itself past the trenches and over the barricades to the east of the city shifted position. Each warrior turned to face laterally and took a step forward. Shambling dead dragged at their feet and bayonet-wielding irregulars stabbed at their faces; beastmen and beastwives fell, but the carnage on the besieging side was even greater.

And the wedge opened through its center and created a passageway.

The messengers leaped onto their horses—shots stopped some in their tracks—and raced through the passageway. Looking southward and northward, Maltres saw the same maneuver in execution. To the north, though, something had gone wrong. The beastkind wedge hadn't opened. Instead, the beastkind warriors were piling up in heaps of dead and wounded. The messengers mounted, but found their way blocked and themselves targets for musket fire.

Two, he thought, managed to jump their mounts over the Imperial trenches and continue. Otherwise, the north side of the city was a failure.

South and east, the messengers galloped through.

And then their horses screamed and fell. Maltres could see no cause for their collapse, but the beasts dropped to the road and thrashed in the mud and snow, great gouts of blood staining the land.

Caltrops? Or some other unseen trap.

They had failed to take the Imperials by surprise.

There was a traitor. Someone had warned the Imperials.

The riders of the fallen horses were bayoneted to death by men in blue, or torn limb from limb by the shambling horrors from the trenches.

But not every rider had fallen. A few, seeing the fate of their comrades, had veered off the road. They rode through the Imperial camp itself, jumping cookfires and trampling tents in their mad dash to get to open space beyond.

Cahokia's riflemen took their second shot, aiming to clear as much road as possible before every messenger. The task was complicated by the fact that the messengers were no longer on the roads, but here and there within the Imperial camp, soldiers fell to Cahokian fire.

The riders galloped on.

Gunshots took down more of them, but the first of the heralds was entirely through the Imperial camp now. South and east, messengers streamed away from Cahokia with a cry for help.

Too few, dammit.

Sir William blew his horn a third time.

The beastkind began to retreat. Imperial irregulars followed them out of the trenches, and so did the dead. Maltres saw not only whole corpses, but detached limbs dragging themselves after the beastkind to give chase.

"Fire!" *BOOM!*

Zorales's third round of cannonfire cut through the larger knots of attackers, south and east. As the beastkind shook off the Imperial fighting them, their retreat gained speed. The third round of musket fire from the walls shook off some of the more persistent pursuit, and then the beastkind raced into a sprint.

More of them were picked off by shots from the trenches.

North, none of the beastkind were returning.

Half, Maltres Korinn thought bleakly. Half of Sarah's beast-kind had fallen.

And most of the heralds.

The surviving beastmen came back through the gates, and then the gates were drawn shut.

Sarah had no intention of ever getting snared within Robert Hooke's death-vortex spell, and if she did get caught, she planned to break out immediately. She squeezed the Heronplow until her knuckles turned white. She siphoned energy through the orb.

She stepped out of her shoes.

"Fugio!"

She saw a wall of reaching hands rising up from the east as the sky darkened from winter blue to pus-amber. She shuffled her feet and willed her mind backward and out of reach of the spell.

The hands pursued, but they didn't close.

Robert Hooke rose into the air, arms spread wide and coat spreading behind him like wings. He laughed, a sound like rattling bones.

Sarah heard the guns begin to fire. Through Sherem's eye she saw plumes of smoke fired from the mouths of the cannons and rifles of her soldiers.

She ignored the sight.

Lost thy nerve, helldropping?

She backpedaled, careful to keep her physical feet rising and falling rather than actually moving back. Death by falling wouldn't serve her cause.

"Thinking you ain't worth my time, Rot-Face."

She saw her beastkind warriors race from the eastern gate in Sherem's gaze. Then the spell-less Polite looked up to the line of Cahokian magicians on the wall. They began to recite the spell they had concocted and rehearsed with Sarah.

"Cruces perdimus." She heard the words with her own natural hearing; they were the ones she had devised, in Latin because her Ophidian was still rudimentary. The Firstborn wizards crossed their hands like the upside-down crucifixes of Hooke's barrier. *"Murus cadit."*

As they chanted, they passed a lead musketball from hand to hand. The ball started with Alzbieta and with each repetition of the words of the spell it shifted one person down the line.

Yedera and Maltres stepped back to let the mana-gathering ball pass without their touch.

Sarah would have liked to contribute power to the spell herself, but she repeatedly saw the face of Thalanes stiffening into a death mask on the rain-battered rooftop of the St. Louis cathedral of New Orleans. She poured the energy into her own spell of flight, instead.

Thou thinkest to outwit me. Hooke laughed, floating in the air above Sarah. *Thou thinkest to distract me so thy messengers may escape.*

Through Sherem's eyes, Sarah saw the first messengers breaking through the Imperial lines at that moment.

Then Sherem poured powder into his musket.

"Looks like it worked to me," she said.

I care not for thy messengers. No help can come to thee in time.

The musketball reached the end of the line of wizards. There Sherem took and dropped the ball into his weapon, tamping it down firmly. Sarah saw the work of loading the musket from close up, as if she were doing it herself.

Sherem had begged for this assignment, along with that of being Sarah's eye.

He wanted to be part of the magic. Sarah couldn't find it in her heart to refuse him. Maltres Korinn, hearing her plan, had suggested a marksman. She had told her Vizier she didn't think accuracy mattered.

Really, Sherem should only have to hit the wall of black fire, and maybe not even that. Maybe a bullet crossing the line of the fire would be enough.

"Well, I guess that's checkmate for you, then, Bob," Sarah said. "Can't fault me for trying."

On the contrary. I find great fault in thee. I find the fault of pride, more than any other.

"Yeah, well, you ain't the first preacher to tell me so." Through Sherem's sight, Sarah watched the Polite rest the musket barrel on the Treewall.

Pride in placing thyself above the good of the Empire. Pride in placing thyself above the good of all the children of Adam. Thou thinkest to stand in the service of life, but it is only mankind's universal death that is preserved by thine actions.

"Hell." Hooke's wall moved closer. Sarah forced more energy into her retreat. "I sound like a real bad seed."

Wouldst thou not see death undone? Eternal life for all mankind? Thou art proud to resist God's appointed redemption. Proud to believe thyself to be a match for the Lord Protector.

Sherem primed the weapon's pan and took aim. He sighted along the barrel at the largest of Robert Hooke's crosses.

"So long, Bob," Sarah said.

Proud to assume that I would be here to face thee alone.

Bang! Sherem fired.

"*Visionem—*" Sarah began the spell she had intended to cut her connection with Robert Hooke, preparing to burn as she forced the ley energy of the Mississippi through herself to do so.

But the second dark aura, sending off wisps of death and evil like Hooke's, reappeared. As if all things about her moved through honey or amber—or the deadly sea of Hooke's evil spell—Sarah saw a person who looked like a child step forward from behind the large cross just as Sherem squeezed the trigger.

She saw this through Sherem's eye.

Through her Eye of Eve, she saw the person's hideous aura.

Through all three of her fields of vision at once, she saw the small person raise its arm—

and the enchanted bullet, hurtling through the air toward the cross and its diminutive defender like a bright blue meteorite, stopped.

Stopped, and hung in mid-air.

Sarah was so astonished, she nearly stopped fleeing. The groping hands of Hooke's spell threatened to encircle her. She leaped back, but stared at the little figure as she did so.

The little figure had, she now saw, a death's head for a face.

Was the wall of black flame higher than it had been? Sarah saw a flash of blue light rolling across the ground outside the Treewall. One of her people had died. A messenger, or someone on the wall. A defender.

The blue light struck the black flame and vanished.

And the flame rose slightly higher.

The deaths of Sarah's people, the Firstborn, added to the strength of the noose around their own neck.

The small person raised an arm and reached toward the hovering bullet—

and the bullet drifted into its hand.

And now thou hast met my Lord Cromwell. Hooke laughed.

Sarah shuddered.

Cromwell, tiny and naked, was immediately the most menacing thing on the field of battle. He raised the bullet in both his hands and Sarah saw the blue light between his fingers swirl and grow cloudy as if with black silt. A terrible thought struck her heart.

"Break the connection!" she shrieked. "Sherem! Maltres!"

She couldn't see any of them to know their reactions.

Oh, look thou at the squirming of Adam's illicit get!

"You're wrong!" she shouted, but stopped herself. Was she going to debate theology with Robert Hooke? Or less likely, tell him her revelatory experience on the Sunrise Mound?

She almost laughed, despite the danger to herself and her people. If she told Robert Hooke that Wisdom was the same person as Eve, only before Her fall, he would at best laugh.

Cromwell laid his right hand back alongside his ear and then hurled his hand forward. A ball of black light launched toward the Treewall.

Sarah turned to face the incoming missile. *"Pallottolas—"* she shouted, to begin a bullet-deflecting spell, but as she tried, hands grabbed her and she was forced again to divert her attention to Robert Hooke.

"Maltres!" she heard Sherem shouting. "I need silver, now!"

Where was Maltres Korinn going to get silver at this moment?

Sarah backed away from Robert Hooke. She needed a way to strike at Cromwell.

She needed more power.

And there was nowhere to get it. Already, the flow of energy moving through her soul threatened to burn her to cinder.

Through Sherem's eye, she saw something unexpected. The Polite turned away from the field of battle and looked down within the Treewall. There, a man in a Cahokian warder's uniform threw something at him. It wasn't an attack, the toss was underhand.

Sherem caught the thrown object—

and it burned his hands.

Abruptly, Sarah's link with Sherem snapped. She staggered away, physically. Arms gripped her, and she heard Maltres Korinn whisper in her ear. "Strength, Beloved."

Her link with the Mississippi ley flickered and disappeared. Her flight from Robert Hooke slowed abruptly. Hands closed about her.

The black sphere hit Sherem and he staggered. Then it spun

about him and struck the next person in line, one of Sarah's wizards. He was tall and pot-bellied, and his face had the dignified expression of a thoughtful scholar.

The orb entered his body and paused, briefly. With a blood-curdling shriek, the man fell from the Treewall. His soul—or ka, or whatever it was—exploded from him in a blue ring.

Strengthening the black flame.

But Sarah dipped into the passing wave of energy as well, and the sudden burst of power pushed her beyond the grasping hands.

Was that Thalanes she saw, in the wall of numb faces?

And Grungle?

The black sphere leaped to the next wizard, a woman with short white hair and the tattoo of a raven on her neck. This time Sarah was ready. She reached forward with her own soul and dipped into the dying woman's spirit.

It broke her heart. She was drinking the souls of her own people.

But the alternative was worse.

Sherem raced past, slapping the magicians as he went. He touched his hand to their bare skin: on their faces, or the backs of their hands.

Some of the woman's energy escaped her, but most poured into Sarah. It felt like cool water after a dry walk under a hot sun. With the power she gleaned, Sarah pushed farther out of Hooke's grasp.

Hooke laughed. *Someone has taught thee Cromwell's own magic, whelp!*

Sarah wanted to vomit. She was pulled away from Hooke, but the black sphere was killing her wizards.

The third was a broad-shouldered woman with a lipless mouth. The sphere rested inside her chest for a second, and then she threw her arms over her head, shaped her mouth like an O, and collapsed where she stood.

Sarah grabbed her energy, sucking in as much as she could before Cromwell could take it.

Sherem was catching up to the sphere, but not nearly fast enough. At this rate, all her wizards might die. How did he know what to do, being a man with no spells?

Then Sarah realized what she had done. In her spell she had said *coniungo, I share.* As she had had Sherem's vision, he had had hers. He had seen Cromwell's aura, and the black sphere coming, and Maltres Korinn had somehow had a piece of silver for him.

With the link broken, he no longer saw what Sarah did, but he was racing from wizard to wizard, trying to get ahead of the death spell he knew was killing them.

Sarah could help him. She felt for the Mississippi through the Orb of Etyles and found it there again.

"Pedes accelero!" she shouted.

She had no coffee to throw or spit, but she hurled all the energy she could at Sherem's feet. The silver in his hands felt like an enormous weight, and she pushed with all her might to speed Sherem up.

His pace redoubled. He fairly flew past two more mages, touching them a split second too late. An elderly man with a posture like a question mark toppled forward, and then a man so young Sarah wanted to call him a *boy*.

Sarah grabbed their energy and poured it into Sherem.

Then it happened. He clapped his hands, holding the bar of silver as they did, onto the next wizard. This was a heavy woman with curly brown hair and multiple iron rings piercing each ear. The sphere entered her body, and then Sherem slapped a hand onto her neck.

Light exploded from this woman too, but it wasn't the blue light of her soul. It was the black light of Cromwell's spell, and it broke in a ring. Sherem was thrown backward as if by an explosion and struck the Treewall's parapet, crying out in pain and surprise. He dropped the silver, and Sarah saw bloody welts on both his hands.

Dead hands grabbed at Sarah and dragged her. Out of sheer inertia, she seized the ring of Cromwell's energy as it passed her and consumed it.

Her link with the Mississippi was suddenly cut off. She faltered. Her soul felt full of tar. Her spirit was drowning.

She tried to will energy into the Heronplow. She knew it was in her hands, but she couldn't find it. She was utterly exhausted of power. She felt limp, body and spirit. She couldn't find Thalanes's brooch, couldn't find the river's ley, couldn't find the orb.

Hands pulled her down and she heard the slow laughter of Robert Hooke.

She lost her view of the Treewall and the battle. She saw dead hands and dead faces, including the dead face of Robert Hooke.

Thou hast saved one or two worthless wizards, the Sorcerer said. *And lost thyself. And in losing thyself, thou hast lost the city of the goddess, Her people, and all else. I shall not visit thee in hell, Ophidian.*

He was right, and Sarah knew it. She'd lost half the beastkind and a quarter of the city's magicians, and now *she* was dying. Who would defend her father's land? Who would protect Nathaniel and Margaret? Who would stop Thomas Penn?

"Beloved!" The voice of Maltres Korinn sounded miles away.

A weight struck her, but she couldn't see what it was.

She fell.

Was she falling into the vortex of dead hands? Fingers and paws brushed at her skin; dead eyes stared. Hooke drifted somewhere above them all. Behind him, Sarah thought she saw a naked youth with white eyes.

Then another blow shook her. Her skin was crisp as paper, and something scaly and rough rasped across her body. She screamed, though she couldn't hear it.

The hands seized her.

"The blanket!" Maltres Korinn shouted. "The blanket, now!"

Fire swept across Sarah, body and soul. She arched her back and screamed again, but the hands and eyes surrounding her were swept away in the purifying flame. The amber sea boiled, and its final wave tossed Hooke and his master both aside.

Sarah struggled to breathe. Something suffocating pressed around her.

"Help!" she croaked.

Then she tumbled out of a blanket and a net in which she'd been tangled. Abruptly, the brilliance of the clear winter sky seared her eyes. She fell on snow, and the chill of it on her skin was a relief.

She was alive.

She had miscalculated. She'd lost soldiers, beastkind, and wizards.

Had she reckoned wrong, though? Was it possible that Oliver Cromwell could snatch a bullet from the air with no warning?

Or were we betrayed?

It seemed likely.

But she was alive.

And messengers were on their way.

—➤◆◄—

CHAPTER ELEVEN

Margarida lit her prison on fire by kicking its Franklin stove.

She didn't know who they were, other than that they were Dutch. Smugglers or pirates, maybe: like her own people, the Catalans, the Igbo and the Dutch were merchants first, but frequently shaded from trading into smuggling when stamp duties became too onerous, and into piracy when customs officers became too well-armed.

Or were they her own people? The Chevalier of New Orleans had called her a princess. And Tia Montse had taken her over and over to Cega Sofía, until the chevalier's men had killed the old woman. The chevalier, at least, seemed to believe that Margarida was someone or something other than a young pirate.

Unless the Quintana lands were considerably more extensive than Margarida had ever been told.

The chevalier had separated Margarida from her Tia Montse and put her in chains on a Dutch ship. She had tried to stay calm, as Montse had urged her to do all her life, but a week's separation had proven too much for her. In rage, she had beaten to death the sailor who brought her food, and then wrecked the ship on which she'd been sailing by tearing the mast right out of the vessel.

Why none of the sailors had simply shot her at that point, she didn't know.

She knew the vessel was Dutch because the men leaping off the ship had been shouting in Dutch. Tia Montse had been very careful to teach Margarida excellent English, somewhat against Margarida's will, but Montse had insisted that this was the language of the empire and it would pay her well to know it. She had picked up French from her time spent in New Orleans and the bayous of Louisiana. She'd learned Igbo and Dutch from other smugglers.

Swimming ashore from the shipwreck, she'd met other Dutch people, from which she had guessed she must be near the Hudson River Republic. But at that point, her memory of events petered out quickly to nothing.

Until she had suddenly awakened in a cellar with a wizard wearing orange trying to keep her prisoner, and two ghosts apparently rescuing her.

She kicked the stove barefoot. She did it in anger, unthinking, and immediately expected a terrible burn to her foot. Perhaps because of the swiftness of the kick, she took no injury, and she put the stove right through the kitchen wall. In its flight, the stove scattered burning embers across upholstered chairs and wooden furniture.

Other Dutchmen attacked her. Again, they didn't shoot her, and instead tried to capture her in nets or throw looped line about her or tackle her and drag her to the ground. She was too strong for all of them. She broke legs; she hurled men out windows into the winter's cold. When one Dutchman shouted, "Pest!" and drew a knife, she grabbed him by the front of his filthy nightshirt and threw him straight up, right through the ceiling. His dangling legs twitched once and then were still.

As she slowly calmed, she regained some control.

She found square-toed shoes that fit her, as well as an orange flannel dress that mostly did, and climbed into them. She was still furious and took out some of her rage on the building. With a single kick, she put a crack in an exterior wall, floor to ceiling; then she marched through the crack, splitting it open and sending planks and splinters in all directions.

She intended to head for the nearest barn, because she remembered that her two rescuing ghosts had told her to do so. When she reached the front porch, though, they were there, waiting for her.

"Hello, Margaret," one said. He was obviously Eldritch, pale-skinned and dark-haired. He wore his coat inside-out and his tricorn hat backward, and he carried a large, two-skinned drum over his shoulder. It looked like an Indian drum, though he was definitely not Indian.

He spoke English.

"Margarida," she said.

The second ghost, a Dutchman, smiled. "We have many things to tell you. But you had better get a coat or something. It's very cold out here, and we have hundreds of miles to go."

"To New Orleans?" She wanted to go home to Tia Montse, and not wherever it was the chevalier had attempted to send her.

Rage still burned in her veins. When she was angry, she was very strong.

"To Cahokia." The strangely dressed boy drummed fingers softly on the wooden cylinder of his instrument. "You don't know me, but I'm your brother. We have a sister, too. I've never met her, but she's Queen of Cahokia."

"That would make me..."

"A princess." The drummer smiled. "But quite a bit more than a princess, really. My name is Nathaniel."

A princess.

"No," Margarida said. "You're wrong about me. I'm Catalan, and I have nothing to do with Cahokia."

A shadow loomed up behind Nathaniel. It was a tall man, made taller by the peaked Covenant Tract-style hat he wore. The orange firelight shining on him gave him a terrifying cast: the skin of his cheeks and forehead was the color of pale ash, his nails and the skin around his eyes were black.

In his hand, he held a raised longsword.

"Look out!" Margarida shouted.

The attacker roared wordlessly and slashed down with his blade. Nathaniel turned and threw himself aside, but not quickly enough—the sword bit into his shoulder and he fell.

Anger surged through Margarida. While the Dutchman cursed and pulled a pistol, she seized a broken timber from the wall of the house and ripped it free. The far end burned like a brand and she swung it at the attacker.

He roared like a beast again, with no words, and leaped back. In the firelight, she saw into his open mouth—not only did he have no tongue, but his mouth was full of dark rot, corrupted flesh, as if he were not a living man, but a corpse.

Serpentspawn! Margarida heard a Yankee voice whisper in her mind.

She swung the enormous timber back the other way and

connected, striking the Yankee in the head. He fell to his knees in the snow, bellowing incoherently and raising his sword to parry another blow.

Margarida took a step back, tucked the timber under her arm like a lance, and charged. The blazing tip of the timber hit the tall man squarely in the center of his chest. She lifted him off his feet and carried him several yards before throwing the timber and man together into the night.

The tongueless Yankee hit the snow of the yard and rolled. When he stood, his rotting cloak had caught fire. He howled, more beast than man, and dropped to roll in the snow again.

Ophidian whelp!

The Dutchman knelt to look at Nathaniel.

Margarida ripped another plank from the side of the burning house and stomped toward the Yankee again. Seeing her approach, he yelped, staggered to his feet, and then loped away into the darkness.

"I can stanch the blood flow," the Dutchman kneeling over Nathaniel said. "But I need to get him to a surgeon. Is there a doctor in the village?"

"I don't know," she said.

"There are doctors in New Amsterdam," the Dutchman said. "But that must be six miles away."

Margarida looked at the wound; it bled, but the Dutchman had bandaged it tightly and that slowed the bleeding. She stooped, picked Nathaniel up, and turned to the Dutchman, who was her height. "Climb on my back."

Promptly, the Dutchman did so. "My name is Jacob Hop. I like to be called Jake."

With the anger and energy that still burned within her, Margarida ran. When she reached the wooden fence at the far end of the field, she took it in a single bound. A groaning shadow shifting in a ditch beside the road showed her where the Yankee was hiding, but if he reached out to grab her he was far too slow.

"You were very quick to climb onto the shoulders of a strange girl," she said.

"I know your sister," Jake said. "This isn't the strangest thing I've seen your family do, not by a long shot. How long can you run like this?"

"Not long. The strength fades when I don't need it. When I

don't feel threatened anymore. When it's over, I'm going to have to sleep. And I'll wake up starving."

"If that Lazar catches us, he'll kill us. He wants your entire family dead."

The Dutchman's words shocked Margarida. She ran faster.

"And your hair," the Dutchman asked. "Does it always stand up like this?"

"My hair stands up with my strength."

"I wonder how much your father knew," Jake murmured. "Turn left at this next crossroads."

"Is this boy really my brother?"

"Yes," Jake said instantly. "You should look into a mirror together, that would tell you instantly. But also, we found you with an enchantment created for us by your sister. I don't think there can be any real doubt."

Margarida looked down at the unconscious face. Was she really as homely as this young man? "My sister is the Queen of Cahokia, you say."

"That is her claim. I don't know how far she has advanced it yet; when I left, she was gathering allies about her and approaching the city. I know she is in the city now, and I understand she had quickened its Treewall. I also understand that she is under siege by more than one enemy. But I accept her claim of right, and I think she'll prevail. You grew up among the Catalans?"

Margarida decided that she didn't quite believe this story of an Eldritch witch who was her sister. "Jo sóc Catalana. My Tia Montse raised me. She's a noblewoman and a pirate." Her curiosity needled her. "What did Nathaniel mean, quite a bit more than a princess?"

"Maybe he was talking about the gift of your strength. Or maybe he was talking about your father and mother."

"You said you wondered how much my father knew." Margarida felt herself slowing. As her legs slowed, she also felt the cold air slapping her face and hands with more force.

"Your gift of strength comes from your father. Your brother has a gift of hearing and your sister a gift of sight. Your father... this is going to sound odd... when your father was dying, he blessed three acorns with his blood. His wife ate those acorns and conceived you three children. Each of you has a magical gift. They didn't come from your mother—she was a powerful woman, but not a magician. I wonder how much your father knew of what he was giving you. Of what you would be."

"That doesn't sound odd." Margarida's breath was coming harder.

Nathaniel groaned.

"No?" Jake asked.

"It sounds insane."

Jake laughed. "Okay, insane, then. Given my own experience, I sometimes have a hard time telling what sounds only strange from what sounds truly mad. Your hair is . . . ah, softening, by the way. Starting to lie flat."

"How far away are we?"

"We're halfway there." His shifting weight on her back suggested that the Dutchman was turning to look behind them. "It's mostly just straight on from here."

"What's your experience that so distorted your perception?"

"I had a god inside me. Not a nice god, either. Not Jesus. A wild and tricky and destructive god."

"That sounds painful."

"At the time, it wasn't. It hurts now."

"And who is my mother supposed to have been, who was so powerful, but not a witch?"

"Hannah Penn."

"Mad Hannah?" This part of the story, somehow, rang true.

"She wasn't mad. Your Tia Montse, as a young woman, was a friend of hers. I believe that when Hannah gave birth and three of her close servants and comrades took the infants and fled, your Tia Montse was the woman who took you. I don't know her, so this is just a guess, but I wager that one reason she has lived as a pirate all your life, rather than in a castle on her family lands, is better to keep you out of sight."

The farms gave way to houses around them, and boardwalks encircling the buildings began to appear.

Margarida's legs faltered. The story was strange and new and foreign, but it made a kind of sense. It explained why she had lived a life in hiding. "Margarida Quintana the orphan pirate might have a safer life than Margaret Penn, daughter of the landholder. If someone powerful was trying to find her."

"You may be the rightful landholder in your own right," the Dutchman said. "I'm not sure which of you three is the oldest."

"I can't go much farther," Margarida gasped.

Jacob Hop leaped from her back. After skidding and nearly falling down in the snow, he regained his balance and ran at her side. "Just a few more streets." He pointed, but Margarida couldn't make out any detail ahead. Window lights stretched out ahead of her in a thick swarm, like a cloud of fireflies descending all the way to the Hudson.

"I'll go with you," Margarida said, "but only on one condition."

"Name it."

"Tia Montse is in prison. The Chevalier of New Orleans has captured her. We have to help her escape." Margarida was not entirely sure, on balance, that she believed the story she was hearing about acorns and gifted children and Hannah Penn. But if these two strangers could rescue her, perhaps they could also rescue Tia Montse.

Jake laughed. "As it happens, I have experience helping people escape the hulks of New Orleans. At least, the god once within me does, and I remember the experience. More or less. Agreed."

Margarida missed a step and fell face-down in the snow. Nathaniel cried out and they tumbled together, rolling to a stop.

"Ambroos!" She heard the Dutchman's feet racing away through the snow as she faded into unconsciousness. "Ambroos, come quick!"

Churchill zieht aus zum Kriege
Die Fahne läßt er wehn
Da reicht zum Kampf und Siege
Die Hand ihm Prinz Eugen

Gert Visser didn't strike Isaiah as a hothead. He seemed like a big, cheerful ox, who wouldn't stop singing dance tunes in German, Dutch, and English, even as he carried on the work of sailing their borrowed craft up the Hudson, work that would have left any two normal men together breathless. He was as broad across the shoulders as any two men, and nearly a hand taller than Isaiah, who was himself a tall man. He was also blond and bearded, with a clear complexion and sparkling blue eyes. His natural facial expression seemed to be a friendly grin.

Adriaan had understated the size and physical presence of his daughter's suitor. No wonder he had been reluctant to notify him of his terminated engagement, or allow his daughter to do so.

Adriaan's letter to Gert was heavy in Isaiah's pocket.

Could he use Kinta Jane Embry's professional skills to defuse the situation? He imagined scenarios in which the Choctaw woman seduced Gert, and Isaiah tricked Gert into breaking off the engagement himself, out of guilt or fear of revelation. Isaiah didn't like the idea of ordering Kinta Jane to do that, but she'd done that much and more already for Franklin and the Conventicle.

And so, for that matter, had he.

And which was really worse—a little professional seduction, or the possibility that Gert, informed of the breakup, would go berserk and have to be put down like a rabid animal?

Isaiah thought, and said nothing. He'd promised he'd tell Gert at Ticonderoga.

Gert was not a fisherman, despite his name, but a merchant. He regularly brought goods up the river to Fort Nassau, so this was the pretext of their journey they'd offer to any casual inquiry. Beneath that lay the real motive, which was that Isaiah and Kinta Jane needed to get to Montreal, and the secondary objective, which was to get Gert Visser out of the way.

At Fort Nassau, they'd switch to canoes that they could portage overland. In the meantime, the Hudson was deep enough to accommodate a small sailing vessel. Isaiah was glad for the rest.

Dockery accompanied them. Adriaan Stuyvesant had insisted, and the Pennslander had nodded and accepted without a word.

English was the language they all had in common, so they spoke English.

"You don't work for Adriaan, then?" Isaiah asked.

Gert shook his head. "Not a Company man. Too much of the old Frisian in me, I guess. I just want to be on my own, in a little coracle out on the sea, you know. Be my own man."

"Not a hansard, either?"

"You know, independent merchants are still the rule in the empire. For one thing, the Hansa towns are strictly river traders. And the Imperial Ohio Company and the Dutch Ohio Company are both, you know, in the Ohio. Here on the Hudson, no one is in charge. You've just got lots of little traders, like me. And in Acadia, Champlain controls trade. You buy a license or you don't sell goods."

Isaiah nodded. He'd been trying to calculate what other loyalties Gert might have. He was tempted to ask whether the big man was a Freemason, but that seemed too obvious. "How did you come to be a brother?"

Gert blushed, his pale skin turning a bright red from the neck up. "That's a little complicated."

"With the Tappan Zee behind us, I gather we still have two days of sailing ahead. I could stand the complication. Kinta Jane?"

"Anything that can make a man the size of an ox embarrassed must be a fascinating story," the Choctaw said.

"Not that fascinating," Gert said. "I'm a simple man, really. But I'm a simple man in love."

Dockery snorted. It was the first sound he'd made in hours. Mostly, he'd stood out of the way, scanning the forested banks with one hand shading his eyes. He still dressed as a frontiersman, with a wool pullover frock thrown over his fringed jacket. A straight Missouri war ax hung at his belt.

"Tell us about that." Kinta Jane's face showed no indication that she knew this already.

"And worse, I'm a poet."

"Dammit." Isaiah grinned. "I thought we had a rule. No artists."

Gert Visser blushed more. "So, I was calling on Miss Julia Stuyvesant."

Dockery spat in the water.

"Any relation to Adriaan?" Isaiah asked mildly.

Gert nodded. "His daughter. She's a brave girl, quite funny, and much smarter than I am. And lovely, of course."

"I may have met her," Isaiah said. "When you say calling, you mean...?"

Gert blushed a still deeper shade, looking more like a lobster than a man. "No! I mean, her father made the same mistake. He found us in her room, and he assumed—"

"You sneaked into her room?" Kinta Jane smiled and clicked her tongue. It was a gesture she had recently relearned, and apparently enjoyed.

"I'm not very good at sneaking. You can't be as big as I am and be hard to notice, you know. But I'm a good climber, and there's a trellis under Julia's window."

"You climbed into Julia's room." Isaiah smiled. "Which action her father *completely* misunderstood, as you had no amorous intention at all."

Was Dockery actually *growling?*

Gert Visser's blush faded and his face grew serious. "No, I didn't say that. My intentions were very amorous. But they were honorable."

"I can't imagine how Adriaan Stuyvesant detected your presence in his daughter's room," Kinta Jane said. "Unless it was possibly the fact that his house shook with your weight on the second story."

"I am almost seven feet tall," Gert said. "But I'm not *ten* feet tall. I stoop to pass under doors, but I can stand under most ceilings. Not Julia's, as it happens, since her room is on the corner of the house, and has a low, sloped roof. I was sitting, and the only place to sit in her room is on her bed."

"I am scandalized already," Kinta Jane said. "I'm afraid any more detail might cause me to faint."

"I'm sorry," Gert said, and fell silent.

"She jests," Isaiah said. "Kinta Jane Embry is such a woman of the world that I don't believe you are even capable of making her faint. Or even feel scandalized."

"It's true, Gert," Kinta Jane said. "Men have sat on my bed before, too."

Gert furrowed his brow and continued. "I don't believe Julia betrayed me. I believe it was her sister Elena. I climbed into Elena's room by mistake the first time, so she knew I was visiting Julia."

"She was jealous?"

"She didn't approve. Maybe because I wasn't rich enough. Maybe because she was the older sister, and believed she should be the one receiving a suitor, before her sister. Maybe because she dislikes poetry."

Kinta Jane's smiled turned down at the corners with wry compassion. "Maybe she saw the seven-foot-tall blond man and wanted you for herself."

Gert shrugged. "I think Elena told her father. Perhaps she told him that we, you know, neuken."

"No, tell me." Kinta Jane smiled like an imp.

Isaiah intervened. "I think we know. Adriaan walked in one night, you were sitting on Julia's bed, he thought more was going on, and he brought you into the Conventicle."

"Don't mistake me," Gert said earnestly. "More was going on than he thought. But all the action was here." He clapped a hand over his sternum. "I love Julia Stuyvesant very much, and I would never do anything to hurt her or make her lose standing with her family. I was reciting poems to her."

Dockery hawked a ball of phlegm from deep in his throat. From the length of time it took and the volume of the sound, the phlegm must have been big enough to play a game of Boston town ball with. When Dockery spat, he somehow missed the water and spat right on the boat, phlegm and brown tobacco juices mixed together in a vile blot.

Visser didn't notice, and Isaiah didn't call it to his attention.

"But Adriaan thought you were...neuken...and brought you into the Conventicle."

Gert nodded. "He forced the issue of the engagement. Demanded I either propose marriage or leave. Of course, I proposed."

This was not the story Adriaan Stuyvesant had told.

And it felt as if there was still something missing from the tale. But looking at Gert's face, he thought it might be something the big trader didn't himself know.

Isaiah suddenly regretted the entire conversation. He couldn't afford to like Gert—it would make the big man's death too painful, if it ever came to that.

"How far to the Wappinger trading post?" he asked.

"U-puku-ipi-sing? We'll be there tomorrow. We'll buy and sell a few things, in case anyone is watching us. Don't worry, they're wild Algonks, but that only means they don't send Electors. They're honest people." Gert grinned. "You see, I'm a poet, but I'm a man of the world, too. I am a trader, and I can be a good follower of the great Franklin."

Isaiah grunted and pulled his tricorn hat down over his eyes so he could pretend to sleep.

Suddenly, Dockery broke into song:

> *A parson preached to his flock one day*
> *On the sins of the mortal race*
> *And the clerk, "Amen," aloud did say,*
> *With the solemnest tone and face*
> *And the pious clerk, on the quiet though*
> *Did venture a bit of remark*
> *"Sin is sweet," said the parson,*
> *"Then sin for me," said the clerk*
> *Amen*
> *"Sin for me," said the clerk*

❖   ❖   ❖

"Wouldn't it be easier to summon a storm and chase all the patrol boats back to shore?" Monsieur Bondí suggested.

"And then cross the water ourselves in a storm?" Etienne asked. "Then I would indeed sleep in the Pontchartrain, as your ditty has it."

"I can't help it if the song is catchy. Besides, you're the hero of the song."

"And that is a mistake," Etienne said. "I'm not the hero. I'm the man who wants revenge."

Bondí shrugged. "What other kind of man do you think can be a hero in a city where everyone believes there is no justice?"

They waited in a fast yacht named *La Bonne Chance* on the far side of the Pontchartrain. The *Bonne Chance* had belonged to August Planchet, and Etienne had seized it for the bishopric, or at least to put to the ends of avenging the bishop's death. It seemed like a reasonable use of the wealth the former beadle had stolen. It was night, and late enough that the moon had sunk. It was only by the gift of Papa Legba that Etienne's sharpened eyes could see the chevalier's guard boats, sailing without lights around the hulks to contain their prisoners and prevent escape by water.

Etienne had considered bribery, but so far, the chevalier appeared to be keeping up with payroll. He'd have to do something about that, and soon. Tax receipts were dwindling, but not fast enough, and the ranks of the chevalier's men were swelling fast. How was the chevalier to keep up with payments? He must have more wealth than Etienne had realized. Perhaps from this secret payment from Thomas Penn.

The growing number of gendarmes ruled out direct assault upon the hulks.

Despite Monsieur Bondí's enthusiasm for the idea of weather magic, the thought exhausted Etienne. He didn't know whether Maitre Carrefour would accomplish such a work for him, and he didn't have any other arcane means of doing it. Weather wasn't the sort of thing the Brides tampered with, for instance.

That left trickery. Etienne had chosen a combination of a distraction and a quick snatch operation.

"We'll do this like a team of pickpockets," he murmured.

"I know the plan, boss," Monsieur Bondí said.

The sailors were Igbo, provided by Onyinye Diokpo. The men worked cheerfully and efficiently, and they bowed deeply to Etienne. This seemed odd at first, since he wore his black and white waistcoat and red sash rather than any episcopal finery, but then he heard one of the men mutter the words Eze-Nri.

Priest-king, the words meant, but he didn't know much more than that. His father had been an urban man and a Christian, like his father before him, and his knowledge of what kind of worship happened in the farms and forests of the Free Cities of the Igbo was very little.

"There's your man Kennedie," Monsieur Bondí said. Fires had appeared abruptly all along the Pontchartrain wharf. You didn't get flame that large and that sudden from a torch—you had to use oil, and maybe bring fire in a closed container to begin with. Monsieur Bondí looked through a telescope. "It's him in person, not just his men. I recognize the limp."

"I understand the man was hurt in the war," Etienne said.

"And there go the chevalier's men. All the more reason for him to stay home and let his underlings do the dirty work."

"You're saying I should stay home, is that it?"

"Yes." Bondí put away his telescope and signaled to the sailors. The Igbos raised sail and anchor, and the ship pulled slowly across the Pontchartrain, toward the hulks. "If you stayed home, I could stay home, and I'm just an accountant. I'm really doing Armand's job, following you around to keep you safe."

"I feel safer for your concern." Etienne took the telescope and watched events on the shore. "Tell me where home is, with the cathedral burned, my father's apartments given to the Polites, the bishopric given to another man, and my casino under constant observation by those mussulman assassins."

"Home could be wherever you want it." Bondí grunted. "Right now, I guess home is with me."

"That's how I think of it, too." As the chevalier's guard vessels sailed in close to the wharfs, the Irish fighters turned from smashing windows and lighting docks on fire to hurling flaming bottles at the ships.

The *Bonne Chance* laid quietly alongside the hulk lying farthest from shore. Onyinye's men leaped quietly from the yacht to the larger ship, then swarmed over the side, long ropes coiled over their shoulders. Etienne and the hôtelière had agreed to use her men because they were all Igbo. That gave them a shared language their target would not understand. Etienne's men were New Orleans mongrels, Creoles, and men of all nations.

"Boss," Monsieur Bondí cajoled, but Etienne ignored him. He kicked his boots off to free his toes—the better to climb with—and went up over the side after Onyinye's cousins.

One great disadvantage to the chevalier of staffing his prison hulks with deaf-mutes and idiots was that they were spectacularly easy to take by surprise, and pitifully bad at spreading any kind of alarm. The Igbo dragged the guards to the planks, held them immobilized, gagged them, and tied them up, backs to the stump mast rotting in the center of the deck.

The other advantage of using Onyinye's men is that the Igbo were famous wrestlers. Etienne's men would have killed the deaf-mutes; letting them live was an outcome much more consistent with the image of the wronged and righteous bishop fighting the tyrannical chevalier.

Etienne took a lantern from the iron nail where it hung, fixed to the mast, and went belowdecks. He found a ring of keys on a table in what had once been the captain's cabin of the former warship, and he set about freeing the prisoners.

"I do this to follow the words of St. Paul," he called loudly, over and over. "'And that they may recover themselves out of the snare of the devil, who are taken captive by him at his will.' I am Bishop Ukwu, and I am here to set you free."

All the prisoners were men. A few had lost their power of speech during their stay on the hulk, and could only wail piteously as they scampered up to see the night sky. Most thanked Etienne courteously, in all the various languages of New Orleans.

The chevalier only kept prisoners of value in the hulks; other enemies and criminals he simply had killed. That meant that many of the men Etienne freed were wealthy and powerful, or had wealthy and powerful connections.

"I am Bishop Ukwu, and I am here to set you free."

He almost missed the final prisoner, an old man lying in the shattered aft cabin of the hulk. Etienne was returning to the steps to exit the ship when he heard the prisoner's cracked but vital voice calling out in Castilian, "Señor! Señor! No me abandone aquí, yo le ruego!"

The man was more skeleton than flesh. Unlocking his manacles, Etienne knelt to help the prisoner stand.

"Je suis l'Évêque Ukwu. Je suis venu pour vous libérer."

"You're not Chinwe Ukwu," the old man said as they hobbled

toward the stairs together. His French was quick and polished. "Chinwe was murdered, the very night I was arrested."

So recently? From the state of his physique, Etienne would have guessed the man had been a prisoner for years. He refrained from making that observation. "No, I am his son."

"Ah, but you are not Chigozie Ukwu, either. Chigozie is taller, though perhaps not so handsome."

Etienne continued to hold the old man as they inched up the stairs. "I hope you are willing to be rescued by Chigozie's brother Ofodile."

"I thought Chigozie's brother was named Etienne. And he was . . . an owner of gaming establishments, among other things, in the Vieux Carré."

"I am that same man."

"And now you are bishop? And rescuing me at night from the chevalier's Pontchartrain dungeon?" The old man began to laugh. "The chevalier must be shitting his trousers."

"I can only hope, Don . . ."

"Don Luis Maria Salvador Sandoval de Burgos," the old man said. "My family and I ship cotton and silver, principally. More recently, I put a knife to the throat of the chevalier."

Interesting.

They emerged on deck. Etienne looked to the shore for signs of the chevalier's guard ships and saw them all burning, wrecked against the land. He turned to the other hulks and saw their staff's backs as they pressed against the far rails to stare at the fires.

"Fais attention!"

A body slammed into Etienne, knocking him to the ground.

He tried to grab his knife, but the man who had knocked him down had managed to sit on his chest to pin both arms. His attacker was large and stank; he howled like a wordless beast as he raised a great splinter of wood over his head to stab Etienne in the face—

another man grabbed the attacker's wrist.

The newcomer was one of Onyinye's Igbo fighters. He neatly hooked the deaf-mute in his nostrils with two fingers. As the brute wailed, the wrestler pulled him backward and off Etienne. It looked like gentle motion, but the bigger Frenchman shrieked in discomfort and then wiggled like a fish trying to escape as the wrestler sat, embraced him from behind, cradled his head in two strong arms, and choked the man into unconsciousness.

The wrestler stood and helped Etienne to his feet. "I'm sorry," he said in Igbo. "I tied a weak knot."

Etienne straightened his clothing. "But you imposed a strong grip. What's your name?"

"Sometimes, I wrestle for the French and the English under the name Lusipher. You may have seen me with red paint on my face and chest." The wrestler grinned. "But I am more truly named Achebe Chibundu."

"I have seen you elsewhere, haven't I?"

Etienne gazed at the man's face until it came to him. "When I first saw you, I took you for a bartender. You were present at the death of the beadle."

Achebe nodded. "I was there to protect Onyinye, if necessary. She's my great-aunt. And when I first met you, I took you for a criminal. It's only since that I have learned you are a man of many gods, a man whose own god is mighty."

Etienne furrowed his brow. "This is what people say about me?"

Achebe smiled. "They do. And what they ask, but do not know for certain, is whether you might be Eze-Nri."

Etienne considered. "I'm the Bishop of New Orleans, at least, and I have lost a bodyguard," he said. "If I speak to Onyinye, would you be willing to consider taking his place? I warn you, it's a dangerous position. When I say I lost my bodyguard, let me be clear—Armand was murdered by my enemies."

Achebe's eyes widened. "For the Bishop of New Orleans? Yes, of course, I would be honored!" He dropped to his knees.

Etienne helped Achebe up. "Excellent. I will speak with my friend Onyinye. In the meantime, we have another half-dozen hulks to clean out. Once we've liberated the chevalier's prisoners, we need to put his men ashore and then burn the ships."

"All New Orleans will see it, Eze-Nri."

Etienne nodded. "That is the point."

He resolved that he would ask Onyinye what this Eze-Nri business was.

Ferpa and Kort, without any appointment or title, became Chigozie's assistants. He deliberately strove to shun all the trappings of leadership: he did not choose who would pray, he dictated no meal times, he waited until others spoke before speaking, he did not assign himself any right to preach.

But the Merciful asked him to speak, requested his advice, and came to him to settle disputes.

Very well. If he was to be the Shepherd, he would be the Shepherd who only led by example, and from the center of the flock.

Watching him, Ferpa and Kort adopted similar behaviors. In a military organization, one might have called them Chigozie's aides-de-camp, and in an ecclesiastical one, his suffragans. Among the Merciful they had no title at all, but the other beastkind looked to them for inspiration and example.

Whether explicitly or not, they arranged that one of them would always be at his side, asleep or awake. The presence of a cow's or bison's head made Chigozie think of the Merciful as a kind of herd, notwithstanding the presence of part-canine and part-reptile members.

The one who wasn't with Chigozie was inevitably working.

The Merciful built a screen at the mouth of their canyon. It wasn't a wall, not a defensible structure of any kind, but a hedge of brush and dead trees that further hid the existence of the canyon. They destroyed trails that led close to the Still Waters, and were careful to follow a ridge of rock themselves in coming and going, so as not to create a new trail.

They brought timber from miles away, again in order not to attract attention to the Still Waters. With the timber, they built. A springhouse protected the springs and also sluiced water out the rock seeps above the springs to make it convenient to drink. Chigozie grew to love the smell and even the taste of the water.

His sleep grew worse. He dreamed of the women he'd killed, begging him not for mercy, but for life. He felt less rested each morning he awoke.

A barracks provided a communal sleeping place. When the Merciful built Chigozie a hut near the waters themselves, he declined, and instead asked that a member of the herd who was then ill be moved into the hut instead.

Organized parties hunted and foraged. A guard was posted above the canyon at all times, and another below the canyon along the stream that flowed from it. Chigozie preached often the necessity of turning the other cheek and not resisting violence with violence, and he was prepared to flee with the Merciful at the first appearance of an attacker.

Ferpa returned from a foraging party with three wounded children of Adam. Chigozie was reciting passages from Isaiah to the Merciful when she arrived—the large amount of holy writ he'd committed to memory at the urging of the Bishop of Miami now proved to be extremely useful. She descended one of the steep entry trails, carrying a man in her arms.

To his astonishment, Chigozie knew the man. He was Naares Stoach, soldier of Zomas, the man who had chased the Merciful out of their first chosen home. There was no sign of either his horse or his hound.

Ferpa laid Stoach down on the much-trampled grass at the edge of the springs and stepped back. The two Merciful with her laid down two other men; all wore the red and black of Zomas, with the cuckoo and crown, over wooden breastplates. All were battered and wounded and unconscious.

Ferpa cleared her throat. "This child of Adam struck me on one cheek."

"He struck us all," Kort said.

A rumble passed through the Merciful. Chigozie saw surprise, anger, and fear on the faces he'd learned with difficulty to read. He also saw something else.

Groaning, Naares Stoach opened his eyes and sat up. He probed the clotting blood in his blond hair with his fingers and squinted at Chigozie. "It stinks. Am I your prisoner?" he looked at his two fellow-soldiers. "Are they dead?"

"They aren't dead," Ferpa lowed.

"We need to decide what to do with you." Chigozie surveyed the Still Waters—most of the Merciful were present.

"I hereby impress you all," Stoach said. "You now serve Turim, Lord Zomas."

Kort laughed, a long, low rasp.

"He is bold," Ferpa said.

"Friends, we must decide." Chigozie addressed the Merciful. "Let us consider some possibilities. We could kill these men. We could tell ourselves that we were only doing it to prevent the loss of another home, that their deaths would not be an act of revenge or anger."

The Merciful watched Chigozie quietly. Ferpa snorted.

Naares Stoach reached for the hilt of his sword and found his scabbard empty.

"We could show mercy," Chigozie said. "We could let these men live and leave our Still Waters alive. To show our generosity, we could even send them away with food and water."

"We could guide them back to their lands," Kort added.

The Merciful still watched in silence.

"Or we could embrace them," Chigozie said. "As long-lost brothers. We could give them food and shelter here, and tend to their wounds, and only when they had recovered and wished to go, we could take them back to the towers of Etzanoa."

"Like the Good Samaritan," Ferpa murmured.

"Like the father of the prodigal son," Kort added.

A murmur of approval ran through the Merciful. Chigozie found that he wanted to test them a little more. "We will put ourselves at risk if we do this," he said. "The warriors of Zomas may attack us. May follow us back to our home. May enslave us and force us to fight against the warriors of Simon Sword."

"Seventy times seven," Kort said.

"We turn the other cheek," Ferpa said.

Chigozie looked to the Merciful and found them nodding in agreement. He nodded as well, and then he offered a hand to Naares Stoach. "We turn the other cheek."

"Is this all there is to the joke?"

CHAPTER TWELVE

"I've seen him heal others," Jake said. "And people in Johnsland told me he healed himself once."

Margarida had awoken from her collapse, but felt in need of some healing herself. Or at least some solid rest. "Is that why you're burning the tobacco? You think it will help him?"

Hop twisted his fingers together and stroked them. He seemed to be fidgeting with a nonexistent object, or remembering toying with something small. Nathaniel—Margarida's brother—lay mumbling and sweating on a pallet in the New Amsterdam house of a Dutch clergyman named Ambroos. Beside him was a china teacup in which smoldered a pile of dried tobacco leaf. From time to time, Jake picked the leaf up and blew on it to keep the flame going.

"Say that I hope, rather than that I think. I have been with Nathaniel in his healing trance, but I understand it very little. But the first time he did it—when he did it and healed himself—he was in a great cloud of tobacco smoke."

"Do you think—or hope—that he's in that trance again now?" Margarida was only half-convinced that this unconscious boy was her brother. In any case he had rescued her. She felt attached.

Jake shook his head. "I don't even hope it."

"Not even hope?"

Jake shook his head again. "There's no bear."

"The deacons are all here." The voice was Lotte's speaking from the door of the room. "I'll keep an eye on your friend, Jacob."

"Dank je, Lotte."

Margarida trailed the Dutchman downstairs and into his cousin's study. In such a room in the French and Catalan homes she knew, she'd expect to see pictures of saints hanging from the walls. You couldn't always tell a saint from her face, but you knew you were looking at a painting of a saint by the other strange items in the picture. In a picture, St. Peter always had a key, St. Paul a sword, and St. Martin a hammer and nail. These weren't pictures of saints, but there was something oddly familiar about the images anyway. One man chased pigs into the sea. Another man touched the eyes of a blind man beside a fountain. A third man chased merchants from the portico of a church. In all the paintings, the figures had Dutch faces and wore Dutch clothing.

The deacons were five serious-faced people. The youngest was middle-aged, and they were a mixed-sex group: three women and two men. With Ambroos, if he was also to be counted as a deacon, they were half and half. They all wore sober black coats and black knickerbockers, and the men wore tall hats with flat brims.

"Should I lie on the floor?" Jake asked. "Or hold a holy wafer in my mouth or something?"

One of the deacons beckoned Jake forward into the center of their circle. Margarida held back, standing beside the door. The deacon, an old man with a twinkle in his eye, handed Jake a large sheet of paper.

"What is this?" Jake asked.

Another deacon, a woman whose blond hair was knotted into a tight bun at the nape of her neck, and who might have been the youngest of all of them, began to read from a large, leather-bound book. Everyone in the room was speaking Dutch, and Margarida understood them perfectly. Nevertheless, the woman's reading had the rote quality of an incantation. Her pronunciation of the words was deliberately archaic; the words felt to Margarida more like deeds, each syllable an act. "En toen zij bij de schare gekomen waren, kwam iemand tot Hem, knielde voor Hem neder, en zeide."

"It's a writ of divorce," the old man said. "Write your name here."

Another deacon presented a bottle of ink and a quill pen. Jake wrote.

The woman kept reading. "Here, heb medelijden met mijn

zoon, want hij is maanziek en hij is er slecht an toe: want dikwijls valt hij in het vuur en dikwijls in het water."

It was the story of one of Jesus' exorcisms, from the Bible.

"And here, write the name of the other party."

"Legion," murmured two of the deacons.

Jake wrote again. Margarida had good enough eyesight to see
that he'd filled in the two blanks in the form with the names
Jacob Hop and *de Reigerkoning*.

"En ik heb hem naar uw discipelen gebracht en zij hebben
hem niet kunnen genezen."

Ambroos shook his head. "Write 'the devil.'"

"But he isn't the devil," Jake said.

"Isn't he?"

Jake hesitated, and then in the white space above *de Reigerkoning* he added *de Duivel*.

"Jezus antwoordde en zeide: O ongelovig en verkeerd geslacht,
hoelang zal Ik u nog verdragen? Breng hem Mij hier."

"Hold the writ," the old man said.

"I don't need to burn it and eat it or anything, do I?" Jake
had half a smile on his face.

"What do you take us for?" the old man chuckled. "Wizards?"

"En Jezus bestrafte hem en de boze geest ging van hem uit,
en de knap was genezen van dat ogenblik af."

"Now kneel," Ambroos said. "Put a prayer in your heart."

"What shall I pray for?" Jake asked.

"What do you want? That God cast out this demon."

"Toen kwamen de discipelen bij Jezus en zeiden, toen zij met
Hem alleen waren: Waaron hebben wij hem niet kunnen uitdri-
jven? Hij zeide tot hen: Venwege uw klein geloof."

Jake nodded and closed his eyes, clutching the writ to his chest.

On the floor above her, Margarida thought she heard Nathaniel moan.

The deacons closed in around Jake, including Ambroos and
the woman who was reading. Other than the reading woman,
each put his or her left hand on the shoulder of the deacon next
in the circle, and his or her right hand on Jake's head.

"Want voorwat, Ik zeg u, indien gij een gleoof hebt al seen
mosterdzaad, zult hij tot deze berg zeggen: Verplaats u vanhier
daarheen en hij zal zich verplaatsen en niets zal u onmogelijk
zijn. Maar dit geslacht vaart niet uit dan doorbidden en vasten."

"Devil," Ambroos intoned. His voice didn't sound like a spell; it had the theatrical boom of a sermon. "By the authority of the priesthood of all true believers, and by our faith, though it be as small as a mustard seed, we command you to come out. Amen."

"Amen," all the deacons intoned.

Jake leaped to his feet, howling. The deacons staggered away, but Jake flung himself after them.

"Stop!" the old man warbled, just before Jake stuffed the writ of divorce into his mouth.

Jake grabbed the heavy bible from the hands of its reader and struck her on top of the head with it. Her bun exploded. She collapsed and lay twitching on the hardwood floor, yellow hair encircling her head like a halo.

Margarida cowered in the hall outside the study. In part, she was afraid of Jake, in his sudden madness. But also, he was her rescuer, and the thought of fighting him was surprising and unpleasant.

"What is happening?" Lotte rattled down the stairs, yelling.

"No, Jake!" Ambroos took decisive action, punching Jake in the jaw—

Jake didn't slow down. He gripped Ambroos by the front of his shirt and hurled him into the next room.

Then he looked at Margarida and roared. Margarida's heart leaped into her throat, cutting off her breath with its berserk pounding.

Behind Margarida, Lotte bellowed. "Get out, Jacob! What are you doing? I will kill you if you have hurt my Ambroos!"

She rushed toward the dining room.

Margarida felt her heart beat faster, and the tingling in her scalp told her her hair was standing on end.

"Lotte, no!" Ambroos shouted, struggling to rise from the floor.

Margarida ducked between two fleeing deacons and looked. In the dining room, a scattergun rested on long nails over the fireplace. Lotte grabbed the weapon and turned to face Jake, cocking the hammer.

"No!" Margarida yelled. She threw herself forward—

Jake jumped at Lotte, snarling—

Lotte squeezed the trigger—

click.

Jake was about to seize Lotte by the neck when Margarida

bowled into him from behind. She didn't want to hurt Jake—he had rescued her—but something was wrong with him and he was not himself. She knocked him into the fireplace.

Ashes and embers scattered across the kitchen floor. Lotte leaped aside but didn't manage to avoid the cloud of soot that billowed into the air. She rushed to the kitchen.

Ambroos tried to stand, but couldn't.

Jake arose from the fireplace, smeared in ash. Great black blotches distorted his face and live embers glowed, tangled in his blond hair. Margarida smelled burning skin, and the Dutchman who had rescued her from captivity picked up an iron poker.

He launched himself at Margarida, swinging the iron.

Lotte returned from the kitchen with a broom. Seeing Jake's attack, she rushed forward, reaching with the broom to intercept him, but she was too far away.

"Jacob, stop!" Ambroos cried.

Jake swung at Margarida's head—

Margarida caught the poker in her left hand.

If it had taken her by surprise in her normal state, the blow would have shattered all the bones in her hand. As it was, she felt the impact, but without pain.

She yanked the poker from Jake's hand.

He roared and leaped forward—

she slapped him in the face, knocking him to the floor and sending him skidding across the dining room.

Lotte adjusted course quickly and began to beat Jake with a broom.

"Zoete Jezus," Ambroos cursed.

Margarida's limbs trembled with strength. Her Tia Montse had told her that this was the result of an old witch's blessing, bestowed on Margarida in the cradle. Now she had been told by strangers that instead it came from her father, a powerful wizard and king.

Sometimes, when her strength was upon her, Margarida lost control. The strength didn't cause her to lose control. It only came upon her in moments of fear, excitement, anger, and danger, and those were moments when she was already close to losing control. When she lost control, she could really hurt people.

She didn't want to hurt Jake.

She tossed the iron to one side. She didn't mean to throw

it with force, but it struck the wall and knocked a head-sized chunk of plaster and brick to the floor.

Jake scrambled to his feet and grabbed Lotte.

Margarida seized Jake by both wrists and yanked his hands from Ambroos's wife. Jake gasped in pain—had she broken his wrist?—and she threw him into the corner of the room, farthest from everyone else.

"Calm down, Jake!" she yelled, in a voice that was anything but calm.

Jake hesitated. "Am I Jake?"

Margarida wished Nathaniel were conscious. This seemed like the sort of thing he could handle well. She grabbed Jake by both arms and pinned him, lifting him and pounding him against the wall. Plaster sifted down into her face.

"You're Jake," she growled.

"Am I?" He slammed his knee into her chin. Some other time, the blow would have cracked her jaw. Now, she didn't even blink.

She punched him in the belly with her free hand. It was reflexive, an act of anger.

"You're Jacob Hop," she said.

He kicked her again and she tossed him across the room. Jake bounced off the top of the dining room table and rolled on the floor.

Calm down. Calm down.

She didn't want to kill her rescuer.

"Do you have a brig?" she called to Ambroos. "A dungeon?"

"What kind of house do you take this for?" Ambroos had picked up the poker, but he held it without confidence. "We have a root cellar in the yard."

Jake staggered to his feet. Blood poured down his chin from his nose, and his eyes rolled wildly in his head.

"You're Jacob Hop," Margarida said again.

Jake jumped for Ambroos's poker.

Margarida dove and managed to grab Jake by the ankle. Both of them hit the floor and rolled—she pushed herself to be up on her feet first. Grabbing Jake by the back of his shirt, she hauled him in her wake.

"Back door!" she hollered.

Lotte led the way, throwing wide a door that led from the kitchen into the rectangular yard behind the house. Outside, snowflakes hung nearly suspended in the air. They sizzled as they touched Margarida's skin, melting into frigid streams that ran into her orange flannel dress, soaking it instantly.

She threw Jake into a snowbank.

He leaped to his feet and she knocked him down again. Part of her raged, wanting to grab the Dutchman in both hands and break his neck. She struggled against that desire as much as she struggled against Jacob Hop.

"Are you Jake?" she yelled.

He tried to stand back up a second time and she jumped on him, knocking him prone. Scooping up a big handful of snow, she shoved it into his face. "Are you Jake?"

The back of her neck felt unprotected. What if the tongueless dead sorcerer was waiting in the yard and attacked her now? The fear raised goosepimples on her flesh, fueled her strength, and added urgency to her question to the Dutchman.

He punched her in the eye, and she ignored it. Standing, she picked him up and threw him headfirst into a deeper drift of snow. His feet kicked aimlessly. He tried to stand, and she held him down.

"Jake!" she roared. "Are you Jake? Are you Jacob Hop?"

"Murmph! Murmple!" His words were trapped by the snow, but his tone had changed.

Shivering suddenly from the cold, Margarida stepped back to let him climb out of the snow. He was bloody and bedraggled, but he wore a rueful smile. "Ja," he said. "I'm Jake. I'm Jacob Hop."

She scrutinized his face. He seemed to be in control of himself again. Her own heartbeat began to slow, and the strength coiled in her limbs faded.

"Are you sure?" she asked. If this was a trick, if her strength left her entirely and she passed out again, she worried he would easily kill Ambroos and Lotte.

Jake nodded. "I don't know what that was, but I'm sorry. And I tell you one thing."

"What's that?"

"I won't be asking for an exorcism again."

Sarah knelt and looked toward the Serpent Throne.

To her side, Alzbieta Torias also knelt.

In Sarah's mortal eye, the throne loomed large and treelike over the floor of the temple below. In her Eye of Eve, she saw . . .

Smoke.

Beneath the smoke, light, but the smoke was thick and oily, clinging to the Serpent Throne, the walls, and the floor of the apse.

She didn't see the goddess sitting in the throne.

She also didn't see the Heron King.

"Something is wrong," she said.

Alzbieta sighed. "You haven't forgotten that Calvin killed a man on the Serpent Throne?"

"I haven't. But that's not what I mean. I can see Eërthes's blood like a pool on the seat itself, like no one ever cleaned it up."

"No one did clean it up," Alzbieta said. "They're afraid to. *We're* afraid to."

"Afraid of the goddess? I thought the blood was a desecration. Wouldn't She want Her throne cleaned?"

"Afraid of the Throne. Onandagos had the throne brought from the Drowned Lands. It sailed on its own ship crewed entirely by priestesses and unprofaned by the presence of any weapons."

"This would have been long before cannons, or muskets."

"The priestesses didn't carry so much as a bow."

"Good thing no one tried to capture it."

"But they did. When the fleet was anchored within sight of the New World, a party of raiders came aboard at night. They killed every priestess, slitting their throats and dropping them in the water. Then they weighed anchor and sailed away.

"In the morning, Onandagos and the rest of the fleet began to search for the missing ship and the Throne. It took a week, but they found it. It had been brought ashore and taken to the village of the people who had taken it. They were an Algonk people, a small nation whose name is now forgotten."

"How did Onandagos get the Throne back?" Sarah asked.

"Everyone in that village was dead," Alzbieta told her.

"The Serpent Throne killed them?"

"Holiness is not some label that means a certain object or place is *nice*," Alzbieta said. "Holiness is not beauty, or fine craftsmanship. Holiness is a power that kills. It requires special people with special preparation to handle holy objects, because a person who is not prepared dies from contact."

Sarah was silent for a moment. "This is part of why I have to be the Beloved before I can become queen? I am prepared by steps for contact with what is most holy, or in other words, contact with what is most lethal?"

Alzbieta nodded. "In fact, not only did the village where the stolen Throne was housed die, but every pirate who had participated in the theft died, too. As did every person who had come into contact with one of those pirates. And so did every person who had come into contact with one of *those* people, and so on, to the seventh degree."

Sarah whistled low. "No wonder no one remembers that nation's name."

"So no one dares clean the Serpent Throne."

"Maybe that's why my father never closed the curtain. He didn't dare sit on the throne."

"Perhaps."

"Well, good. That's just what I want. I want a big dose of power that can kill people seven degrees removed, and I want to dump it on those Imperials out there. Hell, I'd wheel the Serpent Throne out there myself and let it do the job, even if it meant my own death, only I'm afraid Cromwell might actually have the means to turn it to his own ends."

"Tell me how you think you can become mistress of that power, and I will serve you."

Sarah looked sharply at her cousin. "Alzbieta, it's time you told me what you know of coronation rites."

The priestess said nothing.

"I saw the goddess on the Serpent Mound. She was a beacon of living power. I saw Her again on the Sunrise Mound and again She was mighty, but once She had chosen me, She disappeared. I can tell, looking at the Serpent Throne, that it is a source of a great power. I believe that I am supposed to sit on it, and that its power will give me the strength to free this city from the trap of Robert Hooke."

Alzbieta said nothing.

"If I do not do that, I fear that Hooke's spell—Cromwell's spell, because now we know *he's* here, and I suspect his presence is what enables Hooke to cast so large a net—will kill us all. Every death we suffer fuels the net that has us trapped. That black flame out there is a reservoir of energy that belongs to our enemy. When enough of us have died, who can say what he'll do with it?"

Alzbieta looked at the floor. Sarah examined her closely.

"We don't know the procedures for cleaning the Serpent

Throne," the priestess said. "Or at least, we're uncertain and we're afraid that, if we do it wrong, She'll be angry. Or we'll be killed by the throne."

"Good God," Sarah finally said. "You don't *know* the coronation rites."

"I told you early on there were things I didn't know. I always told you that."

"I sort of imagined those would be just the deepest, darkest secrets. What were you thinking, that I'd just figure these things out for myself? What about your oath, Alzbieta? To help me?"

"I *have* helped," Alzbieta protested. "I have tried to give you good hints. And tell you what I know, and what I *think* is relevant."

"In other words, these are riddles that you haven't solved yourself, and you were hoping I could do it for you. But you weren't willing to tell me that you were just ignorant. And what, you were hoping I would figure all these things out, and then you could steal the information and make yourself Queen?"

"No!" Alzbieta looked genuinely shocked. "I have tried to be faithful. I have served your interests from the moment of my vow."

She means it. Sarah inhaled deeply and sighed. What she had taken for oathbound decorum and sacred reticence had been ignorance and pride and fear. "Very well. We do this *my* way."

"What's *your* way?" Alzbieta asked.

"Heart full of fear, and making it up as I go along." Sarah nodded in the direction of the Throne. "But I have a clue. Or a theory. I need lamp oil."

Alzbieta bowed. "I'll have the sept of priestesses with today's tendance duties fill the bowls."

"No," Sarah said. "Bring the oil. I'll do it. If anyone's going to die, let it be me."

Alzbieta's back stiffened. "The people, I am sure, would rather someone else died instead."

"Too damn bad." Sarah stood. "Bring the oil. If you're so hell-bent on putting yourself at risk, you can sit here with me."

Alzbieta Torias herself brought the oil in a simple clay pot from storerooms beneath the temple.

Something, or a series of somethings, had defiled the Temple of the Sun. It didn't shine like the Serpent Mound; it didn't have the palpable presence of the Sunrise Mound. What had happened? Alzbieta might know. So might Zadok, although what the priestess condemned as a defilement, the priest might celebrate as an act of heroism. That history might be useful to her, and she should try to learn it.

But what she really wanted was to activate—or reactivate—the power of the Throne. And if she could do that without sorting through the half-remembered battles of prior generations, so much the better.

She stepped out of her shoes, took the oil, and approached the Serpent Throne.

The smoke she saw through her Eye of Eve grew thicker as she approached. Beneath, she thought she saw blue light, but it was obscured by the black fumes. At the foot of the stairs entering the shrine's apse, she resisted an urge to look back.

Taking another steadying breath, she climbed.

There was a ritual way to do this, and she didn't know it.

But there was a divinity to be honored as well, and she could at least show respect.

At the top of the stairs she knelt, pressing her forearms to the floor. She deliberately held the position for a long time and tried to clear her heart of hesitation and fear, malice and hatred.

She tried to be pure of heart and single and selfless of purpose.

Curiously, she found herself trying to feel in her heart as she imagined Calvin must feel. Not innocent, but trusting, good, and open. Honest with himself and with the world.

"Mother Wisdom," she said. "Forgive Thou my missteps and my arrogance in approaching Thee. And if Thou strike me down, may it be as an atoning sacrifice to cleanse the past misdeeds Thy children have sinned against Thee. I wish to cleanse Thy footstool, that I may save Thy city."

Halfway through, what she had intended as a statement of her intentions had become a prayer. Not the Latin prayer-incantation she had used to activate the Heronplow, but a simpler prayer of the heart.

Also unintentionally, she had fallen into the cadences of Court Speech.

Thank you, Calvin.

Rising, she began to pour the oil. Despite her words, she really didn't want the goddess to strike her down, atoning sacrifice or not. She took measured steps, as if approaching a dangerous predator—a panther or a wolf—and deliberately trying not to startle it. She stepped with flat feet, except when she had to rise onto the balls of her feet to pour oil into the higher bowls.

The goddess didn't strike her down.

Sarah abased herself to the floor again. "Thank you, Mother Wisdom. Mother Eve. Mother of All Living." She wished she'd grown up a little less New Light, so she had more sense of ritual.

Still kneeling, she raised her hands before her, palms up, and repeated a tiny spell she had once used, perfectly timed, to drive away an attacking slaver on the Natchez Trace.

"Ignem mitto."

The spark she sent lit the lowest of the seven bowls. She repeated the spell six more times, each time lighting only one lamp.

When they all burned, the light sprang from the gold-covered Throne, rebounded off the gold-plated walls, and nearly blinded her.

Sarah pressed herself to the floor again.

Then she took the oil and retreated to meet Alzbieta Torias. She knelt beside the priestess and they gazed upon the Serpent Throne together.

"What do you see?" Alzbieta whispered.

Sarah touched a finger to the oil very slightly, anointing her eye and then Alzbieta's, and then she took her cousin's hand. *"Visionem condivido,"* she murmured, and willed their visions to fuse.

The fog still shrouded the Serpent Throne, but in its seven burning lamps now danced seven flaming salamanders.

Alzbieta gasped.

Questions flooded Sarah's mind, and she bit back her tongue. She would let the goddess reveal what She willed.

At least until Sarah felt she wasn't getting the information she wanted.

The salamanders wiggled together and then spoke. Their voice was a chorus of feminine bass tones woven together in a close harmony. "Thou seekest a vision."

Sarah bowed, pressing her forehead to the cold tile of the floor. Alzbieta imitated her immediately. "I am trapped." Her voice boomed very loud in the long hall.

The salamanders danced and the black smoke seemed to part. Still through a haze, but more solidly now, Sarah again saw the Woman sitting on the Throne. She was tall and beautiful and the sun shone from Her face, which seemed to shift between a woman's and a lion's and a gazelle's.

Suddenly, men were in the vision. Men climbed the throne, wrapped ropes about it and tried to drag it, struck it with picks. A priestess in white linen tried to stop them and was run through with a spear, her body thrown onto the seat and left. The Woman sitting on the throne cupped Her face in Her hands and wept, and her weeping was the sound of rain. When the desecrators found they couldn't damage the throne, they defiled it by voiding their bladders and their bowels upon it. The Woman stood and retreated to the space behind the Serpent Throne, still weeping. As a final insult, a man rode a horse up the steps and into the apse. There he circled the throne three times before finally dropping the rotting corpse of a dog onto the throne's seat.

The sound of weeping came from two directions. Sarah looked at the priestess beside her and saw that Alzbieta wept, too.

"And my father?" Sarah asked. "Did my father not cleanse the temple?"

The vision continued. Sarah saw a man with her own face—not her own face, because it was lightly bearded, but obviously the face of someone who was Sarah's kin—climb the Serpent Throne and sit on it. But the stains left by the dog and woman and the attacking men were all still there, the black smoke didn't dissipate, the Woman stood behind the bearded man at arm's length.

"Thy father sat upon the throne," the salamanders hummed. "He was the Beloved of the goddess, and She permitted it. But he was not king."

"What?" Sarah and Alzbieta spoke together. Alzbieta looked as surprised as Sarah felt.

"I saw his coronation in the Basilica," Alzbieta said. "The Metropolitan crowned him. And I know he sat on the throne in the Temple of the Sun. I saw him sit there. I assumed...I mean..."

"He never shut the veil," Sarah said, thinking out loud, "because he never performed the temple enthronement rite. The people made him king, but the goddess didn't. He was Her Beloved son, but he was never King of Cahokia in Her eyes."

Was that what her father was doing at the Serpent Mound when he died? Lacking the Heronplow, he had not been able to meet the goddess on the Sunrise Mound. Instead, he had gone to find Her elsewhere. Was it to be crowned king? Was it to learn *how* to be crowned king?

The vision continued. Sarah saw the Woman watching and

weeping behind the Throne as claimants to the Throne stood in the nave before Her and asked to be chosen. She chose none of them.

She saw the Throne glow with golden light as Maltres Korinn placed her shoulderbag containing the regalia on it. She saw Calvin Calhoun kill Eërthes the poet, and black smoke rose again from the Throne, obscuring her view.

"I would ascend the Throne. Will you teach me?" Sarah asked.

The salamanders were silent.

"Could I use the Heronplow?" Sarah asked, but in her heart she knew the answer: no. The plow might be an important part of consecrating the Temple of the Sun, or re-consecrating it, but there was a pollution to remove first. And mere consecration wouldn't open the way to enthronement.

She needed a rite. A rite she had assumed Alzbieta would be able to help her discover or recreate, but that assumption had been mistaken.

The salamanders said nothing.

"And to cleanse the temple?" she called. She tried to remember her Bible on this point. "Twenty thousand oxen and a hundred thousand sheep, something like that?"

She doubted Cahokia had that large a herd in the entire kingdom. Certainly, such herds and flocks were not within the Treewall.

The salamanders trembled and were silent.

Alzbieta took a breath as if to speak, but then only whispered to Sarah. "Why not the Sunrise Mound? The goddess chose you there. Can She not crown you there as well?"

Sarah hesitated, but it wasn't a bad question. "Would the goddess seat a king on the Sunrise Mound?"

This time, the salamanders spoke. "Would you take the Serpent Throne to the Sunrise Mound and place it before the eyes of all the world, including heretics and Imperial spies? And having done that, how would you then cleanse the pollution you had brought with the Throne?"

Sarah bowed in acknowledgement of the answer.

"I think my father knew more than I do," she said slowly. "I think I'm going to have to visit him and ask what he can teach me about the enthronement rite."

"If he knew it, why wouldn't he have used it?"

"Maybe he couldn't use it because he needed the Heronplow to rededicate the temple," Sarah guessed. "Maybe he couldn't use it because he didn't know how to cleanse the temple. Maybe he only knew part of the rite. In any case, I'm pretty certain he knew more than I do." She laughed softly. "Mostly because I know nothing. If I can learn what my father knew, that'll be two big steps forward."

Alzbieta lowered her voice, as if not to be heard by the salamanders. "What . . . necromancy . . . are you planning?"

"No necromancy," Sarah said. "Anyway, not as you think of it. No Cromwellian nonsense about death winds or Lazars. But I think I can speak with my father at the Serpent Mound."

"You'll leave the city." Alzbieta's face showed uncertainty.

Sarah laughed. "Once, you would have welcomed my disappearance."

"Those days are long past, Beloved. What will we do without you?"

"Fight until I get back, I expect," Sarah said. "Only I really hope you're fighting against the Imperials, and not with each other."

"When will you leave?"

"As soon as I can figure out how. Only we have some burials to attend to first."

Jake awoke with a splitting headache and a powerful feeling of shame. Lotte and Ambroos both stood over his bedside with worried looks on their faces.

"I'm sorry," he said immediately. "I wasn't myself."

"I could see that," Lotte snapped, but then her face softened. "I am pleased you're feeling better now."

"Whatever was wrong with you," Ambroos said, "it's still wrong."

"You think I'm possessed, hey?"

"No." Ambroos shook his head. "I've seen enough possessions to see that your case is . . . something different. For one thing, if you were possessed by a devil, the exorcism should have worked. You would have screamed and resisted, and the devil might have tried to enter into one of us, but we would have forced it into the writ of divorce, and then burned the writ."

"Easy as pie," Jake said.

"No, very difficult. But something we know how to do, something we've done before. Instead, you went berserk."

"Maybe it's because I don't have the devil in me," Jake suggested.

"You mean the Reigerkoning?" Ambroos smiled. "Okay. But you wrote his name down on the writ too, and it's not like any herons flew in the window and asked to participate in the rite."

"That's not what he looks like," Jake said. "He's a giant, and . . ." His voice faltered as a vision of a plain strewed with dead and dying warriors, tall and red-haired and wearing copper breastplates, filled his vision.

Ambroos waved his hand. "I think you're mad, Jacob."

"You don't plan to send me to Roosevelt Island?"

Ambroos looked his cousin in the eye and thought for a moment. "No. But I can't have you do that again. Not around my family, Jacob."

"I'll leave. Is Nathaniel conscious?"

"Not yet."

"Will you watch him for me? I have something I must do in New Amsterdam, but it doesn't require either of the children to come with me. I'd feel safe if I could leave them here." Jake saw looks of apprehension on both their faces. "And I don't even have to come back. I could stay in a hotel. Or in a shed. Or a haystack."

The last image did it; Ambroos laughed. "No, you can come back. But, Jacob . . . if you do that again, I will have to shoot you."

Jake nodded. "Ja, that sounds like a fair deal to me."

Lotte and Ambroos left him, and Jake got up and dressed. He found Margaret standing in the hall.

"I'm coming," she said.

"It's not safe."

"Nothing is safe. And if I stay here, maybe I can protect my brother. But if I come along, maybe I can protect you. And since you're leaving the building, with its light and people and guns, I think maybe you're the one most likely to need protection."

Jake stopped arguing. "I think your sister would say similar things. On the other hand, if you come with me and get hurt, your sister might kill me. But really, at the end of the day, how could I possibly stop you?"

Margaret crossed her arms and smiled.

"Would you be willing to wear a disguise? Just a hat and a coat, breeches, so you look like a Dutch boy instead of like the girl with strange hair and an orange dress who escaped yesterday?"

Margaret nodded.

They both dressed in borrowed clothes—long coats, scarves, and tall hats—so they looked like a couple of short Yonkermen bundling against the cold.

Lacking any better means of finding his quarry, Jake took a blank card from Ambroos, on which he wrote the words I HAVE SOMETHING FOR YOU AND I AM WAITING IN THE LOBBY before tucking it into an envelope. On the outside of the envelope he wrote MR. TEMPLE FRANKLIN.

At the first book-cadger's they passed, Jake stopped to buy a copy of the Tarock. The act of thumbing through the cards brought him a sense of calm; when he drew three cards, they were the City, the Drunkard, and the Emperor.

The familiar riddle, menacing though it was, brought a smile to his face.

When they reached New Amsterdam proper, Jake took them to a street of elegant hotels with marble facades and three or more stories of rooms. Starting at one end of the row, they walked into the hotel doors and told the desk clerks they had a message for Mr. Temple Franklin.

The fourth clerk, at a hotel called *De Republikein*, took the envelope.

Jake debated between asking Margaret to hide and asking her to stick close to him. He settled on the latter, and the two of them sat on a red-upholstered sofa with a view of the stairs as well as the front door.

"We might have to wait hours," Jake said to Margaret. "Stay awake."

They only had to wait minutes. Temple Franklin descended the stairs in waistcoat and slippers, the card in his hand and a curious frown on his face. Jake stood and waved to the emperor's confidant. They met in the center of the room.

Franklin looked Jake and Margaret both carefully in the face with a keenness of eye that made Jake regret he'd come. "You sent this message up to me?"

"Are you Franklin?"

"Yes, as you and the staff of the *Republikein* well know."

"Are you...the *only* Franklin?"

Temple Franklin's eyes narrowed. "To my knowledge, I'm my father's only child, as he was his father's. We both had births that were...less than fully conventional, so I can't guarantee I don't have a sibling somewhere. Why the genealogical inquisition? Who are you, and what do you want? Is this some kind of back channel attempt from Stuyvesant?"

Jake nodded. "In October, I witnessed the death of a man name René du Plessis."

Temple frowned. "That is not an especially uncommon name, if you were in, say, Acadia."

"Du Plessis was the intendant of the Chevalier of New Orleans. The seneschal."

Franklin nodded slowly. "I know the man you speak of."

Jake decided to omit mention of his mistress, though du Plessis's actual dying exhortation had begun *tell the Witchy Eye that she must.* "In his moment of death, he told me to give this to you." Reaching inside his coat, he took out the bronze medallion carved with the Franklin Shield.

Franklin raised his eyebrows. "A cheap trinket, sold all over Philadelphia for pennies. Is this all there is to the joke?"

"No joke, Mr. Franklin," Jake said. Was this the right Franklin? But who else could it be, if he was the only descendant of the Lightning Bishop? "And he said, 'tell Franklin that the sword has gone back.'"

"The sword? Did he say which sword?" Franklin smiled warmly.

"From the context, I think he must have meant the Heronblade. The sword that was once carried by the King of Cahokia, as part of his regalia."

Franklin's eyes narrowed. "And now the sword has gone back to whom?"

Jake hesitated. "To Simon Sword, Mr. Franklin. To the Heron King."

Franklin nodded slowly. "Stay here one moment, would you?" He walked to the front desk.

This was the moment of truth. Despite being an envoy of the emperor, Franklin might also be a leader in the so-called Conventicle, if it existed. He might be an ally for Sarah; maybe his position close to the emperor could be turned to Sarah's advantage.

When he returned, one of the doormen was with him. The doorman held a cocked pistol in each hand and scowled.

"Where did the other fellow go?" Franklin asked. "The one who looked like a wiggly?"

Jake looked about—Margaret had disappeared. "What other fellow?" he asked. "I came to see you alone."

Franklin shook his head and clicked his tongue. "Such a liar."

Margaret reappeared, stepping from behind a column, out of sight of both Franklin and the doorman. In a single fluid movement, she gripped the doorman by his belt—

Jake ducked—

bang! bang! the doorman's pistols both went off—

and tossed him across the lobby.

Franklin spun around in time for the girl to yank the medallion from his hands and knock him to the ground with a tap to the chest that looked gentle.

"Laten we vertrekken!" she bellowed. Without waiting, she marched out of the hotel.

Jake followed. No one tried to stop them.

*"Stick to talk of anointings and burials,
and say nothing about who should rule."*

CHAPTER THIRTEEN

A bonfire burned in a plaza just inside Cahokia's southern gate. The sun had gone down hours earlier. Luman Walters stood in the cold at the edge of the fire's reach, standing beside two gray-caped Cahokian wardens who had just finished twelve hours of standing on the ramparts.

They ignored Luman.

Within the fire's warmth, living beastkind, Sarah Elytharias's bodyguard corps, sat on the frozen ground. The more man-shaped among them sat cross-legged, but some lay like cattle on their flanks. Collectively, they emitted a low-pitched rumbling sound.

Luman shrugged deep into his wizard's coat. He resented not being invited to stand with the Firstborn wizards on the wall, but not because it suggested that Sarah doubted where his loyalties lay. That was a reasonable response, despite whatever it was she saw in her magical eye. Luman hadn't been an employee of the Imperial Ohio Company long, but that was how Sarah had first met him.

He resented his lack of invitation because it meant they saw him as their magical inferior.

And even more than that, he resented the fact that they were clearly right.

"The draug came out at sunset," one of the soldiers said to the other. He had a nasal whine to his voice. "Not just one or two, I mean. All of them."

"To attack?" the other asked in a raspy growl. "I get posted facing the river. I see mostly beastkind, day and night both."

"To take our dead," Nasal said.

"Beastkind?"

"And Firstborn. I feel sick. They dragged them right back into the trenches."

"Don't think about the draug eating them, if it makes you sick. Just imagine they're buried to life, returned to the Virgin."

"That's not it."

The moaning of the beastkind grew, not in response to anything in particular.

"You're Reformed, hetar?"

"I'm not religious at all."

"What is it, then? You're not troubled about the dead beastkind, are you?"

Nasal sighed, a sound like a heavy rattle.

Luman had been listening with a growing sense of dread, and suddenly found himself jumping into the conversation. "He's troubled because the draug didn't *eat* the bodies. They *took* them."

"Exactly." Nasal spat.

"You mean . . ." Rasp fell silent as he realized what Nasal intended.

Suddenly, Sarah Elytharias appeared among the beastkind. She walked slowly, as if stiff or exhausted. The blue Imperial army coat she wore dwarfed her. She wore the ragged bandage that covered her magical eye. The beastkind looked up at her. When she arrived at the center of the group, she stopped and raised the patch.

She was alone. Where was her Cavalier general? The Podebradan warrior who stuck to her like a shadow? Her vizier?

Luman doubted such people would leave Sarah alone, if commanded. So she must have eluded them.

His respect for her, already high, rose another notch.

Sarah looked at her beastkind warriors—had she lost a third? half?—slowly, turning to run her gaze over each of them in turn. She paced about the fire to do it, and the beastkind moved with her. They parted to give her space, then followed her until she stopped. The warriors had regrouped themselves in a cluster around her.

She didn't look once at Luman; nevertheless he felt she was seeing his soul.

She rolled the strip of cloth into a ball, then deliberately threw it into the bonfire.

"My warriors," she said slowly. "Today we lost members of our pack."

A growl passed through the beastkind with a wave of rising fur and clenched fists.

"They're gone," Sarah continued. "If their bodies rise to fight again, know that those are bodies only, animated by the foul will of the Necromancer. It matters not that the husk returns to earth immediately, or that we must first defeat it and lay it down. Our packmates have fulfilled the measure of their creation and are returned to the river."

Beastkind heads nodded on all sides.

Sarah removed her blue coat. Underneath, she wore a thin Appalachee shirt and breeches. The shirt showed her arms and neck, which were covered with red welts. A few of the welts had broken her skin and scabbed over—she looked as if she had been beaten with sticks.

"Across the river, in the Great Green Wood, a chick is born this night who fought by our sides at the Serpent Mound. A cub is whelped who marched with us into the Ohio. A kit yaps for the first time who this day roared her last into the face of Imperial guns."

Luman had no idea what the theology of Sarah's statements was, but the beastkind purred and growled, a noise of contentment and resolution.

"I'm not entirely comfortable with the direction this is going in here, either," Nasal said. He and Rasp both edged away from the fire and the crowd.

Luman stayed where he was.

"We will see them again." For the first time, Sarah's face broke into a smile. "And when we see them, they will be our foes. We'll fight them tooth and nail, for that is the thing we were born to do."

The rumble rose in volume.

The two wardens turned and fled. Watching them go, Luman realized that a ring of Cahokians hid in the shadows around the fire. Their eyes were transfixed, their faces stunned and fascinated.

"Tonight, let us give praise to our fallen companions. Let us celebrate with joy their ferocity and valor, and the success of their lives."

The low rumble broke into a shout of approval.

Luman's knees buckled, but he forced himself to stand still.
Sarah threw back her head and howled like a wolf.

The beastkind roared.

Then they danced. With her warriors, Sarah circled the fire.
She crouched on all fours to leap forward; she pirouetted around
her beastkind; she slunk like a wild cat. She turned and raced
directly at the bonfire, leaping over it and drawing another exuberant cry from her warriors.

The heat of the sweating beastmen and beastwives magnified
the heat of the fire. Luman shrugged out of his own long coat
and laid it aside. He was careful to drape it over a wooden table
that looked as if by day it made part of some tradesman's tent
stall on the plaza. An errant beastwife's hoof would crush valuable arcane supplies; would a watching Cahokian, desperate with
hunger and the pressures of the siege, steal the coat?

He'd take the risk.

Luman Walters stepped into the circle of dancing beastkind.

Luman was familiar with the dances of the German Ohio and
had taken a few steps in the circle dances of the Haudenosaunee,
but he instantly knew that this dance was another thing entirely. It
was a race, but a race in a circle with no apparent end. The racers
took enormous leaps, spun on one leg, and took short cuts across
the bonfire to emulate their queen, either bounding through the
licking flames or stampeding across the coals. Beastkind locked
limbs and whirled together, or threw each other in violent actions
halfway between a wrestling hold and a dance spin.

Luman's shirt came untucked and sweat poured from his body.
He spread his legs as if straddling an invisible horse and barked
in answer to the staccato shrieks of a beastman who danced
opposite the fire. He entwined his elbow through the arm of a
beastwife with a gray, thick-haired hide and eyes like an owl,
and briefly did something like the triple-time gliding German
waltz, cheek pressed to cheek and stalking through the sparks.

After a climax of howling and breathless stamping of feet,
Luman found Sarah's coat in the corner of the plaza. It was
scuffed and dirtied with the tracks of many hooves and feet, so
he offered her his own coat instead.

"That's a bold offer, magician," she said. The word *magician*
made him smile and stand slightly taller. "Aren't you afraid I'd
take your coat and use it to ensorcel you?"

"Yes," he admitted. "But you could just as easily order me shot, or feed me to your beastkind."

At that moment, the beastkind were staggering to the corners of the plaza and flinging themselves down to sleep.

"I don't know whether they'd eat the flesh of men," Sarah said. "Some of them, likely, yes."

"I'm not offering to be the experiment," Luman said. "But I'm in your power."

"I see it hasn't even occurred to you to take my coat and use it to ensorcel me."

It hadn't. Luman felt himself blushing. "Your Majesty," he said, "I have offered you my service. I offer it again now."

Sarah took her own coat. "Tell me what you hope to gain, Luman Walters."

"Power to act," Luman said. "The wisdom to know what to do. An understanding of the nature of the universe."

"You don't want to take your Faculty of Abrac to some village outside Cleveland and just make a decent living, hexing barns against fire and shops against theft? There's honor in that, and enough cash money to keep a person fed."

"That was my mother's hope for me," Luman said. "My father was convinced that if he only woke me up first and kept me in the field longer, my body would eventually develop the muscles that my brothers all sprouted naturally, and I would be a farmer like him. I, on the other hand, was convinced that his plan would kill me from sheer exhaustion. Mother gave him half the contents of her hope chest to get him to agree that I could be apprenticed to the local schoolteacher instead, and the other half to the schoolteacher. He taught reading, writing, and the Elector Songs, but he was also a famous rodsman."

"You didn't follow your mother's plan."

"Once I'd mastered the rod—which was the only arcane art that schoolteacher knew—I went back to my father and offered to use it to help him."

"Let me guess…you failed."

"No, I found water immediately. We dug a fine well, and when I offered to use the rod to ask other questions he might have, and search his farm for buried treasure, my father simply paid me a rodsman's wages and sent me on my way."

"You didn't dig wells for the neighbors?"

"I decided instead I would learn the secrets of the universe. A person who knew the secrets of the universe would never have to dig wells or pull a plow in his life. Or if he did, it wouldn't matter—he would have the peace of mind to endure it. The eyes to see, the ears to hear." He studied Sarah Elytharias's face closely, and she studied him back.

"You're looking for initiation," she said. "Esoteric secrets."

"I have been initiated," Luman answered. "More than once. I'm looking for knowledge."

"From any source?"

"From true messengers," he said, looking into her unnaturally pale eye. "I tend to find that the truest messengers are the strangest-looking ones."

Sarah laughed once, a sharp bark. "I'm looking for knowledge, too," she said. "And initiation. I don't suppose you're already a Grand Master of Cahokian royal throne lore?"

Luman's breath came faster. "No. But I would *like* to know it."

"So would I," Sarah said. "In fact, I think I *need* to know it. And I'm starting to think not only does no one alive know what I want to know, but maybe the dead don't know it, either."

"The dangers of an esoteric tradition," Luman said. "Distortion in transmission. Misunderstanding. Corruption. Failure."

Sarah studied his face with her piercing gaze. "Alright then, Luman Walters. Stick close to me. I'm going on a trip in the morning, and you're coming along."

"Your Majesty," Bill said. "I cannot insist. But I beg you to regard this Zadok as a potential threat. He stands now at the edge of the burial field, shouting things that many another queen would regard as directly seditious."

"I *do* regard him as a threat," Sarah said. "And I will not go to a funeral rite accompanied by a troop of beastkind. Not here, not in my city. Not in Her city. Not in front of my people. Our warriors must stand outside the burial ground."

They stood beside the Temple of the Sun. Behind Sarah stood a file of priestesses. She and they wore simple linen dresses, despite the cold. The only decoration the linen bore was a stitched pattern with thread that was itself white and therefore almost invisible; the thread appeared to create entwined serpents over the priestesses' breasts. *Ceremonial garb*, Bill thought.

"Then *I* will be at your side," he said. "Should half the city attack, at least I will be there to defend you."

"If he incites a mob that size to attack me, General, even you will be powerless to stop them."

"Yes," he agreed. "But I will not be powerless entirely. I will have the power to kill that son of a bitch Zadok."

Sarah hesitated, which was as it should be. Bill wasn't sure her life was at risk, but he didn't want to take any chances.

"Not you, Sir William," she said softly. "Not today, not at this. Whatever you have to do, you stand outside."

"I will stand by your side, then," Yedera offered.

The Podebradan wore her scale mail and rested a hand on the hilt of her scimitar. Bill didn't think the Firstborn warrior looked any less offensive then he did to funerary ritual, but for some reason, Sarah evidently saw it differently.

"Yes, Your Majesty." Bill tried to sound dignified and not stiff. He bowed and descended the mound in advance of the priestesses, clearing the way for the ritual procession. He leaned on two sticks and groaned at each step.

"The pain in your thighs is bearable, suh," he ground through his teeth to himself, but he feared what might be coming. Discreetly, halfway down the Great Mound, he took two swallows from a flask he kept in his coat pocket. The brandy inside was extremely cheap and tasted of cherries, but he had spiked it with Gazelem Zomas's Paracelsian Tincture.

By the time he reached the foot of the mound, the pain in his legs had dulled.

He knew no way to blow the Heron King's horn softly, so he leaned to Chikaak at the foot of the Great Mound. "Softly," he said, "but have the men fall in."

Then he levered himself into the saddle. Chikaak mutely offered a hand, and Bill took it without comment.

Heeding Chikaak's gentle yips, the surviving twenty beastkind marched behind Bill. He threw his chest out proudly, knowing without looking that the beastkind walked in two parallel lines, as crisply as a platoon could whose members didn't all possess the same number of walking limbs.

He didn't look back until they reached the Sunrise Mound. Sarah had designated a flat space beside the low mound as a Field of Life, and an honor guard of wardens stood in a ring that encompassed both the field and the mound. It was as large an honor guard as Bill believed the city could afford, comprised of men not currently on duty on the Treewall, but it didn't create a solid barrier.

Fortunately, most of the city's people—it did seem that the entire city had turned out, packing the open space just within the Treewall on all sides of the field and mound—respected the notional line the wardens created.

A solid minority, though, stood with Zadok. The Metropolitan of Cahokia had positioned himself at the edge of the cleared avenue leading to the field of life, just a few steps from the field. He stood with his back to the avenue now, addressing a wedge of Firstborn who stared at him intently. The Cahokians watching Zadok had marked their faces with ash, and Zadok addressed them.

"The Lord God cannot look with any allowance on such wickedness!" Zadok wailed. "He said unto His servant Amos, 'That drink wine in bowls, and anoint themselves with the chief ointments: but they are not grieved for the affliction of Joseph. Therefore now shall they go captive with the first that go captive, and the banquet of them that stretched themselves shall be removed.'"

"Sergeant." Bill spoke loudly enough to be heard by the priest. "Accommodate the men over there." He indicated a space just across the avenue from Zadok.

"And again, to Ezekiel, 'Son of man, wail for the multitude of Egypt, and cast them down, even her, and the daughters of the famous nations, unto the nether parts of the earth, with them that go down into the pit.'"

The Firstborn, whether out of fear of Sarah's warriors or respect for their sacrifice, made room. They had a strong ability to squeeze tightly together, packed like salted fish in a barrel.

Bill needed someone to hold his mount, and the animal was uncomfortable with the beastkind. He missed Calvin Calhoun and his sergeant Jake, but there was no point pining for what he couldn't have. Bill dismounted and found a young man standing alone in the crowd. "Do you know horses?" he asked.

The young man shook his head, but didn't shrink away.

Bill handed him the horse's reins and two shriveled apples. "Just stay here until I come back. One apple is for the horse."

Then he took one of his walking sticks and stumped over to the priest.

Zadok was still speaking. "But I fear we have a Pharaoh...or a witch...who knows not Joseph. Did Onandagos not say, when he lay upon his deathbed, 'Remember always that the serpent is the conquered one. And when the sons of the conqueror shall willingly wear the yoke of the conquered, then shall their servitude become an eternal burden'?"

The Metropolitan's followers groaned.

"Metropolitan Tarami." Bill leaned over the priest to bully him and put a hand into one of his coat's deep pockets. The feel of the horse pistol butt there was reassuring. "You may say all you like of banquets and ointments, but that is where you must draw your line."

Zadok turned to look up at Bill. He, too, had smeared ash on his face. "Do you presume to silence the words of the Lord?"

"No," Bill said. "Only the words of Mr. Zadok Tarami, and then only when he begins to talk of conquest and servitude. Keep your words to exhortations to repentance, and you and I may remain friends."

"And if the repentance I must preach is the repentance of the queen?" Zadok asked. He didn't look intimidated in the slightest. With the crowd staring at him, Bill suddenly wondered whether he'd chosen a battle he couldn't win.

He didn't lose his nerve. But he doubted his own wisdom.

"Metropolitan." Bill sighed. "We are surrounded by enemies on two sides. More enemies arrive daily. Pray let us be united in our defense of this people and its rightful queen."

"I have anointed no Queen," Zadok said. "But I recognize the Regent-Minister, and I love this people. And I am here because I grieve for my people's idolatry and wish us to repent."

Damned old man looks as if he really means it. "And also, you are here because you grieve for the sacrifice required of some of the noble sons of this fair city. And grieving with them and their families, you would never dream of bringing dishonor on their interment."

"I *do* mourn their deaths," Zadok said, finally giving an inch. "And I celebrate their heroism and willingness to sacrifice."

It would have to do. "I believe I shall watch the procession with you, suh." Bill turned his back to the crowd, forcing several of Zadok's followers to scuttle backward. He gripped his pistol firmly.

Sarah came at the head of her priestesses. They walked in three files; the central file followed directly behind Sarah, and each of them—including Sarah—held an unadorned jar made of fired brown clay and not so much as glazed. The files to the right and left played musical instruments: sistra, flutes, and hand drums. Ancient instruments, it seemed to Bill, and not the guitars or banjos or three-stringed Cahokian lutes that accompanied modern song.

They sang and Bill could make nothing of the words, which were in Ophidian. Sarah sang with them.

Bill shot a glance at Zadok. The cords in the man's neck stood out: was he just that thin, or was his body tensed with anger or the will to strike?

"Remember, Tarami," Bill murmured, loud enough for only Zadok to hear. "We mourn. We only mourn. Tomorrow you can tell your flock what a bunch of pagan bastards we all are."

And maybe, after all, the priest was right. Who could really say what God looked like, and whose hymns He liked the most? But when Bill got his judgment, he'd be content to look his Creator in the eye and swear he'd been a faithful soldier.

Sarah passed Bill. If she wasn't actually in a trance, she looked as if she were. In the center of the Field of Life, a series of pits had been dug in a spiral pattern. The pits were three feet across and four feet deep, surrounded by a crown of loose dirt from the excavation. Sarah walked around the inside of the spiral, slowly, raising the unglazed jar in her hands above her head. The central file of priestesses followed her. Bill now saw that Alzbieta Torias was in that group, as was the Lady Alena. The singers and players peeled away left and right and walked around the edges of the field of life until their leaders met on the far side. That created a cordon around the funeral ground that alternated musician-singer-musician, just within the ring of wardens.

Sarah reached the most inward spot of the spiral, beside the innermost pit, and knelt. After her, Alzbieta knelt beside the first pit, facing it. As each succeeding priestess reached the next following pit she knelt, and each placed the jar in her hands in lap, lid on the jar but facing downward. Or maybe, Bill thought, the jar was next to her womb.

Or perhaps not.

At the rear of the procession, behind all the priestesses, came bearers. Were these men eunuchs, slaves, or volunteers? They walked in pairs, carrying between them a jar identical to the jars carried by the priestesses, only larger, held in a rope sling.

The jars, Bill knew, held his dead soldiers, one man to a jar, curled into fetal position, wounds tended and bodies washed. The Germans of Chicago buried their dead with weapons. Freemasons buried theirs in embroidered aprons and caps. The Firstborn—at least, the Firstborn of Kyres's faith—buried their dead naked.

The bearers traced the spiral from the side opposite that trod by the priestesses. When each pair had arrived beside a pit, they turned and as one bent to lower their jars into the holes. The graves were precisely dug to barely accommodate the burial jars, so the bearers had to push to squeeze the pottery into place. They removed the lids, set them beside the graves, and retraced their steps out of the spiral.

Behind the bearers came the Podebradan Yedera. She came just within the circle of musicians and stood in the corner of the burial ground itself. She gripped the hilt of her scimitar with one hand, prepared to leap into action.

No one paid her any attention.

The priestesses' song changed. The crowd sang along. Bill cast an eye on his beastkind soldiers and was proud to see them hold their ground without so much as a whinny or a stray growl.

Sarah leaned over the innermost grave. Opening her pot, she reached into it with a wooden dipstick and pulled out a gob of golden honey. As the musicians and singers arrived at a verse-ending climax, she reached down to swab honey into the pit.

Into the mouth of the dead soldier, Bill had been told. From where he stood, he couldn't see it himself. But it was no stranger than pennies in the eyes, or ankles stitched together.

The priestess beside the same grave cried aloud as if in pain and leaned away from the grave. At the same moment, she opened her jar and a coiled snake fell into the pit.

"'He removed the high places,'" Zadok Tarami muttered, "'and brake the images, and cut down the groves, and brake in pieces the brasen serpent.'"

"Not today, suh," Bill said. "Today he watched and held his tongue."

The crowd behind the Metropolitan wasn't singing. They murmured and shifted uneasily from foot to foot.

"This is idolatry." Tarami looked up at Bill with a mixture of anger and pleading in his eyes. "Are you not a Christian man?"

"I'm a Cavalier," Bill said. "We take our religion as gentlemen, on whichever side of Byrd's Compromise we stand."

Zadok beat his breast and moaned loudly.

"Those are my soldiers receiving an honorable burial." Bill raised the pistol slightly. The weapon remained within his pocket, but Zadok noticed the gesture and must have realized what Bill held. "I will shoot you, suh, if you cannot show them and their queen respect. And then I'll see to it that you, too, are stuffed into a jar, fed honey, and given a snake to play with."

"They don't *play* with the snake," Zadok growled. "They believe it can pass between worlds—it was in Eden with our first parents, and then came with them in their exile. The serpent is capable of retracing its steps, so it will lead them along the invisible part of the spiral and into the arms of the goddess. Also, the snake is reborn, as the dead are reborn into life."

"Heaven's curtain, suh," Bill said. "To what can you possibly object in that?"

"Have you read your Bible?"

"I've had it read *to* me, at various times."

"The serpent is Satan. The serpent is the tempter of Eve."

There were good snakes in the Bible, too. Bill just couldn't remember what they were. "I'm little interested in and poorly equipped for a theological debate, priest. I dimly recall that the issue is more complex than that, and I invite you to take it up with my queen. *After* the funeral."

"The Revelation of John says, 'He laid hold on the dragon, that old serpent, which is the Devil, and Satan, and bound him a thousand years.' This is Satan-worship, Captain Lee!"

Bill spat on the ground. "*Captain* was my Imperial rank, suh. Here you will find I am *General* Lee."

"And I am Metropolitan of the Basilica!"

The crowd behind Zadok Tarami was muttering openly now. Bill heard words like *wickedness* and *appalling* and *riot*.

"I *did* call you *suh*," he pointed out. "And I believe now is the time for you to get your people under control. Quietly."

"Or you'll shoot me?"

"Yes, suh. With pleasure."

Tarami ground his teeth, but he turned to face his followers and shushed them, a stern expression on his face.

Across the avenue, Bill noticed Maltres Korinn. The vizier

was dressed all in black, as always, but he wasn't holding his staff. And he was looking at Bill.

Bill nodded.

Maltres nodded back and flashed Bill a grimly satisfied smile.

The priestesses shattered the small jars they had carried to the burial ground, dropping the shards into the graves. Then they finished the interments, placing the lids over the corpses and pushing earth into place over the jars with their bare hands. As each buried her dead man, she exited along the inside of the spiral, forming up behind Sarah, who stood holding her jar of honey.

Yedera now stood at Sarah's side.

Sarah looked at Bill and Zadok with her fierce eye. What was she seeing in Bill? His loyalty, he hoped.

And in Zadok Tarami?

With the burials finished, the song changed again. Sarah fixed her eye on the Temple of the Sun and began her march. As she left the burial ground, the musicians and singers formed up to either side of her, and the priestesses filed away from the graveyard in a stately unwinding motion.

Like a snake, uncoiling to move.

As he did at mass, Bill knew he was in the presence of a knot of intertwined symbols to whose meaning he was totally oblivious.

"You see, suh?" Bill said to the Metropolitan as the final priestess passed them. "No orgies, no blood sacrifice, everything carried out with the most solemn decorum. Nothing that couldn't be done before the entire Electoral Assembly in Philadelphia." Except perhaps the part where the ladies gave birth to snakes, but Bill was willing to regard that as a detail. "Now aren't you glad you helped me keep the peace?"

"You cannot stop me from preaching against this. Against her."

Bill sighed. "Nor would I wish to. But I intend to stand here until you leave, suh. And if I catch you preaching against my queen or her goddess on this spot, today or ever, know with a surety that I will shoot you dead immediately and feed you to the dogs."

Chikaak's appearance at Bill's shoulder at that moment was so perfectly timed, Bill wished he'd arranged it in advance.

"You would commit murder? And you think this would be righteousness?"

"No, suh. We are under siege, and I think it would be an

appropriate response to sedition." Bill turned to Chikaak. "Sergeant, post a guard at this spot. If the Metropolitan or any of his people preach here, or interfere with the graves, arrest them immediately and bring them to me."

Zadok Tarami nodded, cold but polite. He addressed his ash-touched followers. "I will now speak at the Basilica. My text will be Second Corinthians, chapter eleven." He looked at Bill as if daring him to respond.

Bill shrugged. "My friend Calvin Calhoun might know the reference. I do not."

Tarami raised his voice nearly to a shout. "'But I fear, lest by any means, as the serpent beguiled Eve through his subtilty, so your minds should be corrupted from the simplicity that is in Christ.'"

Bill was tired. His head ached, and the dull throb in his legs threatened to overcome the calming veil of the laudanum. He drew the long pistol and pointed it at Tarami's belly. "You've been warned, suh. Fly to your Basilica and preach all you like there, but not another word on this spot. And know this: I am watching you. Stick to talk of anointings and burials, and say nothing about who should rule."

Zadok Tarami left the plaza with long, purposeful strides.

Sarah stood with her advisors at the base of the western Treewall. The sun was setting, and the deep shadows the wall cast over this side of the city hid the fire damage from the first night of the beastkind's rampage. She wore her dragoon's coat again against the chill, and Thalanes's shoulder bag.

"I'm not fleeing," she said. "I'm not abandoning you or the city."

"No one thinks you are," Alzbieta answered immediately.

The others nodded agreement. Sarah looked at them in turn: Maltres Korinn, Yedera the Podebradan, Sherem the Polite, Cathy, Bill, Luman Walters, Montserrat Ferrer i Quintana. With her Eye of Eve, Sarah saw fear and doubt, but none of it directed at Sarah herself.

"We all want to come along," Bill said.

"And we are somewhat concerned about your choice of companions," Cathy added.

"For those who do not know me, my name is Montserrat

Ferrer i Quintana." The Catalan bowed deeply, sweeping her hat. "My family lands lie on the Gulf, in Igbo territory. I have been a pirate and a smuggler for fifteen years, but once I was a true friend of Queen Sarah's mother, Hannah."

"You are a true friend still," Sarah said.

Was that a tear in the corner of the pirate queen's eye?

"I'm Luman Walters." The hedge wizard nodded, his hands in the pockets of his long, bulky overcoat. "I've offered my services to Her Majesty, knowing that as a magician I have at best a little talent."

"Recently in the Imperial service," Cathy observed coolly.

"*I* was once in the Imperial service," Sir William muttered.

"A long time ago," she reminded him. "And you rode with Kyres."

Walters shrugged. "I was recently on the staff of a director of the Imperial Ohio Company. Not for very long. She found me to be insufficiently powerful."

"And how will you be of assistance to Sarah, then?" Sherem pressed the wizard.

Sarah intervened. "Like me, Luman seeks light and knowledge. Initiation. He's familiar with various traditions, and I hope he'll be able to help me interpret whatever information I'm able to gather from my father."

Luman nodded deferentially.

"I could send Chikaak and the beastkind with you," Sir William said. "They could open the road before you, at least."

Sarah smiled at him. "They're needed to defend the wall. Sneaking is our best option here, and to sneak I need the smallest number of companions."

"I am captain of a sailing vessel," Montse said. "The ship, she waits downriver. We will not go very far before we signal *La Verge Caníbal* to pick us up and bring us to the Serpent Mound. I only ask that you care for my crewman, Miquel."

Cathy nodded. "We will."

"And I'll come directly back," Sarah added. "In the meantime, Maltres and I are in touch."

The vizier nodded. He had half a broken slate, enchanted as Sarah had once enchanted and broken a slate she'd sent with Jacob Hop.

"I am familiar with Your Majesty's spells of disguise and

concealment. Will you climb down the wall, as the Catalan came up it?" Cathy asked. "Or should we prepare a volley and open the gate?"

"I have a different idea." Sarah set the Heronplow on the ground, pointing directly into the Treewall, and took the Orb of Etyles into her hands. "Montse, Luman—stand as close to me as you can."

The wizard and the smuggler huddled close.

"There," Alzbieta said. "Now you look properly Firstborn, standing shoulder to shoulder like that."

Sarah gazed into the Treewall. She had chosen this spot deliberately, as it was closest to the Mississippi. That might make it easier to draw power through the Orb. More importantly, it meant they had less distance to go.

She saw the wall's roots with her Eye of Eve, deep in the earth, stretching toward the water. She examined them, looking for the longest, thickest, straightest root she could find.

"I'm not sure what I'm seeing," Cathy said.

"I think I know." Sherem's voice was barely a whisper. "She's looking for a way under the river."

She found it. Several of the largest roots stretched all the way across, in fact. She repositioned the Heronplow slightly.

"We'll be back," she said. "Hold on."

Then she knelt and touched the plow. "*Traductum aperio me occultoque*," she said. Her Priestly Ophidian—an archaic dialect that appeared in scripture and ritual—was still rudimentary. For casting spells, anything she had to do on her feet, Sarah needed to rely on Latin.

But she thought that Priestly Ophidian would give her a closer connection to the goddess. In Her city, especially, that seemed important. It seemed powerful. She aimed to master it as soon as she could.

The thought that Thalanes would approve of her incantation made her smile.

The words meant *I open a tunnel and I hide myself.*

The plow moved forward into the Treewall. Where it touched the base of the wall it split the bark, creating a crack. Pushing deeper into the wood, like a lumberman's wedge, the plow widened the crack and split it upward, until it was as tall as a man and two feet wide.

"Join hands," Sarah said. She took the pirate's hand, Montse took Luman's, and Sarah led them into the crack.

She walked several steps forward, just behind the plow as it opened the passage before them. Looking over her shoulder, she saw Montse and Luman and the rest of her friends in the open air behind them—

and then the crack's entrance closed.

"I'm blinded," Luman said.

"I also," Montse agreed.

Sarah's natural eye saw nothing, but through her Eye of Eve she saw the golden-green plow continue forward, opening the way. She saw the contours of the tunnel around them as faint blue-white lines.

"I can see," she told them. "Trust me, and walk slowly."

Once the crack closed, the inside of the passageway was warm.

They inched their way forward. There were no stairs or sense of descent, but after a dozen steps, Sarah felt the throbbing energy of the Mississippi River overhead. She looked up and saw a faint greenish glow above them. Within the light, she saw the brighter green of torpid fish and sleeping frogs.

Suddenly, she was seized by a terrible fear. The river belonged to the Heron King. In some sense, perhaps, it *was* the Heron King. And now she was daring to cross beneath it.

Had she put herself into his power?

She stopped, and Montse bumped into her.

"What is wrong?" the pirate asked.

The wizard muttered something that sounded like Greek.

"I . . . nothing," Sarah said. She pressed forward again.

She looked about as she walked. Over her shoulder, she could see the blue of the Treewall, and also the blue and white auras of people with her city. Outside the wall, she saw greenish glows and black lights of rampaging beastkind and besieging undead.

She saw the smoking black light of Hooke's spell.

Not Hooke's alone, but Cromwell's.

Had she made a mistake? She'd chosen this underground route rather than, say, flying, because she thought she'd be less visible. But was that a miscalculation?

Too late. She was committed.

Ahead, she saw beastkind, but not many. She saw animals,

but only small ones—rabbits, foxes. Presumably the beastkind had eaten the others.

And she saw when the edge of the Mississippi River drew near and they were about to emerge. "One moment."

They stopped. She knelt and found moist earth on the floor of the tunnel. She took a trace amount of it onto her finger and touched it to each cheek, and then also smudged faint rings around both her nostrils. *"Oculos obscuro et nares obturo."*

She added the piece about plugging noses out of fear that if she didn't, wild beastkind might smell them.

"Redundant in here." Luman Walters chuckled. "We must be about to emerge."

"You speak Latin," Sarah said.

"And a smattering of other languages," he agreed affably. "German, some Greek and Hebrew, a little Haudenosaunee. Lack of language ability isn't what holds me back from becoming a gramarist. It's lack of magical talent."

His voice and aura both took on a tint of sorrow.

"Hold on," Sarah said. "We're about to hit the chill again."

She stepped forward, and the plow suddenly split out a doorway into the open air. Sarah emerged from a mound of earth into a narrow gully thick with tree roots, dead leaves, and muddy snow. She pulled her pirate and her wizard out after her, and then the crack closed behind them.

She picked up the Heronplow and put it away.

"We ought to be invisible," she told them. "Unsmellable too, but stick close, just in case. Montse, we'll follow you. Let's go find your ship."

But how will I sleep? Or will I ever sleep again?

*"Hell's Bells. You have had the revelation,
and you have converted it into mere church."*

———⊷•⊶———

CHAPTER FOURTEEN

Maltres Korinn settled into the corner seat of the common room. For the meeting, he'd chosen a nondescript gray tunic and brown leggings, with an undyed matchcoat to keep out the winter's chill. He also wore a broad-brimmed Pennslander's hat, but he made no attempt to hide his face.

The disguise was that he wasn't wearing black.

Naturally, he'd had to borrow the clothing from one of his servants.

He'd left the staff of office behind and was armed with nothing but a long fighting knife and a loaded flintlock pistol, both hanging from his belt and concealed by the matchcoat.

The tavern was called *Mimir's Well*, and it was famous in the Wallenstein quarter of Cahokia—famous for its rough traffic, catering as it did to riverboatmen and traders, as well as travelers from Waukegan and Chicago. For whatever reason, travelers from Zomas and its sole city of Etzanoa often washed up here as well. They generally arrived by river just like the Germans and the Russians from New Muscovy, despite the fact that it was the southern gate of the city that had once commonly been known as the *Zomas Gate*.

The *Well* was an unsurprising place for a meeting with Gazelem Zomas.

"Wine," Maltres said to the serving girl.

"It's watered seven to one," she said.

If she said *seven* to one, that probably meant it was watered *ten* to one. "An auspicious number. Give me two glasses. I'm meeting a friend."

As Maltres thought the name, the man himself sat down.

"Maltres Korinn," Zomas said. "I'm pleased you're willing to venture down into this part of town. I'd have thought you preferred more high-priced eating establishments."

"You mistake me, hetar." Maltres Korinn sighed. "I would rather eat a slice of cheese from my own goats and baked squash from my own garden."

"And then get back behind your plow and till, like the humble son of the earth you are."

"You mock my ambitions."

"Do I?" Zomas laughed. "And yet, the city has a queen... or a princess, who's acting like a queen... and you're still here. I think if you really, really wanted to sit on a stool among your blackberries and pick the banjo, you would be doing it right now."

"I never said I'd pick the banjo."

"Still." Gazelem frowned. "It's harder to relinquish power than to acquire it, perhaps?"

"Not for me." Maltres leaned forward over the small table between them. "But I *saw*, Gazelem. I truly saw."

A ray of doubt and surprise pierced the clouds of Gazelem's face. "You saw Eden?"

"Unfallen. Eternal. I stood in it, and the goddess chose Sarah."

"And for this you stay?"

"For this I stay. And because I love my people, and I think Sarah Elytharias can benefit from some guidance."

Gazelem shrugged. "Less guidance than I would have imagined."

Maltres smiled. "She's growing on you, as well."

"She's brave," Gazelem said. "She's persistent. I think her heart is good."

Was the poisoner prince from Zomas being sincere?

"She isn't always tactful," Maltres said.

"That's true," Gazelem agreed. "But listen... my homeland is under siege. I understand that it's hard to have the beastkind rampaging on your doorstep, as Cahokia does, but they are ravaging *within* Zomas. Every teaspoon of blessing we ever had from building Etzanoa so close to the palaces of the Heron King, we are now paying out in a gallon of blood."

"Etzanoa still stands?"

"Etzanoa stands. The sons of Zomas sow their blood, and I pray the seed sprouts in a crop of dragons." Gazelem sighed. "I would happily come to her aid, if I could. But I think if she could free herself from the forces surrounding her, queen Sarah Elytharias would also come to the aid of Zomas. If she were to become empress, she might come to Zomas at the head of a very large army, indeed."

"Have you considered seeking aid from Lord Thomas and the Empire?"

Maltres watched Gazelem's face closely, though trying himself to appear nonchalant. The Zoman princeling's gaze faltered at the mention of Thomas Penn, and then he looked back at Maltres.

"We aren't exactly allies. Thomas Penn will one day have interest in Zomas," Gazelem said. "When he has crushed the Ohio, consolidated power by doing away with Franklin's Compact, and is looking for his next conquest...there lies Zomas. Her land is more fertile than Texia, her children are less savage than the Free Horse Peoples, her skies are clearer than those over the muddy bogs of the Misaabe, and her summers are longer than those of the frozen north. I believe we would be next."

Might that belief push Gazelem into the arms of Thomas Penn?
The wine arrived.

"I believe you would, too," Maltres said. "Gazelem, I need your help. The city needs your help."

"I can't commit my household troops to the wall, Korinn," Gazelem said. "I already gave you my wizard. I get too many hard looks on the street, and I need them to protect my house from looters. And before you start...it's different, being an outsider. Being Zoman. I get spat on in the street when I don't have my guard."

"I understand." If it came to it, Maltres would requisition Gazelem's small platoon of troops by force. They wore Zomas's queer wooden armor, but they were ferocious fighters. "But it's because you have soldiers...private soldiers...that I need your help."

"Some suicide mission beyond the Treewall? How romantic." Gazelem snorted. "The young prince on the distaff side tried and failed to save his own country, despite his exile. Then, permanently committed to an ideology of Quixotism, he died in a suicide charge on an Imperial trench. Here I had rather hoped that your messengers might actually bring help."

Maltres sipped his wine and changed his guess at the watering ratio from ten to one to twelve to one. He made a mental note to send wardens around to talk with the owner. "I have the same hope. But I have a more urgent problem. Queen Sarah tonight wishes to attempt to contact the goddess."

Gazelem sat upright. "For power? For information? As a symbol?"

"All of the above. And she needs protection. We fear spies and assassins."

"She has the wardens. And her beastmen."

"Her soldiers will be on the wall. Also, there will be a decoy."

A sly smile crept onto Gazelem Zomas's face. "Your decoy queen will be surrounded by wardens, and you wish me and my men to protect the real one. Because we will be less conspicuous."

Maltres finished his cup. "Are you willing?"

Gazelem hesitated. "I should name a price, for the sake of my image. And to extract some vengeance on you for the debacle of the solstice presentation."

"I have little to give. But you can ask."

Gazelem shook his head. "No price. I'll do what you ask. I'll hope that Queen Sarah remembers this service when she comes completely to her throne and I beg for aid on behalf of my country."

"Tonight at sunset. At Alzbieta Torias's residence." Maltres extended his hand and they shook. "Keep your men out of uniform."

He left *Mimir's Well* directly. As he walked out the door he looked back to see Gazelem Zomas staring into his winecup and swirling its contents reflectively.

He had two suspects. Someone had betrayed Cahokia. Someone was passing information to the Imperial forces besieging the city. It could be anyone, but to Maltres Korinn, two men seemed the most likely culprits. Two men who had contributed household magicians to the effort on the wall and therefore knew about the plan to send messengers for aid. Two men who were, or had been, Sarah's rivals, and had desired the Serpent Throne for themselves.

Maltres would test both possibilities.

He had told Sarah, through the enchanted writing slate of which each of them bore half, that he believed they had been betrayed, that he had two suspects, and that he was going to test the possibilities. She had concurred. She hadn't asked who the suspects were.

He made his way directly to his second arranged meeting. This was beside an *actual* well—there was some irony in that, Maltres thought—in the center of a plaza on the northern side of the city. On the way, he bought an empty gourd from a streetside stall whose owner's face brightened so much at the sale that Maltres was sad he couldn't reveal his identity.

Voldrich had similarly disguised himself for the meeting. He wore a patched wool cloak over layers of rough and frayed cotton. He must have borrowed clothing from an employee or a dependent of some kind.

Voldrich's disguise was poverty.

They stood beside the well and pretended to be strangers, engaging in small talk as Voldrich lowered the bucket.

"Voldrich, I need your help," Maltres said. "The city needs your help. Your help and the assistance of your household troops."

"Of course, I'm happy to do anything my city asks," Voldrich said.

Maltres heard the distant *splash* of the bucket hitting water.

"The first Daughters of Podebradas took their vows in the year after Adela was executed by her former husband," Yedera said. It was the most Cathy had ever heard her say, and Cathy herself had prompted it by asking what it meant to be a Podebradan.

Cathy had acquired Yedera as a companion by telling Alzbieta she was going to listen to the preaching at the Basilica. Ostensibly, she'd communicated her intentions to be responsible, to coordinate with the other members of Sarah's party.

Had she also, though, wanted to tweak the priestess's nose? Perhaps.

As they trudged up the steps to the Basilica in the chilly afternoon, they talked.

"Was there a founder? Other than Queen Adela, I mean?"

Yedera shook her head. "No founder, no rule, no organization, no property."

"You're not a nun?" Cathy regarded herself as well-versed in the ecclesiastical organizations of the children of Eve, but of the Firstborn she knew little.

"Does that surprise you?" Yedera smiled. "Did I give the impression of being a nun?"

Cathy chuckled. "No, more like a knight. Like one of the Knights of St. John, or the Swords of Wisdom. But knights have rules, and vows, and orders."

"I have made vows," Yedera said.

"If there's no organization, to whom did you make them?"

"To Mother Adela. To be a Podebradan is a personal vocation, inspired by Queen Adela Podebradas and her life and works. There have been Podebradan poets and singers, mapmakers, architects, magicians, and so on."

"But you're a warrior. Maybe something like the warrior version of a Cetean nun."

Yedera shrugged. "I'm a warrior."

"What stops me from declaring that I'm a Daughter of Podebradas, too?"

"Nothing." Yedera adjusted her scale mail. Despite its obvious weight, she didn't seem to be breaking a sweat on the climb. "The first Podebradan was a poet. His name was Ondres the Blind, and he wrote a song called *The Funeral Lay of Adela*. In the song, he dedicated himself to his people and to his lost queen. Most Podebradans build their oaths and model their commitments on the words Ondres the Blind sang."

"So Ondres was your founder, in a way. Only I thought St. Adela Podebradas had *daughters*."

"He called himself an Unborn Daughter. Many men have done so since."

"Will you share with me your vows?" As they approached the top of the Basilica Mound, they heard the rumbling of many voices. Cathy saw the backs of people standing near the top, watching the Basilica itself.

"No."

"You swore an oath to Sarah, back in Chester."

"On the Sevenfold Crown. I haven't forgotten."

"What if your two vows conflict?"

"Then I believe the power of the Crown will compel me to keep the latter oath."

"And what will that mean?"

Yedera stopped walking and laughed. "I'm not some fairy tale creature, Cathy Filmer. I won't cease to exist if I break my vow. I have no magical powers that depend on my vows. I have no order to be ejected from. I have no sacred penalties hanging over my head. I'm a warrior, and my skill comes from long years of fighting and longer years of training. If I'm forced to break my Podebradan vow, I will be *disappointed*. Then I will recommit myself, and I will move on. But I don't think such a conflict will arise."

"Why is that?"

"Because my commitments are to first, the Elytharias family, second, the people of Cahokia, and third, the children of Wisdom."

"You resisted Sarah at first."

"I didn't believe her claims. I have come to see their rightness."

"And having made those three commitments, you hold yourself outside other rules."

"No bond can hold me but love of the queen," Yedera said. "Yes. That is the essence of being an Unborn Daughter. I bring about a world Adela Podebradas would want, in her honor and memory."

"What moves a person to become a Podebradan?" Cathy asked. "I was educated by the Sisters of St. William Harvey myself, but that was really a decision my parents made. They had enough children to run the farm, and wanted me to develop medical skills to be able to tend to the injured and help birth cattle."

"I was born on a farm, too," Yedera said quietly. "In the Missouri, closer to Etzanoa than to Cahokia. My family raised horses in addition to growing grain. One night, on a full moon, a Comanche raiding party attacked us. They killed my father and my brothers. My sister and my mother and I were captured, along with the horses."

"I'm so sorry," Cathy said.

"They treated the horses better than they treated us. My sister slit her own throat after three days. My mother asked to bury her daughter. In answer they beat her severely, then tied her wrists and made her run behind one of the horses. When she could run no more, she fell and was dragged to her death."

Cathy felt sick. All she could do was shake her head.

"Both my mother and my sister were left to be eaten by vultures. I lived. I was adopted, and I lived for three years with a

Comanche war band. I learned to speak Comanche, and to ride, and to fight."

"Do you still speak Comanche?"

"A little. In summers, when the moon was full, the men would ride to the Cotton Princedoms, Louisiana, Texia, and New Spain to take plunder and slaves. They sold the slaves to Memphis and to Zomas, which brought the tribe most of their wealth. Me they kept, though...not for reasons of kindness."

Yedera told her tale dispassionately, but Cathy knew what rape and intimidation and beating were like. She struggled to hold in tears. "How did you escape?"

"I didn't. That's the point. One full moon, the war band was on its way back from a slave-taking raid when it was ambushed by the Lion of Missouri. He had declared a personal war on the slave trade. He had even threatened to start burning Memphite barges on the Mississippi if they didn't stop buying slaves. He and his men killed the entire war band and then rode into camp. They gave the old men, women, and children who hadn't ridden south fair warning that they would attack the next day unless the tribe released every slave it had."

"Kyres Elytharias freed you."

"I rode to Cahokia on the back of his very horse. I was a girl then, so I dreamed he was carrying me off to marry me. I dreamed it so hard, I convinced myself it was true. I recovered in his home, imagining I was preparing for my wedding. And then two weeks later, it was announced that he was marrying the Empress Hannah."

Cathy chuckled. "That must have been a disappointment."

"I was young." Yedera snorted. "I got over it."

"*Did* you?"

Yedera was silent awhile. "No. No, really, I didn't. When Kyres rode to Philadelphia, I moved into the household of his cousin, Alzbieta Torias. It was there I first read *The Funeral Lay of Adela*. On a night when there was no moon, I climbed onto Alzbieta's roof to face Cassiopeia and sing to her my vows."

"Cassiopeia...were you making vows to the goddess, or to St. Adela?"

"The difference between those two is reasonably clear in my mind. It isn't always very clear in my heart."

"When did you tell Alzbieta?"

"She heard me in the act. I didn't see her until after I had finished singing, but she was on the roof, performing her liturgy for the dark of the moon. She could have laughed at me, but she took me seriously instead. I think she knew I was partly acting out of infatuation with the Lion, maybe because she felt that way herself, and she thought my interest in Mother Adela would pass."

"It didn't."

"I keep my vows."

Cathy hesitated. "I want to hear what's going on above us," she said slowly. "But I want you to know that I honor your life. Thank you for telling me about yourself. And about Mother Adela."

Yedera nodded, and they finished the climb.

Zadok Tarami sat cross-legged in the Basilica's open front door, beneath a cloister of white doves and surrounded by people. Cathy and Yedera pushed their way through the crowd to see the priest. His face was smeared with ash; looking around at the crowd gathered about the Metropolitan, Cathy saw ash on many of their faces, too.

"Should we rise up, Father Tarami?" asked a burly young man in a leather jerkin. "Should we burn the Temple of the Sun?"

"No violence," Zadok said.

"Not against another Cahokian!" added a woman in the front row.

"She's no Cahokian," grumbled a thin man standing right inside the door. "She isn't even properly Firstborn."

"No violence at all," Zadok said.

"But the witch wants to make herself queen!"

"I have no view on who should be king or queen of this land," Zadok said. "I support the Regent-Minister."

"You snake." Cathy hadn't meant to speak, she had come just to see what Tarami was doing and saying to his people. Nevertheless, she felt she had to. "If you tell your people you have no view, it can only mean you don't endorse Sarah Elytharias! It can only mean you're waiting for someone else to present herself... or maybe *himself*. Do you think maybe you should be king, Zadok?"

Zadok turned his eyes on her calmly. "No. I do not wish to be king."

"No, of course not." Cathy crossed her arms over her chest. "Why would you want to be king, when you can hold court just as you are?"

"Why do you think this concerns you, daughter of Eve?" Zadok smiled peaceably, but he showed his teeth.

Several voices in the crowd murmured approval.

Cathy ignored them and barged ahead. "For that matter, when you say you support the Regent-Minister, you're neglecting the fact that he doesn't use that title anymore. He goes by *Vizier*, now, meaning the right-hand man to the queen. If you really supported him, you'd accept the queen as he does. Except that what you really mean is that you support him *as* Regent-Minister, with an empty throne and more power for the Metropolitan and the Basilica to grab."

"I have already said I don't wish to be king." Zadok smiled as he spoke, and damned if he didn't sound sincere.

"And your people here are threatening to destroy the throne itself!"

"I said no violence." Zadok looked around at the crowd, meeting their gazes sternly. "Did everyone hear me? I said no violence against any person, except as needed to defend our home."

"Neat," Cathy said. "You say 'except as needed to defend our home,' and that could mean you advocate fighting against the Imperials...but it could also mean you think Sarah is attacking your homes, and that violence in defense would be acceptable."

Zadok Tarami took a deep breath. "You would have me a sophist and a liar. But I am not the one twisting words here. I'm no lawyer, to build a great case on a distinction of language invisible to everyone else."

"Do you accept Sarah Elytharias as your rightful queen?" Cathy asked.

"She hasn't been crowned by anyone," Tarami protested. "She *isn't* queen."

Yedera interrupted. "Everyone here—everyone not out wandering around the Ohio while the city was being besieged—felt the goddess choose Sarah Elytharias as Her Beloved as the sun dawned on the shortest day of the year. Do you deny that, priest?"

"I dispute nearly every word you've just said, child. I wasn't wandering, I was traveling the Onandagos Road, following the sun on my knees through the deeds of the great prophet toward the site of the serpent's imprisonment. Everyone who belongs to the city felt a great feeling of benevolence toward Sarah that morning, it's true, but that's all. I believe that feeling was in response to our many prayers for deliverance. Do I believe Sarah Elytharias has come to benefit the land? Yes. Do I believe she will be queen? That remains to be seen. Do I believe in your goddess? No, I do not, and neither do these good people. The serpent was an ancient demon that plagued this people until Onandagos put the beast down. If it is the serpent that has chosen Sarah Elytharias for her own—and that might be true, based on the pagan funeral liturgy I witnessed yesterday—then we must beware her, indeed."

"When was there ever a son without a mother?" Yedera snapped.

Zadok pointed at Yedera's weapons. "Are they handing out falchions at divinity school now?"

"I've read the same books as you, Metropolitan," Yedera snarled.

"When was there ever a mother who remained a virgin?" Zadok shrugged. "And yet that is what we read in the gospels."

"Mary didn't push a child out her birth canal and remain a virgin!" Yedera was nearly yelling. It was necessary, given the loud grumbling of the crowd. "What kind of pointless, nonsensical miracle would that be?"

"No more pointless than the Lord's cursing of the fig tree, and yet there it is!" Zadok was red in the face. "We do not believe because we can explain everything, we believe because we read, and because God speaks the truth into our hearts!"

"She was the Virgin because the goddess was with her!" Yedera cried. "You want to talk about what we read, priest? How about the words of Mary herself, 'Behold the Handmaid'!"

"The handmaid of the Lord!" Zadok's voice was more shrill the louder he got. "Not the handmaid of the goddess!"

"That's the same thing!"

"If I say, 'I am your servant,' is that a claim to priesthood?"

"If you say it to me, no!" Cathy half-expected Yedera to draw her scimitar and cut the priest to bits. "But if you say it to a god— or a goddess—then *yes!* What is a priest, but a servant to a deity?"

"Yes, and I serve the god of Heaven!" Zadok lurched to his feet. He flailed a finger in Yedera's direction as his beard whipped about him in the winter wind. "So do not come to me asking for the endorsement of a demon's disciple!"

Yedera abruptly calmed, as if her energy had all been deliberately assumed, as a provocation. "Sarah is no demon's disciple. She is the daughter of Kyres Elytharias, the Lion of Missouri. She is the Beloved of my goddess. I know, because I heard the angel choir. You heard it too, if only in your heart. If anyone can save this city, I believe it is she.

"And will you or nil you, Sarah Elytharias will be queen."

The crowd stared, stunned. Zadok's mouth moved, but no words came out.

Yedera turned and marched back down the mound. Cathy nearly had to run to keep up.

Bill waited behind the bead curtain, leaning on his crutch and controlling his breathing so as not to be noticed. He stood in one of the side passages built into the long wall along the nave of the Temple of the Sun. The curtain separated him from the nave, which was presently dark, but for a faint glow that diffused in through the open door from the stars above and the city below.

Where Bill stood, stairs led up and down. He believed that the rooftop was an astronomical observatory, and that beneath the temple were storerooms and also living quarters for the priestesses. Apparently, many of them didn't live in the city and only came here for the purpose of fulfilling their service. While they did so, they slept beneath their goddess.

Sarah had taken to sleeping beneath the temple, as well.

Bill carried four pistols, loaded and primed, two of them his long horse pistols from his days as a dragoon. Cathy, beside him, also held two pistols. Hers were the Lafitte pistols, taken from above the altar in the St. Louis Cathedral in New Orleans. She had pronounced them especially suited to the setting when she had declared her intention to participate, and Bill had had to agree. He had also been unable to dissuade her.

Bill himself had also insisted on participating when Maltres Korinn had set forth his plan. Korinn had insisted that he needed more mobile forces, and Bill had promptly rearranged their schedules to free up Sarah's entire platoon of beastkind warriors. They crouched in hiding now, preparing to leap into action at the right moment. The only reason the Great Mound's ravens were not sending up an unholy objection at this very moment was that it was nighttime, and the birds were too sleepy.

Bill's thighs hurt. He took a slug of his cherry brandy to be sure.

And then another to be more sure. He might have to run.

Also, the second slug was the one that deadened his heart when he thought of Charles.

"Are you not going to offer a lady a drink?" Cathy asked.

She didn't know about his laudanum. But she would almost certainly taste it if he gave her the flask. Surely, as a Harvite initiate, she had studied the stuff.

"My lady," he said, "This is too rough a cordial for a person of your refinement. Pray let me find you a better vintage, once we have concluded the evening's entertainment."

In the darkness, he couldn't see her expression, but she said nothing.

He wrapped an arm around her and drew her body to him. She would smell the laudanum on his breath or taste it on his kisses, too, so he satisfied himself with a one-armed embrace.

A shorter man might have found himself reaching up to embrace Long Cathy. Bill delighted in her height.

"And when the season's entertainment is done, let us be married." He said it on impulse, but immediately knew it was right. If Bill's wife was not dead, she had long since assumed he *was* and moved on.

"Is that a formal proposal?" Cathy asked.

"No," Bill said quickly. "The formal proposal will be more elaborate. Heralds, fireworks, fountains, a masquerade ball, things of that nature. Or at least something more prepared than a fumbled embrace in the dark."

"I rather like the fumbled embracing in the dark, Bill," Cathy cooed. "It makes me feel young again."

"What does *again* mean in that sentence, my nymph?" Bill squeezed her again. It made him feel younger, too. Too young to have a murdered son.

Dammit.

"Stop trying to distract me, General." Cathy eased out of his grip. "I believe I see lights."

She was right. They each readied a pistol as torches came through the front door and into the nave. Bill counted eight men in dark cloaks and a ninth in red velvet. With them were three young women who lay aside gray cloaks and were wearing long white linen tunics.

"Youins are most kind to think on our safety this evenin'," the young woman in the center said. She had Sarah's face and voice, though her Appalachee twang was overstated.

"She plays the Cracker too hard," Bill whispered.

"She plays it as one for whom it is mostly an imagined accent," Cathy whispered back. "Voldrich is also unlikely to have spent much time in Appalachee."

"Your Majesty." The man in red velvet, Voldrich, bowed. "It is my pleasure to serve my people."

"I doubt it's him," Bill said. "The other fellow looked like an evil star incarnate. This man is merely wealthy."

"Iffen you don't mind watchin' the door, then, I'll commence the ritual."

The priestesses were all volunteers. Bill respected their courage. The same Polite who had hexed Sarah's face onto the priestess that most closely approximated her size and frame had also hexed into invisibility the door through which Bill and Cathy now looked, as well as an identical opening opposite.

Two of Voldrich's men paced down the nave and back. Others stood in the main entrance and looked out. False-Sarah knelt and faced the Serpent Throne, a barely visible bulk in the gloomy apse, and began chanting.

Was it gibberish, or was she reciting some real Ophidian text?

The two adjutant priestesses knelt to either side of False-Sarah and faced the apse with her. If all went well, they'd kneel on the stone for fifteen minutes, pronounce the magic inconclusive, and walk away.

Voldrich stood two paces behind False-Sarah, two men to either side of him. They watched the apse. Bill wished he could see the expressions on their faces. Hopeful? Fearful?

All five men slowly put on gloves.

"Bill," Cathy said. "I believe we're about to see action."

The priestesses' chant droned on.

The men reached into pouches at their belts and filled their hands with something. "I don't see a weapon," Bill said.

The men leaped forward. Three of them fell on False-Sarah, slapping something into her flesh. The priestess in disguise as her Beloved shrieked sharply, and then fell silent. The other two priestesses merited one attacker each. Again, the men pressed unseen objects to the women's flesh, and then the five men trussed the three women up with cords.

"Is this her?" Voldrich asked his men. "Bring the torch over her. I can't see."

A torch was brought, and Voldrich cursed.

"Serpent's tooth, it's not her!"

"It looked like her," one of his men said. "I would have sworn."

"Of course it did!" Voldrich snapped. "That was gramarye, you idiot! The silver we touched to her skin ended her illusion." As he spoke, Voldrich headed for the exit. "This is a trick. Out of here, all of you!"

As the first of Voldrich's men exited the main door, Bill stepped through the beads and fired a pistol.

Bang!

That was the signal. Outside, Oriot, Chikaak, and every other beastman soldier who could fit had hidden crouched on the stylized vine above the door. Given Bill's signal as Voldrich's men exited the building, the beastkind dropped on top of them and attacked.

They were treating the Temple of the Sun in a deeply profane manner. Bill hoped the goddess would forgive him.

The use of a pistol shot as a signal had two virtues. One, it was loud. And two, Bill hadn't fired at the air. He'd shot one of Voldrich's men. The fellow fell to the floor, clutching his side and screaming.

"This way!" Voldrich shrieked to his own men. "There's a door over here!" He turned and bolted to the bead-filled doorway opposite the one where Bill and Cathy had waited. The wall on that side looked like uninterrupted stone and tile, but when Voldrich slapped his silver-filled hand to it, the camouflaged door appeared.

The three remaining inside with Voldrich grabbed False-Sarah and dragged her with them toward the door. They were not especially expert, carrying her to one side rather than as an effective shield.

Bang!

Bill's shot went high, a disappointing error in marksmanship that nevertheless had a satisfactory conclusion as a second man fell to the ground, shot through the head.

Then the two uninjured men followed Voldrich into the doorway.

Bill lumbered across the room. "Hell's Bells!" Lightning struck his legs with each step, despite the laudanum. Passing the first injured man, Bill took a moment to club him in the face with his crutch. The man tried to draw a sword to parry, but didn't get the weapon out in time.

Bill shot a glance out the main doorway and was satisfied to see Chikaak and the others pressing Voldrich's men hard. The fight would last no more than a few minutes.

Still, that meant Bill faced a few minutes without aid. "Cathy!" He continued his dogged run.

Cathy was nowhere to be seen.

Bill had two shots, a heavy wooden crutch, and his cavalry saber. So far, Voldrich's men didn't seem to have firearms. To reload, Bill would need to stop.

Of course, Voldrich's men had no idea how many guns he had.

The bead-blocked doorway loomed large before Bill. If one of the Firstborn warriors waited inside with his sword planted, Bill might impale himself with no effort on their part.

"Damn me," he muttered. Pulling a long horse pistol, he fired into the dark doorway, then hurled himself through.

No one stabbed him immediately. Here too were stairs up and down. Down lay darkness and silence. Up, Bill saw faint starlight partly blocked by the shadows of running men.

The rooftop. Would they jump down? Or had they some mechanism to fly, such as he had experienced with Queen Sarah, leaving New Orleans?

In any case, they had rope.

"Chikaak!" he yelled. "The roof!"

Had the beastman heard him? Bill had no time to wait. Cursing, he threw himself up the stairs.

His legs felt as if they would snap off. Maltres Korinn had given in to Bill's insistence that he participate, but had assigned Bill to the target he thought most likely to be innocent, and had also put him in the location where the target would have less ability to run.

They had underestimated Voldrich.

As he stumbled to the rooftop, Bill took his crutch up into his left hand and his last unfired pistol into his right. A dark shape leaped toward him—

bang!

Bill fired and swung his hard stick at the same time. The attacker's sword grazed Bill's leg, but did little damage. The man fell to the rooftop. Bill smashed his stick down three times, striking tile, then tile, then flesh.

The man's throat.

The scream became a gurgling choke. The former attacker rolled over and crawled away from both his sword and Bill.

The rooftop was a flat rectangle with a low wall around the outside. If it was an observatory, the tools escaped Bill's notice. Cold wind bit Bill's face. From here, the highest point for many miles around, he saw the few and small nighttime fires of Cahokia—wood couldn't be brought into the city any more than food could—and the many and large fires of the surrounding Imperial forces.

Voldrich and his one henchman still standing were near the wall. The henchman held the captive priestess to his chest, protecting his body, and pressed the blade of a long, straight sword to her throat.

In the moonlight, Bill could see the girl's face. She wasn't crying. She had welts like Sarah had had when Maltres Korinn had rescued her from Cromwell by slapping silver all over her body, but she was calm.

Indeed, she was smiling.

Voldrich had tied a rope around some feature of the wall Bill couldn't make out—a crenellation or a knob of some kind—and was throwing the cord down to the plaza. Where were Bill's beastkind? If they were still distracted fighting Voldrich's men, then the traitor might get away.

"Stop there!" Voldrich called to Bill.

Bang!

Bill was surprised by the shot, and even more by the source. Cathy stood a few steps behind Voldrich and his man—she must have come up the other staircase. And she had shot the henchman right through his skull.

He dropped.

"That's no way to treat a lady," Cathy said.

Voldrich raised a leg to climb over the wall—

bang!

Cathy shot the Firstborn with her other pistol. He dropped to the rooftop, cursing. Cathy and Bill both approached.

In the moonlight, Bill saw dark blood on Voldrich's thigh. "Well-aimed, my lady."

"Might I suggest that I reload my pistols while you take the opportunity to beat this man a little."

"I am hesitant to compare myself to the Redeemer," Bill said, "and I believe in the event that He made use of a whip. Still, I am holding a stout staff, and here lies a changer of money who deserves to be driven out of the temple."

Voldrich shrank back and Bill cracked the man with the stick in the ankle. Voldrich screamed. The crunch was loud enough that Bill doubted the man would be jumping up to run away.

He leaned on the crutch. "Keep an eye out for his servants, my lady," he said to Cathy. To Voldrich, he said, "And you, suh. Commence your confession."

"The people will starve!" Voldrich barked. "What is there to confess? I'd have been a hero if you hadn't stopped me!"

"There may be times," Bill said, "when the line between a kidnapper and a hero is a fine one. Tonight is not one of those times. Besides, we have days of food in store, thanks to Queen Sarah. Perhaps weeks. I wonder whether you were not more concerned with your land. Is not much of that land outside the wall yours?"

Voldrich grunted, but said nothing.

"I will take that as a yes. And so you thought to turn Sarah over to her loving uncle in exchange for what? An end to the Pacification? No, I think not, not from a man like you. I think you would ask only that your lands be free of soldiers, or that you be given land elsewhere in exchange. Or perhaps you promised that you would open the gates, invite Imperials to all the meetings, and comply in all respects with the terms of the Pacification if only Tommy Penn would make you King of Cahokia. Am I right?"

"She's not the queen," Voldrich snarled. "She's not even Cahokian. She's only a half-breed usurper."

"I've heard this tune before," Bill mused. "Only it was in the key of Pennslander. You're saying you don't merit punishment?"

"Or in the worst case, a mere slap."

Cathy pressed two loaded pistols into Bill's hands.

"Thank you, my lady," he said.

"You're welcome, my lord." She smiled at him and the pain in his legs vanished. "If I might take the liberty of doing the same with your pistols?" She took his smaller flintlocks, which were the same caliber as the Lafitte guns, and went to work.

"You were saying," Bill mused. "A slap. And yet in addition to attempting to kidnap the goddess's Beloved—I am no jurist, but it is my understanding that generally a man may be convicted and even hanged of *attempting* to do a thing, no matter how egregious his *failure*. Attempted murderers hang. Why not attempted kidnappers? In addition to that, you have assaulted three of Her priestesses. Even if the ablest lawyer in the Cahokian Bottom were to get you off without legal consequence... do you not fear your own goddess, man?"

Voldrich shook his head. "I don't know that Sarah Penn is the goddess's Beloved. I woke up feeling good about Sarah a few weeks ago, but that feeling has faded. I don't know what it was. Maybe it was a spell."

"Maybe it was a spell?" Bill considered shooting the Firstborn on the spot, but held back. "Who suggested that to you?"

Voldrich said nothing.

"Zadok," Bill said. "Hell's Bells. You have had the revelation, and you have converted it into mere church."

*"Don't you go taking liberties, though.
I'm in a vulnerable state."*

———⇌•⇀⇐———

CHAPTER FIFTEEN

Nathaniel opened his eyes to light that was far too bright. Dark curtains were closed over the tall window, but where daylight came in through a crack between the drapes it was blindingly white and had a shimmering halo.

His head hurt. His shoulder hurt worse.

His closed his eyes again, but not before catching a glimpse of Jacob Hop and his sister Margaret, both dressed in black and looking like a Republican meneer and mevrouw.

"What happened?" His mouth was so dry, his cheeks rasped over gritty teeth as he spoke. His tongue tasted of old blood.

"Ezekiel Angleton attacked you," Jake said.

"The Yankee? The sorcerer Ma'iingan called a *wiindigoo?*"

"He cut your shoulder with his sword," Margaret said. "Ambroos and Lotte have been taking care of you."

"Mostly Lotte," Jake said. "Ambroos is a good fellow, but his best skill was always talking."

"Hey now." This was Ambroos. Nathaniel cracked an eyelid and saw Jake's cousin standing in the door. "If you want me to show you the way out, you better be nice to me."

Nathaniel forced himself up into a sitting position. The effort split his head in two. "Way out? Aren't we at your house, Ambroos?" He recognized the tall white plaster walls and the painting on the wall. He was pretty sure it was a picture of John the Baptist and

Salome, just before she had his head cut off. In the background, there were two men, one holding a platter and the other a large axe, but John was dressed like a Dutch burgher. Like Jake and Ambroos, in fact. Salome was dressed like a harem girl from the Caliphate, with a gauzy blouse and pantaloons supplemented by a girdle of large gold coins.

He'd never seen such a painting in Johnsland.

"Ja, natuurlijk," Ambroos said. "Only the front door is not available right now."

"I need to heal," Nathaniel said. "I think... Jake, if you'll help me, I think I can fix my head in an hour or so."

"I'm afraid we don't have time." Jake's expression was concerned. "Can you do something to ease your pain a bit now, and then later, once we get you aboard ship, do the rest?"

"The house is being watched by Imperials," Margaret said. She didn't look troubled by the information. "Soldiers from the local garrison."

Nathaniel pushed himself to his feet and headed for the window, but Jake intercepted him. "Whoa, Nathaniel. The house is watched, front and back. You don't want to be seen."

"Front and back? What way out *is* there, then?" Nathaniel asked. "Jake tells me my sister Sarah can fly and turn people invisible, but I can't do any of those things. I'm a healer." He felt he might vomit and sat down on the bed, taking deep breaths.

"There are only twelve of them," Margaret said. "I can deal with them."

"I don't see your hair standing on end." Ambroos said it as a joke, but he looked uncomfortable at his own words.

"If I walk out there and they try to arrest me, my hair will stand up soon enough."

"This is my fault," Jake said. "I contacted Temple Franklin in town. He's a sort of advisor to the emperor, but I thought... well, I had a message, and I thought it was for him. Apparently, it wasn't. And I think he found out where I was staying."

"Don't worry," Ambroos said. "This is a Dutch house, and it has a Dutch doorway."

Nathaniel laughed; the laughter made his temples throb, and he massaged them. Under his breath he hummed a tune, and that took the sharpest edge off the pain. "I thought that meant a secret passage, for smugglers."

"It does." Ambroos grinned. "And before you ask, no, I'm not a smuggler. But since you know about Dutch doorways, maybe you've also heard this about us Dutch: one Dutchman, a preacher; two Dutchmen, a church; three Dutchmen, a schism."

"I thought that meant you're quarrelsome about religion," Margaret said. "You have lots of little churches, instead of one big one."

"You could say that we're *quarrelsome*, or you could say that we permit every person *liberty of conscience*. But yes," Ambroos agreed, "you're right. Lots of little churches. And so a Dutch doorway is useful for more than just smuggling in unstamped tobacco. It's also good for getting an unpopular preacher in or out of a house."

"Do all the houses of New Amsterdam have Dutch doorways?" Nathaniel asked.

"No," Ambroos said. "But this one does. It used to belong to a smuggler, and the Dutch doorway is one reason I bought it. I knew I'd be holding house meetings here, and I wanted the option of a discreet entrance or exit."

"Do we have to go now?" Nathaniel stood, testing his legs. They wobbled, but held.

"I have arranged passage on a ship." Ambroos smiled. "You see, in addition to being a preacher, I am a director of the Dutch Ohio Company. I have many uses. The ship sails in two hours. That gives you enough time, but not a very large margin for delays."

"I can walk." Nathaniel proved it by walking to the door and shrugging into his long coat, which hung on a peg in the wall. Some well-meaning person had turned the coat rightside-out, so Nathaniel reversed it. Taking his hat from another peg, he settled it backward onto his head.

With his coat and hat in place, the pain lessened considerably.

Then he took his drum from the corner of the room and shrugged under its shoulderstrap. The pain was almost gone. He took a deep breath.

"Yes, you can," Margaret said.

"You won't have to walk far," Ambroos said. "I have a carriage waiting."

They went downstairs. As they passed the kitchen, Lotte handed Ambroos a lit lantern.

Nathaniel thought her glance at Jake looked hard, and maybe resentful.

The walls of Ambroos's basement were of red brick. When

he depressed an innocuous-looking brick in one corner, a section of wall swung inward without a sound, revealing the dark mouth of a passageway.

Ambroos handed the lantern to Jake.

"I'm not saying don't come back," the preacher said to his cousin.

"Ja, I understand," Jake said. "But don't come back for a while."

"She knows it wasn't you."

"Only it *was* me," Jake said. "The Heron King isn't in me. Sarah would see him if he were. But the person he left behind is . . . not stable."

They walked together down a long, brick-lined passage. At its end, Ambroos looked through a peephole and then pulled open a door using an iron handle. The exit opened in an alleyway between two buildings. No windows looked down on the door; at the mouth of the alley, partly veiled by a curtain of falling snow, was a black carriage.

"We'll leave tracks in the snow," Jake said.

Ambroos nodded. "I'll tramp up and down the alley a bit to hide them. And then the new snow will do the rest. The carriage will take you to the ship. She's named *De Zomerwolf,* and her captain is Janssen. They're sailing to Miami."

"Perfect," Jake said. "From there we'll find another ship."

Ambroos hugged Jake, and then shook hands with both Margaret and Nathaniel. "Travel safely."

Nathaniel took long steps to the carriage, conscious of the tracks he was leaving. The carriage was black and sober, with waxed paper curtains that pulled down off a bar hanging over each window. The curtains were already shut, so when Nathaniel scooted across the leather seats, he pushed one sheet aside a fraction of an inch to be able to see where they were going.

With Margaret and Jake aboard, Ambroos shut the door and called to the driver in Dutch. The carriage rolled forward.

Nathaniel saw tall, stone-faced Dutch houses, and two broad streets crossing. Then he saw the houses facing Ambroos's. There were indeed Imperial soldiers. They had lit a fire in a portable iron stove and stood around it in the snow, warming their hands and staring at the preacher's house.

Nathaniel let the curtain drop back into place. "You've succeeded, Jake," he said.

Jake jerked when he heard his name, as if snapping out of some gripping memory. Nathaniel heard the faintest hint of a distant scream. Hop took a deep breath, and then plunged a hand into a jacket pocket. Pulling a deck of Tarocks out, he commenced thumbing through them and looking at their images.

"Yes," the Dutchman said. "Or rather, we *are* succeeding. But you know, we still need to get to Cahokia. Or wherever the right place is."

"Tia Montse," Margaret said. "I need to save my tia."

"We should discuss it with our sister," Nathaniel said. "Maybe once we get aboard ship."

"Your sister," Margaret said.

"Our sister," Nathaniel said, trying to sound inviting. "Sarah."

Margaret's nostrils flared. "What is Cahokia like?"

"I've never been," Nathaniel said.

"Nor have I." Jake laughed. "But I can tell you what your sister is like."

The two Elytharias triplets nodded.

"She's very smart. She's a powerful magician. She has an unusual gift of sight. She sees the person, I think. The soul. And she cares very deeply about things, especially, I think, about family. Kin. More than anything else, I think she cares for her kin. The things she has done, she has done them for you. She learned about your existence, she learned you were in danger, and she decided that to save you she would have to make herself queen."

"She thinks big," Nathaniel said.

"These things are very impressive." Margaret frowned. "She doesn't sound like a real person at all, the way you describe her. She must have some flaws."

"She's mean," Jake said. "She's hard. She's sharp-tongued. She doesn't trust easily. She doesn't always see the full cost of the decisions she makes, especially the prices paid by other people. Do those make her sound like more of a real person?"

Margaret nodded. "They made her sound a bit like my tia."

They rode without talking into New Amsterdam. Jake hummed to himself and occasionally played his drum very faintly. Strength flowed into him from the drum. Ridiculously, he felt like a bear.

Margaret stared at him.

He smiled back.

The *Zomerwolf* was a large sailing ship docked on the west

side of the island. When the coach rolled to a stop, a thin-legged man opened the door. He had large ears and a sunburned face under blond hair, turning gray and pulled back into a tight queue over his neck. He eyed them briefly.

Did he look *surprised* to see Nathaniel?

"Ik ben Janssen," he said. "Komen jullie van mijn vriend Ambroos?"

"Ambroos is my cousin," Jake said.

They piled out of the carriage and followed Janssen up a broad gangplank. The swaying of the ship made Nathaniel's stomach a little queasy—he'd crossed the Hudson before, and the occasional river in Johnsland, but he'd never sailed on the ocean. The thought of this much motion, or even more, made him ill.

He rapped his knuckles on the skin of his drum and hummed. The seasickness vanished, and the pain in his shoulder faded further. It was almost gone.

Janssen led them down steps and to a large cabin at the rear of the vessel. Two shelves of books adorned one wall, and a large bed another. Two tables filled the center of the room, covered with open ledgers and nautical maps.

"I didn't think I'd have a room this large," Nathaniel said.

"Ximple." Margaret laughed. The word sounded like an insult, but her voice was friendly. "This is the captain's room. You and I will be lucky for a bit of net to curl up in."

Janssen laughed too. "You know your ships. But you must be Catalan. Curious, I'd have said you were Firstborn."

Margaret shrugged. "Who can really tell where his great-grandfather came from?"

"Mine came from the Zuiderzee." Janssen opened a hamper nailed to one wall and pulled out a bottle of wine. "But there was more money to be had in the New World, so here I am. If you would open this." He handed the bottle and a corkscrew to Jake and reached into another hamper.

"Mine as well." Jake uncorked the bottle.

Janssen produced four pewter cups. "I hope you will forgive me for not giving you proper glasses. On a sailing ship, it's best to use glass only where you absolutely can't use anything else. It would be a shame to bring elaborate wineglasses and have them all shatter in a storm."

Jake poured four cups of wine and Nathaniel took one. "Thank you for carrying us," he said. "I don't know what Ambroos said, but I'm happy to pay our way."

Janssen shook his head energetically. "Ambroos paid me. He's a preacher, but he's not one of those who expects everything for free just because on Sunday he's the one who reads out of the Bible. Besides, I owe my fortune to the Dutch Ohio Company. I'd to be happy to take you even for free, happy to help any friend of the Company."

Jake raised his glass. "To friends of the Dutch Ohio Company!"

"To friends!"

They drank.

"When do we sail?" Nathaniel asked.

"Tomorrow, with the early tide," the ship's captain said. "Until then, you're welcome to stay inside our...discreet cabin."

Nathaniel grinned. "You mean secret?"

"A Dutch cabin, maybe?" Margaret added.

Janssen chuckled. "I like to call it by its other name, the Hancock. It's not really intended for passengers, so much as for very valuable cargo."

"Which you don't wish to show to Imperial customs agents," Jake said.

"Or any customs agents at all." Janssen nodded. "But one place to enter it is here. Look, this cabinet will be nailed to the floor before we set sail, but right now it moves." He dragged aside another hamper. When he pushed the wall behind, it opened inward.

Nathaniel went first. He felt lightheaded and fatigued, but he didn't try to drum it away—if he *could* sleep, he probably *should*.

The Hancock was long and narrow, more like a passageway than a room. Three straw mattresses lay on the floor, each covered with a wool blanket. Nathaniel quickly lay on the last one, bundling himself inside the blanket and his coat.

"Very good," Janssen said. "Get some sleep. When you wake up..."

Nathaniel slept without dreaming. Sometime later, he drifted nearly back to wakefulness because a light was shining on him. He heard two voices talking. He thought one of them sounded like Temple Franklin's.

✧   ✧   ✧

"Fort van Nassouwen." Gert Visser offered his hand to Kinta Jane and she took it, stepping off on the trading town's docks.

The town was a busy hive of whistling, yelling, and the crunch of rolling cart wheels. Beyond the unpaved streets and tall, narrow houses, Kinta Jane saw rolling hills covered with forests. Some of the trees were scrub oaks, black and naked in the winter, but there were also green pines.

"You might know it better as Fort Nassau." Dockery stepped off the ship and spat onto the wood. "That's the actual fort itself, on that island in the river. Been here near two hundred years. But they call the whole thing after the fort."

"This is the capital of the Republic?" Kinta Jane asked. She knew that it was, but the fact seemed extraordinary enough to bear repeating.

"What you mean to say," Dockery drawled, "is this looks a hell of a lot less important than New Amsterdam. What are those towheads thinking?"

"I do not have a toe for a head," Gert objected.

Dockery laughed. "You're about as towheaded as they come, Gert. Best I can guess, Kinta Jane, the line of logic pursued by those old meneers must have been something like this: government is the least important function of society, so let's put it up at the most arse-end useless place we can find. Or else maybe, government's the ugliest thing we do, let's hide it and make believe it never happens. Kinda like how you put the jakes behind the house, and not out in front by the road."

"You should not talk this way to a lady, you know," Gert said.

"I beg your pardon." Dockery doffed the badger he wore on his head in Gert's direction. "I didn't know you were a lady."

"You apologize." Gert thrust forward his chest and stepped into Dockery's personal space. The frontiersman didn't back down, so they stood chest to chest and stared at each other. "You apologize for calling me a foot-head, and a lady. And also for speaking this way in front of a woman."

"Tow is T-O-W," Isaiah Wilkes said.

"I don't care how it's spelled," Gert growled.

"It doesn't mean foot. It means a person with bright yellow hair. Which is true about you specifically, and often true of Dutch people." Wilkes tugged at Gert's elbow, and Gert retreated a few inches.

"But if you want to go to knives over your inability to spell, Gert, let's do it." Dockery grinned, his teeth yellow, uneven, and vaguely canine.

"You know, you shouldn't behave this way in front of a lady." Gert shook his head and backed away.

"That's your basic problem, Gert Visser. Thinking of women as ladies. If you thought of them as *women*, real people who wanted real things, and not ideal will o' the wisps that a big dumb knight like you carries around to inspire him, you wouldn't be here."

Gert stared, perplexed.

Kinta Jane moved back from the men and placed her hand near her stiletto for easy grabbing.

Isaiah Wilkes stepped into the middle. "Fort van Nassouwen is older than Nieuwe Amsterdam," he said, picking up the explanation to Kinta Jane as if nothing had intervened. "It was located here as an important stop on the road up through Ticonderoga to Acadia, the way we're bound, as a depot for gathering furs. Its location made all the sense in the world commercially. New Amsterdam at the time was nothing but a deep-water bay where Dutch ships anchored to trade with the people on shore. Later, other kinds of trades made New Amsterdam grow into the metropolis it is today, but the Dutch, with their conservative instincts, kept the seat of the Republic up here."

"I like my explanation better," Dockery said.

"Gert," Isaiah suggested, "why don't you sell the boat? The rest of us will go buy canoes."

Gert nodded efficiently and set about prowling the docks looking for a buyer. Isaiah prodded Dockery and got him moving up the hill.

"We ain't gonna buy canoes," Dockery growled once they were out of Gert's earshot. "What are you imagining, some old Mohican running his canoe shop will just knock us up a pair? No, we're gonna make a couple, just like if the snow gets too deep, we'll make shoes to walk across the top of it."

"Shoes to walk across the top of the snow?" Bizarre images filled Kinta Jane's imagination, of slippers made of ice.

Dockery nodded. "Or bone skates for a frozen lake. I know my way around. There's a reason old Stuyvesant sent me off with you folks, and it's got nothing to do with his daughter Julia."

It was Isaiah's turn to confront Dockery, pushing in close and jabbing the other man in the chest. "What do you know?"

Dockery looked away and frowned. "None of your business, Wilkes."

"Everything that happens on this trip is my business, Dockery," Isaiah snarled. "*Everything.* I am the Franklin. Tell me what you know."

Dockery took a deep breath and exhaled slowly. "Old Gert down there is being sent out of the way. Adriaan doesn't want him around to scotch a wedding with little Tommy Penn."

"How did you know that?" Isaiah's eyes narrowed. Was he going to stab his guide right here on a busy street?

"It's not a secret, man!" Dockery yelled, then collected himself and started again, more softly. "I'm around the house all the time, do you understand? It's no secret what's going on."

"Does Gert know?" Kinta Jane asked. She wasn't sure which she preferred—a fiancé who knew he was being sent away and cooperated out of some sense of chivalry, or a fool who could be manipulated.

"That ox?" Dockery's face clouded. "No. Nor does Thomas know that what he's getting ain't exactly what he asked for."

Wilkes frowned. "What do you mean?"

Dockery spat again. "I shouldn't have said anything."

"Is Adriaan going to substitute a different daughter?" Isaiah asked. "Is Julia a foster child?"

Dockery shook his head again and again. "None of that fairy tale shit, no. Come back to the real world, Your Franklinity."

Kinta Jane almost laughed at Dockery's mocking of Wilkes's title. Then she tried to guess what the trapper might mean. "Julia isn't a maid. She's known a man."

Dockery sighed. "She's known a man, and she's kept a little bit of him too."

"Good hell," Isaiah Wilkes said. "She's pregnant. That will rip the marriage deal asunder. If it humiliates Thomas enough, it might do worse. We'll get the Pacification of the Hudson next."

"It will if they don't take care of the thing." Dockery's voice was low and pained. He looked away.

"No wonder Adriaan Stuyvesant wanted him sent away." Isaiah looked back down the hill at Gert Visser, enthusiastically engaged in back and forth with a man in a long canvas jacket.

"And is willing to have him killed," Kinta Jane added.

Dockery looked up, surprise showing in his face along with...
something else.

Isaiah Wilkes sighed. "Look, Dockery. We may have to kill
Gert Visser. Needling him as you do will only make him more
ready for the blow when it comes."

"You're asking me to lay off."

"I'm *ordering* you. Why didn't you tell me that you knew
before now?"

Dockery shrugged. "You didn't ask. And with all due respect...
Wilkes...it still ain't none of your business."

They stayed one night in a nameless inn on the northern
edge of Fort Nassau. Gert, who had immediately reverted to his
bluff good cheer, bought furs and wools with the proceeds of
the ship. Dockery, whose soured mood remained sour the rest
of the day, disappeared into the forest in his wool pullover frock
and badger-pelt hat and didn't reappear until morning. When he
did show up, as the others were drinking hot coffee and eating a
plate of cold cheese and sausage in the common room, he looked
exhausted. His face was pale, his eyes bloodshot, and his hands
skinned from work and red from cold.

"We've got two canoes," he said. "I've hidden them by the river."

"Shall we rent a sledge to take our things there?" Gert asked.

Dockery's eyes flashed, but his voice was measured. "We
only take what we can carry from here. We're going to have to
portage these canoes over a couple of spots, and too much will
sink the canoes."

"Thank you." Kinta Jane touched Dockery's hand and smiled.
His skin was cold as ice. The Pennslander scooped up two sausages and huddled beside the fire, alone.

Gert sold a few last things—items he had apparently expected
to trade in Acadia, and on which he instead took a loss. Dockery
bound all their things into large fur-wrapped bundles, and they
carried them to the canoes.

"The water's cold as ice," Dockery warned them all. "Don't
fall in."

Kinta Jane shivered. "It's winter, and we're traveling north."

"Spring's coming," Dockery said. "I'd like to beat it to Montreal."

"Is that unlikely?" she asked, getting into the front of a canoe
while Dockery held it. Isaiah Wilkes and Gert Visser climbed

into the other. The canoes were neatly made, wooden frames with birch bark wrapped around them.

"We ain't that far," Dockery told her. "I make it four days to where the river turns west at Baker Falls. From there we portage to Lac du Saint-Sacrement—that's the hard part, but it's short. One hard day, maybe two if the snow is deep and we have to wear shoes. If we get weather of any kind other than sunny, we'll hole up, eat pemmican, and wait for it to blow over. From Saint-Sacrement it's easy, down La Chute and on to Montreal, canoes all the way."

"I suppose a ship would have been faster," Kinta Jane said.

Isaiah Wilkes nodded as both canoes pushed out into the river. "But ships' manifests are easy for Imperial customs agents to read. The lonely road is sometimes a safer road."

"Except when there are road agents," Gert added cheerfully.

"That's why I'm grateful to have you and Dockery along," Wilkes said. "Any down-on-his-luck farmer with a scattergun will think twice before beginning his career as a bandit by shooting me in the back."

They paddled north, up the slow-moving current. Kinta Jane thought the trees on the river's banks moved by more slowly than if they'd been walking on solid ground, but there was at least three feet of snow piled up between their trunks. Likely the river was the faster road.

When Gert Visser wasn't singing, he whistled.

Everyone paddled, but Gert and Dockery did most of the work. Gert had the larger muscles, but Dockery's wiry arms were tireless, and at no point did he fall behind. In the afternoon, they chewed on pemmican and boiled water for coffee on a large rock in the river, melted clean of ice by the sun.

Kinta Jane missed the fish, onions, and peppers of New Orleans, but she didn't say anything.

The sun was low in the west, and Kinta Jane's arms were numb, when Gert abruptly stopped singing and began talking to Dockery. The canoes were close, an arm's length apart.

"I think I know what a woman wants," Gert said. "Beauty. Respect, you know. A man who will treat her well."

"You'd be surprised how many women want a man who'll treat them badly," Dockery shot back.

"Are you saying that about my Julia? Are you saying that about me, that I treat her badly?"

"She ain't *your* Julia!" Dockery hesitated. "She's her own Julia. I reckon she's proved that, if nothing else."

"She and I are betrothed, ranger-man. If she will not be my Julia, then I will be her Gert."

"What some women want," Dockery said, "is just to get away from their fathers. No matter what price they have to pay to do that."

"Marriage to me would be a grievous price, eh?"

Dockery laughed. "You don't know what you're in for, any more than Thomas Penn does!"

Gert stopped paddling for a moment. "Thomas Penn!"

"Shut up, Dockery!" Wilkes barked. "Gert, he's just talking. He doesn't mean anything."

"Right." Dockery's voice was bitter. "I never mean anything. I don't tell the truth, and if I open my heart, it's just a trick to get under a girl's bedsheets. Ignore me. I'll just do the work and bite my tongue."

Gert paddled fiercely to catch up.

"Everyone relax." Wilkes raised his hands in a calming gesture.

Gert's canoe caught up. He was red in the face and his nostrils flared like an angry bull's. "So, now we get to the truth!"

"Gert!" Wilkes shouted. "Dockery! Shut up right now, both of you!"

"The child is yours!" Gert shouted.

"You knew she had another man's child and you asked her to marry you?" Dockery yelled.

"To take care of her! To take care of both of them!"

"Did it occur to you, you log-headed nitwit, that the other man might want to care for them?"

"Don't call me a nitwit!" Gert brandished his paddle like an ax. "Is Julia going to marry Thomas Penn? Am I being sent away?"

Bang!

Wilkes had fired a pistol into the air. He held a second in his other hand, pointed it at the space between the quarreling men so he might shoot either one of them with minimal effort. He was twisted around to face backward.

Everyone had stopped paddling. The canoes drifted with the river.

"Yeah," Dockery said quietly. "You've been sent away. You and me both. I ain't the right kind of fellow to stand in Adriaan Stuyvesant's parlor, and however good your poems might be,

they don't weigh nothing in the balance against the coal mines
of Pennsland."

Gert roared without word and stabbed with his paddle.
Dockery raised his own paddle to parry, but Gert wasn't aiming
for the frontiersman—

he slashed a great hole in the bottom of Dockery's canoe.

Icy water flooded Kinta Jane's legs.

Dockery sprang from the canoe, hurling himself through the
air at Gert—

bang! Isaiah Wilkes fired—

Dockery slammed into the Dutchman. Gert, Dockery, and
Wilkes all tipped over and went into the Hudson.

Kinta Jane gasped as the icy water took her. She didn't know
how to swim. She kicked down with her feet, hoping to find
solid ground.

She sank.

Away to her left, she was aware of thrashing men. She heard
their movements as loud *SWOOSH* sounds that seemed very far
away. That struck her ear and the side of her face as physical
force just as much as noise. The world lost all sense of smell,
and time disappeared.

"Dockery!" she thought she heard.

Flailing with her arms, she came to the surface for a moment.
She coughed out freezing water. Already, her body was numb.
She had to make it to shore, but she had no way to move that
direction.

She sank again.

Thrashing, her hand struck something solid. For a moment,
she thought the fur meant a bear was attacking her in the river,
but then her cooling brain remembered the bundles of gear. She
lashed out at it again—

and caught hold of a leather thong.

The bundle was buoyant.

She kicked and moved herself toward the shore. An eddy in
the water worked in her favor, and she found herself standing
in water that was only waist-deep.

Shaking uncontrollably.

She scanned the river. Both canoes were gone. Three bundles
bobbed away down the river. There was no sign of any of the men.

She scanned the shore. No buildings. No smoke.

She lurched away from the river, dragging the bundle. Dry, she had easily carried it on her shoulder. Wet, she could barely move it. The snow was up to her knees. Casting about for any shelter, she saw a stand of pine trees growing close together, a few steps from the water. In their center, beneath their lower boughs, she could see needle-covered ground.

She forced her way into the knot of pine trees with the last of the day's light. Her teeth chattered and she couldn't make them stop. She tried to untie the leather thong binding together the gear, but her fingers were too stiff. Her stiletto, happily, was still in its sheath on her forearm. She cut the strap and pulled the bundle open.

Fur and wool. Fur and wool should retain heat even if they were wet. But her body had lost too much of its warmth already, even if she bundled up, she thought she'd freeze to death.

And then Dockery was there. He bled from a wound in his side and his badger-fur cap was gone. His own skin was the color of a boiled lobster.

"Fire," he muttered. His rattling teeth made the word sound as if it had multiple Ts in it. "I'll light a fire."

The inside of the bundle was mostly dry. Kinta Jane laid a wool blanket on top of the pine needles, then a second blanket, and the fur on top. It was all the covering they had.

Dockery, meanwhile, smashed the dead lower branches from the pine trees and piled them beside the bed Kinta Jane was building. Though his hands shook and his fingers must have been frozen, his stack was impeccable. He added bark he tore from the trunk of a dead pine with his patch knife, and then he shook water off his powder horn and poured a neat pile of powder at the bottom of his fire.

Kinta Jane climbed onto the bed and prepared to burrow into it.

"Your clothes are wet," Dockery mumbled. He handed her the powder horn.

Kinta Jane hesitated, befuddled. "What?"

"Those wet clothes'll kill you. Take 'em off."

Kinta Jane stripped off her wet clothing and flung it onto pine branches, then shoved herself into the wool and fur. She felt no warmer inside.

Dockery fell to his knees and fumbled a small pouch from

around his neck. He took a bit of flint from the pouch—a spare for his rifle, perhaps—and struck it on the blade of his knife.

On the third try, he got a spark that ignited the powder.

"Get in here," Kinta Jane called.

Dockery nodded. Instead of complying, though, he staggered away into the snow.

"Where are you going?" Kinta Jane called.

She felt nothing below the neck. As the tiny fire licked itself into being, she collapsed in the bed and wept.

After a minute, she felt the powder horn digging into her back. Pulling it from beneath her with trembling hands, she looked at it more closely and saw a single word, a name, hidden cunningly within the vines and flowers of the carving.

Julia.

Dockery lurched back into view with an armful of dead wood. He knelt and laid two pieces beside the fire, where the flame would soon reach them, and piled the rest within reach.

Then he stood and pulled off his buckskinner's clothing. In the light of the tiny fire, Kinta Jane saw knotted muscle and many scars as well as tattoos, although it was too dark to make out any details.

"I'm gonna get in with you now, Kinta Jane." He crawled into the bed behind her. The shock of his cold skin felt as if an ice floe had drifted up against her back.

"I guess you better tell me your name."

"We come all this way from New Amsterdam and you don't know my name yet?" He chuckled, a dry rasp. "It's Dockery."

"Your mother called you Dockery?"

Dockery was still and quiet for a moment. Had he died?

"My mother called me Tim. Baptized Timothy, but *nobody* ever called me *that*. A man called *Tim* can't be taken seriously."

"I'll call you Tim, then."

"Don't you go taking liberties, though. I'm in a vulnerable state."

"Shut up," Kinta Jane muttered through rattling teeth. "Shut up and just don't die."

And Gert Visser? And Isaiah Wilkes?

Kinta Jane stared as hard as she could and saw nothing beyond the light of the tiny fire.

"Hey," Dockery said, just before she fell asleep. "Are you missing some toes?"

✧   ✧   ✧

Sarah felt feverish.

She could keep her spells against detection up all day, no problem. In fact, she felt she *had* to keep them in place. Who knew how far south along the Mississippi the beastkind of Simon Sword were ravaging? At least as far as Irra-Zostim, likely farther. Who knew how far down the river the Imperial chokehold extended?

She'd brought a full bag of coffee beans with her from Cahokia, and she used that to accelerate their step, refreshing the spell with a mouthful of roasted beans every few hours. That was also not a challenge for Sarah.

Her problem was power. Energy. She could draw fuel for her gramarye from the Mississippi, but it burned her from the inside.

Hence the fever.

Once or twice, discreetly, when the pirate queen and the hedge wizard weren't looking, she coughed up blood into the snow.

"This look like a good place to you?" she asked Montse. "Best I can tell, there aren't beastkind in sight."

"Hard to be sure with the trees," Luman warned.

The Catalan surveyed the riverbank. A spit of land poked out slightly into the water. It was free of vegetation larger than trampled yellow grass, poking up dispiritedly through a blanket of snow.

"I'll light two fires to signal Josep." Drawing her saber, she stalked out onto the spit of land, watching the trees, just in case.

"I'll watch her back." The wizard drew two pistols from his coat and checked their firing pans. "Unless Your Majesty has more urgent tasks for me."

"Go keep our smuggler safe," Sarah told him. "I'm going to look upriver, see what I can see."

A wave of pure envy washed over Luman Walters. In another man, that might have come with a will to commit acts of violence, but Sarah saw no such thing in him. Envy, humiliation, and a burning desire to know more.

He nodded and followed Montse.

Sarah climbed down as close to the river as she could and took a drop of cold Mississippi water and tipped it into her Eye of Eve. "*Hostes video.*" Gazing deeply into the Orb of Etyles, she sent her gaze into the green life-stream of the mighty river and up.

She saw the black taint of Robert Hooke and his shambling corpses, but it paled beside the darker, blacker taint of Oliver

Cromwell. She watched them from afar, as a frog watching from the river itself. Cromwell's unholy blaze poured from the body of an adolescent boy.

These she knew about. What else might be coming?

Sarah pulled her vision back in and then sent it up the Ohio River. Following her incantation, her spell ignored aid and allies and sought out enemies.

It found them. In a fleet of barges rushing down the Ohio River accompanied by soldiers in Imperial blue, rode guns.

Not muskets, but cannons. Long-barreled, large-mouthed cannons that dwarfed the guns her own renegade Pitchers operated atop the Treewall. Guns that would punch a hole through the wooden palisade and keep firing until every mound in Cahokia was flat.

She grabbed the writing slate. She had no idea how to intervene from this distance, but at least she could warn the city's defenders.

"Maitre Carrefour, I beg you to ride in fire!"

———◦———

CHAPTER SIXTEEN

Young Andy barreled up the hill, yelling. Calhoun Mountain was blanketed with the sort of light snow it got in winter, thicker than usual, and Andy triggered several small avalanches onto his own head by crashing into tree branches on the way. He didn't even slow down, just took the snow dumps with his head down, hunkering under his slouch hat and as deep as he could into the undyed wool coat he'd inherited from his father David.

"We got a visitor!" he hollered. "Hell if it ain't a Fairy!"

Young Andy made a beeline for the Thinkin' Shed, and Cal easily grabbed the boy by the back of his collar. Andy's forward motion spun them both in a circle. Cal had to keep a firm grip to avoid dropping the boy in a snow drift.

"Don't call 'em Fairies," he told his cousin. "Or Unsouled or Serpentborn or Wigglies."

"On account of Aunt Sarah's one?" Young Andy was red in the face from the cold and the exertion, but he wasn't out of breath.

"Also on account of it might give offense. How do you feel about people callin' you Cracker?"

Andy shrugged his indifference.

"Lessen you *mean* to give offense," Cal continued. "And then go right ahead. Also, mebbe don't say 'hell.'"

"Is it your place to tell me what to say, then?" Andy sneered.

"Well," Cal said thoughtfully, "I *am* your kin. I'm older'n you, and iffen I ain't wiser, at least I can whup your ass."

"Grandpa says 'hell.'"

"Grandpa's a war hero and an Elector. You git that kinda stature, I reckon you can say 'hell,' too. For now, what about 'Jumpin' Jehoshaphat' instead?"

"You're gonna make me sound like an old woman," Andy grumbled.

"Iffen you mean polite and wise, that wouldn't be the worst thing in the world. Mebbe 'durnit'? That's shorter, be easier to say."

"Damn...I mean durnit, Cal, they's a...I dunno, what's the polite word for a Wiggly?"

"Firstborn," Cal suggested. "Or I reckon Eldritch ain't too insulting."

"They's a Firstborn arrived at the bottom of the draw. Red Charlie's a-bringin' him up, 'cause he's wounded."

"What's he want?"

"To talk, I reckon. Says he's a messenger, but he ain't yet said what the message is. His horse looks worse'n yours did when you arrived."

"Where's he come from?" Cal didn't want to get his hopes up. "Is he wearin' a gray cape, by any chance?" He was thinking of the wardens who stood on the Treewall and guarded the streets of Cahokia.

"No." Andy shook his head. "Just a dirty brown one. Says he come from Sarah."

"Dammit, Andy!" Cal hurled his young cousin in the direction of the Thinkin' Shed. "You's supposed to say that *first!* Lord hates a man as can't do things in the proper order. Now go on, tell the Elector!"

Cal raced down to the draw. Unreasonably, he hoped the messenger would have a face he recognized: Bill's, or Jake's—though they weren't Firstborn—or Yedera's, or even Chikaak's. He didn't, and Cal felt a tiny pang of loss.

The messenger was haggard. From three steps away, Cal smelled the stink of an infected wound on the man. His Eldritch complexion was so pale, if he lay down in the snow, Cal thought he might disappear entirely. He had his left arm over Red Charlie's shoulder—under a brown cloak, Cal saw that the man's right side was clotted black with blood.

"Hot water!" Charlie yelled. "Food! Aunt Sadie! Aunt Beulah!" Sadie had been a Pitcher in her youth. She didn't have much occasion to fire cannons off the sides of Calhoun Mountain, but she'd never forgotten her medical training. Beulah was a hexer, never as talented as, say, Sarah, but she possessed a healing touch.

"Beer," the Firstborn croaked, and he shot Calvin a ragged wink.

"Can I git under your other arm?" Cal asked him.

The Firstborn groaned.

"Best not," Red Charlie suggested. "He's in a bad way. But iffen you can take him the rest of the way, I'll git my Polly to git a bath and a bed up, quick."

Cal took over the carrying of the messenger. Up close, the wound stank worse. The man was gangrenous. Cal doubted he'd survive, whatever the healing talents of the Calhoun women.

Sarah would be able to save him, but she wasn't here.

"You're from Sarah," he said.

"You're Calvin Calhoun," the messenger grunted.

Cal finally recognized the man. He'd been one of Alzbieta Torias's soldiers. Cal remembered his thin lips and the horizontal scar across his entire forehead. "Olanthes," he said.

"Olanthes Kuta." Olanthes nodded. "Ole, if you prefer. I volunteered to carry the message, but there were many messengers, sent to many places. Her Majesty sent me here specifically because I'd know your face. And I have a message for *you*, in addition to the formal missive I bear for the Elector."

"She's queen, then?" Cal's heart tried the impossible maneuver of simultaneously leaping for joy and plummeting into despair. If Sarah was now queen, that meant she had succeeded, or at least she was succeeding. On the other hand, if she was now queen, there was simply no way she could ever marry Calvin.

"When I left, she hadn't yet been formally crowned. But as Beloved of the goddess, in practice, she rules her father's city."

"What's the message?" Cal asked, half-afraid of the answer.

"She bids me tell you that she loves you. Despite anything that happened in the past, and no matter what happens in the future."

Cal bit his lip so hard it bled. Young Andy reappeared with Caleb and Uncle David in tow, which was good, because suddenly Cal couldn't see for the tears springing to his eyes.

He stepped back, let the others carry Olanthes on, and tried to catch his breath.

It didn't mean what he wanted it to mean, he knew that. She

loved him because he was kin. He'd helped her on her journey, fought at her side and against her enemies. She loved him for all those reasons.

But she was going to be Queen of Cahokia. The last monarch of Cahokia had married the Penn landholder. Sarah wasn't going to marry a penniless cattle rustler from the hills above Nashville.

Iron Andy appeared in the Thinkin' Shed's dog-trot. "Red Charlie's!" he called. "Polly's got a tub a-heatin' right now."

Caleb and David turned toward Charlie's place, cutting through a snow-covered meadow and a small stand of trees to save time.

"We'll have you tended to," Iron Andy said, falling in step beside Olanthes and dropping into Penn's English. "Is there any message you need to give me verbally?"

"You're Andy Calhoun?" Olanthes asked.

"Iffen I ain't, I killed him and I'm wearin' his skin," the Elector quipped.

"Her Majesty bid me tell you you're still her grandpa, and she still carries the staff you carved for her."

"Good girl," Andy muttered.

"I've seen the staff," Olanthes added. "It's true, she carries it. It has become her own staff of office, in a way. She has worked miracles with it. How did you come to decide it should have a horse's head at the tip?"

"I'm old," Andy said. "I *know* shit."

"I also carry a written missive," Olanthes added.

Andy nodded. "I'll want every single detail I can git from you about what Sarah's doing. First, we need to git you taken care of."

Olanthes disappeared into Red Charlie's cabin, carried by many hands. Iron Andy turned and found Calvin. He clapped his grandson on the shoulder. Cal saw a hint of tears in his grandfather's eyes, too.

"Lord hates a man as don't know when to cry," Cal said.

"It warms my heart to hear such wisdom in one so young. Now git on down the mountain to Nashville."

"Where am I a-goin', Grandpa?"

"You know the Harvite convent?"

"By the river." Cal nodded. "I'll bring back a healer?"

"Not jest any healer, boy. They's a Sister Serafina Tate there. She'll say no, she don't lay hands anymore, and mebbe the abbess won't even want you to see her. You insist, you hear me? You tell her Dancin' Andy Calhoun sent you, and he needs the best healer east of the Mississippi. You git her up here."

Dancin' Andy?

But the Elector was gone, disappearing into Red Charlie's with Charlie and his wife Polly and a few of the women.

Grandpa had chosen Cal for a second time.

Cal quickly saddled two horses, sturdy little beasts, scarcely larger than ponies. But they could keep their footing on the steep slopes, and within fifteen minutes he was heading down the mountain.

He had a hard time focusing on the path, so it was a good thing the horses were mountain-bred. Sarah was alive! She was on her way to queendom!

And she hadn't forgotten Cal!

Snow was falling by the time Calvin reached the gates of Free Imperial Nashville. Snow was unusual in Nashville, but more unusual was the fact that it didn't melt off immediately. In the stone corners of the market town, the snow of this bad winter now piled up in dirty drifts. The town watch waved Calvin and his two horses through, and he headed down to the river.

The Harvite convent had a ten-foot tall stone wall surrounding a small complex of buildings. Cal had never been inside because he'd never been hurt enough. He assumed some of the buildings were dormitories for the Sister, and others held patients. Or maybe a library.

The front entrance was shut. It was a single door, four feet wide and eight feet tall, and a big iron knocker hung in the center. Cal knocked.

Almost immediately, a small window set above the knocker and protected by an iron grate opened. A scowling woman's face pressed forward into the window and examined Cal. "Are you looking for healing, my son?"

"Yes, Sister," Cal said.

"You look well," she answered.

"Not for me," he said quickly. "I come down from Calhoun Mountain. We've got an injured man up there, hurt real bad." He showed his purse. "I've brought the customary contribution."

"I'll get a Circulator." The Sister moved to shut her window.

"Sister!" Cal stopped her. "I need a particular Circulator."

"You mean your injured man has an unusual injury?"

"He's in a bad way," Cal agreed, "but what I mean is I's sent to get a specific Circulator."

"Who?" The woman's eyes narrowed in suspicion. "We ordinarily don't permit that, because some patients fall in love with the Circulators who tend them. But perhaps..."

"Sister Serafina Tate," Cal said.

The woman snorted. "Absolutely not. Sister Serafina is half-blind and nearly ninety years old. If I sent her out in this snow, it would be her death."

"But I's sent—"

"No."

"But I—"

"No. Listen, I can get you a Circulator. But not Sister Serafina. Do you want one or not?"

"I'm afraid I have to insist," Cal said.

The woman shut the window.

Cal waited a few minutes. Had he been persuasive enough? Would the woman go ask Sister Serafina, who would then make herself available?

Though if she were really as frail and impotent as this woman made her out to be, Cal wasn't sure she was the best choice.

But the woman didn't come back, in any case.

Cal took a deep breath. He hadn't failed the Elector in taking Sarah away *from* Calhoun Mountain, and he wasn't about to fail his grandpa in bringing Sister Serafina *to* the mountain.

Behind the convent, in a patch of snow between the convent's walls and the taller town walls, Cal found a pine sapling. It wasn't tall enough or sturdy enough to climb, but it was enough tree to hitch the horses to.

Carefully, he climbed onto his horse's back and slowly stood.

"Good boy," he murmured to the beast. "Shh, everything's fine. Everything's normal. I'm jest doin' a little bit of circus acrobatics, on account of I got no other way forward."

Standing on the horse's back, Cal was tall enough to grip the top of the Circulators' wall. He dragged himself up and straddled it.

There was no parapet inside, just a ten-foot drop into a garden. That was unexpected, but nice. If he were ill, Cal might very well enjoy a garden stroll. A stone pathway was shoveled and swept free of snow. Cal saw sick and injured people in white gowns limping about, despite the fat snowflakes coming down.

He saw three buildings inside the enclosure. They all had tall windows, so Cal could see directly inside. One was clearly a hospital, with patient beds side by side. The second held a kitchen on the ground floor and books on the story above that. The third had more windows, but smaller. Through some of the panes, Calvin saw women reading, talking, kneeling to pray, and even sleeping.

That's where he'd find the ninety-year-old woman.

Carefully, he stood again. Taking each step slowly out of fear of unseen ice, Cal walked around the stone wall. Men of the watch standing on the town's wall gestured at him and laughed, but did nothing more.

Cal came to within ten feet of the dormitory wall. If he dropped down and walked into the building, he might run into the wrong Sister and get escorted back out again. Plus, what if the convent had guards? If someone shot at him or chased him inside the wall, he didn't think he'd be able to jump back over.

Nothing for it. Calvin Calhoun started yelling.

"Serafina Tate!" he hollered. "I'm lookin' for Sister Serafina Tate! I got a message for Sister Serafina!"

"Git down! Git down offa there!" This from the same face that had rejected Calvin at the door, but which now appeared with a body in Harvite robes attached. "I told you no!"

"Sister Serafina!" Cal hollered again. The patients strolling in the garden stared at him and the men on the wall stared at him. Now windows in the buildings began to open, and Harvite Sisters stared, too. "Sister Serafina?" Cal implored them.

Did it really have to be Sister Serafina? Could only she treat the Cahokian rider's wound? Maybe that was true; Iron Andy had been emphatically confident about his own knowledge when he had commissioned Cal. And in any case, the Elector had been quite specific. If nothing else, for the Elector, it had to be her.

But none of the nuns looking at Calvin through the windows gave any indication that they planned to help him.

"Pull him down from there!" The Sister from the door shouted. Two men Cal hadn't previously seen, heavy men wearing leather jerkins and carrying cudgels, moved in Cal's direction.

"I'm here for Sister Serafina Tate!" he shouted one last time. "Sister Serafina, Dancin' Andy Calhoun sent me, and he told me not to take no for answer!"

The men in cudgels yelled and Cal inched back, nervous they might jump and hit his ankles.

"Sister Serafina!" he cried. "Dancin' Andy Calhoun sent me!"

A window on the highest floor of the dormitory swung open, and a pale face under wisps of white hair appeared there. "I'm Sister Serafina!" she yelled to Cal. Then she poked her head out the window and yelled at the door-warden, too. "If Dancin' Andy sent this boy, I'm a-goin' with him. Send someone up to fetch me!"

"I'll carry you!" Cal lowered himself into the garden, between the two heavy men who now wore frustrated and baffled expressions. "Gentlemen," he said to them, "iffen you wouldn't mind helpin', I got two horses tethered to an itty-bitty pine tree out back. The patient's in a bad way, so iffen it don't bother you, I'm in a rush. I'll git the nun. You bring the horses around."

"Onandagos had a son and a daughter," Naares Stoach said.

The Zoman captain looked deeply into the small fire, as if it helped him dredge up memories. His two surviving fellow-soldiers of Zomas sat to either side of him, right and left. They drank beer salvaged from a ruined town across the Missouri. Kort and Ferpa had swum the river despite its floes of ice and emerged pink-fleshed and smiling.

Most of the beastkind were highly resistant to cold, as well as to fatigue. They sat farther from the fire than Chigozie or the three Zomans, for whose benefit the blaze had really been kindled. When it got too cold, the beastkind tended to huddle together in piles and just go to sleep.

"Forgive me," Chigozie said. "I am a southerner, and I never learned the Firstborn genealogies. Onandagos was the founding King of Cahokia?"

"Say rather that he built the Great Mound," Naares said, "and that the city was founded after him. As I was about to tell you, he had a son and a daughter. The son was older, and should have been King of Cahokia. But he had the great misfortune of falling in love."

Chigozie laughed. "As a sworn celibate, I have little to say on this matter. I know from observation, though, that some men experience love as slavery."

"Yes," Stoach agreed. "Others experience it as great liberation, as a sudden bolt of clarity that teaches a man what to care about, what to do in his life, and what, as a result, is mere dross, to be ignored."

"And the son who fell in love?" Strangely, the words reminded Chigozie of his brother. "How did he experience love?"

"As the opening of a new world," Naares said. "His love was from one of the so-called Brother Nations."

"An Indian."

"And a princess, of sorts. We understand that her people were relatives of the Caddo, or maybe were Caddo themselves, as the Caddo existed centuries ago."

"That is a new world, indeed, if he came from Germany."

"You are thinking of Podebradas and the Wallensteins. Onandagos came much, much earlier. The land he walked in the Old World is many centuries beneath the waves."

"Of course. Did Onandagos not approve of the Caddo princess?"

Naares's face was grave, dappled orange in the firelight. "By his lights, Onandagos was a wise man and a kind one. But he could not accept that his son Zomas, a prince of the Firstborn, would marry one of the daughters of the Fallen."

"The Fallen," Chigozie repeated. "You mean, the children of Eve."

Naares nodded. "He gave Zomas a choice. Give up his love, or give up the throne."

"A hard choice."

"Zomas refused to do either. He pleaded his case, and when Onandagos's servile priest-judges ruled against the prince, he raised the banner of revolt."

"He must have lost."

Naares shook his head. "When he saw how many of his people had fallen by the spear and by the arrowhead, he withdrew. He never surrendered his claim to the throne of Cahokia, which was his by right of primogeniture."

"I didn't know this was the Cahokian rule."

"It was the rule of the Firstborn until the days of Onandagos. Nor would Zomas surrender his love. Nor would he accept the Cahokian disdain toward the children of Eve, which continues to this day. Cahokia enslaves its own people as severe punishment for grave crimes, crimes against the liberty of the people. But its people freely traffic in slaves descended from Eve. They buy them from Memphis and from the Comanche. In its arrogance, Cahokia believes itself above the Fallen still."

The tale of old wrongs and ongoing grudges made Chigozie feel tired. "Zomas keeps slaves. It is known for it."

"We enslave without regard to race. Children of Adam from both branches, beastkind, even Misaabe. We enslave for debt and as punishments. Slaves are only owned by the state, not by a private individual—private ownership of other people would lead to abuse. Slaves are paid wages fixed by law, and they may buy their freedom."

"It all sounds horrible to me," Chigozie admitted.

"We of Zomas have long lived shoulder to shoulder with the children of Adam. We have intermarried again and again, so much so that it is very difficult to say who is Firstborn and who is Fallen, if that distinction even matters at all."

"In Zomas."

"In Zomas." Naares's face was bitter as he nodded his agreement. "Cahokia still cares, of course. It lives a lofty existence, allied with Peter Plowshare against his son, and prospering from his lore and fertility magic. And the other Sister Kingdoms prosper with her."

"I believe they suffer now."

Naares shrugged. "They eat the fruit of their own rebellion. Meanwhile, the soldiers of Zomas have ever fought with spear and bow—in recent centuries with gunpowder as well—against the tyrant of the Mississippi. He gave *us* no great seed-gifts, raised for *us* no mounds, taught *us* no secret signs to read in the heavens. What magics Peter Plowshare taught our kingdom were for times of war and disaster only. For us there was always the tusk and the tooth, hoof and claw."

"You speak truth," Kort rumbled. His deep voice cut unexpectedly into the conversation, and Chigozie almost jumped. "But only truth of a sort. Truth as you understand it."

"Is there truth other than the one I understand?" Naares asked. "A higher truth than my blood shed in defense of my children and for the liberties of my children's children? Show it to me, beastman."

"You are interlopers on the Heron King's land," Ferpa said. "Onandagos traded with the king for land. Zomas did not. He took land, and so we fought against him and his children."

"*Fought*?" Naares asked. "Do you mean you no longer fight?"

"I am Ferpa. I no longer fight. Other beastkind continue fighting in the Heron King's service."

"If you settle on a land long enough," Naares said, "it is yours. Otherwise, no kingdom could stand and no landowner would sleep at night."

"The Heron King is above this law," Kort said. "The Heron King is the river. All the land that drains into the river belongs to him."

"That's an awful lot of land," Naares said.

"Yes," Kort agreed. "And you have fought a very long war to try to take it. When will you decide that your war is a failure and retreat? There is room in the west and also in the south. Why must you raise your tower so close to the king's?"

"You take this as a very personal issue, beastman," Stoach said.

Kort hung his head and was silent for long moments. Finally, he said, "you are right. I serve a new king now. And my new king does not begrudge you land, wherever you choose to live."

"But *my* king begrudges my absence," Naares said. "Or he believes I'm dead."

"You once said that you impressed us all into your king's army," Chigozie said. "Turim Zomas the second, if I remember right."

Naares leaned away from the fire and said nothing.

"You're not denying or retracting," Chigozie said.

"Turn the other cheek," Ferpa murmured.

Chigozie nodded. "We forgive you for saying that. We understand."

"We forgive you," many animallike voices whispered together.

"But we have renounced violence," Chigozie continued. "We hide here in the Still Waters. We cover our tracks to prevent others from learning where we are. We want only to live in peace."

"I would not raise my club to defend myself," Kort growled. "I will certainly not raise it to defend your king's desire for land."

"Could you swear an oath?" Chigozie asked.

"What kind of oath?" Stoach narrowed his eyes.

"To preserve our secret. To tell no one of this place, or of this people."

"I have sworn other oaths of allegiance," Naares said. "Those oaths come first."

"Perhaps they do not know the way here." Ferpa eyed the three men. Chigozie did the same, trying to gauge their reactions. "Perhaps we can blindfold them and lead them home."

But Chigozie saw in the eyes of the three men that they *did* know where they were. Even before Naares Stoach hesitated in response to Ferpa's suggestion, he knew that if they took the three Zomans to their land of the white towers, sooner or later, Zoman soldiers would return to the Still Waters and enslave his people.

"We will have to move," Kort said. "I do not like it, but what else is there?"

Chigozie studied Naares's face very carefully. "What if we sent an embassy?"

"What sort of embassy?" Naares's expression was noncommittal.

"What if I came to speak with your master, Lord Turim Zomas?" Chigozie asked. "What if I explained who we are and why we cannot fight either for him or against him, and asked to be left alone?"

"I cannot promise you anything," Naares said. "As of now, I'm captain of a skirmisher unit that no longer exists."

"But tell me about Lord Zomas. Is he a reasonable man? Are his judgments wise? Can he be negotiated with?"

Naares considered. "Lord Turim Zomas is a reasonable man, but he lives in an unreasonable time. The war of banked fire he inherited from his father has exploded into a conflagration that threatens to destroy his kingdom. In better times, he might find you a pleasant curiosity. In these days, he will need to draw strength from you."

"We are returning three of his soldiers," Chigozie said. "Three of his men whom we could have killed, or even merely left to die. Instead, we bring you back to the war."

"And still," Naares said. "I don't think it will be enough."

Was the Zoman negotiating on behalf of his sovereign? But Chigozie was unwilling to surrender any of the Merciful into slavery. Better to uproot the community and move again. And again, and again, if necessary.

"I will go alone," he said.

Ferpa and Kort squealed together in protest, a sound like an entire herd provoked to anger.

"I will go alone," he repeated. "If I do not come back, take that as a sign that it is time to move."

"You will not go alone," Kort rumbled.

"Once, you would have had me as your king," Chigozie said. "Will you not obey me in this?"

"You refused to become king," Ferpa said. "You chose to be

the Shepherd, instead. And the shepherd does not travel without his chosen."

Chigozie smiled ruefully. "Very well, then. But only a *few* sheep."

Philippe and François were tough, capable men, with flexible consciences but loyalties as rigid as steel. Achebe the wrestler had curiosity and maybe also a devotion that Etienne didn't understand, but also didn't doubt.

Still, Etienne missed Armand. Especially when dealing with smugglers. He'd have been useful.

The four men stood in the dockmaster's office in Natchez-under-the-Hill. The lights in the office were snuffed and the night outside was dark, but for a few torches and the trickle from very few windows. The dockmaster stood with them, or rather, she leaned against Etienne and purred like a cat.

Her name was Adisalem. She was Amhara, judging by the bones of her face. She spoke English with an accent that was pure Mississippi—a little German inflection, a little Igbo bounce, and a dash of Appalachee twang. She was nearly as tall as Etienne and smelled of cinnamon and tobacco smoke.

Not enough tobacco scent to appease the Brides, however. They toyed with the woman, dominating her and placing her firmly under Etienne's control.

Monsieur Bondí had picked this site. He had done it as only an accountant could, examining the records of the dockmasters of New Orleans and interrogating them as to the origin and points of call of ships that periodically docked there. Many Memphite barges called in New Orleans. Far fewer had come from Youngstown and the northern Ohio River, and fewer still made the journey on a quarterly basis.

One that did was the *Favor of Nephthys*. According to the stevedores Monsieur Bondí asked, she stopped at the Hansa town of Natchez-under-the-Hill.

She was due.

Monsieur Bondí was proving to have talents beyond those merely of an accountant. Or perhaps it was more accurate to say that his accounting skills had uses beyond merely keeping, interpreting, and disguising financial records. Etienne would promote the man, except that his work in keeping the cash flow coming to Etienne was more important and more dangerous and more costly than ever, with the chevalier behind them at every step.

Bondí was needed on the books.

But perhaps he could be persuaded to train some of Etienne's other men in his investigative skills.

"There she is." Adisalem's voice had a metallic twang in it, like a harpsichord.

The *Favor* was a trireme. The narrow, rowed barges moved quickly up and down river regardless of wind and could be sailed in very shallow water, which made them powerful on the Mississippi. The great disadvantage they suffered was cost—since the barge was crewed by two hundred men, most of them rowers, only a person of enormous wealth—or a person commanding many slaves—could afford such a vessel.

Memphis used the barges.

"Why would they not simply beach the ship?" François asked. It wasn't a terrible question; beaching the barges was common enough.

"The beaches here are too wooded," Adisalem said. "The Natchez Trace is infested with road agents. And on the far bank, beastkind. Especially now. The beastkind are rampaging."

"Therefore, they shelter here for the night," Etienne said. "Under the watchful eye of the Hansa."

"They aren't Hansards," Adisalem said. "The captain sails out of Memphis. But he knows whom to pay to buy safety on the river."

"He has a precious cargo," Etienne said.

"I understand your plan better now," Philippe said in French. Once Monsieur Bondí had identified the *Favor of Nephthys*, Philippe had suggested that they seize the barge and its cargo. But the barge was a large one, a trireme, and Etienne didn't have enough men to take it in an assault. Counting now, he thought he saw twenty free sailors, all armed, and as many armed men idling—guards. "But must you come? It would be safer here, I think."

"The vessel will be warded," Etienne said, also in French. "It will be much easier to walk within the warding than to try to send power across it." He spoke in English to Adisalem. "Is it time to go?"

"Come with me," she said.

All five of them exited the dockmaster's office and walked

down the creaking planks. Etienne smelled the fertile Mississippi and the acrid smoke of the few torches that more or less illuminated the river.

The men weren't dressed in Etienne's blacks and whites. Etienne himself wore his scarlet sash, but he wore it underneath his clothing. They all wore quilted jackets against the cold, plain corte-du-roi trousers, and hemp rope shoes.

Etienne felt the comforting tug of the weight of the bottle in his jacket pocket and managed not to pat it.

The trireme, bobbing alongside the dock and bumping against it, let down its gangplank. Etienne heard men inside shouting curses in Amhara, Oromo, English, and German, as well as the crack of a whip—the Memphite sailors were doling out water and driving the rowers from their benches to the floor, where they would sleep.

Adisalem stroked Etienne's arm, breathing hard.

"After you, Dockmaster," he told her.

The *Favor*'s captain might have Adisalem's underlying high, fine bones, but they were hidden beneath layers of gristle. His mate was a scowling Bantu with a knife blade in place of a hand. Etienne avoided making eye contact, reminding himself that he was a dock laborer, a Hansard whose job was menial at best.

The rowers were all men. Etienne could tell, because the Brides were in their full power and looking for women. Unable to find any other than the dockmaster, they poured into her like a fifty-gallon barrel trying to empty itself into a pocket flask.

Adisalem whimpered and shifted from foot to foot.

"Iwi selami newi." The captain spoke to Adisalem in Amharic, and she spoke back.

If he had merely paid off the dockmaster, Etienne would be nervous about the fact that he didn't understand what passed between her and the ship's captain. But he could feel her spirit, taut and yearning, through the fibers of his own body. He knew the need that drove her, and he knew she could not possibly resist.

"I'll send my men below," Adisalem told the captain, switching to English.

"Igbos?" The captain shot Etienne a skeptical look. "You don't find them to be too lazy? Always wanting to laugh and play?"

Etienne grinned and tried to look harmless. "That one is a wrestler," he said, pointing to Achebe. "I'm too lazy even to play."

The captain snorted and the mate sneered.

"No cargo to unload here?" Adisalem asked.

The captain shook his head. "Carrying coal down to New Orleans and cotton back up. Nothing to unload on the way."

Adisalem nodded. "We will be brief."

Ostensibly, Etienne and his men were Hansards and would now check that the *Favor*'s cargo consisted only of coal. Of course, it wasn't true; somewhere buried under the coal was a smaller cargo of gold, sent by the Emperor Thomas Penn to the Chevalier of New Orleans as a blackmail payment.

Probably, Adisalem was bribed by the captain to look the other way. Or maybe she had no idea of the wealth that was being transferred under her nose. Maybe she didn't care.

Etienne nodded to the deck crew as he passed and ignored the uppermost bank of rowers, who were huddling together under wool blankets and squeezing beneath their own rowing benches. He went belowdecks and saw two more banks of rowers similarly bedding down for the night in the long gallery beneath the orange flicker of several torches.

"Maitre Carrefour," he murmured as he walked. "I seek your aid tonight in destroying the murderer of my father. I beg you to appear in your cloak of flame. My Brides, Ezili Freda, Ezili Danto, I feel the power that abounds in you both, and I implore you to direct it toward the master of the crossroads. Maitre Carrefour, come to me tonight!"

Four tall, bearded men in Ferdinandian hats and long black coats beat the rowers out of the central aisle with heavy sticks. Etienne nodded lazily to them, too, and avoided meeting their gaze.

"Cargo?" he asked.

One of the men pointed at an open hatch in the floor and steps leading down the lowest chamber of the ship: the cargo hold.

"I will check the rowers," Philippe said. He and François padded up the gallery, looking left and right under the benches as if they might find anything. Achebe took a torch and descended with Etienne into the darkness.

The cargo hold had no rowing benches, but large wooden boxes. The boxes had no tops and were full of large chunks of black Pennsland coal. In the bottom of one of these boxes, if he guessed right and dug quickly enough, Etienne might find Pennsland gold instead.

"Maitre Carrefour," Etienne murmured, stepping away from the square of torchlight that shone down through the trapdoor. "Tonight I implore you to ride in fire."

Etienne was no horse, to be ridden by any of the loa other than his Brides. But he had brought many worshippers to Papa Legba. He knew what the dark loa needed, and he had the Brides to help him.

He felt the pressure of the bottled-up passion of the Brides, swollen between him and the dockmaster, dissipate suddenly, as it was redirected to the great loa of the crossroads. Etienne took the bottle of gunpowder-infused rum from his pocket, filled his mouth, and spat forward. He spat a second mouthful aft, and then one each to starboard and port. He took the torch from Achebe.

"You're no dockworker."

Etienne turned to face the source of the voice. Two of the tall, bearded men had come down the ladder behind him. But as the one spoke, Etienne realized that his accent wasn't Ferdinandian at all.

"You're the mameluke," Etienne said. They both spoke French.

The mameluke smiled and drew a curved sword. "Did you think we were standing outside your gambling den, O pagan bishop?"

In fact, I did. But now it was clear that the men posted in front of Etienne's casino, the ones Etienne had taken to be mamelukes watching over him, were decoys. The real men were here, guarding the chevalier's life-sustaining gold.

Or rather, guarding the bait; Etienne had walked into a trap. *The chevalier willingly threw away Planchet's life to set the trap. Poor fool.*

"It doesn't matter." Etienne threw the torch onto the coal. It landed atop a pile and lay there guttering.

"What kind of idiot thinks he can ignite a pile of coal so easily?" The second mameluke grinned and also drew a saber.

Achebe squeezed past Etienne and crouched low, his feet and hands wide apart. "I will make you swallow that word," the wrestler said.

"Idiot," the second mameluke said again. "Cretin. Moron."

Etienne took a deep breath, isolating the dockmaster away from himself and feeling the Brides in a mounting frenzy. "Maitre Carrefour!" he shouted. "O Brides, bring the black dog of the crossroads! Maitre Carrefour, I beg you to ride in fire!"

The mamelukes chuckled, but it was a forced sound.

Etienne took a swig of rum into his cheeks and sprayed it on the torch.

A curtain of fire sprang up all around the cargo hold as every single box of coal ignited at the same moment. Etienne heard howling sounds. A blast of air colder than ice blew through the hold as if the ship had disappeared and a wind straight from the pole was burning down the Mississippi.

"Yarob!" The first mameluke shouted, and Achebe hurled himself upon the swordsmen.

They had swords, but their surprise at the sudden ring of fire let the wrestler get inside the blades' reach. Suddenly, he had one man clutched to his own chest, head and shoulders pinned in a lock. He pushed his captive at the second man, forcing them both back and opening the road to the stairs up.

Etienne ran up the stairs. He slipped a small knife from inside his jacket, prepared to fight, but he didn't need it. The fire already licked at the walls of the middle gallery, as well, though there were long lines and circular patches where the fire burned around the wood.

The ship's defensive warding. Naturally, the owner had hexed the vessel against fire, but the spell had been partial. It had assumed an ordinary fire, rather than explosion of the wrath of Maitre Carrefour, fueled by the lust of the Brides, from the ship's own hold.

The deck crew was abandoning ship, and the rowers with them. Etienne saw Adisalem—released by the Brides—staring stunned at the fire roaring up the side of the ship.

Philippe and François lay on the deck, dead. Over them knelt a third mameluke, bloodied and haggard. Etienne didn't see the fourth mussulman, and he didn't wait. He marched down the gangplank, waving away hostile stares of two of the deck crew with a fierce gesture of his knife.

Achebe rejoined him on the dock. The wrestler held a curved sword in his hand and wore a look of grim determination on his face.

They left the pool of light that was Natchez-under-the-Hill and climbed the bluff above, to where Etienne had horses waiting.

"I's led to expect I'd git a dance."

———◆———

CHAPTER SEVENTEEN

Sister Serafina had to be helped onto the horse. She had to be wrapped in three blankets Calvin had brought, and rode up the mountain clutching a ceramic pot containing live coals from a fire to keep her warm. Calvin had to lead her horse—over the rougher parts of the terrain, he even had to dismount and walk beside her to be sure she didn't fall off. Once they finally got up the draw to the meadows atop Calhoun Mountain, she had to be lifted off her horse onto Red Charlie's porch.

But when she saw the Cahokian herald, no one had to tell her what to do. She knelt beside the Firstborn and examined him thoroughly.

Olanthes looked worse. Stripped of his clothing and long boots and bathed, he lay beside the fire on a pallet. An angry red wound gaped in his side—the flesh from his armpit to his hip was blistered, swollen, red, and oozing pus.

"I reckon the pus might be laudable." Red Charlie coughed, probably to avoid gagging. Cal wanted to gag himself from the stench of Olanthes's wound. "We didn't squeeze him none, the pus jest came out on its own. Bearin' away the agents of infection, that's what they taught us in the Foresters."

"Horseshit, boy." Sister Serafina snorted. "Ain't no laudable pus. Pus is pus, means he's infected. That's wet gangrene there, and he's jest about on death's own doorstep right now. Iffen his blood ain't already poisoned, it will be come mornin'."

"This rider come to me from my daughter Sarah," Iron Andy said. "You tell us what you need to treat the feller, and you'll git it."

"Scaldin' hot water, lots of it. Knives, and someone to heat the knives in the fire. Hard liquor for him to drink, iffen he wakes up, and to splash on the flesh, and on the blades. A bucket for the parings. Someone to hold him down iffen he moves."

"The tools are all here," Andy said. "You ain't my first Circulator."

"I'm your best, though." She smiled at him, and Cal saw blue eyes clear as the noon sky flashing at his grandpa.

"True enough. I'll heat the knives myself." Several thin, sharp knives lay on a boiled cloth on a table beside the Cahokian. Iron Andy took one, wrapped its hilt in several layers of cotton blanket to protect his hand, and thrust the blade into the fire.

"We'll hold him," Polly said. Red Charlie nodded, and they positioned themselves near Olanthes's head.

"I'll need a Bible." The Harvite looked around at Red Charlie, Polly, and Calvin. "And a reader."

"We got a Bible," Polly said. "But . . ." She looked at Red Charlie dubiously.

"I'll do it," Cal offered. Polly handed him the book, which was heavy, and which served Red Charlie mostly as a register for recording births, baptisms, weddings, and Masonic rites.

"You got a good, clear voice?" the Circulator asked him.

"I used to read for corn afore I got the New Light." Cal shrugged. "It was clear enough for the farmers, I reckon."

"Then it'll be clear enough for this feller. Start with the third Psalm."

The wound had been washed, but Sister Serafina washed it again with water just shy of boiling. She took a heated blade from the Elector and began cutting into the Firstborn's infected side.

Cal read in his best voice:

Lord, how are they increased that trouble me! many are they that rise up against me. Many there be which say of my soul, There is no help for him in God. Selah. But Thou, O Lord, art a shield for me; my glory, and the lifter up of mine head. I cried unto the Lord with my voice, and He heard me out of His holy hill. Selah. I laid me down and slept; I awaked; for the Lord sustained me. I will not be afraid of ten thousands of people, that have set themselves against me round about. Arise, O Lord; save me, O my God: for Thou hast smitten all mine enemies upon the cheek bone; Thou hast broken the teeth of the ungodly. Salvation belongeth unto the Lord: Thy blessing is upon Thy people. Selah.

He'd had an explanation once about what "selah" meant, but he'd forgotten it. Something like amen, maybe. Whatever it was, Sister Serafina seemed to be listening for it, and as Cal pronounced the word *selah*, she made her deepest cuts.

She dropped the cut bits of flesh into a leather and pine-pitch bucket beside the fire. They hit with soft wet *splat* sounds.

Cal felt ill.

"Good," she said. Following Calvin's gaze, she added, "I'm a-cuttin' out the dead flesh. Iffen we can git all that offa him without him dyin', we might jest save this boy."

She set aside the knife she had just used, and the Elector handed her a new one, freshly scoured by the flames. Sister Serafina seemed untroubled by the heat of the water and the steel. Had age dulled her senses? Or long years of exposure?

"Shall I read it again?" Cal asked.

"Psalm three is the Song of Injuries," Sister Serafina said. "We may git back to it. For now, read the Song of Afflictions. That's Psalm ninety-one."

"He that dwelleth in the secret place of the most High shall abide under the shadow of the Almighty," Cal read. "I will say of the Lord, He is my refuge and my fortress: my God; in Him will I trust. Surely He shall deliver thee from the snare of the fowler, and from the noisome pestilence."

"*Noisome* means *stinky*," Sister Serafina said. "Jerusalem iffen that ain't the truth."

"I know what noisome means," Cal said.

"Keep readin'!"

He shall cover thee with His feathers, and under His wings shalt thou trust: His truth shall be thy shield and buckler. Thou shalt not be afraid for the terror by night; nor for the arrow that flieth by day. Nor for the pestilence that walketh in darkness; nor for the destruction that wasteth at noonday. A thousand shall fall at thy side, and ten thousand at thy right hand; but it shall not come nigh thee. Only with thine eyes shalt thou behold and see the reward of the wicked. Because thou hast made the Lord, which is my refuge, even the most High, thy habitation; There shall no evil befall thee, neither shall any plague come nigh thy dwelling.

"St. William Harvey," Sister Serafina cried, "guide now my knife. As I have stripped my life of all things but service to the children of Adam in the name of Christ Jesus and in thy name, to the restoration of life to all, strip thou from this man his dead flesh, the restoration of *his* life. Amen."

"Amen," Iron Andy said.

Olanthes screamed and tried to sit upright. Red Charlie and Polly both threw themselves onto his shoulders and pinned him.

Cal kept reading.

For He shall give his angels charge over thee, to keep thee in all thy ways. They shall bear thee up in their hands, lest thou dash thy foot against a stone. Thou shalt tread upon the lion and adder: the young lion and the dragon shalt thou trample under feet. Because he hath set his love upon me, therefore will I deliver him: I will set him on high, because he hath known my name. He shall call upon me, and I will answer him: I will be with him in trouble; I will deliver him, and honour him. With long life will I satisfy him, and shew him my salvation.

"We're comin' to it now, son." Sister Serafina's teeth were gritted. She wrestled with Olanthes, splashing a little corn liquor on his bleeding flesh and pouring much more of it into his open mouth. "Psalm twenty-nine is the Seven Voices. Read this one loud."

"Give unto the Lord," Cal read.

"Louder!" Sister Serafina shouted. "Loud as e'er you can, son, so nothin' else in this room gits heard o'er your seven voices." She poured more liquor into Olanthes, and then dug into his side. Strips of flesh and skin fell into the bucket beside the pallet.

"Give unto the Lord, O ye mighty." Cal stood to give his belly and lungs more strength. He raised his voice so he was practically shouting. "Give unto the Lord glory and strength. Give unto the Lord the glory due unto his name; worship the Lord in the beauty of holiness. The voice of the Lord is upon the waters: the God of glory thundereth: the Lord is upon many waters."

"Good!" Sister Serafina cried. "That's one voice!"

"The voice of the Lord is powerful," Cal read. "The voice of the Lord is full of majesty."

"Three voices!"

"The voice of the Lord breaketh the cedars; yea, the Lord breaketh the cedars of Lebanon. He maketh them also to skip like a calf; Lebanon and Sirion like a young unicorn."

"Four!"

Olanthes arched his back and screamed.

"The voice of the Lord divideth the flames of fire. The voice of the Lord shaketh the wilderness; the Lord shaketh the wilderness of Kadesh."

"Five and six!"

"Please!" Olanthes was weeping. "Please stop!"

Cal's hands trembled. "The voice of the Lord maketh the hinds to calve, and discovereth the forests: and in his temple doth every one speak of his glory."

"That's seven voices," Sister Serafina said. "Everything speak of glory, now."

"His be the glory, forever and ever," the Elector said.

"Glory to God!" Polly cried.

"Glory be!" Red Charlie added.

The chapter wasn't quite finished, so Cal kept reading. "The Lord sitteth upon the flood; yea, the Lord sitteth King for ever. The Lord will give strength unto His people; the Lord will bless His people with peace."

At the word *peace*, Olanthes's back flattened out and he fell silent. Tears ran down his cheeks and into his ears, but his breathing became regular. Sister Serafina poured the last of the liquor over his side. She had cut away several pounds of flesh; the Firstborn lay open like a deer in the process of being gutted.

"Shall I keep reading?" Cal asked.

"You done well," Serafina told him, answering a question he hadn't wanted to ask. "Start again with the Song of Injuries, while I bandage this boy up." To the Elector, she said, "Your messenger will live. Burn this flesh, lessen you want to infect more of your people."

"And iffen I want to keep a bit of him, for hexin' purposes?" Cal could tell by his smile the Elector was joking.

"I'll cut you off a finger. Won't nobody else git the gangrene that way. Jest tell me which one you want."

"I reckon I'll do without a finger. How can I repay you?" Iron Andy asked.

"Well, Jerusalem," she told him. "I's led to expect I'd git a dance."

To her surprise, Kinta Jane Embry survived the night. While she slept shivering, slowly coming back to a decent temperature, Dockery somehow managed to act. By the time the sun rose again on the Hudson and she poked her head out of her cocoon of wool and fur, her clothing and most of his all hung dry on a neatly lashed frame that hung over a small but hot fire.

He wore a blue linsey-woolsey shirt and baggy long underwear. His feet were in moccasins. He crouched over the fire, tending with a short stick to several fillets of fish that lay cooking on a low, flat rock surrounded on three sides by hot coals.

"Glad you're awake," he said.

"Glad I'm not dead." She looked around and saw white snow, a broad sheet of brown river, black tree trunks poking vertically from the white, and the dark hint of evergreen boughs hiding under the thick winter mantle. No sign of other people. "Did Wilkes make it?"

"It'd be a miracle." Dockery hung his head. "I'm sorry."

"He wasn't my friend or yours," Kinta Jane said. She meant it, but as the words came out she felt a pang in her chest that told her they weren't quite true. She was shaken and hurt by the loss of Isaiah Wilkes, the man who had given her back her tongue. "But he was our leader, and his loss is . . . serious. You and I have a task to accomplish."

"Yeah," Dockery agreed. "And I don't even know what it is."

"I don't know that I do, either." Kinta Jane took her clothing from the rack and climbed into it. Her motions were awkward because her limbs were all stiff, but the cloth was warm and felt good on her chilled skin. Dockery looked away as she dressed, a gesture that she found gallant. "*I'm* sorry."

"For what?"

"You love Julia Stuyvesant."

"*Loved*, maybe. No more. I was just standing around that house bored forever and she was there, is all."

"You love her *now*, Dockery. I'm not an idiot."

Dockery looked away at the river and a tear rolled down

his unshaven jaw. "They're going to kill the baby. They have to. Maybe poison, maybe a doctor's knife, maybe they let it see the light of day and then they leave it out in the snow."

"Does *she* love *you*?" Kinta Jane asked.

"I doubt it. But what man ever knew, really?"

Kinta Jane sighed. "Maybe they'll put the baby with foster parents. Or in a home."

"Maybe I'll never learn the end of it," Dockery said, "since you and I are bound for the frozen north."

"There are caves beneath Montreal," Kinta Jane told him. "All I know is that Wilkes was going to make some kind of signal to someone living around Montreal, and they would meet us in the caves."

"Someone who?"

"Do you know the story of the three brothers?" Kinta Jane asked.

Dockery shook his head.

"In that case . . . maybe an Algonk ally. I'm not sure."

"I figure you ain't sure about the signal, either."

"If I knew it, I'd tell you." Kinta Jane sighed. "I guess we have a little time to think about what kind of signal to send when we get there."

"I was always partial to fireworks," Dockery said.

Dockery built a canoe. He urged Kinta Jane to stay close while he did it, but she ignored him and wandered downriver.

Was she hoping to find Wilkes alive, huddled over his own fire? Or his corpse, frozen and battered on the rocky shore?

In either case, she was disappointed. But she did find another of the fur bundles. It lay waterlogged in the shallows of the river, but she managed to drag it out of the water and pull it behind her, back to where Dockery crouched beside the fire, finishing up their new boat.

The sun was low in the west. "Maybe we wait until tomorrow to get back in the river?" Kinta Jane suggested.

Dockery agreed and they examined the second fur bundle. It was Wilkes's, which was just as well—Dockery could fit in the actor's clothing, though they'd be slightly loose. And wrapped in a small packet of personal effects—a razor, a bar of soap and shaving brush, a penknife—she found her own dried tongue, pierced and labeled and hanging on a leather thong.

Wetting her finger with spittle, she wiped off the ink writing that identified the tongue as hers and slipped the scrap of leather over her neck.

Dockery laid out the furs and wools from Wilkes's bundle on the far side of the fire. He also loaded and primed a pistol and handed it to Kinta Jane before stretching himself out in Wilkes's bedding. They silently gnawed pemmican, drank melted snow, and then fell asleep.

In the morning, before the sun was up, they were paddling northward. They paddled five days before they left the river, stopping to eat dried meat and twice-baked bread, washed down with water. Twice they had portable soup, boiled over a small fire; the hot broth felt like a luxury. In the mornings they added coffee to the meal and in the evenings a little brandy.

They saw Indians, twice on the river and once on shore. They weren't the Choctaw and Cherokee and Caddo that Kinta Jane knew—Haudenosaunee or Algonk, maybe—but Dockery waved at the Indians and they waved back and everyone went on their way each time.

She and Dockery spoke little. He had jokingly suggested fireworks, but really, what would the Conventicle's planned signal be? Some kind of password, given to the right person? Maybe, as the Franklin, Isaiah Wilkes had known the people in or near Montreal to contact. Or perhaps he knew the location of a blind drop, as Kinta Jane knew a blind drop in Philadelphia in the event that she lost contact with the Conventicle and had something to communicate. As had actually happened. But Kinta Jane didn't know anyone at all in Acadia, and was unaware of any drop location. *Could Wilkes have known a recurring place and time to show up at, to hold a meeting?*

The place could be the caves. But what would be a recurring time? The first of the month? Maybe the seventeenth of the month—hadn't the Lightning Bishop been born on the seventeenth of January? Maybe the meeting date was annual, and was the seventeenth of January.

In which case, she had already missed it, by a month and a half now.

Or it could be something connected to the heavens, rather than the paper calendar. The full moon, the new moon, the rising of a new constellation in the east.

Kinta Jane racked her brain for hours and could remember no reference the Franklin had made that gave her any sort of clue at all.

She would have to devise her own signal.

Dockery was gloomy. He was also helpful, gentle, kind, and hard-working. Obviously, he was trapped in his own thoughts about his unborn child. Or possibly, aborted child, at this point.

Kinta Jane wished she had words to help or distract him. Other streetwalkers from New Orleans surely did, many of them being masters of the arts of small talk and flirtation. But the period in which Kinta Jane had worked as a prostitute was also the period in which she had had no tongue. Pleasant, time-passing, jest-filled chatter was beyond her.

She ventured a song. Not having sung for years meant she had forgotten the words to most tunes, but she did remember an old love song.

> *Bobby Shafto's gone to sea*
> *Silver buckles at his knee*
> *He'll come back and marry me*
> *Bonny Bobby Shafto!*
>
> *Bobby Shafto's bright and fair*
> *Panning out his yellow hair*
> *He's my love for evermore*
> *Bonny Bobby Shafto!*
>
> *Bobby Shafto's got a bairn*
> *For to dangle on his arm*
> *In his arm and on his knee*
> *Bobby Shafto loves me.*

She sang it in her best Scotch accent, which was pretty terrible. She hadn't thought of it as being applicable to their own circumstances until the words came out of her mouth, but the song got Dockery to smile, so it was worth it. They kept paddling.

Jake awoke and found himself tied into a chair, his wrists strapped to its thick wooden arms and his ankles bound to its legs. He felt sick to his stomach. He pushed with his legs, tried to move the chair and fight through the fog that filled his brain at the same time. The chair didn't move.

Nailed to the floor.

He was on a ship.

He felt the sway of the room and realized that was why his stomach was turning. The knowledge of the cause instantly banished his nausea.

He remembered being bound to a stone slab under a sky of fire and smoke. Mortals with iron knives had stabbed at him and plucked out his organs to feed them to his infant son. He cried out, without words.

"You must have terrible dreams." The voice belonged to Temple Franklin. Shaking sleep from his eyes, Jake turned and saw Franklin sitting in a similar chair a few steps away. "Guilty ones. Are you a criminal?"

"You know the saying. I'm one Dutchman, I must be a preacher."

"If I'm to judge by what you say in your sleep, I'd say you were a regicide, parricide, cannibal, sorcerer, priest. Are you *maanziek, meneer?*"

"Just tired. My cousins and I have been walking a long way. Is that why I'm tied up? You think I'm insane?"

"Come now. They're not your cousins. You're tied up for the same reason I keep the two of them drugged and unconscious. Now, you tell me who they are, so that I know you know, and we can have a serious conversation."

Jake hesitated, but only for a moment. He was being interrogated, but he didn't think he was being tricked. "They're the children of Hannah Penn and Kyres Elytharias."

"Two of the children, more properly. The third being the witch who squats on the Serpent Throne and tries to make trouble for Lord Thomas. Ironically, I've been looking for these two. My spy in Johnsland only realized who 'Nathaniel Chapel' was after he had left. And wherever did you find the girl?"

"Acadia," Jake lied.

"Hmm."

"You're planning to give them to Thomas Penn," Jake said.

"Of course."

"He'll kill them, as he killed their mother. As he tries to kill their sister."

"Or if he doesn't kill them, he'll trade them. Maybe he'll give all three Elytharias bastards their lives if they'll go away into quiet retirement. Let us call it the Washington Plan."

"I don't believe in the Washington Plan," Jake said.

"Thomas has no child of his own," Franklin pointed out. "Perhaps he'll take them in, recognize them, and raise them as his heirs."

"This is exactly why there is no Washington Plan," Jake shot back. "If these two are alive, there will always be someone who wants to use them to raise a banner of revolt, even if they themselves do not wish it."

"Thomas might surprise you. We have been seeking these children for months, and I have never been instructed to have them killed. If I had been, they'd be dead right now, rather than sleeping peacefully."

"Drugged."

"Yes."

"The real question," Jake said, "is why you've kept *me* alive. I'm no Elytharias. I'm just a servant who was sent to find two children."

"Hardly children. Perhaps I'll torture you for information."

"I doubt I have any. I haven't seen my queen in weeks. Surely your spies in the Ohio have more current news than I do."

"Perhaps you have information on other subjects."

"The Tarock," Jake suggested. "I know the Tarock pretty well. If you free my hands, I'll do a casting for you."

"Do you know grandfather's cards?" Franklin smiled. "And have you found the puzzles?"

Jake frowned and said nothing. *Puzzles?*

"Grandfather insisted he'd hidden puzzles in the cards. In any case, now we get closer. I'd like you to tell me all you know about Simon Sword."

Jake held his tongue. Was there a lie he could tell to Sarah's advantage here? Maybe if the Imperials believed Simon Sword was on her side, that would put them in fear of her. Or maybe he could deny the existence of Simon Sword, to increase their surprise when they encountered him?

He remembered fording the Mississippi, waters knee-high, with a solemn-faced Eldritch king holding spear and shield waiting on the opposite bank to meet him.

"Let me tell you what I know," Franklin continued. "I come

from something of a peculiar family. I don't mean the fact that I'm a bastard's bastard—don't look shocked, that's a matter of public record—I mean my grandfather. He collected me from the orphanage and bestowed his name on me ... as Thomas might do with that surprisingly strong young woman you travel with. Likely not the young man. I assume that he wears his clothing inside out because he's an idiot. Thomas doesn't need an idiot for an heir."

"Perhaps Thomas can keep him about the court and consult him as an oracle. I heard they do that in Pennsland."

"Divination by consulting idiots, yes. I don't know the theory—I imagine they're believed to be closer to God, or something. If their idiocy is believed to relay the emanated power of the stars, Thomas may be interested. And my grandfather told me the most ludicrous stories. He said, you see, that this land, everything between the Appalachians and the mountains in the far west, the whole great bowl that drains into the Mississippi, belonged to an ancient god. Or, you know, the land *was* the god, or the river *was* the god, might be how the story ran, that being the logic of gods and fairy tales."

"The Heron King," Jake said, without meaning to.

"Yes, that's the one. Folk hero and bugbear. My grandfather, the saintly Lightning Bishop, believed he was real. Ot at least, he claimed to believe. Real, and possessed of two sides that alternated. One side was peaceful. He stopped diseases and taught people how to farm maize."

"Peter Plowshare," Jake murmured. He remembered trampling a thousand miles of rows of beans, corn, and squash planted together, uprooting the plants and sowing in their place the bones of men. "He did those things."

"The other brought war and catastrophe," Franklin said. "He demanded the sacrifice of men; he toppled kingdoms; he made away with virgins, cheated at cards, fixed elections, smoked too much, and committed every other conceivable sin."

"No," Jake said. "You joke, and this isn't a matter for joking. He shatters power and brings civilization crashing down. You mean Simon Sword."

"Fine," Franklin agreed. "He shattered power."

"Shatters," Jake said. "He *shatters* power. He is doing it now."

For once, Franklin hesitated, giving Jake a queer look. "And my grandfather insisted that a cabal of men had been formed to pass on the knowledge of Simon Sword and make preparations for his destructive reign."

"Your grandfather formed this cabal?"

"Others have said that he did, and that he called it his *Conventicle*. But that wasn't how my grandfather told it. He pointed at William Penn as one of the founders. Penn and his allies and their successors existed in a kind of Masonic fraternity, hidden from the eyes of others. But in places of power that would permit them to stand against Simon Sword when he came again."

"That would be a good thing," Jake said. "Did your grandfather tell you where to find them?"

Franklin shook his head. "At a young age, I took to whoring and dice, and my grandfather stopped telling me those stories. I assumed it was because they were fairy tales and I had outgrown them. Lately, I have been given reason to understand that other men believe and still pass on such stories. Whether or not there is such an organization, there are people who believe it exists, and believe themselves to be in it."

"The Conventicle," Jake said. "It's more than a folktale."

"Yes. A man presented himself at Horse Hall. That's the Emperor's palace in Philadelphia. He called himself *the Franklin*. He called Thomas 'Brother Onas,' and begged him to take up his burden and fight Simon Sword."

Jake felt dread. He had come to the wrong man. "You imprisoned this Franklin, of course."

"Oh, we tried to *kill* him. But he escaped us. I can see in your eyes you'd very much like to talk with *that* Franklin, wouldn't you? You must have been carrying a message for him, and by mistake you delivered it to me. How disappointing for you. Do you belong to the Conventicle?"

"I don't know anything about the Conventicle," Jake said. And because he didn't know anything about the Conventicle, he decided he'd try the truth. "Though perhaps I met one of its members. He was a man in the entourage of the Chevalier of New Orleans, and he died. In dying, he gave me the message I gave you."

"That the sword had gone back."

Jake nodded.

"Did he say the message was for *Temple* Franklin, then? Or for *the* Franklin?"

Jake's scalp itched, and he wished he could scratch it. "As far as I can remember, he just said *Franklin*."

"What does it mean, that the sword has gone back?" Temple Franklin leaned forward in his seat, eyes glittering.

Jake found himself unexpectedly eager to answer the question. "I think he wanted the Franklin to know that it was all going to be worse than the Conventicle expected. Much, much worse."

Cahokia was surrounded by tilled farmland. Etzanoa, her unruly sister, rose out of tangled forest.

Chigozie had seen the city coming for miles, or at least, he had seen a ring of white towers looming above the tops of the trees. *Beneath the towers of Etzanoa, I spoke this prayer for Shenandoah*, was a lyric he'd heard traveling up the Mississippi. The white spires gave the words sudden flesh and bone.

Chigozie and Kort walked along a forest path behind the three riders of Zomas. Kort and Ferpa had both asked to come, despite Chigozie's pleading that at least one of them should stay at the Still Waters with the Merciful.

The towers of Etzanoa were built of white stone. Chigozie hadn't seen stone like it anywhere in Missouri—where had it come from? The white stone statues leaning out from the bases of the towers, depicting heroes and monsters in equal measure and in equally ecstatic poses of battle, were worn and crumbled with age. A small city surrounded the towers, and it was ringed about with a wall of white stone. Behind a thin veil of drifting snowflakes and perched on a high bluff above the Missouri River, it almost looked angelic.

Though he had seen it only briefly, Cahokia gave Chigozie the impression that it had sprung from the earth like a plant. In the case of its Treewall, literally. Etzanoa gave the impression that it had been built by an alien hand, perhaps a demonic one.

Men stood on the walls of the city. They wore red and black and held the same long spears Naares's riders had, but there was something odd about them. At first, Chigozie thought they wore helmets without visors. When he got close enough, he realized what it was.

"Why are they facing inward, toward the city?" he asked Naares.

"There has been a death." Naares's mouth was set in a grim line. "Someone mighty has left us."

"You're saying they're watching a funeral procession?"

"No. A powerful ghost has been driven out of the city. The city's defenders turn their backs outward, because they fear their faces would present a familiar sight and welcome the ghost back. They wish to convince the ghost that its home is on this side of the wall now."

Kort snorted, the hot breath from his nostrils melting a thousand snowflakes on the wing.

"How long will they stand like that?" Chigozie asked.

"It depends on the ghost," Naares said.

"And if they are attacked while they stand thus?" Kort rumbled.

"They will turn and fight. And when they have cut their foe to pieces, they will again sacrifice to feed the ghost, again lead it outside the wall, and again stand with their faces averted."

"I would say that you are curious folk," Chigozie said, "only..." He thought of his own father, also buried outside the wall, evidently with Vodun rites. He thought of his brother Etienne, who had used his father's funeral as an attack spell against the dead man's murderer.

And he realized that in his own heart, he did not *entirely* disagree with what Etienne had done. Was this what had driven him into the wilderness? Was this what had led him to make common cause with penitent beastkind? A need to reject his brother's choice, deny that part of him that silently approved? Did he need to prove he was different from his brother? Superior to his brother?

Did he need to exorcise from his own soul the spirits his brother served?

"Only you in New Orleans build palaces for your dead, and that is far stranger," Naares said.

Kort laughed.

"Palaces?" Chigozie asked.

"I have been to New Orleans. Your living huddle crowded in buildings of wood and plaster, buildings that rot and are carried away in heavy rains. Your dead sleep in stone mansions, beyond the grasp of time and its corruption. You worship your dead. You are ruled by them. Yours is a city of the dead, in which the living are only guests. Etzanoa is a city of the living, from which we have driven out the dead."

"Can we enter this city of the living?" Kort asked. "The gates are shut. I presume to keep out the ghost."

They stood in front of one of the city's gates. A steep-walled, V-cut moat surrounded the wall, containing only a thin sliver of ice in its depths. The drawbridge that would give access to the city over it had been drawn up. Shattered muskets and spears and crushed helmets gave testimony of recent battle around the city. Piles of black ash flashed white glints that might have been bone.

Naares cupped his hands around his mouth and bellowed words Chigozie didn't understand.

There was instant reaction on the wall. Still with their backs turned to the outside, two men together took a long horn and blew a ragged, deep, humming note that began in Chigozie's ears and then seemed to pierce the fabric of the world, resonating in his bones and in the earth and in the stars at the same time.

The drawbridge dropped and a portcullis behind it rose at the same moment.

The long horn note continued as Naares limped across the drawbridge and the others followed, Chigozie came last. Behind him the drawbridge rose and the portcullis fell. When the gate was finally shut again, the horn stopped.

"The horn was to scare the ghost away while the door was open," Kort said.

"Not to frighten it," Naares said. "But to make the city alien to it, so it would seek its home outside."

"Why do you fear the spirits of the dead?" Chigozie. "Many would welcome a meeting with a dead loved one, for advice or a final farewell."

Naares shot a stern look at Chigozie. "There are ghostmasters in Etzanoa who can provide such a meeting. But their work is forbidden as well as cursed. The spirits of the dead eat the souls of the living. That brings sickness, fatigue, despair, and madness."

"If you drive all the ghosts into the forest, then," Kort said. "The forest must be a terrifying place."

"It is indeed," Naares said.

They exited the gate into the city. Everywhere he looked, Chigozie saw white stone. The buildings seemed built with no central scheme—he saw houses beside gardens beside inns beside armories beside palaces. Within the wall, there was an open space that would presumably allow soldiers to march and maneuver in defense. Other than that...

"Are there no streets?" he asked.

"None that are straight," Naares said. "A boulevard is an invitation to an enemy to march to the palace and seize the king. The streets of Etzanoa are built according to a careful scheme, and every child is taught to know that scheme by heart. Any child of ten who is native to the city can take you where you want directly. To an invader, the city is a maze."

Naares led them. The city's streets were paved with stone, and square gutters ran along each side of every street. The gutters ran with water and poured into grate-covered openings every fifty feet or so, but the waste water wasn't sewage and didn't stink.

Etzanoa was clean and white.

More than half the people Chigozie saw wore iron collars. Some of them looked as he imagined slaves would. They wore tattered rags and performed heavy labor, repairing damaged streets or dragging carts of waste. But many dressed and walked and behaved like a free person.

"Your city's fashions are strange," Kort growled.

At first, Chigozie thought the beastman was referring to the collars, but then he realized his mistake. The Etzanoans wore clothing inside out. Not all of it, but each wore one piece, conspicuously, reversed. Some a cloak, some a hat, some a pair of breeks.

"It isn't fashion," Chigozie guessed. "It's to fool the dead person."

"It's to fool the ghost," Naares agreed. "I understand you may find us strange, but at least this is a harmless precaution."

"What sort of precaution wouldn't be harmless?" Chigozie asked.

"Once slaves were owned by individual masters," Naares explained, "rather than by the kingdom. At a man's death, all his slaves were also killed. Their bodies were buried outside the walls, so the dead man wouldn't hear their voices and return. Later, when we had given up executing such slaves, for a period we exiled them into the forest instead. Most likely died as a result."

"Only slaves?" Kort asked.

"What do you mean?" Naares looked uncomfortable.

"If the voices of a man's slaves would call back his ghost, what about the voices of his women and his children?"

"There are stories that suggest that, at least among our royalty, living queens once followed dead kings onto their funeral pyres."

"Like the Chicago Germans," Chigozie said.

"But not children?" Kort pressed.

"Not children," Naares said. "Killing the children of a dead man would be madness. You would destroy the kingdom in a single generation."

The center of the city was a loose ring formed by the white towers. A second wall, higher than the first, ran from tower to tower, but this gate was open. These guards faced outward. The men in black wooden armor and red cloaks were reinforced by a dozen thick-shouldered hounds with spiky hair and wolflike ears.

Naares saluted, was recognized, and passed through.

In the center of Etzanoa was a complex of white stone buildings. Without going inside, Chigozie couldn't tell what happened in these buildings, but guessing by the clothing of the people moving around within the inner wall, he'd have said the buildings included a palace, a barracks, and one or more temples.

Naares stopped to talk to a man standing within the gate. The man could have been Naares's double, with his dusky complexion, broad nose, and blond hair. He wore the same armor and uniform, too, though Naares had lost his cloak and looked the worse for wear. This man was polished.

"English, Dolim, if you don't mind," Naares said, indicating Chigozie's presence with a sweep of his arm.

"Welcome back," Dolim said. "You're timely. The seven days of mourning end tomorrow, and we are preparing to mount a counterattack on the Heron's beasts. Your men are wanted."

"My men are dead, save these two," Naares said. Then he looked at Chigozie and Kort slyly. "Though I may have replacements. Wait...did you say seven days?"

Dolim nodded.

Naares grew pale. "Who has died, then?"

"Who else? Lord Turim Zomas the second. The city is now ruled by Turim Zomas the third."

"Who still wears a dress as he is dandled on his mother's knee. Who will be regent?"

"General Varem has taken control, at least for now."

"That's excellent news for the city," Naares said. Then he turned to Chigozie. "But it's terrible news for you."

"I admire him, and now I am going to rob him."

—⊷∘⊶—

CHAPTER EIGHTEEN

When Cathy arrived, Alzbieta Torias was weeping. The priestess knelt beside the ragged holes that comprised a perfect spiral beside the Sunrise Mound. Smashed pottery shards lay about the holes, and the snow had been trampled into mud.

Cathy stepped closer. The jars were shattered, the bodies within had been removed.

"How can the goddess permit this?" she asked Torias.

She had meant to say *your goddess*, but that wasn't how the words came out.

"If the goddess stopped every attempt at desecration," Torias said, her voice trembling, but containing a cold, hard edge, "we would have no words for blasphemy, impiety, and profanity."

Bill hobbled up behind Cathy, arriving last. "No words for profanity would be a loss indeed, ma'am," he said. "Some men would be rendered entirely mute. I, for one, would feel drained of half my color."

They had received Maltres Korinn's summons on the wall where Bill had paced, glaring at the swelling ranks of the Imperial besiegers. It was only a matter of time before their sheer numbers overwhelmed Cahokia. Unless help came, or Sarah returned having mastered the connection with the Serpent Throne she desired, Cathy knew Bill must inevitably be defeated.

How will I get him out of the city before it is sacked?

Cathy herself had been receiving a lecture from a team of Pitchers, rehearsing without powder and shot the actions necessary to load the wall's defensive guns, lay them at a target, and fire.

"In better times, we'd be firing live rounds," the Pitcher team's sergeant had growled. "As it is, the Imperials will likely give us opportunity for better practice soon enough."

Cathy wouldn't leave Bill behind, which made their movement slow, and they arrived last. Alzbieta Torias and other priestesses appeared determined to provide the now-unearthed dead a second round of grieving; Sherem and Korinn stood glaring at the priest Zadok, who scowled back. The dark-skinned Firstborn, Gazelem Zomas, stared at the opened graves with a stunned expression on his face.

"As an initial response to this situation," Bill suggested, "we must impose a consequence commensurate with the offense. We should hang the priest."

"I didn't do this!" Zadok Tarami stepped back, eyeing Bill fearfully.

"Do you *disapprove* the action, suh?" Bill said. "I shall happily accompany you to the pulpit to hear your denunciation of this crime."

Tarami hesitated.

"I won't hang a man without a trial," Maltres said.

"But *I* will," Bill shot back.

"You don't disapprove," Cathy said to the Metropolitan. "That's obvious. Do you know who did it? Do you know where the bodies have been taken?"

"I assume whoever did this was influenced by my sermons." Zadok straightened his back and looked her in the eye. "I am not sorry."

"I regard that as a confession," Bill said. "In peacetime, I would now turn him over to the constables and law-clerks. We do not live in a time of peace, Korinn. Let's hang the bastard, right after we hang Voldrich."

"I don't intend to hang Voldrich." Maltres Korinn looked exhausted. So did Bill, for that matter. The Cavalier looked gaunt, as well. "Not unless I have to."

"He admitted to passing messages to the besiegers. He attempted to kidnap Sarah and hand her over the wall."

"He attempted to kidnap a woman posing as Sarah."

"I doubt even a Philadelphia lawyer would exculpate the viper on such a technicality." Bill's face twisted with rage, an anger Cathy knew was aggravated by the constant pain in both his legs. "And given that *this* blackguard has convinced his followers to uproot my dead soldiers from their graves, depriving them of their eternal rests and insulting their public honor, I regard the fact that he didn't himself wield a shovel as an irrelevant detail."

"They killed the snakes," Alzbieta sobbed.

Cathy peered again into the pit beside which Alzbieta knelt. At the bottom, on shattered baked clay, lay a snake. The head had been neatly severed from its body.

The sight of tears streaming down the priestess's face softened something inside Cathy. "Would you tell me the significance of the serpent?" she asked.

"It is a deliberate desecration," Zadok snarled. "Obviously."

"The serpent passed between worlds," Alzbieta said, "and therefore it could carry the soul of the deceased back to Eden and eternal life."

"Which is obvious nonsense," Zadok said. "A snake has been killed, nothing more. A symbol has been challenged. Aside from the fact that one does not return to Eden, mankind has been barred from Eden forever. Genesis could not be more clear."

"Is it more obvious nonsense than your Christ crucified?" Cathy asked.

"Theology makes my teeth hurt," Bill said. "Since the Metropolitan finds the shattering of symbols to be acceptable, I suggested we respond by breaking some of the precious furniture of his church. I haven't been inside the place, so I'm open to suggestions as to which pieces."

"The vine over the door," Cathy said coolly. "The altar. The astral tree."

"Astral tree?" Bill laughed. "And I thought you were a Christian, Tarami!"

The Metropolitan blushed. "It is a representation of the cross, in the manner of our ancestors. It is the cross as cosmic pillar."

Bill snorted.

"I will break nothing, and I will hang no one." Maltres stabbed a finger at Zadok Tarami. "But realize that Her Majesty may, for her part, feel differently. As your friend...or at least, as a man who is reluctant to see you hanged, Tarami...I advise you to ease up on your crusade. Moderate your rhetoric. Call back your people."

"I will not." Tarami crossed his arms over his chest.

"I've heard enough. Sergeant!" Bill roared.

Chikaak presented himself, hands on a pair of pistols tucked into his belt.

"Sir William!" Korinn shouted.

"Arrest the Metropolitan!" Bill's face was an unhealthy blend of bright red and corpse-like gray.

Chikaak grabbed the priest by his robe. Tarami didn't resist.

Maltres Korinn swung his heavy staff of office. Chikaak didn't see the blow coming, and Maltres caught the beastman alongside his head. Chikaak staggered back, releasing the Metropolitan.

Bill slouched sideways, leaning on one crutch and dropping the other as he drew a pistol—

Korinn raised his staff like a club, as if he wanted to smash in Bill's skull—

"Stop!" Cathy stepped between the two men.

"You would defend this worm?" Bill grunted.

"No," Cathy said.

"Nor I," Maltres added. "But...it is a grave thing to kill a man, Bill. The thought weighs on me."

"Is it?" Bill chuckled. "Hell's Bells, how is it that I am even able to stand, bearing such a mountain on my back as I do? And if I can bear all the deaths I carry now, I assure you I can bear the death of Zadok Tarami, as well. I'll carry that burden for everyone, and gladly."

No one answered him. Cathy moved to his elbow, prepared to catch him if his knees buckled.

"The serpent is no symbol." Alzbieta's tears had dried up, and her voice sounded like the crinkling of a dried corn husk. "Maltres, you have every reason to know that the goddess lives."

"And if not," the Polite Sherem said, speaking up for the first time in the conversation, "I can remind you."

"I need no reminder." Maltres leaned on his staff.

"Do you not see," Zadok Tarami said, "that whoever took these men must have respected them as heroes, too?"

"I never desecrated the grave of *my* hero," Bill drawled. "Barbaric customs your folk have."

"There are more obvious symbols to attack, if one wished to express anger with the goddess and Her priests," Tarami explained.

"The Great Mound," Cathy suggested. "The Sunrise Mound. The Temple of the Sun. The Serpent Throne."

Tarami nodded. "And the graves were not merely disturbed. They have been *emptied*."

"What are you suggesting?" Korinn took a deep breath and stood straight, as if he had suddenly discovered hope.

"They have been reburied elsewhere." Tarami pointed down at the gaping sockets in the ground. "Grateful for the sacrifice of these defenders of Cahokia, someone has interred them in holy ground."

"We can find a fresh grave," Bill snapped. "The city is not that large."

As the drama had played out between Sarah's advisors and friends in this very public space, a crowd had gathered. Thin with hunger and blue with cold, Cahokians in their cloaks stared at the party standing on the burial ground with apprehension and judgment in their eyes.

"Bill," Cathy said softly.

He looked, saw, and nodded. Korinn looked around at the crowd as well, and then the men locked eyes.

"Well, Vizier?" Bill asked. "If we are to find fresh graves, now is the time to do it. Disturbed earth will settle, if it has not been carefully hidden already."

Maltres Korinn shifted his gaze, looking back and forth between Alzbieta and the Metropolitan. "Can I persuade either of you that there is some shared rite that will satisfy both your priesthoods?"

"No," Tarami said flatly.

"It isn't a matter of persuading me," the Handmaid said. "What would you do to persuade the goddess on whose holy hill you stood?"

Korinn's eyes turned and gazed on the Sunrise Mound, as if trying to stare through it.

"These men were fully buried with the goddess's rite," Cathy said. "I saw that myself. Alzbieta, is there no theological case to be made that the burial was sanctified and complete once the burial jars were shut? That whatever happened afterward, however ugly, is irrelevant to the eternal resting place of the dead men?"

"I do not make theological cases." Alzbieta finally stood, and the muddy streaks on her knees and forearms underlined her words. "I sing the goddess's songs, and I ask for Her favor."

Cathy suddenly saw frailty and weakness in Alzbieta's face, and felt moved. *She desired above all things to be the Beloved of her goddess. Instead, she had to serve as mere witness to a rival who received the honor.*

"Could you then ask for Her favor on all our behalf?" Maltres asked, shooting a grateful look at Cathy. "If I join you in signs of penitence, sack cloth and ashes, and we implore the goddess for forgiveness, might She give it to us?"

"She is benevolent," Alzbieta said slowly. "Let us try."

"You are speaking of a demon!" Zadok Tarami snapped.

"It's not too late to hang the cleric," Bill said drily. "Or I can just shoot him where he stands."

Maltres Korinn shook his head. "You do not make me miss my berry brambles less, Metropolitan. For the moment, I will do nothing about the desecration of these graves. We will beg the goddess's forgiveness and understanding. I am tempted to order you to join us."

The look of revulsion on the old man's face almost made Cathy smile.

"But instead," the Vizier continued, "I request you to consider inviting your flock to pray with us for peace and forgiveness from God as you understand Him."

"I'd suggest adding the customary fasting to the prayer," Bill said, "only I expect that they're all in a state of fasting as it is. If you agree to the Vizier's request, Zadok, I will not shoot you on the spot. What do you say?"

"That is not a friendly codicil." Tarami glowered.

Bill shrugged. "I am not your friend."

Zadok Tarami looked up at the iron-gray clouds hanging over the city as if seeking an answer for long moments. Finally, he nodded. "You do as you think right by the ... by your faith. I and mine shall pray to the Lord of Hosts for forgiveness for all our misdeeds, for peace, and for aid."

"*Forgiveness for all our misdeeds* is a fine formulation," Maltres said. "I will have you watched, Tarami. If I hear you pray for forgiveness for worshipping the goddess, the next man to get buried inside a jar with a companion snake shall be you ... only you shall go in alive, and the snake will be a cottonmouth."

"I forgive you both your threats against me," Zadok Tarami said, nodding as if finishing a prayer.

"And the next time we have a public burial?" Cathy asked.

There was an awful silence.

"We're going to fight this out all over again." Sherem shook his head.

"No," Maltres Korinn said slowly. "From now until the siege is lifted, all public burials, including the deaths of all soldiers, will be administered by the Cahokian First Lodge of the Ancient and Accepted Order of Freemasons, Ohio Rite. I shall preside. A soldier's death can also be commemorated privately by his own people in the fashion they prefer, and no one will molest or interfere. Agreed?" He stared Zadok Tarami in the face. "You're a Notary, Tarami. I will have seven Notaries sign this proclamation, to give it the fullest authority I can. Will you sign?"

Tarami looked around at the crowd, then nodded. "I'll sign."

"I'll sign," said a grave-faced woman with pale eyes who stepped forward from the crowd.

Maltres nodded.

"And I." This was from a bone-thin old man leaning on a crutch not too dissimilar to Bill's.

"I'll write the proclamation myself," Maltres said. "And find four more Notaries." He looked to Alzbieta Torias. "Then I and mine, at least, *shall* begin a fast."

Nathaniel awoke slowly, a rocking motion trying to lure him back to sleep while spears of gray light pierced his consciousness and pulled him the other way.

"Come now, boy, tell me your name."

He opened his eyes and looked into the face of Temple Franklin, the man he'd spied on from the starlit plain with Jacob Hop. Franklin's face resembled his grandfather's, but where in all his portraits the Lightning Bishop's eyes twinkled with wit and kindness, Temple Franklin's eyes were cold.

"Nathaniel," Jacob Hop said. "Don't be afraid."

Nathaniel looked and found Jake, sitting tied into a chair on the other side of Franklin. Franklin stepped aside so they could see each other better, and Jake smiled.

"I'm not afraid," Nathaniel said. "I'm tired."

"I drugged you," Temple Franklin said. "Or rather, that Dutch ship's captain did. The tiresome thing about all these merchants and smugglers who clamor for free trade and no tariffs is how many of them turn out to be for sale when you make an offer. Just once, I'd like some Dutchman to bite his thumb at me."

"I'd bite my thumb at you," Jake called with a cheerful grin, "only it's tied down, along with my other fingers."

Temple Franklin chuckled drily.

"Je vuile pannenkoek!" Jake cried. "Je smeerlap!"

"You should let us go," Nathaniel said.

"Ah." Franklin laid a finger alongside his nose. "Or else what? Or else your sister—don't deny it, I can see from your faces that you're siblings—your sister with the strength of a troll will break my legs, is that it?" He laughed.

Nathaniel said nothing.

"I'm aware of her prodigious might. That's why she'll reach the very end of our journey without ever waking up."

"Do you—?" Nathaniel tried to stand, and realized for the first time that he was tied into a chair just as Jake was. The chairs were nailed to the floor, and the floor tilted first one way and then the other.

They were on a ship.

"I'm not going to kill her, relax." Temple smiled. "That's for Lord Thomas to do, if he chooses."

"Please don't." Nathaniel pulled, but couldn't yank his arms from their bindings.

"Nathaniel," Jake said softly. "Don't be afraid."

Nathaniel was afraid. He took deep breaths to try to calm his beating heart, sucking air in and blowing it out through pressed lips to try to disguise it.

"Here's the situation." Franklin stepped back and put his hands into the pockets of a long blue coat. "Lord Thomas doesn't have an heir."

Nathaniel knew what Lord Thomas was doing to try to get an heir—marrying into Dutch wealth.

Which wealth had probably betrayed Nathaniel and his sister into Thomas's hands.

"Are we going to Philadelphia?" Nathaniel asked.

Franklin nodded. "Have you been to Horse Hall?"

"I grew up in Johnsland." Nathaniel shook his head. "I've never been to Philadelphia."

"Except when you were born there, of course. In the Slate Roof House, if Hannah was telling the truth."

"I don't remember that."

"Naturally." Franklin nodded. "I'm taking you to Philadelphia, and to Horse Hall. To meet your uncle Thomas. What do you think about that, Nathaniel?"

Thomas had killed Nathaniel's mother, according to the Earl of Johnsland. And Nathaniel's father, according to Jake and his sister Sarah. Thomas's face and name had been worn by one of the four cosmic ogres that had torn Nathaniel to bits in the Pit of Heaven, before a Sarah-ogre had reconstituted him. The name filled Nathaniel with dread, and he had no intention of showing that fact. "Did Jake tell you my name?"

"He didn't have to. I have an informer in Johnsland. Oh, don't look surprised, I have them all over the Empire. They keep me abreast of the undertakings of the Electors, the ones they don't publish in the news-papers. The only interesting ones, really. We have been looking for you for months. After the events of the recent Yule, with your disappearance, we realized who you had to be. Nathaniel Elytharias Penn. And then this idiot brought you right *to* me."

Nathaniel tried not to show his confusion on his face.

"Perhaps you were sleeping at the time." Franklin smiled. "He and your sister, whose name I have not yet teased out, assaulted me in the lobby of my hotel. From there it was a simple matter to bribe the right people on the docks and wait. You can't leave New Amsterdam except by water."

Jake hung his head.

"Don't judge the Dutchman too harshly." Franklin tut-tutted. "He tried his best. He only thought he was on the trail of a great conspiracy, perhaps one that would help restore you to your family's wealth and lost power. After all, in an extraordinary act of great courage...he *did* call me a pannenkoek."

"I don't want anything from Thomas," Nathaniel said. "Let us go, and we'll go away forever."

"Don't say that," Franklin said. "There's only one way to go away *forever*, and I don't think you really mean it."

"We'll sail to England," Nathaniel pressed. "You'll never see us again."

"I think you're missing the point here." Franklin scratched his chin in thought. "Thomas needs an heir. He will yet try to produce one himself, yes, but he's not such a fool to put all his eggs in one basket, as my grandfather might have preached against. There's an opportunity for you to prove yourself amiable."

"To Thomas?"

Franklin nodded. "And to me."

"What does 'amiable' mean?"

Franklin shrugged. "In this case, it means willing to help. Willing to help Thomas with his plans for the Ohio. Willing to be an ally, not an enemy."

"Nathaniel," Jake said. "Listen to me; there's something you must know."

Nathaniel tried to pay attention to Jacob Hop, but Temple Franklin stepped in the way. "Picking me up and throwing me, for instance, would not be the act of an amiable person."

Margaret must have done that. Which must be why Franklin is talking to me and not to her.

"I have something I must tell your sister," Jake said. "Sarah, I mean."

Franklin spun on his heels, and Nathaniel suddenly saw a knife in his hands. "Shut your mouth, Dutchman."

"Come find me," Jake said. "Tell her to come find me. It's about the Tarocks—"

Temple Franklin lunged forward, slashing with his blade. It was a tiny weapon, but Jake was bound and couldn't dodge. Franklin rose and fell and rose again like a bird of prey, striking with his hand. Great loops of blood rose with him and splattered across the cabin. The Dutchman shuddered and twitched. When Temple Franklin finally stood back, Jake sat dead in the chair.

Temple dropped the knife to the floor. It clattered on hard wood and then bounced away into a corner.

"Now, then," he croaked. "We were discussing amiability."

After Hooke raised the wall of black fire around Cahokia, Notwithstanding Schmidt feared a conflict in leadership. Cromwell's was a name to curse by, but for some it would be a name to follow. But Hooke seized the tent Dadgayadoh had once occupied, posted the shuffling, dull-eyed, dead Haudenosaunee at the door, and hid Cromwell inside.

Schäfer was forced entirely out of the tent. The Youngstown German trader began volunteering for tasks that would keep him away from camp.

Immediately upon seeing Cromwell occupy the body of one of the Parletts, Schmidt had acted to protect the other two, which constituted her quickest communications link to Horse Hall. But was that link now compromised? Assuming the Parletts on the other end of the link still lived, did Cromwell share with them their mind-connecting link?

She tripled the size of Mohuntubby's command, giving him her best militiamen.

She wished she hadn't lost Luman Walters; the Sorcerer Hooke was powerful. Schmidt felt no compunction about being allied with men of dark art, but she wasn't entirely sure Cromwell and her shareholder had the same strategic objectives in mind.

She made Captain Mohuntubby take her Himmelsbrief. She explained it only minimally, but he nodded as if he were accustomed to having to unpick the lining of his coat and then restore it in order to be able to insert letters written in German. She ordered him not to leave the presence of the Parletts other than to go the latrine, and in that instance to leave his coat behind.

Luman's Himmelsbrief drove back Ezekiel Angleton. Will it be enough to stop Oliver Cromwell?

The snow continued to fall. She had the manpower to collect it and have it thrown into melting pots, while scooping the remainder aside. The perpetual task helped her keep discipline in a camp that every day felt less like a trading post and more like a siege.

The spring thaw, when it came, would be brutal.

Encountering Hooke beside a campfire, Schmidt nodded. "Don't worry at our delay," she told the Lazar. "We are only waiting for reinforcements. We are not sending mines under the walls because the ground is so wet. They would fill in, and the engineers would drown."

And because thou canst not fathom the depth of the Treewall's roots. I have seen sieges before, Madam Director, Hooke replied. *Fear not. Thy sole task is to keep the Serpentborn enclosed. Mine and my master's craft will inevitably take their souls in time.*

"Is that the goal, then?" she asked affably. "To take their souls? I had thought it was the suppression of revolt and the defense of the throne of Lord Thomas." The true unification of the Empire: the bringing of a stronger peace; prosperity for all.

Methods she found acceptable; goals she desired.

Yes, he cackled. *Yes, that's it.*

"I had rather hoped that I'd see more battle magic from a magician of your fame," Schmidt said. "Lightning bolts, curses. That was why I was willing to part company with my previous wizard, who was perfectly serviceable."

Thou hast seen the battle magic. Hooke stared at Schmidt with his white eyes, that trembled in black, worm-filled jelly. *And thou shalt see it yet.*

And then he stalked away into the snow.

Two days later, General Sayle arrived.

Theophilus Sayle was whisper thin, with fine strands of white hair that blew distractedly about the sides of his head and dark liver spots on his bald pate. He wore a blue coat in recognition of his position as Thomas's General of the Army of the Ohio, but otherwise was dressed in sad Yankee browns and orange. The effect was like a bright blue sky over an autumn landscape, as incongruous as it was striking.

He arrived with his first scouts ahead of a force that Schmidt's own intelligencer, coming quickly down the Ohio River by canoe, told her numbered ten thousand men. She hadn't thought Thomas had that many soldiers—he must have acted quickly to recruit, once the Electors gave their assent.

Sayle's eyes were a sad brown that matched his trousers. He entered Schmidt's tent airily, as if blown in on the bitter winter air that followed him.

"Madam Director," he said, extending a hand.

"General." They shook. "Whisky?"

"Thank you."

Schmidt poured them each a glass and they sat on stools across her camp table from each other.

"I won't command your forces directly," Sayle said, "but I expect you to report to me."

Not the first time she had heard such a message from such a man. She kept her facial expression carefully neutral. *Do I move now, or later?* "I have no military experience." Schmidt sipped her whisky. "I can feed, organize, and direct, but I am perfectly content to hand the siege over to you."

"The Emperor informs me he wants you to stay. He feels it's very important that Cahokia have a head of *civil* government after the siege ends."

Schmidt nodded. "I'm prepared for the task."

"I'll attempt to leave you as much of the city intact as I may," Sayle offered. "To that end, I would like to consult you regarding the concentration of my fire."

Schmidt set down her glass. "Do you mean artillery?"

"Of course."

"You aren't going to starve them out?" But she knew the answer already.

Sayle snorted. "Giving every chance for aid to come and raise the siege? No, I intend to batter a hole in the wall the size of the Charles River and march through as soon as I possibly can. If the Emperor has selected me, it can be for no other purpose. I am a cannon man. And I'd like you to help me choose the location of the hole."

Schmidt smiled, feigning a contentedness she didn't feel. "When do the guns arrive?"

"In two days."

"I am beginning to admire this priest," Ravi said.

The four surviving mamelukes rode through the streets of New Orleans. It was two hours before dawn and the sky was at its most opaque. Their horses—the third set they'd employed on the ride—were exhausted, and Abd al-Wahid had slowed their pace to a canter that permitted conversation.

"Do not admire him too much," Abd al-Wahid growled. "We are to kill him."

Ravi shrugged. "Those two things have little to do with each other. But still, the man escaped our trap."

"He fell into it easily enough," Omar said. "As the chevalier said he would."

"I thought the two bishops might wind up in cahoots." Ravi said "in cahoots" in English, though they were otherwise speaking the tongue of the Prophet. It was a word he was convinced existed only in the New World. "I admire Ukwu for killing the other man when he got a chance."

"To kill a man is easy," Abd al-Wahid said. "Your admiration is cheaply bought."

"Not so," Ravi disagreed. "This was not just any man, but another priest. His death would be made public, and Ukwu knew it. He was willing to suffer the disapproval and hatred of some to accomplish his ends."

"He wins admiration from others," Omar said.

"Yes," Ravi agreed. "From me, for instance. Consider also that there was gold in play. Ukwu can't have been certain the information he had from Planchet was accurate, but he preferred killing the man to keeping him around to be useful in the future."

"He wants revenge," al-Muhasib said.

"He wants revenge," Ravi agreed.

"August Planchet had already outlived his usefulness," Abd al-Wahid disagreed. "He was a thief, and the bishop knew it. The old bishop, I mean."

"You see?" Ravi said. "You admire the man, too."

It was true. Abd al-Wahid had expected the houngan bishop to try to take the gold ship by force of arms, or possibly replace the pilot and change its course. He had never considered the possibility that the man might prefer to sink the ship, depriving the chevalier of his wealth without taking it for himself.

The gold lay on the bottom of the Mississippi near Natchez-under-the-Hill now. Did the Hansa know about it? Mulling over the events of the night assault, Abd al-Wahid concluded that if he were in the young bishop's place, he'd have offered the Hansa the unimpeded right to salvage the gold in exchange for their cooperation.

But the dockmaster had been a woman, and Ahmed Abd al-Wahid had already seen the ecstatic power Etienne Ukwu could exercise over women.

"I admire him," he admitted, "and now I am going to rob him."

They rode into the plaza holding Etienne Ukwu's casino. Though it was early morning, Abd al-Wahid was surprised to see the building unlit. He had never seen it shut its doors before—the debauched wealthy of New Orleans were apparently willing to gamble, drink, and dance at all hours of the night.

"Arm yourselves," he said.

"Are we ever not prepared?" Omar grumbled, but all four drew their weapons.

They left their horses lashed to a post across the plaza, and Abd al-Wahid led the way. They crept forward beneath the stares of the obscene stained glass, a sure confirmation if ever he had needed one of the wisdom of God's prohibition against images. Despite years of discipline, he struggled not to glance up at the voluptuous, carnal images, making a mockery of mortal society and the divine at the same time.

He spat to steady himself, then moved around to the front of the building.

The lights were out, shutters were closed . . . but the front door was ajar.

"Prince-Capitaine," Ravi said. "Perhaps wisdom would dictate a withdrawal at this point."

"Come in," a voice called from behind the door.

"At least, let me do it," Omar said.

Abd al-Wahid nodded and stepped back from the door, into the mud of the street. Al-Muhasib and Ravi joined him and the three mamelukes stood with scimitars drawn, watching as Omar opened the door.

Within, at the center of the room, lay a pile of bodies. He couldn't see faces, but from the clothing the corpses wore, Abd al-Wahid knew they were the gendarmes who had stood in for the mamelukes, dressed as them, to convince the bishop that his casino was being watched by the chevalier.

Sitting atop the corpses was the bishop. He wore a black waistcoat and trousers and a red sash around his waist, garb which made him resemble a Castilian bullfighter. Standing, he opened his hand and it was filled with a tall red flame.

"Please come in," the bishop said again. "I know you have been looking for me."

"He's alone, Prince-Capitaine," Omar murmured in Arabic.

"What I don't understand," the bishop continued, "is why you are working for the Chevalier of New Orleans. The man is a murderer, but he's also more or less a Christian. Aren't you Napoleon's elite, the famed mamelukes of Paris and Cairo? Why are you willing to serve such a man?"

"Prince-Capitaine," Omar urged.

"Can it be money? Surely not. But in case it is, please allow me now to offer to double whatever the chevalier is paying you." The bishop smiled. "You don't know how much I can afford, but you do know that the chevalier's resources are overtaxed. He has mislaid a little cash flow in recent days."

"Kill him," Abd al-Wahid muttered.

Omar leaped into the casino, scimitar raised—

KABOOM!

The casino erupted in a gout of fire, and Omar al-Talib was gone.

✧   ✧   ✧

Etienne leaped back from the mirror. He had crafted his spell by means of a doll of himself—it was for the best that the doll was now incinerated—perched atop the pile of dead gendarmes he'd stacked in the casino's common room, and two mirrors. One mirror stood in the casino, facing the doll. The second was in a nondescript garret in a lodging house owned by Onyinye Diokpo, not far away. Through the mirrors and his own sweat and blood, he'd projected his image onto the doll. Through the mirrors, he'd also prayed for Maitre Carrefour to ignite the kegs of gunpowder he'd stacked in the casino's basement and under tables in its common room.

"That did it," Achebe Chibundu said. The wrestler wore Etienne's uniform now, black and white. He topped it with a round, flat-brimmed hat, cocked at an angle that was surely meant to be jaunty, but somehow seemed a few degrees off. In the flickering candlelight that illuminated the garret, he smiled.

"Shame to lose the casino." Monsieur Bondí frowned. "That was a fine business."

"It was too visible," Etienne said. "And we took out all the cash there was."

"It gave you more than cash. It gave you cash *flow*."

Etienne shook his head. "It accumulated cash, but in a fixed location. The logic of our battle is such that if I destroy his gold, the chevalier must surely sequester mine in turn. To avoid restoring him to wealth, I had to destroy the casino."

Bondí scratched his chin. "Yes, I see. As also in wrestling, if a man wishes to gouge out my eyeball, clearly the wise maneuver is to gouge it out myself first. Is this not the case, friend Achebe?"

"No." Achebe sounded slightly puzzled.

"No? Peculiar." Bondí frowned.

"Whether it was wise or not, it is done." Etienne felt tired. "Do we have peppers here?"

"I'll get peppers from the publican," Achebe said. He left, his footsteps rumbling heavily down the stairs.

"It's done. I'm only sad because I don't see that you have any need for an accountant now." Bondí smiled.

"Perhaps I don't," Etienne agreed. "But I always have need of a shrewd man. And besides, I don't intend to be poor forever."

"How will you fight this war, then? As a pilgrim, sleeping in tents and wandering from place to place?"

"I could do that. I believe it is the way saints traditionally fight. St. Francis, for example, and if not St. John Gutenberg, then his Wandering Johnnies. But I don't need to fight a war," Etienne said. "I only need to kill one man."

"The richest man in New Orleans," Bondí said. "A man who has set foreign assassins on your trail."

"He's not the richest man," Etienne disagreed. "I've interrupted his taxes and now I've interrupted his silence money, too. And I've done it at a time when he has taken on more obligations than ever before, hiring hundreds or maybe thousands of new soldiers. However big the pile of cash he started with, it is surely dwindling."

"You've impoverished yourself and he has many soldiers." Bondí nodded. "Yes, I see the wisdom of this plan very clearly."

"Those soldiers want to be paid," Etienne said.

Bondí shrugged. "Admit that I see some intelligence in what you are saying. Where will we sleep, boss?"

Etienne smiled. "You have listened too much to your own singing. *Ne sais où dormira*, eh?" Achebe Chibundu re-entered with a bowl containing several pickled peppers. "Very well, Bondí. Let me eat a little to restore my strength, and I will show you where we will lay our heads."

Luman awoke in the night belowdecks in the *Verge Caníbal*, suddenly certain that Reuben Clay had breached his agreement with Notwithstanding Schmidt.

The knowledge came so completely out of nowhere that it shocked a laugh from his lungs and sent his hammock rocking from side to side.

"What you laughin' at, wizard?"

Sarah spoke with a thick accent, but she didn't call him a hedge wizard and she didn't say *my Balaam*. Luman felt respected, though of the two of them, she was clearly the greater mage.

Really, what can I do to help her?

"A spell I set weeks ago for Director Schmidt." Luman knew he couldn't lie. He couldn't even see her in the darkness of the *Verge Caníbal*'s hold, but he knew from experience that she could see him, in unnatural and piercing ways. "An alarm has been tripped."

"Anythin' of consequence to me, you reckon?"

Luman considered carefully before answering. "I doubt it. A Hansard who agreed to betray his fellow-Hansards in order to squeeze the Imperial fist more tightly around Adena's throat has reneged. Somehow."

"Maybe he's loosened up that fist."

"Maybe. Or maybe he's just taken too big a cut. Or maybe he's had Schmidt's man Oldham killed. Or maybe it's something else. Do you want me to try to find out?" It was what he would have done if the Director had been present.

"No," Sarah said quickly. "That'll do. We're almost to the Serpent Mound."

"Are you looking...through the walls?" Luman asked.

Sarah laughed. "I could do that, but no. I can jest *feel* it comin'. I can feel my father, I think. And the goddess."

"I haven't known you long, Your Majesty," Luman said slowly. "But you seem...changed."

"Prettier, I hope."

Luman laughed, and then caught himself. "That was a joke, right?"

"Luman Walters, I gave up hope of bein' good-lookin' the first time I e'er looked into a mirror. Weren't no one but Calvin Calhoun e'er fool enough to think I's a looker, and that man was a plumb fool."

The sudden pang of loss in her voice unsettled Luman, and he tried to change the subject. "I'm sorry you're awake."

"I ain't slept since we left the city," she said.

"Are you...afraid?"

"Hell yes, I'm afraid. But that ain't what's stoppin' my sleep. I can't sleep, except on the Great Mound. I've tried hexin' myself, but it does no good. I feel scratchier and more burned by the day, and I'm leanin' on my gramarye pretty hard. I need to talk to my father quick, and git back home." She laughed, a hollow sound. "By which I mean, Cahokia."

"What do you hope to learn from your father?"

"Well...well, dammit, everything. He ne'er became king, at least not by any rite Alzbieta acknowledges. So why not? He ne'er shut the veil over the Serpent Throne. Why not? Can he give me knowledge to do those two things, so I can draw power from the goddess like I think She wants me to, and save his city? *Her* city. *My* city."

"I'll do what I can do help," Luman promised.

"I know you will." The twang softened out of her voice. "I don't expect miracles, Luman. It's just that...I was raised New Light, more or less, with naught but a pinch of ceremony on the rarest of occasions. Girl that I was, I didn't even get to become a Freemason, like all my uncles. Like Cal, I believe. As a result, I have precious little sense of ceremony, and I'm afraid a sense of ceremony is the thing I might need most right now."

"It's customary for any initiate to have a psychopomp to guide her through the rite." Luman laughed out loud. "Of course, it isn't customary for that psychopomp to be blind himself."

*"Jest don't trust him any further'n you need to.
He's a lawyer, after all."*

—•—

CHAPTER NINETEEN

The chevalier was speaking in low tones with a vistor when the mamelukes arrived. Abd al-Wahid didn't understand all the words, but he caught a few that he recognized.

"No es una retirada," the stranger said. "Es una garantía de su compromiso, una evidencia de su buena fe. Y insistiremos."

With those words, the visitor left. Abd al-Wahid met the man's gaze as he left the chevalier's office. He had a deeply bronzed triangular face, with a wide forehead and a pointed chin. The long nose, up-swept white hair, and steeply arching eyebrows all gave the face a vertical dimension that made the man appear two feet taller than he really was. Only his narrowly slitted, suspicion-filled eyes and a dark black mustache gave the face any horizontal dimension at all. With his lips pressed tightly together, his mouth almost entirely disappeared. He wore a frock coat and riding boots. He nodded at the mamelukes.

"Señores," the man said.

Abd al-Wahid nodded in return.

"Señor," al-Muhasib said.

The stranger disappeared down the hall, bootheels clicking on the stone floor.

"That man is demanding the chevalier withdraw from New Orleans," al-Muhasib muttered in Arabic. "He says it will demonstrate the chevalier's commitment, and it is not negotiable. What is this, Prince-Capitaine?"

Abd al-Wahid reflected for a moment. "Say nothing of it to the chevalier," he said.

They entered the office.

Chevalier Gaspard Le Moyne looked tired and old, small behind the large desk, yellow in the late afternoon light streaming in through the windows. "Gentlemen," he said. "I'm out of money."

Despite all the wealth the mamelukes had brought him. "We have seen the flogged tax evaders," Abd al-Wahid said, "and the paintings disappearing from your walls."

"I've tried confiscating their property," the chevalier said. "No one will buy it from me at a decent price, so it is not worth the effort. And now that I am unable to pay the gendarmes, I fear that they will no longer help me collect taxes or confiscate property at all."

"There is a traditional solution," Abd al-Wahid said. "Give your gendarmes the right to confiscate criminals' property and dispose of it for themselves."

Le Moyne seemed to think about it for a moment, but then shook his head. "This is a traditional solution for an invading army, Prince-Capitaine. It would be tantamount to declaring war on New Orleans. I would be the city's savior, not her oppressor."

"The difference between the two is not always clear," Abd al-Wahid said.

"Merde. You speak a deep truth, Prince-Capitaine. But I am going to take a different path. You saw the Spanish ambassador?"

Abd al-Wahid nodded.

"I am going to invite two armies to invade New Orleans."

Abd al-Wahid held his tongue, but Ravi couldn't. "This is a very subtle plan, My Lord Chevalier. So subtle, I'm not certain I understand it."

"I will be at the head of one of those armies," the chevalier said. "I will come as the city's savior."

"A Spanish army," Abd al-Wahid said.

The chevalier nodded. "You will accompany the mambo Marie north, to provoke the assault of the other army."

"Shreveport?" al-Muhasib asked. "Memphis?"

"I am here to kill Etienne Ukwu," Abd al-Wahid said. "Nothing more."

"This is how we kill him," the chevalier said. "And I need to send the witch with men I trust."

"With men you don't have to pay, you mean." Abd al-Wahid smiled grimly. "Must we take the witch? The prophet commands us to take refuge from those who blow on knots, and I have already spent more time with this sorceress and her tabletop godlings than I would like."

"You must," the chevalier said. "The witch is essential. In fact, the plan is hers."

Maltres Korinn wore the garment Alzbieta Torias provided him. It was a long linen tunic, almost dress-like in falling all the way to his knees. Beneath, he wore a knee-length pair of linen drawers, pulled tight with a linen cord.

Sherem wore a matching outfit, as did Alzbieta herself, and all eight of her former palanquin-bearers. These eleven, without much planning or discussion, had become the platoon of elite fasters and prayers.

They had discussed where to approach the goddess. The Sunrise Mound was an obvious candidate, as was the Temple of the Sun. Less obviously, Sir William offered a military escort if the prayer cadre wished to make their plea in the Basilica.

Finally, they had settled on the Sunrise Mound, for the same reasons for which it had been chosen as the site of burial for the city's soldiers. Sarah had consecrated it, while the Temple of the Sun had been defiled by Calvin Calhoun's killing of the poet Eërthes. The Temple of the Sun was visible all over Cahokia, but its height gave it a forbidding aspect. The Sunrise Mound was low, familiar, public... and surprisingly sacred.

Also, the graves were there at its side.

"What ceremony will you follow?" Cathy Filmer had asked.

"There is none," Alzbieta had said, then blushed. "Or if there is, I don't know it. We'll offer the perfumes and incenses we know to offer at the goddess's home on the Great Mound. We'll light lamps with Her sacred oil. And we'll pray."

The morning was cold, the sun not yet up. If Alzbieta didn't know an appropriate liturgy, she was improvising with great energy.

Korinn held a clay oil lamp, a simple thing such as his ancestors must have used in the Drowned Land thousands of years earlier. He stood within the apse beside the Serpent Throne; coiled, muscular, and sheathed in gold, the presence of the mighty chair made him uncomfortable, as it if were a beast that might unwind and attack at the slightest provocation.

Was that actually a stain he saw on the throne's seat?

A priestess of the day's sept approached him; other priestesses approached the other ten witnesses. She held a length of burning cord in her hand, flame downward. She swung the cord slowly in circles to keep it from burning her hand.

Like a flaming serpent, and a handler who didn't want to get bitten.

The other ten women held similar flaming cords.

She wasn't old, but in the half-light inside the temple, Maltres wasn't sure she was young, either. In the shifting shadows, the woman's face was ageless.

And serpentine.

She lit his lamp and then kissed his face, once on each cheek and once on the forehead. Then she withdrew.

"O Serpent Queen of the Cosmos, O Firstwomb, O Mother of All Living," Alzbieta intoned, lifting her lamp. "We bring you an offering of light. Hear our plea."

The oil was perfumed, and the heady smell of the burning lamps made Maltres's eyes sting. "Hear our plea."

They proceeded from the Temple of the Sun. Alzbieta walked first, with Maltres to one side and behind her, and Sherem to the other side. Behind the two men came two short files of former bearers.

Maltres had published his proclamation, signed by seven Notaries. The faces he saw on the lower reaches of the Great Mound, the eyes that stared at him all along the avenues as he walked to the Sunrise Mound, were informed eyes and knowing faces. Some looked angry—followers of Zadok Tarami? Others, many more, looked apprehensive, confused, or in pain.

But they knew what he was doing.

Maltres chased the thoughts from his mind. Alzbieta was singing an old modal tune, something somber and priestly that he didn't know. His own German and English were better than his Ophidian. He couldn't make out all the words, so he hummed, creating a supporting drone under the priestess's harmonies.

They arrived at the Sunrise Mound. Alzbieta knelt in muddy snow and placed her lamp on the ground in front of her. Then she pressed her forehead into the snow. The rest of the procession did the same.

"O Mother!" This time her voice was louder. She wasn't performing, exactly, but if the crowd standing about the Sunrise Mound was to be included in the liturgy, they would need to hear the words. "We were witnesses to your choice: three and eight, and the one who stood apart!"

Calvin? No, she meant the Podebradan Yedera. Maltres realized that Yedera stood at the edge of the mound now, watching quietly. Why include the Unborn Daughter? Was it to make the number of witnesses come to twelve? But of course, whatever Yedera had seen, Calvin had seen as well, in which case there were *thirteen* witnesses.

Perhaps Calvin didn't count if he wasn't named.

"We are witnesses now to our own grave sin!"

Was she going to name Zadok Tarami and the graverobbers?

"We sin!" the other witnesses cried, and Maltres echoed them.

Alzbieta glossed over the details of the sin. "We are mortal and fall short, O Mother of Life! We ask thee to forgive us our failures, to give us life and health, to rescue us from our oppressor!"

"Rescue us!" Maltres and the others echoed in chorus.

"Thou art more precious than rubies: and all the things we can desire are not to be compared unto thee. Length of days is in thy right hand; and in thy left hand riches and honor. We beg thee to open thy hands, O Mother, and receive the men we laid up in thy womb unto thee!"

"Open thy hands!" Maltres was no scriptorian, but he recognized that Alzbieta had built her plea on one of the Psalms. Or a passage from Proverbs, perhaps.

"Thy ways are ways of pleasantness," Alzbieta continued, "and all thy paths are peace. Thou art a tree of life to them that lay hold upon thee: and happy is every one that retaineth thee. Lay hold upon us as we lay hold upon thee, O goddess, and retain us as we seek to retain thee, now and forever, amen!"

"Amen!"

The crowd murmured along with the witnesses. Alzbieta pressed her forehead to the ground, and the witnesses followed. First one or two, then in the dozens, and then most of the crowd followed.

Maltres felt his heart beat in his chest. Would the goddess hear?

If She heard, She gave no sign. There was no angel choir, no perfume of Eden. Nothing happened, that Maltres could see.

"And forgive *me*, O Great Lady of the Garden," Alzbieta intoned, "for my deceitful and withholding spirit, for my failures with thy Beloved and her companions!"

Saving her personal guilt for last? And what exactly had Alzbieta done that troubled her so?

But still, no response.

Would the goddess only respond if Sarah were present? Was that her role, the attraction of the goddess's attention or presence? Maltres missed Sarah with a sudden painful twinge in his heart.

Or was it possible that the goddess hadn't responded on the solstice, either? Was it possible that Sarah herself had created the manifestations Maltres had seen?

Was it possible there was no goddess?

Maltres chased away the thought.

And if the goddess was indeed a demon, as Zadok Tarami preached?

Maltres took a deep breath to steady the sudden trembling of his hands. He knew what he had seen and felt, and he would bear witness of it still. And if Sarah was such as mighty sorceress that she had created the illusion of Eden and touched the heart of every person in Cahokia and caused the Treewall to sprout, then he longed for her return in her own right.

And if the goddess was a demon, then he hoped She was a demon who could save his city.

Maltres stayed kneeling in the mud a long time. When he finally raised his face, the crowd had gone. Sherem sat back in the mud, knees up and arms crossed over his knees. Alzbieta still lay on her face, softly weeping.

Two days after Sister Serafina Tate cut away the dead flesh from his side as Calvin read out of the Psalms, Olanthes Kuta awoke and asked for water. Polly Calhoun and Red Charlie gave him water and a thin beef broth, and Cal finally took Sister Serafina back down the mountain.

She had spent the entire two days at Olanthes's side, muttering prayers and monitoring his progress. Cal's grandpa had spent much of that time with her. At first Cal thought it was because he was waiting for the messenger to awaken, so Iron Andy could get more information out of the man. But when Olanthes woke up, the Elector made no hurry to speak with him.

He concluded that his grandfather was passing time with Serafina.

As Cal and the Circulator rode the small horses down the ridge, he ventured a query. "Which steps was Dancin' Andy Calhoun most famous *for*, exactly?"

"He's a fine buck dancer, but I most liked to see him dance flat foot," Sister Serafina said. "I ne'er heard as he was a clogger, but I wouldn't put it past him. He had a way with the ladies, and dancin' was key to his mystery. Ladies love a man as can dance. You remember that, young Calvin." She cackled.

"You knew him when he was a young man, then?"

"Knew him? Hell, iffen the war wouldn't a called us in opposite directions, I'd a been your grandmama."

And then she would say no more, but sank into the cocoon of blankets with the pot of embers at their center that kept her warm.

After depositing the Circulator at her convent, Cal rode to another address the Elector had given him. He had a sealed letter and a name. When he arrived at the building, he found it to be in an elegant neighborhood several streets away from the river, where the buildings were stone houses two stories tall, with hitching posts standing in front of each house. The name on a brass plate screwed into a heavy black-painted door above a brass knocker read:

LOGAN HUBER, ESQ.

Cal hitched his beasts. Then he knocked and stepped back to show respect. He knew that *ESQ.* meant *esquire*, which was a lawyer. Though Iron Andy hadn't explained the errand he was sending Cal on, Cal now realized it was something serious.

The man who answered the door was nearly seven feet tall and thin as a stick bug. He wore a waistcoat and trousers both of somber gray, and both polished by wear to a high shine. His face drooped like a tear, from a high, pointed, hairless forehead, down to trembling jowls.

"You ain't got an appointment," the man in gray said.

"No, I ain't," Cal admitted. "But I've got a letter for you, from the Elector Calhoun." He handed over the folded sheet sealed with a blob of wax.

The man in gray stared at the name written under the blob and frowned. "It ain't for me."

"Brown!" bellowed a voice from within the building. "What

is it?"

"A messenger!" Brown looked back at Calvin and sniffed. "From Calhoun!"

"Take the message and give the man a gratuity!"

"I's told I'd have to bring back a response," Cal said.

Brown sniffed again, looked down a long nose whose tear shape matched the shape of the face around it, and shut the door.

Cal looked around the Nashville street. Snowflakes hung in the hair, but not enough to conceal him. A cartload of hides rolled past. Women and men both walked up and down the uncobbled road. He wanted to smash the door open with his tomahawk, but he'd be seen.

"Jerusalem," he muttered. "Why is everythin' always so *difficult*?"

He tried the doorknob, and it turned. Shaking the snow off his shoulders, Cal screwed his best smile into place and walked in.

A long hallway with a hardwood floor ran straight back through the building. Cal shook his feet to throw snow off onto the rag rug that lay inside the door, then marched ahead. "Squire Huber?" he called out.

The man named Brown reappeared in the hallway, his mouth open in an O of shock and disapproval. "Now look here, I *took* your message!"

"You did," Cal agreed. "Only I reckon you thought to keep the gratuity to yourself."

He grabbed Brown by the front of his waistcoat and held him tight. He didn't want to hurt the man, but he didn't want him to go for a hidden knife or a gun over the mantel, either. "Squire Huber!"

"He isn't a squire." Brown squirmed and looked wretched. "What do you think this is, Camelot?"

"Mebbe." Cal dragged the man in gray into a wide room—with several elegant sofas for sitting and a tall bookshelf full of tall books whose spines bore mysterious titles like *The Philadelphia Reporter* and *The Imperial Tribunal Gazette*—and then back again into the hall. "I mean, I thought *esquire* meant a *lawyer*. On the other hand, those look like collections of news-papers. I guess I can't say I *know* jest exactly what kind of place I'm in. But I aim to talk to your Squire Huber. Or *Mr.* Huber, as the case may be."

"Mister!" bellowed the third voice.

It came from above and behind. Cal released Brown, stepped back into the hallway and looked up. He saw a man in a red wool waistcoat leaning on a dark wooden railing and looking down at him. The man was thick without looking fat, and had a face that was blocky without appearing slow. He projected strength, and the abundant whiskers curling down from his ears and halfway along his jaws made him look vaguely animal. In thick fingers he held a smoldering cigar.

"You don't have to call me *mister*," Cal said. "Jest Calvin will do."

The blocky man snorted. "I meant you can call me *Mr.* Huber, and Mr. Huber will certainly do until we get better acquainted. Do you and I have business, Calvin?" He stuck the cigar into the corner of his mouth and chewed on it. His accent was not Appalachee, but might be Pennslander.

"I don't rightly know," Cal admitted. "I come bearin' a message from my grandpa. Your feller Brown here took the message, but he also turned me away, and seein' as my grandpa told me I'd have to wait for a response from you, I jest couldn't accept that."

"I admire determination in a man," Huber said. "Have you considered a career as a process server?"

Cal had a vague idea that Huber was referring to some sort of officer of the court, like a sheriff or a constable. "No," he admitted. "I kinda got recruited to be a sticks and stones man, once."

Huber laughed, a sound like the bark of an angry dog. "Give me the message, Brown. Let's not make the man wait."

The man in gray snorted his disapproval, then took Cal's letter from a basket Cal hadn't noticed, sitting on a shelf just inside the door. He trooped around a corner of the hallway, reappearing moments later beside Huber. The lawyer popped open the Elector's plain seal and his eyes fairly shot across the page. When he finished, he glared down at Calvin.

"If you had told me your name was Calhoun," Huber said, "we could have saved some time."

Cal shrugged. "Up in the hills, Calhoun's a name as'll carry a lot of weight. Down here in Free Imperial Nashville, it ain't everybody who knows us."

"Well, *I* know you. The Elector's been a client for years. Brown, get the coach."

"I brung horses," Cal said.

"Good, we'll need them to get up that pile of rock your grand-father calls his home." Huber called his words over his shoulder as he rattled down the stairs, collected a coat from a rack in the corner of the hallways, and pulled a tall beaver-skin hat down over his ears. "But Andrew Calhoun is an important man, and as far as it's in my power, I'm going to call on him in style."

"I understood you'd jest send back some kinda paper with me," Cal said. "Iffen I bring back an actual lawyer instead of a lawyer's letter, I might could disappoint the old man."

"Yes, the Elector asks me to prepare a legal document. But what he wants is a document that needs to be witnessed and notarized, and I don't think he realizes that. If I send you up the hill with the form he thinks he needs, either he'll sign a piece of paper that is legally void, or he'll send you back down the hill tomorrow to try again. Or worst of all, what he wants to accomplish might fail. Instead, I'll come up with you now, we'll get the document signed by all the witnesses and notarized by me, as a validly licensed notary public under the Notaries and Public Clerks Law of 1807."

Brown had shrugged into his own coat, the thickness of which doubled the man in size, and was heading for a side exit. "Anything else I should bring, Mr. Huber?"

"Lots of extra blankets, brandy, some cold meat and bread." The lawyer chuckled. "You may be sitting in the coach alone for the night. Iron Andy Calhoun doesn't let just anyone up on his mountain. And you're not of the Craft, are you, Brown?"

The doorman sniffed. "I have not been recommended, sir." He exited.

Huber shook his head. "Hard to imagine why."

"This is impressive client service, I reckon," Cal said. "Only it seems an awful lot of ballyhoo. What was it my grandpa wanted?"

"Oh, you don't know?" The lawyer laughed out loud. "Well, son, the Elector must like you, because he wants you to have his proxy."

Proxy was a word Cal knew in various contexts. New Light preachers sometimes used it to talk about Christ and the Atonement, and Cal knew there were proxy weddings, which meant that one of the wedding parties wasn't present, so instead a man might get married to his betrothed's sister, or her hairbrush. He wasn't quite sure what the word might mean in this context.

He must be staring blankly, because Huber clapped him on the arm. "He's going to send you to the Electoral Assembly, Calvin. You get to go vote."

"Jerusalem," Cal managed to say. He thought of Bayard Prideux's letter. Bringing it home, he had imagined Iron Andy Calhoun, war hero and Elector, standing in the Electoral Assembly and waving that letter, demanding justice.

What if it has to be me, instead? Am I up to that?

Brown sat in the front of the coach and drove, Logan Huber rode inside the coach under an enormous bearskin cloak, and Cal rode alongside. The clouds had cleared and the sky was a brilliant liquid blue that reminded Cal of Sarah's natural eye. The white snow blanketing the hills was closer to the color of her unnatural eye. Cal found himself thinking of her face generally, and wondering how Sarah was faring in Cahokia.

"You rustle cattle, Calvin?" the lawyer asked as the coach pulled out of Nashville.

"You see a herd of cows out in front of me, marked with another man's brand?" Cal shot back. He was a little put out that he was being forced to return to the Elector empty-handed. "Or you jest imagine that I might be a rustler, seein' as my name is Calhoun?"

"*My* name is Pennslander German," Huber said. "But I've lived in Nashville nigh on twenty years now, and Andrew Calhoun has been my client that entire time."

"You sayin' you got us hill people figured out?"

The lawyer's eyes twinkled and he adopted an Appalachee twang. "I'm a-sayin' I'm an old friend of the family, a man you can trust, and I'm just tryin' to make small talk."

Cal laughed in spite of himself. "No, sir. If you was *a-sayin'* anythin', that'd make it somethin' you intended to do in the future, and instead it's a thing you already done in the past."

"Are you a poet, Calvin?"

"Only iffen my grandpa asks me to be. Generally, I reckon the occasional reading out of the Bible or a bit of news-paper is enough literary work for me. But seein' as you lived here so long, I reckon you know how it is. I live on the mountain, and precious few folks as live on the mountain can afford to do jest one thing. I hunt, I trade, I grow tobacco. Recently I took up what you might call . . . confidential errandin', I suppose, for the Elector."

"Like exercising his proxy."

"No, that'd be new. I took his...daughter on a journey to the Ohio."

"Your aunt."

"Yeah." Cal ached. "My aunt."

"If he sent you across the dark and bloody ground of old Kentuck, the Elector must trust you."

"I'm his kin," Cal said. "And we went *around*."

The lawyer laughed, his eyes narrowed, and he fell silent.

"What about you?" Cal asked. "Pennslander like you are, it's a mite odd to see you in Free Imperial Nashville. Wasn't they enough lawsuits for you to chase after in Philadelphia?"

"Philadelphia has plenty of lawsuits," Logan Huber agreed. "It also has plenty of lawyers. They hover over the city like a flock of vultures, and at the appearance of the slightest scrap of carrion they all plunge together, clawing and pecking at each other for the work."

"You make the profession sound so romantic," Cal said. "I almost wish I'd taken up the wig and gavel myself."

"You're thinking of judges," Huber said. "They're the ones who wear the wig and bang the gavel on the table."

"Right, judges," Cal agreed. "Ain't they the ones as get to hang lawyers?"

Logan Huber's laughter was forced. "Only if the lawyers misbehave."

"Ain't that what we was talkin' about? Lawyers misbehavin'?"

At the foot of Calhoun Mountain, Huber climbed out of the coach and onto the back of Cal's second horse. The lawyer must have been three times Serafina Tate's weight, but the sturdy mountain animal made no complaint as its bearskin-wrapped bundle made himself comfortable.

Cal whistled on the shorter ride up the ridge. What did the lawyer want? He wished he'd read the Elector's instructions himself before delivering them, but his grandpa had handed the letter over with a seal on it, and the Lord hated a man as opened a sealed book before its time.

Next time, though, he'd ask his grandpa for more information.

To his surprise, Caleb waved both of them up the draw without any kind of challenge. Iron Andy sat in a rocking chair on the porch of his dog-trot, a long Kentucky rifle across his knees, his one hand resting, casually, on the weapon's stock.

"Alright, grandpa," Cal called, reining in his horse. "I brought that lawyer for target practice like you asked. Tell me how many yards you want, and I'll tie him up."

"More fun to shoot at a lawyer when he's runnin'," Iron Andy said, no hint of a smile in his face.

"You want I should give him a headstart, or should I jest shout 'go'?"

"Elector Calhoun," Huber nodded his salute.

Iron Andy pursed his lips. "Calvin, I didn't ask you to bring the lawyer back up with you."

"No." Cal sighed. "On the other hand, you must a reckoned it was a possibility it would play out like this, 'cause you told Caleb in advance to send the lawyer on up."

Andy cracked a smile. "True. And I b'lieve I know you well enough to say that you wouldn't a brought the lawyer up, or done anythin' different from what I instructed, lessen they was exigent circumstances."

Cal hesitated. "Am I right to reckon that 'exigent circumstances' means I had no choice?"

Andrew Calhoun nodded.

"In that case, yes. The exigent circumstances are that the lawyer hisself insisted."

The Elector squinted briefly at the lawyer. "You reckon he's jest runnin' up the bill, chargin' me by the hour while he rides up and down the mountain on the back of one of my own horses, enjoyin' the view?"

"I considered that," Cal admitted. "He's a Nashville lawyer, after all, and you know how they are: a little scrap of lawyerin' work appears, and they all pile on it like buzzards."

Huber chuckled. "You could at least give me credit for the image."

Cal nodded. "That's what Huber hisself told me, about lawyers bein' vultures. He also told me that you jest didn't reckon with the legal technicalities of a proxy, and he needed to come on up the mountain to git the work done here."

"You find that credible, do you?" Andy's jaw jutted out more than usual.

"I do *not*," Cal said. "Ain't a man on Calhoun Mountain knows the Compact better than you do. Technicalities and all."

"I argued over that thing a summer entire," the Elector said.

"Don't I know it," Cal agreed. "And I thought of that when the lawyer told me you might not a understood. And that's when I reckoned, don't the Compact provide legal immunity for Electors?"

"Everythin' but treason," Iron Andy said. "The only thing any court in the land can touch me for is treason, and the jury has to be made up of Electors. Mind you, as a practical matter, if Tommy Penn was ready to start hangin' Electors, I don't expect he'd necessarily hold out for the fig leaf of a magistrate's say-so. Still, it's some protection."

"What I don't know," Cal said, "but mebbe you can tell me, is if proxyholders git the same immunity."

Logan Huber muttered a curse under his breath.

"For the duration of the proxy, yes. They do," the Elector said.

"I reckoned that might be the case," Cal said. "You know, if Walter Fitzroy had only written songs about the Compact instead of listin' out the Electors, I might a known that without askin'."

"Tell me what you're thinkin', then."

"I'm thinkin' the reason we got a Pennslander lawyer in Nashville ain't that they was too many buzzards in the big city so he come out to the hills to find work with less competition. I figure they's a warrant out for his arrest in Pennsland. Likely Philadelphia itself."

"William Penn's bones," the lawyer grumbled. "Did I ever underestimate you."

Cal shrugged. "Mebbe you did. I think he wants to git back to Philadelphia without gittin' hisself arrested, and this is his chance. So he made up his cock-and-bull tale about how he needed to come up the mountain to do what you asked. But instead, I reckon he's goin' to tell you *he* should have the proxy, and not me."

Andy Calhoun turned to his lawyer. Maybe, just maybe, the rifle across his lap shifted position slightly. "That about the size of it?"

Logan Huber had turned red. "I should tell you that I'm not a criminal."

"You lookin' to carry my imprimatur to the Electoral Assembly, you gotta tell me more than that."

"I wasn't going to trick you," Huber said. "I would have told you everything."

"You ain't tellin' me everythin' *now*," the Elector pointed out.

"I had a partner at the bar," Huber said. "Our firm was Becker and Rupp. Business associations, debt proceedings, admiralty, commercial law. We traveled all over Pennsland, the Haudenosaunee country, and the eastern Ohio. We made a good living."

"Which is as much as to say, your name ain't Logan Huber."

"Logan Rupp," the lawyer admitted. "Huber was my mother's name, so it isn't so much a disguise as a change of emphasis."

"It's a disguise," the Elector said.

Logan Rupp sighed. "Becker turned out to be a bigamist. Or rather, since *bigamist* would imply that he had two wives simultaneously—in fact, it turns out he had five—he was a *pentagamist*. When he finally broke down and admitted to me what was going on, he joked that he needed Walter Fitzroy to write him a song to remember his wives' names and the cities they lived in."

"He spent his money on the women."

"And the children." Rupp nodded. "He was, in his way, a sincere family man. I believe he loved each of his families, perhaps equally. And each of them believed they were the only family, and entitled to his full share of the partnership income. He worked like a demon. For years I didn't understand why."

"But it wasn't enough," Cal guessed, "so he stole from you."

"Oh, he stole from me," Rupp agreed, "but that was hardly the problem. No, he stole from *clients*. He took client funds we had won in judgments, or were holding in escrow, and he dispatched them to his wives."

"Intending to pay them back," Andy Calhoun suggested, "only of course he never did."

Rupp's shoulders slumped. "John Hancock himself came after us at law when Becker failed to pay him the proceeds of an insurance claim for a shipwreck. He had all our partnership assets, which at that point were nearly zero, and then he commenced actions against both of us personally, for fraud."

"And did you commit fraud?" Iron Andy asked sternly.

"No!" Rupp nearly shouted. "Becker was the senior partner, and I trusted him to handle the money. I knew he was delaying payments to me, but I assumed he was merely tardy. If I had known..."

"Where's Becker now?" Cal asked.

"Dead." Rupp's face was glum. "He hanged himself and burned

all his papers shortly after Hancock commenced his suit. I think he saw it as the only way to protect his families from shame and impoverishment."

"Did it work?" Cal asked.

"I doubt it. John Hancock was a ruthless man. I imagine he hunted down those women and took what he believed was his."

"And you ran," the Elector said. "And changed the emphasis of your name."

"Even so." Rupp nodded.

"All of which don't really explain why you want to go back," Cal said.

Rupp hesitated. "I was also married. I suppose I *am* married. Though for all I know, she has taken another man by now, my daughters have a new father, and I have forced her into unwitting bigamy."

"She thinks you're dead?"

Rupp nodded. "I still send her money but I do it through a Beguine cloister, so she can't know where it's really coming from."

"But mebbe," Cal guessed slowly, "you're hopin' she *has* figured it out. Mebbe you're hopin' she's figured you're alive and hasn't remarried."

Rupp hung his head.

The Elector stared at the gray horizon for long moments and then spat a stream of tobacco juice off his porch. Finally, he stood and leaned his long rifle against the wall.

"I ain't givin' you my proxy, Huber," he said to the lawyer.

"I understand. I'm a fraud."

"That ain't it. It's got to be Calvin as goes on this errand I need done. But iffen you want to go along with him, I'll write you a letter of credit and protection."

Rupp looked up and frowned. "I don't know that legal document."

Calhoun cracked into a smile. "It ain't a legal document, you ninny. It's a letter as'll say you're under my protection, and iffen anybody has any claims against you, I invite them to take the claims up with me so's we can negotiate a settlement."

Rupp gasped. "Hancock's losses alone were enormous. With the other creditors—"

"Don't let that horse gallop off jest yet, counselor," the Elector said. "I ain't a-promisin' to pay, jest invitin' any creditor of yours to calm down and come negotiate with me. And I'll pay you a daily rate, though if I end up havin' to pay John Hancock or some other disappointed shipowner, I'll take the settlement amount out of what I owe you."

"I accept," Rupp said. "Gladly. Thank you, sir. That's more than fair."

The Elector nodded at the Thinkin' Shed. "I expect you'll want to git set up in there. They's a table. I'll have Cal here go collect Polly and Red Charlie and Ole Kuta to come witness."

Rupp tumbled off his horse in a pile of rucked-up bearskin and climbed onto the porch. As he tossed the skin aside, Cal saw for the first time that he carried a wide, shallow wooden box with a hinged handle attached to it, as well as a small green book whose cover read ELECTORAL FORMS. "I'll get this drafted directly. We'll be ready to witness in ten minutes."

The lawyer let himself into the Thinkin' Shed.

Andy stepped to the edge of his porch and leaned out. With Cal mounted, the two men stood eye to eye. "Huber, or Rupp—or whatever his name is—will come in handy. Truth is, I expected him to come runnin' up the hill with an offer to accompany you for a fee. This story about an ex-partner is all a surprise."

"I don't mind havin' someone as knows Philadelphia at my side," Cal said. "Not to mention the law, and the Compact."

The Elector nodded. "Jest don't trust him any further'n you need to. He's a lawyer, after all."

"That's Fort Schuyler." Dockery nodded at the angular walls of the castle above them. Kinta Jane knew that the triangular sections of stone wall that jutted out and gave the castle its vaguely starlike shape were intended to expose attackers to the maximum possible gunfire, while forcing them to shoot at the fortress from far away. "The Republic built it, back before the Compact."

"Acadia starts here, then?" Kinta Jane asked.

"This is the boundary," Dockery agreed. Mist rose from the water around them and veiled the steep, snow-covered hills frowning down at the canoe. "Lake Ticonderoga."

"I am thinking a news-paper article might get us what we want," Kinta Jane said tentatively.

Dockery paddled in silence.

"What do you think?"

"You mean, print something that will attract the attention of the right people. An invitation."

"Of course, the trick will be doing that without attracting any of the *wrong* people," Kinta Jane quickly acknowledged.

"Who *are* the wrong people, exactly?" Dockery asked.

"The *right* people are whoever answers to the name Brother Odishkwa." Kinta Jane remembered her confrontation with the Emperor Thomas Penn in his library in Horse Hall. "Which might be no one at all. Maybe the rightful Odishkwa has completely forgotten."

"Or has laid down his burden," Dockery said bitterly, "and in preference is chasing his own personal wealth."

"I'm sorry about Julia," Kinta Jane said.

"I'm sorry about Wilkes," Dockery shot back. "I'm sorry about Julia, too. I'm sorry about all of it. Except I'm not sorry I drowned Gert Visser like a rat. That's nothing but what he deserved."

Kinta Jane watched the mountains and the gray clouds above them through the mists. It was pure illusion, but the mist made her imagine that the waters over which she paddled, which were nearly freezing, were instead warm. The long lake valley had a mystical, ghostlike feel to it. She half-expected King Arthur and his knights to sally out of Fort Schuyler and ride down the mountain to her rescue.

If it came to it, she wouldn't say no.

"The *wrong* people is anyone else," she said.

"And especially the Heron King."

"Do you think he sees here?" Kinta Jane had assumed they were beyond the reach of Simon Sword once they'd crossed the mountains and begun descending toward Philadelphia.

Dockery shrugged. "Beastkind ain't common on the coast, but you do see them occasionally. I assume if there's beastkind, there can be Simon Sword."

"I was imagining that the old allies would be watching and waiting, and that we'd be beyond the Heron King's reach. Think about the geography of it: William Penn, the Algonks, and the Anaks. All those lands lie on the edge of the Ohio. They *border* it, but they're not *in* it. If you wanted allies who would act to contain Simon Sword, this is who you would choose."

"Not Memphis, or the Appalachee? Not the Ohio Kingdoms themselves?"

Kinta Jane thought about that. "I don't know. But the story is about three brothers I know that one of them is the Penn Landholder, and I'm pretty sure the other two are an Algonk leader and one of the giants. Maybe that's just who was available. Or who agreed to join."

"The Appalachee are a fractious lot," Dockery agreed, "and Memphis is aloof."

"Or maybe it's who was there at the time key events happened."

They paddled in silence for a time. Thunder rolled, and Dockery laughed.

"There's old Hendrick," he said.

"You mean... one of the three brothers?"

"No, I mean the thunder," Dockery said. "When thunder rolls within earshot of the Hudson, it's supposed to be the ghost of old Hendrick Hudson himself, playing at ninepins with the skulls and bones of his dead crewmen."

"That doesn't sound like the behavior of a good leader."

"Who can say what makes a good leader? You lead our expedition well enough, there might come a time I'm happy enough for you to play ninepins with my skeleton."

Kinta Jane laughed. "Well, I believe I know the place where Brother Odishkwa would expect to meet. All I need to do is send the signal."

"I think it's a reasonable bet," Dockery said. "Though you don't need my agreement."

"Yes I do," she said.

"This is your mission," he said. "I'll do what you say. I'm a faithful man, however rough I may appear."

"I'm not Wilkes," Kinta Jane said. "He knew everything, had spies and contacts everywhere, and kept his own counsel. I have only a vague idea of what I'm doing, the thought of which nearly makes me choke, since I fear the end of the world as I know it. You've traveled this part of the Empire; I never have. I value your advice, Dockery. I *need* it."

"You can have it," Dockery said. "For starters, I think a newspaper is a fine vehicle for reaching out to our allies. It allows us to speak in the kind of double-talk old Ben Franklin loved. But we're going to need to figure out a message that's a little more eye-catching than: *Brother Odishkwa, it's time to meet.*"

✧   ✧   ✧

Monsieur Bondí entered Etienne's room nearly at a run. "They've left New Orleans!"

They were not staying at one of Onyinye's many hotels, because Etienne didn't want to be too much in debt to that single ally. Instead, he and Bondí and Achebe were staying at a house belonging to Don Sandoval, a Spaniard merchant they'd rescued from the hulks.

Not the Don's actual home, which remained occupied by his family, and possibly watched by the gendarmes.

Though possibly not. With the chevalier's increasing failure to pay, many recent gendarme recruits had deserted. Those without the wit or the means to escape into the bayous or upriver were to be seen bolted into the stocks or chained to whipping posts at busy intersections around the city.

Monsieur Bondí had reported rumors of crucifixions in the cases where fleeing recruits had also stolen the chevalier's property (that is to say, taken their new rifle with them), but so far, they had only been rumors.

In any case, Etienne's men had not seen any gendarmes watching the Don's family home. Nevertheless, it was too obvious a place to choose as a retreat. Instead, Etienne and his men and the Don himself stayed in a discreet apartment in a narrow alley not far from the opera house. The Don said nothing to the effect, but it was the sort of apartment where a wealthy man might meet his mistress.

"Who are they?" Etienne asked. "Who has left?"

"It is the chevalier." Don Sandoval looked up from poring over an account ledger. His nephew had brought the book to him to allow the Don to learn what had happened in his enterprises during his period of confinement. "He has heard of my release, and now he flees in terror." The old man's bold words conflicted comically with his haggard and bone-thin appearance.

"Doubtless," Etienne said.

"No," Bondí said. "But you are closer than you might think. His Egyptians."

"The mamelukes," Etienne said.

Don Sandoval blinked.

Bondí nodded. "They have taken a Memphite barge northward, and they've taken the mambo with them."

"Are you certain?" Etienne asked. "For weeks, I believed the same men were standing guard around my casino, and that turned out not to be true."

Bondí nodded again. "When I learned they had booked passage, I waited to watch them board with my own eyes."

"Good." Though eyes could be deceived. "Perhaps they take the girl along with them to try to fetch their money again. Perhaps they think she will be an effective charm against fire."

Bondí shook his head. "The girl wore her finery, boss. She carried a broom, and she had a snake in a basket."

Don Sandoval scratched the tip of his nose with an ink-stained finger, leaving a black smudge. "I do not understand the meaning of this."

"It's a wedding, Don Sandoval," Etienne said. "They're taking the girl somewhere to be married."

"I assume you are proposing to command this verloren hoop?"

———◆———

CHAPTER TWENTY

Luman stood beside Sarah at the foot of Wisdom's Bluff. He'd never been here before, and the sheer size of the hill surprised him. Snow fell and blanketed the hill and its trees, but through the mantle of white Luman could still see the obvious line of a road that climbed the mountain.

The *Verge Caníbal* rode at anchor below the bluff, where the limpid waters of the Ohio poured into the muddy flow of the Mississippi. The pirate lieutenant Josep had cheerfully praised the clear lines of sight such a position would give him for his cannons, both downriver as well as up in two directions.

The navigator-gramarist Piet had gone below to sleep. He looked exhausted from the effort of bringing the ship to this point. Sarah, who looked even more exhausted, had gone ashore.

Montse, the smuggler captain, had come ashore with Sarah and Luman.

Luman carried two loaded pistols (a weapon with which he rarely fought, and used principally for magical purposes) and a loaded long rifle (a weapon he'd used as a boy to hunt wild hogs). He had no confidence in his ability to hit a target in any kind of motion at all, but he also felt exposed and vulnerable. He kept his right hand near the rifle's trigger, ready to raise the weapon and quickly fire.

Sarah was sketching something in the snow at her feet with

the tip of her staff. The expression on her face was one of concentration and distraction at the same time.

"Ten circles," Luman said. "Cabalistic lore?"

Sarah's head yanked up sharply. "You're talking about Jewish
magic?"

Luman nodded. "The *cabala* are the received things, in Hebrew.
They're passed down in a tradition, as the brauchers and the
Memphites do, and everyone else, really. Cabalists are workers
in that tradition, and if I'm not mistaken, they know a tree of
life shaped much like the array of circles you've drawn there."

Sarah's eyes bugged open and she glared at Luman's face.
"You said *tree of life*."

"Perhaps I'm remembering it wrong. I'm not a member of the
tradition." *Or of any tradition, you fraud.* Luman's heart ached.
"And there's another name for it: the *emanations*. I think the
Hebrew word is 'sefirot.'"

Sarah looked up at the top of Wisdom's Bluff. What was
she seeing through that unnatural eye? "Did you know that the
Ophidians build their libraries in just such a shape? And that
they call them *palaces of life*?"

"I didn't know either of those things." Luman inclined his head
respectfully. "I'm from Haudenosaunee territory, Your Majesty.
Though I've wandered in this life, it's mostly been east and south."

"Once, a..." Sarah started, but then looked thoughtful. "I was
about to say *a wise man*, but that isn't right. It isn't that Jacob
Hop is wise, it's more that he sometimes seems a borderline idiot,
maybe on account of his having been deaf and dumb most of his
life. Only, then once in a while he says the most insightful things."

"He sounds like a useful friend to have," Montse said. The
pirate captain wore a long wool coat, and of the three of them
seemed to be suffering the cold the worst. Despite burrowing
deep into the wool, she shivered and her teeth rattled.

"He is," Sarah agreed. "And he once pointed out that the map
of a palace of life makes a sort of tree." With the tip of her staff,
she connected the circles with a central line and then with three
branches on either side of it.

"Not just any sort of tree," Luman said, "but a seven-branched
tree of life, as the Serpent Throne is a seven-branched tree on
which the Mother of All Living sits. And there is a seven-branched
tree echoing the throne in the apse of the Basilica."

"There is?" Sarah looked surprised.

Luman nodded. "As there are seven planets: the moon, Mercury, Venus, the sun, Mars, Jupiter, and Saturn."

Sarah granted. "If you're counting the moon as a planet, you're talking astrology."

"Say rather *cosmology*," Luman said. "And *all* magic is cosmology. How can you produce effects in the world, if you don't know the world's structure and its laws? A planet is a 'wanderer' in Greek, a visible object in the sky that changes its position against the background of the stars."

Sarah nodded. "Arcturus is always in Boötes. But Mars moves."

"I am also reminded of the creation in Genesis."

Sarah stared at her own drawing, and then shook her head. "How?"

"Your ten circles make a tree with seven branches. In the first chapter of Genesis, God makes ten creative utterances, and the result is seven days of creation. What makes you draw this now?" Luman asked. "Do you think there's a connection with what you've come to learn?"

Sarah sighed. With the dark sleep circles under her eyes, she looked like a much older woman. "I dunno, wizard. I'd like there to be, I guess. I'd like to see more and more connections, and fewer and fewer strange surprises. I reckon if that started about now, I might actually understand the world before I die. Just for once, I'd really like someone else to know the answers, and to be happy to tell them to me."

Luman examined the sefirotic tree. "I must repeat that this is not my tradition. Neither what the Jews hand down, nor what the Firstborn know. But if I were to read this tree as an initiatic map..."

"There it is," Sarah said. "Read the map and tell me what you think it's saying."

Luman reflected. "There are surprising commonalities across initiatic traditions. One of them is the number three, especially manifesting as three worlds. Or, in old Solomon's temple, three chambers."

"Lack of imagination?" Sarah asked.

Luman chuckled, and then shrugged. "Perhaps they share sources. Perhaps they commonly derive from the structure of the universe. I haven't read it, but Agrippa's *Three Books of Occult Philosophy* are three precisely because he believes that there are three worlds. I have heard it whispered that the book itself, for one who reads with open eyes, constitutes an initiatory path through the three worlds, leading the reader to become the philosopher's stone."

"Did you mean *possess* the stone?" Montse asked.

"If you prefer." Luman shrugged. "There many things that are ... Hebraic about the Firstborn ways. Shared scriptures, a temple that looks like Solomon's might have looked, shared deities. In Hebrew heaven is 'shamayim,' which is a grammatical dual. Literally, it means 'the two heavens.' For Jacob there were earth and two heavens above it, reached by a ladder, just as apparently there were for Henry Cornelius Agrippa. Looking at what you're showing me now, I'd have to guess that for old Onandagos as well, a threefold world would not be surprising."

Sarah whistled. "Luman Walters, I knew there was something I liked about you."

"You wish to ascend the throne," Luman continued. "The throne is a tree. This map is a tree."

"Every library in Cahokia is a map," Sarah said.

"Apparently." Luman reflected on the map. "You likely see three levels here. You start at the base of the tree and wish to climb. There are three levels you will ascend."

Sarah nodded. "Anything else?"

"Three levels and three worlds should mean three guides," Luman said. "Moses, Elijah, and the Lord."

"You mean like the Mount of Transfiguration?"

"Or Malachi."

"Guides. You said that before once," Sarah said. "Why do I need guides?"

Luman pointed with the butt of his rifle. "If this is a map, it shows not only three levels, but alternate roads. More than one road implies that you can make a misstep. Fall into the abyss, enter the open mouth of hell, get lost in mists of darkness, and so on. Or maybe the three lines forward tell of three guides, while the three horizontal levels speak of three worlds."

"Three guides."

"Also, three gates. A passage to enter each new world. Perils along the road. Secret teachings to be delivered by the guides. Commitments. Judgments."

"This feels like an awful lot to do, just to be able to sit on the throne." Sarah cracked a bitter grin.

Luman took a step back. "For you to sit on a throne, you have to become the kind of being that sits a throne. And a heavenly throne, at that. This road is no formality, but a process of changing the person you are in order to become... a better person. A more powerful person, a more permanent person." He caught a sob in the back of his throat and wrangled it into a cough, turned his head away to hide the mist in his eyes. "A road such as the one I see mapped here also reveals the structure of the cosmos and gives those who walk it models for their behavior in everyday life."

Sarah looked down at the sefirotic tree. "You're awfully ambitious for those ten little circles."

Luman shrugged. "I could be wrong."

"I think you told me more in ten minutes than my priestess cousin told me in ten weeks. And candidly, maybe more than she knows." Sarah looked up the bluff. "How do you feel about a little walk, Luman?"

The leaves of the trees on Wisdom's Bluff had been red and gold when Sarah had seen them. Now they had fallen and either had blown away or else lay clumped under the piles of snow carpeting the hill.

Other than the leaves on *her* tree. The tree that had sprouted from the acorn Sarah had carried in her eye socket the first fifteen years of her life, the tree that had delivered to her the Cahokian regalia, the tree that in some sense was her father. That tree still looked like an invincible spring oak sprouting from the eye of the Serpent Mound, its leaves bright green and free of snow, the ground beneath and around it in a broad ring also clear.

"I didn't expect *this*," Luman Walters said.

Montse saw the green blaze of the tree and knelt, crossing herself in the snow. Sarah knelt beside her and Luman followed. They rested a moment, looking at the tree.

Through her Eye of Eve, Sarah also saw the bright blue-white presence of the Serpent lying within the mound. Now it seemed familiar to her; something in its color or in the pitch at which it hummed remind her of the goddess, something of the smell of the hill reminded her of Eden.

Some of the cloak of fatigue she bore, heavy on her neck and shoulders, fell away. She breathed in deeply, and then exhaled.

"Luman," she said. "I would like to contact my father."

Luman nodded.

"You're not telling me that that's necromancy."

"You don't need me along to say stupid and obvious things to you, Your Majesty."

"Do you know any spells for speaking with the dead?"

Luman shook his head. "I think I could doctor one up. Or I could put together a charm that would let you speak with your father in dream."

Sarah put a restraining hand on the magician's forearm. "Don't trouble yourself with it, Luman. My brother can help, I believe." She looked at each of her companions in turn. "Will you two defend me while I make the attempt?"

They both nodded.

Rising, they walked to the tree. Sarah knelt in the tall, soft grass growing within the Serpent's eye, over the roots of her father-tree. The earth was warm. She laid the Elector's staff beside her and took the Orb of Etyles into her hands.

Luman Walters laid a pistol in the grass to either side of her. Then he stepped back and stood on the ridge of the Serpent's eye. He held the rifle in his left hand, butt on the earth, as if it were a staff. He reached his right hand within his long, many-pocketed coat, reciting something Sarah didn't know. *Greek?*

Montserrat Ferrer i Quintana stood beside Luman, naked saber in one hand and an elegant pistol in the other.

A sudden urge gripped Sarah to check in with Maltres Korinn, but she set that aside for the moment. With her Eye of Eve, she gazed a long time at the tree, looking for the spirit of her father.

She saw the tree, which was the right color, but no sign of the man.

"Father?" she murmured.

No answer.

Nathaniel would help her.

Reaching into the orb, she drew energy from the Mississippi ley and channeled it into her eye. *"Fratrem quaeso."*

Her vision raced along the Ohio River's ley, past keelboats and Memphite barges. It abandoned the river for fainter leys on footpaths over the mountains, then raced along another large river Sarah didn't immediately identify—

and found Nathaniel.

He sat tied in a wooden chair. The chair was nailed to the floor.

The floor belonged to the cabin of a ship. Late afternoon light shone in through glass windows. Sitting in another chair, also tied, was Jacob Hop.

Both Jake and Nathaniel slumped forward, heads lolling sideways.

Jake was covered in blood. Dead?

Sarah's heart pounded. She took deep breaths to still her panic, knowing that Luman and Montse were staring at her.

"Nathaniel," she whispered. "Nathaniel."

He stirred and murmured without words.

"Nathaniel!"

His head jerked up and he stared about with wild eyes. The whites of his eyes were red and the skin around them was puffy from weeping.

Jake must be dead.

"Sarah?" Nathaniel asked.

"I need your help," she said.

He laughed, but his laughter collapsed into a sob. "Sarah," he said, "I can't help anyone. I'm tied here."

"I'll untie you," Sarah said. "I'll help you escape." She wasn't sure she really had the ability to do that—just maintaining a visual and auditory link with her brother felt burdensome, never mind the effort it would require to sink a ship at that distance. "But I need you to connect me with our father."

"Our father?" Nathaniel frowned. "But what . . . how . . . ?" Realization dawned on his face. "He's dead."

"He's dead," Sarah agreed. "But I think he has things he wants to tell me."

"Maybe I can help," Nathaniel said. "If you can untie me."

"Luman!" Sarah called. Her eyes were entirely absorbed in her vision of Nathaniel aboard ship, somewhere in the east, so she couldn't see Luman. She knew he was there, though, and she held out her hands. "You have a knife. Can I borrow—"

Before she could finish her request, the hilt of a knife was pressed into her hands.

"Thank you," she murmured.

"I haven't done anything yet," Nathaniel murmured.

"*Fratrem libero,*" Sarah murmured. "*Funem seco.*"

She ran Luman's blade along her wrists, miming cutting bonds away from her arms while at the same time projecting her will along the network of leys to where her brother was captured. She attacked the ropes at his wrists.

They slid off.

She repeated her words and mimed the same actions at her ankles. The last ropes holding Nathaniel in place dropped to the floor.

Nathaniel stood. Sarah didn't see where it had come from, but suddenly there was a drum over his shoulder, primitive and simple-looking, though elegant. "Our father is near you?"

"I'm not sure quite what the concepts *near* and *far* mean in this manner of thinking," Sarah said. "But I'm kneeling beneath a tree he made of his own blood and soul, so I think the answer is probably yes."

"Can you wake our sister?" Nathaniel asked. "I think she's on the same ship with me, and I believe she's been drugged into unconsciousness. You should be able to see her now."

"I'll do that immediately," Sarah said.

"I'll get our father and bring him to you," Nathaniel said. "And Sarah?"

"Yes?"

"Jacob Hop said there was something he had to tell you. Just before he died."

The words yanked at Sarah's heart. "Did he say what it was about?"

Nathaniel shook his head. "The Tarocks, maybe?"

That was unexpected. "I'll see you soon," Sarah said. "*Sororem quaeso.*"

This time her Eye of Eve found its object almost immediately, in a room that had to be adjacent to Nathaniel's. She looked like their sibling, with pale skin and dark hair, except that where Sarah's was still growing out from having been shaved a couple of months earlier, her sister's was long and extravagantly curly.

She lay on a narrow net hammock. Her wrists were shackled together, as were her ankles. Her aura was the color Sarah had come to expect of all her family, but there was a sick patina to it—something was wrong with her.

Sarah didn't think her sister was restrained by a spell, but the young woman might indeed be kept deep in sleep by a drug.

"Margaret!" she yelled.

Her sister didn't move. Gripping Luman's dagger, Sarah poked its tip into the palm of her hand until it bled. *"Pharmacum extraho."* She willed her own soul to act like a siphon drawing the noxious substance from her sister's veins and then her own. Margaret's aura slowly changed to an acceptable color, like Nathaniel's, like Sarah's own. Sarah looked down and saw black liquid the thickness of molasses drip from her own hand into the grass.

Margaret stirred.

"Sororem evigilo," Sarah incanted. Reversing the knife, she stabbed her other palm.

Margaret shrieked and threw herself forward. The chains on her wrists and ankles limited her movement, but they didn't fix her in place, and her sudden motion hurled her sideways. The hammock spun and opened, dropping her onto a wooden floor.

"Margaret!" Sarah shouted. "Margaret!"

But Margaret didn't hear her. Margaret had neither her eye, nor her brother's ear, and she and Sarah were in a one-way contact only. What did Margaret have, then?

Sarah's sister lurched to her feet. She tottered back and forth, wrestling with the chains at her wrist and grunting. Sarah gripped the knife in her hands, preparing to help her sister with her chains—

when she noticed her sister's hair.

It was rising. The curly hair slithered upward and outward, until Margaret Elytharias Penn looked like a black-spored dandelion ready to explode on the autumn wind.

Her face was twisted into a red snarl.

Margaret gripped the manacle on her left wrist with her right hand. Ripping suddenly, she tore it from her flesh, the iron peeling apart like the skin of an orange. Just as quickly, she yanked off the other manacle.

She didn't even stop to waste effort on the chains on her ankles. Leaping forward, she shattered them with the force of her stride.

With one swing of a balled fist, Margaret shattered the door to her cabin. "Nathaniel!" she roared. "Jake!"

She didn't need Sarah anymore, and Sarah had other things to do.

Also, Sarah was faint from sleeplessness and effort.

"Visionem termino." She returned to Wisdom's Bluff.

✦ ✦ ✦

Nathaniel sprang upward into the grassy plain of the sky, drumming and singing:

> *I ride upon four horses, to heaven I ride*
> *I ride to seek my father, all iron inside*
> *A king of the Ohio, a Penn his bride*
> *O Lion of Missouri, where do you ride?*

He listened first for any sound of the Sorcerer Robert Hooke. The man was away in the west, and near him was the heavy creaking sound of something enormous being moved by cart. Men cursed and whips cracked. In his heart, Nathaniel felt dread.

Was this an act of healing, or would this journey leave him feeling ill?

He listened for his father.

He wasn't sure what he was listening for, exactly. He tried listening for a voice that sounded like his own. He thought he heard more than one, wisps of unknown family members coming to him from multiple directions over the astral breeze.

But Sarah had said that their father was near her, in some sense. He listened for Sarah instead. He heard her immediately.

His horses carried him across the plain quickly, the silver breeze of starlight filling his hair and pooling in his tricorn hat. In the west, at a junction of two creeks, he found a low, rocky hill. Two strangers stood at the bottom of the hill in long coats. One was a woman with long red hair and a saber in her hand; the other was a man with curly dark hair, spectacles, and a trumpet-propelled hymn that leaked from his sleeves and collar.

Nathaniel rode to the top of the hill and found three more people. Two he knew, or at least, he'd seen them before. His sister Sarah knelt and held an iron ball in both her hands. Behind Sarah rose a tree wrapped in a serpent; a spring bubbled from the tree's roots and a barefoot woman stood, cooling her toes in the spring's water. He had last seen that woman mourning alone on a hill—her expression now was one of contentment, like a woman at rest, watching her happy children play.

The third person was a warrior. He was a tall man with sharply Cahokian features—a long nose, a complexion the color of china, and long, black hair. He wore a Cahokian tunic and cape, boots rising to above his knees, with crossed pistols on his belt and an empty scabbard at his hip.

He looked like Sarah and Margaret. And like Nathaniel.

Sarah looked at Nathaniel and smiled. "Welcome, brother."

"Thank you for freeing me."

"Can you find our father?"

"He's standing right beside you."

Sarah shivered. "I don't see him."

"He sees you," Nathaniel said. "He's smiling."

"I want to talk to him."

Nathaniel considered. He held out his hand and Sarah took it, putting away the iron sphere she carried and rising to her feet. Then he held out his other hand to his father.

Kyres Elytharias, the Lion of Missouri.

Kyres took Nathaniel's hand. A tingle of life and energy rushed through his arm. The feeling made him want to leap and run for joy. It startled him so much he almost dropped his father's hand.

Sarah's mouth dropped open. Then she extended her free hand—

and Kyres took it.

"Father," she said.

~What did your mother name you?~ the Lion of Missouri asked.

"I'm Sarah." Tears streamed down her cheeks. "Sarah Elytharias Penn. I was raised as a foster child by Iron Andy Calhoun."

"I'm Nathaniel Elytharias Penn," Nathaniel said. "I was fostered by Earl Isham of Johnsland. Noah Carter Isham."

Kyres Elytharias nodded. ~Good men.~

"You have a third child," Nathaniel added. "She's with me."

"Margaret Elytharias Penn." Joy shone in Sarah's face, and pride in being the bearer of a welcome message. "She grew up as a Catalan, with Montserrat Ferrer i Quintana."

~Another friend,~ the Lion said.

Far away, Nathaniel heard a rumbling sound. It resembled thunder, only it had a basso note of wickedness and despair. He frowned.

"I have so many questions," Sarah said.

~I can try to answer them,~ their father replied. ~But, living or dead, I am but a man. And there are some questions I can only answer in the right time and place.~

Sarah laughed, a sweet rolling sound with a bitter note in

it. "Alzbieta Torias said a similar thing. And it turned out, she was mostly bluffing. She knew very little of the royal secrets."

~*I only ever knew very little of them myself,*~ Kyres said. ~*In life.*~

"And now?" Nathaniel asked. The line between life and death had come to seem thin and arbitrary to him. If the dead knew vastly more than the living, could Nathaniel access that information?

~*Some limitations fall away with the mortal coil,*~ Kyres said. ~*Time. The veil of ignorance.*~

"Were you ever King of Cahokia?" Sarah asked.

~*I was crowned and anointed by the Metropolitan in the Basilica, in full view of all the city and beneath the Lady's doves. In a sense, that crowning and anointing was a lie.*~

"The lamp in the Basilica is a stand-in for the Serpent Throne," Sarah said. "A symbol, a proxy. Being crowned and anointed in the presence of that lamp is a statement to the kingdom that you have ascended the Throne and sat on it."

~*Say rather that it is a promise to the people that you will ascend the Throne.*~ Kyres's voice was sorrowful.

"Only you never did."

Kyres shook his head. ~*I never was crowned and anointed beneath the Lady's ravens. My failure didn't matter in the eyes of the other Electors, or the Empress. For the secular world, I was the King of Cahokia.*~

"And for the goddess?"

~*I was Her Beloved. But I never became more than that.*~

"You were a great king," Sarah said. "You're a legend."

~*I worked hard to make up for my failure. If I couldn't put myself into the proper place in the cosmos, I could put other wrongs right. I fought for justice. I sacrificed for peace. I do not regret my failure to be anointed.*~

"How could you regret anything?" Sarah asked. "You did so much."

~*I should have forgiven more.*~

Sarah looked surprised. She was silent for a moment. "Do you mean Bayard?"

The Lion smiled. ~*In death, I have forgiven Bayard. In life, I had nothing to forgive him. I mean my brother Thomas. I mean my wife Hannah. I mean myself. I mean everyone. Forgiveness is eternal life.*~

"Your people miss you," Sarah said.

~They have you now,~ he answered. ~They are much the better for it.~

"It was your lack of knowledge of the royal secrets," Nathaniel said. "That's why you never ascended the Throne."

Kyres nodded. ~I looked long and hard. I gathered scraps of old poetry. My mother taught me what she could. She was never the Beloved, but her husband had been in his youth. And therefore she knew very little, too. Her husband, my father, came to manhood under the influence of the Metropolitan. He was a man who hated the goddess and all Her gifts. He did everything he could to destroy the royal lore wherever he found it.~

"And now?" Sarah asked. "Now that the veil of ignorance has fallen away, do you know the royal secrets?"

Kyres nodded.

"Will you teach them to me?"

~When you reach me, I will,~ Kyres said. ~In the right time and place.~

"At the Throne," Sarah said.

~At the Throne. You will need two guides to bring you to me there, across the forest of the world and over the abyss of hell.~

"You're my third guide," Sarah said. "Three worlds, three guides. Luman Walters was right."

Kyres nodded.

"How do I cleanse the Throne?" Sarah asked. "It's polluted. Things have happened."

~The Throne was attacked and deliberately befouled.~

"Because the Serpent Throne is the goddess," Sarah said.

~Yes. You have the power to do what I could not. You can enclose the space again, make it sacred. Draw the veil.~

"I have the Heronplow."

~I entered Peter Plowshare's kingdom and asked to borrow it. As I rode my borders, dispensing justice, I was also riding his. In his old age, he was weakened, and his grip over the beastkind was slipping, so I was his great ally in the Missouri. There are other rites, older rites, that could consecrate the Great Mound, but I didn't know them. I knew the golden plow could do the work, but Peter Plowshare wouldn't relinquish it.~

"I thought he was the great giver of gifts," Sarah said. "Dispenser of civilization and all that. Seems stingy not to share the plow a bit."

~He was too weak to come plow the bounds himself. And he was afraid that if I gave him the Heronblade in exchange, he would die holding the sword.~

"Empowering his destroyer son-self." Sarah's shoulders drooped. "Father, I . . ."

~I know.~ Kyres gripped both their hands fiercely. *~I know. You did what you had to do. You did the right thing. It wasn't a perfect choice, because there is no perfect choice, but you restored the starved Treewall and the desecrated Sunrise Mound. You became the Beloved. You fed your people.~*

"I walked through a tree root, too," Sarah said. "Kinda proud of that one."

~So am I.~

"I'm afraid if I just run the plow around the Great Mound now, it will be . . . wrong," Sarah said. "And dangerous. Like, I should be enclosing sanctity, but instead I'd be enclosing a pollution."

Nathaniel felt awe at his sister's words. He found himself barely able to follow the conversation with his father, much less contribute to it. Sarah, on the other hand, seemed completely comfortable with all the talk of sanctity, ritual magic, enthronement, desecration, and divine rebellion.

He felt proud of Sarah, too.

~The Serpent Throne is cleansed by sacrifice.~

Sarah was so still she seemed not to be breathing. "I've heard . . . rumors. You don't mean a blood sacrifice? I don't have to kill someone?"

Kyres shook his head. *~The goddess doesn't call you to kill. You must decide your sacrifice. And as what you ask is great, what you give must be great.~*

Sarah looked thoughtful. "I understand. And . . . two guides?"

~I cannot help you.~ Kyres shifted and looked into Nathaniel's face. His father's eyes were deep as time itself, and at the bottom, stars twinkled. *~But Nathaniel can.~*

"I don't know any royal secrets," Nathaniel said.

~The royal secrets never go away,~ Kyres said. *~To say that they are lost only means that those who should know them do not. But they are dispersed in the world, and lie buried under fallen logs and written in flaming letters on the hilltops. Who has ears, can always hear.~*

"You mean they're hidden in plain sight," Sarah said.

"Jacob Hop," Nathaniel said.

"The Tarocks?" Sarah's astonishment showed on her face.

The Lion of Missouri said nothing.

"But who else?" Nathaniel's mind raced. Ma'iingan, maybe, the Ojibwe man who had rescued Nathaniel and set him, with the help of Ma'iingan's own manidoo, his personal guardian spirit, on the trail of transformation and healing?

Or Ma'iingan's manidoo, perhaps?

"Thalanes?" Sarah's face was hopeful. "Our mother? You don't mean . . . Zadok? The Metropolitan?"

Kyres shook his head patiently, and he looked into Nathaniel's eyes again. *~You will find your sister's guides.~*

"I'll do it," Nathaniel agreed. Could Kyres be referring to their third sibling, Margaret? That didn't seem likely.

Temple Franklin? He shuddered at the thought.

The thunder-like sound cracked again, louder this time, and Nathaniel shrank at the horror of it, nearly losing his grip on his father's and his sister's hands. "What's that?"

~The goddess is under attack in Her own city,~ Kyres Elytharias said. *~She needs you.~*

He released their hands and stepped back.

The feeling of energy flowing through Nathaniel's body vanished, and he gasped. Sarah looked as if she had been struck.

"Sarah?"

"Go," she said. "You and Margaret, get yourselves off that ship."

"What will you do?"

"Save my city." Sarah smiled. "Only really, I think all I can do is hold out until you figure out who my guides are supposed to be."

"What about the Luman Walters person you talked about?"

"Maybe. Only the Lion said *you* would find the person." Sarah shrugged. "Someone hidden in plain sight, I guess. Let me know when you figure out who it is."

With a heart heavy with doubt, Nathaniel turned and raced his horse-drum across the starlit plain.

Bill's heart sank. The end was approaching.

Sarah hadn't returned. The food supplies were beginning to run low. Now the Imperials had cannons.

And not just any cannons.

The guns were long and elaborately carved. Even looking through a spyglass, Bill couldn't make out the writing around the guns' mouths, but he knew it was there. The weapons and their inscriptions were as famous as their commander.

General Theophilus Sayle had been an artillery captain in the Spanish War. In the retaking of New Orleans, he had been frustrated by a series of gun misfires, and had ordered a new cannon cast. To give it more power, it was said, he had had a New Testament verse forged into the gun's metal: *I will give unto thee the keys of the kingdom of heaven.*

Some men understood that inscription as an act of magic, or of faith. To Bill, it looked like a soldier's joke—Captain Sayle had been ordered to get inside the City of New Orleans. Lacking a key, he forged himself one.

Not that the city of New Orleans was often mistaken for the kingdom of heaven.

Regardless, since the Bible verse in question was (apparently) a reference to St. Peter, the gun came to be called the Peter. Before the siege was over, he had forged the James (*he surnamed them Boanerges, which is, The sons of thunder*) and the Matthew (*there shall not be left here one stone upon another*).

Now all Twelve Apostles stared at Bill, lined up on the eastern city of the city, all laid at the eastern wall.

"Our own guns don't have the range to touch them," Jaleta Zorales said.

Bill sighed. "Thank you."

"They're beyond the Necromancer's screen of black fire," Sherem added. "I don't think we can penetrate that shield with an arcane attack."

"And thank *you*," Bill said.

"The cannons arrived with a mob of reinforcements," Valia Sharelas said. "Those trenches are packed with Imperial troops."

Bill couldn't force himself to utter another word of thanks. Instead, he grunted.

"I have ordered boats built of all available wood," Maltres Korinn said. "If our soldiers can give our people cover in a sustained volley from the western wall, we can put as many of our people as possible in the river to escape."

"I do not like running away," Bill grumbled. "And there are the beastkind. But I prefer it to certain death."

"The other priests and I are all fasting and praying for deliverance," Zadok Tarami said.

Bill turned from surveying the enemy to glare at the priest. "As little as I like hearing bad news, I prefer it to useless air."

Tarami frowned. "Do you find God—"

"Get down off the wall," Bill growled, "or I'll shoot you."

"Help may yet arrive," Cathy said softly. "Messengers *did* get through the cordon."

Bill favored his lady with a gentle smile. "Some of my riders did get past the trenches," he agreed. "For all we know, they were shot down a mile further on. Still, of course, you're right. And the moment any relief force arrives, I will offer up every sheep and goat I can find in thanks to that force's guiding totem. *Cuius auxilium, eius deus,* as you might say."

He laughed out loud at his own bon mot. *In Latin, no less!*

"Also," Alzbieta Torias said, "Sarah may yet return. Her Majesty has proved to be a resourceful magician."

"And yet, we must prepare as if those things will not happen." Maltres Korinn's voice was gloomy.

"Build the boats," Bill said. "We will send as many baby Moseses into the water as we can, and hopefully none into the bellies of the angry beastkind that prowl there."

Maltres nodded and climbed down off the wall.

The Podebradan Yedera stared at the cannons.

"What are you thinking?" he asked her. Her presence with the city's leadership on the wall was not strictly regular, but no one criticized or defended it. She simply *was*, and seemed to stand at all times outside the rules.

"A small force," she said. "Highly protected and fast."

"Magic could be worked that would provide protection at least until such a force reached the black flame," Sherem said thoughtfully. "It would require a large amount of power, but it could be done."

Yedera looked at the Polite and something unspoken seemed to pass between them. Yedera nodded.

"Perhaps the queen's beastkind," Bill suggested. "They are terrifying and fast, and make for excellent shock troops."

"I had in mind another force," Yedera said. "I had been thinking that such a force might target the Necromancer himself, but I think our more urgent need is to eliminate the guns."

"Such a force would suffer serious casualties," Bill said. He had the uneasy feeling that Yedera wasn't going to ask his permission. At least he could offer advice. "But if it could spike those guns, it would buy us time."

Yedera frowned. "I don't know guns. Do you mean stop up their mouths?"

Jaleta Zorales stepped in; this was her métier. "The charge in the gun is ignited by combustion that passes through a touch hole. That's a small hole at the base of the cannon, at the opposite end from its mouth."

Yedera nodded. "I think I understand."

"I'll show you," Zorales said. "If you jam a spike through that touch hole, the Imperials might take hours, even days, to get the spike out. In the meantime, the cannon is useless."

"If you have the spike forged with barbs," Bill added, "it becomes even harder to remove."

"Do we have such barbs?" Yedera asked.

Jaleta Zorales nodded. "We have a few ready made at all times. In case of retreat, we spike our own guns so they can't be turned against us."

"I'll have more made," Bill said. "I'll have sixty by sundown. I assume you are proposing to command this verloren hoop? That's what the Dutch would call such an expedition."

"It sounds like *forlorn hope*," Alzbieta said.

"It's worse than that," Bill said. "It means 'lost troop.'" He looked gravely at Yedera. "Shall I task the beastkind?"

"No," Yedera said. "I have my companions already. Give me the spikes by sundown."

"I'll be ready," Sherem said.

Was the wizard going to run out with the Podebradan to spike the Twelve Apostles? That didn't seem quite right to Bill, but having lost his magic, perhaps the man was anxious to make his mark some other way.

"Tell me what else you will require," Bill said.

Yedera shook her head. "Nothing, General. I have sworn my oaths, and I will do my duty."

BOOM! The first of the Twelve Apostles began to fire on the eastern wall.

*"It seems that there's a fine line
between the living and the dead."*

CHAPTER TWENTY-ONE

Dockery had been whistling incessantly. He and Kinta Jane Embry stood in a slanted crack between two walls of gray striated rock. Ahead of them lay the entrance down which they had come, the entrance Isaiah Wilkes had taught her. Behind them lay a pool of crystal clear water.

In the light that shone when Kinta Jane cracked open her darklantern, she saw white, eyeless things wriggling in the pool. Some of them looked like fish. She hoped they weren't venomous; she and Dockery might have to flee in that direction. She hadn't crossed the pool, but Wilkes had said there was a back way out. That had to be it.

> *On a warm night in May*
> *All the girls came out to play*
> *And dance, as far I could see*
> *I said to myself*
> *She's an angel, or an elf*
> *You'd put on your red dress for me*

Who would answer their signal? After much debate, she and Dockery had written a news-paper story together. Cracking the lantern a little wider, she unfolded the sheet of paper and read it again.

ONAS AT THE SIGN OF THE CENTAUR

*At the Centaur tavern this week, famed Pennslander story-
teller BROTHER ONAS performed his much-loved tale, "The
Three Brothers and the Landlord Gone Mad." Brother Onas
can be reached evenings at the Centaur all this week and
next, warming himself by the chimney, should there be any
audience desirous of a second performance.*

It had the advantage of being slightly less obvious than
Brother Onas wants to meet, while at the same time being short.
Montreal news-papers, it turned out, charged by the word, and
when individual words became too long, the editors sometimes
counted them double. They had paid to run the English-language
version of the message in *The Tattler* and *The Herald*. They had
also prepared a French version for *Le Courier* and *Le Mercure*.
Kinta Jane had paid for the ads by selling rings she had taken
off the fingers of an Imperial thug named Joss. Joss had assaulted
Kinta Jane in the Ohio, and she'd killed him for it; it pleased her
to think that her assailant's wealth now aided her in her mission.

Is my message too obvious?

Too clumsy an approach might not attract the people Kinta
Jane wanted, or might draw the attention of enemies.

There was no *Centaur* beside a chimney by which they could
warm themselves. Indeed, the chimney in the article was a sly
hint, referring to the chimney of rock in which they stood, the
appointed meeting place Isaiah Wilkes had known.

They had found the rock formation eventually, riding past it
twice before passing it at exactly the right angle to be able to see
the centaur within. The chimney and cave, which took only an hour
of climbing to find, had confirmed that they were in the right spot.

Each night for a week and a half following publication of their
notice, Dockery and Kinta Jane had come down into the chimney.
By day they slept in a rat-infested boarding house called *Le Baiser
du Roi*, eating what food they could gather in the late afternoon
and buying lantern oil to get them through another night.

*Not a month had gone by
With a tear in my eye
I came on bended knee*

I could see you were touched
I said, I can't promise much
Would you put on your white dress for me?

The words disappeared into the echo, which lingered long, drifting back down the stone chimney in reflected, lugubrious snatches.

Kinta Jane shivered. "This is the last night."

"That's it, then?" Dockery spat. The corner of the cave where his brown saliva and soaked tobacco plugs had accumulated over the week they'd spent underground reeked, but at least he had the decency to keep using the same corner. "We're just finished? The Conventicle failed?"

"I don't know," Kinta Jane said. "I don't know what else the Conventicle is trying to accomplish. But I came here to meet Brother Odishkwa, and Brother Odishkwa never showed up."

"You and I failed, then." Dockery's voice was bitter.

First the first time in weeks, Kinta Jane Embry couldn't find her tongue.

As they had for ten days, they climbed back out the stone crack at dawn and loped back toward the boarding house. Cold gnawed at Kinta Jane's fingers and toes, burrowing through her flesh to pinch her bones.

Montreal was a city of a handful of stone buildings within a stone wall encircling a three-peaked hill on an island. The sun cracking over the eastern horizon lit those structures and tinted them pink, as if they had come directly from a fairy story. The southern hills through which Kinta Jane and Dockery had come by canoe were blue-gray at their base and wrapped in white around their upper two-thirds.

The morning light revealed the bulletins and broadsheets that covered every empty brick and protruded from beneath snow and mud. Montreal was a city of competing missives, especially now—some sort of public debate was taking place, over the replacement of a dead elector. *La Fayette soutient l'évêque*, began one broadsheet, while another countered, *Le sieur de Champlain témoigne de la valeur de l'abbé*, and a third forcefully argued for a kind of compromise: *L'heure est venue pour un chaman haude-nosaunee.* None of the pamphlets were in English, but some were in a mixed patois with a few words that looked to be of French origin: Michif, Kinta Jane thought. In Acadia, they called Creoles *Métis*, and Michif was their own language.

Maybe she should take up praying to St. Jean Nicollet and ask for the gift of tongues.

Champlain and La Fayette were to choose an ecclesiastical elector between them, and they could not agree.

Kinta Jane sucked cold air into her lungs and exhaled a small cloud of steam. The carts of the morning's pedlars and shopkeepers, trundling off to set up their work, raised a comfortable din around her. Coureurs du bois, trappers and traders who dressed and held themselves like Dockery did, moved to and from the river with a purposefulness that suggested they wouldn't stay long in the city if they could help it.

"We could go find Brother Anak," she suggested experimentally.

"Yes." Dockery nodded. "Where would we do that?"

"North," she said. "Somewhere."

"As far as I know, everything north of here is wild Algonk land. If you go far enough, you get to places so cold, nobody owns 'em and their bears are white."

"That sounds like a fable."

"No, I've seen one myself. You want to see Anakim in any kind of numbers, you gotta go west. But I think maybe we ought to try to talk to Champlain or La Fayette. I don't expect they're Brother Odishkwa, but maybe they're in on the secret."

Kinta Jane hesitated. "They seem a little busy right now."

"Man like that is always busy. But they won't make time unless we ask them to."

"Do you know either one of them?"

"Did Isaiah Wilkes know Thomas Penn?"

"He rescued Thomas from a fire. He himself set the fire, I believe."

Dockery laughed. "There you are, then. One thing you know I can do well, rain or shine, is start a fire."

Kinta Jane looked at the stone walls of the city's center and shook her head.

"You don't look like Brother Onas. Neither of you does."

The words were spoken by a new voice, which came from behind Kinta Jane. She jerked in surprise, then tried to keep her knees from wobbling as she turned to look at the speaker—

and found herself staring into his sternum.

"Hellfire," Dockery muttered. He spat tobacco juice into the snow.

"In the woodcuts and the puppet shows," the stranger continued, "Brother Onas always has one of those broad hats they like in Pennsylvania. And long, curly hair. Mind you, I think they're just trying to portray William Penn."

The speaker was a giant, literally. At first guess, Kinta Jane would have said half again the height of a normal man, though after a few exchanges of dialog, she'd have brought her estimate down to eight feet. Give or take a few inches. He had a broad face with wide nose and cheeks, a chin so small she might have called it recessive, and deep-set dark eyes that twinkled beneath a rocky outcrop of forehead. His eyebrows were large enough for a small bird to nest in, and a thatch of red hair hung down around his neck.

He wore layers of fur and wool draped over his enormous body, with broad leather belts buckled around his chest and shoulders to hold them in place. Above his shoulder she saw a crude, leather-wrapped hilt that suggested a sword hanging on the man's back. A quiver of arrows too long and too big around to be useful to a man of normal size was strapped to one thigh, and he carried cradled in his arms a long staff that tapered and was notched at both ends.

A long bow, Kinta Jane realized.

Of enormous size.

"Mind you," the giant said, "I speak only out of my own knowledge, which is miserably inadequate. Persons of your culture and sophistication are likely well-advised to ignore me entirely."

"You're Misaabe," Dockery said.

The giant nodded. "That's what our Chippewa neighbors would call me. But old Will Penn spoke the language of the Bible." The giant cracked a grin that seemed to split his entire head in half, revealing yellowed teeth the size of eyeballs. "Maybe that's why he went to heaven, like the song says."

"You ain't in the empire," Dockery said. "You know the Elector Songs?"

"We ain't." The giant shook his head. "But I've traveled, and the songs that stick in your head aren't necessarily the best ones. Sometimes they're the catchiest, or the shortest, or just the ones you hear most often. I know about the *three from Philadelphioo*, although I don't really know what they're for. But because he was a Bible man, Penn called us the *Anakim*. The sons of Anak.

Anyway, that's what I've been told, but I'm too unlettered to have confirmed it for myself."

"Or Brother Anak," Kinta Jane said.

"In the woodcuts, Brother Anak is usually twice the size of Brother Onas and Brother Odishkwa." The giant smiled again. He seemed unable to grin with closed lips, so every smile cracked his maw wide open and sent his eyebrows into a merry dance. "You will have noticed that that's an exaggeration."

"Would you say you're...large for your kind?" Dockery asked.

"No," the giant answered. "Nor am I small."

"A more important question," Kinta Jane said, "is why are you talking to us?"

The laughter that exploded out of the Misaabe startled a passing horse, causing it to throw its rider into the snow. The man rolled to his feet cursing and shaking snow from his three-cocked hat, but when he saw the giant, he spun on his heels, grabbed the animal's bridle, and ran.

"Really?" the giant countered.

Kinta Jane crossed her arms.

The giant dug beneath a thick fur on his chest and found a piece of paper. It was a page from *Le Mercure*. "My French wouldn't stand the scrutiny of a deaf man, miserable untutored pig that I am, but I know pretty well what *Frère Onas* means. I've been watching you."

"How long?" Dockery looked surprised.

"Since the day this was published." The giant leaned down to look more closely at the scrap. "A week."

"I never saw you," Dockery said.

"Either you're calling me a liar, or you're expressing admiration for my woodcraft." The giant grinned, and Kinta Jane stepped back in surprise at the sudden flashing of teeth. "Don't worry, you'll have plenty of chance to see me in action. I expect you'll find me terribly inadequate. Head like an oak trunk, that's me. No boring through it, no climbing over, you just have to go around. Obviously, I have to take you back to my people." He smiled again. "Put your witness to the test."

"I saw no tracks in the cave other than our own," Dockery said. "You might be quick and quiet, but a fellow your size leaves a mark in the dirt."

"I came in the other entrance," the giant said. "I watched you both. *And* listened."

Dockery looked mortified. "Listened?"

The giant sang:

> *Now, if the sergeant is right*
> *We won't last the night*
> *And the river is as deep as the sea*
> *So pray one more time*
> *Kiss the children good-bye*
> *And put on your black dress for me.*

"I think I've heard it before," he said when he'd finished. "It's about your Spanish War, isn't it?"

"I guess no one invited the Misaabe to that one." Dockery looked distinctly uncomfortable.

"We're on the far side of your Empire. I think mostly you were grateful we didn't take the opportunity to cause trouble."

"You look like you could cause a lot of trouble, if you wanted," Kinta Jane said.

The giant snorted. "No, we're peaceful people. The great advantage to being bigger than everyone else is you're never forced to fight, because others leave you alone. That lets you cultivate a mentality of harmony. It's little people who are aggressive."

Dockery opened his mouth and shut it again.

"You were waiting here," Kinta Jane said.

"We've been watching for years," the giant answered. "We lost contact with Brother Onas when the Empire was formed. Brother Odishkwa stopped talking to us ten years ago. We've been watching for signs of either ever since."

"We'll go with you," Kinta Jane said. "Only I suppose you'd better tell us your name."

"Chu-Roto-Sha-Meshu, son of Shoru-Me-Racha," the giant said.

"My name is Kinta Jane."

"Dockery. That's a long name you've got."

"And I do not deserve it." The giant showed all his teeth in his still-terrifying grin. "Call me Mesh."

"Shall I bind you?" General Varem asked. He had a receding jaw and a receding hairline, and two glittering eyes set close in beside a pointed nose. His black wooden armor showed several long cracks and his red cloak was filthy.

Chigozie shook his head. "Why would you want to do that?"

Chigozie, Ferpa, and Kort stood before the General on a street in Etzanoa. The general stood on the back of a cart, from which he had been shouting orders to a succession of messengers and junior officers. He had fallen into a silence when he'd seen Chigozie and his beastkind approach. The hounds standing around the cart had growled, baring long teeth as spiky as their fur.

"I have to decide what to do with you," the general said. "I've received interesting intelligence, news that may present an unparalleled opportunity in our war with the Heron King, or possibly may herald an unprecedented threat."

"You should let me go, with my people." Chigozie spread his hands apart to show that he was unarmed. "My people are the Merciful. We have no wish to fight with Zomas. Indeed, we would gladly trade with your people. So far, though, your outriders have chased us from our first home and threatened to chase us from our second."

"I know the terms our outriders offered," Varem said. "You could have chosen to join us."

"As slaves," Chigozie said. "But the gospel of John teaches us that the truth shall make us free."

"Only some of you would be slaves," Varem said. "The others would join us to fight."

"We aren't fighters," Chigozie answered. "My people have retired from the rampaging of their kind. They have chosen peace. They have chosen to give mercy, in the hope of receiving mercy."

"That is Matthew." Varem smiled without humor. "You see, I know scripture, too. There was a time when I thought to take orders and become a monk. A Cetean of all things, would you credit it? I had enough of coercion, I believed my father and the king were wrong, and I knew better than they."

"What changed your mind?"

"My father was killed. And my mother. They were eaten, in fact, by rampaging beastkind. And that was years ago, and long before the beastkind began to rage *en masse*."

Ferpa slowly knelt in the snow. "I grieve with you." Kort followed her example.

"I rejoice in your fellow feeling." Varem's face showed no emotion.

"We are peaceful people," Chigozie said. "Let us go."

"Other than *you*, I understand that you are not *people* at all." Kort and Ferpa made no response to the Zoman's insult. "Tell me how a New Orleans priest comes to make his home with the children of the Heron King?"

Chigozie shrugged. "It is where I feel God has called me."

"You see that we are entirely aligned. You feel God has called you here. Your friend with the cow's head shares my grief at my people's suffering. And you are all in a position to help me. To fulfill your calling, priest. To show mercy to Zomas, a land eminently in need of it. You do one thing for me, and I will let you and your people live in peace. I will protect you, with such protection as I can offer. I will extend trade recognition to your Merciful, and the right to come and go in Zomas as you please."

"These are great boons." Chigozie was wary. "What do you need?"

"I need you to rescue a woman."

Unbidden, memories of the women he had killed—to save them from a longer and more painful death at the hands of Kort and other beastkind—flooded into Chigozie's mind.

"I would gladly rescue a woman," Kort said. He must be remembering the same episode. "Without any promise of recompense."

Naares Stoach grunted an objection. "Are our own men grown so weak that we can't mount a rescue raid to seize a prisoner?"

"This would not be a raid," Varem said. "At least, you would not ride to the rescue in open hostility. Instead, you would sneak. Having found the woman, you would bring her here."

"I repeat my question," Stoach said. "What about *our* men? What about *me*?"

Varem's eyes flared, but then softened into something that looked like exhaustion. "You should go. I will send other aid. But not warriors, not outriders. They are needed in battle."

"And having rescued the woman?" Ferpa asked.

"We run," Chigozie said.

Varem nodded. "I imagine so."

"You want the help of my people because they are beastkind."

General Varem nodded. "That will be useful where I need them to go. And I also want their help because they give the impression that they can be reasoned with. Or at least, *you* can be."

"You don't need to reason with me." Kort rose to his feet. "You need to tell me how to find the woman."

"Here is how we'll proceed," Varem said. "I'll send men to your valley to watch over the remainder of the...what did you call yourselves? The Merciful. If you fail, or if you attempt to flee your duty, I'll have your people massacred."

"No," Kort murmured.

Ferpa stood, a look of pain in her eyes.

"We have a witness, someone who knows where the woman is being kept. And also, one who has the art to find her. Your party here, and Naares Stoach, will go along. As prisoners."

"The beastkind don't take prisoners," Chigozie objected. He tried not to think about what exactly the beastkind *did* do to their victims. He looked at Kort.

Kort bowed his head.

Chigozie thought through what he knew about the Heron King and his people. "When do the beastkind take prisoners, Kort?"

"If Simon Sword's warriors are taking prisoners, it is for a sacrifice." Kort's face was expressionless. "Simon Sword drinks the blood of men."

"In large quantities," Ferpa added.

"I can tell you from personal experience that the beastkind are taking prisoners." General Varem scrutinized Kort's face as he spoke. "What do you say, priest? You walk alongside these beast-kind and you call them your friends. Do you trust them enough to wear bonds and walk into the presence of their former god?"

Chigozie didn't hesitate. "I trust them. I know Ferpa and Kort want mercy." He looked at the beastkind and felt tears sting his eyes. "And I know they can have it."

"They can indeed," General Varem said. "As can all your people. Mercy, and your little land in perpetuity, by whatever deed or pact you require. Only bring me the woman."

"If the Shepherd trusts his flock, then I trust them, too," Naares said.

"Good." Varem nodded. "Five beastkind leading prisoners to the sacrificial altars of the blood god of the Mississippi and the Ohio Rivers. This will be easily accounted for."

"Flight will be less easily explained," Naares said.

"Then be ingenious in your explanations," the general told him. "Or be very, very fast."

"I understand your king has died," Chigozie said. "Who is the woman? Someone in the royal family? A princess, a queen? Or someone you need for your war effort?"

"The woman comes from New Orleans," Varem said. "She's a witch. A *mambo*, they would have called her there. And my seers and stargazers tell me that it is imperative for our war effort that we take her out of Simon Sword's hands."

"When you say the woman is a prisoner..." Chigozie said slowly.

"I *hope* she is a prisoner. It is possible she regards herself as Simon Sword's ally." Varem's face was stony.

"And if we cannot persuade her to come, you will tell us to compel her to come." Chigozie shook his head.

"And if we can't compel her?" Naares asked.

"Kill her," General Varem said simply.

"You got a spell that'll ward off bullets?" Sarah asked.

The Pennslander wizard nodded. "I've got a strong braucher charm for the purpose."

"Good." Sarah nodded. "It's gonna take all my energy to fly this boat."

After the unsettling conversation between Sarah and thin air, in which Sarah had appeared to hold hands with invisible people and weep at their inaudible words, Montse had followed Sarah and Luman Walters back down the mountain. Josep had sent a boat for them, but on return to the *Verge Caníbal*, Sarah had stayed in the boat and held back her two companions.

Josep laughed as if Sarah had told a joke, but when he realized she was serious, his face fell flat and he nodded vigorously.

"I could turn us into birds," Sarah said, "only it's a bit of a flight, and I don't know how many hungry raptors there are between here and there. Or hungry Missourian refugees with scatterguns. And I suppose I could just fly us all individually, but then I have to worry about holding us together as well as keeping us in the air and moving the right direction. If we all sit in the boat, then I only have to worry about the boat."

"Why not *La Verge*?" Josep grinned and swept in the ship with a gesture.

"Too big," Sarah shot back. "Obviously."

"The boat is an excellent solution," Luman Walters said.

"Montserrat Ferrer i Quintana," Sarah said.

Montse didn't love hearing her full name enunciated. Had she made some mistake and earned a dressing-down? "Yes, Your Majesty?"

"My sister Margaret lives."

"Margarida." Montse found her eyes suddenly full of tears.

"Margarida viu!" Josep shouted.

"Margarida!" the smugglers cheered.

"Visca Margarida!" Josep shouted again.

Sarah smiled.

"Is she out of danger?" Montse asked.

"No," Sarah said. "But she's out of her bonds. She's with my brother, so I think they'll soon be headed my direction."

"Thank you, Your Majesty."

"I'm going into danger. No oath binds you to me. I would understand if you preferred to climb aboard your ship and sail south."

Montse wiped tears from her cheeks. "No, Your Majesty. Your mother was the greatest friend of my life. I won't abandon either of her daughters now. And Margarida...I raised her as my neboda, my niece. I don't think that's changed."

Sarah nodded, and then turned to the magician. "Luman?"

Luman shook his head slightly and grimaced, as if saying something he didn't think needed to be communicated. "All my life, I've been looking for the great initiation into the mysteries of the universe. Your Majesty is penetrating deeper and faster than I ever did, deeper and faster than I ever thought possible. There's nowhere else I would want to go."

"You ready with that spell, then?"

Luman made the sign of the cross as he began to speak, first over himself, then over Sarah and then Montse.

Die himmlischen und heiligen Posaunen, die blasen alle Kugeln und Unglück von uns. Wir fliehen under den Baum des Lebens, der zwölferley Früchte trägt. Wir stehen hinter dem heiligen Altar der Christlichen Kirche. Wir befehlen uns der Heiligen Dreyfaltigkeit. Wir alles verbergen uns hinter des Fronleichnams Jesu Christi. Wir befehlen uns in die Wunden Jesu Christi, daß uns von keines Menschen Hand werde gefangen noch gebunden, nicht gehauen, nicht geschossen, nicht gestochen, nicht geworfen, nicht geschlagen, eben überhaupt nicht verwundet werde; das helf' uns.

He produced a tiny toy trumpet from one of his many pockets and touched it to his lips, pantomiming blowing notes.

Sarah was staring. "I was tempted to crack a joke about you using too many words, Luman. My charm against bullets takes exactly two. On the other hand, I like your *Baum des Lebens* very much."

"And I like yours," Luman said.

"But watch me do this with just one word." Sarah winked at Luman. "And hold on tight."

Josep waved. Montse and Luman both gripped the sides of the small boat. Sarah took feathers from her leather shoulder bag and touched them to the boat's prow. *"Vola!"* she shouted at the vessel.

Smoothly, at a gentle incline, the boat rose from the water. Montse laughed, to cover her nerves as well as from delight. The craft moved forward, passing *La Verge* and then leaving the ship behind. Wisdom's Bluff seemed to shrink and sink into the earth as the boat continued its rise. It pivoted around the hill, turning into the course of the Mississippi.

A bitter wind struck Montse in the face. Perhaps ironically, it made her feel more comfortable, as if she were leaning forward into a storm, hanging off *La Verge*'s ratlines.

"I don't have any spells to do *this*," Luman said.

"Accelera!" Sarah shouted at the boat.

The boat rose again and shot forward, punching into a thick bank of cloud that obscured the land and the river below them. Now Montse truly felt as if she were sailing, with the icy crystals of winter stinging the skin of her face and hands.

Sarah sat in the front of the boat and Luman in the rear. Montse could hear Luman's breathing, occasionally felt the faintest warmth of a breath that touched the back of her own neck. Sarah threw off heat like a fire. Her breathing was rapid and shallow, as if she were fighting a fever. Montse wanted to touch the girl, reassure her as she might have reassured Margarida during a bad storm, but it was not her place.

"Once you land, we're going to have to get inside the walls." Montse shouted, to be heard over the wind whipping through her hair and around her ears. She wanted to include Luman, too. "Will we go underground, as we did before?"

Sarah said nothing.

"Sarah?" Montse touched the girl's shoulder. The heat blazing through the witch's wool dragoon's coat nearly burned Montse's finger, and she pulled back.

"Sorry," Sarah gasped. "I'm concentrating. I was exhausted before. Now I'm trying not to throw up or bleed."

"Will we travel under the river again?" Montse asked. "To get inside the Treewall?"

Sarah shook her head, a stiff motion. "When this spell ends, I think I'll pass out, so I'm aiming to land inside the walls. I'll do it as gently as I can, but they'll be shooting at us, so we'll be approaching fast. Be prepared to be knocked about."

Montse wasn't accustomed to being a mere passenger. "Anything else I can do?"

Sarah laughed drily. "Be ready to shoot back."

"Nathaniel!" Margarida yelled.

She knew her hair was standing on end. She could feel it, not in her scalp alone, but all along the strands of hair. The air she moved through struck the tips of her hair as an irritant. Her feeling of annoyance, wounded indignation, and wrath grew with each step.

She stalked across a wooden-walled chamber she knew must be belowdecks on a ship, because the floor rolled like a ship, and a mast sank through the room from floor to ceiling. She threw open two doors, looking for her brother.

Nothing.

Somewhere, she heard an animal roar.

A file of soldiers clattered down the ladder into the room with her. Three of them held clubs, two came at the rear holding a net between them, and one advanced in front, hands open placatingly.

"Relax, girl," he said in Dutch. "We're all friends here."

Then he tried to grab her.

Margarida caught both his hands in hers, fingers interlaced as if to play pat-a-cake. She squeezed her fists together and shattered bones in his hand. He screamed and stumbled, sinking toward the floor—

but she picked him up and threw him—

into the spread net. The two men holding the net fell together around the screaming man.

The other three charged, clubs swinging.

Margarida ignored the clubs. They thumped her head and shoulders, and the irritation of the blows made her blood boil. She didn't feel wounded; she wasn't going to fall down—she felt as if a cat with a rough tongue were licking her face and body, and she wanted it to stop.

She grabbed one of the three by the throat. Her attack caught him by surprise, and his eyes bulged as she squeezed.

"Nathaniel!" she yelled.

"Alsjeblieft!" the sailor gasped.

She slammed him to the boards with such violence that they shattered, then raised him a second time into the air and hurled him down through the floor.

"Kanker!" A second sailor with a club dropped it and ran.

The third man swung at Margarida again, face full of anger. She grabbed his weapon arm, took two long steps to get the leverage she wanted—

and flung him against the mast.

His spine snapped in two with a wet sound and a scream that ended abruptly.

The two men holding the net dropped it and ran back abovedecks.

"Please, please," begged the man with shattered hands. She ignored him.

Roooooar!

She heard the animal bellow again and followed the sound.

A door standing in her way was no impediment. With a single kick, she reduced it to splinters.

In the room on the other side, she saw her brother Nathaniel, lying on the floor beside a chair. Over him crouched a shadowy apparition that had the shape of a bear and emitted bearlike growls.

In a second chair, tied, bloody, and still, was the Dutchman Jacob Hop.

Standing and facing her in a corner of the room was the man she'd tossed across the hotel lobby in New Amsterdam. Temple Franklin wore a narrow, smug smile on his face. He held a pistol in each hand. Both were pointed at her.

"Perhaps you should—" he started to say.

She charged.

Bang! Bang! Both guns fired at once. Bullets struck the left side of her body, one in her hip and one in her side. She spun sideways with the combined force of the blow, landing flat on her back on the floor.

Roar! The bear-shadow swiped with its paw, not at her, but at Temple.

"Foolish girl," Temple Franklin said.

Margarida rolled over and stood up. "No es fote mai amb una catalana," she growled.

Then she grabbed him and threw him against the wall.

When he struck the heavy beams of the ship's hull, Margarida saw a dull white flash. Franklin bounced off the wall, then struck the floor and rolled to his feet. He didn't look hurt.

Franklin jammed his hands into his coat pockets. He might be grabbing for a gun or something equally pointless, but Margarida had no patience in this state. She punched him in the chest, twice, blows that should have crushed his ribcage and left him drowning in his own blood.

Instead, he just took a step back to recover his balance.

Roar!

Margarida grabbed the empty chair. It was nailed to the floor but she yanked it free with no effort, then swung it at the old man's shoulder. The chair came apart in a cloud of dust and splinters, but Franklin only staggered slightly from the force of the blow.

Then he stabbed Margarida.

The split second of surprise she felt at the sensation of her skin being pierced was immediately followed by a much larger pain. The knife Franklin Temple held in his hand was tiny, but it felt like a lance. He stabbed her in her side, but she felt completely impaled and transfixed.

Someone was screaming.

It was her, she realized.

She dropped to her knees, sliding off his blade. Throughout her body, her blood pulsated. She felt poisoned; she felt suddenly slowed.

The dull glint of the blade in Franklin's hand wasn't steel, but silver.

"I admit, I've never seen anyone quite like you," Franklin said. "But this is not the first time I've had to tangle with an Ophidian."

His coat. His coat must be enchanted. It had been stopping her blows.

She had lost feeling in her hair. As much as the silver blade had hurt, the other thing it had done was take her out of her combat rage.

"I still want to take you to Thomas alive," Franklin said. "Are you ready to cooperate?"

Suddenly, Nathaniel was standing behind the old man. He looked ridiculous with his backward hat, his drum over his shoulder, and his purple coat inside out. But he reached around Franklin from behind, grabbed both lapels of his coat, and jerked them back and down—

exposing Franklin's chest, and pinning his arms to his side.

Franklin shook his head as if he was mildly inconvenienced.

Margarida's strength was gone, but she picked up a leg of the broken chair and stood.

Franklin struggled, but couldn't get free of Nathaniel's grip. The old man's facial expression grew suddenly alarmed. "You won't get past the crew!"

She pummeled him in the face. Her arm was weak, but the blow felt good, so she did it again.

And again. And again.

He dropped the knife. His nose split and blood spattered over the floor.

Margarida picked up the blade. Its handle was silver, the mere touch annoyed the skin of her fingers, but she gripped the weapon firmly and stabbed the Emperor's man through the fabric of his coat.

A blinding flash of light sent her reeling back, and she dropped the blade. Nathaniel fell back as well, dropping Franklin heavily to the floor.

The old man lay still.

"Jake!" Margarida gasped.

Nathaniel leaned over the Dutchman to lay a finger along his neck. "He's dead." He frowned, but it was the frown of someone with a problem to solve, rather than a frown of mourning or loss.

"I can't carry him."

"Let's get out of here," he said. "The body doesn't matter."

"My strength is gone," she whispered.

"They don't know that." He grinned. "Look angry."

He picked up Temple Franklin's pistols and cocked them.

"Those are empty," she whispered.

"They don't know that, either," he whispered back. "But we have to take advantage of the surprise and go right now."

There were sailors with clubs belowdecks, but Nathaniel snarled at them. Margarida brandished a chair leg in each hand and made barking noises in the back of her throat. They climbed the ladder unmolested and found the Dutch ship captain waiting for them on deck. He stood with his back stiffly arced, and behind him lurked two officers. They held pistols, but pointed them at the deck. Around the ship, sailors were armed with boathooks, cutlasses, knives, or clubs, but they held back.

And eyed Margarida nervously.

"We don't want trouble," the captain said.

"No," Nathaniel agreed. "You want the Emperor's guilty money, and you're happy to kidnap innocent people to get it."

"Life is complicated," the Dutchman said.

She tried not to be distracted by it, but there was shoreline visible in the east. Margarida didn't recognize it, but she saw silver strands of beach and gray forest jumbled under white snow.

"Let me simplify it for you," Nathaniel said. "You let us down in a boat, right now, or she'll tear the masts right out of this ship and send it to the bottom."

Margarida hunched her shoulders and took half a step toward the captain. She growled low in her throat.

"That is simple," the Dutchman agreed. "You can have a boat."

Margarida continued her pantomime of rage while the ship's crew quickly lowered a boat. Then she and her brother scrambled down the sides of the ship.

Settling onto the benches, Nathaniel said, "I'll row."

"I'll row," Margarida told him. "I know how to do it."

Nathaniel laughed softly, and sat facing the Dutch ship as Margarida worked the oars and they pulled away. He held the empty pistols with their butts on his lap and their open mouths pointed up at the ship.

If at any point, the Dutchmen decided to start shooting, Margarida and Nathaniel were doomed.

But whether it was out of fatigue, disinterest, or fear, the sailors watched them go and did nothing.

Having had many years of practice, Margarida had the knack of rowing with her legs and back. This spared her arms and shoulders, and very quickly sent the wooden boat skidding toward the beach.

"This is much better than the last time I escaped a ship," she said.

"You mean, in some smuggler adventure you once had?"

"I mean, when I discovered the chevalier had sent me from New Orleans to prevent my rescue. That time, I *did* tear the mast out of the ship."

Nathaniel stared.

"It was a small ship. Tearing out the mast sank it, and then the next thing I remember, I was talking to you and Jake."

They arrived at the beach and stepped into the freezing surf. Out of habit, Margarida dragged the boat up the beach and out of the reach of high tide. "Where are we?" she asked.

"I think this is Pennsland," Nathaniel said. "Franklin must have been taking us to Philadelphia. A little farther south, and I think we'd have turned north and west into the Delaware Bay and then the Delaware River."

"These are *our* trees." She smiled at her brother.

"Or Sarah's, maybe? I'm not sure what Pennsland law says. Or the terms of the grant." Nathaniel shrugged.

"I'm sorry about Jake," she said.

They trudged into the trees.

"So am I," Nathaniel said. "We need to find somewhere warm and dry and safe. So I can talk to him."

"Did I hear you right?" Margarida stopped walking and looked back at the Dutch ship. It had resumed its course southward. "You want to talk to Jake?"

Nathaniel nodded. "He had something to tell Sarah. Sarah wants to hear it, because . . . well, because she thinks Jake has figured out something that will help Sarah ascend the Serpent Throne. Something our father never did. And obviously, I'm the only one who can connect them."

"What do you mean, 'obviously'?" Margarida felt concerned. "Are you some kind of necromancer?"

Nathaniel laughed. "No, I'm not. Only in what I do . . . it seems that there's a fine line between the living and the dead. Or maybe the line isn't what it appears to be to mortals. But you make an interesting point. Cromwell might be able to do it, too, I suppose. Though I don't think he'd want to."

Margarida sighed and resumed walking. "Family was so much simpler when it was just me and my tia."

"Onandagos's staff was carved of this same sacred wood."

CHAPTER TWENTY-TWO

After sunset, the booming of the cannons grew louder and the shuddering of the Treewall with every impact was greater.

Cathy followed the Polite Sherem into a residential mound not far from the eastern wall of the city. At a knock, they were admitted into a room lit by few candles and ripe with the scent of children of Adam.

He hadn't invited her to follow him, but once she'd realized what he was planning, she had begun, and he hadn't stopped her.

"Don't do this," she'd said to him in the street.

"How great is my witness," he'd mused in response, "if I'm not willing to die for it?"

"To die is one thing. To kill one's self is another."

"Didn't St. William Harvey write in his *Exercitationes* that it is acceptable to kill when mercy requires it?"

"Yes, he did."

"I read that he even attempted self-slaughter at one point, using an overdose of the Paracelsian Tincture."

"He suffered from disease," Cathy said. "He was in great pain. You are whole."

"My city and my people are *not* whole." Sherem shrugged. "And I am driven by the requirements of mercy. I have given my charms, my tools of gramarye to those who may still use them. Today I will give more. Today my testimony will be sealed with my blood, my commitment to the goddess and Her city will be written on the face of the land itself, and my people will be saved."

"Will gain respite," Cathy said. "For perhaps a day."

"In a day, Queen Sarah may have returned and ascended the Serpent Throne. In a day, the longships of Chicago or the long rifles of Appalachee may have arrived. And if the city falls in one day, then I have given all the goddess's children here another day of glorious life."

"Dammit," Cathy grumbled, "that's the logic of a fanatic."

"Of a committed man. And I'm not alone. You can't stop us. We're going to save you in spite of yourself."

So she had followed.

Now she pushed through the crowd into what must ordinarily have been a living room, but the furnishings had all been removed. A circle of women and men stood around the edges of the chamber. Within the circle, sitting on the floor cross-legged, was a second ring.

Cathy realized she'd seen the standing circle before—they were the wizards with whom Sarah had mounted her attack on Robert Hooke's wall of black flame. The attack that had failed.

Sherem pushed through the wizards and took his place at the last vacancy of those seated cross-legged.

"Don't do this."

The voice shocked Cathy; it belonged to Zadok Tarami.

Zadok stood on the far side of the room, behind standing wizards. He pushed forward slightly to become more visible, without penetrating either ring of people. The Metropolitan looked exhausted.

"Greater love hath no man than this, that a man lay down his life for his friends." The words were spoken by a thin man who stood in the ring of magicians. His shoulders hunched forward, which gave him the appearance of a feeding animal, and his large eyes seemed to glow in the dim light.

"Josiah," Zadok said. "You will be excommunicated for this. You've already been stripped of your priesthood."

"Your messengers reached me." The man shrugged. "Every saint is seen first as a heretic."

Zadok snorted. "St. Josiah Dazarin, is that it?"

Josiah shook his head anxiously. "St. Jock of Cripplegate. But if in my humble way I can help bring forth St. Jock's miracles, then I will be grateful to have had a ministry."

"St. Jock will perform the miracle of self-murder?"

"St. Jock will save this people. Greater love hath no man."

"You pervert the word of God," Tarami said.

Sherem shook his head. "I find that I can't tell where the word of God stops and the word of man begins."

Zadok turned his attention back to the Polite. "*I* can tell."

"Lucky you." Sherem laughed, unexpectedly. "And yet, luckier me."

"I baptized you," Zadok said. "I saw the joy in your parents' eyes when you were born again unto Christ. Don't do this thing."

"And I shall see joy again in their faces," Sherem answered. "Soon."

"In death you escape nothing," Zadok said. "In death you will have to face the consequences of all your sins, including the self-slaughter you now perpetrate."

Sherem ignored his words. "Lucky me, for I have stood on the goddess's holy hill. I bear you this witness, Zadok Tarami. There was an Eden that fell, but there is an Eden that is eternal. I have breathed its scented air and heard the buzzing of its bees."

The Metropolitan's face looked sunken under the weight of grief. He said nothing.

"There is a goddess there who knows you as Her child, and who waits eagerly for your return." Sherem looked shockingly serene; Cathy found her own breath coming in ragged gasps, as if she were fighting back tears. "And I offer you this blessing, Zadok Tarami, if I have any blessing to give. A blessing for you, and also for all this people: you, Zadok, will witness what I have witnessed. You will see the spring and the tree that are forever, and you shall have eternal life."

"If you are determined," Zadok said slowly, "then let *me* give *you* one final blessing."

"Gladly," Sherem said.

"God forgive you."

The two men locked eyes for long moments, and finally the Metropolitan of Cahokia nodded. He ignored Josiah Dazarin entirely. Stepping back, he sank into the crowd.

Four others stepped forward, into the center of the two rings. One was Yedera, the oathbound Podebradan, but Cathy didn't know the others. In total, two women and two men. They all wore armor of no particular consistency. Each carried a sword unsheathed, and each was festooned with pistols and powder horns.

"We are ready," Yedera said.

One of the standing ring-members was a woman with short gray hair and sleepy eyes. She held out her hand, and each of the four warriors unbuckled their sword belt and handed belt and scabbard over to the woman.

The woman kept one of the scabbards herself and passed the others to her left around the circle. They passed from hand to hand and when they came to rest, they were held at four equidistant points around the circle.

Then the standing outer circle—comprised of wizards, Cathy now saw—joined hands. Those holding a sword belt looped it over their own hand and the hand of a neighbor, so that the belts and scabbards became part of the ring of magicians. Then they chanted.

Cathy didn't know the words, but she felt them resonate deep inside her chest.

Yedera and her three warrior companions—were they all Podebradan Daughters?—bowed deeply. Then they left. The wizards didn't break their circle, raising their arms to permit the warriors to pass beneath.

"I have written a song." Josiah looked at Zadok Tarami as he spoke. "Or, if it isn't too impudent to say it, a hymn. I hoped you would all sing it with me while the warriors travel to their positions."

There was a murmur of approval, and Josiah began to sing. At the end of each line he stopped, so the others in the room could echo his lyric and melody. Sherem's voice was the loudest in the chorus. Cathy found herself singing along.

> *Every man a murderer*
> *Every man a thief*
> *Every man a malefactor*
> *In need of sweet relief*
>
> *Poor St. Jock of Cripplegate*
> *Hear my words I pray*
> *And bear my soul to Eden fair*
> *A sacrifice this day*

It wasn't long, and its melody could have come from any New Light hymnal, but music and words together were effective. Cathy desperately wished she could walk out of the mound, because she knew what was coming and she didn't want to see it.

But she owed it to Sherem to stay.

"It is time," the short-haired woman said. She and her fellow gramarists began chanting again. The words must be Ophidian, but whatever they were, the sounds were guttural and brutish.

In the background, someone took up Sherem's hymn again and the crowd joined.

"This is my witness!" Sherem cried. "As I live, She lives! As She lives forever, I shall live forever, in the Eden that cannot be destroyed!"

Cathy never saw the knife, but suddenly Sherem's wrists both bled from long, deep gashes. He rolled his head back and opened his eyes, staring at the ceiling. "St. Jock!" he cried. "Take my gift, and let my people live!"

The others sitting on the floor were bleeding, too.

Cathy half-expected the blood the fly through the air, into the circle of magicians or perhaps into the scabbards they held. That didn't happen; the blood poured onto the floor. But as the blood flowed, as the willing sacrifices grew paler and paler, and one by one toppled to the floor, the wizards' chant grew louder, faster, and more rhythmic.

Cathy wished she had Sarah's gifts. What would the Beloved of the goddess see here? Light flowing around the room? Light flowing from the dying into the circle of wizards and then along an unseen line toward Yedera and her squad?

Sherem the Polite fell over last of all the sacrifices to St. Jock of Cripplegate. He landed facing Cathy, with a smile on his face. On striking the floor, air was forced from his lungs; Cathy thought his last word sounded like "Sarah."

Zadok Tarami sobbed.

Director Notwithstanding Schmidt posted herself near one of General Sayle's long guns. The inscription around the gun's mouth—she had looked before the firing began and the sun set—read: *Let us also go, that we may die with him.* Did that make the gun Thomas? Or Philip?

She stood near the gun, near Sayle, to observe. The Yankee artillery commander sat still astride his horse now with shoulders thrust back, hands on his hips, and a riding crop in one hand, staring at the Treewall. From time to time, he shouted orders to his men to adjust their aim or rate of fire. The artillerists sang sea shanties to time their work together, punctuating the verses of "Oh, Shenandoah" and "Drunken Sailor" with the explosive firing of the Apostles.

Reason suggested that, under the relentless salvo Sayle had begun pouring against the walls of Cahokia, the city couldn't last long. Schmidt didn't want the walls to fall while she slept. She would participate in the Emperor's victory, if only by being awake and watching.

The barrage had another silent observer: the crucified Parlett who held the shade of Oliver Cromwell stalked along behind the firing guns, observing keenly. Where the child-Lazar trod, the gun crews shrank away, but Sayle rode up and down the line with his riding crop in hand, and didn't hesitate to crack it as encouragement for his gunners.

Behind Oliver Cromwell shuffled Dadgayadoh. Whatever the poor Haudenosaunee had become didn't have the wit of a Lazar, or of Cromwell, if Cromwell were something different. Like the other Imperial dead, like the Cahokian beastkind killed during their herald-launching sortie, Dadgayadoh was a moaning, shuffling thing, He was strong, he was sleepless, and he was slowly falling apart.

Something is wrong here.

Hooke appeared at Schmidt's shoulder.

"I don't know," Schmidt said. "I favor forcing the issue quickly over a siege. A siege wastes life and everyone's time. If Cahokia will just surrender, we can quickly get back to business as usual."

But it was true: she didn't want Sayle to get the credit. She'd rather have it herself.

Is that what thou wantest, Director? Business as usual?

"*Madam Director*, if you want the technical right of it. Yes. War is a waste. Trade is life. I want to get this little war over with, and get back to living."

Hooke seemed not to be listening. Instead, he stared at Cahokia, through the sheet of black flame he himself had erected. *Something is happening in there.*

"I'd be disappointed to learn nothing was happening. Killing all the Cahokians can't be the goal."

Can it not? Hooke grinned.

A shadow suddenly appeared high over the Twelve Apostles, moving fast.

"Watch out—" Schmidt tried to warn the gun crew of the Thomas, but something glinting and metallic bowled out of the sky and struck the crew. They scattered in all directions.

It's an attack! Hooke strode toward the Thomas.

The metallic projectile unfolded and stood, revealing itself as a warrior in plate armor. Hooke picked up his pace, but the warrior ignored him. Instead, he calmly walked to the butt of the Thomas, held something against the gun, and then with a mallet at his belt, hammered the object into the gun.

Into the vent. The object, Schmidt realized, was a handspike.

She had little experience with big guns herself, but enough to know that a handspike pounded in through the cannon's vent would put the gun out of commission, at least temporarily.

The crew recovering, they charged the man in plate. He calmly pulled a sword and dispatched two of them. When the others fell back, he charged toward the next nearest gun.

"The Apostles!" Schmidt fired her pistol into the air, but it was indistinguishable against the firing of the cannons. "The big guns are under attack!"

The man in plate mail ignored the crew of the second gun entirely, and simply ran forward, slamming his handspike into the gun's vent, and then hammering it home.

General Sayle, several guns down the line, saw the commotion and rode toward Schmidt, cracking his whip. "Stop that man!"

Schmidt reloaded her pistol.

The interruption of the guns meant that less din was being made than before, rather than more. Some of the traders were beginning to notice. More fires were being lit.

Another armored figure jumped up from the shadows. Was it a woman? She, or he, wore scale mail, and vaulted from the top of a barrel of powder right into the general. She dragged the general and his mount over, dropping them to the ground.

Startled, the gun crews scattered, and the man in plate mail escaped and ran on to the next gun.

Kill him! Hooke screamed.

The general's horse rose screaming in protest onto all fours again, but now its rider was the woman in scale mail. "Podebradas!" she screamed, galloping directly at Robert Hooke.

Hooke raised his hand defensively and the woman slashed, shattering the long nails of the Sorcerer's hand. Hooke stumbled aside and the woman—an Unborn Daughter of Podebradas, apparently—swept past the gun crew, forcing them to scatter.

The man in plate mail spiked a third gun.

Sayle lay still. Was he dead?

Schmidt rushed toward him, loaded pistol ready.

The mounted woman rode back at Hooke again. Over the horse's protests, she forced the animal to trample the Sorcerer several times.

Cries of dismay from near the other Apostles suggested that they, too, were under attack.

Schmidt reached Sayle. The man was breathing, but unconscious, and bleeding from a deep gash in his forehead. She stuck her pistol in her belt, knelt, and shoveled the general onto her shoulders to carry him away.

She stood. The ground was wet and cold, but she forced herself to take a single step. Then a second.

She fixed her eye on her destination, her own tent. There were blankets and brandy there, and she could have a surgeon sent.

She heard a fierce neigh before she saw anything, and suddenly Sayle's horse was looming over her, the rider slashing at her with a long scimitar. Schmidt felt steel bite into her shoulder—had Sayle also been cut again? She sank to one knee and fumbled, trying to get her gun back out.

The horse reared and kicked forward with its hooves. Schmidt fell back, rolling with Sayle in cold mud.

Suddenly men stood over her with torches and guns. The horse neighed another objection, several shots were fired, and then the horse galloped away.

Two men stooped to pick her up. One was Captain Mohuntubby. The other was her trader, Schäfer.

"Mohuntubby," she gasped. "The Parletts."

"All my men are still at the Parletts' tent," Mohuntubby said. "And once you're out of the fighting, I'll go back there again, myself."

"I can walk," she said. "Sayle needs help."

Mohuntubby handed his rifle to Schäfer and easily slung the wounded general onto his back. As Schäfer dragged her away, Schmidt watched the rest of the raid play out.

The man in plate armor died when three gunners from a crew ambushed him, one man holding him at bay with the ramrod while the other two crept up behind and shot him with carbines.

Another armored raider, a man, after spiking one of the Apostles, turned and made a run back toward the Treewall. He was sprinting past the Imperial trench when arms reached from the ditch and dragged him into it. Schmidt saw cadaverous, bloated beastkind, animated corpses like Dadgayadoh, but with the jaws of wolves and the tails of scorpions, tear the man's armor from his body and rend his flesh.

A third raider—she only saw four in total, which was a pitifully small force, given what they accomplished—was tackled by two gun crews together and dragged toward the fire. They were intercepted by Robert Hooke. The Sorcerer stood awkwardly, shoulders hunched, one arm at his side, one leg dragging. But he stood.

Whatever the Sorcerer said to them made the gun crews shrink in fear. The raider—a woman—stared calmly at Hooke, and then spat in his face.

He slashed a knife through her throat, and then he and the Parlett boy and Dadgayadoh fell on her together. Her legs kicked and trembled for a full minute before they finally stopped.

The fourth raider was the woman with Sayle's horse. She was the last to spike a gun, leaping to the earth just long enough to pound in a spike, and then driving away the objecting crew with her scimitar before leaping onto the horse again.

She raced at the Sorcerer and the Necromancer again. Dadgayadoh rose to defend them, and for his troubles the poor former trader lost his head to a ferocious sweep of the scimitar, powered by the muscles of General Sayle's horse.

Then the raider galloped away. She rode through the Imperials' camp rather than toward the besieged city, but she was quickly beyond the center of the commotion and crashing through quiet parts of camp where no one challenged her.

Angling toward the river like that, would she turn and reenter Cahokia? Perhaps, but Notwithstanding Schmidt didn't see it. Mohuntubby and Schäfer brought her into her tent, and Schäfer stayed with her while Captain Mohuntubby left to check on his command and the two living Parletts.

Schmidt discovered that she had a high-pitched ringing in

her ears. She took several swallows of brandy, which lessened the noise only the slightest amount. She could hear the ringing because the guns had fallen silent.

"The Twelve Apostles?" she croaked.

Schäfer shook his head. "As far as I know, they got them all."

Bill watched through a spyglass as Yedera and three other Podebradans sprang down from the Treewall into the open space before the Empire's cannons. Gramarye was obviously at work. Maltres Korinn whispered into his ear that they had been rendered invisible to the enemy with the same magic, but that Cahokia's wizards expected their spell to fall when the Podebradans crossed the black-fire curtain.

Which is why the Podebradans had leaped across that curtain with great final synchronized jumps that carried them twenty feet into the air and threw them sixty feet forward. The black fire would make the raiders reappear, but it wouldn't pluck them out of the air or claw them down.

Each of the four carried six spikes. Bill's best hope was that they might spike half the guns, and give his people an easier day or two. The Podebradans exceeded his expectations by far, silencing every one of the Twelve Apostles.

The cost was high, though. Bill watched them fall, one by one.

Except Yedera, who ended up on an officer's horse. After a circuitous loop around to the north, half an hour after the raid ended, she was being hauled up the Treewall with a rope.

Bill was at the top to greet her, along with Alzbieta Torias.

Yedera's face was shockingly calm as she came over the wall. The priestess pulled her bodyguard to safety and embraced her.

"The others gave their lives." Yedera frowned, slightly.

"We saw," Bill said. "*I* saw. Your courage was extraordinary."

Yedera shook his head. "I do not matter. I fulfilled my oath. But the Daughters who died must be buried."

"Maltres Korinn will perform a ceremony," Alzbieta said. "He insists it should be him. If we do it soon, we can perform a memorial without the accompaniment of cannon music."

"Just before dawn," Yedera said. "And Sherem and the other followers of St. Jock?"

It was Bill's turn to frown. "Who is St. Jock? Sherem was a follower of St. Reginald Pole."

"He was," Yedera agreed. "But he, and others, chose to give their lives tonight. Sherem lost his ability to cast spells when he resisted Queen Sarah. Tonight, he gave his life to fuel the spells that sent us over the enemy line and silenced their cannons."

Bill rocked back onto his heels, suddenly short of breath.

Alzbieta broke into tears.

"You bear no blame, Holiness," Yedera said.

"She's right," Bill added.

Alzbieta said nothing.

Scant hours later, Bill sat in a wooden chair on a low wooden stand beside Yedera, Alzbieta, Maltres, Cathy, Yedera, and Gazelem. Following his vindication—or rather, following the discovery that the city's traitor was Voldrich—the Zoman prince had pressed to be included in Sarah's inner ring.

There remained one empty seat with them on the stand. The vacant space before them, in which a temporary wooden marker had been raised—a signboard with a cannon painted on it, looking for all the world as if it had been stolen from an inn—had no special significance. The field had not previously been a burial ground.

That was its attraction.

A large crowd had gathered. When did these people sleep?

The bodies of Sherem and his fellow Jockites, or Jockians—both terrible names, but no one had yet had time to formulate a good one—were dressed in white linen and laid in graves. Each also wore a gold and green apron.

A line of men in similar garb stood at the edge of the field, and a second line at a right angle to the first.

This was not the goddess's method of burial; nor was it what Zadok Tarami would have wanted.

It was the compromise.

Maltres stepped to the edge of the platform.

He left his staff of office behind. In his hands he held a scroll.

As if this were his cue, the Metropolitan of Cahokia shuffled forward from the crowd. His step was slow and his shoulders bowed, but he engaged in none of the theatrics Bill had seen from the man previously: ashes on the face, or crawling on hands and knees.

He looked truly grief-stricken.

Another man tried to follow Zadok from the crowd, but he was held back, Bill couldn't see by whom. He stood at the edge of the burial ground, standing on tiptoe and staring at the proceedings.

Maltres held his tongue while the Metropolitan walked around the graves and joined the Vizier on the stand. Despite his short height and sleight frame, Zadok Tarami settled into the last empty seat with the creaking of a heavy man.

Then Maltres spoke.

"Brethren and friends. It has ever been the custom of the Ohio Rite, from the days when Onandagos himself presided as Grand Riverine Master, at the request of a departed Brother or his family, to assemble and, with the solemn formalities of the Craft, to offer up before the world a final tribute."

A murmur of uncertain agreement rippled through the crowd.

He continued. "Today, we bury dead whose bodies we have, and we honor dead who fell on the field and whose bodies we may never see. In life, not all of these dead were brothers. Pursuant to the rules of the Rite and a duly-ordered vote, every one of them has been made a brother in death. And we will remember them all accordingly."

More of the crowd was nodding. They couldn't all be Freemasons, could they? But they could approve of Maltres's tone of reconciliation and inclusion.

"Our brothers have reached the terminus of their earthly suffering. The end came for our brothers not by illness or age, but as the sacrifices demanded by war with a merciless enemy. Our brothers have entered the forgotten lands ahead of us, and they have done it for our sake. The dust has returned to the earth as it was, and the spirit has returned whence it came."

Bill had no idea whether Maltres was following a specific liturgy, but he noticed that the words chosen didn't antagonize either Alzbieta Torias and her priestesses or the follows of Zadok Tarami.

Tarami looked thoughtful and sad.

The two connected lines of men in Masonic garb broke into singing. It was a dirge consisting of two modal threads stitched at strange intervals to each other, with the occasional third note thrown in to create a chord.

Either it was wordless, or Bill couldn't hear the words.

Maltres opened the scroll in his hands and began to read. "Brother Sherem Tauridas, Hierophant Minor of the Humble

Order of St. Reginald Pole, a Master Mason. Member of the Royal Onandagos Lodge, number one. Entered into rest today, the nineteenth of March, in the Year of our Lord eighteen-sixteen, age thirty-eight years, six months, and two days."

Bill had never known Sherem's family name, and now he felt embarrassed by the fact.

Tears streamed down Zadok Tarami's cheeks.

Maltres kept reading. "Sister Iyara Zulodem, a Master Mason." A gasp burst from the crowd, and Bill himself sucked cold early morning air through his teeth. Masons were men. Always, as far as Bill knew, even in the Ohio. The crowd stared at Maltres, and some of the men in the line of singers shifted from foot to foot nervously. "Master Mason," Maltres repeated firmly. "Member of the Royal Onandagos Lodge, number one. Entered into rest today, the nineteenth of March, in the Year of our Lord eighteen-sixteen, age forty-five years and fourteen days."

He continued on with the names. Maltres was so hell-bent on recognizing and including everyone that he was flouting Masonic tradition to do it. He seemed to be a high-ranking member of the Royal Onandagos Lodge; would it be enough to protect him?

Or will there be consequences?

Bill almost laughed at himself. He was besieged in a city of wooden walls by an army that grew larger every day, with food supplies running out, and he was worried about whether Maltres Korinn might offend some masons.

No doubt Korinn had made a similar calculus.

Maltres Korinn had reached the end of the list of names. "Almighty Heaven!" He cried. "Into Your hands we commend the souls of our beloved Sisters and Brothers."

By the artifice of clever timing, and perhaps with a certain amount of luck, the sun chose that exact moment to crack its orange face over the horizon. In minutes, it would disappear again behind the sheet of clouds overhead, but for a brief space, it seemed to be smiling on the proceedings of Maltres Korinn.

"Heaven, in its infinite wisdom, removed our Sisters and Brothers from the cares and troubles of this earthly life. Let we who survive be yet more strongly cemented by the ties of love, to one another, to our Sisters and Brothers in the forgotten lands, and to our Sisters and Brothers who have not yet come to us from eternal Eden."

Zadok Tarami looked as if he might vomit. He leaned forward and buried his face in his hands.

"Let us not forget," Maltres said, "that we, too, are mortal; and that our spirits, too, must return to the great land from which they came. 'Man that is born of a woman is of few days, and full of trouble. He cometh forth like a flower, and is cut down; he fleeth also as a shadow, and continueth not.'

"Seeing then, my sisters and brothers, that mortal life is so uncertain, and Heaven knows that our lives in particular lie within the mailed fist of a hostile oppressor, let us no longer postpone the all-important concern of preparing for that life which is forever. Let us embrace *this* moment, because it is the only moment we have, and because it is *every* moment. These trials will pass, but in the Eden we will make for ourselves, there is comfort. Acting well, we shall be prepared to enter into our definitive judgment, in which all the secrets of our hearts shall be known; and on the great day of reckoning we shall be ready to give a good account of our stewardship while here on earth."

Maltres's voice was firm, but Bill was far enough to the side to be able to see tears trickling down his pock-marked cheek.

"With becoming reverence let us supplicate the Divine Grace, whose goodness and power know no bounds. That, on the arrival of the momentous hour, our faith may remove the clouds of doubt, draw aside the sable curtains of the hidden world beyond, and bid hope sustain and cheer the departing spirit on its journey into the world of undying love.

"Zadok Tarami, Metropolitan of the Basilica of Cahokia, has agreed to offer up a prayer in the capacity of chaplain *pro tempore*."

Maltres stepped slowly back from the edge of the platform and sat.

Zadok Tarami stood. In the stiffness of his motions and the slow, hobbling speed of his walk, he looked to Bill as if he'd aged twenty years in twenty minutes. The old man gazed slowly at all the faces before him. At first, his eyes looked wary, but as he looked, he grew in confidence and started to nod. Finally, he raised both arms skyward and began to declaim.

"Most glorious Father! Author of all good, and Giver of all mercy! Pour down Thy blessing upon us, we beseech Thee, and strengthen our solemn engagements with the ties of sincere affection! Endue us with fortitude and resignation in this hour of sorrow, and grant that this dispensation from Thy hands may be sanctified in its results upon the hearts of those who now meet to mourn! May the present instance of mortality draw our attention toward Thee, the only refuge in time of need. Enable us to look with eyes of Faith toward that realm whose skies are never darkened by sorrow; and after our departure hence in peace and in Thy favor, may we be received into Thy everlasting kingdom, to enjoy the just reward of a virtuous and well-spent life. Amen!"

"Amen," the crowd answered.

"May we always remember, Father, the words of Thy son, when the lawyer tempted him. 'Master,' the trap-setting hypocrite said, 'which is the great commandment in the law?' Jesus said unto him, 'Thou shalt love the Lord thy God with all thy heart, and with all thy soul, and with all thy mind. This is the first and great commandment. And the second is like unto it, Thou shalt love thy neighbour as thyself.'" Tarami paused. The crowd seemed to be holding its breath. "Not, we notice, 'the second is almost as important,' but 'like unto it.' May we always remember in our hearts that the second commandment and the first are equals. That the second commandment is a helpmeet for the first. May we love our neighbor as ourself, O God, from this day forth. Amen!"

"Amen!" The crowd's answer rose in volume and enthusiasm.

"And may it be fitting in Thy sight," Tarami continued, "that we *not* enter into Thy kingdom at this time. Our brothers and sisters have laid their lives down on the altar. Can there be greater love than this? Your eternal word, O Father, assures us that there cannot! May their final sacrifice, and may all the sacrifices we have made to this great and terrible day, be sufficient in Thy sight! We are sinners, Father, and we repent! We beg thee to turn away from us the face of Thy wrath, and direct it instead toward those who would rob of us our wealth, tear from us our lives, and pry peace from our hearts with their acts of terror! Liberate us from the destroyer, O glorious God! As our brothers and sisters died to give us life, may we live to give You glory! Amen!"

"Amen!" the crowd shouted.

Tarami moved back, vigor again in his step. Maltres rose and put his arm around the priest's shoulders. Despite their difference in height, the priest didn't appear small standing beside the vizier. "So mote it be!" Korinn cried.

The singers, and many men in the crowd, responded as one. "So mote it be!"

The choir broke into another song, this time in English, and more melodic:

> *Blest morning, whose young dawning rays*
> *Beheld our rising God,*
> *That saw Him triumph o'er the dust,*
> *And leave His dark abode!*

The song continued for several verses. Tarami sat, and Bill looked at the priest's face. The man beamed, but not with the smug energy of fanaticism. He looked relaxed and happy.

Noticing Bill's gaze, Tarami reached across and patted his knee.

When the singing ended, Maltres resumed. Having set aside the scroll, he now held a wooden box. "Our sisters and brothers have been raised in that eternal Lodge which no time can close. In that Heavenly Sanctuary, the Unbroken Light, unmingled with darkness, will reign unbroken and perpetual. There, under the protection of the All-Seeing Eye, amid the smiles of Immutable Love, in that house not made with hands, eternal in the heavens—there, my brethren, may Almighty God in His infinite mercy grant that we may meet again, to part no more."

He removed a masonic apron from the box and turned from left to right, displaying it to the crowd. "Those of you who have not been raised within the Craft may have wondered at the aprons we have placed upon our dead. The Apron of Eden is an emblem of innocence and the badge of a Mason; we of the Ohio Rite make them of green and gold. Green for the leaves of the tree of life, and gold for the crowns that Eve and Adam wore. More ancient than the Golden Fleece or the Roman Eagle, more honorable than the Star or Garter or any distinction that can be conferred by king, prince, potentate or any other person, the apron was worn by our first parents in their first home. By it we are continually reminded of that purity of life and conduct so essentially necessary to gain admission into the great lodge above, the Royal Celestial Lodge, number one, where the Supreme Grand Master of the Universe forever presides."

Korinn replaced the apron and pulled out an evergreen sprig, which he in turn showed the crowd. "Moses furnished his

tabernacle with gold and acacia wood. The great ark of Israel was
built of acacia. Onandagos's staff was carved of this same sacred
wood. This evergreen is an emblem of our enduring faith in the
Immortality of the Soul. By it we are reminded that we have
an imperishable part within us, which shall survive all earthly
existence, and which will never, never die. Through the loving
goodness of our Supreme Grand Master, we may confidently
hope that, like this Evergreen, our souls will hereafter flourish
in eternal spring.

"We shall ever cherish in our hearts the memory of our
departed sisters and brothers. They sacrificed their lives for us.
Commending their spirits to Almighty Heaven, we leave them in
the hands of those Beneficent Beings who have done all things
well; who are glorious in Their Holiness, wondrous in Their Power,
and boundless in Their Goodness; and it should always be our
endeavor so to live that we too may be found worthy to inherit
the land prepared for us from the foundation of the world."

Maltres again retreated, and Alzbieta Torias rose. She walked
forward to the edge of the platform and knelt, touching her forehead to the wood. When she raised her face again, she looked
skyward and prayed.

"O Mother of All Living, hear Thou our prayer! We came into
this Thy world through Thy womb, and we know we live here at
Thy sufferance. We are grateful for every breath, for every falling drop of rain, for every mouthful of corn that we have from
Thee. In all that we do, may the glory be Thine!"

Zadok Tarami stood, and Bill felt his own muscles tighten.
He didn't see a weapon on the old man, but he didn't put it past
the priest to attack Alzbieta with his bare hands. Out of respect
for the funeral, Bill had climbed the platform without a weapon.
He regretted it now.

"O Mother of All Living, hear Thou our prayer!" Alzbieta
continued. Zadok Tarami knelt beside her, but she continued as
if she didn't see him. "We return our loved ones now into Thy
womb. What rebirths they shall experience, in this life and with
Thee in Thine Unfallen Eden, give us joy. We are grateful for their
lives and for their final gift, and we ask Thee to receive them."

Tarami joined her for her final line, raising his hands to the sky
just as she did: "O Mother of All Living, hear Thou our prayer!"

The chorus had somehow obtained shovels. Alzbieta and Zadok

stood, and all the others on the platform with them joined them in standing, Bill included. They bowed their heads, and so did the crowd. Bill removed his hat and held it to his chest as the chorus solemnly approached the graves, three men per grave, and methodically shoveled in dirt until the bodies were covered and the holes were filled.

Everyone on the platform remained standing, but Maltres spoke again. "Soft and safe, my sisters and brothers, be your resting place! Bright and glorious be your rising from it, now and in the eternities! Fragrant be the acacia sprig that there shall flourish! May the earliest buds of spring unfold their beauties over your resting place, and there may the sweetness of the summer's last rose linger longest! Though the winds of Autumn may destroy the loveliness of their existence, yet the destruction is not final, and in the springtime, they shall surely bloom again. So, in the bright morning of the resurrection, thy spirit shall spring into newness of life and expand in immortal beauty, in realms beyond the skies. Until then, dear sisters and brothers, until then, farewell!"

"The Lord bless us and keep us!" Yedera said, speaking for the first time. Her face was serene. "The Lady make Her face to shine upon us, and be gracious unto us! Heaven lift upon us the light of Its countenance and give us peace! Amen!"

"Amen!" the crowd repeated.

"So mote it be!" cried Maltres and the other masons.

"One people," Bill muttered to himself. "Many ways, but one people."

The crowd fell silent. The sun finally disappeared behind the cloud cover above, and the fiery orange light that had accompanied most of the funeral winked instantly into a cold blue.

Sorrow anchored Bill's legs into place, but he also found a kind of relief. Alzbieta and Zadok seemed reconciled, and somehow it was thanks to Maltres Korinn and the authority of his Freemasonry. At the same time, the cost had been high, both in lives lost and, for Bill, a growing sense of dread.

The self-slaughter of Sherem and a few like-minded souls had given Cahokia brief respite from her besiegers. What would happen the next time the guns began to fire?

Would others volunteer to sacrifice themselves?

And if they didn't, would the city command sacrifices? Would it slaughter its slaves, at least the ones who were Firstborn?

Bill had the uncomfortable sensation that a dark line had been crossed. An ancient taboo had been broken. He feared there was worse to come.

"General," Gazelem Zomas murmured in his ear. "What's that?"

Gazelem pointed, and Bill saw something that might have been a bird, only it was coming on too fast and getting too large. It might be a projectile weapon, only he'd heard no cannon fire.

It was headed right for the crowd.

He hated to break the charm that had ended the funeral, but he had no choice. "Take cover!" he bellowed. "Step aside!"

He grabbed the Heron King's horn at his side and blew a three-tone sequence, three times, to summon Sarah's beastkind.

The flying object shifted angle. Was it a board? It seemed to be slowing, as well.

Chikaak entered the clearing at a run, with several beastkind at his heels. Bill nodded at them and rejoined Cathy in the crowd. His lady had been holding his pistols in a carpet bag, and she now handed it over.

"If this is an attack," Bill told her, "be prepared to take cover."

"With you to defend me?" Cathy smiled. "Never."

The object missed the actual graves and came to earth in the street. It struck and then skidded a hundred feet, digging a furrow and throwing shattered cobblestones in all directions. Bill shielded his eyes from the flying debris with his hand. When the grinding sound stopped and he looked again, what he saw made his heart leap.

The object was a rowboat.

Sarah stepped out of the boat. She wobbled on her feet from fatigue. Luman Walters and Montserrat Ferrer i Quintana emerged from the boat with her and held her up, one to each side.

Sarah looked around. "I am glad you're all here," she said. "I'm going to need your help."

Then she fainted.

"Believe it or not, that was the easy part."

⊰•⊱

CHAPTER TWENTY-THREE

Sarah awoke to bright daylight and the smell of squash cooked with raisins and molasses. She recognized the room; she lay in her sleeping chamber beneath the Temple of the Sun.

She sat up—too quickly, and it made her head spin. She rolled over and pressed her forehead to the cool stone of the wall, breathing in deeply.

"I need Zarok Tarami," she said. She could hear other people in the room, though her vision spun too wildly for her to actually look and see who they were. "And Maltres Korinn."

"They're both waiting above." The voice was Alzbieta Torias's. "Though I'd feel better if you took some food, or maybe a little wine, and went back to sleep."

"I'm fasting." Sarah snaked an uncertain foot to the floor, pressed to confirm that the world had stopped revolving, and then stood. She wore a linen sleeping gown. "I can't have slept long. I feel like if I just shut my eyes I could sleep a whole year, right now."

"Two hours," Alzbieta said.

"Take me to the Vizier and the Metropolitan," Sarah said. "I want to see both of them together. Please."

Alzbieta herself looked tired, her face lined with deep grooves. She nodded with something like a faint smile of recognition playing around the corners of her mouth, then handed Sarah her dragoon's coat. With slow steps, Sarah shuffled along the corridor and up the steps that took her into the long nave of the Temple of the Sun. There Alzbieta helped her into a wooden chair that seemed to have been placed there for the purpose. Then the priestess led in the two men Sarah wanted to see.

"Gentlemen." She had intended to stand, which would at least put her eye to eye with Tarami, though she'd still have to look up to meet the eyes of the Duke of Na'avu. But she found she didn't have the strength. "I came expecting cannon fire, and instead I walk in on Freemasonry. You gittin' yourself raised in the Ohio Rite, Father Tarami?"

Zadok smiled. "Not yet. But after this morning, I'm thinking about it."

"Imperial artillery arrived and began bombarding us," Maltres said. "Your Majesty's gift of sight showed you that."

Sarah nodded.

"A party of raiders, four Unborn Daughters of Podebradas, went over the wall in the middle of the night and spiked the guns. With their sacrifice, we have gained time. Perhaps as little as a day, perhaps more. This morning, we buried the three who died."

Sarah's mouth was dry as cured tobacco. "Yedera?"

"Yedera is the one who lived, Your Majesty." Maltres bowed slightly.

Sarah nodded.

"And there are others who gave their lives, as well."

"Killed on the wall?" Sarah asked.

Maltres shook his head, opened his mouth, and then closed it again. No tears trickled down his cheeks, but his face twisted into a mask of anguish.

"They sacrificed themselves," Zadok Tarami said slowly. "Following with great courage in the footsteps of the Lord Christ. Their deaths gave power to the spells that sent the Daughters over the wall, disguised them and propelled them against the Imperial guns."

A wave of nausea took Sarah. She leaned forward, grateful to be sitting, and coughed and retched. "Sherem?"

Maltres nodded. "Did he tell you he planned this?"

Sarah shook her head. "But he was thinking about it. He and others. They were aiming to sanctify Jock of Cripplegate. Who, as I understood it, was a burglar and deserved the hanging he got."

"There are painful ironies here." Zadok nodded heavily.

Something was troubling Maltres Korinn; she saw a cloud on his aura. "What is it, Vizier?"

Maltres smiled ruefully. "I cannot conceal my thoughts from you, Beloved. We have arrested a traitor in your absence. You will remember Voldrich? He was one of the candidates—"

"I remember," Sarah said. "The landowner. Was he the one who told the Imperials we were going to send out messengers?"

Maltres nodded.

"You haven't killed him yet, so you're waiting for me to decide?"

The Vizier nodded again. "There is a faction that would happily hang him without trial. While I sympathize, I have merely detained him."

Sarah hesitated.

Forgiveness, her father had said. He wished he had forgiven more.

"Send him over to his friends," she said. "Tell him all his lands are forfeit, and all his other wealth. We're taking it all. If he sets foot in the city, I'll have him hanged. You need Notaries to back you up on this?"

"I'll get them."

"I'll sign," Zadok said. "This is an act of great mercy."

Sarah sat silently. She felt time slide past her like honey, slow and nearly opaque. Finally, she had to give word to her thoughts. "I must make a sacrifice."

The two men held their breaths.

"I asked Alzbieta to bring you in because I need both of you. All three of you. Alzbieta, stop hiding back there and join the conversation."

"Your Majesty." Alzbieta stepped forward.

"I need the power of the Serpent Throne," Sarah said. "I can see the power there. Great as the power of the Mississippi is, the power in the Serpent Throne is just as mighty. Perhaps mightier. My father never tapped into that power, because the temple was unconsecrated in his day."

Zadok Tarami hung his head. Was that a good sign? Had the sharp edges of his zeal rubbed off?

"I have met and spoken with my father," Sarah said.

Alzbieta gasped. Sarah remembered that the priestess had once been an intimate of her father, and maybe his lover.

"His shade, at least," Sarah said. "My brother connected me with my father on the Serpent Mound."

"Who is your brother?" Maltres's expression bordered on awe.

"He . . . I don't know quite how to explain this, but Nathaniel can hear things, and he can travel to strange places. Including places where the spirits of the dead linger. My father gave me some of the advice I needed about the Temple of the Sun. Though I reckon I could just as easily have read my Homer, or the Book of Kings. I need to offer a sacrifice."

The look on all three of her advisors' faces was one of surprise, fear, and anxiety.

"What sacrifice?" Maltres Korinn asked.

Sarah's heart was heavy. "I hadn't considered the . . . Jock of Cripplegate option. But perhaps I should."

"I regret that Sherem and his fellows didn't wait a day," Maltres said. "Perhaps then you could have availed yourself of the energy they freely gave, to perform the sanctification you plan."

"Your Majesty could . . . ask if there are others," Alzbieta said slowly. "Who are willing. Maybe who are sick or dying."

"No!" Zadok Tarami's voice thundered in the small room. "Please, no, Your Majesty. I beg you to see the difference between someone who voluntarily gives up his life to save his fellows, and someone who is ordered to commit self-murder."

"It doesn't have to be an order," Maltres murmured. "It could be a request."

"That is a blurry line at best," the Metropolitan said.

"All the lines here are blurry," Sarah said, "even to me, and I'm famous for my sight. When I ordered a sally to protect and send out messengers, I knew some of them would die. Show me the line between that order and the query whether someone might be willing to sacrifice herself, like Isaac, like Christ."

"When you sent out soldiers to protect your messengers," Zadok said fiercely, "you hoped they would all live."

"That's true." Sarah remembered their deaths and her chest was cold.

"To me, that is a clear line."

Sarah nodded slowly.

"You would offer sacrifice," Tarami continued, "because you must sanctify your . . . the goddess's enclosure. You would clean the throne of the taint that blocks you from accessing it. Do you need mana, or do you wish to offer sacrifice for sacred, priestly reasons?"

"Both," Sarah said. "Mostly, the latter. I think I have the power I need to run the plow. Hell, I've done it before."

"Please, then, do not make your sacrifices with the blood of men." Zadok Tarami lowered himself to his knees and clasped his hands in front of himself. "I will not stop you from worshipping the goddess. But make Her a goddess indeed, and not a demon. There are enough old stories of blood spilled to thirsty monsters living on mountaintops—let us not make a new story in the same vein."

Zadok's words lightened Sarah's heart. "You're right, Metropolitan. But if we are not to sacrifice our comrades, what can we give the goddess to show our devotion?"

"Our food," Maltres said.

There was a moment of silence. Then Tarami nodded.

"There is little enough of it left," Maltres continued. "Mostly in storehouses owned by Your Majesty and guarded by my men."

"If we burn the last of our food, we give *all* our lives *entirely* to the goddess," Alzbieta said.

"We risk revolt," Maltres added. "I could not do it. I have the people's respect, I think, but I do not have their love."

"You are the Beloved," Alzbieta told Sarah. "They would do it for you."

"Some of them would," Sarah agreed. "Others would be reluctant. But they might do it if the Metropolitan helped."

She looked at Zadok Tarami. His face was impassive, but through her Eye of Eve she saw coils of doubt and fear, hard kernels of hatred, and murky pools of pride.

And then, suddenly, a spring of hope, welling up within him.

"I will help," he said.

"Thank you," Maltres said.

"Yes. Thank you," Sarah added. "I need more than just your approval. To undertake this sanctification of the mound, I need to be crowned and anointed. By your hand, naturally. And I want to do it in the Basilica."

Zadok hesitated. "Will my flock still follow me, if I anoint you?"

"Don't be foolish," Maltres told him. "Sarah isn't asking you for a concession, she's giving you one. Your public crowning of her will be seen as essential to her ascension of the Serpent

Throne. Your stature grows, because you become a gatekeeper to the kingdom."

"I'm not offering any kind of concession at all," Sarah disagreed. "Nor am I asking for one. The time for bargaining is past. I need to be crowned queen so that I can approach the goddess in Her home and repair its damaged walls. Will you help me or not, Zadok Tarami?"

"I offer you the use of my men," Sir William said.

"Specifically, Sarah's beastkind?" Maltres asked.

The two men stood at the door of the Hall of Onandagos. Maltres had been emerging with his chosen detail of soldiers to go collect the city's remaining food and transport it to the Great Mound, and he'd met Sir William at the door. At the general's side stood the coyote-headed beastman Chikaak. Behind him in a tight file waited the remainder of the beastkind.

"You are asking people who fear death from cannons and enemy bayonets to also face imminent starvation." Sir William's voice was hard, but Maltres saw compassion in his eyes. "It would be reasonable on their part to resist."

"That's why I have chosen these men."

Sir William looked at Maltres's force and sighed. Maltres knew what the Cavalier saw—old men, spry and determined, but not vigorous, not in their flower.

"Are they Freemasons, then? Will they give their neighbors the grip in exchange for the surrender of a loaf of bread or a rasher of bacon?"

"Or a baked squash, or a pot of beans?" Maltres smiled faintly. "Some of them are, in fact, brothers. And if they have to, I expect they may turn to the persuasive and reassuring tools of the Craft. But no, I've chosen these men because they are Swords of Wisdom."

The general's mouth hung open.

"You rode with Kyres Elytharias," Maltres said. "Do you know—"

"I know he was one of the Swords of Wisdom," Sir William said. "I hadn't heard of them in recent years."

"They still exist," Maltres said.

"You are giving the requisitioned food an honor guard," Sir William said.

"It's to be a sacrifice. I send consecrated men to collect it."

"Very good, suh." Bill hobbled to his horse, mounted, and rode away.

Bathed, her hair neatly combed, and clothed in a white linen dress, Sarah felt like a person again. To the exhaustion that dragged at every limb she now added a mouth full of sand and a rumbling belly, but she felt that what she had to do today should be done in a state of fasting.

If this had been a strictly political act, she would have liked to give her people longer notice. Perhaps there was additional pomp and further spectacle that could have been incorporated to give people more joy and confidence. Maybe she could have thought through a rite that would include more actions by her people.

Still, they were involved.

Sarah walked on bare feet to the Basilica Mound. The winter wind gnawed at her flesh until it was numb. The steps up the eastern face of the mound were lined with the people of Cahokia, each holding a branch of an evergreen tree. Standing at the foot of the mound was Gazelem Zomas, the dark-skinned prince of the schismatic kingdom on the other side of the Missouri. To Sarah's surprise, Gazelem raised his evergreen branch and shouted.

"Hosanna to the Daughter of Onandagos! Blessed is she that cometh in the name of Heaven! Hosanna to the Beloved of the goddess! Hosanna in the highest!"

At the end of each phrase he paused, and the crowd shouted his words. The hosannas rippled up the mound, and with them rippled the waving evergreen branches, giving the mound the appearance of being alive and moving.

Sarah began to climb. Gazelem continued shouting.

"The earth is the Lord's, and the fulness thereof; the world, and they that dwell therein. For he hath founded it upon the seas, and established it upon the floods. Who shall ascend into the hill of the Lord? Or who shall stand in his holy place? He that hath clean hands, and a pure heart; who hath not lifted up his soul unto vanity, nor sworn deceitfully. Hosanna! Hosanna! Hosanna!"

"Hosanna!" The crowd shouted and waved its branches.

The pumping action of her legs moved Sarah's blood and warmed her, but the hard stone of the steps bit into the soles of her feet, and she stubbed a toe.

Gazelem followed her. He had good strong lungs, to be able to walk up the steps and shout at the same time. As she neared the top of the mound, Sarah saw Alzbieta Torias. The priestess stood in the open door of the Basilica holding the Sevenfold Crown, the Orb of Etyles, and the Heronplow on a large, silk pillow.

"He shall receive the blessing from the Lord, and righteousness from the God of his salvation," Gazelem called out. "This is the generation of them that seek him, that seek thy face, O Jacob. Lift up your heads, O ye gates; and be ye lift up, ye everlasting doors; and the King of glory shall come in."

Sarah entered the Basilica, hearing the hosanna shouts behind her.

She walked the length of the nave slowly. She didn't know most of the faces in the church, but she saw the Lady Alena, Maltres Korinn, and Cathy. She saw old men she understood to be the Swords of Wisdom, the knightly order to which her father belonged, and which had gathered up the city's food for the sacrifice that would shortly take place. She saw people she knew were generally dressed in velvet and silk, but everyone in the hall today wore white linen.

Except Zadok Tarami. The priest was arrayed in his full liturgical garb, with shawls, scarves, aprons, and a tall hat that looked somewhat like a crown. He stood waiting beside a seat that had been placed for the purpose near the altar and the seven-armed treelike candelabrum on the apse. The Basilica was lit with candles; the gold thread and gems in Tarami's clothing sparkled and made him look angelic, more than mortal.

His face showed concentration and humility.

Alzbieta followed at Sarah's right shoulder, matching her step for step. Gazelem continued at her left, and was still shouting.

"Who is this King of glory? The Lord strong and mighty, the Lord mighty in battle. Lift up your heads, O ye gates; even lift them up, ye everlasting doors; and the King of glory shall come in. Who is this King of glory? The Lord of hosts, he is the King of glory. Hosanna! Hosanna! Hosanna!"

The crowd within the Basilica shouted the hosannas with Gazelem. Through her Eye of Eve—was she perhaps deceived by her fatigue and hunger, and by the staging and the light?—Sarah saw the crowd for a moment as an angelic host. White, winged, and singing, they waved their branches from the tree of paradise and ushered her onward.

Sarah reached the front and stopped. From this position, she saw priests—clothed in white linen like the ordinary attendees, but also wearing turbans that marked their special status—standing to either side of the altar. One held an elaborate brocaded and gem-covered robe. The other held a basin of water and a towel over each arm.

The echo of the hosannas died away. Slowly, Zadok Tarami stepped out of his sandals and seated himself on the chair.

The chair was wood—acacia, Sarah had been told—and covered with gold foil. It was tall, sturdy, and unadorned, other than a leaf-and-branch motif in its carving that ran up all four legs and in a braid around the seat back.

Sarah knelt. The priest with the basin knelt beside her and offered it to her. She took it, and also one of the towels.

"Lady, dost thou wash my feet?" Tarami asked.

In truth, his feet were already clean. But the point of the liturgy was not actually to clean one's feet. Sarah took water in her cupped hands and poured it first over one foot, then over the other.

"What I do thou knowest not now," she recited, "but thou shalt know hereafter. If I wash thee not, thou hast no part with me."

"Lady," Tarami said, "not my feet only, but also my hands and my head."

Sarah took one of the towels and dried the Metropolitan's feet. "He that is washed needeth not save to wash his feet, but is clean every whit: and ye are clean."

She stood and stepped slightly back; not too far, because her father's people stood close to each other at all times.

The Metropolitan arose and stepped back into his sandals. Sarah sat and the priest knelt. Without words he repeated her actions, washed and dried her feet.

The basin-priest left and Sarah remained sitting. Zadok Tarami—with Luman Walters listening, eyes keenly focused—had walked her through the ritual beforehand. He had assured her that he'd give her any promptings she needed, and she had assured him in turn that she wouldn't need any.

The garment-priest handed Zadok a pair of gold-threaded

slippers. The Metropolitan placed them on Sarah's feet. She stood, and Gazelem Zomas began to recite again.

"The Lord reigneth, he is clothed with majesty; the Lord is clothed with strength, wherewith he hath girded himself: the world also is stablished, that it cannot be moved. Hosanna!"

"Hosanna!" the crowd shouted.

Zadok took the robe from the garment-priest and hung it over Sarah's shoulders. The sudden weight of the gold and gems nearly knocked her to the floor. She staggered, and Zadok grabbed her forearm to steady her.

His wiry arms were surprisingly strong, and his smile was warm.

"Thy throne is established of old: thou art from everlasting. Hosanna!" Gazelem cried.

"Hosanna!" the crowd cried with him.

Zadok took a white, gold-stitched stole from the garment-priest and laid it over Sarah's shoulders.

"The floods have lifted up, O Lord, the floods have lifted up their voice; the floods lift up their waves. Hosanna!"

"Hosanna!"

Zadok took the Orb of Etyles and the Heronplow from Alzbieta and placed them one at a time into Sarah's hands.

"The Lord on high is mightier than the noise of many waters, yea, than the mighty waves of the sea. Hosanna!"

"Hosanna!"

The basin-priest returned and held forth an ivory horn, bound in gold. Zadok took the horn and walked around to stand behind Sarah, so they both faced the crowd.

Through her Eye of Eve, Sarah saw angels. Angels stood on the floor in white linen, glowing blue and white. Angels hovered above the floor in the same garb, shining the same shades. The word *hosanna* rang from the stones of the Basilica's pillars and floods, as if the building itself were celebrating the moment.

Oil poured onto Sarah's scalp. She felt it run down both cheeks and her jaw. Then Zadok took the Sevenfold Crown from Alzbieta Torias and settled it onto Sarah's head.

"Thy testimonies are very sure: holiness becometh thine house, O Lord, forever. Hosanna!"

"Hosanna!" the crowd cried.

"Hosanna!" the angels shouted.

"Hosanna!" roared the Basilica itself.

Zadok Tarami walked around Sarah again to stand in front of her. "Your Majesty." He knelt and touched his forehead to the floor.

The crowd knelt, as did Sarah, Gazelem, and the two assisting priests. "Your Majesty!"

Sarah helped Zadok to stand. "Thou shalt know hereafter," she whispered to him.

The gathered food stores of Cahokia stood heaped in a pile at the foot of the great mound. Looking at what there was, Maltres experienced a moment of doubt.

Had his people in fact refused to surrender their stores? How could there be so little?

But no, the answer to that question was that the divine-magical abundance Sarah had produced a few days earlier had been consumed. The city was its own plague of locusts. Without a countryside to produce its food, or a goddess to fill the deficit, it would starve.

The crowds standing around the plaza at the foot of the mound, though, were not looking at the food. They were looking at Sarah, who stood on the lower steps, facing them.

The Swords of Wisdom had performed another duty for Sarah while they were gathering food. At Maltres's order they had gathered all the silver they could, and that silver had been cast into bullets.

Also, the Swords had found and collected twelve stones. Sarah had specified that the stones must never have known chisel or dressing; they must be natural and uncut. This would have been easy enough, if the Swords had been able to go the riverbank, or out into the flat land of the Cahokian Bottom. As it was, the stones were of unequal size, some as large as a man's head and others as small as his fist. But Sarah had examined them each carefully and pronounced them all fit.

Maltres wasn't exactly sure what she intended. God had commanded Moses not to use "hewn stone" in the altars of ancient Israel, so Sarah must mean to build an altar. On the other hand, if she intended to burn the mound of collected food on a heap made of *those* twelve stones, it would take days, perhaps weeks.

Sarah had walked to the Great Mound directly from the

Basilica, with the crowd following. She still wore her coronation robe and crown and carried the regalia in her hands. Per her instructions, Maltres and Alzbieta and the eight former bearers who were her other witnesses had gathered at the foot of the Great Mound with her.

Maltres thought of Sherem, remembered the glories of Eden, and felt a pang of loss.

"Zadok Tarami," Sarah called.

Her voice rolled like thunder across the plaza. Tarami, who had just arrived, once again dressed in a simple woolen tunic, looked surprised.

"Step forward, Zadok," Sarah called again. "Join my witnesses."

The Metropolitan looked at the assembled ten, hesitated, and then moved to join their number.

Sarah shifted the Orb of Etyles into the same arm that carried the Heronplow, then stooped and picked up the smallest of the twelve stones. "Witnesses," she said. "Take up the burden of your witness."

Maltres picked up a stone. The bearers took the largest of them so his was small, roughly rectangular, and jagged. It still bore dirt on one side, showing it had been pried from the earth just hours earlier.

"Follow me." Sarah turned and walked up the Great Mound.

Alzbieta Torias followed first. Then Zadok Tarami, with a look of wonder on his face, and then Maltres. Behind him came the bearers.

He focused on his steps, making them solemn and steady. He focused on his hands also, willing them to bear the rock, small as it was, without fatigue or complaint. Maltres thought of the crowd below—how were they receiving this? Zadok Tarami had anointed and crowned Sarah Queen of Cahokia, and they had cheered. As Sarah included the Metropolitan in a sacrifice to the city's ancient goddess, would they cheer again? Was the city ready for this?

At the top of the Great Mound, Sarah stopped, turned, and waited. Alzbieta reached her first. Sarah touched the priestess's forearm and said, "Here."

Then Sarah walked twelve paces—Maltres counted—toward the Temple of the Sun. When Zadok Tarami reached her at that spot, she again said, "Here."

Alzbieta and Zadok stood waiting in the places assigned them, at compass points east and west. Sarah assigned Maltres himself a spot to the north. As the bearers arrived, she placed them on the points between the cardinal directions. Finally she herself stood at the southern spot.

"Place your stone!" she called.

Maltres stooped to place his stone on the earth. The others, except Sarah, did the same.

"Mother of All Living!" Sarah cried. "Hear our prayer! We consecrate these stones and the earth within to Thee. All that we place on this altar, we give to Thee. Amen!"

"Amen," the other eleven said.

Sarah placed her stone.

She walked to the edge of the mound. "Swords of Wisdom!" she called to the old men waiting below. "Bring the sacrifice!"

One armload at a time, the men carried up the last of the city's food. Squash, corn, beans—staples of the Cahokian diet. Dried fruits, green vegetables. A very small amount of cheese, beef, and pork.

One man at a time, the Swords entered the delimited space of the altar, set down the food, and returned.

Three trips up and down the mountain by each man—with the crowd silently waiting and watching—and all the food had been transferred. The Swords of Wisdom arrayed themselves in a circle around the compass-altar.

Sarah addressed the crowd below the mound. "People of the city of the goddess, join me now in prayer!"

She knelt. Below, the entire city knelt. She faced them and they faced her, and beyond her, her altar and the Temple of the Sun.

"O Mother of All Living," Sarah cried, "O Serpent of the Sun, O Unfallen Eve!"

The crowed repeated her words.

"We have life from Thee in three worlds, O Goddess. The world before, the world now, and the world after. We would unite the worlds in one, O Virgin of Eternities! We offer this sacrifice, the blood of all our lives, to Thee! We ask Thee to cleanse this mount of all pollution and sin, that we may offer the mountain itself to Thee, amen!"

The crowd repeated every line in turn, including the last. "Amen!"

Sarah returned to her stone at edge of the altar of earth. There, she knelt and pushed the cutting blade of the Heronplow into the soil. *"Sacrificium damus."*

The blade moved. Maltres was unsurprised at the motion, but he hadn't expected the tingling feeling that ran up and down his spine at the sight. The Heronplow cut a perfect circle around the uncut stones, and as it came around again to the first stone, it cut inward and continued, making a spiral.

As the moving plow touched the piles of food, the food evaporated into blue light. The light rose into the sky, a blue curtain of splendor that trailed behind the Heronplow and visibly marked the city's sacrifice.

Below, Maltres heard the crowd gasp.

The Swords of Wisdom broke into a wordless song. Was this spontaneous? Were they following some traditional sense of liturgy Maltres didn't know? Had Sarah agreed to this in advance?

The Heronplow touched the center of the altar and the light changed. It grew more diffuse, washed out, but at the same time it spread. As the blue glow expanded out from the altar and encompassed Maltres, he felt it as warmth.

And love.

He took a deep breath, his heart full of blackberry brambles and the sound of water running past his home.

The light spread until it covered the entire top of the Great Mound. The crowd below began to hum, not the same melody the Swords sang, but oddly, one that harmonized with it. Maltres felt as if he were flying.

The trees atop the Great Mound sprouted leaves and burst into flower.

Sarah knelt to pick up the Heronplow, then carried it to the southeast corner of the Temple of the Sun. Kneeling again, she placed the plow against the foundation stone of the building.

"Magna mater," he heard her say, *"maxima mater. Rogo ut hoc aratrum pelleas."*

He knew the words; he'd heard her use them to revive the Treewall, and to consecrate the Sunrise Mound. Now, they sent the Heronplow into the stone of the Temple of the Sun.

Sarah staggered. Maltres wanted to run to her aid, but he'd been set into place by her, and didn't dare. Two Swords of Wisdom evidently felt no such limitation; the old men caught her before she fell and held her by her upper arms.

The universe stood still. Though it was late afternoon, Maltres looked up and thought he saw both the sun and also a full field of stars in the sky. Breath passed in and out of his lungs like electric ice, invigorating him and shocking him at the same time.

Sarah stooped to recover the Heronplow.

"Alzbieta Torias," she said. Her voice rang like a deep bass. "Zadok Tarami. It's time."

Alzbieta stepped out of her place. Together, the queen, the priestess, and the priest entered the Temple of the Sun.

Sarah's own muscles had already failed her. What held her up were the two Swords of Wisdom at her side and some force that came directly out of the earth, stiffening her legs and pushing her forward.

She stepped into the Temple of the Sun. Through her mortal eye, she saw the same mosaics she had always seen before, the long nave, the elevated apse, the empty throne.

Through her Eye of Eve, everything had changed. The dark mists she had seen around the throne before had dissipated. The mosaics seemed to have sprung into three dimensions, so that she saw the Serpent Throne across a long and rugged landscape. Between her and the high mountain on which the throne rested, she saw forested hills, a bleak desert, and a storm-shattered ocean. The sky overhead shone with stars, spinning around the plane of the ecliptic.

The Swords of Wisdom, Alzbieta, and Zadok all stepped out of their shoes. "Hallowed ground," one of the Swords murmured.

"Your father would be proud," the other whispered into her ear.

"I know." Sarah sobbed once, and then took a deep breath. "I know."

"My God," Zadok Tarami murmured. "Was it always like this?"

Sarah, too, stepped out of her coronation shoes. "Is the Lady Alena here?"

It was Alena's day of tendance. The priestess with the vow of silence appeared from Sarah's left; she held a primitive clay jug, which Sarah knew to contain the goddess's sacred lamp oil.

"I'll follow you," Sarah said.

They crossed the length of the nave. Sarah half-closed her Eye of Eve—it was distracting, to swoop at lightning-like speeds across the strange terrain, but she couldn't shut it out entirely, either. It was too beautiful, its colors too vivid, its details too perfect. Stepping across the ocean, she climbed the steps to the apse.

At the top, she halted. She looked back over her shoulder at Alzbieta, Zadok, and the two Swords. All four of them knelt and faced her. She turned to face the Serpent Throne—it rose enormous before her, dwarfing her with its sheer physical presence.

Sarah cracked open her Eye of Eve. Did she see the flicker of a person sitting on the throne? Just the hint of an image?

She couldn't be sure.

She knelt, too, before the Serpent Throne. She nodded to the Lady Alena.

Alena moved forward alone into the apse, holding the jug of oil.

Sarah hesitated, uncertain of the right order. Close the veil, then light the lamps? But the lamps were ordinarily lit only behind the closed veil.

Curiosity won.

"Fill the lamps," she said.

The Lady Alena nodded. She poured oil slowly into the seven bowls, starting with the lowest and rising to the highest. Through her Eye of Eve, Sarah saw the bowls as planets that with their anointing began to spin and sing.

She took a deep breath. The Lady Alena stepped to one side and waited, jug in her hands.

Will and the strength of the earth alone held Sarah up, even on her knees. She gripped the Orb of Etyles tightly. Reaching into its depths, she found the green glow of the Mississippi River and tapped into it. *"Septem lucernas accendo!"*

The lamps burst into bright flame. The planets revolved, ignited, and became seven salamanders, all dancing in their golden bowls and looking intently at Sarah. The light of the seven lamps struck the Serpent Throne and caromed off greatly amplified—the throne itself shone like an enormous light, like the sun for which the temple was named.

Someone sat on the throne. A woman. Sarah found she couldn't look at Her; the Woman Herself shone like the sun, Her brightness stinging Sarah's eyes and the tears blinding Sarah. Sarah looked away.

She heard a voice she knew, a voice she had heard in Eden.

You are my Beloved daughter. I await you on my holy mountain. Come to me.

The words had physical force that shook Sarah's frame. A warm wind smelling of cinnamon and citrus blew from the Serpent Throne, warping through Sarah's hair and clothing and filling the nave.

It was too much. She couldn't handle the power of standing directly face to face with the goddess, even looking away. Her body trembled and burned. And what of those who were not as prepared and defended as she? Zadok Tarami? Alzbieta Torias?

"*Velaman occludo,*" she incanted, reaching one more time into the Orb of Etyles.

Power flowed through her again and struck the veil. With a hissing sound like a thousand singing snakes, the veil slid shut, drawing from both sides and meeting in the middle, closing the Lady Alena inside.

Through the curtain, with her Eye of Eve, Sarah could still see the seven dancing salamanders and the burning blue outline of the Mother of All Living.

She retreated backward down the steps to the floor of the nave. Weakly, she stood and turned to see her priestess and priest. Alzbieta's face wore an expression of sheer joy, but the joy in Zadok's eyes was woven through with terror and surprise.

"Was it always like this?" he asked again.

Sarah took a deep breath. "Believe it or not, that was the easy part."

The Orb of Etyles made a loud *clang* as it struck the floor. The sound caught Sarah by surprise; she hadn't realized she'd dropped it. Then the floor rushed up to meet Sarah and struck her in the face.

Luman Walters watched the coronation from the shadows of the Basilica. He wore the linen tunic the priests offered him, and found himself standing beside the Cetean, Mother Hylia.

They said nothing, but as the ceremony finished and Sarah strode slowly out of the Basilica in her royal garb, Hylia laid a gentle hand on Luman's arm and smiled.

He watched the building of the altar and the sacrifice of the city's food from the top of the Treewall. The Cavalier Sir William

Johnston Lee allowed him up and then joined him in watching, together with the queen's confidant, Cathy Filmer. From their height, they could see the proceedings reasonably well—they were still a little below the Great Mound, but high enough that they could tell roughly where people atop it were standing.

They watched without comment.

After the great flashing blue spiral that launched light into the sky with the diffuse blue glow, the Treewall itself seemed to hum.

"You're the wizard, suh," Bill said to Luman. "What do you make of this?"

Luman scanned the city and then examined the wall. He saw leaves sprouting here and there, shoots of plants rising tentatively from the snow-covered earth. As each leaf unfurled, though, and as each tender sprout tried to open a flower, it died. The leaves dropped brown and lifeless to the snow. The sprouts withered into yellow-brown wisps and blew away.

The Treewall, too, sprouted leaves, but each reached maturity and died, drifting away from the city's wall in a slow cloud of dull, dead brown.

"The goddess seems to be again attempting to bestow Her bounty upon the city," Luman said.

"The city could certainly use it," Bill grumbled.

"It would be a remarkably direct miracle," Cathy added. "We surrender our food, and She immediately returns it."

"Only something is in the way," Luman said. "Something is stopping Her."

"Hell's Bells, no," Bill cursed. "The miracle isn't being blocked, it's being stolen."

All three of them turned in the same moment to look at their besiegers. The circle of black flame that surrounded the city throbbed.

And grew.

"Heaven's footstool!"

"Sarah fuels her enemy," Cathy said. "Did she know? Did she expect it?"

"Does she know now?" Bill asked.

"I'll tell her," Luman said. "I know she intends more, she... has asked me to be part of it. I'll tell her she's feeding the Sorcerer Robert Hooke. Perhaps that will make her accelerate her plan, or change it."

He turned to descend the nearest steps, and a loud *BOOM* cracked the air.

The Treewall shook again, this time not from a magical attempt to grow or bear fruit, but because a cannonball had struck it. Luman's knees buckled; he fell onto all fours and nearly tumbled off the wall.

Bill threw himself to the edge of the Treewall, pressing his eye to a spyglass. "Is it just one gun they've unspiked?"

As if in answer, a second *BOOM* split the air.

"Go," Cathy said to Luman Walters. "Go quickly."

"You shouldn't ought to overestimate my kin, though.
Most of 'em don't know how to take orders."

———◆———

CHAPTER TWENTY-FOUR

"I don't like this place, Prince-Capitaine," al-Muhasib said. He spoke in Arabic; was he trying to keep his words secret from the witch, or was he afraid of their guides?

"I didn't bring any cowards with me from Paris," Abd al-Wahid responded.

"Thank you," Ravi said. "I've been waiting for you to say that."

"I did, however, bring a nitpicking Jew."

"Because you know excellence in a man when you see it," Ravi said. "And perhaps because you are covered in nits."

They rode through a forest unlike any Abd al-Wahid had ever seen. Trees he didn't know rose like stately columns, their higher boughs interlaced almost densely enough to form a pavilion, despite the fact that winter had stripped the trees of their foliage.

The fallen leaves lay in humps on the ground, flashes of orange and gold showing through gaps in the snow cover. The snow lay two feet thick in places. Only a large traffic of hooves and feet had worn the track they walked to frozen dirt.

One of their guides, the man with the badger's head whose name sounded like "Fftwarik," looked back over his shoulder at them. "We are arriving imminently," he said in clear French.

The other guide, a man with a crab's claw for one hand and a snake's head in place of the other, grunted.

A dozen howling beastkind had met the mamelukes and their charge when Abd al-Wahid was aimlessly trying to cut a road

438

through the wilderness of Shreveport. When told the mamelukes bore a message and a gift for the Heron King from the Chevalier of New Orleans, the beastkind had quickly placed them on this path, and then introduced them to Fftwarik and his companion, Croom.

They had been walking for two days since. Abd al-Wahid guessed, from his occasional glimpses of stars overhead, that something about the path itself caused them to move unnaturally fast.

In the forest to either side, Abd al-Wahid had heard an extraordinary range of sounds, all along the journey: hoots and howls, shrieks and whispers, cries that sounded like the distant screams of men. Tree branches rustled, piles of leaves erupted beneath the snow, and occasionally he spied paw- or hoofprints that crossed the track, but the road itself was undisturbed.

A building hove into view. Not a building but a stone pyramid, stepped like the pyramid of Djoser at Saqqara, but much larger. The trees around it gave way to a clearing as the mamelukes approached; smoke rose, as if the clearing had only been created by burning the trees away that same morning.

"Are these the great mounds of the Ohio?" Abd al-Wahid asked. "We have structures like these in Egypt."

"You're not in the Ohio," the mambo Marie said. She carried a broomstick in one arm and a basket on the other, as she had all the way from New Orleans. A snake hissed in the basket now, accenting her words. "You're on the Missouri side, somewhere in the Great Green Wood, if you are even any longer on earth at all."

The thought sobered Abd al-Wahid, but he persisted. "Then like his neighbors across the river, the Heron King enjoys towers."

Croom laughed. "It is a very old style of architecture. It was old when the pharaohs of your Egypt adopted it."

Abd al-Wahid resisted the temptation to respond. He wanted to point out that the pharaohs were dead, that *his* Egypt began with the prophet, and that mankind had created many wonders since that were much greater than the simple pyramids, including the glory that was Arabic calligraphy and the writings of the poet.

Mindful that he did not know what lurked in the forest, he said none of those things.

The mambo sat upright in her saddle. "The Heron King will see us."

Fftwarik spat yellow saliva into the snow. "Wishing it won't make it so."

A deer with a crocodile's head atop its neck and the face of a woman protruding awkwardly from it, bounded to a stop. "The King will see you."

Fftwarik grunted in surprise.

Abd al-Wahid stared at the strange messenger. "Truly the poet says, the garden of the world has no limits, except in your mind."

"The audience hall?" Croom asked.

The deer nodded and raced away in long leaps.

Fftwarik led them on, directly toward the pyramid. As he drew closer, Abd al-Wahid's estimate of the structure's size grew. He also saw increasingly more detail: buttresses rising from lower levels to shore up higher ones, faces twisted in terror carved into the stone; windows and staircases; columns that appeared to support stone blocks above them as well as columns that looked merely painted on. He saw flaking paint, too—at some point, the entire structure appeared to have been painted in bright colors, but only splotches and flakes remained of that life.

Multiple holes gaped in the lower few levels of the stone pile; Fftwarik and Croom led the mamelukes up a crumbling staircase and into one of the openings. At no point did the beastkind suggest the Franco-Egyptian warriors should dismount.

The interior of the tunnel they entered was dark, warm, and wet. Their horses' hooves, crisp on the frozen ground for days, now sounded with wet splashes. The tunnel seemed interminable...time passed, the splashing of hooves...and then a light appeared at its end.

A green light.

They emerged into a long hall. Here too, straight tree trunks rose like pillars as far as the eye could see, and overhead their branches grew together. But strangely, in this forest, there was no snow. Leaves filled the canopy overhead completely. Beneath the hooves of the mamelukes' horses, springy green grass carpeted the ground.

Beyond the trees, Abd al-Wahid saw bees the size of horses. They had barbed stingers and cruel eyes, and they watched the mamelukes advance. Grotesque goats, with staggered pairs of horns sprouting from their shoulders and their backs, lurched from one bramble to the next.

The air was thick with the smell of cinnamon and blood.

The trees grew farther apart, the track rapidly becoming a

hall. Abd al-Wahid rode past a broad pool with a stone fountain at its center, spouting tall plumes of water.

He had the curious sensation that there were more people with him now than he had brought with him into the hall. Beyond the trees he saw a white rhinoceros, covered in thick fur. Beside it frolicked a herd of horses no taller than Abd al-Wahid's knee. On his other side, a creature like an ape, but with a low, rounded head and long nails, slowly crept down the trunk of an immense tree.

Am I riding my horse, or is this horse riding me?

The gigantic bees buzzed; they were distant, but the sound rang in his ear. The hum of the strange pollinators and the warm feel of the sunlight, however green, on his skin, made Abd al-Wahid doze in his saddle until he felt his mount stop. The abrupt bump opened his eyes.

On thrones of green water, flowing, filled with moving fishes, and yet impossibly holding their shape, sat the Heron King and two other creatures. To Abd al-Wahid's left sat a goat with a sad mouth; to his right, lying back in the throne with his legs up over one arm, sat a man with the golden eyes of an owl.

The Heron King was a giant. He was twice the height of a man and very muscular. Fine feathers that might have been white or might have been iridescent and shining with an array of colors covered his entire body, which was man-shaped, but for his head. Mounted above immense, powerful shoulders, was a head the shape of a heron's, with impenetrable eyes.

I know the Chevalier of New Orleans. The words pierced Abd al-Wahid's heart directly, but the look in the Heron King's eyes suggested that he was their source. *I met him. He did not strike me as a giver of gifts.*

"And yet he has sent us to offer you that which you most desire," Abd al-Wahid said. He was standing, as were Ravi, al-Muhasib, and the mambo. He didn't remember dismounting. Where had the horses gone?

The destruction of the world of men? The Heron King stood; in his hand he held a golden sword as long as a man's body.

"An heir."

You're mistaken. I don't want an heir. Simon Sword's body trembled as he spoke.

The mambo Marie spoke up. "Yes, you do. You want an heir who is not Peter Plowshare."

The bird-giant looked at the mambo with glittering eyes. *What do you know of my desires, witch?*

"You are a god," the witch said coolly. "You envy men their freedom, because you can only do the things you were made to do. And the two things you were made to do are destroy and mate."

You're wrong. I do not mate. I breed.

"But to create an heir is to create Peter Plowshare, who will destroy you. For this reason, you have held off assailing Cahokia, and have instead fought her estranged sister in the woods."

Abd al-Wahid marveled at the witch's words. They must be informed by intelligence from the Chevalier. *Or perhaps from her dark Africk gods?*

Zomas is ever a thorn in my side, the Heron King insisted. *It is a thorn to my father as well, when he reigns, though it is a thorn he coddles and tolerates.*

"You fear the Serpent Queen, Sarah Calhoun. You fear her, and you are attracted to her."

Enough! The Heron King sprang down from his throne and leaped among the mamelukes. With a single blow of his golden sword, he sliced al-Muhasib in two, from top to bottom. Without drawing a weapon, maybe without even seeing his death coming, the mameluke collapsed to the ground in two bloody halves. *Make your offer, witch. I will accept, or I will kill you all.*

Abd al-Wahid trembled, shocked. Al-Muhasib's death had happened too quickly for him to even react, much less defend his man. Now he feared the Heron King's words would be an irresistible lure to Ravi, who would respond with a joke, the timing of which would result in their immediate deaths.

But Ravi held his tongue.

This new world was blighted by its wicked gods.

"I am the gift the Chevalier sends you." The woman held her head high. "And I am no slave; I offer myself of my free will. I have come to bear your heir, a son who will not be a child of the river and will not carry within him the taint of Eden. My womb is hexed and ready, O King, to bear you the child you *wish* to have."

You cannot survive such a feat.

The mambo turned her chin upward. "My loa have given me great fertility magic, and have assured me that I will live to see the child born. This child . . . and its father . . . will save my people."

The Heron King nodded slowly. Abd al-Wahid found that his hands were shaking. *This is indeed a gift. And there was a message, you said. Perhaps an indication of what the chevalier would wish to have in return?*

The witch nodded. "He invites you to invade New Orleans."

Nathaniel and Margaret found a house that would take them in. They looked at an inn called the *King Canute*, at first—Nathaniel wanted to get in out of the cold, especially for Margaret's sake, who would be left behind with Nathaniel's body while Nathaniel went looking for Jake—but then Margaret wondered out loud whether the innkeeper would give them up to any Imperial soldiers who came asking.

They considered space in a half-filled stable alongside the *King Canute*, too. The bodies of horses, dogs, and one cow filled the stable with enough warmth to make the evening comfortable, if redolent. But at the last moment, Nathaniel worried that a traveler on the road might stable his horse here and find them.

Including a traveler who might be an Imperial officer.

Or someone in the pay of Temple Franklin.

Franklin had said he had an informer in Johnsland. Who could that be? The earl's godi? One of the earl's farmers? His pig-keeper, Murphy?

They trudged through snow to a farm a mile off the track. Margaret's teeth were chattering loud enough by the time they reached the long farmhouse that Nathaniel had resolved to make this location work, even if meant using their stables. As it happened, the woman who answered the door heard Margaret's teeth and admitted them at once.

Which turned out to be good, in that there were no separate stables. Three children dozed under furs on a wooden platform against one wall, and furs on a second platform were likely where the farmer and her husband slept. The house was a single long room, with the far end given over to two horses, two cows, and about a dozen chickens.

"My name is Sigrid Andersdottir," the woman said. "My man there is Sören Håkansson."

The man sat beside a hearth full of coals that lay on the short wall of the house, effectively heating both piles of sleeping furs.

"Thank you," Margaret said.

"Chicago German?" Nathaniel asked. Sigrid and Sören both looked like the stories told of Albrecht von Wallenstein might be told of them instead. He thought that a small puppetlike sculpture of a man riding in a goat-cart, that sat on the mantel above the hearth, might represent Thor. If he was to the Chicago Germans what Thunor was to the Cavalier followers of the old gods, then he was here to bless the house and the marriage and the farm.

Sören grunted. "We could be. If we were in Chicago." He laughed at his own joke with great merriment, despite the fact that no one else joined him.

"We were both born in the old world," Sigrid said. "We came thinking we'd go to Waukegan, but once we landed, we found people who spoke our language right here in Pennsland. It was just easier to stay."

"What about you?" Sören asked. "You speak with the long vowels of the Crown Lands, but she's from the gulf and you both *look* like Yggdrasslinga. Are you married? You look alike, but they say that happens to married people over a long period of time."

"It doesn't," Sigrid said. "If it did, you'd be handsome."

Sören laughed even longer at Sigrid's joke than at his own.

"Besides, look at them," Sigrid continued. "They can't be older than twenty. There is no long period of time with these children."

"We're sister and brother," Nathaniel said. "But we were raised apart."

Sören raised his eyebrows. "Raised *that* far apart? It's an interesting family that has the resources to do that. Or is that broken."

"We're orphans," Margaret said. "But a friend of the family recently found us both."

"And musicians?" Sören pointed at Nathaniel's drum. "Or some kind of clown that wears his clothing the wrong way?"

"That's exactly right," Nathaniel said. "A clown."

That seemed to end Sören's curiosity. At the same moment, he finished sharpening the ax. He stood, hung the ax from pegs on the wall, and stretched his back. "I rise early. It's the cows. They have no mercy, and they don't care what the weather is. But it means I must a-bed now."

"Please," Sigrid added. "We have milk and bread to share, and this humble bed will keep you warm. Sören and I will sleep with the children tonight."

Nathaniel wanted to protest the hospitality, which seemed

too much, but the truth was that he thought the bed would do very nicely for what he needed.

"You stuff these guests with bread and milk," Sören said, "and I'll go explore that queer little building behind the long house. We can eat them when I get back."

Margaret laughed politely. Nathaniel feigned nervousness while Sören laughed.

"I'm joking," the tall man finally said. "We don't eat children. Anymore."

Nathaniel and Margaret drank the warm milk with bread dipped in it and lay down directly. Nathaniel fought fatigue to stay awake; with his injuries still healing, it seemed even harder.

Where was the wiindiigo, the Yankee sorcerer who served the Necromancer and had attacked him in Johnsland, tonight? Could *he* possibly be Temple Franklin's spy in Johnsland? That didn't seem likely.

Soon the Germans had settled under the covers with their children. Within moments, one of them was breathing deeply and regularly, and fifteen minutes hadn't passed before Nathaniel heard two adult snores from the shifting pile of arms and legs.

"Margaret?" he whispered.

"I'm awake," she whispered back.

"I'm going to go find Jake."

She had come to terms with the strangeness of this suggestion. Perhaps she connected it with her own experience of seeing Jake and Nathaniel in a dreamlike state and being freed from her bonds by them.

"There's going to be a bear," Nathaniel warned her.

"I've seen it."

"His name is Makwa. He is...part of me. He *is* me. I don't think he'll hurt you, because I wouldn't hurt you. But he's there to defend me while I...look for Jake, so be careful."

"Understood."

Nathaniel drew his drum close by his side. With gentle fingers, he drummed a rhythm and sang:

> *I ride upon four horses, to heaven I ride*
> *I seek my lost companion, a friend who's died*
> *I can ride two worlds, I will not be denied*
> *I ride upon four horses, to heaven I ride*

The seven-stepped ladder descended through a ceiling that faded into stars. Nathaniel sprang up the steps on horseback and found himself on the starlit plain.

He listened for his friend Jacob Hop, and heard nothing.

Terror stabbed him in his heart. Sarah—her city under siege, her life at risk—was counting on him to find a dead man and enlist his aid. And he was counting on Jake to help him interpret whatever he could learn from Isaiah Wilkes.

Thinking of the second man, Nathaniel held still and listened for Wilkes.

Nothing.

Panic seized him. Was Wilkes dead also?

What would Nathaniel do?

He assumed he'd find it as easy as it was to locate a living person. He'd spoken with the shade of Charles Lee, for instance.

But he hadn't tracked Charles Lee. He'd found him because Charles was with the Earl. Nathaniel pondered the implications. If he was going to find deceased spirits, he was going to have to learn a new skill.

But to start with, he could try looking for Temple Franklin.

He listened.

Quickly enough, he heard Franklin yelling. Behind the Lightning Bishop's grandson, Nathaniel heard the cry of a gull. Franklin was still aboard the ship.

Nathaniel followed the sound. He quickly descended a steep bluff onto white sand, and there he found Temple Franklin. The Emperor's advisor stood on a raft, floating in a large pond. Three Dutchmen stood on the raft with him, holding a body. Franklin was cursing out the Dutchmen.

~I understand failure, Captain!~ Franklin snapped. ~What I don't understand is your decision not even to try!~

The body was Jake's. His eyes were open, but they darted back and forth and rolled wildly in his head.

The captain remained calm. ~I don't answer to you and your Emperor. Maybe one day I will. But in the meantime, I am happy to explain to the Board of Directors that, in light of all the damage that young woman caused to my ship and crew, I made what I thought to be the prudent decision, and let them leave.~

Franklin shouted wordlessly and stomped off to the far corner of the raft.

The Dutchmen threw Jake into the pond and poled the raft away.

Jake stood. Water poured down his face and soaked his clothing, but he didn't seem to notice. Whatever he was looking at was entirely invisible to Nathaniel—his eyes shot and rolled in all directions, and he whimpered.

What was wrong?

Nathaniel took a deep breath. First, in case Wilkes was in fact dead, Nathaniel should learn as much as he could about death from Jake. He turned his head slightly and listened as hard as he could.

The same background harmony that he heard on earth filled his ear here. He focused and tuned it out.

He heard Jake's whimpers. There was something strange about them. He listened closer. He heard an echo when Jake made noise. He heard something else, too...

No, something was missing. Some piece was taken out of Jake's voice, as if certain timbres had been suppressed.

The world harmony. Nathaniel relaxed, listened again, and realized what he was hearing. Jake's voice was fading into the harmony of the world. That made it less distinct, but only across part of what Nathaniel heard. The middle part, the part that normally gave Jake's voice its character. If Nathaniel listened to the high parts, and also to the low parts of Jake's voice, he heard the Dutchman just fine.

He took another deep breath and relaxed further.

Stepping back, he listened experimentally for Isaiah Wilkes. He'd heard the man's voice only a few times, but for whatever reason—maybe it had to do with his ear—Nathaniel had a wonderful memory for sound. He listened for the chiming high tones and the rolling baritone underpinnings, and he heard Wilkes.

The other man was close.

Nathaniel saw a stream that fed into a pond. Not far away, just up a slight slope, Wilkes sat in that creek, rocking himself backward and forward and singing Elector songs.

> *The German duchies are sisters three*
> *Chicago, Minneapolis, and Milwaukee*
> *The Earl of Waukegan and the Knight of Green Bay*
> *Five Electors speak High German today*

Nathaniel would deal with Wilkes in time. First, he had to help Jake.

He drew close to his friend, hip-deep in water. Though they stood nose to nose, Jake didn't respond to his presence at all.

Jake was seeing something else.

His spirit was here. Nathaniel was interacting with his spirit.

What was causing him to see something else, then? His mind? His eyes? His memory?

> *Six Electors from the people of the longhouse*
> *Six great sachems from Erie's shore*
> *Mohawk, Oneida, Onondaga*
> *Cayuga, Seneca, Tuscarora*
> *Six Electors from the people of the longhouse*
> *Six mighty nations forevermore*

Jake said he remembered another life, other lives. Lives that weren't his, lives in which the Heron King, as the reaver Simon Sword, wreaked great destruction. After death, he was still experiencing those memories. Now—perhaps because his physical flesh was no longer softening the impact of the memories?—the memories were incapacitating him entirely.

But what could Nathaniel do about memories?

He sat at the edge of the pond and thought, while Wilkes sang through the Elector Songs for the Imperial Towns, the Free Cities of the Igbo, and then the Algonks.

Finally, he resolved on a course of action. To call it a plan would be too much—he had an intuition about how he might help Jake.

Taking his friend's hand, he tried to drag Jake out of the water. Jake wouldn't budge.

Nathaniel played his drum and sang:

> *I ride upon four horses, at the water's side*
> *To free my friend of memories, lodged deep inside*
> *My horses are as strong as heaven is wide*
> *To save my true companion, through heaven I ride*

Leaping atop the horses as they appeared, he grabbed Jake's arm and tried to drag the Dutchman's spirit with him. He nearly yanked his own arm out of its socket. Again, Jake wouldn't move.

Time to try something more drastic.

Nathaniel rode his horses a short distance away, to the shore of the pond, and then rode them directly at Jake, trampling the Dutchman. As the foremost horse's hoof struck him, Jake split open.

What erupted out of Jake was full of fire and noise and blood. Nathaniel and his horses tumbled into the pond, the cool water sheltering him slightly from the sudden hot wind that blasted across the plain. Smoke billowed from Jake's body and the screams of a multitude of sufferers exploded from his lips. Stone pyramids exploded upward. Jake's body had become a world, and it was a world in pain.

Above it all, laughing and shrieking, loomed a giant with the head of a crested bird.

"Jake!" Nathaniel yelled. "Jake, this is not real! It's only in your heart!"

But is that true? What is real? Are only physical, tangible things real, after all?

Jake thrashed in the pond, sucking in water as if the water could douse the fire that burned in him. The giant tore the heart from Jake and ate it, tore out his entrails and bound him with them, shattered his bones, tore out his heart again.

The giant *was* Jake, with a crest of feathers.

"Jake!"

But the Dutchman didn't hear.

Nathaniel scrambled onto his horses. He needed to reach Jake, but how?

He drummed his fingers against the horses and sang:

> *I ride upon four horses, my friend is near*
> *He cannot hear me calling, he rolls in fear*
> *To touch his broken heart, I must catch his ear*
> *I ride upon four horses, Jake, help is here*

Nathaniel slapped his own head, opposite the side into which the four ogres in the Pit of the Sky had inserted a quartz acorn, when they had torn Nathaniel apart and then rebuilt him. That acorn now popped out of Nathaniel's head and fell into his palm.

Order disappeared from the universe. The stars overhead whirled at ten times the speed they should. The blades of grass around Nathaniel whipped like tigers' tails. Frenzied for blood, the pond began to boil.

Nathaniel raced again toward Jake. Holding the acorn in his fist, he leaned down in the saddle—

the giant grabbed for him, but he swerved aside—

then swung low and slammed the acorn into the side of Jake's head.

The giant whirled and swung at Nathaniel again. This time his enormous fists connected, and Nathaniel and his horses went tumbling across the frenetic grass. The giant stretched his arms, reared back, and laughed a laugh like an earthquake.

Jake still thrashed in the pond.

"Jake!" Nathaniel cried.

This time, Jake looked at him.

"Jake! That's not real!"

"It's in me!" Jake's eyes were wide.

"But it's only fear! Get rid of the fear!"

"Where can I put it!"

"Throw it away!" Nathaniel scrambled back onto his horses. They were uncomplaining beasts, being some combination of a drum and the ghosts of dead animals and Nathaniel's own will.

Jake lurched to his feet. He burst his own entrails standing, and the cavity of his chest gaped wide as he tried to stagger away from the gigantic Heron King. The monster leaped after him, flames jetting from eyes and beak and crest. In the flames Nathaniel saw hidden echoes of Jake's own face.

The Heron King seized Jake in his grip.

"Drop him!" Nathaniel galloped to his friend's rescue. Fire fell from the sky all around him. Blood and shrieking sprang from the soil with each touch of his horse's hooves.

Jake threw something into the tall grass.

Nathaniel kicked his horse's flanks and leaped directly at the giant. They collided, a blow that knocked all the air out of Nathaniel's body and filled his mind with fire and fear. But it also knocked the Heron King back. Jake dropped onto Nathaniel's horses.

Nathaniel splashed back onto the whipping grass on the far side of the pond.

"I've made a place!" Jake shouted into Nathaniel's ear. Nathaniel barely heard him over the shrieks of pain and the crackle of the world on fire. "We'll throw him into it!"

Nathaniel kicked his horses forward again, shouting without words. He veered left, then left again, then leaped directly at the giant—

feather-covered arms wrapped around him, Jake, and the horses, and squeezed—

Nathaniel heard himself screaming in pain—

ahead of him, looming in the grass, he saw a blond boy with an oversized sword—

all of them crashed together into the boy—

and then Jake and Nathaniel alone tumbled in the grass on the other side, as Nathaniel's horses galloped away.

Grunting in pain, Nathaniel dragged himself to his feet. He gingerly gave Jake a hand, then reached up to pluck the quartz from Jake's ear and return it to his own.

The grass stopped moving. The stars slowed. The fire and screaming were gone.

There was no sign of the feathered giant.

"What happened?" Nathaniel asked.

Jake stooped and picked up something from the ground to show to Nathaniel. It was a single Tarock, the card for Simon Sword. Behind the blond, sword-wielding boy who customarily represented Simon Sword, Nathaniel saw within the card a bird-headed giant. "I put Simon Sword into the Tarock."

Nathaniel sighed. "You mean, you put your memories of him into the Tarock. Your memories of being him. The things he left behind in your soul after he vacated your body."

Jake seemed to think about that. "Ja, that's what I mean. Ambroos is not going to be very happy when I tell him the Tarocks worked when he and all his Deacons couldn't do anything."

"Maybe don't tell him," Nathaniel suggested.

There was an awkward silence.

"I think I'm dead," Jake said.

"Yes," Nathaniel agreed. "But Sarah needs your help."

"I have nothing else to do." Jake grinned. "What does she need?"

"Wait a minute," Nathaniel said. "There's someone else. Come with me."

They walked along the edge of the pond and upstream, until they came to Isaiah Wilkes. The man had stopped singing. He looked at the two of them with wide-open eyes.

"Who are you?" Wilkes asked.

"My name is Nathaniel. I'm a healer."

"What did you just do with Simon Sword?"

"Unfortunately, that wasn't really Simon Sword. It was more a shadow. Not really memories of him, but his memories, trapped inside someone else."

"Trapped inside *me*," Jake said.

Wilkes's eyes narrowed. "I think I've heard of you. You met a friend of mine."

"I've met a lot of people."

"You would have known her as a tongueless Choctaw whore."

Jake smiled. "Who visited the prison hulks of the Chevalier of New Orleans? I remember her well."

"You gave her a coin."

Jake shrugged. "Simon Sword gave her a coin, but he was inside my body at the time."

"We need your help," Nathaniel said to Wilkes.

"What with?" Wilkes asked. "I'm dead. And even if it was only a shadow you were dealing with, I saw what you just did. I couldn't have done it."

"You're an actor, right?" Nathaniel asked. "You do the Philadelphia Mystery Plays?"

"And other plays," Wilkes said.

"And you're the head of a conspiracy that exists to stop Simon Sword's reappearance in the world," Jake added.

"I would say a *senior figure* of an *esoteric coalition*," Wilkes said. "Yes."

"My sister is Sarah Elytharias Penn," Nathaniel said. "She has taken the throne of Cahokia, and she is besieged there by both the Emperor and the Heron King. She is attempting to reconstruct the enthronement ritual of the Mother of All Living, because she believes that if she can ascend the throne, that will give her the power she needs to defeat her enemies. She needs help with the reconstruction. She also needs two people who...have ears to hear...to participate in the liturgy as guides. I think, on both counts, you two are the best help I can possibly find her."

Isaiah Wilkes nodded. "I'll do it, on one condition."

Nathaniel smiled. "I think you'll do it anyway, because we want the same thing. But tell me what your condition is."

"That afterward, you check on my friend. Her name is Kinta Jane Embry. If she's alive, she's headed north to Montreal."

Nathaniel nodded. "Agreed. Now, let's look at those Tarocks."

At Logan Rupp's suggestion, Calvin booked seats for the two of them and Olanthes Kuta on an Imperial mail coach. "We'll make fifty miles a day, riding on stone-paved Imperial pikes all the way. It'll take us twice as long if we ride our own horses. With the snow, four times as long on some other road."

Cal objected that he felt uncomfortable in the presence of Imperial officers, even if they were just carrying the post.

"You think too much of yourself," Rupp said. "No one knows who you are."

"Yet." Olanthes smiled. The expression made the scar on his face turn white.

Rupp shrugged. "Fine, yet. This is why you're going, and not the Elector. If he tried to ride the mails, he'd be noticed for sure. If Thomas Penn has given instructions to stop any person from coming up from Nashville, it's Andrew Calhoun."

The three men sat bundled in an Imperial mail coach, Cal and Rupp watching the white-cloaked mountains rattle past through fogged glass windows. Olanthes mostly slept. They rode through Knoxville, past the turnoff to Asheville, and through Blacksburg, all Free Imperial Towns. In each city, Cal huddled down inside his gray coat and tried to look inconspicuous.

"Stop it," Rupp muttered to him as they climbed back into the coach, shaking Blacksburg snow off their boots.

"Stop what?"

"Stop looking guilty. You carry an Elector's proxy, and you're going into the Electoral Assembly to make a formal motion. You can't do that skulking like a thief."

Cal's laugh was dry and short. "I reckon mebbe I'm a cattle rustler, after all."

"Well, that just makes you Hermes, doesn't it?"

"I know my Bible pretty well," Cal said. "Can't say as I remember a feller named Hermes."

"He's not in the Bible," Olanthes said. "He was a Greek god."

"He was a messenger." Rupp smiled cheerfully, the cold and the sips of brandy with which he was warming himself every half hour gave a rosy glow to his cheeks. "So that's you. As a baby, he got up out of his crib and stole a herd of cows belonging to his brother Apollo."

"Alright, I reckon there's a passing resemblance," Cal allowed.

"You'll like this, wait." The coach rattled on. "He walked the cattle out of their pasture backward. That way, it would look like someone else had driven a second herd into the same pasture as Apollo's cattle, and that both herds had somehow disappeared."

"Lord hates a man as tells a fib, counselor," Cal said. "Everyone knows you can't git a cow to walk backward, not for love or money. Even the Lightning Bishop wouldn't tell a tall tale like that one."

"Do you want to hear the rest of the story or not?" Rupp glared.

Cal shrugged. "It's a long way to Philadelphia. I reckon I might as well."

"Apollo figured out the trick," Rupp said. "By the time he had found his brother and the herd, though, young Hermes had killed two of the cows and converted their guts and bones into the first lyre. That's a bit like a banjo—it's a musical instrument."

"More like a harp," Cal said.

"Oh, yes. Well, Apollo was so fascinated by the lyre that he agreed to let Hermes keep the cows if he'd give Apollo the instrument."

"More fool Apollo." Cal felt sour. He wasn't sure what the lawyer was going to do to help him on this trip, but he had definitely been manipulated into bringing the man along. He didn't trust him, either, not after he learned all the business about his bankruptcy. "He could have taken back ninety-eight cows, slaughtered two, and made his own lyre. Would have still had ninety-six cows, then."

"Not everyone is as confident in his ability to make things as you are," Rupp said.

"See, now you got me wrong all o'er the place. Yeah, I rustled cattle. But I ain't some woodcarver, that's my grandpa. I'm a trader and a tracker. I can fight and I can find my way jest about anywhere. I seen my share of strange things and I ain't afraid to stand up and tell the truth, when tellin' the truth is what's necessary. But I ain't a harp-maker and I ain't a harp player and I ain't a messenger, except by accident. I reckon iffen Andy felt confident he could trust you entirely, Huber—or Rupp, or whatever your name is—then you'd be here alone and I'd be up in the high valleys, keepin' an eye out for Donelsens with a hankerin' for beef."

The lawyer was stiff and silent for a moment. The postal carriers sat atop the carriage, wrapped in furs and watching for outlaws the Foresters didn't manage to deal with. Cal, Rupp, and Olanthes were alone with canvas bags full of mail.

"I understand that the Elector was surprised to learn of my prior life," the lawyer said slowly. "My name is Rupp. And given the time that has passed, and the Elector's letter, I intend to be called *Rupp* in public in Philadelphia. So please, let's get used to that now."

"Fine," Cal agreed. "Rupp."

"And I don't believe that the Elector mistrusts me. I don't think he'd have sent me along at all if he didn't trust me really well. I think if he thought I'd betray you or fail you, he'd have had me thrown off the top of Calhoun Mountain without a second thought."

Cal laughed. "Mebbe."

"I admit to ambition. I admit to wanting to get back to Philadelphia and, Calvin, I did try to outmaneuver you. But I thought you were just an errand boy, one of the Elector's many kin who didn't know how to do more than take orders. I thought I'd serve the Elector better than you could."

"You thought I was Hermes," Cal said. "Jest a messenger."

"Touché," Rupp said. "I apologize for the story and I retract it entirely. Calvin, you're your own man and I respect you."

"You shouldn't ought to overestimate my kin, though," Cal said. "Most of 'em *don't* know how to take orders."

"Let's be allies, Calvin." Rupp smiled broadly and stuck out a hand.

Cal took it, trying not to show the wariness he felt.

"While we're all agreeing to be allies," Olanthes said, "can you tell me the plan?"

"I'm sorry," Cal said. "I thought the Elector—"

"He told me he was sending all the men he could to Cahokia." Olanthes was very pale. Cal wasn't sure whether that was just his complexion, or because of his recent tangle with death. "I said I'd return with them, and he asked me to go with you to Philadelphia as a witness instead."

"I'm gonna need your testimony about the siege of Cahokia," Cal said. "I ain't seen that part with my own eyes."

"Are we going to try to get the Electoral Assembly to end the Pacification of the Ohio?"

Rupp laughed. "That sounds like a *good* idea. We're going to attempt something much less prudent."

Olanthes's face showed mild surprise. "What's that?"

"We're going to try to get Electors to vote to impeach the Emperor," Cal said, "and then remove him from office."

Rupp positively cackled and began to count grounds off on his fingers. "One, conspiring to murder Kyres Elytharias, an Elector. Two, conspiring to keep that crime secret, including by paying blackmail with funds raised from Imperial taxes. Three, contriving a war against Kyres's daughter Sarah, in order further to conceal his crime and its consequences. Four, the sequestering on false grounds of his sister, at the time the Penn Landholder as well as an Elector. Five, her murder. Six, the Pacification of the Ohio and specifically the siege of Cahokia. Of course, we may allege fewer formal grounds—easier to prove—but the Electors will be considering all of these."

"How does this work?" Olanthes asked. "I barely know my Elector Songs, much less the technical details of the Compact. Is there some list of deeds for which the Emperor can be removed from office?"

"I wish it were that simple," Cal said glumly, and returned to staring out the window.

"Simple, no," Rupp said. "But it will be exciting!"

"It is a grim business."

———— ➤◆◄ ————

CHAPTER TWENTY-FIVE

A few miles north of the city, in a thick stand of pine trees, Mesh brought Kinta Jane and Dockery to his camp. The first sign Kinta Jane noticed of the camp was a deep growling sound.

"Chak! 'Uutz!" Mesh snapped, but the growling only increased.

"I apologize for my dogs," the giant said. "I live a lonely sort of life, despicable person of no social standing that I am, and they keep me company. Like me, they're not civilized. At least, not by your standards."

"I'm from New Orleans," Kinta Jane said. "My standards as to what's civilized might surprise you."

She walked forward toward the camp, pushing through snow up to her knees.

"Kinta Jane!" Dockery tried to grab her arm to stop her, but she was already past him and entering the grove.

The dogs stopped barking just as they came into Kinta Jane's view.

Only they weren't dogs. They looked like dogs, of a breed that had a significant amount of wolf in its ancestry, but their shoulders were as high off the ground as Kinta Jane's waist. As Kinta Jane stepped forward, they strained on their chains and opened their mouths...

And then looked at each other, puzzled.

"Good boys," Kinta Jane said. She held out her hands for the dogs to smell her, but they slunk away in shame and defeat.

"That's quite a trick," Dockery said.

"They're not boys," Mesh said. "'Chak' means flower and ''Uutz' is a kind of poetic stanza."

"You have a bitch the size of a pony and mean as hell," Dockery said. "And you named her *flower*."

Mesh laughed, flashing his teeth at the trees. "What should I name her? Fang? Wolf? Dog? Rex? Dockery?"

"Well, I wouldn't have said we were friends, but I admit that hurts a mite."

"Be careful around my dogs," Mesh said. "Don't try to pet them or feed them, and if you're bleeding, stay out of their way. We use only bitches for our fighting animals. Our trainers make them mean and angry by being cruel to their puppies. Then they are taught to trust only one person, who will be their master. In the case of these dogs, that's me."

The giant reached into a leather satchel hanging from one of the trees and pulled out several strips of red, raw meat. He flung these to the beasts, who shrank away from Kinta Jane, eyeing her resentfully as they settled down to eat.

The camp consisted of a snow cave with two entrances, at one of which was a small fireplace, a sheltered spot within reach of their tethers where the dogs lay on a pile of tattered wool blankets. There was also a large backpack, propped up against a tree. Standing up in the snow were multiple oval frames, some three feet long and others closer to five, with hide and thongs stretched within the frame. Kinta Jane stared at them for a minute before she managed to puzzle them out.

"Those are for walking on snow," she said to Dockery. "Like you were talking about."

The giant looked at Dockery with curiosity in his eyes. "You know the art of walking with the aagimag?"

Dockery shrugged. "I walked in snowshoes before. I expect I could use a little practice, if we're planning to walk much in this snow."

"We may do some walking," Mesh said. "We will also ride beasts. It's hard to pass unnoticed on the river."

"Beasts?" Dockery asked.

Mesh ignored him.

"Why do you have to be so cruel to the dogs?" Kinta Jane asked.

"I'm not cruel to them. I'm loving. The trainer was cruel."

"But why? Why do you need such a large dog to be so ferocious?"

"We keep these dogs to fight bear," Mesh said. "And hunt elk. And warn us of strangers. And chase away the wiindigoo and beastkind that have strayed too far to the north. And we take the dogs to war. They would serve us nothing if they were not ferocious and also ferociously loyal. What did you do to them? Why are they sad?"

Kinta Jane shrugged. "Dogs react that way to me." It wasn't a lie, but something about the way Dockery was acting made her uncomfortable around the giant. There was no need to tell the whole truth this early in their relationship.

"You have beastkind blood?"

Kinta Jane was startled. "Is that a possibility?"

Mesh shrugged. "It happens. Sometimes people with such ancestry don't even know it. Some beastkind have only very subtle features. And really, who can ever know for sure whether their grandmother has a cat's tail, or not? And dogs sometimes react badly to beastkind."

"I don't think that's it, though," Kinta Jane said.

Mesh shrugged. "Well, unless you like your meat raw, we need food. Why don't you stay here, and I'll go find us a nice bit of elk? I am a terrible hunter, loud as a herd of bison in heat when I tromp through the woods, but this land is so thick with game, even a fool as I will be able to bring back a deer."

"Or a bear." Dockery nodded. "Bear chops are worth eating."

Mesh nodded. "Maybe you get a nice fire started. It will keep you warm until I get back, and then we can roast the meat."

By the time Mesh had strung his bow and strapped his feet into two of the longer snowshoes, the dogs had finished gulping down their meat. He stooped to disconnect the chains that held them from their collars—which Kinta Jane now saw were of broad, thick leather, with iron spikes studding them. Mesh rubbed both animals behind the ears, and then barked several syllables of his guttural language at them.

Smiling at Kinta Jane and Dockery as if he'd made a hilarious joke and they should be laughing, Mesh shuffled out of camp.

The dogs followed him. The shadows were getting long.

Dockery stepped close to Kinta Jane to whisper. "We need to get out of here."

"Why?"

"Look at his snowshoes. Notice anything about them that makes you nervous?"

"That he has a whole bunch of snowshoes?"

Dockery nodded. "Yeah, that's one thing. Also, look at them. Those big ones are Misaabe make, you can tell by their long, tapering, pointed heels."

"The smaller ones are different," Kinta Jane said. "More rounded. Who made those?"

"Algonks of some kind, I expect."

"He was waiting for us, so he bought snowshoes."

"You don't *buy* snowshoes, Kinta Jane," Dockery said. "You make 'em. He might have made those three big pairs, but it seems a hell of a thing to do for the sake of boredom. But he didn't make the smaller ones."

"You think he killed someone," Kinta Jane said.

"I think it's a distinct possibility that whoever Brother Odish-kwa is, or was...our man Mesh killed him. I think maybe he even killed Brother Anak, too. And I might be wrong, but I want to get out of this camp right now, and figure out later just who Mesh is and what he wants."

Kinta Jane didn't wait for more. She turned and trudged out of camp, heading back to Montreal. There she could get a room in an inn, under an assumed name if she had to. Maybe she could even seek help from La Fayette or Champlain. She regretted they hadn't gone to the Acadian Electors in the first place.

At the edge of the camp, the dogs waited for her. They bared their teeth, snarling in all but the actual emission of sound.

Their eyes were full of hate and vengeance.

"That thing you do with dogs," Dockery said. "Any chance it will stop them from biting *both* of us?"

"I don't think it will even stop them from biting *me*."

"Then we got two choices. We kill the dogs right now and run. Or we wait for a better opportunity."

"Mesh can't be a hundred yards away," Kinta Jane said. "With those long legs, and him wearing the snowshoes, he'd catch us for sure."

"Dammit," Dockery said, "but I think you're right."

Kinta Jane eased back from the edge of camp several steps. "In that case, I think we should probably start a fire."

"Keep your weapons handy." Dockery took sticks from a small pile of wood near the fire and began to build them into a pyramid. "It might not be an elk he's bringing back."

"Ye've changed staff somewhat, Your Grace." Eoin Kennedie smiled at the form of address, but it wasn't a hostile smile. "Was your old bodyguard eaten by lions, or borne into heaven on a chariot of fire?"

Etienne, Onyinye, and Eoin sat in the corner room above a tavern called *Grissot's* in the Vieux Carré. The room had windows facing in two directions, and each of them had a pair of companions to stand on the iron-railed balcony outside and watch the drizzle-soaked streets. Eoin had his two jackanapes brothers, Roibeard and Teodoir; Onyinye had a pair of burly men Etienne vaguely thought might be her cousins; and Etienne himself had Monsieur Bondí and the wrestler Achebe.

Bondí was the only one of the six companions to sit at the table with the principals.

Etienne himself had cast quick looks down both directions before joining his allies at their table. He'd seen three gendarme deserters whipped bloody and hugging the posts to which they were chained, but otherwise none of the chevalier's men.

"The thing about lions," Etienne said, "is that once they've eaten a Christian or two, they become convinced they're kings. But at the end of the day, they're still just beasts in the bottom of a pit."

"You've stopped the lion's meat," Onyinye said. "Now what? Throw in more Christians? See if they can overwhelm the hungry cat?"

Etienne laughed. "Let's drop the allegory to avoid confusion. The chevalier recruited huge numbers of men. We hurt his income in a few different ways, so paying his large army has caused him to run out of wealth. Now he can no longer pay them. This results in desertions, punishments, low morale, poor behavior, lawlessness, and unhappy citizens even less willing to collect and pay their taxes."

"The lawless citizens are my favorite part." Eoin picked at something in his teeth with a long fingernail. "I must tell ye, my business is booming."

"And all the while," Etienne continued, "I appear from time

to time on a street corner, or in a house meeting, or even at a Vodun congregation, to preach disobedience to the unrighteous chevalier."

"You are making the city ungovernable." Onyinye smiled.

"That is the goal." Etienne touched his mother's locket with thumb and forefinger. *Well done, my son.*

"I admire the ruthlessness of a man who was seeking to replace his father as bishop while his father yet lived," Onyinye said.

"I admire a woman who will kill her own cousin to get what she wants," Etienne answered.

"Well, you both bloody well scare the shit out of me." Eoin chuckled.

"I didn't kill him." Onyinye's face had an unusual softness to it. "The mameluke fought back and killed my cousin. We made his death appear to be at the hand of the same assassin, to throw the prince-capitaine off the track."

"And I was not seeking to replace my father. I was seeking to succeed him, and I was doing it because my mother bid it."

"Your gede loa. Your personal goddess."

Etienne hesitated, but nodded. "One of them."

"Ain't that sweet?" Eoin Kennedie chuckled. "I'd tell ye both my sentimental secrets, cement our alliance and our friendship, only I don't have any."

"Keep your secrets." Etienne cleared his throat. "Monsieur Bondí has been working with all the pawnbrokers within the walls of New Orleans on a related project."

"That's a terrible business, if you do it honestly." Eoin grinned. *Pawnbroker* was a euphemism and sometimes a cover for Eoin's very business, which was fencing stolen goods.

"It is indeed a hard business," Bondí agreed. "Low margins, slow turnover. It turns out that if you're willing to buy a few items, pawnbrokers will talk to you."

Etienne feigned displeasure. "Monsieur Bondí, please tell me you're not storing all this junk in my tent."

Bondí shook his head. "I throw it all into the Pontchartrain. And it's not junk, it's good swords men inherited from their grandfathers, fathers' pistols, antique powder horns. Soldiers' things. The sorts of things a successful soldier fallen on hard times—say, an officer who hasn't been paid in weeks—might pawn."

"Or a gendarme," Eoin said.

"You devious bastard." Onyinye smiled at Etienne. Was that respect in her face?

"It isn't me," Etienne admitted. "Monsieur Bondí would have made an excellent lawyer, or judge, or witchfinder."

Bondí shrugged. "I think through the consequences. I like to ask myself, *if this were true, what sort of evidence would I see for it?* It's all forensic accounting, really."

"I don't know what forensic accounting is," Eoin admitted, "but if ye ever want a job, Bondí, ye've only to say the word."

"I won't trade him for Roibeard, if that's what you're thinking," Etienne said. "Or for him and Teodoir both."

"No, you don't trade away your kin. I'd just have to pay my new forensic accountant an ungodly excellent wage."

"I can certainly match *ungodly.*" Etienne smiled. "I'll have to let him speak to the *excellence* of the wages."

"This is very flattering," Bondí said, "But I'd like to tell you more about what I've been up to. I've been looking for gendarme officers who are dissatisfied. Frustrated ambition, poverty rather than wealth."

"The ones complaining the loudest," Eoin said.

"No," Bondí said.

"Not the loudest," Onyinye explained. "They're the most likely to be planted by the chevalier himself as spies."

"Correct," Etienne said.

"Or else the most likely to just be useless loudmouths," Bondí added. "No, I wanted men of honor unhappy with the current situation. Men with a history of decisive action. Veterans of a war, preferably. The Spanish War, or Jackson's invasion, more likely. Men of resolution."

"If you've brought us here, it's because you've found such a man." Eoin spoke to Bondí, but he looked closely at Etienne.

"Three such men," Bondí said. "They'll be arriving momentarily."

Etienne passed out the simple black hoods he'd brought. "The men know they're coming to meet me. They've been given hoods like these, as well. But there's no reason to expose *your* identities."

Onyinye promptly pulled on the mask. Eoin shrugged as if indifferent, but then put his on as well. Etienne lit the oil lantern sitting on the table and Monsieur Bondí closed the shutters to discreetly conceal the faces of the men on the balcony.

"I trust we're all armed," Etienne said. "Just in case any of

the three has second thoughts and wants to become the chevalier's darling?"

"Of course," Onyinye said.

Eoin only snorted and rapped a knuckle against one of the
plates sewn into his leather coat.

There came a knock at the door. "I shall play Papa Legba,"
Etienne said, "and admit those who are to be admitted. Or at
least, my man shall do so."

Bondí whispered at the door while Etienne smiled reassurance at his two partners. It was a little disconcerting not to be
able to read their facial expressions in return.

A man came in and sat. He was tall and heavy, and the skin of
his hands was dark brown. "Nous attendons des autres?" he asked.

"Oui," Etienne said. "Moi, je suis l'évêque."

"Monseigneur." The man nodded his head. "Je connaissais
votre père."

Etienne was caught by surprise, though given Monsieur Bondí's
description of the sort of men he'd been looking for, he shouldn't
have been. He merely nodded, fighting a surprising flood of emotion.

He reached into his waistcoat and rubbed his thumb on the
edge of his mother's locket.

Bondí admitted a second man, as tall as the first, but with
paler-skinned hands and a long black queue of hair that fell down
out of his mask and between his shoulderblades. The man wore his
gendarme's uniform, and his boots and belt were highly polished.
He clicked his heels together and bowed toward the entire table.

"Bonjour," Etienne said.

"Thank you," the man said in English.

"Ah, a rarity," Etienne said. "An English-speaking gendarme.
And was that a Pennslander accent I heard?"

The man with the queue coughed as if embarrassed. "It may
be, Your Grace. I've never paid all that much attention to accents."

The third man followed close on the second's heels. This man
was shorter than the other two, broad-shouldered and stocky. He
dressed as if he were a sailor, in a white blouse and blue canvas
pants, with rope sandals on his feet.

Nodding to the rest, he sat down.

Monsieur Bondí took up a position to the side of the table.
"Allow me to make introductions," he said. "This is my master,
the Bishop of New Orleans."

The first gendarme chuckled. "And devotee of Maitre Carrefour, and gangster."

Etienne arched an eyebrow.

"I knew your father," the gendarme said. "And your brother, Chigozie. And I know you as well, Etienne Ukwu."

Etienne decided not to respond.

"Your Grace." The other two gendarmes bobbed their heads.

"You're all here for the same reason," Bondí said. "The chevalier is failing the city."

The second gendarme, the man with his hair in a queue, cleared his throat as if in alarm. "Perhaps we can speak in more general terms than that."

"You were rather specific when you and I were alone," Bondí said.

"We're not alone now," the gendarme said. "And I have heard of the Bishop here, but I don't know who his companions are, and I don't know these gentlemen."

"Think of us as the bishop's angel choir," Onyinye said.

"Or altar boys," Eoin added. "Or deacons. Or—what do ye call 'em—suffragans."

Queue laughed, but uneasily. "I appreciate the humor. But I feel that I've gone very quickly from a casual conversation in which things were said that I might not have said if I had been a little less drunk, and that I might not really have meant, to an invitation that I commit myself to revolt in front of masked strangers."

"Cold feet, eh?" The first gendarme chuckled softly. "That's not what they call you around the barracks, is it? Cold Feet Hollings?"

"Cold *Heart*," Queue snarled, then hesitated. "You know me."

"Everyone knows you, Hollings. Don't you recognize *me*?"

Hollings tore off his mask and stared at the other man. "Yes!"

The first gendarme chuckled. "Liar. You never had an eye for anyone who wasn't a superior officer or a lady. Preferably the wife or daughter of a superior officer."

"The time has come to take off your masks, gentlemen," Etienne said. "If we're going to work together, we must know each other."

The two gendarmes removed their masks.

"I've introduced myself," Etienne said. "You, sir, are Cold Heart Hollings."

"Lieutenant Gerald Hollings," the gendarme said. "I fought against Jackson. I shot him at least once myself."

"While he was shooting back at you?" the first gendarme asked. "Or do you mean while you wandered the Place d'Armes, drunk, and he was already dead and harmless in his iron cage?"

"Do not mock me..." Hollings trailed off, flailing to remember a name.

"Eggbert Bailey," the other man said.

"I don't know the name *Eggbert*," Etienne said. Bondí's hand was close to a pistol he'd hidden behind the window shutters, but Etienne wanted to defuse the situation if he could. "It almost sounds English."

"Might be Jamaican," Eggbert said. His head matched his torso, enormous and solid, framed within a shock of tightly curled braids, and he seemed to wear a permanent confident grin. "I've got some of that in me. Some Igbo, too, maybe some Cherokee, who knows what else?"

"A good New Orleans Creole," Bondí said. "Like me."

Eggbert laughed. "We could be brothers."

"My name is Alexandre Durand," the third volunteered. He looked less cocksure than Bailey, but had a cheerful smile.

"My God," Hollings said, "I know these men."

"Of course you do." Eggbert snorted. "Do you think you're going to start a revolt with *strangers*?"

Hollings stood up. "No. But if I were ever to do anything of the sort—and I'm not saying I would, I'm only saying in *theory*—then I'd do it with men I honored. Men who honored *me*. Not naysayers and scoundrels."

"Nobody has said anybody else here is a scoundrel," Durand said. "You are overreacting, Hollings."

"Yes," Eggbert agreed. "You're out of line, Hollings. Sit down."

"I'm finished." Hollings spun on his heel, as if to make for the door.

Eggbert caught his wrist. "I think you really want to consider that carefully, friend."

"Unhand me," Hollings said.

Eggbert released the other man, but didn't move his hand far. "I've seen your face, and you've also seen mine. If you're not with us, I can't really let you leave here with the ability to speak."

"The ability to..." Hollings's face turned an ashen gray color. "You're threatening me."

"No," Eggbert said. "I'm only explaining the logic of the

situation. Monsieur Bondí has forced our hand. Either we all leave together, wanting nothing to do with this, and we go directly to the chevalier to tell him all the details, or we're all in together."

"I'm in," Durand said.

"You see?" Eggbert said to Hollings. "Now you and I, either we kill Durand and leave here as loyal gendarmes of the chevalier, or we join him."

Without a flash of warning, Hollings sprang around the table. He scooped up Etienne before Etienne could react, and pressed a cold knife blade to Etienne's throat.

Bondí had his pistol in his hand, but he wasn't a great shot, and Etienne wasn't sure his accountant could hit the big gendarme without shooting Etienne.

"I've got another suggestion!" Hollings snarled. "For starters, I don't like the fact that the two of you are still wearing your masks. It doesn't show a lot of trust."

"Easy, lad," Eoin Kennedie said. "Ye don't want to do this, I promise ye."

"Take them off," Hollings said coldly.

Suddenly, the knife blade disappeared from Etienne's throat and went flying across the room. In the next instant, Hollings went spinning after it, screaming and clutching at his elbow, which had been smashed so forcefully it was bent backward. With the abrupt movement, Etienne stumbled, but Achebe was there to catch him.

Eggbert Bailey was nearly as fast as the Igbo wrestler. Springing to his feet, he pulled a long knife from his boot. As Hollings caught his balance and turned to face Etienne again, still screaming, Bailey knocked him against the wall with a shoulder and then sank the knife blade into his neck.

The scream cut off with a sudden gurgle and the blade sank all the way into the plaster of the wall. Hollings squirmed, but only for the two seconds it took Bailey to get a firm grip on his weapon's handle and jerk the blade sideways, cutting Hollings's head clean off.

Hollings collapsed in blood, his head bouncing and rolling across the room until it stopped at Durand's chair, eyes and mouth gaping at the ceiling.

Durand turned and smiled at Etienne, still calm and cheerful. "You want a revolt. It seems you have your men."

Eggbert stepped lightly across the room and switched his grip on his knife. Raising the blade, he stabbed Durand downward, through the other man's clavicle and into his chest. The blade sank all the way up to the hilt; Durand opened his mouth and spewed purple blood in a fountain into his own lap.

Bondí pointed his pistol at Bailey, who raised his hands to show peaceful intention and stepped back. "The problem with Alexandre Durand," he said, "is that the man was an informer. So you have to ask yourself, *what does the chevalier know about this meeting already?*"

"Very little," Bondí said, speaking to Etienne, Onyinye, and Eoin. "I told him to expect a message. He was handed this address on a scrap of paper only an hour before arriving here."

"An hour is a long time for determined men." Bailey pointed to his weapon. "May I take my knife back?"

Etienne nodded. "But first, take this." He tossed a purse to Bailey, who caught it and looked inside.

Bondí kept his pistol trained on Bailey.

"Revenue from your casino?" the gendarme asked.

Etienne shook his head. "That money is the gift of certain wealthy New Orleans families. The chevalier had suggested that a ransom would be necessary to procure the liberation of their loved ones. Since we freed their loved ones instead, the grateful families gave *us* the cash."

Bailey laughed harshly. "Or more likely, gave you half what old Gaspard asked for. Good. This will help persuade men to join me, and buy weapons that can be stashed away from the chevalier's official armories."

Bondí relaxed his aim.

Eggbert extracted his weapon, wiped it clean on Durand's sailor's blouse, and then resheathed it. "We should meet again later. We should go our separate ways immediately, and watch for signs that we are followed."

"How do we know we can trust you?" Onyinye asked.

Bondí looked shaken at the hotelier's question, which was reasonable. But the implication was that two of the three men Bondí had chosen had already proved problematic.

"I fought in eighteen-ten," Eggbert Bailey said. "But I didn't fight for the chevalier. I fought for Jackson. I marched on those pirate Lafittes and their criminal militia with freedom and liberation in my heart. Many of Le Moyne's gendarmes died, and in the hectic days after Jackson was killed, it was easy to claim I had been part of the New Orleans militia defending the city. A big man like me, who could fight? They'd have been crazy to turn me away. I said what I had to say and I did what I had to do. To survive."

"Are ye some sort of Jackson revivalist?" Eoin asked. "Are ye hoping to make yourself King of the Mississippi?"

"No," Etienne said. "He's hoping to regain his honor."

Eggbert Bailey smiled. "With all due respect, You Grace, you're mistaken, too. I'm hoping to regain my *soul*."

"Tell me what to do, General!"

Luman stayed low on the wall, conscious of the bullets that whizzed over its top as well as the cannonballs—slowly becoming more frequent—that slammed into its length.

Bill was haggard, his complexion gray even in the torchlight that should have left him looking orange. "Can you join the wizards in their effort?"

The Polites, family magicians, priestesses, and other high magicians of Cahokia stood interspersed among Cahokia's guns. Luman wasn't sure he knew entirely what they were doing, but he thought that as Cahokians died—struck by musket- or cannon-ball, or falling off the wall, or for any other reason—the wizards were capturing the soul-energy that was released and preventing it from being sucked into the Sorcerer Hooke's ring of black fire.

And maybe also using the energy to deflect bullets.

Luman held up open hands. "I'm not a gramarist. I don't have the power or the flexibility to do what they do, weaving together spells out of thin air. I have spells I've memorized, to do specific things."

"I don't need a girl to fall in love with me today." Bill squinted through his spyglass at the Imperial trenches. Dawn was still hours away, so what glints of light the Cavalier might be catching through his seeing tube, Luman couldn't guess. "Or to find a lost object, or dig a well, or any such country wizard stuff. Can you heal?"

"I can help you see better," Luman said. "Then I'll join Mrs. Filmer."

"Do that," Bill said. "Only perhaps call her *Cathy*. She likes that better."

A bullet plucked Bill's sleeve to the side, neatly perforating his cuff on two sides.

"May I borrow the glass?" Luman asked.

Bill handed it over and turned, shouting at the Pitcher commander Zorales, fifty feet away. "No shots fired until you can kill a hell of a lot of them! When they come, I want to see bloody furrows!"

Zorales waved in acknowledgement.

Bill turned the other direction and bellowed at a woman with short hair dressed in Polite red. "Protect the cannons if you can, but above all, the wall must stand. As long as we can possibly manage it, the wall must stand!"

Strictly speaking, the powwow Luman was about to attempt was a remedy for poor eyesight. Also strictly speaking, he knew he should repeat the prayer and action over several days. Also, he should use running water.

But he had none of those luxuries.

"May I borrow a handful of water?" he asked the women sighting alongside the nearest cannon.

They dipped a wooden ladle into a bucket beside their gun— whether it was intended for use in cooling in cleaning the gun, or for the gunners to drink, Luman couldn't tell—and handed him the ladle.

Please, God of Heaven, let this work. My intent is pure; I wish to save life; I have nothing else to gain by this but service to your creatures.

Trapping the spyglass under one arm, he washed the larger lens with his left hand five times. Each time, he repeated the same prayer:

"Wie dieses Salz wird vergehen; sollen meine Augen heller sehen; Christus ist der helfen kann; hiermit fangt der Seegen an."

After each prayer, he dropped a pinch of salt from a bottle taken from a breast pocket of his coat and dissolved it into the water. After the fifth washing, he poured out the remaining water onto the Treewall. Then he handed the ladle back to the Pitchers and the glass to the Cavalier.

"You may not have the flexibility or power of the Polites," Bill said, "but I'll give you this: you have considerably more theatrical flair. I believe I might pay to watch you perform, in better circumstances."

"Thank you," Luman said. "I think."

He carefully took seven steps backward, as required by the working, and then turned and walked toward the stairs. Ideally, he should now walk to his own home to complete the charm.

But where was his home now, anyway? Where had it ever been?

Cahokia didn't have a Harvite convent. It did have an assortment of herbalists, cunning women, family healers, former ship's surgeons, and volunteers, who were all organized under Cathy Filmer. Luman found Cathy in the gap between the Treewall and a dense block of residential mounds. She knelt over a man who lay with a twisted back. She was holding his hand and talking to him earnestly.

Gazelem Zomas stood at her shoulder.

"You may die, my friend," Cathy said. "This is terrible news, and I am sorry. We'll do everything we can, but the bad news is that our best wizards are occupied catching bullets and throwing them back at the enemy."

The man with the twisted back wore the gray cloak and tunic of a Cahokian warden, over knee-high boots. He grinned, blood on his lips. "I hope they hit the bastards in the eye."

"Your duty to your queen now," Cathy continued gravely, "is to live absolutely as long as you can. We'll try our best to heal you. We'll try our best to dull your pain. You focus on living."

Gazelem knelt beside the broken man. "This won't heal you, but it will help with the pain." He tilted a metal flask to the man's lips and poured several drops of some liquid into the man's mouth.

Luman recognized the smell of laudanum.

"Our best wizards are on the wall," Luman said. "However, we do have a few completely mediocre wizards down here among the injured. Let me see what I can do."

To Bill's surprise, the hedge wizard's abracadabra over the spyglass worked. Looking through it, despite the darkness that reigned more than an hour before the dawn, he saw Robert Hooke. Hooke stood well behind the Imperial trench, immobile and staring. The unnatural posture made Bill uncomfortable— what was Hooke doing?

Was it possible that Cahokia's magicians were failing, and that the energy of the city's deaths was, in fact, being stolen by Hooke and his spell?

Bill examined the throbbing wall of black fire and found himself uncomfortably unable to pronounce one way or the other on the subject.

Following the line of the wall of fire, his eye fell on a boy, or maybe a short young man. He might be Sarah's age. Despite the cold, he stood naked in the snow.

"Another cannon has joined the shooting." This observation came from Montserrat Ferrer i Quintana, who stood at Bill's side.

Bill listened, and then nodded stiffly. "We earned damnably little time with our sacrifices."

"Was there ever a loss in war that did not earn a damnably small return?" Montse's smile was rueful.

"I knew you for a hellcat and an adventuress," Bill said. "It was even money at Hannah's court whether you would wind up conquering and then dominating some Elector husband, or become openly acknowledged as Hannah's lover."

Montse's response was gentle and quiet. "When you say *openly acknowledged*, you assume far too much."

"I do." Movement in the corner of Bill's field of vision caught his attention, and he followed it. Something was happening in the trench. "I also *pre*sume too much. Your relationship with the Empress, or with the Imperial Consort, is none of my affair. If you will forgive the turn of phrase."

"I don't think I will forgive it," Montse said. "You are saying things about my Empress that should not be spoken."

"Because they're not true?"

"Because they should not be spoken. What makes you so envious, Captain Lee? That I had a relationship with Hanna so close as to inspire such rumors? Or that you did not have such a relationship with Kyres?"

"I am not . . . I am not the sort of man." Bill felt discomfited. "Hell's Bells."

"Yes," Montse agreed. "Hell's Bells. I think they will toll today."

"Not for our queen." Bill clenched his jaw.

"For many of us, I am sure. May they not toll for Sarah." Montse looked abruptly sad. "Or Margarida."

"Or Nathaniel." Bill looked at the angular, copper-haired Catalan woman, as if remembering for the first time that she had saved Sarah's sister, as Bill had saved her brother.

"No one at court would have wagered on my becoming a

smuggler. Curious, in that it is my family business. The Quintanas, at least. The Ferrers own land—it's from them I have a castle."

"You have a castle?" Bill whistled. Something was definitely moving inside the ditch, clambering to get out. "I don't think the ballroom crowd of Philadelphia knows the Quintanas."

"No doubt the Quintanas prefer it that way. Though they are well known in Louisiana and in New Spain. I have had three uncles hanged by Spanish alcaldes."

"After your uncles killed how many Spaniards?"

"Considerably more than three. Though I think my uncles' downfall was due more to the robbery, smuggling, counterfeiting, and theft than the mere killing of a few soldiers and revenue men. Even under the Bourbons, Spain and New Spain have many, many sons to sow into the ground, hoping to find they can grow an empire."

"It is a grim business." Bill sighed. "Is it more grim than what you and I do?"

"Yes," Montse said.

"Why do you fight, then?" he asked her. "And smuggle, and rob, if not to build your own kind of empire? Surely you, too, have thrown the corpses of customs officers into bayous full of gators, or taken the lives of gendarmes who came too close to finding you."

"Bread and gold are far too easy to come by, for a person of enterprise," Montse said. "I fight for love."

"Love?"

Montse nodded. "I always have. I always will. It won't guarantee that I make no mistakes, but if I kill a man who didn't deserve it, it wasn't so I could eat basilisk etouffé or wear a new silk blouse. It was because I was trying to protect the ones close to me."

"Did your uncles teach you that?"

"My mother and my father. She was Mireia Quintana, born and bred outside the law, and she was a holy terror in the dance halls and customs booths of Louisiana as a young woman. Her family's home was in the bayous and aboard small ships without names. Then she married Jaume Ferrer, a landed gentleman, a farmer and a scholar, a man who was an advocate and had a career in politics. It was said in his time that Jaume Ferrer spoke every language of the Empire, and as many languages again as were not at home in the New World. In his day, he was expected to be elected to the City Council of New Orleans, though his family lands were closer to Ferdinandia. For his sake, Mireia Quintana swore off the family trade. She loved him more than she loved wealth and fame."

"That's very bucolic." Bill saw men begin to march out of the Imperial trench and, if he wasn't mistaken, still another cannon joined the firing. "One moment." He yelled to Jaleta Zorales. "Infantry approaching! Hold your fire until you can shoot into the mass of them!" They just didn't have that much powder and shot.

"It was lovely," Montse said. "Until my uncles were accused of stealing a ship called *La Flor de Andalucia*. It was the pleasure yacht of a New Spanish merchant who traded in slaves, silver, and rum."

"A false accusation?"

"The accusation was true. The ship had been full of silver and rum, and was left unattended."

"Completely unattended? That seems like a shocking dereliction of common sense in a successful merchant."

"Let us say, barely guarded. Who could be expected to resist such a temptation? Not someone surnamed Quintana. My uncles could not be found, so the chevalier threatened to hang my father if he didn't turn them over. He refused to do it, because he loved his wife and her family more than he loved his life. The chevalier hanged him."

Bill had never known. "The current chevalier?"

"His grandfather. And so my mother took up the family trade again, because she loved her husband and her family more than she loved her oath. She sailed *La Flor de Andalucia* as her vessel, only she had it rechristened with a different name. I was born on that ship, three weeks after my father was thrown into a pauper's grave. If I had had a daughter, I would have given it to her."

"*La Verge Caníbal*. Heaven's jawbone, you sail your mother's ship."

"In her wake, and in the wake of my father, and in the wake of Hannah and Kyres both. I sail for love."

"And will you give the ship to your foster child? To Margaret?"

"I have promised it to Josep. I have sailed and smuggled and pirated for fifteen years in part to give Margarida a good life, so that she would not have to sail and smuggle." Montse smiled. "For love, I do not *want* her to inherit *La Verge*."

Bill considered. "I'm glad Margaret has been in your care these last fifteen years. I can scarcely conceive of anyone who might have offered her a better refuge."

"I can only hope Hannah feels the same way."

"I have no line to the dead," Bill said. "Though I must say, it appears that they wish to have a line to us."

"What? May I borrow the spyglass?"

Bill handed the glass over to Montse. What she saw, what he had been looking only moments earlier, was a shambling column of men and beastkind that approached the Treewall with lurching step. They left behind fragments of themselves, including whole limbs. Behind them came more conventional Imperial forces: soldiers and militiamen and armed traders.

"We come to it now," Bill said. He called down the line again, this time to Valia Sharelas. "Prepare to fire silver shot!"

"Prepare silver shot!" Sharelas passed the instruction to her troops.

"I have no silver shot prepared," Montserrat Ferrer i Quintana said.

"Can you find a source of fire?"

"It's good mystery-logic.
We take the path that would seem forbidden to the uninitiated,
because they do not know the deeper truth."

CHAPTER TWENTY-SIX

By the time Luman had finished his prayer and rubbed the burnt, ground calves' bone he carried in a pocket into the wound, some combination of the man's fatigue, his injury, and the tincture of laudanum had knocked him unconscious.

Luman was therefore shocked when the man opened his eyes and spoke.

"Luman Walters," the man said.

Luman hadn't mentioned his name. He touched his coat to feel the reassuring crinkle of the Himmelsbrief inside.

"What if I am?"

"I know you are," the wounded soldier said. His voice sounded mechanical, as if a bellows were squeezing air over reeds constructed to sound like a voice. "I'm Sarah's brother."

Luman sat back on his heels and thought. "Are you dead?"

"No. But there are ... well, look, that doesn't matter. It's time for you to join us."

"Coming from the lips of a man with a broken spine and blood spiked with the juice of the poppy, you'll understand why I feel some trepidation."

The man was silent for a moment. "Sarah wants you to join her on the Great Mound."

Luman looked around the field hospital Cathy was running. There were other workers dealing with the injured; he could

476

leave without being too much missed. And besides, he was being summoned.

He climbed the Great Mound, looking over his shoulder at the eastern horizon. Flashes of light told him the Imperials' cannons were busily firing at the wall. The defenders, much less frequently, were firing back.

The swarming patterns of the defenders atop the Treewall suggested that attackers were coming up the wall on ladders, as well. Or maybe climbing or jumping.

The black birds of the Great Mound objected as Luman disturbed their sanctuary. Standing within the door was Sarah, wearing a white linen shift and holding a tiny clay lamp, unlit, in one hand. Over her other arm she carried what looked like a blue wool blanket. Her horse-headed staff leaned against the door frame beside a single bracket, whose torch lit the scene.

"Your Majesty." Luman knelt.

"I am going to ascend the Serpent Throne," Sarah said. "I'm going to walk my own Onandagos Road, and get that grip of peace. I will access the throne's power, or die trying."

"On the twenty-first of March, the vernal equinox, at dawn? Propitious timing to enter the Temple of the Sun. But I think you should seriously consider the possibility that death might indeed be a result of the attempt." Luman looked into his queen's eyes. Was she serious? Was she committed?

She seems to be.

Sarah nodded. "I believe it. I've convened a kind of committee to help me."

Luman looked around. "Am I the only member of the committee? That's an honor, but it may be a mistake."

"The others are convened elsewhere. You're here, so I assume you've heard from Nathaniel."

"He assures me he's not a ghost."

"Did he speak to you through someone else's body?"

Luman laughed. "He's done it before, I gather."

Sarah nodded. "I need you to join them because of your ritual knowledge. And I think the only way for you to do that is to be asleep. Nathaniel can reach me while I'm awake, I think because of our blood, but also because of my Eye of Eve. But others need to be unconscious to see him. To be where he is."

"Where is that, exactly?" Luman asked.

"I can't explain it. But it's a place of spirits. I think it's within space and time, but it's upside down, and things work differently. Nathaniel is powerful there. He's a healer."

Luman was unsure how any of this fitted together, though it sounded vaguely like some of the things the Ojibwe said about their Midewiwin healers. He confined himself to nodding.

"If you had told me earlier, Your Majesty, I could have brought some laudanum to knock myself out."

Sarah laughed, a sound that was sharp and free and utterly lacked music. "I need you asleep but alert, Luman. Don't worry, I'll ring your bell myself, no problem. But there's something else."

Luman bowed and waited.

"I think the way this is going to work is that you're going to be my liaison. I'll talk with you, you will talk with Nathaniel and the others, and they will...operate the liturgy."

"Who are the others?" Luman asked.

"They're dead," Sarah said. "Jacob Hop was in my service, and was killed by the Emperor's henchman. The other man is named Isaiah Wilkes. Apparently, he's an actor from Philadelphia."

"Ah, yes." Luman chuckled. "How often I have said, what I need most right now is an actor to guide me." An idea occurred to him, and he checked himself. "Wait...is he one of the Lightning Mummers?"

"I ain't sure what that is." Sarah dropped into her Appalachee accent without warning, but then pulled back out again. "But he's one of those who act out the Philadelphia Mystery Cycle. Franklin's Players."

Luman nodded. "That's who I had in mind. I take it back. I'm very interested in meeting both these men."

"I think the easiest way for us to stay in touch," Sarah said, "is for you to wear my coat."

Luman shrugged out of his own long coat, and then hesitated. "Your Majesty, I don't know what's about to happen, but may I ask you to bear a talisman with you where you go?"

Sarah hesitated, but then nodded. "You mean the angels in your pocket?"

Luman laughed. "I do. It's a Himmelsbrief, a kind of amulet of protection. It's a letter from heaven. If you just wear my coat, you will have it with you. Shall I...can I open the coat's lining and show you?"

Sarah looked at him with her unnatural eye. "No, I believe you."
Luman nodded.

"Did you write it?" Sarah asked.

"I copied it out. The words themselves are believed to come from heaven. This is their power."

Sarah shrugged into Luman's coat. "It's German work, isn't it? What do I do with it? How do you know it will work?"

"Ohio German. You shouldn't have to do anything, just don't take off the coat. And I know that such letters work, because I have experienced their power. You've seen the angels yourself, in my pocket. And I have faith that this letter will accomplish its task."

"I have faith, too."

Luman put on Sarah's coat. It was a blue Imperial military coat, too wide and too long on Sarah, but on Luman it fit reasonably well.

Sarah gripped both lapels of the coat Luman wore. "*Hoc est corpus meum,*" she said, her voice taking on a commanding vigor, "*quod tibi do.*"

Luman shivered at the words. Were they a deliberate echo? Should he repeat them in turn?

"*Accipio,*" his Latin was good enough to say.

The shiver along his spine enveloped his whole body. Luman tingled, and then had the strangest sensation of being in two places at once. He was standing inside his own body, looking at Sarah, but he was also standing inside Sarah's body, looking at Luman.

Sarah smiled. "I can see it worked."

Luman nodded, afraid that if he moved too much, he'd upset the spell.

"*Dormi.*"

Luman fell to the ground in deep sleep.

Isaiah Wilkes was dead. The chill water of the Hudson had stunned him. He'd sunk beneath the surface and died quickly, with little pain.

And then he had come back above the surface and found himself standing in a creek, under a sky full of stars, but no moon. He hadn't recognized the place, and had been reciting all the geographical knowledge he possessed in an attempt to identify it, when Nathaniel Penn and Jacob Hop—the latter also dead—had approached him and asked him to help them recon-struct the Cahokian enthronement rite.

Being dead didn't feel much different from being alive. The land about him seemed fluid, as if the distance between two points could be now long and now short, depending on ... Isaiah didn't know what. That fluidity seemed to harden when Nathaniel Penn was around.

When he rode away on his four horses—or were they a drum?—leaving Wilkes and Hop alone together, the land again seemed to melt, stretch, and bend.

The stars, oddly enough, were constant. If he squinted at them, he could make out the stars he knew, and their familiar rotation around the celestial pole. But if he relaxed his vision, the shapes they made together were not the shapes he was accustomed to.

"How did you die?" Hop asked conversationally.

"Drowned. Two men in love with the same girl were riding in different canoes. When they started fighting, all of us fell into the water."

"Have you seen the others here?"

"No," Isaiah said. "I assume they must not be dead. And you?"

"Stabbed repeatedly by the Emperor's Machiavel."

"Temple Franklin?"

"Yes."

"I know the man. I'm not surprised he has murder in his heart."

"And now on his hands." Jacob Hop grinned affably.

It was altogether the strangest conversation Isaiah Wilkes had ever had, and he'd had more than his share of odd ones.

Nathaniel returned, and on his horse—or on a horse following his?—rode a man with curly dark hair and spectacles. Nathaniel and the new arrival dismounted, and the horses leaped onto Nathaniel's shoulder, where they became a drum.

"I'm Luman Walters," the new man said. "Hedge wizard, dabbler in braucherei and Memphite magic, among other disciplines. Formerly in the employ of the Imperial Ohio Company. From the Haudenosaunee territory. Physically in the city of Cahokia, which is besieged by Simon Sword's beastkind and by the Emperor's soldiers."

"Jacob Hop. Formerly a deaf-mute, and after that, briefly possessed by the spirit of Simon Sword. Dead. Physically, maybe lying on the bottom of the ocean. I have an idea about the Tarocks."

"Isaiah Wilkes. In life, I was the Franklin of the Conventicle, and also the head of Franklin's Players." Somewhat to his own surprise, Isaiah felt comfortable speaking openly about subjects on which he'd been sworn to secrecy in life. "Former apprentice printer, actor, and musician. I am committed to ending the reign of Simon Sword by any means possible. Also dead. Frozen at the bottom of the Hudson River."

"Nathaniel Elytharias Penn. Son of Hannah Penn and Kyres Elytharias. I'm a healer. I have…the ability to travel this land. I'm alive, and in Pennsland somewhere. Simon Sword is attacking my father's land, and my sister."

"This is an odd crew." Hop smiled.

"I should tell you that I can see what Sarah sees," Luman Walters said. "She can hear me. I don't know if she can hear the rest of you." He paused. "Sarah, can you hear the others?" Another pause. "No, she only hears me. But I will be the link to her as we reconstruct this rite."

Isaiah Wilkes studied the other men. "I assume you are all at least Freemasons."

They looked at each other blankly.

"What exactly will we reconstruct this lost rite *from*?" Wilkes asked.

Jacob Hop produced a deck of Tarocks and spread them before him. "I have a theory about the Tarocks."

Isaiah raised his eyebrows. "Another man than I might express skepticism. But those cards were designed by my master Ben Franklin. If you tell me they encode esoteric information, I'm inclined to believe."

"I think they do," Hop said. "Look, if I choose the minor arcana and spread the cards out, each suit appears to tell a story."

"A story is essential," Luman said. "Many stories encode memories of lost mystery rites. The Hymn to Demeter, for instance, is known to tell the ordinances of Eleusis, if only one knows how to read it."

"The Hymn to Demeter is *thought* to record memories of Eleusis," Isaiah said. "But in fact, no one *does* know how to read it."

"A salutary reminder," Luman said. "Apuleius's Golden Ass is another, with respect to the mysteries of Isis. The Chemical Wedding of Christian Rosenkreutz. The oldest versions of the grail legend. The stories of Orpheus."

"The Philadelphia Mystery Plays," Isaiah added quietly. "Allegedly."

"What do they have in common?" Nathaniel asked.

"They show features of initiatory experience," Isaiah said. "A journey, either in a circle or else in a direct line to the center. Trials, by which the initiate gains wounds and also wisdom. Transformation from one state to another. Healing or empowerment."

Nathaniel was staring at him. "A journey into the sky, where one is torn to pieces by monsters and reassembled with iron bones, healed of the falling sickness?"

Isaiah smiled. "That is a colorful example. But yes, maybe."

"And if there is a story, then in the liturgy, the initiate must reenact the story." Jacob Hop gazed thoughtfully at his cards.

"It is the essence of liturgy to repeat the deeds of the gods," Luman said. "Paul teaches us as much. 'Therefore we are buried with him by baptism into death: that like as Christ was raised up from the dead by the glory of the Father, even so we also should walk in newness of life.' Baptism is a simple initiation, imitating the death and resurrection of Christ."

"The gods or the heroes," Jacob said.

Luman nodded. "Christian Rosenkreutz is not a god. Nor are the grail knights."

"Nor was Onandagos," Jacob said.

"That is a provocative choice," Isaiah said. "Why do you think of the Firstborn prophet?"

Jacob showed the Tarocks. "I believe this person's journey involved Simon Sword, Peter Plowshare, and the Serpent Throne. A journey along a mighty road, arrival at a great river, and the Temple of the Sun. The building of a great city, and a staff with a horse's head. Who but Onandagos would that be?"

"It might be every man, properly understood," Isaiah said.

"Agreed," Luman said. "And yet, it's not a bad guess. Sarah herself has described what she is attempting as her own Onandagos Road."

"The pilgrim road," Isaiah said. "And the Haudenosaunee who are called the Onandaga...their name means 'mountaintops,' in their language. Is Onandagos the man of the mountaintops? The man who ascends?"

"Do they take their name from him, or the reverse?" Jacob asked.

"What do we get, then, if we lay out the ten cards in a suit?" Nathaniel asked. "Not counting the face cards."

Jacob frowned. "It depends on the suit."

"Two of these suits show women wayfarers," Nathaniel pointed out, "and two show men. Do we assume that's significant?"

"Yes." Jake pocketed all the minor arcana bearing the sigils for sword or lightning bolt. Nathaniel stood his drum upright on the ground and Jake spread the cards out. "Sex is meaningful to the goddess, who chooses Her Beloved in part based on an alternation between women and men." He looked around at the other three. "If I understand the theology correctly."

The other three men shrugged.

"Ten numbered cards to a suit," Luman said. "Ten rooms in the palace of life."

"What's a palace of life?" Nathaniel asked.

"A Cahokian library," Luman explained. "They traditionally follow a standard architectural plan of ten rooms in a distinctive pattern. Sarah taught me this. I think she intuited that the libraries—which are called *palaces of life*—had something to do with her planned ascent."

"Are you saying that the ascent should really take place in a library?" Isaiah asked.

Luman pondered the question. "I don't think so. I think a literal ascent of the throne is intended, and that implies a location in the Temple of the Sun. But perhaps the purpose of the palace of life's structure is as a didactic tool. Perhaps students are taught subliminally through some course of instruction in the palace, prepared without their own awareness for a future initiation. Or perhaps the subjects of volumes stored in each room of the library is determined by the initiatic schema."

"Or the writing system," Jacob Hop said.

The wizard narrowed his eyes. "What do you mean?"

"I mean that each of the Major Arcana is bordered with a letter of the Cahokian writing system. Also, each room of a palace of life contains books determined by both the Adam and the Eve form of the letter."

Isaiah took the Major Arcana from Jake and thumbed through them, pointing at the patterns around the borders. "These knots, you mean."

Jake nodded.

"Each room of the palace of life is associated with two letters, two cards of the Major Arcana, and we think a card of the Minor Arcana?" Luman asked. "Or maybe as many as four numbered cards, one from each suit?"

"A Philadelphia physician once told me that assigning meaning to all things was a sign of madness." Isaiah laughed. "He called it over-determination. This conversation would give the poor fellow the vapors."

"Which of us speaks Cahokian?" Nathaniel asked.

Each of the other three shook his head *no*.

"Pity." Luman examined the cards, laying them out in numerical order. "Is it possible that we have here two separate journeys, two separate liturgies? Or rather four, two for a female initiate and two for a man?"

"We are attempting to reconstruct a throne ascension rite, and already we are making wild guesses," Isaiah said.

"Say rather *intuitive leaps*," Luman suggested.

"What would this other liturgy be for?" Isaiah asked.

"Was there a liturgy when my sister became the Beloved of the Goddess?" Nathaniel asked.

"Let me ask." Luman looked out into space. "Your Majesty, was there a liturgy you followed when the goddess chose you?"

"I don't expect there was," Isaiah murmured. "Christ was chosen as the Beloved, and as far as the gospels record, he was baptized, at most. I see no baptism card here."

"King David's name means *Beloved*," Jake said. "And he was merely anointed by Samuel."

Luman nodded. "She says she knelt and there was an angel choir."

"Could it be that the cups and shields represent a journey in and a journey out?" Nathaniel asked. "A circle, like you were saying?"

"It's certainly possible." Luman considered. "But the throne stands in the apse, elevated, at the back of a long nave. Conceptually, that makes it the center of the universe, the sacred mountain of the gods. It seems more likely to me that the liturgy we are looking for progresses from the outside to the center and stops. Consider Exodus twenty-four."

"I was raised by followers of the old gods," Nathaniel said. "What happens in Exodus twenty-four?"

"Moses, Joshua, and the elders of Israel start at the bottom of the sacred mountain. That's the first level. They ascend one level, and God comes down to meet them halfway. That's level two. They see God, they eat a meal with Him, but on them God 'laid not his hand.' Moses and Joshua alone then are invited to go up once more, to level three, or as Exodus says, 'into the mount.'"

"And did God lay His hand on Moses and Joshua in the mount?" Isaiah asked.

"Maybe." Luman nodded. "A cloud covered the mount when Moses went up, perhaps telling us we shouldn't ask too many questions."

"What are we here for, if not to ask questions?" Isaiah pointed out.

Luman nodded again. "But scripture never says Moses came down. It does say he spent forty days and nights up there, under the cloud. A straight liturgy. Whereas a circular liturgy might go the other way—from the village into the wilderness, and then back. Or think of Christian Rosenkreutz, whose straight-line journey of ascent also passed through three levels: the outside world, the castle, and then the tower."

"Forty days and nights is a provocative number," Isaiah said.

"Everything is provocative," Nathaniel said. "Everything corresponds."

"You have touched on an entire world view," Luman said.

"But we don't need everything to correspond," Nathaniel said. "We need to know what to do to help Sarah ascend the throne. And we need it now."

"We need to know the drama," Isaiah said, "to be able to perform it for an audience of one."

"Could we access a Cahokian palace of life?" Luman asked. "If the letters are indicated on the spines of the books, maybe that would help us lay out the cards in the right order."

"You don't think the numerical order is the performative order?" Isaiah asked.

"Maybe, for the Minor Arcana," Luman said. "But if each stage of the journey also corresponds to one of the Major Arcana, I don't know how to identify that correspondence. There are hints here and there—is that a horse-headed staff? is that blond face with no apparent body attached Simon Sword?—but some cards in the Minor Arcana don't appear to have any hints of the Major Arcana in them."

"There is a palace of life in Irra-Zostim by the river." Jacob

Hop turned to Nathaniel. "That's a sort of country home, owned by your family. If I direct you, could you take us there?"

Nathaniel shrugged. "I can try."

Jake swept the cards into his pocket. Nathaniel thumped the skin of his drum with a ragged pattern and it exploded into four horses. The four men mounted up, and then Jake pointed westward. "Irra-Zostim lies close to the Mississippi, south of Cahokia."

The ride was short and Isaiah marveled again that this shadow of the world seemed to be completely elastic, sensitive to the presence of Nathaniel Penn. When they reached a grassy rise above a broad, slow, green river, Nathaniel reined in his beast and all four horses stopped. "What does Irra-Zostim look like?"

"It is a conical mount with thirteen standing stones at its peak," Jake said. "Maybe what you would call Eve Stones."

"I don't know what an Eve Stone is." Nathaniel shrugged.

Jake closed his eyes as if to visualize the place. "It stands in an enclosure at the edge of a forest. Within the enclosure are two buildings: a residence and the library. West of the enclosure are farmed fields leading down to the river."

"I don't think all of that exists in this place," Nathaniel said. "But I see the mound."

They rode again. When they stopped they were in a clearing shielded from the river by tall nut-bearing trees, with broad avenues leading between their smooth trunks. From the center of the clearing rose a tall tower with sheer walls. In the bottom of the tower was an open doorway.

"Is this it?" Nathaniel asked.

Jake hesitated. "I think maybe it is," he agreed. "Follow me."

They dismounted and entered the door.

Isaiah had never been in a Cahokian library, and he didn't feel he was in one now. He stood in a roughly circular room. One passage led forward, one led leftward at a forty-five degree angle, and at a forty-five degree angle on the right side was a third exit.

"No books," he said.

"But look at the floor." Luman pointed.

Two of the knot-like patterns were written on the floor in glowing light.

"I don't know this realm," Isaiah said. "Doesn't it seem unlikely that a mere library would have such glyphs?"

"Everything here is a shadow of the physical world," Jake said.

"Or the other way around," Nathaniel added.

"I think the mere fact that this place exists tends to suggest we're following a good trail," Jake suggested. "Also, I'm encouraged by the fact that the palace of life manifests here as a tower."

Luman took two steps up the leftward passage to look along the series of rooms that lay beyond it, then up the rightward passage to do the same. "The letters on the floor of each room are different. This may be the guide we are looking for."

"Except that we still have a problem," Jake said. "What order do we walk the rooms? Up the left, then right, then center?"

"Sarah," Luman asked. "We're at the palace of life in Irra-Zostim, looking for guidance as to the order of the rite. Do you have any advice?"

Moments later, he shook his head *no*.

They all thought in silence. "We believe we seek a journey to the mountain of the gods, at the center of the universe," Isaiah said.

"Eden," Nathaniel added.

"Can the palace of life be walked in a spiral fashion, ending in the center?" he asked.

"Aha!" Luman snapped his fingers and leaped forward. At a brisk walk, he tested the question. They walked up the right side of the structure, turned left, then coiled around and into the building's center. They could walk the room in an elongated spiral pattern, passing through each room exactly one time.

When they stood in the central room, staring at each other, Isaiah felt exhilaration.

"That's it, then," Nathaniel said.

Luman addressed Sarah. "We think we should walk it in a spiral," he said. Then he turned to face the others. "She reminds me that the spiral is an ancient symbol of the goddess. I admit I feel a little bit the fool."

"But which way?" Isaiah asked. "Do we turn left from the start, or right?"

"Surely, we must take the right-hand path," Luman said. "A child in his first Latin lessons can tell you that the left hand is sinister."

They were all nodding their agreement when Luman began to laugh. "You are of course right, Your Majesty."

"Well?" Isaiah felt a pang of envy at Luman Walters's connection with the witch-queen of Cahokia, and the words she was whispering into his ear.

"Her Majesty suggests that the question isn't left or right," Luman said.

Jake frowned. "It felt like left or right to me. Does she suggest we should go straight from the beginning?"

Luman shook his head. "She points out that the choice is whether we follow the sun, or go widdershins."

Jake laughed. "We follow the sun."

"Left it is," Isaiah said. "It's good mystery-logic. We take the path that would seem forbidden to the uninitiated, because they do not know the deeper truth."

"But how do we know which cards to lay out? Which of the Minor Arcana, I mean?" Nathaniel asked.

Jake held up the tens of cups and shields. "The ten of cups shows a hand emerging from behind a cloud, reaching out to the traveler. The ten of shields shows a woman flying over a city."

"Is she flying because she is on the sacred mountain?" Jake asked.

"Remember Exodus twenty-four," Luman said. "The cloud over the mountain. Could it be the veil that covers the Serpent Throne?"

"It could," Isaiah agreed. "Look at the floor in the tenth room. What are the two possible Major Arcana in the room?"

"The Serpent Throne and the City," Jake said.

"Clearly our path, however eclectic and surprising, leads somewhere." Isaiah tried to contain his excitement. Was this how he would fulfill his duty as the Franklin? Not raising the Alliance of the Three Brothers, but raising Sarah Elytharias Penn to the Serpent Throne?

"I think the journey of the shields must end somehow with the city," Luman said. "Which means that the journey of the cups ends with a hand coming out of the cloud, and the Major Arcanum of the Serpent Throne. Also, I believe the cup, being the symbol of a vessel that needs to be filled, is appropriate as the suit of supplication."

They cut directly back to the first room, and Jake dropped the one of cups face-up in the center of the floor. "The road begins. We know where it ends. Our job is to help our queen survive the journey. But how will we know which of the Major Arcana to play in each room?" Jake asked. "In each case, we have a choice of two."

Isaiah scratched his chin.

"That's a good question," Luman agreed. "Your Majesty, how do you think we should choose which Major Arcanum to play in each room? Wait ... stop. Your Majesty, have you considered this carefully? Sarah?"

"What's wrong?" Nathaniel looked alarmed.

Luman's face was pale. "She says she can't wait on us slow-pokes. She's going in."

The Treewall broke, and Montse nearly fell off.

While dawn was gray in the east, it became clear that all twelve Imperial guns were firing. It also became clear that Cahokia's magicians were tiring. The city's defenders were being struck by bullets and falling from the wall. The black ring of fire was growing and constricting, threatening to block entirely the imminent sunrise. Every Cahokian death gave its defenders a jolt of energy, but the jolts were smaller and smaller as they became more and more frequent.

Several of the mages themselves were dead.

Once the undead beastkind and the Imperial soldiers advanced in wide enough ranks out of their trenches, Jaleta Zorales and her guns began to fire at them. When a gun crew near Montse lost one of its members, Montse stepped in. She knew how to lay a gun, sight accurately on a target, fire, swab, and load. The shouted commands the Cahokian Pitchers used were slightly different than the Catalan cries aboard *La Verge*, but she knew the rhythms and quickly mastered the syllables.

She and her crew fired shot after shot into the densest masses of enemy bodies they could reach, massing at what they judged to be the edges of the defenders' guns' reach. When the crew's captain fell, Montse took over, shouting the orders and also aiming.

The attackers rushed forward with oil and torches and lit the base of the Treewall on fire. For a time, the spells of the Cahokian gramarists dampened the fire. But as the wizards fell one by one, this fire also grew.

Montse and others defended the wall with small arms, firing onto the Imperials who charged with oil and fire. Where attackers fell, here and there across the field, small fires grew.

Once all the Imperial guns were in operation and the wall shook at every blow, the undead emerged. Shuffling, hopping, and dragging themselves forward, they emitted a piteous collective racket that was part roar and part wail of the damned. It was at this moment that Montse and her crew, following the bellowed orders of Jaleta Zorales, fired the last of their shot, though not the last of their powder. The balls tore through the ranks of the dead. Where it struck the front ranks, it shattered men and beastkind and hurled their skulls and ribs further into the massed ranks as shrapnel. Each hit tore a cone of devastation through the ranks of the attackers.

But those who weren't hit continued forward.

So did those who had lost limbs, now dragging themselves or lurching, but moving with no less speed or determination.

So did some of the detached limbs.

When the undead reached the wall, they briefly scrabbled there, as if thwarted in their plan and unable to change direction. Montse and the defenders threw oil down on the assailants. It added to the fire, but as long as the Treewall held, the fires could be put out.

Two minutes later, the Treewall broke and the shuffling dead climbed through.

"The gun!" Zorales shouted. "Throw it!"

Throw the gun? Montse looked down inside the wall and saw what the Pitcher commander saw—that directly in the path of the walking dead was a field of wounded. A hospital. Cathy Filmer, the former Harvite, held a lit torch in her hand, and Gazelem Zomas, the outlander Ophidian, gripped a spear; they stood between the undead and the wounded.

"The powder!" Montse shouted to her crew. She wasn't disobeying an instruction so much as carrying it out with creativity. "Put a fuse to it!"

Her gun had a single barrel of powder left. The barrels were packed tight and sealed against water—if she introduced a spark into it, it should explode. One of the survivors of her crew, a thin Ophidian woman with large hands and nose and the mouth of a child, gouged a quick hole in the wood and worked in a fuse.

Montse waved her arms at Cathy and Gazelem until the Ophidian looked up. "Get back!" she shouted. "Move the wounded! Run!"

Beside the gun stood a small coal fire with pitch-infused torches for lighting fuses. She lit the fuse attached to the barrel. The cord threw sparks against her face as she hefted the cask.

A cart rolled up, pulled by a horse that looked as thin as a ten-year-old boy and no stronger. Gazelem and Cathy, with the aid of other healers, began shifting the wounded from the ground into the cart.

And then she saw that one of the healers aiding them was Miquel. The boy limped, but he sang cheerfully as he hoisted wounded men into the cart.

The first of the walking dead shuffled through the hole in the wall. They were beastkind with misshapen limbs, animal heads, and mismatched body parts. Ichor oozed from their white flesh, and a confused animal din groaned from their beast-lips.

When the third one dragged itself into view, Montse dropped the cask. A beastman with the head of an antelope caught it and looked at it, confused.

"Cut out the stops!" she shouted at her crew. "Prepare to drop the gun in front of that hole, inside the wall!"

BOOM!

The hot wind from the explosion scorched the skin of Montse's face and ruffled her hair. The beastman holding the cask was blown to bits, as were the two in front of him. His body shielded those behind him from the worst of the blast. Montse drew her saber, grabbed the fire and torches in her free hand, and ran down the nearest steps.

She skidded to a halt in a slime of blood, mud, snow, and rotting flesh. The city stank. She positioned herself in front of the opening.

It was large enough to drive a wagon through. Fortunately, since the Imperial troops were now trying to pass through, the guns had stopped firing on the spot.

Likely, they were being repositioned elsewhere.

The next ranks of undead shuffling into the breach had been men once.

Beyond them, Montse saw files of men in blue marching toward the walls.

"Fire!" she heard Jaleta Zorales call from above, but few of the cannons responded—most had exhausted their shot, as Montse's had.

"Fire!" Bill yelled, and muskets answered. Through the gap, Montse saw soldiers in blue drop, dead and wounded. Their files struggled to march over and around them without losing integrity.

Living dead shambled toward her.

She waved to her crew. "Drop the gun!"

Two of the zaambi—a beastman and a man—had come fully through the gap and were out of reach when the cannon dropped off the wall. They didn't even turn around as the iron tube and its wood and iron carriage fell with a loud *thud*, crushing three walking dead behind them into paste.

The beastman was terrifying. Covered in fur, it had the head of a horse, three legs, and only one arm. Montse stepped forward and hurled the burning coal and pitch into the creature's face, spattering it with flaming asphalt.

The stink of burning, rotten flesh billowed immediately into Montse's lungs, nearly choking her. She staggered back, but couldn't seem to get out of the cloud. The beastman emitted a hissing sound. Montse saw the creature's flesh blister, swell, and split open. When it cracked, black ichor belched out in waves like molasses glugging from the side of a toppled jug. The stench got infinitely worse.

It ran at her.

Its improbable geometry made it surprisingly fast. In a sudden sprint it leaped at Montse, one flaming arm raised to clutch her in a hellish embrace. She slashed and stepped aside, but it rolled around and lurched at her again. If she impaled it, it would trample her. But it was faster than she was.

She ducked once more, surely the last time she'd be able to evade it. The beastman spun and leaped at her—

and Gazelem Zomas stepped into its path.

He held a spear. High on the spear's pole, just below the blade, the spear had a strong crossbar. Gazelem stepped on the butt of his spear, crouched, and rammed the spear tip into the zaambi beastman's chest, just below its thick, horselike clavicle.

The monster shrieked, took another step forward, and collapsed. It flailed, trying to grab Montse or Gazelem with its one fiery arm, but Gazelem and his spear held it firmly in place while it twitched its last.

Bill staggered down the steps. He leaned on one crutch as he moved, and his steps were ragged. Behind him came Cahokian wardens with muskets, bayonets, and longbows. At the foot of the stairs he slipped, catching himself against the wall.

"The ambulance cart!" Bill shouted.

Montse had been distracted. She turned and saw the other zaambi who had got through. The man wore a tall black beaver hat, a red blanket over one shoulder and belted around his waist, and he had the shaved head and scalp lock of one of the Indians of the northeast. As Cathy Filmer shoved a torch into his side, he ignored her. Flesh sizzling, he hacked at a wounded soldier in a gray cape with a war ax.

With his first swing, he crushed the wounded man's shoulder.

With his second, he lopped away a slice of the man's skull.

The soldier screamed once, shrilly, sat up, and then died.

Miquel sprang at the zaambi, with nothing but a knife in his hand.

Montse raced for the dead man. "His eyes!" she shouted to Cathy Filmer. "Burn his eyes!"

As the zaambi raised his ax to strike at Miqui, Cathy shoved the torch into his eyes.

He missed his blow, the ax biting into the edge of the cart. Howling in rage, he swung at Cathy—

hitting her in the shoulder and knocking her down.

Miquel stabbed the dead man, to no effect.

"Cathy!" Bill's voice came from too far away for him to do anything. "Fire!" he yelled next, and the sound of guns that resulted suggested that his men were shooting into the breach in the Treewall.

The zaambi raised his ax again—

Montse ran him through, pushing with all the strength in her legs and heaving herself against the dead man. She pushed until her sword bit into the wood of the cart and pinned him, off-balance and squirming.

With her other hand, she yanked the ax from his grip.

The zaambi groaned. With both hands he reached for a patient and missed. Then he groped in Cathy's direction and got his fingers into her long hair—

Montse swung down with the borrowed ax with all her might. With her first blow, she chopped through his elbow, and with her second she severed his forearm. Cathy stumbled backward, kicking the two disembodied forearms away from her, fingers opening and shutting and still trying to grab.

Montse settled into a better stance and swung the ax at the dead man's neck. She hit squarely where she aimed. His head toppled from his shoulders, rolled over three times in the muddy snow, and came to rest looking at Montse.

His face was confused and terrified.

She swung the ax one last time, shattering the skull into fragments.

*"Perhaps from this very spot. Leaning out
one of the chevalier's own windows, for instance."*

—◆—

CHAPTER TWENTY-SEVEN

Chigozie was hard pressed to keep up. A few short months earlier, he'd have been unable to, given Kort's long, loping pace, but
winter in the Missouri had hardened the muscles of his legs and
given his stride ambition.

Naares Stoach seemed to struggle with the pace, too. That
surprised Chigozie, given how comfortable the outrider seemed
to be generally in this frontier land, but then he reflected that
the Zoman was probably accustomed to traveling it horseback.

The second Zoman accompanying them might have been
chosen for speed: she had long legs packed with lean muscle, and
the face and torso of a racing greyhound. Her long brown hair
blew wildly behind her as she ran, like a horse's mane, but in
fact she was a magician. Her name was Ya'alu. Chigozie didn't
know magic and didn't trust it. It had always been his brother's
art, and even when it had seemed more innocuous than pervert-
ing their father's funeral into a curse spell, Chigozie had never
really liked it. This wizard was here to build on the Caddo boy's
testimony and find the prisoner they were to rescue.

Or, possibly, the servant they were to kidnap.

Kort and Ferpa traveled with long, quick paces. The other Merciful had no trouble, but they all seemed to have been assembled
by a creator who wanted them to have fast legs. One had some
kind of long tail, belly pouch, and powerful hindquarters that

494

kicked her forward in ten-foot leaps and bounds. The second was the closest thing Chigozie had seen to a centaur: he had the body of a lizard that ran on all fours, though he could stand on his hind legs to elevate his man's face when he wanted to look around. The third had the legs of a running bird and could easily pull ahead of all the others when it came to a contest.

The last member of the party that sneaked into the Great Green Wood was a Caddo boy named Ba'tshush. He was thin, with all the hair of his head shaved except for a narrow strip that ran down the center, front to back.

Whatever they were going into the Great Green Wood to retrieve, it was something the boy had seen.

Chigozie felt profoundly unsettled, but he also felt he had no choice. He had accepted the call of the Merciful to be their Shepherd. "The good shepherd giveth his life for the sheep," and Chigozie was undertaking an insane risk in order to protect the Still Waters and its people from the soldiers of Zomas.

Chigozie, Ba'tshush, Ya'alu, and Naares all pretended to be the prisoners of Kort. To give veracity to the fraud, each ran with his hands loosely tied with the same long cord, a string of prisoners behind the bison-headed giant.

The deception also required that Naares Stoach let Kort carry his weapons, concealed in a sack along with a few other items that might conceivably be plunder, including a box of colored chalks and a doll. Some of the paraphernalia belonged to the wizard, who would furtively consult a polished white stone by laying it over a leather map and peering into it when they took breaks from running, or cut the palm of Ba'tshush's hand with a flake of obsidian and throw the liquid into the air when the wind was still, carefully observing which direction the drops flew. The wizard also anointed all their knees—or in the case of some of the beastkind, other joints that approximated the function of knees—at every stop with a thick reddish ointment taken from a stone jar.

"Will it make me faster?" Ferpa asked, the first time her knees received the unguent.

"You won't tire," the Zoman wizard said.

Ferpa grunted his acceptance.

It was a lie, though. Chigozie grew weary early on in their run. But somehow, despite a weariness that seemed to get simply worse and worse, beyond any fatigue Chigozie had ever endured, he had the strength to continue. He was exhausted, he knew it, but it didn't matter to him.

They passed other travelers on the paths they trod, mostly beastkind. The children of Adam they saw were either prisoners— some looked Cahokian, some had the rough and ready look of Missourian Children of Eve, others still were Bantu or German—or people in flight. A Comanche band of two men and four women, with a handful of skinny children behind, rode past at nearly a gallop.

Between what the Caddo whispered and what the Zoman mage saw, the party reached a stone pyramid, rising above the snow-painted forest. They had traveled non-stop for three days, and Chigozie was unsure where they were. He'd faced into three sunrises and run generally downhill on a long, gradual decline, so they might be near the river, but he saw no sign of river birds and he didn't smell the Mississippi.

Ya'alu again consulted her stone and map. "We go through the pyramid."

Kort snorted and shifted from foot to foot.

"What do you mean, 'through the pyramid'?" Naares asked. "Do you mean *around* it?"

"That's not what the scrying stone tells me." Ya'alu shrugged. "Through."

"There is a place on the other side," Kort said slowly. "It is on the river, but not the river as you know it."

"Something like another world?" Ya'alu asked.

"There is no other world," Kort said. "Not that I know. Though my Shepherd preaches a Heaven, and I want to believe. But I do know that this world is more complicated than it appears to the mortal eye. The Heron King lives beside the great river, in a place where no mortal foot can arrive unaided. This pyramid is the aid. It is a gate."

"Do you feel uncomfortable going in there?" Chigozie asked the beastman.

"No," Kort said. "I feel afraid."

Ferpa lowed her mournful agreement.

The pyramid had openings in it like gaping mouths. Beast-kind emerged from some and entered from others. Some of the beastkind moving into the pyramid had prisoners, either led on a string like Chigozie and his companions, carried over shoulders, or dragged along in carts.

None of the beastkind *emerging* from the pyramid had children of Adam with them.

Chigozie decided not to mention the fact.

Naares seemed to notice it, though. "Getting in seems easy enough. What about getting out?"

"We will have a hostage," Ya'alu said. "If it comes to that."

"I don't like the idea of taking a hostage," Chigozie said.

"Do you like the idea of being killed by an angry demigod?" Naares asked.

He didn't, of course. Nor did he like the idea of kidnapping anyone in the first place. He liked nothing about what he was currently going through. "He's not a demigod," he protested weakly.

Naares snorted. "Say that to me again when he's killed twenty thousand of your people, priest."

Chigozie lowered his head, unwilling to either fight or concede.

"I have spells that will camouflage our flight," Ya'alu said. "I have been preparing for this day."

"You're a specialist in kidnapping allies of the Heron King?" Chigozie asked.

"More or less," she said.

"This is not the first Simon Sword my people have known," Naares said. "Only we are not protected by the covenants of the Serpent Throne and the magics of the Heronblade. Onandagos's other children stole those from us and left us naked in the woods to fend for ourselves as best we could."

"Like Adam and Eve." Ferpa looked at Chigozie as if confirming her understanding.

Chigozie nodded.

"No," Naares Stoach said. "More like Ishmael, abandoned to die. Only an angel took care of that foundling. But over the centuries, we have learned to be our own angels, because we have had to. Someday, we'll take back our birthright."

"Not today?" Kort asked.

"No." Naares pointed at the pyramid. "Today we're going to take a hostage."

They moved forward again, run now slowed to a march. Chigozie was full of questions for the Zoman outrider, but he was careful to ask them when they weren't passing packs of beastkind.

"What are you going to do with this hostage?" he asked.

"A good strategist has more than one plan."

"Will you tell Simon Sword that you'll kill the hostage?"

"That's a possibility. Another is that the mambo will...will empower us."

"With her magic?" Chigozie asked. How much worse could this expedition get?

"Not exactly," Naares said.

They followed a dark tunnel through the pyramid, and the space into which they emerged on the other side was free of snow and much warmer. The trees here still held their leaves; multiple avenues led off between the tree trunks in different directions. A flock of beasts that looked like alpacas—but three times the size, and with impossibly long necks—strode past, munching leaves well over Chigozie's head.

And somewhere, to what should have been the east, Chigozie heard drums and chanting.

"I fear you will have us approach the drums," he said. As he voiced the idea, he watched three beastmen with the heads of wolves drag a sledge full of children toward the rhythmic sounds.

Ya'alu consulted her map and stone. "No." She pointed to the right, which felt to Chigozie like south. "This way."

The land was flat and the soil moist and spongelike, as if it were built of millennia of river silt and rotting leaves. Just the touch of his heel in the soil made scents spring up that made Chigozie think of fertile farmland. Was this soil the reason the trees were so tall and strong, apparently bearing their leaves through the winter?

But no, that was obviously wrong. Whatever Kort said, this place was not the earth Chigozie knew.

To his right, moving silently through the forest in a line parallel to his own, Chigozie saw a tiger twice the size it should be, with teeth like scimitars. The beast noticed Chigozie's gaze and slunk deeper into the woods, disappearing from view.

They followed the right-hand path for a mile or two. Chigozie saw beastkind such as he'd rarely seen before, dressed in elegant robes or wearing gold and silver jewelry, adorned with bits of amber and lapis lazuli. Some wore long feathers plaited into their hair or fur, or had their own feathers waxed or painted.

Most of the beastkind, and all of the children of Adam, were moving east. Chigozie's breath came more thickly in his throat, the thicker the traffic became.

Ya'alu stopped their journey with a raised hand in a thick copse of trees. "It's time to take a precaution."

"The precaution I'd like to take is to bring along a cavalry squad," Naares Stoach said. "Or more than one."

"You have better than that." Ya'alu winked at him. "You have me."

Naares snorted playfully.

"I will gladly see whatever precaution you have for us," Chigozie said.

At Ya'alu's direction, Kort opened his sack. She extracted five small skulls from the sack and handed one each to Naares, Chigozie, and the Caddo boy. She herself took the doll. Chigozie examined his skull: it was small, the skull of a gopher, or something similar. An iron staple had been pounded into its top, and a loop of twine passed through the staple.

"Each of you, touch your skull to one of our beastkind," the wizard directed.

"They are not ours," Chigozie said, "except in the sense that they are *our* friends and *our* companions. And they are not beastkind. They are the Merciful."

"My name is Kort."

The wizard sighed. "Please, now is not the time to complicate things."

Chigozie turned to Kort. "May I?"

Kort smiled and laid a hand on the gopher skull.

The Zoman wizard chanted briefly, and then Kort laughed. "You have become like me," he told Chigozie.

Chigozie wished he had a mirror, but he could see that each of the three other children of Adam in the group had become a perfect visual replica of one of the Merciful. Naares looked like Ferpa.

"We'll attract less attention like this," Ya'alu said.

Chigozie shrugged out of the lead cord, the others following his lead. Then they continued on their road.

After two slow curves in the road, they arrived at another stone pyramid. This one was considerably smaller than the immense tower through which they'd entered this queer realm, but also finer. Its stone had crisp corners and lines of gold tracing elaborate patterns on every surface. On some level, Chigozie expected hieroglyphs, wall-carvings or paintings, but the patterns resisted such easy analysis. Other than one obvious, recurring image: the pyramid was covered with images of skulls. Within whorls and square frames, precious stone panels sparkled, supplementing the shine of the gold. As greenish rays of light filtered down through the organic canopy above, they struck the stone and gave it the brilliant green hue of emerald, shading into the more somber greens of jade.

Ya'alu took the lead, climbing the steps up the front of the pyramid. Near the top was a square opening. As Ya'alu reached the last of the steps, two beastmen emerged. One had the head of a mantis. The other looked like a man, but with tusks like a wild boar's.

"The king sent us," she said.

Chigozie realized with some part of his mind that what he was hearing was not in fact French, but a beastkind mode of communication. Still, it sounded like French to him.

He looked to Naares Stoach to comment on his surprise, and saw Stoach calmly pluck the skull from the Caddo boy's chest. "Son of Adam!" Naares roared.

"Son of Adam!" roared the two guards at the top of the pyramid.

A look of intense fear and sudden comprehension broke into the boy's face, and he ran.

Kort bellowed, a sound of distress. Did the bison-headed Merciful wish to rush and save the boy?

Chigozie put an arm on Kort's shoulder. He couldn't restrain the giant, but his touch reminded Kort of Chigozie's presence, and maybe also of what was at stake—the survival of all the Merciful at the Still Waters.

Kort flinched.

The pyramid guards bounded down the stone steps. As they raced past Kort, the beastman lurched forward, as if he, too, were bounding after the Caddo guide...

only he leaped into the path of the guards.

The three of them tumbled to the ground. The other two dragged Kort to his feet, snorting and pawing the earth. Kort shrank back, head and shoulders dropping. It was a strange and unnatural motion when performed by such a ferocious and formidable person, and it worked—the guards threw him to the ground and raced after the Caddo boy.

"I am humbled," Chigozie whispered to Kort. "Your courage humbles me."

"No, Shepherd," Kort said. "I am not braver than you are. I am only larger."

Ya'alu waved from the top of the pyramid and they climbed the steps to join her. "We don't have long," she warned.

Within the pyramid, the stone glowed green, a soft light emanating from the floor, walls, and ceiling. The drumming and chanting sound faded, muffled by the stone walls. The structure contained only three chambers—a room with rough pallets that smelled of beastkind near the entrance, and then, down a flight of stairs, a bedroom and a chamber with a pool of warm water. Green light reflected from its surface and dappled the ceiling.

On the bed lay a woman.

She wore green and gold over skin the color of cinnamon. She was young, she was beautiful, and she was very pregnant. When Chigozie and Kort followed the Zoman magician into the room, she sat up on the edge of the bed.

On the floor beside the bed, Chigozie saw a wicker basket torn to shreds and a wooden broom whose handle was snapped in two.

"I will be missed immediately," the young woman said.

"You will be missed," Ya'alu agreed. "But not in time. Show me your knees."

The young woman hiked up her skirt to show her knees. Removing the cap from the stone jar, Ya'alu anointed her kneecaps.

"For stamina?" the young woman asked.

"You are a witch?" Ya'alu countered.

"Who else?" the girl said. "Whose art should a woman trust to hex her womb, if not her own, and the strength of her loa?"

She had the strong French-Creole accent of someone who had lived in New Orleans, probably the Vieux Carré or the Faubourg Marigny.

Ya'alu reached inside the girl's dress with two fingers of ointment to anoint her belly.

"You're a mambo," Chigozie said.

She looked at him with narrowed eyes. "I know you."

"I am no one special, that you should know me." Chigozie

shrugged. "But I assisted my father when he was Bishop of New Orleans."

The mambo's eyes opened wide and she laughed, her voice becoming suddenly musical. "I *don't* know you," she said. "I didn't know your father. But I know your brother, Etienne Ukwu."

"My name is Chigozie."

"I'm Marie."

Chigozie wanted to sit down. "Dare I ask in what capacity you know my brother?" Etienne himself was a houngan, an initiated Vodun priest. Did the girl know him from some dark cavorting in the name of Papa Legba?

"He's the bishop now."

Chigozie felt as if he'd been punched in the stomach. He wanted to throw up, and he also wanted to weep. "Yes, I knew that."

"Did you know that the chevalier destroyed the cathedral?"

Chigozie felt lightheaded. "No." He thought of his brother's wicked, and maybe blasphemous, preparations to curse the chevalier. "Does Chevalier Le Moyne still live?"

"They both live, as far as I know. They attack each other in turn, destroying allies, wealth, health."

Chigozie longed for a chair to sit down in. He leaned against the wall and inhaled deeply as his vision blurred. "But Etienne lives."

"Yes."

"The chevalier sent you here. What for?"

"We have no time for this now. Get up!" Ya'alu pulled Marie to her feet and handed her to Chigozie.

"I can walk," Marie said.

"I believe you." He took her arm anyway.

"Do not let go of her." Ya'alu took another dab of the ointment from the stone jar and rubbed it on the knees and belly of the brown doll. She chanted, and Chigozie blinked. The Zoman magician had been transformed into...himself. And the doll on her arm had become the mambo Marie.

"Where did you learn these magics?" Chigozie asked, feeling a little envious despite his general mistrust of wizardry.

"From my master, an old man who was half-Sioux. But he told me that originally they came from Peter Plowshare. Once the Heron King taught us what we would need to know when the day arrived that we would have occasion to enter his king-dom unawares."

"I thought Zomas and Peter Plowshare were enemies," Chigozie said.

"Every border has tense moments," Ya'alu said. "And we have had our share of ours with the Heron King. And yet Peter Plowshare gave us this gift."

Naares Stoach entered the room. "Where is the witch?"

Ya'alu pointed at Chigozie. Naares peered, and after a moment saw Chigozie. "Very good. We go now. Stay close."

They exited to the renewed booming of drums and screech-ing of alien voices.

They fled the pyramid at a speed that was nearly running. Chigozie was shocked at himself, dragging along a pregnant woman as he was doing, but Marie didn't complain. They didn't retrace their steps, but followed another path, one that seemed to be dictated by things Ya'alu said after placing her stone to Marie's belly and listening through it.

But that was the illusion. The magician must be consulting her map, as she had before.

Chigozie had more questions for Marie, but their speed took his breath away. He took Ya'alu's instruction to mean that he should be quiet and focus on holding the witch, that if he did, they would remain unseen.

They arrived at the pyramid gate abruptly, a screen of trees giving way to a steep stone wall. Naares—who looked like one of two beastkind with a lizard's body—raced up a crumbing stone slope to the shelf above. Chigozie dragged Marie as close behind as he could. The Merciful followed, then Ya'alu.

How was she so slow now? She had been faster than Chigozie until the mambo's pyramid, and now she lagged.

Chigozie shot a glance at the Zoman magician and found her farther behind still, looking up and behind her.

The drumming suddenly stopped, and there was a moment of silence—Chigozie heard birds in the unreal forest, and the whistling of a soft breeze.

He was higher on the large pyramid now than he had been earlier, so he took the opportunity to look eastward. There he saw not the river, but another pyramid. One face of the pyra-mid had been scalloped away and carved into the shape of an immense throne. Sitting on that throne and facing south was a giant, covered with white feathers, whose head bore the crest of an enormous bird.

Stairs winding up the other three sides of the pyramid crawled with beastkind in gray robes. They moved between enormous flaming salamanders whose flickering tongues of fire mostly passed between the robed figures, but occasionally scorched and killed them. A hum emanated from the reptiles. It rose in volume with the emergence of jetting tongues; the tone was bass, but feminine. The beastkind in robes passed bundles up the steps from hand to hand. Chigozie had to squint, but after a moment, he realized what the bundles were.

Bound children of Adam.

At the peak of the pyramid, above the head of the seated giant, was a U-shaped stone bar or table. As Chigozie watched, straining to see detail with the distance, the gray-robed beast-kind at the top of the pyramid laid children of Adam across the stone . . . and killed them.

Chigozie didn't quite see how they died, but he guessed it must have been by a blade, because red began to stream down the stone and onto the bird-headed giant's white feathers. Or were the feathers colored like the rainbow, and iridescent?

From this distance, Chigozie couldn't tell.

The small amount of blood that poured onto the giant was barely an anointing, enough to speckle his head and shoulders. But then the beastkind in gray killed another three, and then another, and another, and the speckles became a coat.

The beastkind threw the corpses down the altar. Where they struck Simon Sword, or landed within his reach, the giant seized the bodies of men, women, and children, and tore their limbs from their dead bodies with his enormous beak.

Chigozie vomited, but managed not to let go of the witch.

"There!"

He heard the word in French, but the sort of French that sounded like it was a translation of beastkind speech. Straightening up and wiping vomit from his mouth, he saw the two pyramid guards emerge from the trees and charge.

Not toward Chigozie, who was above them on the large pyramid, but toward the false-Chigozie, Ya'alu and her doll, who were on ground level and had drifted somewhat into the forest.

Ya'alu turned and ran away from the pyramid.

Chigozie froze, watching. The Zoman magician ran and the beastkind chased her. Within moments the trees began to obscure that contest. Chigozie was unable to tear away his eyes, until Naares grabbed him and the mambo Marie both by the napes of their necks and propelled them up the pyramid again, toward an open passage.

Chigozie kept looking over his own shoulder. He saw an image of himself running through the woods. The image hid briefly behind a tree trunk bigger around than the pillars of the St. Louis Cathedral.

The former St. Louis Cathedral.

He saw the image of himself and the mambo Marie running across a clearing toward a silver ribbon of flowing water.

He saw himself torn to pieces and the witch snatched from his bloody corpse in triumph.

Then Ferpa and Naares dragged him into the tunnel.

"Don't dishonor her sacrifice," Naares said. "She gave her life to save your people."

"You are the ones threatening my people." Chigozie's eyes stung. "She gave her life to save her own kind. I am not so stupid that I don't see the difference."

Achebe woke Etienne from a deep sleep. Etienne opened his eyes with the awareness that he had spent the night with the Brides—drained, exhilarated, slightly disoriented.

"The city is attacked, Your Grace," Achebe said.

Etienne rose immediately. "Get Bondí."

"I'm here, boss." Monsieur Bondí stood in the corner of the room, unnoticed because of the darkness. One of the shutters of Etienne's bedroom was open the slightest crack, and a very faint light crept in from the street outside.

"The money?" Etienne asked.

"What little we have in cash." Bondí patted a leather satchel. "It's here."

The rest of Etienne's wealth—dwindling and under attack, as the chevalier directed his gendarmes to persecute Etienne, Ony-inye Diokpo, and the Kennedies, rather than enforce good law and order in the city—continued with the businesses themselves, hidden behind proxy names and joint-stock companies hard to trace to Etienne, or had been banked under assumed names, with Monsieur Bondí designated to the banks as the accountholder's proxy.

"Who attacks?" Etienne asked.

"I don't know, but the city burns."

Etienne considered. *Could it be Eggbert Bailey's revolt?*

He needed a vantage point from which to observe the city, but there was none.

"To the *Victoire*, gentlemen. Bring pistols."

They were staying at Don Sandoval's opera-house apartment, which was in a tall building on a fashionable street. Behind the apartment building stretched a wide stable, and there Etienne kept a number of horses.

These were under Achebe's name.

Don Sandoval himself was away, having left for New Spain. By the time Etienne and his aides were saddling their sleepy beasts, he no longer longed for a vantage point. The opera house was on fire. Dark shapes raced through the red-carpeted lobby, shattering glass and tearing furniture to pieces. Their silhouettes were swollen, misshapen, grotesque.

"Beastkind," Etienne said grimly. "The Heron King has come to New Orleans."

August Planchet's ship *La Bonne Chance*—its hull repainted to christen it *La Victoire*—rested at anchor at the docks nearest the Vieux Carré. On an ordinary night, the ride to the docks would have been a cool, fifteen-minute saunter through quiet streets. Looking over the iron, plaster, and wisteria that made up the New Orleans maze between himself and the river, Etienne now saw mostly fire.

"This way!" Etienne called.

Bondí was a clever investigator, but he was a man of books and didn't know the city the way Bishop de Bienville's former leg-breaker did. Achebe wasn't from New Orleans at all. After several weeks, he still looked around with the wide eyes of surprise wherever he went. Both men followed Etienne without hesitation and without question, and he led them by the route that looked to be the least on fire.

He skirted the northern edge of the Vieux Carré, crossed the Esplanade, and entered the Faubourg Marigny. He heard shooting in the Vieux Carré—not the infrequent shots of looters, robbers, or shopkeepers defending their investments, but the sustained shooting of battle.

The chevalier's men defending the city? The chevalier's men and Eggbert Bailey, battling?

He didn't dare ride closer to see.

They were shot at while crossing the Esplanade, which forced them off Etienne's planned route, but the Faubourg was intact. Its inhabitants swarmed like ants under boiling water, fleeing the fires, running toward them, or hiding behind barricades to prepare for whatever was attacking the city. Etienne tried to cut back through the Vieux Carré toward the docks and saw gendarmes crouching behind barricades.

He'd go farther around.

The Franklin Gate was abandoned and dark, the gate itself open, the guards gone.

Strange voices called from the Spanish moss-draped oaks outside.

"If we ride out that way, boss," Bondí said, "we're not taking the *Victoire*."

"We could ride to Mobile," Achebe said.

"Yes," Etienne agreed. "But that's longer than I want to go in the saddle." He was no horseman, and already his legs were sore. "We abandon the horses here."

"Pity," Achebe said, "I had come to enjoy owning such fine beasts."

They turned the animals loose and sent them out of the city, Etienne guessing that was the beasts' best chance for survival. Then they climbed within the guard tower of the Franklin Gate and stepped onto the wall.

Now Etienne had his vantage point.

Two thirds of the city burned. Etienne kept an eye on New Orleans as he crossed back toward the docks high on the stone wall; he saw marching and shooting gendarmes in blue uniforms, but nowhere did he see gendarmes fighting gendarmes.

Had Bailey's revolt failed?

There were no guards over the Mississippi Gate, either. Before going into the gatehouse, he looked for the Palais du Chevalier. The windows of the great palace were dark, though fire burned in its gardens.

Where was the chevalier?

"I've found the mechanism for lowering the gate," Bondí said.

"No," Etienne said.

"No...what?" Bondí stood inside the gatehouse and examined a pair of long levers. "Do you want to just jump down, instead? Whoever is lighting fires, they haven't done it on the docks. I can see the *Victoire* from here."

"No, we're not leaving," Etienne said.

"Shall we retrace our steps?" Achebe asked. "Take shelter in Don Sandoval's apartment?"

Etienne shook his head slowly. "We don't need to take shelter. We need to *give* shelter."

Immediately, he felt the desire of the Brides well up within him.

"Like a king," Achebe said.

Bondí looked up. "But you are a king without a palace, boss."

"Not sure where to sleep, eh? Not to worry. New Orleans has a palace for the taking."

What did it mean? Why would the Chevalier of New Orleans abandon the city that made him wealthy and powerful, an Elector and a force to be reckoned with? Had he simply tired of the battle?

Etienne himself had withdrawn from his cathedral and from his gaming establishment, and not because he wished to surrender or had lost the will to fight. He had been forced to change strategy, and he had adapted. Perhaps the chevalier was dodging Etienne's attack, preparing a counterstrike.

Where was the chevalier, and what was he doing?

Etienne sang as they walked:

> *Il se cachera de jour*
> *Mironton, mironton, mirontaine*
> *Il se cachera de jour*
> *De nuit il va voler*
> *De nuit il va voler*

They descended within the gate complex itself, then crossed through the corner of the Place d'Armes. There, Etienne saw four men in gendarme uniforms dragging an old man from a burning storefront.

"Eggbert Bailey!" Etienne cried. The four gendarmes all looked quickly at him, then looked away, as if uncomfortable. "I'm the Bishop of New Orleans!" Etienne snapped. When that also failed to produce a response, he elaborated. "I am no friend to the chevalier. When you see Eggbert Bailey, please tell him that Bishop Ukwu is requisitioning the Palais. Invite him to please send refugees there."

The gendarmes stared in astonishment, then faintly nodded their heads, as if barely comprehending.

Etienne led his two men to the Palais. It was located north and west of the Vieux Carré, in a neighborhood of lovely old homes. Here, too, was a high wall and a gatehouse.

"It looks empty," Bondí said. "It also looks locked."

"You are not of my faith, Monsieur Bondí."

"Either of them."

"Nor I," Achebe said. "Will you ask your god Jesus to help you?"

"Jesus is not generally understood as a god of opening doors," Etienne said. "But Maitre Carrefour is."

"Your Bible tells me my god is called Mammon," Bondí said jovially. "He can open doors, but generally only when there is someone inside to do the physical work of opening."

"Maitre Carrefour is not so constrained."

Etienne examined the gatehouse. It had a portcullis designed to be large enough for carriages to enter. Absent miraculous physical strength, there was no way to lift the portcullis from the outside. But there was also a small door, made for a person to walk through; that door was of heavy planks and had a large, iron lock mechanism.

"My Brides, come to me," he murmured.

He felt them awakening to life within him. If only he had brought hot peppers for the Brides, or gunpowder-infused rum, for Maitre Carrefour. But he hadn't.

"My Brides, I beg you to bring with you Maitre Carrefour, the king of all crossroads, the opener of every way."

Etienne felt heat and motion within him, swelling as if to a crescendo and then stopping. He took his powder horn, small and elegant as befit a gentleman who shot only rarely, and poured powder into the lock's keyhole.

"I don't think you can burn down the door that way," Achebe said. "But if you tell me it's possible, I'll believe."

"Shh," Bondí said. "He's not going to burn it down."

The sensation of heat and power abruptly returned, snatching away Etienne's breath. Alongside Ezili Freda and Ezili Danto there was now a third presence, dangerous and definitely masculine.

"My Brides," Etienne said, "give me strength. Maitre Carrefour, I stand before a way that is blocked. I would move forward, not for myself, but for all the poor of this city. I beg you now, open this door."

Etienne crouched and blew into the lock.

As if he had just spat a stream of fire, the powder inside the lock ignited. In a bright red flash, the powder erupted and disappeared. Smoke scattered in curling puffs away from the lock, and Etienne stood.

Bondí and Achebe were both watching him, the former with calm confidence and the latter with nervous faith. Behind them now stood others.

Eggbert Bailey, musket in hand, stood at the head of twenty gendarmes with bayonets on their muskets and heavy coats on their backs. Behind them were men, women, and children. They were scorched and bandaged, their eyes exhausted and doubtful.

Beside Eggbert waited several men with light pistols in their hands and light cotton jackets on their backs. They looked impatient—messengers, probably.

"You said to come here," Eggbert Bailey pointed out. "You said you would give refuge. That's a timely offer, Your Grace. New Orleans has many who have need of shelter this night."

"Strait is the gate," Etienne said, "and narrow is the way, which leadeth unto life." He opened the door.

It opened, revealing the cobbled courtyard within and the hulking shadowed Palais.

Etienne stepped aside and ushered in the poor of New Orleans. Some rushed straight in, but others stopped to kiss Etienne's hand, throw themselves around his neck to embrace him, or kneel to touch their foreheads to his feet.

"Go with them," Etienne said to Monsieur Bondí. "See what food has been left in the pantries. Feed them and get them back into bed, if you can do it."

Bondí went.

"They will shoot you for looting," Eggbert Bailey said.

"If the chevalier begins to shoot looters for actions taken on this night," Etienne said. "He will have to shoot half the city, at least."

"Including me." Eggbert laughed. "It warms my heart that you and I are in the same predicament."

"Is this the revolt of the gendarmes?" Etienne asked.

"It started as the revolt," Eggbert said. "We stole rifles, we burned barracks. But then the city was attacked by a horde of beastmen from the Great Green Wood. Our revolt has become the defense of New Orleans. Perhaps they will sing such songs of *us* as they now sing of Jackson."

"Perhaps we too will be executed by firing squad," Etienne suggested, "and then allowed to molder in iron cages on the Place d'Armes."

"You are so cheerful."

"Did the chevalier hear in advance of the revolt?" Etienne asked, gesturing at the dark house. "I worry we have an informer, someone who allowed the chevalier to escape."

Eggbert shrugged. "Maybe we do. But isn't the other possibility worse?"

"You mean the possibility that he knew in advance about the attack of the beastkind."

Eggbert nodded solemnly.

Etienne considered. "I hope the chevalier knew the beastkind were coming. We should certainly put that story about, whether it is true or not. New Orleans is loyal to its own, and a man who would throw the rest of the city into the fire in such a manner would lose a great deal of respect. He might not be able to return."

Bailey smiled. "Perhaps, once the fire is under control, you might consider preaching a sermon. Perhaps from this very spot. Leaning out one of the chevalier's own windows, for instance."

"It would be effective proof that the man was gone," Etienne agreed. "Get me gendarmes to keep the fires from the Palais tonight, and send me refugees to fill the chevalier's beds. I will consider a fitting sermon for the morning."

Eggbert Bailey bowed slightly, and then bellowed orders to turn his men around and head north into the city. As he ran, he rattled off instructions to the runners, sending them flying in other directions.

"Come," Etienne said to Achebe. "Let's get a view of this revolt."

There was no central staircase within the Palais, but with enough wandering around by lantern light, Etienne and the wrestler found their way up five flights of stairs, to the top of something like a tower that jutted out on the north side of the building. The tower had a walkway around its circular perimeter. Standing on the walkway, Etienne felt a cool breeze blow through his hair. The Mississippi and the city were far enough below that he couldn't smell the stink of either.

Walking around the tower, he could see great distances north, east, and west; to the south, the bulk of the Palais itself blocked out anything else. The forest east of the city was dark, as it should be. To the north, within the city walls and beyond them, fires burned. The raging, uncontrolled flames burned buildings and leaped from tree to tree. The beastkind.

Why would the beastkind rise up to smash New Orleans? It seemed too formal, too much effort. Mere feral rampaging would leave them farther north, in the Cotton Princedoms, or the Ohio, or Memphis.

This was organized.

Mulling over the questions these thoughts sparked in his mind, Etienne almost didn't look westward. When he did, he was stunned.

To the west burned additional fires. These were not the wild fires of looting and destruction, though, but the organized fires of a marching company. A large marching company. On the far side of Bishopsbridge and strung out for miles, Etienne saw torches, lanterns, campfires.

An army.

No army that large ever marched out of Texia; the Texians were fierce, but simply not that organized. Texians resisted being told what to do even by their own leaders. This was an army fielded by a large and wealthy power.

The Empire was a possibility.

But New Spain was much more likely. The army approached by land, from the west.

"What is that?" Achebe asked at his shoulder.

"I believe we have found the chevalier," Etienne said. "And I'm afraid it is up to you and me to stop him."

"Fools. Peter Plowshare makes the bounds, yes.
And Simon Sword breaks them."

———◆———

CHAPTER TWENTY-EIGHT

Boom!

The big Imperial guns punched a second hole in the Treewall.
"To the breach!" Bill shouted.

He was gratified that Cathy and the other healers had withdrawn farther from the fighting. He was grateful to Montserrat
for saving Cathy directly from the shuffling, undead Voldrich.

Maltres Korinn ran toward the new gap, a group of wardens at his heels. The hole was too big, there were too many
Imperials—living men in blue coats now, as well as the rotting,
mobile dead—and Maltres and his men were too few. But he had
a gray banner tied to his horsehead-tipped staff of office and he
raised it high, charging into the face of the foe.

Two birds were on the banner, one black and one white.

A curious choice.

Then a third gap opened in the wall.

Sharelas saw it. Shouting, she sent soldiers down the steps
toward the new breach, and others toward where Sarah's beastkind drove back the earliest incursion of damned corpses. They
were few, though, and men in blue coats battered their way past
the first Cahokians—

to be met abruptly by the Podebradan Yedera.

Flashing her scimitar and emitting a blood-curdling yell, the
Unborn Daughter hurled herself into the Imperial soldiers from

the side. Closing to such proximity that their bayonets became an awkward liability, she held her weapon laid alongside her own forearm; in her other hand, she held a dagger.

Spinning and leaping, she seemed to be battering the advancing soldiers with her fists and elbows. In her wake, men fell screaming or dead.

The Imperial tide rose, a wall of blue surging through the gap in the Treewall, pushing Yedera out ahead of it—

and another squad sent by Sharelas arrived to reinforce her, setting spears and halting the charge.

Bill blew *fall in* on the Heron King's horn. Chikaak, blood on his muzzle and on his sword, withdrew from the fighting and presented himself for orders.

"Help me get on this horse, Sergeant," Bill grunted.

Chikaak was man-sized but stronger than any child of Adam Bill had ever known. He hoisted Bill up and into the saddle. Bill snapped his spyglass to his eye and looked at the Temple of the Sun.

No sign of Sarah. The Imperial hedge wizard Luman Walters had also disappeared.

"Her Majesty," Chikaak said.

"My thoughts exactly." Bill blew *fall in* again, and rode toward the Great Mound.

Sarah's beastkind responded with enthusiasm. Despite their unequal speed, they duly fell in and followed together. Bill was certain that some of those warriors were capable of outracing his horse. They were ragged and wounded, but their discipline held, and they marched double-time as a unit.

He let Chikaak bring them up, and rode ahead to the top of the mound.

Once, not long ago, horses had ridden on the top of the Great Mound, and even into the Temple of the Sun. Now his mount shied back, whinnying uncomfortably, as Bill approached the peak. Several lengths short of the summit, he lowered himself to the ground.

There was nothing to lash the animal to, so he let it go. It bolted.

He hobbled around the top of the mound quickly on his canes, surveying the battle below. Another hole had pierced the Treewall on the north, and yet another on its south side. The wall was giving way.

A body wearing a long blue coat, such as the Philadelphia

Blues wore, lay slumped in the temple's doorway. Sarah had such a coat.

Bill lurched toward the body, and then caught himself short.

A feeling of dread and awe seized him two steps from the doorway. He shook his head and inhaled deeply, but it didn't fade.

It felt like...like the sensations he'd felt as a much younger man, at the outset of his earliest battles in the service of the Earl of Johnsland. A grim and transcendent sense that he stood in the presence of a mighty power, something that could strike him dead and would do so without a second thought.

Was this the feeling that had driven off his horse?

The prone person lay with face turned away from the daylight, but the curly hair and heavy shoes told Bill it wasn't Sarah. It was Walters, the magician.

Only he was wearing Sarah's coat.

The open space behind the doors of the Temple of the Sun was dark, and no sound escaped it.

Bill took another deep breath, planning to bellow into the temple, to ascertain that Sarah was safe. The feeling of dread stopped him.

Sarah was in the arms of her father's goddess now, and whatever she was doing, Bill was of no use to her.

"Serve her well," he grumbled to the sleeping wizard, and then returned to the eastern face of the mound. For his part, Bill would serve Sarah by buying her all the time he could.

The beastkind had nearly reached the peak. Below, Maltres Korinn and his men had stopped up one gap in the Treewall. The unhallowed dead shambled steadily in through the others.

Chikaak stepped to the top of the mound at the head of the file of beastkind and saluted.

"Sergeant," Bill growled, "we are too few to surround the mound with an unbroken square. Should it come to it, we will make a last stand in the doorway of the temple. For now, post scouts on every corner of the mound. Three men at each corner, and skirmishers prepared to respond to any enemy that attempts to ascend."

Bill didn't have nearly the combination of calls on the Heron King's horn he would need to give such complex orders. He thanked God in his heart for his coyote-headed sergeant as Chikaak barked out a series of instructions in tones Bill didn't know. The fastest of the beastkind split out in groups of three and headed for the corners.

The slowest remained with Bill and Chikaak, facing east.

"Your eyes are keen, Sergeant."

Chikaak nodded, a growl low in his throat.

"Keep an eye out for my lady," Bill said. "I believe she is with the healers. You and I will die here, but if there is anything we can do to save her, consistent with our duties to our queen, we will."

Chikaak nodded again.

"Now have every man who can shoot lie on his belly. The mound itself will afford us our best protection."

Bill himself stretched out on the cold ground, carefully setting his hat beside him and laying his powder inside it.

Below, dead men were climbing the base of the mound. Mingled in their ranks were dead beastkind, with limbs and snouts Bill recognized.

Sarah's own warriors, turned against her by the foul power of Robert Hooke.

He checked his firing pans. "Don't waste your ammunition. Hold your fire until you can see their eyes."

Sarah walked through a dark forest. Somewhere behind her, in some space, she knew that Luman Walters lay asleep on the ground. But Luman Walters also walked beside her. She wore his coat and he wore hers, but it felt as if they standing together inside a single long woolen garment.

For the first time in months, she looked with both eyes and saw a single, unified view of everything.

That fact made her uncomfortable.

She stepped on a path. The ground beneath her feet was rocky and pitted, as if it had been carved through the earth against the earth's will. Twisted boles of pine trees leaned in close against her on either side, casting shadows deep and dark enough to make her doubt her eyes even as to the very existence of a path. Her horse-headed staff was useful, giving her in effect a third leg to balance with. It saved her from falling more than once.

The sky above her was pure white. The sun shone from directly ahead of her, as if lying on the horizon in a permanent dawn. She heard the buzzing of bees, a comforting sound. The air was tinged slightly with the smell of spice and citrus.

"The first trump card is the Highway," Luman Walters said. "Or else possibly the Widow."

Sarah shook her head. "Iffen you're seein' what I'm seein', Walters, you know this ain't no Highway."

"It's no Widow, either."

Sarah laughed sharply. "Dammit, I like you, Luman."

Luman Walters bowed his head. "But maybe our guess is wrong. Maybe there's no connection with the Tarock, after all."

Sarah shook her head. "I feel you're on a good track. Everything is connected, I think. And this is a kind of a highway we're on." She heard the lonely hooting and growling of unseen beasts in the forest around her. "What should we expect to see coming up?"

Luman turned and spoke to the empty air beside him. "What's in the next room?"

She kept walking.

"Peter Plowshare," Luman reported. "The Drunkard. The Horseman. The Bird. These are the trumps indicated by the characters on the shelves in the second and third room. Assuming, also, we're right to walk this path sunwise."

"I don't see any of that," Sarah said, but as she said it, the path turned toward a thick knot of evergreen trees and abruptly forked. One branch of the path shot right at a ninety-degree angle, and the other shot left, at the square.

Above the path to her right, perching on a branch directly over the rocky trail, a white dove stared at Sarah with its yellow eyes. Clinging to a branch over the path on her left hand, a black raven stared at her.

A man lay slumped on the ground, just before the fork. He leaned up against an object that Sarah took at first to be a boulder, but after a moment she saw that it was a barrel. The man wore stained gray travel woolens. In his hand he clutched a powder horn, flat against his belly.

No, a drinking horn, like something they'd pass around the banquet hall in Chicago.

"The Drunkard," she said. "The Highway, the Drunkard, the Bird."

Luman said nothing. His expression was both astonished and pleased.

"Or birds, rather," Sarah said. "But I reckon that's okay, since the highway don't look too much like the card, either."

She heard a faint burbling sound. Looking, she saw a trickle of water emerging from a spring. It flowed from the ground between the leftward and rightward paths, crossed the track, and then disappeared into the pine forest. A pair of antelope stood drinking from the water; as Sarah looked at them, they noticed her and bounded away into the forest.

"Go to hell," the man leaning against the barrel said. "I'm not drunk, I'm wounded."

"There's not a wounded man in the deck, is there?" Sarah asked Luman.

He shook his head.

"What wounded you, then?" Sarah asked the man on the ground.

"The monsters in the forest," he said.

"What monsters?"

"Haven't you read?" he pressed. "Cherubim and a flaming sword."

"To keep me out of Eden." A shiver ran down Sarah's spine. "And did you encounter the cherubim and the flaming sword down one of these paths, then?" She looked down both; within a few paces, each path twisted and threw itself out of her sight.

"I did."

"Which one?" she asked.

He glared at her with a sour eye. "It hardly matters."

She felt it did matter, immensely. "Will you try to stop me if I walk down one of these paths? Or both?"

"Do I *look* like cherubim and a flaming sword?"

"No." Sarah stood and considered. "Luman," she said. "What can you tell me about the Drunkard in the Tarock?"

Luman answered immediately. "The picture looks like him. Complete with barrel and horn."

"Anything else you can tell me about that card?"

"There's another object in the image," Luman said. "It looks metallic, copper. Maybe it's a coin or a nugget."

The Drunkard snorted.

Sarah frowned. Luman seemed to be right, and the path she was walking—into the spiritual space inside the Temple of the Sun—was in some way marked by Franklin's Tarock. Surely, then, the Drunkard was here for a reason. "If you won't try to impede my progress," she said to the man leaning against the barrel, "are you here to *help* me? Will you tell me which path to take?"

"Why should I help you?" The Drunkard sneered.

Sarah nearly took her bag off her shoulder to batter him with it, out of sheer irritation.

Only then she noticed his choice of words. The Drunkard hadn't said *no*, he'd asked a question. Why *should* he help her, indeed?

"I could command you," she said.

"If you are walking this path, then you are not yet queen." He smiled, a hint of sorrow in his eyes. "And you may never become queen."

"I bear my father's sevenfold crown!" she snapped. "I could command you, queen or not!"

"Your father's crown." The Drunkard nodded. "Once, the crown belonged to Onandagos himself. But on me, even the mighty Onandagos would have no hold. Not on me, and in here, not on anyone."

In her heart, Sarah knew he was telling the truth. Whatever he was, the Drunkard wasn't a man. Wasn't a person, not in the ordinary sense of that word.

If I am walking the Onandagos Road, am I Onandagos?

"Would you trade with me?" she asked. "Can I give you something?"

"What could you possibly give me?"

Her heart sank. "Would you *please* help me?" Sarah forced her voice to sound as humble and polite as she could. It cracked with the effort.

The Drunkard looked at her and blinked.

Sarah's chest felt tight and her eyes stung as if she were about to cry, and then she realized she had almost missed it.

What could you possibly give to me?

Again, the Drunkard hadn't said *no*.

He had asked a question.

What *could* she possibly give to him?

Slowly, Sarah knelt beside the drunk man. His eyes met hers. They were deeply familiar, though she couldn't place them. She took the horn in both hands.

It was empty, of course. Lying as it had on his belly, any liquid in it would have spilled out immediately.

What she could give the Drunkard was wine.

"I have no wine," she murmured.

The Drunkard said nothing.

"I also have no wine," Luman said.

Sarah stood and looked around her. The forest was dark, and again she heard the echo of hooting and snorting in the trees. Cherubim and a flaming sword, the Drunkard had said. Was she meant now to enter the forest, braving the monsters that lurked therein to find wine for the Drunkard?

Was she meant to leave the path and return, bringing wine? Sarah looked back the way she'd come. If she did leave, would she be allowed to return? And if she did return, could she bring such a mundane object as a bottle of wine with her?

She doubted it.

She sighed.

She was the Beloved. She was supposed to be here, on this path, making this climb to the Serpent Throne and Unfallen Eden. If this was a riddle, it was a riddle she was *meant* to solve.

She was the Beloved.

There was water.

Sarah knelt beside the spring. This felt like a sacramental act, so she moved slowly. She knelt in a posture that was as dignified as she could manage, and pressed her knees into pine needles and mud.

She filled the horn and stood.

Looking down into the horn, she saw sparkling, clear water.

She needed something more. She needed an incantation.

"What have I to do with thee?" she asked. The words were from the Gospel of John, and they came out of her almost automatically. "Mine hour is not yet come."

Energy flowed through her, but it didn't come from her, and it didn't come with the burning feeling of a ley's power. Instead, the mana seemed to flow from the trees all around her and from the path, and it flowed into the horn.

The spring water changed color and became dark. The sharp, fruity smell of wine filled Sarah's nostrils.

She turned and knelt again, offering the horn to the Drunkard. He took it and drank, and then he held it out to her.

Sarah took the horn and sipped from it. As she drank, the Drunkard's face and disheveled traveling clothing seemed to fall away like a fog whipped off by the wind. The person Sarah saw was someone else entirely.

She saw her father.

But then she swallowed, and the Drunkard returned.

He stood, all the languor and torpor gone instantly from his body, and smiled at Sarah.

"Tell me your name," he said.

"Sarah."

The Drunkard nodded. "I have two things to give you, Sarah. The first is a warning."

Sarah's limbs trembled. "I'm listening."

Luman Walters was also listening. His face shone with excitement and he leaned in close.

He held the Drunkard's horn in his hands. Had Sarah handed it to him without meaning to?

Had he drunk from it?

"One road leads to great danger, Sarah," the Drunkard said. "One road leads to Eden."

Sarah listened in silence for a moment longer, thinking the Drunkard had more to say, but he had finished. She refrained from cursing. "That's the warning?"

The Drunkard nodded.

"And what's the other thing you have for me?"

The Drunkard stooped and picked up the barrel against which he had been leaning. In his hands it suddenly seemed to be a small cask, almost a little basket, like a music box. When he opened it, Sarah saw a flash of copper.

Inside lay a metal disk like a coin. The Drunkard pressed it into Sarah's hands. "Here is a token for your journey."

Sarah looked down at the token. It was smooth around the edges, like an old-fashioned stamped coin, before they became milled to prevent shaving. On one side was a horse's head and on the other a circle. The sun, maybe?

She looked up from her hand to ask the Drunkard, but he was gone.

"Did you see him leave?" she asked Luman.

Walters shook his head. "I . . . no, Your Majesty. I'm sorry."

Sarah snorted. "Don't be sorry. Luman Walters, I think you've figured this trail out. Or part of it, at least. Does this token mean anything to you?"

She rotated it, showing him both the obverse and the reverse sides. He shook his head.

"At least you didn't say you're sorry this time." Sarah grinned at the wizard. "What do you make of his warning?"

"There are two paths," Luman said. "One leads to danger, and the other leads to Eden. You have to pick the correct path."

Sarah tucked the copper token into her shoulderbag. "Hmm." She stepped forward and into the center of the fork, looking at length down the right and then down the left. "A dove and a raven. Like the Basilica and the Temple of the Sun."

"Are you being asked to choose between those two?" Luman suggested.

"Surely, if that's the choice, then it's an easy one. I have to choose the Temple of the Sun, as it's the building I'm standing inside."

"Hmm." Luman rubbed his chin.

"You're thinking that's the obvious choice, and therefore the wrong one." Sarah blew air past her teeth. "So am I, Luman."

"But choosing the dove seems just as wrong, doesn't it? Could you really come here into the goddess's temple and choose the chapel instead?"

"What was it you called it? Mystery-logic? Choosing the left hand, which appears to be the wrong answer, but is in fact the right answer for some non-obvious reason?"

"Yes," Luman agreed. "Only I'd feel much more comfortable if I could see what the non-obvious reason was. I really do not relish the thought of you and me being attacked by cherubim with a flaming sword."

"You and me?" she challenged him. "I left you asleep at the door, Luman."

"Are you sure about that?" His smile was gentle. "I think if a flaming sword cut you in half right now, the damage done to my coat—the coat you're wearing—would be done to my body."

"I'm sorry, Luman," she said. "You're right."

"You never have to apologize to me," he said. "I've chosen you for my queen."

Sarah looked down both forks again. "Maybe we're not thinking about this the right way. What does the card show?"

"What does the card show?" Luman asked.

"Which one?" Isaiah Wilkes held all three in his hand. "The Highway, the Drunkard, or the Bird?"

Something was bothering him about the cards, and he wasn't quite sure what it was.

"Any of them," Luman said. "We need a hint, an indication.

Which fork does Sarah need to travel down: left and the raven, or right and the dove?"

"We're turning left, sunwise, around the palace of life," Jacob Hop pointed out. "Maybe it's that simple. Maybe the answer isn't in the cards at all. Turn left."

"What, constantly?" Wilkes shook his head. "That doesn't sound right. Besides, here the sun is directly ahead of us. And look, the Highway in the picture goes right."

"Nonsense," Nathaniel said. "It goes both directions. No road only goes one way."

"But look at the travelers painted on the card." Wilkes touched them one by one with his fingertip. "They're all traveling to the right."

"That seems like a thin reed," Hop said.

"Besides," Nathaniel added, "Maybe this is Luman's mystery-logic. Everyone in the normal world goes to the right, so Sarah should travel left."

"That's a thinner reed," Hop said.

"The bird is a dove," Luman said. "Can the answer be that simple?"

There was a dreadful silence as they all contemplated the question.

"But look," Wilkes said, pointing. "The dove isn't above a path. If Sarah is meant to walk a path to the dove, shouldn't there be a picture of the path in the painting?"

Was that what troubled him?

Nathaniel took the Tarocks from him and tried to lay them out together, aligning the Highway so that it pointed at the Bird. The action revealed nothing.

Luman stared at the Bird. "The Bird isn't over a path. It perches on a branch, but it perches over a stream."

But that wasn't what was bothering Wilkes; suddenly, he realized what had niggled at him so.

"No, that's not what's wrong with the picture. Look at it closely. That Bird isn't a dove at all. It's a raven, but it's been painted white."

"A misprint?" Jacob suggested.

"The raven is white," Luman said.

"The raven is white," Luman said, and Sarah knew the answer.

"What was it you said about the two paths?" she asked him again.

"One leads to danger, and the other leads to Eden."

Eden. The bird in the Tarock was over a spring, not over a path.

"And a river went out of Eden," she said.

"What?"

Sarah laughed. "Only that isn't what the Drunkard said. He never said 'the other road.'"

"No?" Luman looked taken aback.

Sarah shook her head. "He said, 'One road leads to danger, one road leads to Eden.'"

Luman narrowed his eyes in thought. "I don't understand."

"Luman Walters," she said. "There is only one road."

"But which..." He stopped and nodded.

Sarah walked directly at the spring of water, bubbling from the woods at the edge of the path right where the road forked right and left. Luman followed her. She continued straight, ignoring the two paths, and stepped over the top of the bubbling water—

the pine trees seemed to reach for her with malevolent hands, the hooting in the forest ahead grew to abrupt sharp shrieks—

and her foot came down on a broad, flat path.

The woods around her were suddenly brighter, the trees deciduous. The wider path had a narrow grassy fringe. The trees that had moments earlier seemed to be about to wrap themselves about Sarah now stood several paces back.

She gazed back the way she had come. There was no path right and no path left, only a broad, smooth path that led straight back, as far as her eye could see. On a branch overhead perched a single bird—a white raven.

Sarah tapped the road at her feet with the tip of her staff. "Welcome to the Highway, Luman Walters."

Luman whistled a low note of appreciation and nodded slowly. "Indeed. Only remember one thing, Your Majesty."

"Yes?"

"If there is only one road, then you and I are walking into great danger, even *as* we approach Eden."

"Cherubim and a flaming sword." Sarah laughed. "Hell, Luman. Tell me something I *don't* know."

Together, they walked down the Highway. In the distance, above the trees and silhouetted against the perpetually dawning sun, Sarah saw low, forested mountains.

✧   ✧   ✧

Though he hid in thick forest, crouched behind a bramble, Chigozie felt naked and exposed.

Naares Stoach and the mambo Marie were with him, along with Kort and Ferpa; the other Merciful hung back deeper in the forest. *Are they more afraid to be seen?*

Stoach also crouched, while Marie sat with her back propped against the trunk of a tree, holding her belly.

Had her belly grown since they'd brought her out of the Heron King's land?

Chigozie felt horror at the implications of that thought, but he was plagued by greater horrors still.

The Merciful stood, but somehow, their presence in the forest seemed natural. Looking directly at them, Chigozie felt he almost didn't see them, as if they were grazing deer, and could only be observed if you were looking for them and thinking of them consciously.

They were gathered on a long, low ridge. Below them was the white city of Etzanoa, the great city of Zomas, rebel sister of Cahokia, the only metropolis of the Missouri.

Under thick cloud cover, Etzanoa burned.

Even at this distance, Chigozie knew what the wailing and the smoke meant. Beastkind rampaged through the city of white stone, shattering walls and scattering fires across rooftops. He knew, because he had seen it in the Missouri. Rape, murder, and the eating of the flesh of mankind traveled in the wake of those fires. The thought made him shudder.

How much guilt did he bear for not stopping Kort when Kort and his band were doing the rampaging? He had put victims out of their misery and he had called it mercy, but it was a poor sort of mercy that could only offer death as a release from pain. Could he have resisted in some more effective way?

He should have tried.

He looked at Kort's face. The beastman had the head of a bison, and Chigozie could read no emotion in it. Kort's dark, glittering eyes were fixed unflinchingly on the destruction of Etzanoa.

Scattered bands of Firstborn fighters still resisted within the city's maze. For every warrior in a lacquered breastplate, firing muskets or stabbing with long lances, Chigozie saw five men with wolf's heads, or ox horns, or the tusks of elephants, ripping the city apart stone by stone.

"They have General Varem," Naares Stoach said. Stoach's face was drained of color and the lines of his mouth barely moved as he spoke.

Chigozie followed the Zoman's line of sight and saw General Varem. Three beastkind so encumbered with animal parts that he could scarcely find any humanity in them dragged Varem from a collapsing alley into a broad square whose once-white stone was now painted red with blood.

They dragged him because he was missing a leg and an arm, both on the same side. From this distance, Chigozie could see no bandages; some magic, either of his own or of his captors, was keeping the man alive.

From a sagging gate, Simon Sword emerged. He towered over his minions and the sunlight scattered off his feathers like light through a crystal, shedding flecks of color on the city's walls all about him. In his hand he held an enormous golden sword. As he spoke, the god alternately clenched and unclenched his empty hand, or swung the sword in great, emphatic arcs.

Chigozie flinched instinctively, but Stoach put a hand on his shoulder. "Steady, Shepherd," the outrider said. "Ya'alu's art comes from Peter Plowshare himself, and will hold."

The words gave Chigozie little comfort.

"I wish I could hear," he said.

"Ya'alu would have amplified the words for us." Stoach turned to Marie and glared at her with disdain. "What say you, witch? Will you ask your Africk spirits to wing your husband's words to us?"

Marie spat.

Good God of Heaven, her belly was definitely swollen.

Stoach shrugged. "It matters not. He asks the general where we are. Since the general doesn't know, he will either bluff or tell the god of the Missouri and the Ohio Rivers to go bugger himself."

Chigozie stared. Simon Sword prowled about the pinioned general like a large cat stalking a small and helpless animal. The general stared dully ahead.

Simon Sword circled the general twice, his gestures becoming larger and more energetic. Beastkind dragged Zomans into the square and killed them in front of the general, disemboweling them, tearing off their heads, and rending their flesh with beastlike teeth.

The general sagged, defeated.

Simon Sword circled a third time, and then abruptly wheeled on the general. With a single downward swing of his golden sword, he split the Firstborn commander in half.

Lightning flashed and the earth shuddered. Moments later, the sky groaned.

A knot of beastkind pounced, devouring the remains of General Varem. Chigozie looked away.

"You are next," the mambo Marie muttered.

"Your loving bridegroom is unable to find us," Naares Stoach said. "Peter Plowshare makes the bounds, and by ancient covenant with Zomas and Etzanoa of the White Towers, he taught us the arts to enforce them."

Marie's laugh was hollow and sounded more like choking. "Fools. Peter Plowshare makes the bounds, yes. And Simon Sword breaks them. For all his father does, in all his decades of work, Simon Sword breaks them. He breaks them all."

Naares Stoach growled. "You carry a monster in your womb and you rejoice in it?"

She gazed at him coolly. "Père Loko and Mère Ayizan permit it. And I do it because this is how I will have my revenge."

"On *Zomas*?" Stoach howled. His voice was so loud, Chigozie turned and looked toward Etzanoa, half-expecting the Heron King to come charging their direction.

"On mankind," Marie said. "On men. On the chevalier, who imprisoned me. On his mamelukes, who dragged me to the Heron King's bed. And yes on Zomas, and on Memphis, and on every other power that has enslaved my people!"

"I will kill the child in your womb." Stoach drew a pistol from his belt, checking the firing pan. "I was sent to bring that child back to Zomas, to be held as a bargaining chip against the Heron King, but Zomas has fallen. I will shoot you in the belly and destroy you and your madness now."

Thunder rolled and the earth shook again.

"I will die." Marie sneered. "And my newborn son will kill you where you stand."

"We shall see." Stoach raised his pistol and pulled back the hammer.

"Stop!" Kort bellowed.

Chigozie flinched again, uncertain where to turn. A glance at the funeral pyre of Zomas reassured him that the Heron King still hadn't noticed him, but a look at Kort's face gave no reassurance whatsoever. Why was the beastman interfering?

Had his conversion and faith fallen away? Had it been feigned? Was he now intervening to save the child of his true god, the Heron King?

Kort moved between Stoach and Marie, towering over them both.

"She speaks the truth," Ferpa said softly. "She doesn't speak it kindly, but she speaks the truth."

"As she knows it." Naares Stoach ground his words out through clenched teeth, but he lowered his pistol.

"There is a balm in Gilead," Kort said slowly. The big beastman turned and looked at Chigozie. "I have learned this from the Shepherd of Still Waters."

"No," Stoach said.

"If there is a balm that can heal my wounds, then it can heal the wounds of this witch, and of her child," Kort said.

Marie laughed. "But I am a good Christian already! And more than that, I am mambo asogwe of la Société la Belle Aphrodite of the Faubourg Marigny!"

Stoach shook his head, but his words were words of surrender. "I have nowhere else to go. It's worth a try."

Kort looked at Chigozie. Chigozie took a deep breath and nodded.

Marie continued to rave. "And I am the *bride of a god*, the great mystère of this continent, the *Heron King!* You cannot give me *more religion*, beastman!"

"No," Kort said. "But I can give you mercy."

Marie shut her mouth, but still showed her teeth in a snarl.

Chigozie turned away from the burning city and looked northward. "Let's go. We will lead these lost souls, too, beside the still waters."

"Lead me where you will," Marie murmured. "Simon Sword will find me."

Kort picked the mambo up, and they walked northward. The earth continued to shake and the sky to rumble, as if the world itself were protesting.

Sören and Sigrid continued to sleep soundly as Nathaniel collapsed into a trance. As he had predicted, a shadow rose from the furs about his sleeping form and took the shape of a bear.

"Makwa," Margarida said in friendly greeting, and fell asleep.

She dreamed of golden light on the waters of Pensacola Bay, the ancestral lands of Montserrat Ferrer i Quintana, which she had once believed were *her* family demesne. In the dream, she still believed, but a lawyer in a three-cocked hat followed her about, trying to persuade her otherwise. He presented a birth certificate, written in blood on a plank of oak, that showed her to be a child of the Penn family. He tried to press into her hands affidavits of witnesses to her birth, though they were all in the form of transcriptions of torture sessions. Each statement verified that she was Margaret Elytharias Penn, daughter of the Empress Hannah Penn and her husband Kyres Elytharias, and was accompanied by a notation as to the sort of torture that had produced the statement. "Spoken through the slot of the iron maiden," one said. "Given upon the rack," said another.

Each time the lawyer approached with such a document, Margarida fled, first down to the beach, and then out onto a long dock that trembled at every step. Finally she leaped into a waiting boat and rowed herself out into the water.

The last time the lawyer appeared, he emerged directly from the waters of the bay. Salt water sluiced off his hat, which, for the first time, he was wearing backward on his head.

As the lawyer climbed out of the water on the invisible rungs of a ladder, Margarida saw his faded purplish coat, which was worn inside out, and recognized his face as the face of her brother, Nathaniel Elytharias Penn.

Nathaniel shook himself like a wet dog, throwing off water, and stepped into the boat. "You need to wake up. You're about to be attacked."

"But Makwa," she said.

"Makwa will fight." Nathaniel frowned, looking very serious. "I don't know if Makwa alone is strong enough to defend us."

"Who is it?" Margarida asked. "The Emperor's man, Franklin?"

Nathaniel shook his head. "Cromwell's man. Ezekiel Angleton, the Martinite. The wiindigoo."

"How am I going to stop him?" The sunlight was gone, the waters of the bay scowling the gray reflection of a cloud-filled sky that now seemed to threaten rain.

"Seize the initiative," Nathaniel said. "Take the fight to him. Surprise him if you can. I'll do everything I can to help. But I'm needed here."

"Where is *here*?" she asked him. "Where *are* you?"

Nathaniel hesitated, then frowned. "*Here* seems to be many places at once, and some of them may not even fit the ordinary definition of a place. Here is a thing that is happening, and I have to be part of it because I am holding some of the pieces together. We're helping our sister Sarah. But I think I can be with you, too."

"You can be in two places at once?"

"At least two," Nathaniel said. "I am Makwa, for instance, as much as I am the boy sleeping beneath."

"You're the bear?" But he had already told her that he was.

"Wake up now. Take a weapon, and I will come with you. Let's find the wiindigoo. And maybe you could get a little angry. Not all the way, not so you lose complete control, but enough so that you can rip the masts out of ships."

Margarida woke up.

Makwa stood on the packed earth floor of the longhouse, nodding at her. Margarida shrugged back into her wool coat. The hair on the top of her head began to rise and her scalp tingled as she lifted Sören's ax from the pegs where it rested and crept to the door.

She listened at the planks and heard nothing. Lifting the leather-thong latch, she slipped out into the winter night.

Makwa followed her.

What stars and moon there might be were obscured by thick clouds. Margaret crouched beside the longhouse, wishing suddenly that instead of her own gift she had the gifts of her sister and brother. Where she saw a dark thicket of leafless trees, rolling fields under snow, and ditches thick with impenetrable shadow, Sarah might see the Yankee necromancer, plain as day.

And Nathaniel might hear him.

As if prodded by her thought of Nathaniel, the shadow-bear Makwa nudged Margaret's side. It felt warm and substantial, despite its appearance. It turned and slunk past the outhouse behind the longhouse, heading for a line of fenceposts and a creek bed beyond.

Ax gripped tightly in both hands, Margarida followed.

"I'd wet my breeks at the sight of you."

⊰•⊱

CHAPTER TWENTY-NINE

They were losing.

Bill saw Maltres Korinn fall back from the wall with a shrinking knot of Cahokian wardens and the Podebradan Yedera. They retreated to the Hall of Onandagos through bloody streets as a hundred-foot length of the Treewall crumbled. South of the Duke of Na'avu, Joleta Zorales and Valia Sharelas beat a similar retreat, abandoning their guns on the walls and falling back to one of the city's larger private homes.

Here and there, other homes made defensive stands. Maltres had requisitioned all of Cahokia's bodyguards, retinues, and family troops. The women and men standing atop wooden walls and firing down at the Imperial soldiers wore no uniforms and carried irregular and uneven weapons.

The blue soldiers streaming in through the gaps flooded across the plain below him.

Shuffling dead flooded up the Great Mound. Some were men in ragged blue Imperial colors, but more daunting than those were the dead beastkind, Sarah's own former troops. More daunting, larger, and in front.

Bill needed a barrier.

He needed fire.

"Sergeant," Bill growled, "we need to send soldiers into the temple and requisition wood and oil. Anything we can get that will burn."

Chikaak didn't answer; he had disappeared.

"Sergeant!" Bill bellowed, but there was no answer.

He dragged himself, wincing, to his knees, and turned just in time to see the coyote-headed beastman come over the lip of the mound. With him came two of Sarah's larger beastman warriors, grunting and roaring. Between them, they dragged a cart.

The cart was piled high with wounded warriors. Those lively enough to do so loaded and fired weapons down the slope of the mound behind them. Montse's young pirate protégé was among them, shouting and singing as he fired.

Cathy Filmer, Montserrat Ferrer i Quintana, and Gazelem Zomas staggered up in the cart's wake.

His heart nearly exploded in relief, but Bill had no time.

"Sergeant!" he shouted to Chikaak. "Well done! Now take those men into the temple and get me all the flammable material you find. Furniture, oil, sheets—anything you can get!"

Cathy and Gazelem both looked as if Bill had struck them. Chikaak nodded and barked to the two beastmen at the cart. The three of them charged toward the temple door—

and froze, just as they reached the opening.

"They can't do it." Gazelem Zomas's voice was filled with awe. "They can't go in."

Hell's Bells. We are caught between the hammer and the anvil, and the anvil is Sarah's own goddess. "Unload the men from that cart!" Bill shouted. "Get every man who can fire a gun into position. Get ready to light that cart on fire and send it down the hill!"

Chikaak raced to obey Bill's orders. Cathy worked with the wounded men, helping them down off the groaning wagon. Montse and Gazelem returned with Bill to the edge of the mound. All three of them crouched to present small targets to the Imperial soldiers below.

The dead warriors ascending the hill were slow but tireless, and they had nearly arrived.

"I can see their eyes!" Bill barked. He took the Heron King's horn in his hand and blew the signal for *fire.*

The volley crashed through the lumbering beastmen. Two fell, knocked down by the impetus of the bullets, but the others moaned and wailed and kept running.

"Load silver shot, if you have it!" Bill bellowed.

He noticed the black fire surrounding the city; after the first few days, it had become such a normal sight, it escaped his notice.

He saw it now because it had doubled in height, and it was drawing nearer.

It had crossed the Treewall.

"I'll ignite the wagon." Gazelem slipped away.

"What I wouldn't give for a few of those big guns and the Pitchers to work them," Montse murmured. She loaded a brace of pistols with silver bullets.

"The small guns do virtually nothing," Bill grunted. He blew one signal advising his warriors to arm themselves with bayonets, and a second, summoning them to form up beside him. "We will have to break this charge with a counter-charge. Hell's Bells, I need barrels of black powder. Or a few hundred more soldiers."

Beastkind warriors rejoined Bill from the other corners of the mound. They were pitifully few in numbers, but their eyes were fierce.

The last of them came with Gazelem Zomas, dragging the hospital cart. Somehow, he'd managed to ignite it. Flames licked up the cart's walls.

"Before the wheels burn," Gazelem advised with a resolute nod.

"Great God of Heaven," Bill said, grinning at his men. Not all of them could understand his words, but the peeled-back lips, bared fangs, and joyous panting he got in return told him they could understand his smile. "If I were one of Thomas's wage-boys, I'd wet my breeks at the sight of you."

Chikaak saluted, straightening his spine and snapping one furry hand to his coyote brow. Following his example, the other beastmen all saluted in turn.

General William Lee saluted back.

He lacked an appropriate horn signal. "Chikaak, the Imperial soldiers approaching the top of the mound must surely be fatigued. Let us send them an appropriate conveyance."

"Perhaps a wagon?" Gazelem Zomas suggested.

"I believe it would be the very thing, suh."

Chikaak and three of the other beastkind stepped forward and hurled the cart down the steps of the mound. The dead beastkind warriors, formerly their fellows, were within moments of the peak, and the flaming cart caught them by surprise. Several were trampled and lay still. Others were knocked down. Some were caught up and rode hissing and shrieking down the mound, igniting with the wood.

The Imperial charge was broken.

Form up, Bill blew, then *fire*, and then *charge*.

A mixed volley of lead and silver slammed into the undead creeping up the mound. Many of them dropped, and some of them stopped moving entirely. Then Sarah's beastkind warriors thundered down Cahokia's great mound, roaring as they went.

"Cahokia and Elytharias!" Bill shouted. It was an improvisation, but Gazelem and Montse took it up immediately.

"Cahokia and Elytharias!"

Bill couldn't run, but he fired his pistols over the heads of his men into the oncoming mass of Imperials.

The beastmen collided fifty feet below the top of the mound. The Imperials were fatigueless dead, but the living flesh and bone of Bill's warriors was driven by courage, devotion, and gravity, and it followed a racing fenceline of bayonets.

The beastmen rolled over their former fellows and the shambling dead men who climbed in their wake. Beyond that was a gap, caused by the weariness of the living leg muscles of the Imperial soldiers following. As his men entered the gap, Bill blew *retreat* to summon them back to the height of the mound.

"Give them covering fire!" he shouted.

Cathy was there, and Montse and Gazelem and half a dozen wounded Firstborn soldiers. They fired and reloaded over the heads of the beastmen.

From below, the Imperial soldiers also fired and reloaded into the mass of living beastmen.

Sarah's beastkind soldiers struggled back up the hill. Tired from battle, weak from rationing, and wounded, they didn't make it. Chikaak fell ten feet from the top of the mound, dropping first to his knees as bullets struck him in the back, and then falling away to one side.

His dying face wore the grin of a faithful dog.

One of the Firstborn, a man Bill had seen in drill but whose name he didn't know, rose to his knees to try to retrieve Chikaak. A bullet passed through his throat, killing the Cahokian instantly.

As the man dropped, Bill had the distinct impression of seeing his soul leave his eyes, not fading into nowhere, as he had seen so many times on the battlefield, but sucked away into the atmosphere—

and into the wall of black fire.

Was it a trick of his mind that made the ring of fire seem to constrict slightly more around the dying city?

And was that ring centered on this very mound?

With a twist of pain like a stab wound in the pit of his stomach, Bill knew that every death of his own men strengthened the enemy's sorcery.

Two figures ascended the mound. They did not walk on it, but floated above it, as if they were birds wearing the shape of men.

One was the Sorcerer Robert Hooke. The other seemed to be a naked child.

"I'd give both my legs for more silver bullets right now," Cathy Filmer said. She fired anyway, and so did Bill, but if they hit Hooke or the child, the targets gave no sign of it.

"Gentlemen," Bill said. "This is the end. It has been an honor."

There was a rumble of general agreement.

Hooke and the child stopped above the scorched, bloodied, and mangled heap of beastkind flesh. Hooke laughed, a dry, rasping sound.

"You still have time to surrender!" Bill roared.

So very droll. Hooke smiled. *But my lord shall not give thee the same opportunity. He has come to perform his great sacrifice.*

The child had white eyes, and his skin was deathly pale. He spoke into Bill's mind, Hooke-fashion, and his voice was a grating jangle, as if two church bells were being slammed together to their mutual destruction.

Son of man, can these bones live?

Hooke's lord? Bill stared at the floating child.

"It's Oliver Cromwell," Cathy murmured. "The Necromancer."

Gazelem spat.

"What you offer isn't life!" Bill shouted.

The child-Cromwell stared at him, his mouth a flat line. Then he raised one hand, palm-down and level with his own shoulder. *Rise,* he said in his hideous shriek of a voice. *Take up your weapons and walk.*

Chikaak stood first. The coyote-headed beastman stared at Bill with flat, lightless eyes, and his canine jaw hung slackly.

Behind him, the other dead beastmen stood. Each picked up

his bayonet, and they staggered up the mound toward its last defenders.

"Damn you!" Bill fired twice at Cromwell, and he was certain he hit the boy-Necromancer. The dead flesh showed no sign of the attacks.

Cromwell and Hooke rose together vertically and turned their attention toward the Temple of the Sun. The black fire loomed closer. It was now as tall as the Great Mound. The flames licked in, as if trying to enclose the city under a dome of dark flame.

Sarah's former beastkind, now dead, charged.

Behind them and almost caught up, rose a wave of Imperial blue.

"Fire!" Bill yelled.

On horseback, Etienne, Achebe, and Monsieur Bondí rode east of the city. Loud shadows under the moss-draped oaks hinted at beastkind on this side of New Orleans as well, but the two men rode fast and didn't stop until they arrived at Bishopsbridge.

On the other side of the Mississippi, a string of lights trailed out to the east and south. At this distance, they looked like fireflies, but they must have been fires. Torches and campfires.

"Stay here." Etienne slipped off the back of his horse and ran up the stone. As he rose toward its height, he hunched down to keep out of sight of whatever approached from the other side.

Behind him, he heard the running feet of his two men. He shook his head at their disobedience, but their loyalty lightened his heart.

Ahead, the clatter of hooves on stone. Two horses, he thought.

Etienne straightened to his full height and raised his chin.

The two men approaching on horseback wore Spanish colors: blue jackets and red trousers. They weren't lancers, but some kind of scout, armed with pistols and sabers.

"Stop!" Etienne shouted.

The two riders reined in their animals. "Who goes there?"

"I am Etienne Ukwu. Identify yourselves."

"We are the allies of the Chevalier of New Orleans," one man said. He was the heavier of the two, and the shorter. With the lights at their backs, Etienne couldn't see the men's faces.

If only they were women, the Brides would give him power over them.

"Your accent is Spanish," Etienne said slowly. "And you say you are the chevalier's allies, not his servants. Has the Gaspard Le Moyne sold himself to New Spain, then? I believe that would be an act of treason under the Compact. Levying war against the Empire."

The second rider grabbed for his pistol, and Etienne heard the crack of a firearm at his ear. The rider flopped from his saddle, but one foot remained tangled in his stirrup. When he hit the ground, his horse bolted. The startled animal galloped past Etienne, dragging the dead Spaniard with it.

Etienne kept his eyes fixed on the living rider. The other man didn't reach for a weapon. Etienne forced himself to trust that Achebe and Monsieur Bondí were behind him with weapons, giving him support.

"The chevalier has returned to bring order to his city," the Spaniard said.

"The chevalier left, and the city has found order without him," Etienne said. "You may tell the chevalier and his other allies that the Le Moyne family is no longer welcome in the City of New Orleans."

The rider hesitated. "Who are you?"

"I am Etienne Ukwu," Etienne said again. "Gaspard will know my name, since he had my father murdered, and also destroyed the cathedral in which my father and I both served. I am the Bishop of New Orleans, my father's successor. I hold this bridge in the name of the Bishopric and the city of New Orleans and the Empire. You and all your slaves shall not pass."

The rider snorted. "There are three of you."

"That you *see*." Etienne was bluffing. Where would he get additional troops to hold the bridge?

Or could he destroy the bridge? Where could he find enough gunpowder to blast Bishopsbridge to rubble? It wouldn't stop the Spaniards, but it would slow them. Or if he couldn't find the gunpowder, would Maitre Carrefour destroy a stone bridge for him?

After a brief hesitation, the Spanish scout nodded, wheeled his horse around, and rode back to the torches.

"There must be thousands of them," Bondí estimated.

"How you long to count," Etienne said.

"I didn't know there were that many Spaniards in the world," Achebe added.

"There will be Aztecs among them," Etienne said. "Apache

scouts. Conscripts from Jamaica and Haiti. Celestials. Mercenaries from elsewhere in their empire, or from around the world."

"What do you intend to do?" Bondí asked.

Etienne sighed. "Stop them."

The highway led Sarah to a clearing and the bank of a river.

The sun still lay on the horizon, directly ahead of her, but the sky—without her noticing it—had become a bright crimson. The smell of cinnamon and citrus had grown stronger.

"I'm not intimate with the Tarocks," she said to Luman, "but there's a River, isn't there?"

He hesitated, then nodded. "There's a River. And it appears to be in the right place."

"You mean the letter framing the trump card appears next, or in the next group, in the palace of life."

"That's right."

"In the…wherever it is you and Nathaniel and the others are."

"*Wherever it is* is all the language I have to describe where I am, too." Walters shrugged, and then smiled. "But it seems to be working. We've climbed to a second story in the palace of life, for one thing. At the end of the day, *working* or *not working* is really all there is to magic. At least, to the magic I know."

"Really?" Sarah asked. "To me, magic is one damn surprise after another." She exhaled and looked at the River.

Its muddy waters moved fast and swirled around jagged rocks. It looked nothing like the clear freshet she had stepped across to enter the Highway; could these be the same waters?

A haze obscured the far bank, but Sarah saw the green of trees and bushes, and also flashes of something large, opaque, and white. It flashed in the light like a wall made of quartz.

"You see a city over there, Luman?" she asked.

"On the other side of the river? I only see haze," he said. "But on this side, there's a corpse."

His words made Sarah start. Turning, she saw Luman standing beside a gallows. The gallows was a simple one, tall, and built of plain, thick wood. Notches were hacked into the gallows a hand's length apart. From the gallows hung a noose. The rope was coiled around the neck of a dead man who hung there, swaying slightly, as if there were a breeze, or as if he had been hanged so recently he hadn't yet come to rest.

His eyes were puffed and bulging and his tongue hung from the corner of his mouth, but there was something familiar about the hanged man's appearance.

Beyond the gallows prowled lions. Were they hungry? But they watched in silence, and didn't advance.

"This man, too, is a trump," Luman said gravely. "And this trump also appears to be in the correct place."

"You're doing a good job not sounding too smug about being right," Sarah said.

"I can't feel smug." Luman laughed softly. "I'm much too busy feeling astonished."

"Wait a moment," Jacob Hop said.

Isaiah Wilkes looked over the other dead man's shoulder. Hop was shuffling the suit of coins in his hands. "Wait, for what?" the Franklin asked.

Luman Walters was distracted in some conversation with Sarah. Nathaniel Penn had gone quiet, too; he was also communicating with his sister, apparently. That left the two shades to discuss.

Hop held up the one of cups. It depicted a woman entering a forest. "She entered a wood, a forest, hey?"

"Yes."

Hop showed the two of the suit, portraying the same woman walking a twisted forest path, pushing aside a bramble and a low-hanging bough. "She walked a tangled path?"

"I think so." Wilkes jogged the hedge wizard's elbow. "Luman, pay attention."

Walters shook his head and focused on the two cards. His eyes opened wide. "Yes."

Hop showed the three of cups. "A junction of three paths. And look, one of the cups is in the path, away from all the others, which are up in the tops of the trees."

"What's next?" Luman asked.

"Maybe the page." Hop showed the page of cups. "See, he's holding one cup in his hand."

"You think the page meets the traveler at the junction of three paths and delivers one token," Luman Walters said.

"I'm not seeing what you see inside the temple," Jacob said. "What do you think?"

"I think the Lightning Bishop knew much more that he was

credited with." Luman Walters turned to look Isaiah in the eyes. "What do you have to tell us about this?"

Isaiah shook his head, a flood of emotion nearly overcoming him. "This is new to me. Franklin...my old master...organized his Conventicle as a secret alliance to support the forces that would need to stand together upon the return of Simon Sword. I knew he created the Tarocks, and many have speculated that they contain secret information encoded in their images or their sequences, but...this is a surprise."

"What's next?" Luman asked.

"In the minor arcana, there's a clearing, then a...I don't know, is this a bridge?"

"Or a boat?" Luman asked.

"Or a balcony?" Isaiah shook his head. "It just looks like a handrailing."

"And then six is a single tree. And look at the six. The tree. Again, there are two cups at the base of it."

"And the knight of cups?" Isaiah asked.

Hop showed the card. "Holding one cup in each hand."

"You think someone is going to appear at a tree to give Sarah a second token," Luman said.

Hop shrugged. "I think the cards say that."

"Only there is no tree," Luman said.

Hop shrugged, and Wilkes did the same. "Wait," Wilkes said. "What are the possibilities now for the major arcana?"

Hop tucked the minor arcana into one pocket of his brown coat and dug the major arcana from another. He ran through the next three rooms of the palace of life, Wilkes and Luman trailing behind, staring down at the cards. When he stopped, he raised his voice in an abrupt yell.

"Warn her!" he shouted.

"What *of*?" Luman asked.

"Simon Sword!" the Dutchman cried. "I fear the next trump is Simon Sword!"

Nathaniel, who had been quiet, as if his thoughts were focused elsewhere, snapped out of his reverie. "This is the same deck?"

"Yes!" Hop looked frantic.

"What's wrong?"

Nathaniel took a deep breath. "We may have...put the real Simon Sword into that card."

Hop dropped the other cards, gripping the Simon Sword trump with both hands. He tore at it, but it didn't rend. Grunting, he tore again—

the card burst open, green light blazed from it—

a presence like a giant—but smelling of river moss, mud, and bird feathers—passed through the room, knocking all four men to the ground.

And then disappeared.

"Oh no," Luman Walters said.

The Heron King burst from the trees, iridescent, muscular, and enormous. He shattered branches in passing, throwing leaves and bark around him in an arboreal cloud.

Sarah staggered back and raised her staff defensively, then relaxed.

Simon Sword was a trump, a card in the Major Arcana of the New World Tarock. This wasn't the real Simon Sword.

Simon Sword couldn't possibly be part of the Cahokian ascent rite she was experiencing. Could he?

And could the Heron King possibly have entered the Temple of the Sun, other than as conqueror?

Or did his presence indeed mean that Sarah's people were defeated, and victory belonged to the rampaging beastkind?

No. He was in the Tarock. If Luman and Jake and the others were right—and so far, they seemed to be—then she could reasonably expect to encounter him in this place. And maybe Peter Plowshare, for that matter.

That would be interesting.

But something was wrong. Simon Sword strode toward her, growing larger and larger. He raised his hands, and in them he held the Heronsword that Sarah had given him. In her hands it had been a manageable sword, the size such that any child of Adam might wield it. In the hands of Simon Sword, it seemed twelve feet long. He raised the blade above his head.

This was no riddle; this was an attack.

"Watch out!" Luman Walters shouted.

Sarah leaped aside, but too late. The gigantic golden blade rushed down—

all she could think, in the impossibly long moments during which the blade descended toward her, was what a mistake she had made at the Serpent Mound, arming one of her worst foes with the weapon he most desired—

the blade struck her shoulder, and rebounded.

Simon Sword flew backward into the trees in an explosion. The coat she wore—the coat she had borrowed from Luman Walters—split open and golden salamanders leaped from it. They swam in a stream of golden light, light that smelled of citrus and cinnamon and filled her mouth with the taste of honey. Bees, too, seemed to swarm around her, and the cloud of reptiles and honey-spinners hurled Simon Sword into the trees with a sound like a thousand gongs rung together in perfect harmony. She heard words in the chord, though she could not decipher them. The bees buzzed around her for a moment longer while the salamanders scampered into the woods, and then were gone.

The music lingered for long seconds afterward.

Luman rushed forward to catch her, but she waved him off, leaning on her staff.

"Angels in your pockets." She laughed. "In *my* pockets, then. And I'm glad I had them. And you were right, it worked. But what the hell *was* that, Luman?"

Luman shrugged. "Whatever it was that troubled Jacob Hop... memories? A demonic residue? Contamination? Hop and your brother Nathaniel put it into the Simon Sword trump of their deck. And I think it just escaped and attacked you."

"Is it defeated now?" Sarah asked.

As if in answer, Simon Sword emerged again from the woods. He was tall, but this time tall as a tall man might be, rather than tall as a giant. And in his hands, he held no weapon.

Sarah held her staff up again. "What are you doing here, demon?" she challenged him.

"Say *god*, rather." This Simon Sword spoke with vocal cords, and not with the mind-voice she had heard in the Heron King's hall. "But *demon* if you will, because even in calling me *demon*, you acknowledge this: that I am alive."

What was this?

"If you have a token, I demand it," Sarah called. "Of right. Otherwise, stand aside."

Simon Sword laughed. "What right do you have, witch? You have been crowned queen by a faithless zealot who reckons the Serpent Throne a thing of naught. Do you believe *that* anointing will carry you over the river and into the walled garden of the goddess? No, you have no right. Stay with me and choose life."

Sarah tightened her grip on her staff. This was not the Heron King. This was some sort of riddle, or trial.

She was reasonably sure.

"I have the right from my father," she said. "He was king before me, and his father before him."

"*His* father was godless entirely. He let the destroyers run free in the kingdom, wore a Christian shell to appease John Penn, and made his entire kingdom forsake the language of their fathers for mere *English*." Simon Sword snorted. "And *your* father never sat on the Serpent Throne, not by right and not even by audacity. He was a king to the outward world only."

The words stung, but Sarah knew they were true.

Did she have any right at all?

"I am the Beloved of the goddess," she said. "I was chosen by Her."

"And yet Unfallen Eden does not lie open before you, does it?" The Heron King sneered. "You are Her Beloved, and yet you wander the same choked trails as all the children of Adam. Your father was Her Beloved, as well. Did that bring him to the Serpent Throne?"

It had not.

Sarah's heart fell.

"Stay with me," Simon Sword urged her. "Choose real life, the life that lives by eating other living things, not the perfect vision of a life no mortal flesh can ever have. Mortal life is red and hot and violent, and it is yours, if you want it. You have become a mortal queen. *Be* that queen."

"Don't listen to him," Luman whispered. "He's a liar."

Sarah shook her head slowly. "In this place, I don't think you can tell lies. He's telling the truth. I have no right to enter."

Simon Sword laughed, a sound like a waterfall.

And Sarah knew.

She turned her back on the Heron King and looked across the river. She took a deep breath. "I have no right to enter, because *no* mortal flesh has a right to enter."

Behind her, Simon Sword laughed.

"But I have *seen* Eden," Sarah said. "I have stood within the veil and seen my goddess face to face. I know I have no right to enter Her palace, but I have hope that She will let me enter, nonetheless. I will act on that hope. And if I am wrong, then I will lie on my belly outside Her palace and beg Her to help my people."

Luman Walters looked abashed, but he nodded.

Sarah waded into the river.

In the ordinary mortal world, the act would have been suicide; the weight of her regalia alone would have pulled her to her death by drowning. Even here, in this strange place that was the threshold of Eden, she thought she might be making a grave mistake. She might be guessing wrong. Maybe Simon Sword *did* have a token to give her, and she hadn't successfully cajoled it from him.

But she didn't look back. She swam.

The current was fast and strong, but not as strong as it appeared from the bank. Sarah found that for much of the crossing, she was standing on the river's solid bottom. Though the flow pressed her against rocks, it never did so hard enough to wound her.

The rocks, as she saw them from up close, reminded her of other stones. *Where have I seen these before? Irra-Zostim*, she realized.

Were these then Eve Stones? If Adam Stones marked the boundaries of the kingdoms of men, did Eve Stones mark the boundaries where the kingdoms of men met the kingdoms of the gods?

She climbed from the other side and found herself standing, queerly, at the foot of another gallows.

Or rather, the same gallows, with the same corpse hanging from it. Though she had definitely crossed the river, because on this side there was no forest, and a short distance away, a wall built of quartz rose from the black soil. Towers punctuated the wall periodically, and there was a single gate of black wood.

Light radiated through the quartz, or maybe from the quartz itself. If the wall was not the sun, it held the sun within it.

Luman climbed out of the river. His eyes were wide and he hummed a tune Sarah didn't know, something that sounded vaguely hymnlike.

Sarah looked back across the river. On the far bank, she saw the clearing she had left behind and the tangled woods beyond. But there was no sign of Simon Sword, and no gallows.

She turned to look at the gallows on the near side of the river. It was gone.

In its place was a single tree, just beginning to bud.

Standing beside the tree was her father. He wore the noose around his neck, though the length of rope attached to the noose had disappeared. It was a masonic image, though Sarah had stopped paying much attention to the Freemasons when she learned they didn't admit women, so she couldn't say much about it.

Her father took the noose from his neck and laid it around Sarah's. As he did, his face was replaced again with the face Sarah didn't know.

"You are invited," the Hanged Man said to her. "You must come properly dressed."

He pressed a second coin into her hand.

"Are you my father?" she asked him.

"Yes," he said, but it didn't seem to be a complete answer.

"Are you Onandagos?" she asked.

He nodded.

"Are you Adam?"

He smiled, then turned away.

"Am *I*?" she asked.

Without another word, the man walked down the dark soil of the river's bank until he disappeared into the haze and the distance.

Luman Walters stared.

"Well, Luman," Sarah said. "I'm inclined to go up to the door and knock. Maybe we ought to ask first: are there any more secrets waiting for us in the deck? Simon Sword was bad enough, but I'd hate to have, I don't know, flesh and blood rampaging beastkind come out. Or Peter Plowshare. No guarantee he's the grinnin' Johnny everyone always wants to make him out to be."

Luman laughed drily. "No more surprises in the deck, Jake swears."

The ax was heavy in Margarida's hand.

She was not afraid. Makwa the bear padded silently ahead of her, disappearing often in the darkness that covered the farm like a spiderweb shroud. Makwa was Nathaniel, she reminded herself.

Her brother.

It didn't seem possible, on the one hand. How could she have a brother—and sister—she had never known, that her guardian had concealed from her? How could she be the secret child of the Empress herself, not to mention the half-wild, foreign King of Cahokia, whose name was still a byword for resolution and military cunning in the lands around Mobile?

Margarida had guessed instead that, whether Montserrat was really her aunt, or perhaps her mother, there was some shame connected with Margarida's birth. She must be illegitimate, tainted, problematic.

But the bedtime stories and cançones de bressol that her Tia Montse had told and sung to her had often featured miraculous children: saints, witches, changelings. Margarida had believed of herself from an early age that she was different from her few playmates. That belief had been confirmed when her adolescence had brought more than ordinary moodiness, and when she had learned for the first time that she had extraordinary strength.

A young man named Arnau, a carter's lad, had been trying to catch her attention for weeks. At the festival of Sant Jordi, he had dressed as a devil to play the correfoc, tossing fireworks into every open patch of street and playfully prodding the burghers in their bottoms with his nearly blunt pitchfork. He had tormented Tia Montse at particular length, winking at Margarida with good humor even when the smuggler lost her patience entirely and snatched the fork from him, shattering it over her knee.

Tia Montse had chased him away, but not before Arnau had given Margarida a time and a place—the carter's shop, one hour after sunset, when the fireworks were in full flower—for an assignation.

When she had arrived, two young men she didn't recognize were beating Arnau. "Robbers! Run!" he had shouted to her.

Instead of running, she had broken the legs of both boys, grabbing their thighs and snapping them with her bare hands. In her nearly blind rage, she might have broken more, but the sight of Arnau's shocked face had caused her such sudden shame that she had turned and fled.

The next day, Arnau was gone.

Since then, Margarida had been prepared to learn mysterious things about her origin. The visits she and Tia Montse regularly made to the seeress Cega Sofía had come to make more sense. Though she teased her aunt that Montse should use the witch's gifts to further her career, Margarida suspected she herself had a great past and perhaps, if she was lucky, a great destiny.

But she had expected that past and that destiny to revolve around New Orleans, around the Catalan villages of the Gulf, around the lower Mississippi and the Free Cities of the Igbo.

Not cold Pennsland.

Not queer Ohio.

But a boy who could leave his body to travel through dreams and contact dead spirits, a young man who could heal any wound and be in two places at once, a youth who had a second form as a bear made of darkness... that was a person Margarida could see as her brother.

And the witch-queen Sarah Calhoun, who sounded just as easily angered as Margarida herself, and who could see the very souls of men... such a woman could be Margarida's kin, as well.

Which meant that Kyres Elytharias, who had driven off the Spanish when all hope was lost and all allies had failed with a ruse that, depending on whose version you believed, involved sending false messages from New Spain into the Spanish camp, or perhaps sailing the same five ships time and again past the Spanish on land, painting their sides each time to make them appear to be a large fleet, or tricking a Spanish spy into believing that a single barrel of beans—the city's remaining food supply—was an entire warehouse full, was her father. Such a man could be her kin.

Though it meant she was not herself a Catalan.

Was she even a child of Eve? She had to think about it. She was a daughter of Adam, but if her father was Serpentborn and her mother was a child of Eve, Margarida wasn't quite sure where that left her.

Nor was she quite sure that it mattered.

But as she crept forth from the longhouse, fingers wrapped around the cold wood of the ax handle, she became more certain with every step that this was indeed her family. Why else would the Emperor Thomas send his creatures after her? Why else would Tia Montse, who always spoke so reverently of the Empress Hannah, go to such lengths to care for Margarida? Why else had Tia Montse taken her to sea, and kept her at sea, or in the bayous, hidden from prying eyes, since the day her hair had first risen of its own accord, filling her limbs with strength, and she had broken the two robbers' legs?

With certainty came anger.

Thomas had stolen what was hers.

Thomas had killed her mother and her father.

Thomas had tried to kill her sister.

Her spine trembled as she felt the hair on her neck and scalp stand up.

Ani gibbor.

She heard the voice in her mind only, but she recognized it as the voice of the Yankee wiindigoo. Hearing a footfall, she spun and lashed out with the ax—

and the Yankee caught the weapon. The full force of her swing rocked him, but didn't knock him down.

There was just enough light for Margarida to see the Yankee's waxy dead skin and the dark hollows around his eyes. There was just enough light that when he flashed an open-mouthed, leering grin, she could see black gums and long, yellow teeth.

And she could see that he lacked a tongue.

Margarida. He sneered.

"Margaret," she said.

Grabbing the Yankee by the front of his coat, she lifted him off his feet and ran.

"It is about to be over. But not in the way that you think."

———※◆※———

CHAPTER THIRTY

Sarah approached the black door. Steps climbed up to it in a straight ascent, carved of single slabs of the same shining white quartz of which the wall was built. As Sarah reached the bottom stair, she noticed a man standing beside the door. He wore a long robe that was white, but beside the quartz appeared gray. For a moment, Sarah felt she was seeing Thalanes, smiling and nodding, with his hands clasped in front of him.

The feeling took her breath away, and she stopped to get control of herself.

Behind her, Luman was murmuring. He stopped.

"Is something wrong?" he asked.

"What do the cards tell us?" she countered.

"There is a hill," he said. "Then a ditch. Then a hand reaching out of a hollow tree. Then an embrace with an unseen person."

Sarah tried to remember the suit of cups, and failed. "How do you paint a picture of a hug with an invisible person?"

"We see the whole traveler. But of the other person, we only see the arms."

"The traveler." Sarah liked that. She felt like a traveler. "And I reckon that there's the Priest, ain't it? He looks friendly. What are the other possible trumps we might meet?"

Luman conferred with his unseen partners. "The Revenant, the Lovers, the Widow, the Tree."

"The Lovers sound nice," Sarah said. "A Revenant—isn't that some kind of Lazar?"

At that moment, the sky cracked. A fissure split the bright red sky directly over the gate and within moments stretched back to the horizon from which Sarah had come.

"I don't see *that* in the cards," Luman murmured.

"Keep lookin'."

Capillary streaks of darkness shot out from the fissure, spreading across the sky like a net. From the smaller strands, a gray cloud spread, then darkened, shading into charcoal and then black.

Sarah could still see. There was light, but where it came from, she couldn't have said. Within seconds, the entire sky was black.

Sarah gripped the Orb of Etyles in her shoulderbag. "I expect you're going to tell me that the heavenly letter in this jacket only works once."

"Unfortunately," Luman said, "that has been my experience."

Two figures descended from the spot where the sky had first cracked. One, Sarah recognized immediately as the Sorcerer Robert Hooke.

"There's your Revenant," she said. "I feel some exasperation at the fact that my *personal* enemies seem to be taking an outsized role in this ascent."

"I'm not sure . . . I'm not sure that we are doing this strictly by the book," Luman said.

The second figure was a young boy, and he was naked. The descending personages alighted beside the Priest, whose smile transformed instantly into a stern look of challenge.

"Who dares approach?" the Priest asked.

The naked boy spoke with a voice like Robert Hooke's, sounding directly in Sarah's mind, but had the tonal qualities of glass shattering and metal being snapped in two. *I am Oliver Cromwell, and I am here to take possession of this city.*

"*Ignem mitto!*" Sarah shouted. She reached down into the Orb, pulled out a stream of green fire, and launched it at the Sorcerer and the Necromancer.

Robert Hooke stepped in front of the boy-Cromwell and raised his hand. Sarah's green lance struck his palm and entered his body. The Sorcerer's china-white skin took on a faint greenish cast, then a brighter green, and his eyes began to glow.

Sarah's body burned, and she had to drop the fire. She raised her staff defensively, expecting Hooke to throw the fire back at her . . .

But Hooke merely smiled.

"Sarah!" Luman Walters shouted.

Sarah whirled in time to see a wall of hands grab the hedge wizard and drag him out of her view. The air took on an amber cast, and hands grabbed at her body, as well.

"You're not permitted here," the Priest said to Cromwell. As he spoke, he looked at Sarah with an expression of concern.

"*Ignem—*" Sarah shouted, but hands tore the shoulderbag from her, more hands clamped over her mouth, and she lost the incantation.

I am permitted where I please. The boy-Cromwell plunged his hand into the Priest's chest, passing through the white cassock without marking it with blood, and into the man's flesh, if he had any.

The Priest stared at Cromwell, mouth gaping.

Cromwell ripped his hand back out and the Priest collapsed on the steps.

Darkness filled Sarah's eyes.

"Luman," Isaiah asked. "What's happening?"

Luman Walters had slapped his arms and legs ferociously for several long seconds, then froze in place, staring at the wall. "Am I dead?" he asked.

Jacob Hop laughed. "Join the club, hey?"

That snapped Luman out of his frozen posture, drawing a dry chuckle from the hedge wizard. "Sarah?"

"Don't tell me Sarah is dead." Isaiah's heart sank.

"I don't know," Luman said. "Robert Hooke, he . . . cast a spell. Sarah and I are lying in darkness. In a dark, cold place."

"Nathaniel," Jake said. "Can you find them?"

But Nathaniel now was fixed in his vision of some other place.

"Maybe you're in a ditch," Isaiah said. "Like on the card. Maybe this is supposed to happen. Maybe this is part of the ascent."

"I hope so," Luman said. "There seems to be a fine line between the ascent rite Sarah hoped to engineer and her actual conflict with her enemies."

"That's good," Hop said. "She's performing the ascent for real, it's not just drama."

"I would like to agree," Luman said. "But I may be dead."

"Just remember," Isaiah told him, "death is not the end."

Hop looked through his suit of cups. "The token appears to be in the ditch. You are supposed to do something there. Be given a token by someone."

"There's no one here," Luman shot back. "Well, there are hands trying to break in, I think. But they're not friendly. And who would have given her a token, in any case? The Revenant—Cromwell? Hooke?"

"The priest," Isaiah said. "You told us there was a Priest."

Hop held up the Priest trump. A black-edged hole had been punched right through the card, as if a burning cigar had been pressed against the Priest's chest.

"What happened?" Hop asked.

A brief silence. "Sarah says Cromwell killed him."

"Dammit," Wilkes and Hop cursed together.

"Wait," Luman said. "Hand me that trump card. Sarah says she knows another priest."

Etienne was staring at the lights when they began to move in his direction. Still some distance away, it would take them time to reach Bishopsbridge. He had nothing.

"Come on, boss," Monsieur Bondí said.

Achebe agreed. "If we live, we can fight again."

"There is no better barrier," Etienne said. "If we fall back to the walls, then Eggbert Bailey's men are outnumbered, ten to one at least. Probably more. Look at the size of that host."

The Biblical word felt appropriate. If God fought with the host of heaven—the stars—at his side, then the chevalier had brought earthly constellations with him, the host of New Spain.

Etienne sighed. He had nothing.

As he exhaled, a tingle ran up his spine. He felt charged, alive, filled with energy. The Brides were speaking to him.

But there were no women. Or were there? Had the chevalier somehow brought an army of Spanish amazons to fight him?

Etienne laughed at the thought, but his breath came short. Waves of ecstasy rocked his limbs and he fell to his knees.

"Boss?" Bondí grabbed his shoulder.

Etienne fell over sideways.

✧   ✧   ✧

Sarah could not even guess what strange space she was in now. She and Luman lay flat on their backs on cold earth, with a ceiling of earth just above their noses.

A ditch? A grave?

Hands poked repeatedly down from the earth above and up from the earth below to grope at them. She ignored them, but Luman punched them with both his fists, until his knuckles were skinned and bleeding.

She was glad she had him along.

"This is my fault," he said.

She laughed out loud. "In a pig's eye."

"I summoned Hooke." He punched at a groping hand. "I didn't mean to, but when I was with the Imperial Ohio, I cast a spell and he came."

Sarah felt tired. "You didn't mean to."

"But it's still my fault. How can I make amends?"

"You're holding the Priest trump?" she asked him.

"In the palace of life, I am."

Sarah took a deep breath and drew power through the Orb. Wherever she was—and with Cromwell's and Hooke's appearance, she feared she was knocked off the trail of her ascent, and risking a terrible and permanent fate—she could still reach into the Mississippi Ley.

"You're gonna help me work a little gramarye. *Sacerdotem quaeso.*" Touching Luman with her other hand, she reached through him to grab the Priest trump. She fixed that trump—burnt hole and all—in her mind as her navigating star, then sailed down the great river, looking for Etienne Ukwu.

"*Sacerdotem quaeso,*" she incanted again.

She had to hope he was close to the Mississippi. Probably anywhere in New Orleans would be good enough, but she doubted she could reach any great distance over dry land.

She found him on the river itself, standing in the middle of the water and staring off to the west. To her surprise, he stood beside three dark-skinned women. One was scarred and whip-thin, with a look of rage in her eye; the second was young, shaped of soft curves, and smiled flirtatiously; the third was heavy, with long gray hair.

"Will you come with me?" she asked them.

The women smiled. Each of the three put a hand on the

houngan, and he fell into their arms. Sarah joined them. Lifting together, the four women carried Etienne back into the ditch.

The earth chamber had grown in Sarah's absence. Its ceiling was now high enough that she, the three women, Luman, and Etienne could all stand. Luman continued to punch and kick at hands that tried to pierce the chamber and grab Sarah. With each hand that broke through, more cool dark dirt piled up on the chamber floor. The room became larger and more shapeless.

The scarred woman looked at the hands, snarled, and drew a wicked, hooked knife. She leaped into action at Luman's side, slashing at the bodiless hands and driving them back.

Etienne Ukwu now wore a gray cassock with a charcoal smudge across the chest. He opened his eyes and looked down at himself in surprise. Then he looked at Sarah.

"Sarah Carpenter," he said. "And I am to be cast in the role of your father confessor. What is his name? The Ohioan, Thalanes."

Rage welled up in Sarah, at Thomas Penn, at Oliver Cromwell, and at the Heron King. She swallowed it.

"Father Thalanes is dead, and I have need of a priest. You're a houngan, and I figure that counts."

Etienne nodded. "I will be what help I can. Remember that you already owe me."

The gray-haired woman touched Etienne's shoulder. He turned to her and sucked in a sharp breath. "Mother."

Her smile was proud and sad. Etienne took her hand in his and knelt, kissing her knuckles.

"If I don't survive this," Sarah said, "I'll be in no position to do anything. If I do survive, I will do my best to repay you."

Etienne looked up to his mother. She nodded. He stood and turned to face Sarah.

"And I am in great need of help right now." The houngan's face broke into a weary smile. "Though I do not know how you can possibly be of any aid."

Sarah hesitated. How to explain? "I need a token."

"A token of what?" Etienne frowned. "You mean a sign?"

Sarah shook her head. "I don't know. Here—and where is here, you'll want to ask me. I don't know exactly. But I will tell you this: I entered the Temple of the Sun with the intent of ascending the Serpent Throne, and I found myself on a twisted road full of strange characters who try to trick and bully me."

"La diritta via era smarrita," Etienne said.

"What?"

"Dante," he told her. "The Divine Comedy. The road of trials that leads to heaven."

"I guess."

"I am a houngan asogwe of the Société du Mars Vengeur, and I know something of such roads of trials. I am also a Christian priest—this is a recent development, since you and I met—and at least one of those apparently is relevant. Tell me about the tokens so far."

Sarah considered. "There was a drunkard at a fork in the road. I gave him wine and he gave me a token."

Etienne stroked his chin. "And which turn did you take?"

"Neither," she said. "I calculated that the fork was an illusion. To go forward, I had to step into the woods where there was no path. And there I found a highway."

"A highway and a drunkard?" Etienne asked.

"You know the Tarock? Apparently, it has something to do with this road of trials. It's a kind of a map. There were birds at the fork, too."

"I'm from New Orleans. I know Franklin's Tarock." Etienne nodded. "Go on."

"The Highway took me to a River. And there was Simon Sword, and he told me I had no right to continue."

"Did you believe him?" Etienne asked.

"I did. But I told him I had been shown the destination before, and even though I had no right, I had hope I would be allowed in."

"And he accepted this?"

"He disappeared. I swam the river. A Hanged Man on the other side gave me a second token."

"These tokens," Etienne said, "what are they? Something like a masonic grip?"

"Coins," Sarah said. "And the road seems to be mapped by half the Major Arcana, but also the suit of cups, if that helps. And the Major Arcana piece seems to be also mapped out on Cahokia's palaces of life, if you know what those are."

"I don't," Etienne admitted.

Sarah took a deep breath. Etienne might not be able to help her, after all.

"And then?" the houngan prompted her.

"Three trials," Luman said.

"Who are you?" Etienne asked.

"Luman Walters." Luman stomped on groping hands. Dirt fell onto his shoulders. Behind him, the scarred woman crouched to plunge her knife repeatedly into the floor of the chamber.

Still hands came on, and still the earth collapsed.

"He's one of my guides," Sarah said. "Like Dante had Virgil."

"Naturally," Etienne agreed. "Three trials. What happened in the third trial?"

"This is it," Sarah said, "I think. Only I was supposed to climb the steps of the City and talk to the Priest, and my best guess is he was supposed to give me the token."

"Although the cards suggest that maybe he was supposed to give it to her in a ditch," Luman added.

"You are now in the ditch, and you have summoned me to give you a token." Etienne smiled. "What happened to the other priest?"

"One of the final trumps in the sequence was the Revenant," Sarah said. "A Lazar. And Robert Hooke and Oliver Cromwell appeared and killed the Priest."

"That sounds as if the rite is not following its ordinary course." Etienne whistled. "You play a game with high stakes, Sarah Carpenter."

"I didn't choose it," Sarah said. "But I'm playing to win."

"I wish I could help you," Etienne said. "But I do not see how. I have no coins; I know no passwords; I am unfamiliar with this liturgy."

Sarah tried very hard not to look down at her feet. She was not going to die. She wouldn't let herself. She owed it to her siblings, to her father, to Thalanes, to Iron Andy Calhoun, and to her mother. She took a deep breath and looked into Etienne Ukwu's sorrowful eyes. "I understand. If I live, I will do my best to repay you the favor I owe you."

"I do have one observation to make." Etienne wove his fingers together and held them before his face—a contemplative gesture. "Yours is a road of three trials, as there are three worlds."

"Yes," Luman said. "Dante again."

Etienne continued. "Speaking not as a houngan asogwe, but as a Christian priest—if a very *bad* one—I would suggest that you should see your first trial as a trial of faith. To advance, you had to step beyond the visible path, will yourself to take the action for which there was only evidence of goodness, and not proof."

"The evidence of things not seen," Sarah said. "Hebrews." She furrowed her brow; was it possible?

Luman had stopped punching the attacking hands and openly stared at Sarah and the houngan.

Etienne nodded. "Your second trial, even in your own words, was a trial of hope. 'We have access by faith into this grace wherein we stand, and rejoice in hope of the glory of God.' St. Paul's words. You hoped to be admitted into the glory, and in that hope you advanced."

"Charity is next," Sarah said. "This is a trial of my charity."

"'And now abideth faith, hope, charity, these three; but the greatest of these is charity.' I believe this is a trial of your charity. Of your capacity to love."

"Capacity to love ain't exactly my strong suit," Sarah grumbled. "Capacity to keep goin', capacity to fight back, capacity to be a cantankerous beast as never says die, sure. Love?"

She had chosen things other than love. She had driven Calvin away, choosing not to love him.

But was that entirely fair? She had chosen her own hard roads for the love of family. Love for the Elector Calhoun and respect for his sacrifice, love for her unknown siblings and her mysterious parents.

She had been driven by love at every turn.

Forgiveness, her father had said. He wished he had forgiven more.

Forgiveness is eternal life.

Etienne shrugged ruefully. "I wish I had more to tell you, Queen Sarah. Go with God, and with all the loa."

Sarah nodded.

Etienne and his three women disappeared.

Sarah had tried to choose love, and her enemies had responded only with hatred. Her own uncle had killed her parents out of hatred. The Necromancer Cromwell and the Sorcerer Hooke, on Cromwell's orders, had tried to kill Sarah and her siblings out of hatred. The Chevalier of New Orleans, Gaspard Le Moyne, had tried to force her into marriage and had then attacked her out of hatred, and had taken her sister prisoner. Bayard Prideux had murdered her father out of hatred.

But was that really true?

"Sarah," Luman Walters said. "We're running out of time."

Hands dragged him left and right. Dirt cascaded down around his head and hers.

Bayard hadn't hated her father. He'd been desperate for money, and ordered by a superior.

And the chevalier didn't hate Sarah. He didn't respect her, he saw her as a means to an end and an inferior, but he wasn't acting out of hatred. Pride, maybe. Ambition. She just happened to be in his way.

And Cromwell? What was Cromwell doing?

Was it possible that Cromwell was acting out of something like love? That in this case, too, Sarah had the bad fortune to be in his way, but that he maybe saw himself as a benefactor, as a person of good will?

Life, Hooke had said. Cromwell wanted to bring life to all mankind, and Sarah was standing in the way.

Was the Necromancer acting out of love, even if badly misguided?

"Sarah!" Luman disappeared in an avalanche of moist dirt.

She reached into the earth, found his coat (*her* coat, which he was still wearing), and grabbed it. She would have liked to touch the Orb of Etyles, but she only had two hands, and didn't want to drop her staff.

"*Inimicum quaeso!*"

She leaped upward.

Hands dragged at her and she pushed forward. They clutched at her ankles and she beat them back with the Elector's staff.

"*Inimicum quaeso!*" she shouted again, dirt filling her mouth.

Hands tore Luman from her grip. She reached for him again and couldn't find him. Hands clawed at her face and throat and she tore them away by force.

"*Inimicum quaeso!*"

Then suddenly, she was standing at the top of the quartz stairs, face to face with the boy-Cromwell. Cromwell stared at her, surprised, and then he grinned.

Thou hast opened my road, Unsouled hag. I thank thee.

She embraced him.

She did it quickly, before he could react or she could change her mind.

"I don't hate you," she murmured.

He tried to pull back, and she squeezed him tight.

"I don't understand you," she continued, "but I don't hate you. I forgive you."

She willed it to be true. She reached down inside her heart, as if she were reaching into the Orb, and looked for her capacity to love.

Her staff, the horse-headed staff carved by Iron Andy Calhoun, burst suddenly into green leaves.

Witch! Cromwell shouted, and struck her in the face.

"You believe that you are seeking good in the world." And it was true. It was easy to see death as Cromwell's great weapon, but it was more true to see it as his great enemy. Sarah continued to hold on to him, turning her face aside and closing her eyes. The leaves felt cool to the touch. "I do not hate you."

He struck her again. As she rocked back from the blow, she found a place inside her heart where she truly did not hate Oliver Cromwell.

If the world were as Cromwell wants, my mother would be alive.

"I love you," she said.

Light and heat blasted past her. She opened her eyes.

Sarah stood in the open doorway. She was no longer embracing the shorter Cromwell, but a man who was taller than she was. Without relinquishing the embrace, she turned to look outside the walls.

Cromwell and Hooke stood in the full light that flowed through the open gate of Eden. It struck their forms like fire, burning their flesh, but they didn't flee. Rooted in place, mouths open, they howled without words.

In seconds, the light and heat reduced them to ashes.

Seconds later, the light burned away the blackness of the tainted sky, coloring it gold. The entire sky became a single blazing sun, joyous, triumphant, life-giving.

Luman Walters stood halfway up the quartz steps. The light of Eden burned away the dirt that still clung to the blue dragoon coat he wore, purifying him.

He took one step forward, then stopped.

He smiled at Sarah, but shook his head ruefully.

And took off her coat.

She nodded back at her guide. Without relinquishing her

embrace, she managed to climb out of her borrowed coat and let it drop. She stood wearing just the white linen dress and the noose about her neck.

When Luman's garment hit the ground, Luman himself disappeared, along with both coats.

The man embracing her spoke. "What is your name?"

"Sarah."

"And what is your family name?"

"I am Elytharias," she said. "And I am Penn."

"And by what token do you seek admittance into Eden?"

"By the three tokens of faith, hope, and charity," she said. "And the greatest of these is charity."

Her embracer withdrew, keeping an arm around her shoulders. She looked up into the man's face and saw that he was her father; and he was Onandagos, the great prophet-leader of her people; and he was Adam, father of all mankind.

"Welcome home," he said. Turning, he gestured inward, toward a garden of light, perfume, and honey.

In the center of the garden, a mighty tree.

And as Sarah stepped within the gates of the garden, leaves began to sprout from her body.

Bill backed onto sacred ground, knowing his mere presence was a desecration. He hoped Sarah's goddess would forgive him.

Or take Her wrath out on the walking dead who pushed him back, desecrating the hallowed ground even more foully.

But if She was going to act, either against Bill or against his undead foes, She showed no immediate sign of it. His pistols emptied and his powder gone, Bill lurched back one step at a time.

The wounded Firstborn soldiers were little help. Once their powder was gone, futilely spent plugging lead balls into dead flesh without noticeable effect, they were virtually defenseless. Injured and unable to run or fight, they were cut down as Bill's former soldiers crawled over the lip and onto the top of the mound.

Chikaak, eyes dead and one arm hanging detached at his side, tore a screaming Cahokian warrior's throat open with his teeth.

"Damn you, Sergeant!" Bill shouted.

But of course, it wasn't Chikaak anymore.

The Catalan pirate fought fiercely at Bill's side, with a saber in one hand and a long knife in the other. Gazelem Zomas, whom

Bill had thought to be a kind of spy or assassin, proved quite able with a long spear.

They gave ground slowly. Had Sarah failed?

Had Cromwell and Hooke found her inside the Temple of the Sun and killed her already? Was Bill backing toward a greater enemy even as he was backing away from lesser foes?

He could accept death, an old foe he had known for many years.

But death for Cathy was a thought that chilled his heart.

And death without seeing his son or wife again?

"Cathy!" he called to her.

No answer.

"Cathy?"

He wanted to turn and look at where he expected her to be, but the hulking wave of dead crashed against him again, knocking him off balance and forcing him to expend his precious attention on his enemies.

"There!" Gazelem shouted. He hurled himself toward the edge of the mound. Bill was able to strip a moment's focus from his foe and with it he saw Cathy, unconscious—dead?—being dragged away by Chikaak.

"Damn you, Sergeant!" he howled again, uselessly.

They had feared that some magic, or something as simple as silver applied to their skin, would turn Sarah's beastkind troops against her. Instead, the work of Oliver Cromwell had turned them against life itself.

Staggering from a wound to his shoulder, Gazelem Zomas got through the enemy line. He ran with long leaps, like a gazelle. At his approach, Chikaak raised his coyote head.

Gazelem ran the beastman through. The force of the Zoman's charge shattered the crossbar that ordinarily would have stopped the spear's forward motion, and sank the spear a further six feet into Chikaak's chest. The spear tip finally struck the trunk of one of the goddess's trees and stopped moving. The shock of impact threw Gazelem to the ground.

Cathy fell from the beastman's grip, unmoving.

Bill fought to watch even as he parried horn attacks and lopped off an assailing claw. Chikaak writhed, mouth opening and closing, pinned to the tree like a butterfly on display. Gazelem had hurt himself; he rolled back and forth on the ground clutching an ankle, his face twisted.

And then Chikaak began to drag himself forward. One step at a time, red-black ichor spewing from his wound, the coyote-headed monster lurched toward Cathy again.

Bill roared. He meant to shout *Cahokia and Elytharias*, but what came out of his throat was considerably less articulate. Dropping a shoulder, he knocked aside the beastman attacking him and dodged past a second. His legs screamed at him.

"Noooo!" he roared.

Chikaak ripped himself free in a final spatter of gore.

Gazelem lunged and tried to grab the beastman's hind leg, but missed.

Two beastkind grabbed Bill and threw him to the ground.

Chikaak leaped for Cathy, jaws open wide—

and a large, bald man tackled him.

And then a second large, bald man threw oil or liquor or something on Chikaak and applied a torch.

Over the top of the mound came more bald men, and with them Alzbieta Torias. The Podebradan Yedera danced and spun like a dervish at Torias's side, her scimitar casting a web of protective steel around the priestess. The priestess and her former bearers, in turn, had fire and flammable liquid, and they crashed into a wave of undead just as it reached Cathy's unconscious body. Bill saw Alzbieta standing over Cathy Filmer with a torch in hand, waving the flame in the faces of two dead men in long blue coats, and then he was dragged away.

Montse decapitated a charging beastman, slicing off its ape head with a single blow of her saber. Its forward motion continued, knocking her to the ground.

When her breath returned a minute later and she was able to roll the now-still corpse from atop her, she saw chaos. Living and dead in blue uniforms streamed across the top of Cahokia's Great Mound. She grabbed her saber from the ground and looked for her friends.

Bill, kicking and roaring, was being dragged down one side of the mound.

A pile of wrestling and rending bodies struggled back and forth around the spot where Cathy, Alzbieta, and Yedera had been moments earlier. Whether either was still alive, Montse couldn't tell. She saw no sign of Gazelem Zomas, either.

Nor of beautiful young Miquel.

Living men in blue uniforms charged toward the front entrance of the Temple of the Sun.

If Margarida were here, she would be Montse's first priority.

In her absence, the best Montse could do was to defend the other children of Hannah Penn.

She snatched up a flaming torch from the dead hands of one of Alzbieta's former palanquin bearers and attacked the men about to enter the temple from behind. She impaled one through the lower torso—when his comrade turned in surprise, she shoved the flame into his eyes. He dropped to the ground, shrieking.

"Cahokia and Elytharias!" she roared. Her own blade now stuck in a dead Imperial soldier, she stooped on the run to grab his weapon instead. Holding the man's heavy Brown Bess under her arm, she fired it on the run, aiming at the center of mass of a third man.

Bang!

He dropped.

The fourth tried to pivot his bayonet into position and nearly succeeded. He cut a long gash alongside Montse's arm—

and she ran her bayonet through his lung.

He fell sideways, dragging the Brown Bess down with him.

The remaining three men faced her, muskets aimed. And she was unarmed.

She inhaled and was about to spring to the attack one final time, with teeth and bare fists, when the men squeezed their triggers.

Click.

All three hammers fell. None of the weapons fired.

And then there was a man standing behind the soldiers. It was Luman Walters, the short, dark-haired, former Imperial, the hedge wizard. He clapped a small-caliber pistol to the temple of one of the soldiers.

"In the name of Her Majesty Queen Sarah of Cahokia, I demand your surrender."

The soldier snorted his derision. "I know you. You used to dissect toads and make little wax models for Director Schmidt. You weren't much good to her, and I don't see as you've done any better by your new Wiggly friends. Look around you, Walters. Cahokia has fallen."

Montse turned to look.

The top of the mound was the scene of Imperial victory, blue coats everywhere.

Only as she looked, a wave of fighters came over the top of the Great Mound. They weren't soldiers, and their arms were irregular; mismatched old muskets, the occasional pistol, spears, farm implements, even clubs. They wore no uniform.

At their head raced Zadok Tarami. He swung a long staff and cracked an Imperial soldier in the head with it. Behind him, a woman in a nun's habit carried a tall, thin cross, and sang a battle hymn.

Tarami's mob—it *was* a mob, not a military unit—converged on the spot where Montse had last seen Alzbieta Torias.

"Too little, too late," the Imperial soldier beside Luman sneered. He spun, trying to stab Luman with his bayonet.

Bang!

Luman shot the man through the temple, dropping him where he stood.

Then the hedge wizard flung himself on the second of the three men. He had a small, black-handled knife, and before the soldier could get his musket rotated into place, Luman had cut his throat. Blood spattered Luman's face and glasses.

Montse tackled the third man, tearing his bayonet from his hands. When he tried to tear it back, she gutted him with it, like a fish.

Standing briefly in the eye of the storm, she met Luman Walters's gaze.

"You stopped up their rifles," she said.

"A cantrip." He shrugged. "Nothing."

"Is it over?" A bleak feeling gripped Montse's heart. Maybe Margarida could escape, whatever happened here.

Maybe Montse could survive, find her way to Margarida, and continue in that way to keep her vow to Hannah Penn, even as Hannah's other child was destroyed by the forces of Thomas Penn.

Montse sighed.

Luman grinned. Hair mussed, blood on his face, and his long coat missing, he looked wildly out of his element. "It is about to be over. But not in the way you think."

From behind him, in the depths of the Temple of the Sun, burst a blaze of light. It struck Luman and Montse with a force that seemed physical, knocking them both to their knees.

The light rolled like the waves of an earthquake, outward in a concentric ring. As it passed each tree on the top of the Great Mound, the trees burst into flower. Snow melted as the light touched it. The golden ring crossed two shambling Imperial zaambis as they lurched toward Montse and Luman, and they both crumbled. Maggots surged from the earth in large numbers to consume their dead flesh. Living Imperial soldiers saw the light, looked up at the Temple of the Sun, and fled.

The stones of the temple began to glow.

Overhead and around the Great Mound, the black fire rolled back and shrank with the advancing of the light. Above the fire, the heavy gray clouds dissipated.

Montse thought she heard the singing of angels.

Suddenly released as his captors literally disappeared, William Lee dragged himself up again to the top of the Great Mound. Montse and Luman rushed to join him at the pile of bodies, to sort through the living and the dead.

Gazelem was alive and conscious, pinned beneath two dead palanquin bearers. Yedera was alive and apparently unharmed. She sprang to her feet snarling when the heap of dead Imperial soldiers trapping her had been pulled away.

All eight palanquin bearers were dead. The last they found was crouched over Alzbieta Torias, trying to shield her. But multiple bullets and bayonets had pierced both their bodies simultaneously, and the priestess was dead, as well.

Despite being curled into a ball and impaled, her face looked peaceful.

Zadok Tarami, showing surprising strength in his wiry frame, gathered the dead priestess in both arms. Tears streamed into his beard.

Cathy was unconscious, but alive.

Miquel had a leg that was badly mangled—beastkind had torn it with tooth and claw—but Zadok's people were bandaging him, and he looked as though he would live.

Montse helped gather the wounded and the dead, dragging them away from the glowing edifice to the edge of the Great Mound. In Cahokia below, the light continued to set off explosions of blossom and fruit.

Maltres Korinn and a small knot of his wardens emerged from the Hall of Onandagos, alive and surprised.

Jaleta Zorales and many of her Pitchers lived.

Valia Sharelas was dead.

As the Imperials fled, stunned and fearful, no force rallied them.

"The Sorcerer?" Montse asked Luman Walters. "The Necromancer?"

"Gone." He smiled. "For now, at least."

No Cahokian defender pursued their former attackers, either.

"Father Tarami." Bill groaned, dragging himself on two Brown Besses as if they were two crutches. "We will see to our dead in time. Would you please see to the wounded?"

As the expanding circle of golden light touched the upside-down crosses surrounding Cahokia, the crosses burst into flame. They burned quickly, disappearing entirely within minutes.

The Imperial gunners manning the Twelve Apostles abandoned the big guns. Just as Montse began to contemplate the thought of dragging the enormous cannons within the Treewall and finding a way to mount and use them defensively, she realized that the cannons were to have another fate.

Rapidly, as if decades were passing in minutes, a tree sprouted beneath each of the Twelve Apostles. Each gun rose slowly into the air, borne on a platform of leaf and branch, and then the trees grew around the cannons. The wood never swallowed the guns entirely, but when the trees stopped growing, the Twelve Apostles were thirty feet off the ground, perfectly preserved and also perfectly unusable.

From the moment of first contact with the light, the Treewall began to mend.

Montse gathered up Cathy Filmer and woke her. By the time the two women and Luman Walters had reached the bottom of the Great Mound, gathering up wounded and bringing them to the Hall of Onandagos or the Basilica for treatment, all the biggest holes had grown over, and the leaves and bark were beginning to return.

"Sarah?" Montse finally asked the magician. She'd been distracted by wonders, including the sight of children plucking fresh fruit from newly green trees in the city's streets, but she hadn't forgotten Hannah's queer-eyed daughter.

Luman Walters puffed out his cheeks and shook his head. "I don't really know."

"Here I thought you would prefer to go in a fire."

———⟍•⟋———

CHAPTER THIRTY-ONE

"Pick him up."

Hands grabbed Etienne, awakening him with their vigor.

"No." He waved away the hands, which belonged to Achebe, who had been trying to lift him.

Frogs croaked in the darkness. Monsieur Bondí pointed. The splash of yellow light on his face reminded Etienne that he was on Bishopsbridge, and that a large Spanish army was approaching from the west. "You really made them angry, Your Grace. They're sending a whole brigade."

Etienne stood. He sorrowed for the witch Sarah Penn, and his failure to help her. But then, with the best will in the world, how could she possibly have repaid him his favor? Even if she sent a mounted army, or an armed flotilla—and the Ohio was not famous for either cavalry or marines—they could not possibly arrive in time.

"If the Spanish are sending a brigade," he said, "it's not because they're angry. It's because they fear us."

"You," Achebe Chibundu said. "They fear *you*." There was a note of curiosity in the wrestler's voice.

"They are right to fear me," Etienne said. "They are allied with the Chevalier of New Orleans, a man I have sworn to destroy. Let us try to count their fear."

Torches approached the bridge. Fire in the west suggested

that the Bishopric's Westwego plantations were burning. With the lights came a bass chanting in a language Etienne couldn't understand.

"Ordinarily, I do the mathematics, rather than the actual counting," Bondí said. "The miracle of St. Bernardo is in the balance sheet and in the statement of earnings, rather than in the mere *number* of things. But, looking at those lights, I think there are perhaps two thousand men coming this way."

"Five times that many are still in camp," Achebe added. "Though I do not know who St. Bernardo is. Is he the one who trains dogs?"

"Ah, you Igbo." Bondí clucked his tongue. "This is what you get for believing that every man has his own god inside him. No culture."

"But having my own god who created me means that I don't have to rely on a dog-trainer to teach me to count." Achebe bowed his head to Etienne deferentially. "Your Grace, we should go. You are a mighty man, but you are not mightier than the thousands of New Spain."

Etienne took his mother's locket from his waistcoat pocket and looked at it sadly. He hadn't failed her yet, could not fail her unless he died before he destroyed the chevalier, but he felt shame that he had not yet succeeded.

Stay, son.

"Boss?" Bondí prompted him.

Your help comes.

Etienne frowned, looking down at the locket. What help? What help could there possibly be? He looked back over his shoulder to New Orleans and was reminded that it, too, was in flames.

Could Eggbert Bailey spare him troops?

But if every single gendarme in the city joined Eggbert, they would not number enough to stand against the Spanish.

"Gunpowder," he said. "Do we have gunpowder?"

"Enough to throw a few lead balls at the Spanish," Bondí said. "Not nearly enough to destroy the bridge."

"We can come back later," Achebe offered. "With casks of gunpowder and a boat. They won't expect us."

He was brave. If it came to that, his plan, desperate as it sounded, might be the best there was.

Etienne looked at the locket.

Stay. The Serpent Queen sends aid.

He remembered his mother's face—he had just seen it in vision, or trance, or ecstasy. He had seen Sarah in that same transport; Sarah had summoned him, had arranged for him to see his mother.

His mother had never lied to him.

"I am staying," he told his companions. "I suggest you leave."

"I shall stay as well." Achebe Chibundu placed himself at Etienne's left, planting his feet shoulder-width apart and facing the oncoming torches.

"I go with you, Etienne," Bondí said. "But I'd feel much better if we were going somewhere else."

"I'm staying." Etienne softened his expression into a gentle smile. "It will be all right."

Monsieur Bondí took a deep breath and settled himself on Etienne's right.

The first of the Spanish troops reached the bridge. They were not the mounted lancers for which the Spanish themselves were famous, but a division of warriors from their southern lands. The torchlight added exaggerated shadows to an appearance that was already ferocious; they had skin the color of burnt umber, noses like birds of prey, and powerful shoulders. They wore kilts made of the skins of cats, and on their shoulders they rested heavy wooden clubs embedded with glittering black shards of stone. Their cheeks bulged with something that they were chewing—when they spat on the stone, their spittle was dark red.

"Aztecs?" Achebe asked.

No one answered.

The chant came from these men. As they reached the far end of the bridge, it rose in volume and pitch—

and then they broke ranks and charged.

Bondí fired pistols into their attackers, injuring two but stopping neither of them.

"Papa Legba," Etienne prayed, his eyes fixed on the charging, berserk mass. "Jesus. Mother. *Now* is the time."

The chant disintegrated into an animal howl, reminiscent of panther cries. Etienne rubbed his mother's locket with his thumb. *Has she misled me?*

Achebe Chibundu settled into a wrestler's stance, one foot back and both hands ready to grab. "Come feel the grip of Lusipher Charpile!" he bellowed.

One of the charging Aztecs raced out in front. Etienne saw the smears of paint on his face, the expression of animal rage, the torchlight glinting off the long shards of obsidian in his upraised club—

and then the man fell to the ground, screaming.

The man behind him dropped, too, slapping at his own flesh.

"Boss?" Monsieur Bondí said.

Farther back, where the stone of Bishopsbridge met the land, berserkers fell to the ground.

"Snakes!" Achebe hissed.

"No." Etienne smiled grimly. "Basilisks. The *flying* snakes of the lower Mississippi."

"We should run from the basilisks!" Bondí whispered urgently.

Flying serpents winged up from the river's banks and plunged into the mass of Aztec warriors. They bit exposed necks and thighs. The men shrieked in pain or choked on their berserker-weed as they died.

Etienne shook his head. "They won't harm us. They have come to our aid."

A basilisk whipped up from beneath the bridge and hovered directly before Etienne's face. Its wings were white and feathered. Etienne understood that there was another subspecies, with leathery wings like those of a bat. Scales shimmered with a rainbow of color as the serpent flitted back and forth before Etienne. It regarded him with dark reptile eyes that were anything but cool, and a thin tongue that flickered in and out of its mouth. Its tail coiled several times, running a loop along its own back, as if the creature were stroking itself.

Then it turned and darted toward the Spanish.

The Aztecs broke into flight. In their charge, they scattered the ranks behind them. Etienne watched with satisfaction as the line of lights stretching back for miles snapped, and then fell apart into a fainter cloud. Shouts of confusion and fear reached him from the far bank.

"Even the serpents fight the chevalier." Monsieur Bondí chuckled.

"Tonight they do," Etienne agreed.

Tomorrow, he might need another plan. But tonight, Queen Sarah had kept her promise. He looked up the dark, flat mass of the nighttime Mississippi, and felt happy that the queer-eyed Firstborn witch lived.

Lived and had triumphed, apparently.

He resolved to send her an emissary. And a gift. Perhaps a bottle of good rum.

He looked back at the bridge to find Achebe kneeling at his feet. "Eze-Nri," Achebe said. "Eze-Nri."

"What's happening?" Jacob Hop asked.

The actor Wilkes gazed blandly at him and shrugged.

Nathaniel stood with them, but his attention was absorbed elsewhere. He cringed, extended his neck, swatted hands in front of his face, and shuffled from side to side as if he were fighting tiny invisible enemies.

Luman Walters stared into the void and said nothing.

"I don't know whether we've won or lost," Hop said.

"All in all, I'd rather win, since my life's work has been to prepare for the return of Simon Sword and defend against him. It seems that Sarah Penn may be one of the Empire's best bulwarks against his advance. But in either case, I suppose I'm dead."

"Ja, me too." Jake laughed.

Wilkes looked around. "What, then? Is there a path to take us onward? Or is this it? Do we stay here?"

"Is this heaven, do you mean?"

Wilkes gestured at the empty rooms, the characters written on the floor. "If heaven is a library with no books in it, then old Bishop Franklin was badly deceived. And he was not one to be deceived easily."

Jake laughed.

Isaiah Wilkes frowned. "What's happening with the wizard's coat?"

Luman's coat began to glow. It moved, too, flapping as if in a breeze, though the air was still. The space around the magician grew warmer.

"I don't think he's in danger." Jake raised a hand to hold back the other man. "Let's wait and see."

The warm golden glow filling the coat suddenly overflowed it. Brilliant blazing fire filled the room and Jake was blinded. He felt submerged, his skin warmed and caressed as if had sunk into a tub of warm water.

No, a vat of warm, sweet honey.

He opened his mouth, tasting the sweetness. He smelled

cinnamon and lemons, or maybe oranges. He was reminded of his youth on his uncle's ship, buying citruses for the sailors at the market in Barbados while his uncle bought sugar cane from the Spanish traders.

His feet felt nothing. Extending his toes experimentally, he couldn't find a floor beneath him.

Indeed, it felt as if he'd lost his shoes and socks.

Then the light was gone, and the wizard and Nathaniel were gone, and Jake and Isaiah Wilkes stood alone in the palace of life.

Margaret had caught the Yankee by surprise. Her charge carried him along fifty feet before he could react.

Then he hit her with the ax handle.

He was much stronger than she remembered. Her charge ended in chaos, Margaret tumbling one direction and the Yankee skidding back through the snow until he came to rest at the base of a leafless tree.

Margaret leaped to her feet. The pain in her shoulder, where she'd been hit, made her angrier, and she let the anger carry her into a forward charge again. She would rip the Yankee's head off. She would tear him limb from limb.

"Leave my family alone!"

The Yankee raised and arm and swung down over his head, as if cracking a horsewhip. He ended the motion with a single finger crooked at Margaret. Something sticky struck her in the face.

She ignored it and jumped, hands extended—

Mot tamutun! the Yankee mind-shouted—

pain engulfed Margaret's body like fire. She missed her attack and crashed to the ground, sliding through snow.

The Yankee cackled in triumph. Margaret lurched to her feet and wiped at the sticky substance on her face. Looking at it in the palm of her hand in the dim light, she saw only a thick black liquid. It stank of blood, but blood that was infected, corrupted.

Her hand was shriveling.

Anger pulsed through her. Gripping the nearest tree trunk, she yanked it from the ground in a single motion. The Yankee staggered away, raising an arm in defense, and she threw the tree at him.

He disappeared in a tangle of cracked and splintered wood.

Margaret hurt, but she had to be sure the Yankee was dead. She grabbed the tree and dragged it aside, temples throbbing.

The Yankee rose to his feet.

Mot tamutun! he howled again.

The pain knocked Margaret to her knees. She leaned forward onto one balled fist, sucking in frozen air.

The Yankee stepped closer. *You are freakishly strong. Your gift from your abomination of a father. You resist my lord's spell. But you will die.*

She sprang from her knees, butting him in the belly with her head. He didn't exhale, but the impetus knocked him to the ground. Roaring, Margaret picked up the tree, raised it over her head, and slammed it to the ground on top of him again.

Fire. She needed fire.

She turned and ran back toward the longhouse, the faint orange in the glass windows giving her hope. Her steps were ragged and uneven, and her eyelids dragged heavily downward from exhaustion and pain. If she could get brands from the fire before the Yankee freed himself, she could ignite the wood.

A cracking sound at her heels told her he'd escaped. She was still a hundred feet from the building.

Echabeh esh!

The orange glow disappeared.

Margaret tumbled to the ground, hitting on her knees and then rolling forward over her shoulder before sliding to a stop. Holding her hand before her eyes, she saw it wizened and mottled, as if she were aging by the second.

The Yankee stepped to her side, stooped, and picked her up. *My spell will kill you in minutes, but I find I have no patience.*

In his hand, the tall man held a longsword. He pulled back the weapon and pointed its sharp tip at her belly to run her through—

Makwa knocked them both down.

Margaret fell to the ground and couldn't move. Her breath came in slow, strangling gasps, as if her lungs were shrinking. She coughed and spat in the snow, seeing black ichor rather than spittle.

The Yankee stood and Makwa barreled into him again. They rolled together down a gentle slope and into the ditch at its bottom. The Yankee shouted words Margaret couldn't hear. Nathaniel's bear-spirit presence rose into the air and fell again, landing heavily on the ground.

The Yankee leaped on him, sword raised high, and then drove the blade down through the bear and into the earth below, pinning the bear to the ground.

Makwa uttered a shriek, a piercing wail, in the voice of Margaret's brother. The bear's limbs spasmed and its head trembled, as if it were suffering a fit, or experiencing death tremors.

The light faded from Margaret's vision.

You are both so obsessed with family. The Yankee looked from one immobilized sibling to the other and laughed. *Know that your Serpentspawn deaths will make your uncle happy. Yaas, very happy, indeed.*

Rage pushed Margaret to her feet one final time. She saw astonishment on the Yankee's face, and a hint of fear. Between his spell and her rage, she could barely see. Hurling herself from one shaky footstep to the next, she lunged at him.

He stepped back, tongueless mouth open in alarm.

Then she collapsed. She landed on her knees, her hands wrapped around the hilt of the Yankee's longsword.

Makwa trembled beside her, warmth leaking from his body. "I'm sorry," she said.

Rage faded. Strength ebbed. Life slipped away.

Light burst from Makwa's form. It was more than light, because it was sweet on Margaret's tongue and smelled of spice and citrus, like some Christmas drink, or an Arab delicacy in a Ferdinandian orange grove. Her skin prickled with sudden warmth and vitality.

The light came out of Nathaniel's spirit-double. Makwa's back arched and the bear howled again, this time in surprise and anger.

Sudden strength raised Margaret's head. Standing, she pulled the Yankee's sword from the earth, and from her brother. She turned to find her enemy stumbling back, raising his hands to shield his face from the light.

Where the light touched his pallid flesh, smoke rose.

The Yankee shrieked.

Margaret roared and struck the Yankee with his own sword, lopping one arm off in a single blow.

He fled.

She picked up his severed arm. Its fingers contracted as if the arm were attempting to form a fist. She hurled it into the night, after the fleeing necromancer.

Makwa rolled to his feet. The scented, sweet light that had exploded from the bear was fading, and he began to look like a shadow once more. Her own strength had returned; she looked at her hand. Even in the darkness of the night, she could see that it was rosy and healthy.

Her rage subsided.

Makwa nudged her with his nose, pushing her back toward the longhouse. She stared after the departing Yankee for a few seconds. She could pursue him, but did she really want to catch him?

Not tonight, she decided.

She turned back toward the longhouse; Makwa had already disappeared. She had a hearth to relight, and a story to share with her brother.

Isaiah Wilkes was surprised that he was still in the palace of life.

He met the Dutchman's gaze and they both shrugged.

Nathaniel Penn entered the palace, smiling. "Thank you both."

"Is that it?" Wilkes asked.

Nathaniel cocked his head, as if listening to his own ear, or to a sound no one else could hear. "It doesn't have to be."

"You don't mean you can bring us back to life, though, hey?" Jake said.

Nathaniel shook his head. "I'm not that kind of healer. Maybe no one is. But I mean . . . you don't have to leave."

"We can stay in this place?" Isaiah looked around at the palace of life and at the clearing and the woods beyond, and suddenly he knew he had a choice. He *could* stay. "But to what end?"

"I would like to have your help in the future," Nathaniel said modestly.

"You could compel us," Jake pointed out.

Nathaniel shrugged.

"You could remind me of my loyalty to Sarah and order me to stay," the Dutchman said.

Nathaniel nodded slowly, then shrugged again. "I'd rather not. I'm a healer. I'd rather not do things that way."

"Sitting around in this palace of life, waiting for you to call us, sounds . . . dull." Wilkes found that he wanted to help the young man, for the sake of the Conventicle, and for Nathaniel's own sake.

He *liked* the boy.

"And you don't have to do that." Nathaniel waved his arms expansively. "Go wherever you like. Explore the realm; you may learn things that are useful to me."

"I need to find Kinta Jane," Isaiah said without thinking.

Nathaniel nodded.

"How will you find us when you need us?" Jake asked.

Nathaniel frowned. "I think I'll be able to hear you. But if not... I can use these." He showed them two Tarock cards, the Drunkard and the Hanged Man. The cards looked as they had always looked, except that the face of the Drunkard was Jacob Hop's face, and the face of the Hanged Man clearly showed the features of Isaiah Wilkes.

Jake laughed out loud and produced a deck from his own pocket. "And look, we can find *you* with this one."

The Serpent had the face of Nathaniel Elytharias Penn.

"I've become a familiar spirit," Isaiah Wilkes said.

"As you told me," Nathaniel answered him, "death is not the end."

Captain Mohuntubby presented himself in Director Notwithstanding Schmidt's tent, clicking his heels together and saluting. The Cherokee soldier looked sleepless; they all were, the day after the battle.

His face was also scratched; she hadn't noticed that the day before.

And his coat was scorched in strange patterns: the burn marks seemed to have the shapes of letters.

Schmidt sighed and set down her pen. Writing was slow and painful in any case, with the shoulder wound she'd received from the Ophidian warrior in the gun-spiking raid. She hadn't asked Robert Hooke to heal it, because she didn't want his deathly arts to touch her person.

She was writing reports and correspondence, making an account of the day's events. The Imperial forces had *won* the battle, battering down the famed Treewall and entering the city. They'd have taken it, and she liked to think they'd have taken it without the Necromancer's and the Sorcerer's aid.

She missed Luman Walters.

She forced the thought from her mind. She couldn't afford regrets.

Schäfer had care of the surviving Parletts on this end of the connection. In the wake of the battle and its strange conclusion, the Firstborn weren't pursuing her and her forces. But it was wise to have someone keep an eye on the children, just in case.

The Imperials had won the military engagement, unequivocally. An honest record would reflect that.

But Director Schmidt had no use for an honest record, not in this case. An honest record would make Sayle out to be a successful artillery commander and general who had been defeated by an unexplained act of sorcery on the part of the defenders, an act so powerful, it appeared to have destroyed Oliver Cromwell himself.

Appeared, Schmidt reminded herself.

In such an account, Schmidt would be a valiant underling to a bold man who happened to be defeated. Instead, she would be certain that the record indicated that Sayle failed. That he did not defend his famous guns, that in the final analysis, he failed.

She must also not give credit to Hooke or Cromwell, who had disappeared. The battle had been won by the brave men of the Imperial Ohio Company and the Imperial Army, but the victory transformed into defeat by the failure of supporting magicians. The fact that all the shambling dead had been obliterated by the blast of yellow light that had brought an abrupt end to the battle would help the story. That was a moment that would only grow in the telling, from mouth to mouth.

If victory belonged to the Imperial Ohio Company by right, then it also belonged to the company's director on the field.

To be certain the history was written her way, Schmidt had spent this morning, the morning of the day after the battle, sending dispatches and writing letters to every friendly Memphite, Ohioan, Pennslander, and Appalachee news-paper she knew.

The fact that the Twelve Apostles were now perched on top of trees would support her account of the battle. But Sayle would commit his own version to paper.

She hadn't seen Sayle since the breaching of the wall. At that point, she had accompanied Ohio Company irregulars within the wall, where, following the information her informant Voldrich had given her, she and her men had excavated Voldrich's fortune out of the wall of a warehouse cellar.

Voldrich had accompanied them as a guarantee of the truth of his information. As the battle had turned, he'd tried to run.

Schmidt had shot him herself, in the back.

"Captain Mohuntubby," she said. "Surely you haven't come back to report failure."

"No, Madam Director," Mohuntubby said. "Nearly three hundred men collected."

"Happy to be alive and paid, I take it?"

"Happy to be in the employ of the Imperial Ohio Company."

Mohuntubby and his men had been rounding up fleeing Imperials. Schmidt had sent Voldrich's gold with him; he was to pay the fleeing men and remind them that they worked for her. If they returned, well and good.

If they persisted in fleeing, that was an act of desertion, and Mohuntubby was to kill them.

"Have you had to shoot many?"

Mohuntubby looked briefly troubled, but shook it off. "Very few." He pointed at the scorch marks on his coat. "One had some kind of arcane shield. It exploded, and your charm saved me."

Luman's Himmelsbrief. Schmidt nodded. "Is the money all gone?"

"We still have cash." The Cherokee captain took a deep breath and plunged ahead, cutting off more questions from the Director. "We've found Sayle. He's dead."

Schmidt considered. Should she order Mohuntubby to burn the body and make no official report? The resulting ambiguity and rumors would make Sayle a figure of suspicion and doubt. But she decided she wanted to see for herself.

She mounted and followed Mohuntubby into the woods. The Imperial Ohio Company camp, as Schmidt was rebuilding it, was twenty miles from the Mississippi, and located on a small river whose name she didn't know. Soon, she would write dispatches to the agents she had installed in the Hansa towns along the Ohio, requisitioning water, draft animals, and wagons, sending out foraging parties; for the moment, the river and their existing supplies were enough.

Three miles' ride brought them to a small clearing around a single tall tree. Sayle dangled there by his neck from a noose that wasn't exactly a rope. Schmidt squinted at it.

"Riding crop?" she asked. "Wrapped around his neck...and the handle jammed into that branch?"

"That's what it looks like to me." Captain Mohuntubby nodded solemnly.

"And what happened to General Sayle's coat?" The front of the artillerist's coat, and the shirt beneath, were scorched and burned away.

In peculiar patterns. That seemed to have the shapes of letters.

Mohuntubby shrugged, his face totally blank.

"I see."

Captain Onacona Mohuntubby, you sly bastard. You did this, and you want me to know.

Schmidt examined the ground. Even here, twenty miles from Cahokia, the snow was melting in an unseasonal thaw. That left the ground of the clearing muddy. The mud bore only a single set of hoofprints.

"He rode here alone," she said, continuing the fiction. "And hanged himself. His horse?"

"My men and I found the animal over that hill." Mohuntubby pointed. "Its tracks were what brought us here."

"Poor man," Schmidt said. "He tried and failed. The shame of failure led him to this tragedy."

Sayle had made it too easy for her. Sayle and Mohuntubby.

Mohuntubby nodded. "Indeed."

"You'll go far, Mohuntubby. Have you considered employment with the Company?"

"My term with the Army is up in a year."

"I suspect I could have you transferred to the Company now, if you like."

Mohuntubby looked her in the eye and smiled. "I suspect you will effectively be the head of the Army in western Ohio for the next year."

"We'll want to bring General Sayle's body back to camp, so the men can see him. Probably don't want them to see him too closely."

A flicker of recognition touched Mohuntubby's face. He smiled, saluted, and then cut the general's body down.

Abd al-Wahid had not seen such an array of warriors since he'd left Cairo. Not even Paris with her teeming multitudes hosted such a spectacular range of fighting men.

The Spanish warriors included horse-mounted lancers, arque-busiers, and artillerymen from the capital. In addition, there were militia units raised by the dons of the far western lands of New

Spain, armed with sword, spear, and breastplate as well as pistol, and trained to march and fight on foot.

There were warriors from the south of New Spain, dark and fierce-eyed, whose hatchet-like faces matched the sharpness of their obsidian clubs. After one of their companies was routed at Bishopsbridge—by the sorcerous Bishop himself, if their accounts were to be believed—they boiled with vindictive pride, anxious for a second chance. They chewed a weed Abd al-Wahid didn't know, that allowed them to sleep only four hours a night, march on an empty stomach, and enter at short notice into a berserker trance. It also caused them to spit red. Abd al-Wahid wanted to know the secret of the weed.

The Old Man of the Mountain, it was said, had used similar devices on his men.

Several companies of Texians rode for New Spain, though as far as Abd al-Wahid could tell, they spent most of their time riding out to fight, defend against, or hunt down the parties of other Texians who dogged the Spanish army. "Texian" seemed to mean any person who lived in the vast, unruled space between New Orleans and New Spain, and who didn't otherwise belong to a people. Some of the Texians were Irish or German immigrants from the Old World; others were runaway slaves and servants from the Spanish plantations; others still were Indians.

What seemed to mark them as Texian was an unwillingness to bear any other name or any other ruler.

There were scouts and small bands of mounted fighting men from the Free Horse Peoples: Apache, Comanche, Tonkawa. Abd al-Wahid didn't know these names and couldn't tell the men apart, but the differences were important to them—especially to the Apache and Tonkawa, who seemed to regard the Comanche as dangerous and untrustworthy. Slavers, they said. From time to time, a Comanche would disappear, and it became a matter of debate whether he'd been killed (and, some said, eaten) by the Tonkawa, or whether he'd taken some Texian or bayou woman as his slave and ridden at night to his homeland in the north.

Slave soldiers fought for the Spanish, too. These were men of Africk origin, mostly, brought to land from the islands where the Spanish worked them to death growing and cutting cane. The men chosen for this cadre were large and bore many scars; the chevalier hinted that they fought with the promise of their freedom if they triumphed, and the freedom of their families if they died. They glared at Abd al-Wahid with resentful eyes. When anyone not of their company walked too close, they shook their chains and shouted.

Smaller, stranger groups fought under the Spanish banner. There were men who wore a djellaba-like garment they called a kimono, and two-toed sandals. They wore their hair in topknots, quilted armor on their bodies, and they fought with a pair of slightly curved swords: one long and one short. They said their homeland was Nihon, where the sun came from.

Abd al-Wahid didn't know Nihon, but he was familiar with Cathay. The Middle Kingdom provided no soldiers, but a cadre of magicians. There were men and women among them, but they wore identical dresses and long hair so that Abd al-Wahid couldn't tell one from the other. They called themselves *nanwu* and *wuyu*. Since the defeat at Bishopsbridge, they had been intent on summoning rain, apparently to flush out the serpents.

But for now, the serpents remained. They were like an insect cloud, stretching over the bottom of the Mississippi all the way to the mouth and inland for as many miles as the Spanish had yet managed to send riders. Their venom killed quickly and with incredible pain, to judge by the throes of the dying.

Ships were being summoned from all New Spain's islands, in a bid to move around the serpents, but some of the Indian fighters whispered that the expedition was doomed already, with the feathered serpent arrayed on the other side.

"Did you poison this drink, Ravi?" Abd al-Wahid took another long sip from the drink Ravi had brought him. It was a cold black tea over ice, sweetened, he guessed from the taste, with prodigious amounts of sugar.

The two men stood beneath the canvas of their shared tent, looking down toward the Mississippi River and Bishopsbridge. The day's heavy rains had tempted one Spanish commander to order across a platoon of men in archaic plate and chain armor.

The basilisks had proved quite adept at finding unprotected gaps in armor, under the arm and inside the thigh. If anything, the twenty brave men willing to attempt the crossing had died in more pain than those who had attempted it before them.

"I'm drinking from the same bottle as you, Prince-Capitaine." It wasn't an answer, but Ravi also took a long sip.

They listened in silence to the rain.

"I have written my first song in English," Ravi said.

It was a delaying tactic, but Abd al-Wahid accepted it. "Sing, O Jew."

> *Bishopsbridge is falling down*
> *Falling down, falling down*
> *Bishopsbridge is falling down*
> *My fair lady*
>
> *Hold the bridge with flying snakes*
> *Flying snakes, flying snakes*
> *Hold the bridge with flying snakes*
> *My fair lady*

"I have heard this song before," Abd al-Wahid said.

"You have heard another song, a song whose melody and words I have cheerfully plundered. I will say, if pressed, that I have done so because the existing song was very nearly on point, and has a compelling tune."

"But in fact, it is because you are a terrible poet who cannot be bothered to do his own work."

"That is correct."

They both laughed, then fell silent.

"You know what I have come to discuss," Ravi said.

His words chosen carefully, Jew-fashion. Ravi said neither *what I have come to ask you*, which might bestow upon Abd al-Wahid permission to deny him, nor *what I have come to tell you*, which might provoke Abd al-Wahid by trespassing against his sense of prerogative.

What I have come to discuss.

All in all, perhaps such careful speech was warranted.

And I know what he wants.

"You love this land. Its languages, its peoples. Who would not?" Abd al-Wahid sipped and considered. If the tea *was* poisoned, it was a subtle dose, hidden by the bitterness of the tea or the power of the sugar. "This land has such a heady sense of possibilities. Always something new, always something surprising. Always hope for a better future."

He found it was true in his own heart.

And he also found, abruptly, that his affection for this new world, with all its horrifying gods, made him hate Bishop Ukwu. The houngan Elector had killed his men—all but this last one, who now wished to leave. He had made this large and exciting land into a pit of death for the prince-capitaine.

He sipped his sweet tea.

"You are married," Ravi said. "You have high office to return to, and land, and children."

"You could have those things," Abd al-Wahid said.

"I could have them here."

Abd al-Wahid considered. "Is there a woman, then?"

"No." Ravi laughed. "I have scarcely been out of your sight, O Prince-Capitaine. When do you imagine I would find, much less court, a daughter of Abraham?"

Abd al-Wahid grunted. "You are resourceful, O Jew."

They both laughed, gently.

"I have lost so many men." Abd al-Wahid set down his tea and looked steadily into Ravi's face. He knew he was going to lose this one, too, but he could not lose Ravi as he had lost the others. "I think if I am to write to Paris to tell them of your death, I would prefer the letter to be a lie."

My alternative, now that we have come this far, is to kill you where you stand.

Ravi nodded solemnly, understanding in his eyes. "And you— will you continue to hunt this bishop?"

"Yes," Abd al-Wahid said simply. No need to explain that he felt that his honor and the honor of the order were pledged. If Ravi did not feel the same himself, Abd al-Wahid would not try to force the feeling on him.

He had seen too many companions die in this New World.

No need to explain that the mere thought of Bishop Ukwu now caused Abd al-Wahid to feel rage.

Ravi smiled. "I would never come back to Paris to give the lie to your words."

"You have no one to visit?"

Ravi shook his head.

Abd al-Wahid smiled. "Does not the poet say, 'Be grateful for whoever comes, because each has been sent as a guide from beyond'? You have ever been my conscience, Ravi. Perhaps one day I will follow you in choosing to stay in this new world."

"I have not known many men to kick their consciences so thoroughly." Ravi smiled.

"Very few consciences deserve it so well."

"Perhaps Bishop Franklin was mistaken."

"Oh?"

Ravi smiled. "Perhaps two may keep a secret, and both live."

"If they are friends." Abd al-Wahid smiled again.

Ravi nodded. "*When* they are friends."

Abd al-Wahid clapped his last comrade across the shoulder. "I will make your death ambiguous in the telling, so that if you do by some chance return to Paris, both our honors may be salvaged."

"I am not leaving while it rains, in any case." Ravi sat on a folding camp chair. "Come, let us devise the story of my death together."

"You know you cannot go to New Orleans."

"That seems obvious."

"And to the north, the beastkind are ravaging the Cotton League."

Ravi waved away the concern with a hand. "But Texia is large, Prince-Capitaine. And New Spain is larger." He drank the last of his tea. "I would suggest a drowning. Perhaps with an appropriately suggestive final glimpse of my hand sinking beneath the waves of the Pontchartrain Sea."

"Oh? Here I thought you would prefer to go in a fire, disappearing as the burning building collapses, you having entered to rescue an elderly widow and her eligible young daughter."

"Let us make the tale refer only to a widow, Prince-Capitaine. That way I sound less self-interested. More heroic."

"I'm afraid the answer might be Eden."

⟐

CHAPTER THIRTY-TWO

Since his journey with Sarah—since he'd entered the strange landscape within the Temple of the Sun and traveled all the way to the gates of Eden—Luman had felt like a different man. He looked no different in the mirror. His limbs, his stature, his weight, his hair were all unchanged.

But something was different.

Not *wrong*, different. Something was *new*, and he couldn't tell what.

Alzbieta Torias's city palace had burned in the battle. At Sarah's direction, the building had been razed. In its place was a burial ground consecrated to the goddess. Alzbieta and her bearers were the first to be interred there.

Cathy Filmer participated in the rite as a priestess. As Luman and a crowd watched, she simulated giving birth to the snake that she then placed inside Alzbieta's burial jar. It was her first public action on behalf of the goddess; the day after the battle, apparently at Sarah's insistence, the Lady Alena and other priestesses had taken Cathy into the Temple of the Sun. They had stayed for hours. When Cathy had emerged, she had a look of surprise on her face and the title *Handmaid*.

Sarah had not yet emerged from the temple.

Because she cannot? Or because she has come to a place too wonderful to leave?

Luman stood watching the rite, trying to ascertain what had happened to him.

He had chosen not to follow Sarah into the precincts of Eden. She had chosen it at the same time, so he was glad to have spared himself the humiliation of asking for admittance and being denied. He had made his decision because, really, he hadn't belonged there.

Sarah *had* been invited; he had *not*.

Still, he itched with curiosity. What would he have seen within that quartz wall? A tree of light? A goddess a-swarm with bees? Might he someday receive an invitation, not being Firstborn, or a member of the Elytharias family, or a eunuch?

Should he think of himself as a partial initiate? Was this a new thing, that he had become a semi-priest? He didn't think so.

Yedera the Unborn Daughter of Podebradas stood with him. She stared intently at the proceedings, her face a steel mask. Yedera had served Alzbieta, but the priestess was dead. Alzbieta had died in Yedera's presence. Would the Podebradan serve Sarah exclusively now? Could a Podebradan lay down her oaths and choose an unconsecrated life?

Would Yedera see Alzbieta's death as a failure on her part?

Luman resolved to ask her those questions once the funeral was over. To speak now seemed an impiety.

Zadok Tarami stood on Luman's other side. The Metropolitan looked exhausted, the lines of his face noticeably deeper and darker. He had conducted dozens of burial rites in his own tradition in the previous two days. He didn't chant with the chanters or sing the funerary lays, but he wasn't at the head of an angry mob, either. He stood with his head bowed, looking respectful. His lips moved; was he praying for the dead priestess who had been his rival?

If Sarah looked at Luman, she'd be able to tell him what was different.

Pocket full of angels. She had seen the Himmelsbrief, through his coat, not knowing what it was. Luman's Himmelsbrief had saved her life, when the Simon Sword of the ascent had turned out to have within it too much of the real Simon Sword.

He felt pride at the memory.

Also, it reminded him that he needed to write out a new Himmelsbrief for his coat.

He hadn't seen or heard from Nathaniel Penn since.

Wilkes and Hop were dead, of course. Although...if the events of that night had left Luman Walters feeling like a different person, might they have had an effect on the two shades, as well?

Luman sighed. The funeral ended with the retreat of the priestesses. He thought Cathy smiled at him as she passed, so he smiled back.

As the crowd broke up, he lost track of Yedera. He didn't ask her his questions, after all.

He returned to the *King's Head*, deep in inchoate thought. Opening the two windows of his garret to let in the warm breeze of the unnatural spring, he sat at the table to draw out the new heavenly letter. After several deep breaths to clear his mind and a brief prayer of preparation, he lit the candle on the shelf above his work space and began to write.

He concentrated on the letters; he knew the text by heart, and the act of replicating it put him in a state of mind like a light trance. From time to time he touched the Homer amulet around his neck. When his quill needed sharpening, he used his athame, consecrated for this and other magical purposes.

The world seemed to fade away, simplifying itself down to the light of the candle, the light in Luman's heart, and the light of the Himmelsbrief. All three melted together in the focused devotional act of preparing the amulet.

Faith, hope, and charity. Sarah had heard it from a Vodun houngan, no less. Luman was chagrined not to have made the connections himself, but proud to have been there, and full of wonder at the memories of the experience.

So perhaps he and the houngan had been, in the end, Sarah's psychopomps. Her spirit guides.

Or perhaps an exact count didn't really matter.

He had nearly finished the letter and was deep in the concentrated, effortless flow of the act when a gust of warm air, smelling of the river, blew out the candle.

Luman looked at the candle and smiled. He felt one with its light, the light of the candle not under a bushel, the holy light of creation, the light of the sun.

He pointed his pen at the candle. *"Fiat lux."*

A warm feeling spread through his body. The candle burst

into flame. Luman smiled at the candle for several long seconds before he realized what he had done.

He dropped the pen.

It spattered ink all over the Himmelsbrief, spoiling it, shattering his trancelike state of well-being like a brick dropped into a still pond.

He didn't care.

He stared at the candle, feeling his heart beat inside his chest. He had lit the candle. Not with a braucher prayer, not with a Memphite incantation, not with a cantrip begged, borrowed, or stolen in some dark corner under false pretenses...

...but with an act of will and the creative word.

Gramarye.

Luman Walters had never been able to perform gramarye. He lacked the talent, and his ten thousand efforts had never produced a single result.

Until now.

The glow within was the same glow he had felt standing on the threshold of Unfallen Eden, watching Sarah embrace the bearded man in the door. Warm light had poured over him then, and then again when he had stood in front of the temple with Montse.

His first act of gramarye had given him a similar feeling.

He *was* different. He was not an initiate, or wasn't fully initiated. Whatever Sarah had finally seen and done within Eden's walls, he had no part of it.

But the goddess had given him a different gift.

He laughed out loud with joy. *But can I be sure?*

He licked his fingertips and snuffed the candle.

"Fiat lux."

The candle sprang again into flame.

He snuffed it again and relit it.

And again.

Then he stood and danced around the room, holding an imaginary partner in his arms until the innkeeper banged on his door and demanded that he keep down the noise.

Tamping down the giddy delight with a series of deep breaths, he crumpled up the wrecked Himmelsbrief and sat down to draw out another.

✧   ✧   ✧

Montse found Bill. At his insistence, he lay on a cot in the same building with wounded rank and file. Miquel was in the next room, sleeping soundly in an herb-induced trance. Montse expected to find Bill surrounded by surviving officers and leaders of the city—the artillerywoman Jaleta Zorales, or Vizier Maltres Korinn.

Instead, Gazelem Zomas sat on the stool beside the cot. A conversation between the two men was just ending.

"I will arrange payment as soon as I can, suh."

Zomas waved Bill's promise away. "Please don't." He stood and nodded at Montse before making his way out.

Montse had planned to stand—it seemed the right gesture of respect for the wounded general—but Bill pushed the stool in her direction with a groan, and she sat.

"What is this place?" she asked. From the outside, it had seemed like the home of one of Cahokia's wealthier residents, a low, multi-chambered mound dug into a hill, with a wooden building crowning the top of it.

Bill looked around at the white-washed walls and the large open windows. "This belonged to a man named Voldrich. He held it, along with much land outside the city walls, by some sort of feudal tenure. Sarah has revoked his rights and taken back the land. For now, this building will serve as a hospital."

"Later, she'll give it as a reward to a faithful retainer," Montse suggested. "Perhaps to you?"

Bill grunted. "Much as I might like to own a city house, I don't believe Sarah is that kind of monarch. Nor do I want it. Would you want to be given a house for your service to Hannah Penn?"

Montse was quiet for a moment. "You know I did nothing for Hannah for which I expected to be paid."

Bill nodded instantly. "I know. But you did it. You saved her daughter."

"And you saved her son."

Bill nodded again. "Hopefully we'll see them both soon. But Sarah needs us here."

This was the crux of the interview. "You command her army. What does Sarah need from me?"

Bill looked out the window. "There is nothing but the river between this city and the mad god Simon Sword. If we are to defend ourselves, we must hold that river."

Montse nodded. "I will do it."

"It won't be with sailboats." Bill cleared his throat. "The river isn't deep enough. It will be with barges and flatboats and keelboats and, Hell's Bells, what do I know? Shallops, is that the word? What the French call *bateaux*?"

"I'll do it."

"Canoes, I suppose. Perhaps we can purchase barges from the Memphites. If we don't have enough slaves, we can get volunteers to work the oars. We'll need to train some marines. I don't know how to fight on a ship, but I suppose *you* must."

Montse laughed. "I said I'll do it already. Do you have more prepared speech you'd like to deliver before I go and get started?"

Bill shook his head. "May I drink a toast with you, then . . . Admiral?"

"Of course."

A clay pitcher sat on a table beside Bill's cot. He filled two small wooden cups with water. His hands shook—age?—but he managed not to spill any as he handed one cup to Montse.

"Many ways." Bill raised his cup. "One people."

Montse repeated the words, and they drank.

"It feels good to find a toast for Cahokia's officers," Bill said.

"A new toast and a new flag as well," Montse said. "Not to mention a navy. These are heady days in Cahokia."

"New flag?"

"Have you not seen it? I believe it was made at Her Majesty's direction. It's a white bird."

"A dove?" Bill suggested.

"A white raven, I think." Montse stood. "On a field of Cahokian gray."

"Thank you," Bill said.

Director Notwithstanding Schmidt sat at her desk, opposite one of the surviving Parletts. The Parlett spoke in a passable imitation of Lord Thomas's voice, his eyebrows raised and his face elongated into a gentle sneer.

"MADAM DIRECTOR, THE OTHER FOUR DIRECTORS OF THE IMPERIAL OHIO COMPANY ARE HERE, IN MY PRESENCE. WE NOT ONLY HAVE A QUORUM, WE HAVE EVERYONE."

"My colleagues are all in Philadelphia?" Schmidt kept her facial expression carefully neutral, knowing that the Parletts would relay an impression of that as well as of her voice. "I gather there is much work to be done in the capital."

"VERY TO THE POINT, MADAM DIRECTOR. VERY TO THE POINT. NOW BEAR WITH ME WHILE I READ THIS COMPANY ACTION INTO THE MINUTES. MY LAWYER HAS DRAFTED IT, AND HE WANTS ME TO GET THE WORDS EXACTLY RIGHT.

"I, THE UNDERSIGNED SOLE SHAREHOLDER OF THE IMPERIAL OHIO COMPANY, DO TAKE THE FOLLOWING ACTIONS.

"ONE: I HEREBY REQUIRE AND ACCEPT THE RESIGNATIONS OF ALL CURRENT DIRECTORS OF THE IMPERIAL OHIO COMPANY."

The Parlett then made yelping noises, which must surely imitate the cries of dismay that were being emitted in Philadelphia. Schmidt continued to keep a neutral expression; she wanted to howl with laughter.

"TWO: I HEREBY AMEND THE CHARTER OF THE IMPERIAL OHIO COMPANY TO REPLACE ITS FORMER BOARD OF FIVE DIRECTORS WITH A SOLE DIRECTOR, TO SERVE AT MY PLEASURE.

"THREE: I HEREBY APPOINT NOTWITHSTANDING SCHMIDT THE SOLE DIRECTOR OF THE IMPERIAL OHIO COMPANY. SIGNED: THOMAS PENN, SHAREHOLDER."

"Thank you, My Lord President," Schmidt said. "I am honored, and I am committed to doing my best in your service."

"I KNOW YOU ARE," Thomas said through the Parletts. "YOU AND I WILL SPEAK LATER ABOUT MY EXPECTATIONS, MADAM DIRECTOR. THIS MEETING IS ADJOURNED."

Only after she had had Schäfer return the Parlett boy to his tent did Notwithstanding Schmidt permit herself to smile.

Maltres Korinn sat in his office in the unassuming building beneath the Hall of Onandagos, reviewing lists of the dead and wounded. When he could talk to Sarah—*if* he could talk to her—he would propose pensions and honors. He wasn't sure where the money would come from, except that maybe he could sell the lands that had once belonged to the traitor Voldrich.

Or Alzbieta Torias's lands? The priestess was without heir.

Though it seemed more fitting, perhaps, that those should come into Sarah's possession.

And should he, as Vizier, talk to Sarah about commencing lawsuits to make her claims to the Penn land fortune? Even if it was not his place to manage that suit, Sarah's taking ownership of even a small portion of that wealth would be a great boon to Cahokia.

But where was it proper to bring such a lawsuit? Maltres was no lawyer, but he vaguely thought that the Philadelphia Compact must address such questions. Maybe the Electoral Assembly, or a tribunal of Electors, could hear claims against the Emperor.

He sighed. This would be another year in which his berry patches grew wild and untended.

"Vizier."

Maltres looked up. A soldier named Lughan, formerly a warden, stood in the door. He had one arm in a sling and a bandage around his head, but he stood with his back straight and proud, not leaning on his spear at all.

"Yes?"

"There are visitors to speak with you."

"Here?"

"At the Hall of Onandagos."

The Hall was consecrated space, but consecrated for public uses and open to all. It was the right place. Maltres closed his eyes. He was so tired that the act of shutting out the light nearly put him to sleep, so he forced his eyelids open again. He could tell them to come back tomorrow.

But no. "Orphans and widows?" he asked. "Aggrieved land-owners?"

He stood, preparing to climb the mound with the soldier.

"Emissaries," Lughan said.

"Not beastkind?" Maltres thought Simon Sword was done sending emissaries. Indeed, he was unsure why Cahokia hadn't been attacked more than it had.

"The kingdoms of the Ohio," Lughan said. "An earl from Chicago. Johnsland. The Sioux. The Algonks."

"Our riders." Maltres's voice cracked.

Lughan nodded. "Some of them got through."

Maltres ascended a hidden stair to the Hall of Onandagos and walked directly to the audience hall. The scene there resembled a ball, after dinner and before the dancing commenced, when all the guests stood about to talk, sharing news and gossip. He saw Ohioan tunics and boots, Igbo caps, and the rugged fur capes of Chicago.

Tears stung his eyes.

A young man in Johnsland purple bowed, sweeping his three-cocked hat low beneath his breast.

"Good morning," Maltres said. "I'm Maltres Korinn."

"Duke of Na'avu," the young man said. "Vizier of Cahokia and First Minister of the Serpent Throne."

"Yes," Maltres admitted. "Did the Earl of Johnsland receive our courier?"

"No. But he received the messenger of Andrew Calhoun of Nashville. My name is Landon Chapel, and I'm here with three hundred men."

Three hundred wasn't many, objectively speaking, but the Earl of Johnsland would have to defend his own lands against attack from the north, if he went to war against Pennsland. "The earl is generous."

"The earl is concerned." Chapel swept an arm to indicate the other people gathered in the room. "Many Electors are. What Thomas Penn can do to one of us, he can do to any of us."

Maltres Korinn wanted to scream, *Why now? Why was no Elector concerned during the long and brutal Pacification, when our rights were slowly ground away?*

But he was too tired, and too grateful to have any help he could.

"Welcome," he said.

The guns failed, Oliver Cromwell said.

Cromwell had also failed, Thomas knew. But he wasn't going to say that, not to Cromwell's face.

He knelt before the Shackamaxon Throne, head spinning. "The guns failed," he agreed. "Notwithstanding Schmidt tells me that Sayle has already paid for his failure."

Thou hast promoted her to sole Director of thy company, Cromwell said. Cromwell stood beside the Shackamaxon Throne, in the body of one of the Parlett boys. Three others survived: one here in Horse Hall, and two with Schmidt, in the Ohio.

"She does what I tell her," Thomas said. "With energy and imagination. I should have left the siege in her hand. I'm going to give her more control over the Pacification of the Ohio in the west. She's already having Trustworthiness Certificates printed up."

Trustworthiness Certificates? Cromwell laughed.

"Affidavits of good conduct and cooperation, sworn by Imperial officers or officers of the Ohio Company. Ophidians will require them to travel the Imperial highways and main rivers, enter universities, enter the Imperial towns, publish books, so on. She's suggested passports, too, for traveling from one Power to the next, only I don't see how that can possibly be policed."

Random enforcement, Cromwell said. *Stop travelers on the road.*

Thomas nodded. "She said the same."

The war is only beginning, Cromwell said. *We have failed to take but a single hill. Our risen dead were also defeated in the field, but they are cheaply made.*

"You will need bodies," Thomas said.

Thou hast bodies.

Thomas nodded. "I'm not dismayed. My bride arrives tomorrow. With the Dutch on my side, and both Ohio Companies under my control, how can I fail?"

Thou actest with energy and imagination, my son. Rise thou, and come to me.

Thomas stood and approached the Shackamaxon Throne. His limbs trembled and his breath caught short in his lungs.

Parlett-Cromwell held in his hands a yellowed horn, sharply curved and capped with gold. *Sit thou, my son.*

Thomas sat. The corners of Shackamaxon Hall were deep with the gloom of night, but the act of resting on this seat suddenly lightened his heart.

Dost thou know the anointing of David?

"He was anointed by Samuel, while Saul was yet king."

Samuel was led by the Lord God to the house of Jesse. "Jesse made seven of his sons to pass before Samuel. And Samuel said unto Jesse, The Lord hath not chosen these."

"He didn't choose the seven." Somehow, the words comforted Thomas. "He chose the one."

As the Lord Protector Oliver Cromwell poured oil onto the crown of Thomas's head, the shadows in the far corners of the hall faded and disappeared. Light shone through Shackamaxon Hall's tall windows, and the painting of William Penn, kneeling in a patch of sand to receive a similar anointing, seemed to smile.

✧   ✧   ✧

The witch Marie was in labor. She had been in labor for two days.

"This is a bad way to birth a calf," Ferpa said.

Naares Stoach had not left the side of the birthing couch—a pile of dried grass beneath a lean-to, beside the Still Waters—since Marie's pains had begun. The blond man looked something like an anxious expectant father, if expectant fathers stood poised and prepared to murder their children upon birth. He held his spear and pistol and glared.

Kort and Ferpa also stayed by Marie. Since there were two of them, they could take turns eating and sleeping. They looked intent and alert, but well, whereas Stoach looked more ragged and maniacal by the hour.

"It's a bad calf," Stoach said.

"You do not know that." Ferpa lowed, a sound like a growl in the depths of her throat.

"Even a bad calf can repent," Kort added.

"This child has one value," Stoach said. "The Heron King wants him."

"The child could be a daughter," Chigozie said. They all ignored him and continued bickering.

Marie ignored them all.

"Simon Sword wants the child," Stoach said, "and we can trade him to Simon Sword. Except that the only thing worth having in exchange for the child has already been destroyed."

"You care too much for your city," Kort said. "It was only walls. Walls may be rebuilt. This soul is worth more than all the walls in the world."

"A city is the people living in it as well." Stoach glared at the beastman. "Will you rebuild my people? And what of the worth of their souls? Are you certain that the child of Simon Sword will have a soul?"

"There is life after this life," Ferpa said.

"For you." Naares Stoach snarled.

Marie groaned and kicked at the ground with her heels.

"Simon Sword is the destroyer," Chigozie said. "Why would you think you can trust any bargain you make with him?"

"Simon Sword is a god," Kort said. "He is bound by the pacts he makes."

"He is not bound by his father's pacts," Ferpa added, nodding.

"Save one," Kort said.

"Why would Simon Sword want this child?" Chigozie thought of the sacrifices he had seen, and the blood of the victims. "He does not seem to me to have parental inclinations. He does not seem fatherly."

"Simon Sword must have a child," Ferpa said. "That is not a *pact*, it is his *nature*. He will fight to have a child, and only a very powerful woman can bear the child of a god. A very powerful woman, or a bride who is herself assisted by divine powers. If Simon Sword can have a living child by this woman, then perhaps he will be free from the drive that would compel him to have a child by another woman."

"By a woman who might oppose him?" Chigozie tried to imagine what the beastkind were talking about.

Kort nodded. "By a woman who might be mother to Peter Plowshare."

"You mean," Chigozie said, thinking through the information, "the reign of Simon Sword might last forever?"

Marie screamed. Chigozie looked about the valley of Still Waters; the Merciful turned toward the birthing hut, fear and uncertainty on their faces.

"The child is coming," Ferpa said.

The birth happened then, in a gush of blood. Kort pointedly stood between Naares Stoach and the mother; Ferpa knelt to catch the child and ease it out.

Chigozie felt uneasy. Was it because he, as a priest, had no experience of childbirth?

Or did his uneasiness spring from the words of Ferpa and Kort?

The child was far too large and did not slide out, as a newborn child of Adam might. A beak emerged first from its mother's birth matrix, and then talons, as if the creature emerging from its mother's belly were trying to open a door rather than slide out a birth canal.

And then the talons tore in one direction and the beak in another.

Marie screamed as her body was torn open, and then collapsed back onto blankets soaked with her sweat and gore and amniotic fluid.

"My child!" she gasped.

The creature being born *stood up* in the ruins of its own mother's flesh, tore the caul away from its beak, and emitted a hideous shriek of triumph that rang off the canyon walls. It had the body of a boy, though covered with fine white feathers from calf to neck. Its feet and head were both those of a heron.

The child was covered in blood.

He turned and pecked at his mother's body, gulping a chunk of bloody flesh from Marie's throat before anyone could stop him. Her arms flailed once and then she was still.

Ferpa pulled the newborn from his dead mother and gathered him into her arms. He punched and bit at her, but she persisted, wrapping a muscular embrace around him and then covering him with a soiled wool blanket. He chirped and croaked, and she made shushing noises until he calmed down.

"This is a mistake!" Stoach glared at Chigozie.

Chigozie felt weary and afraid. The Zoman outrider might well be right. "We took *you* in. We will take in the child. We will take in all who seek mercy."

"And when this son of Simon Sword takes your mercy in his jaws and rends it apart, as he has just now rent his mother, because what he seeks is not mercy but conquest and the satisfaction of a bottomless lust? What then, Shepherd of the Merciful?"

Chigozie looked down at the dead mambo Marie and realized that tears were coursing down his face. "It is required of me that I show mercy," he said. "The promise I have of God is that He will show mercy to me, as I am merciful to others. I have no other promise."

It took two nuns to lever Bill into position on his knees. He expected Cathy's arrival at the hospital because she had promised she'd come, but at the appointed hour he wasn't in his bed at all. He was kneeling opposite it, in the corner of the room.

To take her by surprise.

"Sister?" Cathy called when she saw Bill's empty bed.

Bill fired his pistol. *Bang!* With no ball in the weapon, he achieved a flash and a loud noise.

Cathy wheeled, stared at him, and then smiled a slow and cautious smile.

"The fireworks, my lady," Bill explained. "And this is the fountain."

He threw a bowlful of clean water into the air—not splashing it on her, of course.

"Bill?" she asked.

"The masquerade ball." He had offered Gazelem Zomas any price the man would name, but the foreign Firstborn prince had been unable to find a Venetian mask. In a rough imitation of what he would have liked to have, Bill raised a patch of gray-dyed wool over his eyes, tying it into place.

The wool had holes cut into it for his eyes, but his vision was blurred by tears.

"My, but you look like a fierce road agent," Cathy said.

"I have lived in stations high and low, in this life," Bill admitted.

"I rather like the idea of being romanced by a road agent."

"And my herald."

The young Catalan smuggler, Miqui, had stood waiting in a different corner. Now he approached and bowed deeply. "My Lady. General Sir William Lee begs that you will do him the honor of marrying him."

Cathy flew across the room to draw Bill to his feet. He bit his tongue to avoid yelping as pain shot through both legs.

"Oh, Sir William," she said. "I have said yes already. I have been saying yes for years."

"Psst."

Kinta Jane opened her eyes. The air within the snow cave was close, starlight leaking in faintly through the doors.

A broad-shouldered man knelt over her and she started; why would the giant wake her at night?

"Psst."

But it was Gert Visser, not the giant Chu-Roto-Sha-Meshu, who liked to be called Mesh.

Kinta Jane eased up on one elbow, to look around. She saw no sign of Mesh. She lay under one fur and Dockery lay under another. He breathed deeply.

"The giant is gone," Gert said. "We should go."

"The dogs," she whispered.

"They won't bother us."

Kinta Jane heard canine whimpering outside the camp. "What did you do?"

"Poison." Gert shrugged and began backing out of the cave. "We need to go now. I don't know when the giant will be back."

Kinta Jane climbed to her knees. She had slept in her coat,

so she dug around under the fur, looking for her boots. "Wake Dockery," she said.

Suddenly, a long knife glinted in Gert's hand, reflecting cold starlight. "Dockery stays."

Was it worth fighting for? Kinta Jane looked into her heart and found that it was. Dockery was competent; it was Gert who had upset the canoes on the Hudson. Dockery also had self-control—he had slept beside her without touching her, while Gert had sunk them with his hot temper.

"Dockery," she said loudly.

"I been awake all this while," Dockery said. "And lest you decide you want to stab one of us with that needle you got, Visser, I should tell you that I have a loaded pistol in each hand at this moment."

Visser snarled and exited the cave. Standing, he spat into the fire.

"If you're coming, you come now." The big Dutchman turned away from the others—

a huge spearhead suddenly sprouted in his lower back, and he was hoisted into the air.

Mesh loomed out of the darkness. With two hands he held the spear that raised Visser six feet off the ground. The red light from the fading fire's embers glowed infernally on his disconcertingly broad smile.

"Shoot! Shoot!" Visser screamed, his legs kicking spasmodically.

Mesh shoved the spear into the thick trunk of a pine tree and stepped back. The giant crouched and looked into the snow cave at Dockery. "Will you shoot me?"

"I guess you heard what I said to Gert there," Dockery said. "I was bluffing. You want me to show you?"

Mesh threw back his head, opened his mouth, and laughed long and hard as Gert Visser kicked out the last of his life.

"Come," he said, when Gert was still. "We are being followed and must go."

"Gert Visser wasn't your enemy." Kinta Jane staggered from the cave and stood, numb. "He was our friend. He was trying to...he thought he was rescuing us."

"He wasn't *Dockery's* friend," Mesh said. "And if he wanted to take you off alone into the storm that's coming, I don't think he was your friend, either. Besides, he hurt my dogs. Miserable, worthless person that I am, I have always taken good care of my beasts." The giant shrugged, a gesture that blocked out multiple stars. "But if you want to try to save him, I'll take him down."

Kinta Jane tugged at Gert's hand and got no response. In the frozen winter air, the Dutchman was already growing cold.

"No." Kinta Jane gathered her pack. "Do we put on snowshoes?"

"I am already wearing mine," Mesh said. "You will ride the shu-shu."

Dockery had his moccasins on, and climbed out of the snow cave. "Is that some Anak word for mule?"

Mesh chuckled, a sound like thunder on the horizon. "There," he told them. "Beyond the trees. You will see."

Kinta Jane led the way. Beyond the trees the giant indicated, she smelled a musky animal scent. All she saw was an enormous ridge, a length of stone that raised the horizon several hands.

Until the horizon moved.

Her eyes adjusted, and she saw the shu-shu.

Kinta Jane had seen elephants once. A wealthy Ferdinandian planter had brought a brace of them to New Orleans to exhibit, when she was a child. They both sickened and died, no one knew of what, but not before they had led several marching parades through the Vieux Carré and the Faubourg Marigny. Kinta Jane had watched through the wrought iron railing of a balcony alongside her half-brother, René.

What she saw now were two elephants, only covered with thick hair, and their tusks were longer and curled.

"Shu-shu," she said.

"Mastodon," Dockery said. "Damn. I thought they were a folk tale, made up to frighten Anishinaabe children into eating their walleye."

The nearer mastodon turned and snuffled at Kinta Jane, sniffing her all over with the warm, moist tip of his long trunk. Then it raised its trunk to the sky and bellowed a long and obstreperous complaint.

"He doesn't like that it's cold," Mesh said. "That's Uchu, he's a whiner. The other one is Shash. She's more patient...what do you call it, stoic? But don't get her angry. She gets really violent when she's mad. You don't want to see that."

"No, we don't," Dockery agreed.

Mesh shouted guttural syllables and both mastodons knelt.

"Climb on," he told them. "One on each. I'll hand you each a dog to hold until they've stopped throwing up, and then I've got to put snow on the fire. We'll be gone in three minutes."

Kinta Jane climbed onto Shash's neck and the beast stood back up. She found a harness strapped around the creature's neck that gave her long stirrups into which to slide each leg; they were giant-sized, too big for her, but she made them work. She gripped the harness with one hand, and with the other received the dog Mesh handed her.

The warmth radiating up from the mastodon was better than the fire had been.

They started out, Mesh walking ahead on his snowshoes and leading both mastodons on a long rope.

Kinta Jane looked back over her shoulder. She wasn't sure, but she thought maybe she saw a thin string of lights, like a traveling party with lamps or torches, a few miles behind.

This was not what the Franklin had planned. What had happened to Brother Odishkwa?

And could she still meet Brother Anak?

Or, more terrifying, had she in fact already met him?

The Assembly Hall of the Electoral Assembly was not the most impressive room Calvin Calhoun had ever been in; many rooms of the Palais du Chevalier in New Orleans were more ornately furnished, more opulent, more beautiful.

But they weren't larger. The Hall fell steeply toward a speaking platform, and its bare walls made for a stark appearance that was itself daunting. Behind the speaker's podium was a small table. At that table sat Thomas Penn.

He was taller than Cal would have guessed, and more handsome. He looked surprisingly youthful, for a man who must be, what, fifty years old? William Lee, for instance, looked much more weathered and lined than Thomas Penn.

Penn had given Cal a glance when Calvin had first come in. Cal had then been questioned by a pair of clerks about the Elector's Proxy papers he presented. They hadn't asked at all about the paper Cal kept inside his fine red linsey-woolsey shirt, against his skin.

The lawyer Rupp had written the secret document by candlelight at night in wayside inns.

Not secret for long.

The clerks interrogated Cal and then admitted him, at which point Cal had left Rupp and the Cahokian soldier Olanthes Kuta behind and entered the Assembly Hall. His knees knocked. He had traveled from east to west and back across the empire, had stood toe to toe and fought Lazars, and had killed a man in the Temple of the Sun on the Great Mound of Cahokia, but this... this was something else.

He felt like a child, about to play the most outrageous game of make-believe ever. Only the stakes were high, the rules barely known to Calvin, and the other players were some of the most powerful men and women in the Empire.

Or, like him, their proxies.

He and Rupp had talked through the procedure repeatedly, and now Cal followed it to the letter. After Thomas banged his gavel and said the session was open, Cal kept raising his hand. Three times he was slow to the punch, so he listened to a short, formal motion that merged the Imperial and Dutch Ohio Companies (passed), the announcement of the impending wedding of Thomas Penn (informational only, no vote required, Cal sat out the smatter of polite Electoral applause), and a proposal to create three new Imperial towns (fiercely debated, with the vote postponed until a committee of five Electors, including Polk, could come back and report more detail on the matter).

Finally, Cal was recognized, as "the Proxyholder of the Elector Calhoun, of Appalachee." As he walked the high steps down to the speaker's platform, Charlie Donelsen caught his eye and nodded.

Calvin's throat and mouth felt full of sand, but Lord hates a man as can't talk when talking is what's called for. He stood at the podium, unfolded his sheet of paper, raised his voice to its best, high-pitched tent-preaching note, and began to read.

"As holder of the proxy of Andrew Calhoun, and at his direction, I hereby offer the following motions of impeachment under the Philadelphia Compact of 1784. First, that both Thomas Penn and Gaspard Le Moyne be removed as Electors of this Assembly, pursuant to article one, section seven of the Compact. Second, that pursuant to article two, section two, following his conviction and removal from this assembly, Thomas Penn be removed from the office of Emperor. Third, that a suitable candidate for Emperor be chosen by this body to replace Thomas Penn. So moved."

"Seconded!" Charlie Donelsen howled, gripping the desk before him so tightly his knuckles showed white, a hundred feet away.

"Seconded!" called another voice. Cal looked, surprised, and saw an old man he didn't know. Was purple the color of Johnsland? Could that be the earl?

A roar went up from the Electors. Cal was conscious that Thomas Penn sat behind him, but he couldn't turn his back. Raising the volume of his voice as loud as it would go, he shouted. If he didn't read the particulars now, he might not be allowed to read them later.

"In support of the motions, I allege the following particulars. First, that Thomas Penn ordered the murder of the then-Imperial Consort, King of Cahokia, and member in good standing of this assembly, Kyres Elytharias. Second, that Gaspard Le Moyne knew the foregoing, concealed it from this assembly, and extorted money from Thomas Penn in exchange for his silence. And third, that Thomas Penn personally murdered Hannah Penn, then Empress and member in good standing of this assembly. Which facts I will undertake to prove in any trial ordered and conducted by this body. I move that such a trial be held at the earliest possible opportunity, and I call for a vote."

"Seconded!" Charlie Donelsen yelled again. Half the Electors yelled with him, while the other half looked stunned.

Behind Cal, he heard a gavel fall repeatedly onto wood, until the roar of the Electors fell to a manageable tumult.

"Well, well, well," Thomas Penn drawled in a gravelly, feline voice. "Appalachee squawks. Let us have a voice vote, then, one Elector at a time."

Pulled through the veil in an embrace from the Lady Alena, Cathy froze in awe.

Seven flames burned in the seven bowls of the Serpent Throne. Were there reptiles dancing in each of the seven flames?

Light from the seven flames reflected off the polished gold of all four walls and the ceiling, off the throne, and off the walls— simple gold in which all light shone seemed dark by comparison. Cathy stood in a galaxy of stars. Was herself one of the stars.

"Please leave her with me, Alena." The voice was Sarah's, and it came from the throne.

Alena bowed and exited through the veil.

Sarah descended from the throne. Was it a trick of the light, or did she *detach herself from* the throne, and then descend? She wore a simple linen dress, though the golden light shone on her dress as it burned in all the walls and the ceiling and the throne.

Deep lines cut into Sarah's face, but she smiled.

"Your Majesty." Cathy began to curtsy, but Sarah caught her arm and stopped her.

"Please. In here, you are Cathy, and I am Sarah."

"You look...at home." Cathy wanted to say *tired* or *older*, but thought better of it. And it was true, Sarah looked strangely in her element, standing before the Serpent Throne.

Sarah laughed sharply. "I know what I look like. You're kind."

"Come sleep," Cathy said. "You haven't left the throne in three days."

Sarah looked into the corner of the room, where Cathy saw only blank, gold-covered wall, and shuddered. "I don't think I can."

Cathy controlled her breathing, and kept her composure, though she felt her heart race. "But you haven't eaten. You aren't sleeping."

"The throne feeds me," Sarah said. "And she gives me rest. And she...connects me. Enlarges me."

Was the throne itself a woman, or did Sarah mean someone else? "I don't understand."

"I *am* the throne," Sarah said. "I *am* the city."

Cathy tried not to show her puzzlement. "You mean you can sense what is happening in the city."

Sarah hesitated, then nodded. "Every inch," she said. "This city is mine, and I am hers."

Cathy wasn't sure what to feel. Compassion? Fear? Surprise? Bafflement? *Keep your composure.* "Tell me if you need anything else, Your...Sarah."

Sarah smiled, her face becoming unexpectedly warm. "I offer my congratulations, Cathy."

"What do you mean?" Cathy felt herself blush. "How do you know? Can you see it...looking at me?"

Sarah shook her head. "I experienced Bill's proposal to you."

Cathy felt tears in the corners of her eyes. "That man has a tender heart, beneath everything."

"I know." Sarah's voice contained a sad note.

"And you...sensed these interactions? What else do you... sense?"

"Within the Treewall, everything." Sarah nodded. "And on the throne, I can truly see."

"You had a gift of vision from your father."

Sarah kept talking, as if she hadn't heard Cathy. "I see the Heron King's realm, Cathy. It is not far from here. Or rather, it is both just across the river, and also in another world entirely. I think he doesn't see me. No, I *know* he doesn't see me. But he has destroyed Cahokia's sister realm, Zomas with its city Etzanoa of the white towers, and now he will turn his attention to us. He rides upon an earthquake, cloaked in thunder and lightning. His land is bloody, a kingdom of slaves and murder, and he would have us part of it."

"What is his land called?" Cathy asked. "What is that world?"

Sarah stared into her face. "I am afraid to ask."

"Afraid...of knowledge?" That didn't seem like Sarah at all.

Sarah took a deep breath. "I'm afraid the answer might be *Eden*."

Cathy took both Sarah's hands in her own and looked deeply into the girl-queen's eyes, both the pale natural iris and the paler one, the eye that had been her witchy eye, but became her Eye of Eden. "Tell me what you need from me, Sarah."

"My councilors," Sarah said. "Maltres Korinn, Sir William, Zadok Tarami. They will not be able to come in here. But with anointings that I now know—that I can teach to you—you will be able to bring them before the veil. I will see and hear you from here, and you will hear me through the curtain."

"We have many things to discuss. Ambassadors are arriving."

"I have seen them," Sarah said. "And...I am sorry."

"Sorry?" Cathy's heart beat louder.

"Steel yourself, Cathy. One of them will break your heart."

Cathy frowned, perplexed, but had nothing to say.

"I have seen the Imperial camp," Sarah continued. "They are not gone, and the war is not over. And I have seen the Electoral Assembly." She smiled suddenly, and again looked like the fifteen-year-old girl she ought to be permitted to be. "I've seen Cal."

Cathy laughed. "In the Electoral Assembly? In Philadelphia?"

Sarah nodded, and then tears trickled to her chin. "Calvin Calhoun of all people, God love him, has presented a motion of impeachment to remove Thomas Penn as Emperor."

Cathy gasped. Sarah smiled, seemingly finished speaking, so Cathy turned to go, saying, "I'll arrange a meeting tonight."

"Tomorrow," Sarah said. "I'll need to teach you the anointing. And, Cathy..." Sarah looked again into the corner of the apse. "Do you see that door, there in the corner?"

Cathy shook her head. "There's no door."

"Are you *sure*?"

Cathy looked carefully. "There's nothing there. Just a corner."

Sarah climbed slowly onto the Serpent Throne, her motions suddenly clumsy, as if she carried heavy weights. "And yet, there *is* a door. There's a door there, and I'm the only one who can see it. And I'm very much afraid of what might be on the other side."